'A troubled meditation on the soul
tinent in light of current British po
Above all, it is a phenomenal feat of storytelling
of characters and scores of ideas woven into one gripping whole.'

Andrzej Lukowski, *Metro*

'This is a novel by the other Murakami. Not Haruki… If Haruki is
The Beatles of Japanese literature, Ryu is its Rolling Stones… [*From
the Fatherland, with Love*] has a Tolstoyan cast of characters, from crack
North Korean commandos and hapless Japanese bureaucrats to a
gang of hoodlums who eventually decide to save Japan. It unfolds
with the pace of a thriller…'

David Pilling, *Financial Times*

'Massively ambitious and uncompromising… Prescient in unexpected
ways… The story reels towards its inevitable climax in the manner
of a Hollywood Blockbuster.'

Joanne Hayden, *Sunday Business Post*

'[Mixes] the thrills of a spy novel with some national soul-searching'

Lionel Barber, *Financial Times, Summer Books*

'An impressive feat.'

*TLS*

'Definitely edgier and darker than Haruki [Ryu Murakami] has a
worldwide following and is regarded by many as one of the most
thrilling writers of contemporary Japanese fiction… [He] offers a
thrilling insight with a geopolitical panoramic view into national
character, human relationships, chaos and disorder'

Tatevik Sargsyan, *Hunger Magazine*

'Godfather to the dark heart of modern Japanese fiction'

*Guardian*

'You may not have heard of "the other Murakami", but he deserves
the huge acclaim he already commands in Japan.'

*Diverse Japan*

Born in 1952 in Nagasaki prefecture, RYU MURAKAMI is the *enfant terrible* of contemporary Japanese literature. Awarded the prestigious Akutagawa Prize in 1976 for his first book, he has gone on to explore with cinematic intensity the themes of violence and technology in contemporary Japanese society. His novels include *Coin Locker Babies*, *Sixty-Nine*, *From the Fatherland, with Love* and *Popular Hits of the Showa Era*, all published by Pushkin Press, as well as *Audition* and *In the Miso Soup*. Murakami is also a screenwriter and director; among his films are *Tokyo Decadence*, *Audition* and *Because of You*.

# FROM THE FATHERLAND, WITH LOVE

RYU MURAKAMI

# FROM THE
# FATHERLAND,
# WITH LOVE

Translated from the Japanese
by Ralph McCarthy, Charles De Wolf,
and Ginny Tapley Takemori

PUSHKIN PRESS
LONDON

Pushkin Press
71–75 Shelton Street,
London, WC2H 9JQ

Original text © Ryu Murakami, 2005
English translation © Ralph McCarthy, Ginny
Tapley Takemori, Charles De Wolf, 2013

First published by Pushkin Press in 2013
This edition published in 2013

008

ISBN 978 1 908968 49 4

This book has been selected by the Japanese Literature Publishing
Project (JLPP), an initiative of the Agency for Cultural Affairs of Japan

Set in Monotype Baskerville by Tetragon, London
Printed and bound by CPI Group (UK) Ltd, Croydon, CR0 4YY

www.pushkinpress.com

# CONTENTS

# PROMINENT CHARACTERS

## TOKYO

*Cabinet Intelligence and Research Office (CIRO)*

**Suzuki Norikazu**, Deputy Leader, General Affairs Section, Cabinet Crisis-Management Center
**Yoshida**, Exchange Section, International Division
**Kawai Hideaki**, Korean Affairs Section, International Division
**Iwata**, Chief of Domestic Division

*The Cabinet's crisis-management room*
*(located under PM's official residence)*

**Kido Masaaki**, Prime Minister
**Shigemitsu Takashi**, Chief Cabinet Secretary
**Yamagiwa Kiyotaka**, Deputy Chief Cabinet Secretary
**Tsuboi**, from Foreign Affairs Division of Foreign Affairs and Intelligence Department at Security Bureau, National Police Agency (NPA)
**Katsurayama**, from Security Division at Security Bureau, NPA
**Ohashi**, Minister for Foreign Affairs
**Umezu**, Minister for Economy, Trade, and Industry
**Minami**, Minister of Health, Labor, and Welfare
**Araki Yukie**, Minister for Home Affairs
**Shimada**, Minister of State for Defense
**Oikawa**, Commissioner General, NPA
**Sadakata**, member of National Public Safety Commission
**Doihara**, Minister for Land, Infrastructure and Transport

**Kai Tomonori**, Director General of Local Government Wide Area Network (LGWAN), Home Affairs Ministry

*Akasaka*

**Sanjo Masahiro**, owner of bar in Akasaka

# NORTH KOREA

*Korean Workers Party, Building 3*

**Pak Yong Su**, Professor of Japanese at Kim Jong Il Political-Military University

**Jang Jin Myeong**, Vice-Minister for Culture

**Kim Gweon Cheol**, Deputy Director of Fourth Section of KWP Secretariat's Organization and Guidance Department

**Kang Deok Sang**, instructor in the General Political Bureau; training supervisor for the advance team commandos

*Advance Team Commandos*

**Han Seung Jin** (39), colonel and leader of commandos; political officer attached to People's Army's General Staff's Light Infantry Guidance Bureau; Trusted commanding officer of Koryo Expeditionary Force (KEF). Right ear is clump of scar tissue

**Kim Hak Su** (37), major and deputy leader of commandos. Tall and powerfully built, with piercing gaze. Bayonet scar from corner of right eye to temple

**Choi Hyo Il** (32), captain. Master of the martial art *gyeoksul*. Head of KEF Special Police. Tall and ferocious-looking, with bulging muscles and knife scar on cheek

**Jo Su Ryeon** (33), first lieutenant. Heads propaganda and guidance section of KEF. Accomplished writer. Tall, slim, and handsome, with resonant voice

**Jang Bong Su** (29), first lieutenant. Serves in intelligence section of KEF. Scar on neck

**Pak Myeong** (29), first lieutenant. In charge of day-to-day operations of KEF provisional government. Elite background. Tall and thin, with refined but mask-like features

**Kim Hyang Mok** (27, female), second lieutenant. Accomplished at languages, finance, commercial theory, and sabotage. Heads logistics and supplies section of KEF. Grandfather was killed by the Japanese in Manchuria. Petite and pretty, with mischievous eyes

**Ri Gwi Hui** (28, female), second lieutenant. Expert in electronic communications and sabotage. Serves in intelligence section of the KEF. Lithe and athletic, with even features

**Cho Seong Rae** (30), second lieutenant. Son of restaurant cook. Tall and gentle-looking

## *Koryo Expeditionary Force*

**Ri Hui Cheol**, staff major. Second-in-command to Colonel Han. Specialist in international law

**Ra Jae Gong**, major. Responsible for economic administration; manages funding in Fukuoka

**Heo Jip**, captain. Army doctor with thorough knowledge of chemical warfare. Short and slightly stooped, with deep-set eyes, pointed nose, thin lips

**Ri Gyu Yeong**, female warrant officer and army doctor. Pretty eyes, plump cheeks, small nose

**Kim Sun I**, female warrant officer. Serves in electronic intelligence under Ri Gwi Hui. Fair-skinned and tall, with gymnast's build

**Pak Il Su**, second lieutenant. Heads Squadron #2 of the Special Police

**Choi Rak Gi**, warrant officer. Serves in logistics and supplies section under Second Lieutenant Kim Hyang Mok

**Ri Seong Su**, warrant officer. Serves in the Special Police. In charge of First Lieutenant Jo Su Ryeon's security

**Tak Cheol Hwan**, warrant officer. Heads Squadron #1 of the Special Police, second-in-command to Captain Choi Hyo Il

**Ra Yong Hak**, warrant officer. Renowned sharpshooter. Subordinate of Captain Choi Hyo Il, Squadron #1 of the Special Police

11

# FUKUOKA

*Local government and media*

**Yoshioka Masaru**, governor of Fukuoka Prefecture

**Tenzan Toshiyuki**, mayor of Fukuoka City

**Onoe Chikako**, senior staff member of Public Facility Projects Section of Construction Bureau at Fukuoka City Hall. Mother of Risako and Kenta

**Mizuki Nobuyuki**, Onoe Chikako's former boss, head of Ports and Harbors at City Hall

**Okiyama Hiroto**, chief of Kyushu Regional Police Bureau

**Yokogawa Shigeto**, reporter from city-news desk, *Nishi Nippon Shinbun*. Married to Yokogawa Naeko

**Hosoda Sakiko**, NHK Fukuoka announcer, cohosts TV program with Jo Su Ryeon

*The National Kyushu Medical Center*

**Kuroda Genji**, Deputy Director of Respiratory Medicine

**Seragi Katsuhiko**, honorary consultant. Specialist in autoimmune diseases

**Seragi Yoko**, dermatologist. Granddaughter of Seragi Katsuhiko

**Koshida**, head of security

**Takahashi**, Director of Respiratory Medicine

**Tsuchiya**, Deputy Director of Hematology

*Criminals arrested by KEF*

#2 **Maezono Yoshio**, charged with forced prostitution and loan sharking

#9 **Otsuka Seiji**, lawyer for crime syndicates, charged with money-laundering and tax evasion

#10 **Omura Kikuo**, physician, charged with fraud and bribery

#12 **Kuzuta Shinsaku**, former prefectural parliamentarian, charged with smuggling

*Speed Tribe*

**The Chief** (37), head of Bosozoku group the Hakatakko Devils

**Koizumi** (33), Deputy Chief of the Hakatakko Devils. Son of bean-jam-bun maker

*Ishihara Group*

**Tateno** (16), master of lethally modified boomerangs. At the age of thirteen, witnessed his father, a building contractor, surreptitiously burying a body. Slight of build, long bangs

**Shinohara** (18), breeds large numbers of poisonous frogs and insects. Face as smooth as a hard-boiled egg

**Hino** (18), expert on ductwork and plumbing. When he was seven, his mentally disturbed mother stabbed his father to death. At thirteen, set fire to the institution he'd been placed in, killing four people. Face like that of a roadside Jizo statue—round and expressionless

**Yamada** (17), has tattoo of Mickey Mouse on left shoulder. At thirteen, discovered the corpse of his father, a proponent of "honest poverty," hanging from suicide noose. Has rabbit-like features

**Mori** (17), has tattoo of Minnie Mouse on right shoulder. When he was thirteen, his older brother stabbed his parents to death. Resembles an owl, or an Ewok

**Ando** (18), at thirteen, murdered and dismembered female classmate. Lean and handsome

**Fukuda** (23), bomb-making expert. Claims to be only child of members of religious cult that carried out large-scale terrorist operations. At fifteen, blew up a "rub and tug" massage parlor. Pale and thin

**Takeguchi** (18), expert in high explosives. When he was ten, his father strapped dynamite to waist and burst into offices of the company that had just laid him off but succeeded only in blowing himself up. Pretty face

**Takei** (48), former bank employee. Makes use of connections with Islamic Yemen-based guerrilla group to smuggle weapons into Japan. Small, frail, and nearsighted

**Kaneshiro** (age and background unknown), obsessed with plans to commit terror on grand scale. Has countless suicide scars on both wrists. Thin face, penetrating eyes

13

**Matsuyama** (19), at fourteen, became convinced that radio waves were controlling his mind, burst into TV station, and murdered two with homemade pistol. Long hair, long face

**Toyohara** (17), at twelve, hijacked a bullet train, wielding grandfather's antique samurai sword, and cut down conductor. Short, beefy, and hairy, with shaved head

**Felix** (age unknown), raised by homosexual hacker after parents were killed by armed robber in Colombia. Full-blooded Japanese citizen, in spite of this nickname. Shaved head, with build like a silverback gorilla

**Okubo** (20), committed forty-six acts of arson in hometown of Iwate. Was famous child actor until age of twelve or so. Skull-faced

**Orihara** (18), member of group of five so-called Satanists. Has brown teeth and face of old man

**Kondo** (17), member of group of five so-called Satanists. Thin and weedy

**Sato** (16), member of group of five so-called Satanists. Big eyes, sweet face

**Miyazaki** (17), member of group of five so-called Satanists. Expressionless, Moai statue face

**Shibata** (17), member of group of five so-called Satanists. Short and chubby, with lots of pimples

**Ishihara** (49), provides housing for all young men in the group. Accomplished poet and winner of Kyushu Prefecture Cultural Award for Literary Excellence

**Nobue** (55), Ishihara's close friend. Previously lived in Fukuoka but currently homeless and residing in Ryokuchi Park in Tokyo

# FROM THE
# FATHERLAND,
# WITH LOVE

# THE BOOMERANG BOY

*December 14, 2010*
*Kawasaki, Japan*

N OBUE AWOKE on his American army-surplus cot to the squawk-ing of a chicken. The bird was inside his tent, pecking at scraps of food on the ground. He took his time opening his eyes, then raised his left wrist to his face and squinted at his watch. The little hand pointed at eleven, but that didn't necessarily mean anything. Ishihara had given him this watch more than twenty years ago, and even back then it had never kept time properly. Nobue couldn't say how many hundreds of times he'd considered throwing it away, but buying a new one would have required more effort than he cared to expend, and besides, ever since he and Ishihara had gone their separate ways he'd come to think of it as a sort of memento. His memories of the time they'd spent together were intense, though usually as hazy as daydreams. When he focused on them they were clear enough, but for the most part they lay buried somewhere deep in his brain, like corpses sunk in the muck of a swamp. There had been other members of their little group as well. Sugioka, Yano, Kato... and one other guy. Nobue wasn't much good at remembering names, but Ishihara's was one he would never forget. The watch had been made half a century before, in Switzerland, and the silvery minute

17

hand was stuck to the white dial. He felt a bit sentimental whenever he looked at the thing.

The blue vinyl tarp was lit with the pale glow of daylight outside. Nobue's tent was of the most basic design—a tarp folded double, draped over a support, and staked to the ground at three points. There were no windows, of course, so he couldn't see what the weather was like or what was going on outside. It was noisy, with people chattering away all around him, but that was always the case and no indication of the time or weather. *What the hell's a chicken doing in my tent?* He tried to sit up, grunting as pain shot through his right shoulder. He couldn't lift his right arm, and his left elbow was creaky and numb. He folded his arms protectively and rolled onto his side, then pressed his palm against the edge of the cot to ease himself up. The chicken was pecking alternately at a scrap of sweet-potato skin and a small wooden skewer to which were attached tiny bits of chicken meatballs. In the oilcan on the ground beside the cot, sticks of firewood still smoldered. That would account for the irritation in his eyes and throat. Lots of the homeless had died of carbon-monoxide poisoning recently, and the so-called non-profit organization that ran the place had issued a warning about leaving stoves burning inside tents and huts. Going to bed without heat in the tent would have been out of the question last night, however. December had been shockingly cold so far, and without a fire Nobue's joints and lower back would have seized up completely. The pain would have forced him awake before dawn.

"Nobue-san, sorry to bother you. Did my Ken-chan come barging in here?"

A man folded back the double layer of vinyl at the entrance and smiled in through the flap, showing all four of his teeth. It was the guy everyone called Kuri, his real name being Kurita or Kuriyama or something. He'd once worked at a bank. Or was it a trading company?

"Who the hell is Ken-chan?" Nobue growled. "You don't mean this chicken, do you?"

"Yessir, that's him all right. I keep telling him he's not to go into other people's houses, but... Ken-chan, come on! You're bothering Nobue-san. Come out of there."

The man leaned in through the flap and reached for his rooster.

"You expect him to understand what you tell him?" Nobue said, coughing. "He's a chicken, for fuck's sake. And this isn't somebody's house. It's a homeless guy's tent."

The man named Kuri tensed visibly. Everyone in the park was wary of Nobue, including the NPO staff, who were drawn from the ranks of the yakuza. He was, after all, something of a legend. There were stories about him killing several people with a reconstructed model gun, or building a thermobaric bomb and, partly for sheer amusement, blowing up a large section of Fuchu City. It had all happened a long time ago, and Nobue himself didn't care one way or the other about his "legend." But there remained a certain menacing power in his startling features and in the sound of his laughter—a hacking cackle that pulled the rug out from under everything the world deemed most important, like peace and happiness and security. It was his ability to project this menace—without ever seeming to try—that won him the respect of both residents and the tough guys in charge of them.

"Ken-chan, come here! Can't you see you're not welcome?" Kuri slipped his hand under the rooster's breast, lifted him, and set him back down outside the tent. "I'm very sorry, Nobue-san. I'll give him a good piece of my mind," he said, glancing nervously at Nobue's face as he backed out of the tent.

"Give him a good piece of my mind," Nobue mimicked, chuckling to himself. "What's a chicken going to do with a piece of your fucking mind?" The more he thought about it, the more hilarious it seemed. First came a pigeon-like *ku-ku-ku-ku-ku-ku*, and then laughter began to roll through him in uncontrollable waves. As he doubled over with it, holding his stomach, his face twitched and contorted and tears filled his eyes. It was laughter of the sort he'd often shared with Ishihara back in the old days, and it always helped him forget the pain in his joints.

When the laughter had finally run its course he stood up, his head pressing against the vinyl ceiling. He wiped away the tears, bent down to pick up the hand mirror that lay on the ground at his feet, and looked at his face, studying for the millionth time the scar on his right cheek—a ten-centimeter zipper that ran from the cheekbone down to the jaw. He used to think that with age and wrinkles the scar would become less noticeable, but several years ago the flesh bordering it had begun to cave in, making it all the more prominent. The mirror was the sort women use, an oval-shaped affair with a white wooden handle, and reflected in it was the face of a man in his fifties whose hair, skin, and general vitality were all beginning to sag. He hadn't been to a barber in a decade or more, and what little hair still sprouted from the top of his head hung over his face like the unraveled threads of an old sweater, or cobwebs. His smile, both top and bottom, was missing approximately every other tooth. Those that remained were gray with tartar and decay, and his gums were nearly black. Though he inspected his face every day, this time Nobue couldn't help thinking: *What a kisser! No wonder I scare people. A scar like that on a mug like this...* He draped himself in the long down coat that doubled as his blanket and stepped outside, absently stroking the scar with his finger.

The winter sunlight filtering through the branches of the trees cast a shifting pattern of shadows on his face. It was still well before noon, he reckoned. By afternoon this entire corner would be in the shade of the towering fence that separated the western edge of the park from the highway. The city had erected the fence, explaining that it was to prevent drunks wandering onto the highway and getting themselves killed. If that were really their concern, however, a simple guardrail would have done the job—no need for a fence six meters high. Ryokuchi Park was surrounded by massive housing developments constructed by a consortium of private railway corporations. No doubt the city had been pressured by local residents to hide from view the army of people who called the park home.

"Nobue-san!" someone called out from behind him. "Good morning!" Nobue grunted a non-reply without bothering to turn and see who it was. He'd been living in Ryokuchi Park for a year and a half now. It was a vast swath of ground straddling the border between Yokohama and Kawasaki, and was one of the more prominent of the nation's designated "habitation zones" for the homeless. The six-meter-high fence stretched some three kilometers along one edge of a grassy space the size of three or four soccer fields and criss-crossed with walking paths and a cycling course. To the north and south, the park was bordered by woods, beyond which were the developments. Sports fields had covered the eastern section before the homeless took over, but now only vague outlines were left of them. All the goalposts and nets, ropes, and bolts had been liberated for use in the construction of huts and shanties. The eastern edge was a steep slope, at the top of which was a narrow stretch that had once been lined with benches to provide a scenic viewpoint. Now it was lined with the tents of the NPO staff supervising the homeless.

Nobue's immediate plans were to visit a toilet and then get something hot to drink. He set off, sidestepping a Log who lay sprawled out on the grass. That was what they called the new arrivals who had no sleeping bags or tents or acquaintances here and had to spread cardboard or old newspapers on the bare ground to lie on—given that name, of course, because they lay around like fallen timber, ripe with the smell of decay and excreta, and displaying few discernible signs of life. There was a place in the park's open market where you could buy the bare necessities for sleeping outdoors—cardboard and old newspapers and vinyl tarps—but the proprietor insisted on being paid in cash. The public restrooms required coins, and the portable toilets administered by the NPO and scattered throughout the park weren't free either. All the same, people were still flocking to Ryokuchi. Right now the population was at about four thousand and rising fast. With the presence of the NPO, there was no danger of any trouble from outside, and at the so-called People's Market you could buy anything you needed—provided you could come up with the money. The homeless living on the street or in other parks were often targeted by gangs of teenagers, and fatal attacks occurred almost daily.

Losing his balance as he swerved to avoid a turd in his path, Nobue accidentally stepped on a Log's hair. But he (or she—it was impossible to tell) didn't even move. Most people, shortly after arriving there, fell into a kind of unresponsive funk, their bodies and nervous systems shutting down from a combination of exhaustion and an odd sense of relief.

There were restrooms near what used to be the entrance to the park, and portable toilets had been placed alongside them. Close by were water fountains and two shops that served coffee and tea. As Nobue approached, a middle-aged man called out to him, asking if he had a minute.

"I was just on my way to your tent," the man said.

He was one of the NPO staff in charge of the toilets. He was wearing a vinyl windbreaker, on the back of which were printed the words HARMONY AND SECURITY ARE UP TO YOU AND ME and a picture of two small animals shaking hands. The man's head and eyebrows were shaved, and he had the English words LOVE & PEACE tattooed in red and green on one temple. The NPO staff at Ryokuchi were all associated with either yakuza or foreign mafia. In the beginning it had been a proper organization that provided the homeless with medical treatment and checkups, as well as employment services, but as the park's population had grown to such massive proportions that even the police shied away, the underworld had begun moving in and taking over.

"What is it?" Nobue said irritably. "I just got up, dammit. Gotta take a shit."

The middle-aged skinhead apologized, bowing deeply.

"I'll wait for you here," he said. "Take your time. Enjoy."

The man turned to a youth with long hair, jerked his head toward the queue for the restrooms, and said, "Nobue wants to take a dump." The longhair cleared a path through the queue, gruffly ordering people to step aside, and yanked open the door to one of the portables. A guy of about sixty was sitting on the toilet, coughing like mad. "Out," the longhair told him. "Yes, sir," said the coughing man in a timid voice. He was trying to pull up his pants as he stumbled out of the fiberglass stall. "Go ahead, Nobue-san, it's all yours," said the longhair. He was about to tear off a few sheets from the roll of toilet paper he was holding, when the skinhead shouted at him: "What're you doing, asshole? Give him the whole roll!" The longhair apologized and handed it over. People waiting in line were watching all this with empty eyes. None of them complained or displayed any emotion. The man who'd been evicted stood bent over, still fiddling with his pants.

Nobue was pleased to find the just-vacated toilet seat still warm—cold seats always made his hip hurt. The cream-colored walls were covered with graffiti. Written neatly in felt pen was a poem that featured the word "terrorist." He began reading it aloud in a low growl. *Know ye the compassionate heart of the terrorist / Betrayed by the nation, deprived of wealth / Know ye, sheeple, that we are one / Know that those who robbed us of property and kin / Shall not go unpunished / Revenge is nigh / Know ye the broken heart of the terrorist.* As he read, Nobue was thinking what an idiot the anonymous poet was—another fool who got relieved of his life savings. The more he thought about it, the funnier it seemed, and soon he was rocking back and forth with laughter. The laughter burbled up from his bowels and burst out of his throat with such force that the entire Porta Potti shook.

At about the time when that mentally challenged American president was compelled to admit that his attempt to force democracy on the Middle East had failed, the dollar had begun to fall precipitously. The yen rose for a while, then sank as rapidly as the dollar had. Municipal and semi-government bonds went into free fall, investors began dumping the yen, and finally national bonds went to hell, along with the stock market. An emergency was declared, and trading was suspended on the stock market. Soon banks were failing as well. Institutions with large holdings in national bonds went under, and debt decimated the economy. Further depreciation of the yen resulted in shortages of food and fuel, and it was openly declared that people would die that winter of cold and starvation.

Nobue believed it was back in the spring of '07 when the Prime Minister and the Minister of Finance had gone on television, bowing their heads as they tearfully delivered speeches to the effect that there was simply no other way to save Japan: all ATMs were being shut down, effective immediately. Limits were put on how much cash people could extract from their own bank deposits and savings accounts; they were allowed to withdraw only a minimal, predetermined amount deemed necessary for living expenses. Next a law was passed to prevent the yen from being freely traded for the dollar or euro. People with savings in these currencies ended up with assets they couldn't use. Meanwhile, the sales tax was steadily increased until it topped out at 17.5 per cent. This was inevitable, according to the mournful explanations of the Minister of Finance, or the yen would become virtually worthless, the nation would face bankruptcy, foreigners would buy up the corporations and the land, and Japan would cease to be Japan. Before long, serious inflation set in, and the net result was that the nation succeeded in relieving its citizens of some forty per cent of their wealth.

At this point, the Prime Minister and the Minister of Finance had at least had the sense to resign. When the dollar began its steep decline, Japan held an enormous quantity of US Treasury bonds but was put under pressure not to sell them. Yet even as they wheedled Japan into keeping these, the Americans maintained a high-handed approach toward their creditor. They raised the price of corn, on which Japanese livestock depended, by nearly thirty per cent; brazenly sold weapons to China; and unilaterally began negotiations with North Korea toward a non-aggression pact. As a result, everyone in the country—the politicians, the media, the intellectuals, the masses—soon began to lose any lingering affection for the United States.

It was, many of them thought, as if the faithful old dog had not only been suddenly denied its daily dishful but beaten with a stick into the bargain. A long-harbored, vague antipathy toward the US quickly turned into a seething hatred. Impoverished, Japan came to despise and be despised by its neighbors, and only stumbled further down the road to ruin. Ultimately, it was of no consequence to these other nations whether Japan liked them or opposed them. Japan was simply ignored. Left to its own devices by Asia, America, and Europe, the nation grew increasingly bitter and insular. A growing number of politicians, cheered on by street-corner crowds, loudly argued that Japan had nearly forty tons of plutonium and that producing atomic weapons would be a breeze. Apparently this was true. Thanks to the eccentric method of atomic-power generation known as a "closed nuclear-fuel cycle," the country had stored up mounds of weapons-grade plutonium.

Nations that are down on their luck and bitter about it are generally disliked and shunned by their neighbors, just as individual people in that position are. Those that are both impoverished and embittered tend to lose the ability to control themselves. They get angry easily. They snap and resort to violence or threaten to slit their wrists—or really do slit their wrists. When the NPO thugs found people like that here at Ryokuchi, they beat them half to death. People who couldn't control themselves were dangerous unless you neutralized them by beating them hollow, beating them till they couldn't stand or move. The targets of such attacks would end up unable even to obtain proper food. They had to scavenge for leftovers and grew steadily less careful about hygiene. Denied access even to the portable toilets, they had to relieve themselves in holes dug in the ground; and without paper to wipe themselves they soon gave off a stench that could be detected even at a distance. Body odor was like a badge of homelessness, but nobody wanted anything to do with people who also smelled of shit. When the NPO discovered real stinkers of this kind, they'd work them over mercilessly, until they were driven from the park for good. And what was true for individuals was also true for nations—once they lost control of themselves, they became objects of scorn, isolated and ultimately excluded from the world community.

Sitting on the toilet, Nobue reflected that he'd still been hanging out with Ishihara in Fukuoka when his fellow countrymen surrendered forty per cent of their money to the government. Straining his abdominal muscles exacerbated the pain in his hip, and his shoulder hurt when he reached down to wipe himself. Standing up slowly so as not to strain his lower back, he wondered how fast he could run the hundred meters now. From middle school up until the time he enjoyed those meaningless massacres in the company of Ishihara and the others, he'd been able to run the hundred in just over eleven seconds. He sure as hell couldn't do that now. His hip, his shoulder, his elbow—all his joints were wobbly and barely functional; if he ever did manage to run as fast as he used to, he'd probably fall apart like a disassembled doll. He pictured his various limbs literally coming undone at every joint, an image that made him start laughing again.

The young NPO guy with the long hair was waiting for him outside and addressed him in a ringing voice as he emerged:

"Nobue-san! I hope everything came out all—"

Seeing Nobue in spasms of laughter, he swallowed the rest of the words and just held out a hot hand towel for him to use. Bent double with laughter now, Nobue took it and peered up at the longhair, his face contorted and his cobweb hair flapping in the wind. "You know what?" he said. "If I tried to run right now, I'd come apart at the joints! Like the old GI Joe doll!" He then grabbed hold of the guy's shoulder for support and began cleaning himself with the towel in his free hand, wiping first his face, then his neck and under his arms, and finally his crotch, reaching inside his pants and scrubbing away. The hand towel went from white to brown to nearly black in the process. Nobue paused from time to time to inspect it, to sniff it, and to wave it about like a banner. The longhair, stunned by this performance, was still at a loss for words. People waiting in line to use the toilets watched the two of them in gaping silence.

"There's a new one here who looks like trouble. I'm wondering if I can ask you to have a talk with him."

The middle-aged skinhead was walking alongside Nobue as he spoke. "Whaddaya mean, trouble?" Nobue said. The two of them were crossing the fields toward the southern woods. They came to the section of land surrounded by paths and a cycling course that was known as the People's Market. This, the lower half of the vast

26

grounds, was packed with shops selling a variety of goods at cheap prices. Even people from outside Ryokuchi sometimes came here to shop. Merchandise was sold from open-air stands, tents, huts, and even a few prefab structures. And most of them had speakers in front blasting music and ads and what have you. Nobue loved the chaos of it all. The hubbub of people milling about made him feel as if he was on some undiscovered planet crawling with bizarre life forms. But the skinhead didn't seem to enjoy the atmosphere: he began scowling the moment they arrived.

"Whaddaya mean, trouble?" Nobue asked again, leaning to one side to speak right into his ear.

"He won't say anything. And he's got these weird-ass weapons with him."

"So throw him out."

"We already beat the shit out of him twice, but he won't leave. And he doesn't even flinch when you hit him or kick him. It's creepy."

Strange characters did show up now and then. About two years ago, a pale, skinny kid named Shinohara had arrived with a large trunk. Inside the trunk were hundreds of poisonous centipedes and millipedes, and out of boredom he'd sometimes have one of them bite a homeless guy, just to watch him go into convulsions. Several of the victims came down with horrific rashes and high fevers and nearly died, creating a panic among health-department workers, who mistook the symptoms for the outbreak of some sort of epidemic. The NPO, led by this same skinhead, had wanted to kick Shinohara out of the park, but they were all too scared of his centipedes to dare even approach him. Shinohara was a kid with dead eyes who would occasionally snicker to himself for no apparent reason, but wouldn't react at all when you spoke to him or asked him a question. But Nobue, simply by walking up and sitting beside him for a while, eventually elicited a boyish smile from the kid, who then began to open up about his parents and his upbringing. "They told me you wouldn't talk to anybody—how come you're talking to me?" Nobue asked him. "It's that face of yours," said the kid. "Anybody who looks that much like an alien has got to be all right."

27

Shinohara had been living in Setagaya with his parents and his little sister, an aspiring cellist. His father was a scholar of some sort, his mother a translator. Since early childhood he'd been fascinated by poisonous creatures, and by the time he entered middle school he was using his allowance to buy frogs, spiders, and scorpions over the Internet. He began raising centipedes and millipedes and bringing them to school in his third year, and ended up being blamed for a classmate's partial paralysis. Just before the police arrived at his house, Shinohara made an unsuccessful attempt to murder his own family. His parents had always doted on their daughter, the cello prodigy, and he felt ignored by the three of them. When he was released from the juvenile detention center he had nowhere to go. A probation officer was assigned to his case, but the man was afraid of insects and stayed away. Shinohara had been quite an expert on poisons even before being locked up, but inside he increased his knowledge to doctorate level by studying biochemistry and pharmacology. "They're such buttheads in that place," he told Nobue. "They won't let you read books about poison, but pharmacology is just the flip side of toxicology—they're basically the same thing. The morons don't even know that much."

"Why are there getting to be so many weirdos around?" the skinhead asked, but Nobue didn't reply. The question made no sense to him. He'd always thought that people who blindly followed society's norms and conventions were the weird ones. One of his friends back in the old days, a guy named Sugioka, in an extremely bad mood one morning from lack of sleep, happened to be walking along behind a fortyish divorcée whose jiggling ass, he said, was just begging to be touched. When he gave it a poke, however, he was rebuked by its owner in such an ear-splitting way that he'd felt compelled to use a commando knife he happened to be carrying. Everybody was capable of murder. The really strange ones were those who thought it strange that people like Sugioka and Shinohara existed. Human beings had the freedom and potential to do anything whatsoever; that was what made them so scary.

People like Sugioka and Shinohara were dangerous, no doubt about it. But they weren't as big a pain in the ass as most of the inhabitants of Ryokuchi. Expelled by a society that found them an inconvenience, turned out of house and home, robbed by the nation of their savings, these people were still looking for something to believe in. Not because they wanted to believe, but simply because they were afraid of not having anything to cling to or lean on. Compared to people like Sugioka and Shinohara and Ishihara, the Ryokuchi crowd had a vacancy about them, something insubstantial about their faces and attitudes and behavior. The whole scene had the quality of a daydream.

"And he doesn't have a code. It's not that he sold it, either—supposedly he never had one. No telling what a nutter like that might do."

The resident-register code was an eleven-digit number, programmed into a chip or encrypted in a mobile communication device, that was used to verify one's identity. Some of the homeless at Ryokuchi sold their codes to members of the Chinese mafia in the NPO. The creation of the Basic Resident-Register Network—or Juki Net, as everyone called it—had been entrusted to a select number of private firms, some of whom outsourced the work to companies in China and India. Once in possession of an individual's code, the Chinese mafia were able to enter the Juki Net and change the personal information. They could then sell the code for serious money to foreigners or people who wanted a new life. There were, however, some Japanese who didn't have a code. Shinohara didn't have one, and neither, for that matter, did Nobue or Ishihara.

It wasn't because of their criminal records, however. You couldn't lose your code by committing a crime, but some people were left out of the national system at the time it was created—those who'd been removed from their family registers, for example, or children of radical cult members who refused to register them; and if they had no desire to be let in, they effectively relinquished their codes. Nobue had never seen his. He'd been registered at his parents' address in Hachioji, Tokyo, but after his arrest along with Ishihara for blowing up a section of Fuchu City, his parents had disowned him. He had no smart cards or credit cards or driver's license or national-health card. And he didn't even know his own code number, which was essentially the same as not having one.

"That's him, Nobue-san. You talk to him, all right? Tell him he has to leave."

The kid was sitting on a lawn chair some distance away, between a meat shop and a stand selling old newspapers and magazines. Nobue left the skinhead and walked toward him. All sorts of shops were crammed together here, and the spaces between them, when there were spaces, served as alleyways. Smoke rose from a stovepipe protruding from a dining tent with a sign that read UDON & SOBA. Noodles had been distributed here free as part of a food-assistance program until two years earlier, when the yakuza-connected NPO arrived. Nothing was free anymore, but prices in Ryokuchi were about half what they were outside. A bowl of udon noodles in broth was three hundred yen. A homeless couple was sharing a bowl now, carefully lifting one noodle to their mouths at a time with disposable chopsticks that had seen better days.

The noodle stall stood next to a place selling little camping lanterns and candles, and across from that was a tent where you could buy lamp fuel and gasoline. Next to that were stacks of used tires for sale, and then a little stand where a skinny man was refilling pre-owned disposable lighters. Squeezed into a space about two meters wide were four different shops, including a place that repaired portable generators, a used pantyhose emporium, and a stand where you could purchase handmade lip balm. Manning the pantyhose booth was a young woman with a bad complexion and the body of a baby dinosaur. Behind the hut that sold vegetables and pickles stood a pile of raw garbage, which an old man wearing about five sweaters was picking through. As Nobue walked along, the cold seeped into his bones; his hip began to hurt again, and he was conscious of a desire for something hot to drink. He remembered now that he'd been planning to get something right after taking that dump. The warm hand towel had felt so good he'd forgotten all about it.

"Morning, Nobue-san," said a man who'd been bellowing through a loudspeaker, hawking Scotch whiskey—*Two bottles, only ten thousand yen!* He was in his late twenties, had a pretty face, and was wearing the same vinyl windbreaker the middle-aged skinhead had on, with the HARMONY AND SECURITY motto emblazoned on the back. He was half Japanese and half Colombian. "I need a hot drink," Nobue told him. The man put the loudspeaker on top of the whiskey cabinet and stood at attention. "Yes, sir! What can I get you?" he said. "Anything'll do," said Nobue. "Cocoa or whatever. Two of 'em." It had occurred to him that the kid might like some too. "What if they don't have cocoa?" the pretty-faced half-Colombian said as he turned to go and fetch the order. "You deaf?" Nobue shouted, scowling. "I said anything'll do, dammit. Anything's fine, as long as it's hot." Noting the look of displeasure on Nobue's face, the man dived into the crowd and came running back in a matter of seconds, panting for breath, with two paper cups full of steaming hot chocolate.

The kid was gazing off into the distance with unfocused eyes. There was a pink swelling on his lip where a cut had festered. The black-leather backpack on his shoulders was of a strange design—flat and L-shaped. Fine, soft-looking hair spilled over his forehead. His age was hard to determine—he could have passed for thirteen or, depending on the angle, late twenties. Nobue held out one of the paper cups, and the focus of the kid's eyes shifted from far away to the cup, then to Nobue's hand, and up his arm and shoulder to his face. He looked as if he couldn't compute what was happening.

Across the way was a place selling batteries of all sizes, and scattered on the ground in front of it were dozens of pamphlets advertising a sperm bank and declaring, in big red letters: GRADUATES OF TOKYO UNIVERSITY, KYOTO UNIVERSITY, HITOTSUBASHI UNIVERSITY—GUARANTEED IN WRITING ¥30,000. About ten meters behind the battery shop, in the direction of the south woods, were some makeshift latrines that consisted of cardboard screens placed around holes in the ground, for people who couldn't afford proper toilets. A fat woman with her hair bleached yellow was doing her business in one of them, struggling with her ragged knit skirt,

31

her fleshy buttocks visible through a gap in the cardboard screen. After a while she stood up, exposing blubbery arms and legs to the world as she wiped herself, but none of the people milling around so much as glanced her way.

The kid took the cocoa. "Mind if I sit down?" Nobue asked. The kid peered at him for some seconds, then nodded.

"What's up with that backpack?" Nobue asked him. "Strange shape. Whatcha got in there?"

The kid mumbled something, peering down at the ground. "I can't hear you. Speak up a little, willya? Just a little will do," Nobue said, and began to laugh, making the cocoa ripple in his cup. In front of the meat shop, pork cutlets, meatballs, and croquettes sizzled in a deep fryer, emitting a smell of boiling oil and scorched flour. Two middle-aged men were eating breaded-meatball sandwiches, crumbs falling from the corners of their mouths as they watched Nobue laugh. "Did I say something funny?" the kid asked. His voice was low and hoarse. "Hell, boy, nobody could understand a mumble like that. It's like you're shy or somethin'. No point in bein' shy in a place like this, where a fat lady's takin' a shit right out in the open." The laughter only seemed to swell with each word he uttered and continued rolling through him for some time. "I'm sorry," the kid said when it finally subsided. Nobue wiped the tears from his eyes and said, "You don't need to apologize. Just tell me what's in the—"

"Boomerangs," the kid said, speaking clearly this time.

"Oh yeah?" Nobue had only a vague idea what a boomerang was. The kid stood up and walked toward the woods, cutting through the alley beside the meat shop, and Nobue followed. Perhaps there'd been a frost: the ground was muddy, and the dew on the grass soaked his sneakers and the hem of his long down coat. From the marketplace to the south woods was vacant land, with only a garbage dump and any number of latrine holes surrounded by cardboard. No one set up tents or huts in the woods because the NPO didn't allow it, and anyone who tried to was roughed up and sent packing. There was nobody else around, only a crow perched on the rim of an oil-drum garbage can. A crew of homeless people employed by the NPO were supposed to collect the excrement and garbage, but since it was winter they hadn't bothered to do so lately. This was a service paid for by people who lived in the residential area beyond the trees. The woods were on a gentle slope, and at the top, where the vegetation thinned out, was a barbed-wire fence. The residential district began just on the other side. Sometimes residents out walking their dogs would linger at the fence and survey the park with binoculars.

The kid stopped short of the woods. He took off his backpack and extracted a crescent-shaped, silvery metal blade. From tip to tip it was about as long as a whiskey bottle. The grip was wound with thread, and the inner edge was honed to a gleaming razor sharpness. The kid adjusted and readjusted his grip and pointed at the oil drum off in the distance. So a boomerang's something you throw, Nobue was thinking, when the air was cut by a sound like whistling wind, and the blade was skimming low over the grass and rising. It picked up speed as it went, until it was going so fast that Nobue couldn't follow it with his eyes. All he could see was an occasional flash when the blade caught the sunlight, so that it seemed to be blinking on and off as it whipped across the field, making straight for the oil drum. Nothing flew like this—not birds or planes or bullets or arrows. The thing apparently gained speed from the way it rotated in the air. Something burst apart on top of the oil drum like a popped black balloon. The boomerang appeared to pause in mid-air, then came spinning and blinking back this way at what seemed even greater speed, to stab into the ground at the kid's feet.

"It's a weapon, then?" Nobue asked when they reached the oil drum, where the crow lay on the ground in two blood-drenched sections. "Correct," said the kid. He wiped the gore and dirt off the blade before returning it to his backpack. His eyes were different now. They had the same look Sugioka's had had after he murdered the woman with the jiggly ass. This kid probably only really feels alive when he's bringing something down with that boomer-thang, Nobue thought to himself. Best to send him to Ishihara's place down in Fukuoka. If he stays here, he's sure to end up killing somebody.

## PROLOGUE 2

# FROM THE FATHERLAND

*March 21, 2010*
*Pyongyang, Democratic People's Republic of Korea*

P AK YONG SU had been told late the evening before that he was to report to Building 3, which housed the Party Secretariat's Frontline Bureau for National Unification, the body responsible for operations directed against the South. To be given an order after ten at night was in itself a bad omen. Moreover, the summons had been delivered personally by Jang Jin Myeong, second-in-command at the Ministry of Culture. While Jang had been Pak's classmate at Kim Jong Il Political-Military University many years ago, this was quite unprecedented. Over the thirty years that Pak had spent in the harsh world of politics, he had learned to be wary of anything out of the ordinary. Jang had specialized in Eastern European Art Theory, and after entering the Party's Organization and Guidance Department had been handpicked for a position in the Ministry of Culture. For his part, Pak had studied philosophy and English before joining the General Political Bureau of the People's Army. Attached to the Fifth Division of the Special Operations Forces Guidance Bureau, he had studied Japanese for sixteen years. For the past four years he had been teaching the language at his alma mater.

"It's been quite a while," said Jang as he entered the room. "You seem to be doing well." These warm words of greeting were contradicted by the cold expression in the eyes behind his glasses. It had been perhaps as long as ten years since the two had last met. Jang was normally a man who never let down his guard, but Pak couldn't remember ever having seen him so disconcertingly tense. His blue jacket was of the too-tight sort worn by film comedians, his polyester necktie was scarlet, and on his shirt, above a bulging belly that made him look a bit like the famous giant lizard in Pyongyang Zoo, was a yellow stain. He was mopping perspiration from his forehead and cheeks with a handkerchief, although the temperature in Pak's office wasn't nearly sufficient to make even a man as fat as Jang sweat.

When informed by a security guard via his telephone extension that Jang was on his way, Pak had hastily switched off the laptop computer on his desk. He'd been reading the homepage of the Japanese Cabinet Office, but though obviously entitled to do this, having official access to all such sites, he couldn't assume that his colleagues were necessarily allies. It had recently become all the more imperative to be cautious about everything one did or said within the GPB. Over the last three years, the United States, under a Democratic administration, had softened its position toward the Republic; and with the rapprochement, political interests vis-à-vis the US had subtly shifted, resulting in the rise of a reformist faction and the fall from grace of the hardliners. Those advocating dramatic change and economic liberalization had likewise been purged.

There had been recurring rumors that the Dear Leader, Comrade General Kim Jong Il, might relinquish power, but handing it over to the hawkish military was out of the question, and among the reformist leaders there was no one with any charisma. Neither the Americans nor the Chinese wanted whatever shift occurred to trigger turmoil. Whether the reformists moved forward to take the reins or the hardliners staged a comeback, the replacement of Kim Jong Il by a collective leadership was still a distant prospect. The Dear Leader had himself stated twice, in the press and on television, that "the spring thaw is still far off." He had also referred to the saying:

"The mushrooms of March are poisonous," meaning that acting or speaking prematurely could well be harmful to the body politic. Some had engaged in loose talk about it now being Japan and no longer the United States that was the national nemesis, but Pak needed no reminding how dangerous this could be. Aligning oneself with either the reformists or the traditionalists was equally hazardous. Maybe Jang had at this late hour, without going through their respective secretaries, come looking for a sacrificial goat, one that was stuck in the middle of the road; maybe he was there to ferret out from Pak's work or attitudes some surreptitious link with the Americans.

"Comrade Pak, I apologize for my sudden visit at this time of night," said Jang, still wiping his forehead as he looked at his watch. It was a silver Rolex, with the Dear Leader's initials inscribed on the rim. Thanks to Jang's contacts in the world of European cinema, the Fatherland had received technical assistance from a Swedish semiconductor maker, along with some Rolex watches.

"No trouble at all," replied Pak. "As you know, I'm still a bachelor, even at my age. Besides, as they say, 'winter butterflies are rare visitors.'"

Though this flattery was born of wariness, he felt a twinge of shame as he compared his visitor—fiftyish, fat, and ugly—to a butterfly.

"Thank you. And old acquaintances matter most of all. But what a splendid view you have of the Taedong River! The lights are finally back on Chungsong Bridge. They may still be a bit dim, but one should see them as a symbol of the last decade—and of the soundness of our Comrade General's leadership."

The curtains at the window were half open to the moist March air. From there Jang had a view of the gently flowing river and, hazily illuminated by the streetlights, the bridge that for ten years had languished in the dark. Recently there even seemed to be a modest increase in the number of boats plying the river during the day. Perhaps, as Jang suggested, the worst was over, even if this wasn't because the economy had improved but because assistance had come from the United States and China, both concerned that the Republic was on the verge of collapse.

"By the way, Comrade Pak. Do you always work so late? I've heard your eyesight isn't what it used to be."

Was he teasing him for being unmarried and remaining at heart a sort of eternal student? Or was this veiled criticism aimed at his use of the computer late at night, despite a state of national destitution that included chronic power shortages?

Jang was a Pyongyang native, whereas Pak was from a small village at the foot of the Puksu and Paek mountains in the northeast. Since primary school, the hardworking Pak had not slept more than four hours a night. His reason for never marrying was Ri Sol Su, a classmate with whom he'd fallen in love, only to lose her to tuberculosis. Born in Kaesong, she had been a clear-headed, affectionate girl. The conviction that there was no one to match her had kept him single. It was true, as Jang had hinted, that Pak's eyesight had rapidly deteriorated since he had begun using the computer. But the GPB had been providing him with costly lamprey-liver oil to combat the problem. Why was Jang, who was obviously aware of all this, probing the reasons behind Pak's obsession with his work?

"I live on my own," Pak replied with an artificial smile. "I have no other purpose in life."

There was a knock on the door, and a security guard came in with tea. The cluttered desk left him not knowing where to put the cups. He nonetheless kept his gaze unfocused, aware that it was strictly forbidden to look around the room or pay any attention to visitors or the computer. Pak pushed some papers aside to make space. The guard put down the cups and slipped out of the room as soundlessly as a shadow on the wall.

Pak took a sip of his tea, then remarked, "Recently there has been an overwhelming amount of material to be read and analyzed." This was true. Since the American presidential election, the situation in East Asia had drastically changed.

"I'd like to hear about your research," said Jang, turning away from the window and looking at him with a serious expression on his face. "What should we make of trends in Japan?"

Pak could well understand Jang's interest in the subject, but he was puzzled why it was necessary to conduct this discussion so late in the evening. Besides, wasn't Japan's ongoing collapse being constantly monitored by that country's mass media? Perhaps, thought Pak, this was simply a leading question.

"I was just looking at the Japanese Cabinet Office's homepage. This week their government has decided on a plan to raise the consumption tax by another 2.5 per cent, bringing it to 17.5 per cent. They also apparently intend to announce that a massive expansion of the military is possible without amending the Constitution. The opposition parties have come up with a slogan that calls for replacing US lapdog patriotism with anti-US patriotism. And this general mood is spreading, not only among the poor but also the hard-pressed middle class and even segments of the upper-class intelligentsia. The government is apparently feeling the pinch and so is desperately looking for a compromise with the opposition and its supporters by acquiescing on the constitutional issue.

"According to the *Asahi Shinbun*, right-wing members of the defunct Liberal Democratic Party, the core of that opposition, are calling for the sale of foreign reserves to finance the militarization effort, and that idea is also gaining widespread backing. But another major newspaper, the *Mainichi Shinbun*, holds the view that in fact Japan's foreign capital, including bonds, has been exhausted by attempts to shore up the yen. The more pessimistic Japanese economists are saying that the government is already powerless to prevent a collapse, and this isn't necessarily an exaggeration."

Pak was speaking guardedly, saying only what was generally known to everyone.

"In my view—limited as it is—Japan, with its economy in ruins, stands at a major crossroads. The opposition, which is demanding a more powerful, nuclearized military, is gaining strength, while the liberal administration now in power is allowing its base to slip away. If Japan leans toward the hardliners, it will bypass the constitutional matter and immediately go nuclear. But even though the Japanese have the technological capacity to produce nuclear weapons, they lack a delivery system, a fact that the media have shut their eyes to. They're seriously behind in rocket technology, and they have no long-range bombers. As a result, there's been absolutely no discussion about the risks involved in possessing even deterrent weapons, to say nothing of a first-strike capacity.

"In any case, the effects of inflation have been severe, and financial resources, both public and private, have been decimated. Since the collapse of the yen, they've slapped a 'Japan premium' on imports not only of oil but of feed grain. The public are concerned that food and oil imports might run out altogether, and this concern only strengthens the hand of those advocating military expansion. On a calorie basis, Japan's self-sufficiency for all foodstuffs stands at forty per cent, but for grain, including animal feed, it's less than thirty per cent, lower than in the Republic. As the yen continues to fall, Japan will inevitably face food and energy shortages. And even as rumors of such a food crisis have spread, the US has raised the price of feed grain by a third. This has only goaded the major media into a unanimous outcry against America. The *Yomiuri Shinbun* said just today that many homeless people may freeze or starve to death in the coming winter."

Jang Jin Myeong listened to this intently. He had still not explained the purpose for his late visit. Pak wondered whether it all might simply be a preliminary test, with the essential topic of the evening yet to follow.

"I would be interested to know your views on where relations between China and Japan are going."

Perhaps now, thought Pak, bracing himself, we're finally getting down to brass tacks. The Republic was in a quandary over its own ties to China, and Sino-Japanese relations were no less sensitive an issue. If the Democratic administration in Washington continued to move toward friendlier relations with the Republic—aid in food and fuel, for example, being offered in exchange for the dismantling of nuclear facilities—the roadmap to reunification might at last be revealed. China, however, would do whatever necessary to oppose the long-sought realization of that dream, as reunification would eliminate the buffer zone between it and the United States, bringing the two countries face-to-face across a single border. Moreover, the fact that a reunified Korean military would be supplied by the US arms industry would be difficult for China to counter. The Republic's relationship with China had thus become an Achilles heel. Rumors had spread as far as Pak's own classrooms that, as part of efforts to create a more compatible puppet regime, the Chinese government was preparing to move the Dear Leader to an estate in Beijing once he relinquished power. But even if that were to happen, the Republic would still be subject to power struggles, secret denunciations, and surveillance. Never had the Dear Leader looked more intently at shifting currents within the People's Army for telltale signs of rebellious elements. But hardliners would have an allergic reaction to the slightest glimpse of any peaceful reunification strategy. Giving up on an invasion of the South was for them tantamount to automatic submission to the US military.

"Comrade Jang," Pak said, "any discussion of China requires very careful thought. I think you understand my meaning. There is a good deal in my research that I can't speak about lightly, even with an old friend and prominent comrade within the inner circle."

Jang nodded emphatically, apparently quite satisfied with this reply. Sitting up straighter in the chair, as though to adopt a more formal pose, he finally came to the purpose of his visit. He spoke with a certain tension on his face, pronouncing each word in a distinct and oddly stilted manner.

"I have been assigned the task of informing you that you are to report to Building 3 at ten o'clock tomorrow morning. As to who has issued this order, I have only been told that this will be clarified when you arrive. A car from the Organization and Guidance Department will come for you. More than this I do not know."

In the morning, skylarks were singing, though the air was still cold. The cycads planted in front of the entrance to the building that housed his office were covered with frost. As he stood outside, Pak swept his eyes over the campus. The Kim Jong Il Political-Military

University, surrounded by a wall some six meters in height, didn't look like most institutes of higher education. There were no sports grounds, and the entire complex rather resembled the headquarters of a corporation. What went on inside was, of course, quite unknown to the general public. Though it was originally established as a training school for agents working against the South, the university had in recent years shifted its emphasis to the study of foreign languages, computer technology, and state-of-the-art economic theory. At the urging of his secretary, Pak had taken along his quilt-lined overcoat. The sky looked threatening, and a drop in temperature had been forecast.

The woolen overcoat, a gift from his mother, dated from the year he joined the General Political Bureau. He had worn it ever since, having it resewn every three or four years. Each time he put his arms through the sleeves, he thought of her. She was looking after a small plot of farmland back at home. His father had died in the War for the Unification of the Fatherland. Though families of the fallen were classified as "revolutionary cadres" and granted preference for Party membership, Pak's mother had raised her son and two daughters on her own—a life of constant struggle and deprivation. Several times a year during the famine-plagued 1990s, he had sent her food coupons, rice, and pork, but it seemed she invariably donated these to the local Workers Party headquarters. Making do with dumplings consisting mainly of pine bark, she described herself as a mere root to the great and compassionate tree that was the Dear Leader, providing what sustenance she could for its precious trunk. She would despise the sort of people who sold salvaged copper wiring on the free market to keep themselves from starving. His mother was as pure as the whitest spun silk and would be absolutely horrified if her son were denounced for some crime today in Building 3.

The guard, a recent graduate, stood at attention at the gate. He was wearing a thin, unpadded uniform. Seeing Pak, he raised his rifle in salute. The car that was to take him arrived thirty minutes early, stopping in front of the covered entrance; no civilian vehicles were allowed on campus. The car was a German model, bearing

41

the license-plate number 216 in honor of the Comrade General's birthday and suggesting that it had been a gift from on high to a top-ranking official. A man stepped out from the passenger seat and opened the rear door with the words: "Professor Pak, I have come to escort you." This assistant, whose face was unfamiliar to Pak, appeared to be in his late thirties. He sat in front, while Pak settled into the leather-upholstered seat behind him, crossing his arms and closing his eyes. With whispers of a thaw between the Republic and America as well as with the South, what business could the Frontline Bureau for National Unification have with a Japanese-language researcher? His unease only increased as the car pulled away.

The broad sidewalk beside the Taedong was largely deserted. With Yangkak Island visible ahead of them, they moved at speed along the riverbank road toward Chang Gwang Avenue. Soon a mass of commuters would be emerging from the underground stations and heading for their various workplaces, and in another two hours or so tourist buses from the countryside would be filling the parking lot in front of the Juche Tower. Pak was quite fond of the scenery here. Amidst the concrete buildings, which he somehow still found alien after more than thirty years in Pyongyang, there was this soothing view along the river. The willows planted beside the path waved their new shoots in the gentle morning breeze. Pak enjoyed sitting on a bench, watching the boats on the river, and gazing vacantly at the far bank—or, when time permitted, taking a solitary stroll there.

In spring, mist hung over the river's surface; in summer, rainbows appeared after sudden showers. In autumn there were tinted leaves, and in winter the clarity of the air gave one a pleasant sense of everything merging with the river itself. When they were both still only twenty years old, he and Ri Sol Su had often walked together here. Back then, in the early 1970s, there had been food stands along the footpath that sold candied apples and deep-fried *karakjippang* sweet rolls. The two of them would buy a snack and sit on a bench to eat it and talk about the future or their hometowns. They had never even held hands, much less kissed.

42

The bronze statue of Kim Il Sung appeared, and Pak felt invigorated by it. Compared with the immense monument newly erected in Mangyongdae, it seemed a truer representation of the Great Comrade Leader. As he gazed at the statue rising out of the mist, he reminded himself that this was no time for sentimentality, or for memories of Ri Sol Su. He was merely one man, a tiny part of a revolutionary work in progress. He was on his way to Building 3. He had to compose himself, to be prepared for whatever was awaiting him.

As they entered the heart of the city, the car slowed down. Traffic controllers and sentries stationed at strategic points saluted as it passed. Inside no one spoke. The secretarial assistant had said nothing further, and Pak himself, not knowing why he had been summoned, was hardly in the mood to initiate a conversation. But when they stopped at a traffic light next to the Okryugwan, the Republic's largest and most famous restaurant, the man turned around and shyly inquired whether he might ask a question. There was something unaffected about his tone of voice, and Pak found himself taking a liking to him. "Go ahead," he said. But what came next was unexpected.

"Have you ever tasted a brand of beer called Kirin?"

"Yes," Pak replied with a smile. "A few times. Why do you ask?"

"I know it may sound decadent, but I hope that someday my allegiance to the Party will give me an opportunity to order that beer in the Okryugwan."

He gave a shy laugh as he said this, with the driver joining in. An ordinary worker making a remark like that might easily wind up in a re-education work camp. But a secretary to a high-ranking official in Building 3 enjoyed a degree of freedom denied to most citizens. Pak assured him that if he remained steadfastly loyal and did his utmost for the Party, that hope would probably be realized. He said this with his gaze on the Okryugwan. He could see a queue in front of the restaurant, though it was still four hours before the lunch break. Those not in the Party, the army, or the higher echelons who wanted to eat there had to be in possession of a meal coupon issued at their place of work. Some two hundred such coupons, good only for cold noodles, were handed out daily in the capital's offices and factories, which meant that the chances of getting one on any given day were one in a thousand. Those without might wait outside in the hope of buying a coupon from scalpers, a few of whom, all disabled, had bought coupons on the black market, which they were now selling outside for inflated prices. Public Security agents turned a blind eye to this, as they were raking off part of the profits.

Arriving at Building 3, Pak was escorted by the secretarial assistant to the reception desk and from there by a sharp-featured People's Army officer to an elevator that took them down to Basement 2. The officer led the way along a dark and narrow corridor to a plain gray steel door, which was opened by Kim Gweon Cheol, Deputy Director of the Organization and Guidance Department's Fourth Section.

"Thank you for taking the trouble to visit us, Professor Pak. I hope we can dispense with formalities. Please come in and sit down."

Kim Gweon Cheol was a legendary figure who had attained his present position at the tender age of thirty-eight, having been a trusted associate of Jang Sung Taek, the Dear Leader's brother-in-law. Even after the latter had been purged for pushing too eagerly for economic liberalization, Kim had survived by playing his cards shrewdly and by successfully managing the Kaesong Special Economic Zone. He had a reputation for being cold-blooded and having a razor-sharp mind. He now escorted Pak to Projection Room 1. The room was subtly different from similar facilities in other government buildings, or in art institutions and guesthouses. A little over fifty square meters in size, it had three rows of seats arranged in a fan shape facing a small screen. Pak sat down in the third row on the far right. The walls and floor were covered with thick gray linoleum; the crimson leather seats had large backs, with aluminum ashtrays on the armrests. There were a dozen other men, all wearing military uniforms and puffing away on filtered cigarettes. From the aroma Pak knew they must be Japanese Seven Stars. The tension he was feeling made him want to smoke too, but as he was reaching for the cigarettes in his uniform pocket he remembered that they were of the pungent Chinese variety and abandoned the idea. The men in this projection room probably all smoked Seven Stars on a daily basis.

Other than a desk in front of the screen, there were no other furnishings. The floor was spotless. The oddest thing of all was the absence on the walls of any photographs of the Great Leader and his son. It was the first time Pak had ever been in a room that lacked them. Preparations for evacuation in the event of an invasion from the South called for rescuing these images first. The fact that there were none present here suggested that this was a place where no such ritual items were necessary.

"We are about to show you a rather unusual film."

From the projector came a whirring sound, as the presentation began. A stout man on Pak's left cleared his throat and stubbed out a cigarette. Glancing casually at his face, he recognized Choi Deok Cheol. Choi was now dressed in a military uniform, but three years earlier, when Pak had seen him at a banquet held at the special events hall in the Taesong District of the Workers Party, he had been wearing a smart and expensive double-breasted suit like nothing Pak had ever seen before. People who could risk wearing that sort of thing in the Republic were few and far between. Choi had for a long time been in charge of operations against the South for the Party Secretariat's External Liaison Office and also ran the Moran Trading Company, which came under the jurisdiction of the General Staff Office Operations Department of the People's Army. Pak's palms had begun to sweat as the screen lit up and the film began.

The story, set during World War II, involved a special-operations scheme initiated by the Nazis. The language was English, with no Korean subtitles or dubbing. The opening scene featured a long-faced American performing some comical stunt with a dog, and then saying that training a dog was much like training a woman. At this, all of the men in the room guffawed. This, Pak noted, meant that

45

they all understood spoken English—a rare skill in the Republic. He didn't puzzle over this, however, as he soon became engrossed in the film. The story was an interesting one.

It began with the hatching of a zany idea by a low-ranking Nazi staff officer. The idea, though summarily rejected by the general staff, happens to come to the attention of Hitler himself, who arranges for it to be made immediately operational. A company of Sonderkommandos is embedded in a group of Jewish refugees on a passenger ship to New York, where they land and occupy Manhattan. They are wearing army uniforms but proclaim themselves to be anti-Nazi activists who have escaped from Hitler's rule and come to New York to establish a new regime. Hitler declares that they are indeed rebels and informs the Allies that it is of no concern to him if they shoot them all as spies. But a number of citizens are being held as virtual hostages, and the American military can do nothing. Hitler, meanwhile, has a hidden agenda for the "rebels." A group of preselected men within the corps, volunteers willing to sacrifice their lives, are sent to Washington to assassinate Roosevelt and other prominent politicians. One of the group falls in love with a cafe waitress, is taken prisoner, and goes over to the other side. The insurgent unit is crushed and its members killed. At the end of the movie, Hitler is seen laughing as he tells the story to those in his inner circle, his only regret being that such a promising operation did not succeed.

The end credits rolled and the lights in the room came on, followed by the sound of the film being rewound. Kim Gweon Cheol took up a position in front of the screen.

"Comrade Ri Dong Ho, what did you think of it?" he said to a thin man in his early fifties, who was sitting in the middle of the first row. Ri, a leading figure in the Party Secretariat's Operations Department, had control of investment banks and trading companies in Rajin, Sonbong, and Sinuiju. Stroking his chin, he replied that he'd found the film very entertaining.

"But I wonder if I might ask why this particular group of comrades has been selected to view it."

Ri turned in his seat and looked at Pak Yong Su as he said this. Pak realized now that he was, in fact, the focus of attention for everyone around him. All their faces were familiar: men with whom he had been at university, men with whom he had worked as a political officer in the GPB. What all of them, including Ri and Choi, had in common was involvement in one form or another in external sabotage operations. In the first row were Gong Chang Su, former director of the foreign section of the Policy Affairs Institute concerned with the printing of counterfeit US dollars and money-laundering; Kim Su Gweon, formerly of the GPB's socio-cultural department, who had devised the plan for the mausoleum bombing in Rangoon; and Hwang Pung Gu, a political officer attached to the command center of the Capital Air Defense Corps and the director of a training school for anti-Japanese operations. In the second row was Ri Hyeong Sup, head of the Academy of Sciences' Central Communications Company and chief administrator of all of the Republic's Internet servers. To Ri's right sat Kim Chang Bok, who gathered and analyzed information on the American military presence in Japan and the Japanese Self-Defense Force as a political officer in the Fourth Department of the People's Army's Main Intelligence and Reconnaissance Bureau; and to his left sat Yim Gang San, a political officer attached to MIRB's Yellow Sea Fleet Command Center, where he managed the smuggling of shipbuilding materials through the Chinese and Russian mafia. Next to Pak was Choi Ho Gyeong, who served on the nuclear-negotiations team with the US State Department in the 1990s while covertly reporting on the proceedings to the External Liaison Office for which he worked. And next to Choi was Shin Dong Won of the KPA Defense Security Command who worked in a section primarily responsible for the stationing and transfer of troops.

Such was the gathering here in the projection room. It was the crème de la crème, men in their forties and fifties, representative of those members of the reformist faction who had survived the pressure of the anti-American hardliners. With the eyes of all these men upon him, Pak felt gooseflesh creeping up his back and down both arms. It was a sensation quite unlike any he'd ever experienced before: as if his very skin had suddenly grasped the reason this group had been brought together. Pak Yong Su probably possessed the most complete command of the Japanese language of anyone in the Republic, and everybody here knew that. He felt as though, when they looked at him, what they saw *was* Japan.

"A rebel army faction that isn't a rebel army faction," said Kim Gweon Cheol from his place in front of the screen. "The Organization and Guidance Department has approved the plan to send such a combat team to a city overseas."

Someone in the audience struck a match. A city overseas... that could only mean a city in Japan. Pak now realized that he was present at the birth of a momentous operation. He was sure of this, and it filled him with the same sort of anxiety and excitement the birth of a child would. As a political officer in the Fifth Division of the Special Operations Forces Guidance Bureau, he had been involved in more sabotage operations than he could count, but they had been planned by the People's Army, not by those in Building 3.

*A rebel army faction that isn't a rebel army faction.* Everyone was muttering and thinking about these words. They seemed to have struck a chord. The twelve men assembled here were now at the center of an epoch-making stratagem. As men, as soldiers, as Party members, privileged to have been born in the Republic, what could be a greater thrill than this? All sabotage projects were nominally subject to authorization by the Party Central Committee, but in practice, formal procedures were bypassed. This was because every agency involved in such operations had its own troops and funding. Moreover, as a universal principle, authorization was inimical to successful intrigue: nowhere did parliaments or cabinets debate the advisability or justification of clandestine undertakings and then approve them. Plotters loved to conceal and loathed to reveal, and their plans were thus never the work of the national body as a whole. Nor was there ever a clear or unified chain of command. The constant risk of disclosure ruled out any elaborate hierarchy, while absolutely requiring the cooperative interaction of a complex network of lateral organizations.

A case in point was the Kennedy assassination, in which a number of rightist groups were thought to have been involved, including conservatives in the government, the Department of Defense, the military, retired members of the military, the CIA, and the FBI, as well as the mafia, Cuban refugees, local police, and foreign mercenaries. That is to say that there was neither a single, unified organization, nor a chain of command. Everything was compartmentalized, each group being responsible for its own role and unaware of who was leading other groups and even what they were doing. It was basically the same for Islamic extremists and other international terrorist organizations. There were groups that did the groundwork, groups that collected data, groups that constructed bombs, groups that transported fuses, groups that rehearsed the actual bombings, groups that housed the perpetrators until the day of the operation, groups that arranged for vehicles, groups that rigged the explosives to the vehicles, and so on, with the tasks of each parceled out in great detail. Each group did only what it was assigned to do and had nothing to do with the others. On the day itself, the only ones present were those who carried out the actual bombing; everyone else had left the country.

"Now then, Professor Pak," said Kim Gweon Cheol. "How many members of the Special Operations Forces have a thorough knowledge of Japanese?"

Pak thought for a moment what the definition of "thorough" might be. Rephrasing the question, he replied, "If by that you mean those who can pass for native speakers of the language, I'm afraid there are none, unless we begin training some of our Chongryon compatriots. Do you intend to infiltrate deep-cover agents?"

Chongryon was the General Association of Korean Residents in Japan, commonly perceived as the de facto North Korean embassy there. Kim explained that this was not what he meant, that what was called for was good comprehension, not flawless speech. It was not to be a deep-cover operation; the commandos would be operating in secret until landing, but from that point on they would be relying on force of arms. In other words, he added, they would not have to be able to impersonate Japanese. All that was needed was a sufficient grasp of the language to allow them to carry out their mission.

The first man Pak thought of was Han Seung Jin. Han was exceptionally talented, as shown not only in his command of Japanese but in his fighting prowess and, above all, his leadership skills. Eight other current SOF members came to mind, all former students of his with some expertise in the language. "One short of ten," he replied to the initial question. "Only nine?" Kim muttered and then, smiling wryly: "Well, it can't be helped. We'll have to make do with what we've got." An officer from the Defense Security Command brought Kim a map, which he unfolded on the desk in front of him. It was on a scale of a million to one and displayed the northern half of Kyushu and the Korean Peninsula. "The operation will consist of three phases," Kim explained. "In Phase One, the nine commandos will slip into the country and occupy certain facilities. Phase Two begins two hours later, when we drop in four SOF companies by air and secure a beachhead. This will involve not sandbags or trenches but rather the blood and lives of Japanese."

"Which city are we talking about?" Ri Dong Ho asked. Hwang Pung Gu pointed at the tip of Kyushu on the map.

"Probably there: Fukuoka."

The four units were to establish a foothold in a residential district and secure it until the arrival of the main force, which would carry out Phase Three: one hundred and twenty thousand troops landing in Hakata Bay by sea. The figure caused a ripple of excited murmurs and a general fumbling for cigarettes. "A rebel army faction that isn't a rebel army faction." Kim Chang Bok, on Pak's right, repeated the words as he slowly exhaled the smoke of a Seven Stars cigarette. "If it's a rebel army faction, neither the Americans nor the South can justifiably attack the Republic," he said, nodding repeatedly. "The Republic will announce that this isn't the work of the People's Army but rather a terrorist attack by a mutinous faction. The South and the US will have to hold back, and since Japan's own constitution renounces war, the Self-Defense Force won't be able to attack us either. If by some accident Pyongyang should come under attack, there would be full-scale war, and Seoul would be a sea of fire within thirty minutes. No one wants that—not the South, not the US, and equally not China or Russia." It was a well-founded plan, and Pak Yong Su could not contain his excitement. Their southern neighbors would not be harmed, and the homeland would go unscathed. The battle was to take place overseas. Blood might flow, and towns might be destroyed, but only in the country that had once ruled the Fatherland and forcibly displaced countless numbers of people, creating the cause for their partition: that hated land, Japan.

"Will we need the cooperation of our compatriots over there?"

This question came from Gong Chang Su. He was referring to the General Association of Korean Residents in Japan. Kim Gweon Cheol shook his head.

"Even if Chongryon offers its assistance after the four companies have occupied Fukuoka, we will refuse. Any further attempt to link up with us will be forcibly blocked. Let me remind you: this plan has already been approved by the Organization and Guidance Department. In the first place, there is the danger of leaks. Chongryon is under constant surveillance by the Japanese intelligence agencies and has been infiltrated. Also, since first-generation Korean residents have all but disappeared, the character of the organization has changed. Most of the younger generation have much the same mentality now as the Japanese and as a result of public outrage over the abduction of Japanese citizens have been losing any loyalty they felt toward the Fatherland, especially since the Pyongyang Declaration. Just as the Dear Leader is always saying: 'The wolf raised by dogs becomes a dog.' Members of Chongryon will consequently be given no special privileges whatsoever; they will be treated in the same way as the Japanese.

"I will go over this with each of you later, but the operation will differ in each phase; leaders will be selected, as will a temporary command structure, and from the moment that the hundred and twenty thousand troops enter Hakata Bay, the job is done. The crucial point to remember is that it is not the Republic that is invading Japan."

Shin Dong Won, nodding vigorously, whispered to Choi Ho Gyeong, "I wonder which division will be sent to Fukuoka in Phase Three." Choi considered for a moment, then smiled meaningfully and muttered: "Perhaps the Fourth Division, or the SOF Eighth Corps." The two units he mentioned, both led by officers of the conservative, hardline faction, were seen as possible barriers to future reunification. There had been endless rumors of a possible *coup d'état*, with the SOF Eighth Corps prominent in the intrigue; and the Party leadership was intent on keeping these divisions in check. The corps commander sent to Fukuoka would be assured that calling it a rebel army faction was only a subterfuge to prevent counterattack and that if the Republic labeled him a traitor it was only for purposes of deception. Hardline officers who feared that reunification would leave them out in the cold ought to be thrilled to be entrusted with the grand and noble task of invading Fukuoka.

"What is the goal of the mission?" asked Yim Gang San, but Ri Hyeong Sup said that perhaps there was no need to decide on one, and both Kim Gweon Cheol and Choi Deok Cheol loudly concurred.

If the rebel army faction and the United States wound up in a standoff, Pak reflected, that would be an accomplishment in itself. To succeed in transferring the buffer zone between China and the United States from the Peninsula to Kyushu would be enough. There was little risk of fighting the US forces stationed in Japan. And the Japanese government would have neither the strategy nor the courage to start a war embroiling the citizens of Fukuoka. Japan might even let Fukuoka go, severing all ties with it. "If Japan hadn't mismanaged its economy, this operation would not have been possible," Ri Dong Ho said under his breath. "Japan didn't mismanage its economy," replied Choi Ho Gyeong, displaying the discernment he'd cultivated in Washington. "But in any country, once vested interests have gone bad, it's very difficult to revitalize an economy. In Japan's case, it was critical to close down the financially draining quasi-government corporations, but when this proved impossible, the much easier path of constitutional revision was chosen. To use an analogy, it's similar to when a corporation is unable to produce profits and simply gives up on that and turns to fiddling with its corporate philosophy. Japan is a dying elephant that lacked the will to heal itself."

Hwang Pung Gu raised his hand to ask if a name had been chosen for the operation. Kim Gweon Cheol spread both arms to call for quiet and said, with a smile, "It has." There was only one man in the Republic who could give this operation a name. Kim puffed out his chest and looked around the room as he proudly revealed it: "From the Fatherland, with Love."

# A MISSED SIGN

*March 3, 2011*
*Tokyo*

S uzuki norikazu flinched at the cold air outside the exit to Kasumigaseki subway station. Feeling the chill on his neck, he sneezed as he set off down the road. The government district was thronged with demonstrators, from right-wingers in their campaign trucks to civil-rights groups and labor unionists, all yelling through bullhorns, vying with one another to be heard. Awfully cold for March, Suzuki thought to himself. He felt like joining in the shouting. He hadn't been getting enough sleep lately and could feel himself coming down with a cold. He should have worn a muffler. That morning he'd sent his thirteen-year-old daughter a bouquet of flowers complete with a free *hina* doll via an Internet florist. She had remained with his ex-wife after the divorce five years ago, and Suzuki had resolved to send her flowers every year on her birthday. Ever since elementary school she had grumbled about it being on March 3, coinciding with the Doll Festival held for Girls' Day, which meant she had to make do with one celebration instead of two. Each time he sent the flowers, he was reminded that it was already March and spring had almost arrived. Over the years the connection had become fixed in his mind, and although the weather forecast that morning had warned that the temperature was ten degrees lower than normal for the time of year, he'd left home without a scarf.

Suzuki worked in the Cabinet Intelligence and Research Office, commonly known as CIRO. For the past few years they had been steadily cutting back on staff, suspending new recruitment, and transferring some existing personnel, so that by last April the workforce had shrunk from more than a hundred and fifty to fewer than a hundred and twenty. Taking time off work for a cold now would merely add to the flak already being directed at employees like himself who had come from the private sector. All the ministries and government offices in Kasumigaseki were being restructured, not just the Cabinet Office and the Home Affairs Ministry. Whenever he got together with colleagues, the conversation would always turn gloomily to rumors of the retirement fund drying up within five years.

Hunching against the wind, he joined the swarm making its way toward the various government buildings. On opposite sides of the road outside the Cabinet Office, right-wingers and labor unionists were trying to outshout each other in their tirades against the government and bureaucrats. The rightists were calling for Japan to arm itself with nuclear weapons and revive the military draft, so that it could stop kowtowing to America and China and become a truly sovereign nation. The unions, meanwhile, howled that adhering to Article Nine of the Constitution was essential to maintain peace and protect jobs. Both sides, however, were united in their hatred of the present administration.

The herd of civil servants, Suzuki among them, scurried along to their various offices, trying to ignore the blaring loudspeakers. For a number of years the economy had been in sharp decline, leading to an unprecedented recession coupled with inflation. As a last resort bank accounts had been frozen to save the financial system, but this had devastated the money markets. A regulated economy was anathema to foreign investors, and they had abandoned the Japanese market in droves. Businesses had undergone ruthless downsizing in an attempt to survive, and the number of suicides among middle-aged and senior citizens had almost doubled. It wasn't only the rightists and labor unions that loathed the bureaucrats, whose jobs and monthly salaries were secure.

"Good morning," Suzuki greeted the security guard at the entrance to the Ministry, sneezing again as he showed his pass.

"You all right, sir?" asked the elderly guard, his familiar face creasing in a concerned smile. "I always use these meself," he added, pulling out several pocket warmers from his jacket. "With those guys around, it somehow feels a whole lot colder." Behind him was an armored vehicle and several Self-Defense Force soldiers in combat gear. The thick steel panels of the heavy camouflaged truck really did seem to emanate a chill. Following the freeze on bank deposits, Molotov cocktails had been thrown at the Ministry of Finance, a bomb was planted in the Prime Minister's official residence, and last summer there had been an Islamic fundamentalist-style suicide bombing outside the National Diet building. The explosion hadn't been large enough to cause a major tragedy, but it had led to emergency legislation allowing deployment of the SDF to guard the Diet, government offices, and other key facilities such as nuclear power stations.

The Self-Defense Force was isolated in its relations with East Asia and the wider international community, and even its dealings with US forces stationed in Japan had soured. The freeze on bank accounts had been precipitated by the pensions crisis as the baby-boomer generation of civil servants began reaching retirement age. Local government bonds together with investment and loan bonds had gone into free fall, and interest rates on national bonds had shot up. Inflation and recession hit at the same time, anxiety and discontent spiraled, and resentment simmered nationwide. In order to stay in power, last year the government had tilted toward expanding the military, provoking strong warnings and opposition from America and Europe as well as China, Russia, and South Korea. Many who had lost their life savings, and the politicians who depended on their support, were in favor of amending the Constitution to allow a military build-up and nuclear armament as a means of salvaging national pride. This faction held sway despite calls for international

56

cooperation from financial circles and liberal politicians. The more isolated Japan became, the more people disillusioned by financial hardship were drawn to a hardline point of view.

For the past five years, the United States had been redeploying its overseas armed forces, and the number of its troops based in Japan had already been halved. The financial and trade deficits had ballooned under the War on Terror, causing the dollar to plummet and effectively ending American global hegemony. The new administration formed by the Democrats sought more collaborative ties with Europe, China, and Russia. It joined China and Russia in expressing grave concern over Japan's nuclear armament, and hinted at revoking the Japan-US Security Treaty while also indicating its willingness to end the embargo on weapons sales to China and abandon the Japan-US joint missile defense system. It then announced a hike in the price of feed grain to Japan, which was still reeling from depleted foreign reserves due to the drop in value of the yen. This was taken to mean that America would not give any aid to Japan in the event of food or energy crises—which were in fact already happening. This sudden U-turn provoked indignation even among the most pro-American politicians and media, and Japan-US relations cooled almost overnight. The reality was, however, that the US had been unable for some time now to maintain its position as the world's single economic and military superpower, and it had effectively given up its role as the world's policeman. It was also pushing for collective-security agreements in East Asia between China, South Korea, and Japan, and even North Korea and Russia, but in Japan this was misinterpreted by the media and a large portion of the population, who felt that they'd been abandoned. Politicians found themselves unable to check the rising tide of anti-Americanism.

The SDF soldiers stood with their Type 89 assault rifles at the ready, making no attempt at eye contact with the stream of employees entering the building. It was as if they were cut-outs. Suzuki had come to recognize some of them, but they never responded to his greetings. Soon after they'd been deployed, he had tried asking one young soldier, who remained standing motionless in the same spot every morning for hours, where he went for lunch. The soldier hadn't answered—hadn't even looked at him. There was strong opposition amongst employees to being guarded by the SDF, and many in the mass media were also critical. Suzuki thought that some minimal communication might help matters. They didn't need to go so far as sharing a joke or anything, but as it was the soldiers were just too unnaturally distant from those they were guarding. If a terrorist attack did happen, some level of cooperation would be necessary; establishing some basic connection from the start would make things easier.

On reflection, though, it wasn't just the relationship between the SDF guards and employees that was unnatural. Even politicians and bureaucrats in the various ministries and agencies, not to mention in CIRO itself, seemed incapable of maintaining normal civility and communicating appropriately among themselves. It wasn't that they were openly hostile to one another, but their relationships tended to be either generally uncooperative or artificially chummy.

"Suzuki-san, would you mind handing this up to the Chief?" No sooner had he sat down at his desk than Yoshida, of the International Division's Exchange Section, passed him a printout of an email from the US National Security Agency. "What's it say?" Suzuki asked, then sneezed three times in succession. "Caught a cold?" The huge office, some fifty square meters in size, was freezing. "Forgot my muffler," he said. "Chilly in here, isn't it?" Yoshida nodded. "They're getting mean with the heating. It's the cost-cutting drive." He opened his mouth and sent out a puff of white breath to prove his point. Suzuki decided to keep his coat on.

The email Yoshida had given him confirmed that the US NSA had officially admitted the existence of the major surveillance network known as ECHELON. "Handing it up" was office jargon for the process of sending information up through the various stages of the hierarchy. At just thirty years old, Yoshida was ten years Suzuki's junior, and like Suzuki he had come from the private sector. Suzuki agreed to pass the email on, but Yoshida remained standing there.

"I dunno," he muttered, glancing at the Chief sitting at his big desk by the window. Suzuki looked at him questioningly. "What's up?"

"Think about it," Yoshida said, pretending they were discussing some papers on Suzuki's desk. "The budget for our own IGS Center was approved on the basis of ECHELON."

"I suppose it was." Suzuki knew what he was getting at. ECHELON was the vast surveillance system operated by government agencies in five countries: America's NSA, the UK's GCHQ, Canada's CSE, Australia's ADSCS, and New Zealand's GCSB. Telephone calls, faxes, and emails worldwide were intercepted and analyzed for certain specified keywords, and transferred to a database. A super-computer known as Dictionary automatically logged the sender and recipient of any emails containing words such as "US President," "assassination," "bomb," "Hamas," and so forth. These key words covered everything related to the national interests of the countries concerned, from politics, public security, the UN, and the economy, to campaigns by environmentalists and civil-rights activists. This involved an enormous amount of data. It had been manageable when email was still only used by a limited number of people, but with the growth of the Net in China, India, and other developing countries, costs had snowballed. Even just inputting different languages into Dictionary cost a fortune—and then armies of translators were needed to decipher the results. Plus there were cases of civil-rights and anti-US/UK organizations sending out mass spam emails containing terms that would be picked up by Dictionary so that it overloaded and crashed—which happened frequently, each time incurring major costs to get it up and running again.

And now the NSA had not only blown the cover of ECHELON but also announced they would henceforth be limiting the range of intercepted communications. It was common knowledge that the high-tech system at Japan's Information Gathering Satellite Center was modeled on ECHELON at the urging of the US. It had been heralded as the world's newest IGS system, with antennas erected in a vast tract of land east of Tomakomai, Hokkaido, with technical assistance from American corporations. It had cost a whopping thirty billion yen, but here it was, not yet even fully functioning and now faced with the main ECHELON network being made obsolete.

"We won't be able to laugh this one off. It will get handed up to the Chief Cabinet Secretary, won't it?"

"Well, that's not for me to say," Suzuki replied. He collated information from the various sections and handed anything important to the International Division Chief, who in turn passed it on to CIRO's Director of Communications, who again vetted it before sending it on to the Chief Cabinet Secretary. As had long been the custom, the International Division Chief had come from the National Police Agency. What Yoshida was getting at was that this information, which was bound to complicate matters in the global community, would end up in the hands of old-timers who still saw any threat to the nation only in terms of the extreme right or extreme left.

"The sooner you become Chief, the better—that's what everyone my age thinks."

"All right, all right. Get back to work," said Suzuki, aware of the Chief's eye on them. The Chief was in his fifties and had followed an elite career path through Tokyo University and the NPA's Security Bureau, but unlike Suzuki and Yoshida he had few overseas connections and was weak on foreign languages, aside from a smattering of Chinese that he'd picked up as a hobby. In this age of international terrorist networks, it was obvious that the anti-terrorist authorities also needed international knowledge and experience, yet Kasumigaseki hadn't changed one bit in the last thirty years—even the old seniority system was still in place. The Chief himself was well aware of all this and prickly about the obvious fact that Suzuki was more suited to the job than him. Suzuki was from a family with three generations of police officers, starting with his great-grandfather, but had broken with tradition to start out in a major trading company, dealing first in paper pulp from Alaska and Latin America, and then Middle Eastern oil. He had come under the spotlight when he won a prize for his analysis of the Israel-Palestine deadlock at a conference attended by delegates from think tanks around the world, and subsequently, at his father's prompting, he had taken a post in Kasumigaseki.

He was no longer sneezing; perhaps he hadn't caught a cold after all. He spent the morning sorting through all the reports handed up to him by the various sections in charge of trade, exchange, Southeast Asia, the Americas, and so on. There were also a few from the Domestic Division and Economics Department. As deputy leader of the Cabinet Crisis-Management Center's General Affairs Section, Suzuki's job consisted essentially of collecting, analyzing, and classifying information. He vetted reports from the domestic and international media, and handed anything important up through the hierarchy.

Within CIRO, Suzuki was generally considered an expert on foreign affairs, although he hadn't in fact spent all that much time abroad other than short business trips. His couple of months in Chile and half a year in Bahrain hardly compared, for example, to Yoshida's two years in Frankfurt, year and a half in New York, two and a half years in Geneva, and stays in Southeast Asia and West Africa. Suzuki himself thought that he wasn't so much an authority on foreign matters as simply very good at gathering and analyzing information. You could grasp pretty much everything that was going on through data that was publicly available. Especially in America and Western Europe, almost everything you needed to know could be picked up from magazines, newspapers, and the Internet. It was only in movies and novels that spies risked their lives to steal important secrets behind enemy lines. Page one of training manuals for new recruits in many intelligence agencies around the world stated that you could get ninety-nine per cent of the necessary information about a country just by sifting through its magazines and newspapers, and it was true.

"Suzuki, have you got a moment?" He was just digging into a sandwich for lunch when the Chief called him over to his desk by the window. He peered through his thick glasses at the reports Suzuki had handed up that morning, while the latter gazed in distaste at his superior's tie, with its oversized white polka dots. "In simple terms, what is this about?" The Chief held up the email from the NSA. It was in English, but there was of course a Japanese translation attached. The word "tapping" had been used instead of "surveillance," but the important thing was that the existence of the vast spy network ECHELON, until now top secret, had been acknowledged by the most secretive organ of the US government, the NSA. This, in and of itself, was evidence that the network had ceased to be effective. Suzuki explained this to the Chief, choosing his words carefully to avoid sounding patronizing. The trick was to precede his comments with phrases such as "As you know," or "As I'm sure you're aware…"

"How come it's marked Top Priority?"

The idiot doesn't want to hand it up to the Cabinet, thought Suzuki. Any fool could immediately infer from the email that ECHELON was now obsolete. Some of the Cabinet and bureaucrats responsible for approving the Japanese IGS system were still in government and in CIRO itself, and while the thirty billion yen would not be entirely wasted, the news, if leaked, would be grist to the mill of the factions within the government that had been against it, as well as the opposition parties and the media. And if there was anything to be gained by leaking information, you could be sure someone would leak it.

"Well, it's from the NSA and it's about ECHELON, so I believe it is of some urgency," Suzuki said, hoping the other would see that ignoring the matter now could lead to trouble later.

The Chief made a sour face and was about to deliver a rebuttal, when a black object swooped into the edge of Suzuki's field of vision. Turning toward the window he saw a large black bird gliding through the gap in the buildings opposite and heading for them at breakneck speed. It frantically flapped its wings and long gray tail in an attempt to avoid crashing, but hit the window with the sound of a plastic water bottle being crushed underfoot. A new girl in the economics section who sat at a desk by the window shrieked and jumped to her feet. It must have sounded to her like a gunshot.

FROM THE FATHERLAND, WITH LOVE

"Another bird?" muttered the Chief looking up briefly, before immediately returning to the document.

Suzuki went over to the window and watched the bird, now some distance below, flying groggily away. The rooftop garden of a private building diagonally opposite CIRO was reflected in the window, and birds would crash into it from time to time, leaving splattered stains on the glass. The new girl came over and stood next to him. "What was *that*?"

The Chief decided the email about ECHELON should remain on file in the General Affairs Section. When Suzuki emailed Yoshida to this effect, he received a one-word reply: *Shit!* As the US was fond of pointing out, the various intelligence services in Japan had no history of sharing information, and there was no system in place for integrating intelligence. In the event of an emergency or major disaster, it fell to the Security Council to collate information and direct the appropriate response to the crisis, but the various intelligence agencies lacked the channels for passing information to the Council in the first place. Why didn't the Japanese government take intelligence seriously? Foreigners often asked Suzuki this question, but he was unable to give a good answer.

With the number of homeless people having increased fourfold, a rapidly rising suicide rate, unemployment approaching ten per cent, and an enormous jump in youth crime, civil order was expected to continue to deteriorate, but the budgets of the intelligence services had been the first to be cut. The most talented bureaucrats in Kasumigaseki were basically concentrated in the agencies dealing with economic affairs. This might be due to the constitutional renunciation of war and the post-war drive for economic development, or possibly even to the indelible association of the words "intelligence" and "civil order" with the dark image of the pre-war special police. But Suzuki thought there was a simpler reason for it: that it simply wasn't seen as necessary and therefore wasn't considered important. Japan had no history of invasion by foreign countries, and was not composed of different ethnic groups with conflicting interests. For centuries domestic relations had been far more important than foreign ones, and the country was simply unable to adapt to the changed circumstances.

By the afternoon, documents were piling up on Suzuki's desk. There was a summary of a report from a British newspaper on the three-way split between the Sunnis, Shia, and Kurds in Iraq; a Macao newspaper article about armed Islamic-militant groups in the Philippines; a report from the homepage of a US West Coast radio station on a number of shooting rampages; an exposé in an Italian magazine of the Israeli source of funds for the Russian mafia controlling the world of professional sports; a newspaper published by North Korean refugees living in north-eastern China; an article in a weekly magazine about the spread of extremist groups amongst Japan's homeless; a Qatar newspaper report on alliances between extremists in Egypt and Saudi Arabia; the newsletter of an NGO that was digging wells in Afghanistan; an essay on Pakistan's secret police by a British university professor; and a printout of an American electric-power company's website that had been taken over by a Brazilian hacker who'd uploaded photos of a morbidly obese woman engaged in bestial sex. Suzuki's stomach churned at the images of the fat woman tangling with a stallion's penis.

Next was a report in a right-wing South Korean tabloid that was known for its scathing criticism of North Korea but occasionally ran information on the North that you couldn't find in mainstream papers. It was this same minor publication that had shocked the world with a scoop on North Korea's sudden acceptance of the inspection of its nuclear facilities. Now it was claiming that North Korea was up to something, even if its only proof for this was that no military activity at all had been observed there for the past two months. Kim Jong Il was known to regularly move troops around, although it was unclear whether he did this to maintain a state of alert or to forestall any attempt at a *coup d'état*. But according to the tabloid there had been no movements or maneuvers whatsoever for the past couple of months. "It's probably just too cold," muttered

Suzuki with a wry smile, recalling that North Korea was currently in the grip of its coldest winter for thirty years.

An article on the back page of the tabloid caught his eye. He read it, and then read it again, his head tilted to one side. Something about it bothered him. It was a report on spy boats shipping out of North Korean ports in large numbers over the past two weeks. But why should this catch his attention? There was nothing very unusual about it.

"Kawai, could I have a word?"

Kawai, of the Korean Affairs Section, had studied contemporary East Asian history, Mandarin, and Korean at universities in China and South Korea. He also had connections with an NPO that provided assistance to refugees from North Korea.

"This came from you, right?" Suzuki said, indicating the paper in his hand.

"Yes." Kawai was short and skinny and gave the impression of being rather weak, but his attitude was vaguely defiant. His was the type of personality least suited to the work of a bureaucrat.

"This isn't the first time there's been a concentration of spy boats in and around ports over a particular period, is it?"

"No, it isn't," Kawai said, adding that there had been similar incidents on at least eight occasions in the last five years. He even specified when and for how long.

Suzuki wondered what it was about this report that made him feel uneasy. Something had caught his eye, but he couldn't say what or why.

"It's just that this time it's a little different," said Kawai.

"How's that?"

"Every time this has happened before, a number of the spy boats have zigzagged in and out of Japanese waters, checking the timing of the patrol boats and keeping an eye on Coast Guard movements. This time, they haven't done any of that."

"So what do you make of it?"

Kawai looked up at the ceiling and was quiet for a while, but finally shook his head. "I don't know."

"But you're sure that it's something new?"

"Yes. Although it's also possible that the Coast Guard just failed to spot such activity. This is the high season for fishing off our west coast, and there are a lot of fishing boats out. If North Korean boats blend in with all the others around the fishing grounds, there's no way of telling them apart. What's more, there've been a lot of days with poor visibility recently, because of the weather."

Listening to this plausible-sounding explanation, Suzuki felt his doubts recede. He often felt uneasy about something or other in the vast amount of information he processed every day. Sometimes his unease was justified, sometimes it proved groundless.

"Thank you," he said. Kawai bowed and went back to his desk.

Suzuki quickly glanced over at the Chief's desk by the window to check if he'd been seen talking to Kawai, but the desk was empty. His gaze moved to the window next to it, and suddenly he realized what it was that had been nagging at him just now. There were stains on the glass from where birds had flown into it. When a bird had hit the window at lunchtime while he was talking to the Chief, the only person who had shown any surprise was the new girl in the economics section. Nobody, least of all the Chief, had paid any attention to it; they were all used to seeing birds crashing into the glass. If you encounter the same situation over and over again, it becomes so familiar you no longer notice. It occurred to Suzuki that something similar might be at work here. Perhaps the North Koreans were deliberately repeating the same actions in order to cover up something else, allaying suspicion by frequently dispatching large numbers of ships. It was just a hunch, however, and the Chief was unlikely to take it seriously. He sighed and put the report in the "done" tray.

INTRODUCTION 2

# THOSE WHO WAIT

*March 19, 2011*
*Fukuoka City, Kyushu*

"HEY, TATENO!"

He wasn't used to hearing his name spoken. Since leaving home, he'd rarely even told anyone what it was. In police stations and reformatories, it was always the first thing they asked him. *What's your name? What do they call you? A kid your age, you don't know your own name?* He wouldn't reveal it even when they threatened or beat him, which made them decide he wasn't right in the head. Not wanting to tell people your name—was that really so strange? It must scare them. Stating your name was the first step to submission.

"Tateno!" It was Shinohara, a guy who kept poisonous frogs and spiders and scorpions and things. None of the people here, from Ishihara down, had ever asked Tateno his name. Whenever one of them paused in the course of conversation, as if wondering what to call him, he'd simply say, "I'm Tateno"—information he hadn't offered freely to anyone since elementary school. Within three months everyone knew what his name was, and he had absorbed everyone else's in the same informal way.

Now that he thought about it, that man Nobue—the one in the homeless park with the ugly scar who'd told him about this place—hadn't asked his name either. The man had given him Ishihara's phone number, and Tateno had hitchhiked and sneaked free rides on trains all the way to Fukuoka. "I was sent here by a guy named Nobue," he'd announced. All Ishihara said in reply was, "Oh yeah?" Nobody stared at him. Nobody asked his age or where he was from, or anything else. No one here had much interest in things like that.

Tateno was sixteen and figured Shinohara was two or three years older. But he had no idea how old Ishihara might be. Ishihara was a small person who at times might have passed for a high-school student and at others looked seventy. His eyes were always sleepy, but there was something absolutely magnetic about him. According to Shinohara, he was a poet who'd won several big awards. Tateno thought he'd like to read his poems sometime. It was Ishihara who had shown him to this room that first day and said, "You'll have to share the place, but you can handle that, right?" He wouldn't have to pay any rent, of course, and he could always get something to eat over in Ishihara's quarters. Apparently a lot of the guys living here had part-time jobs or other ways of earning a little spare cash. Tateno knew he'd been accepted into the group because of Nobue's introduction. It was clear that Ishihara wouldn't let just anyone in.

"Hey, Tateno!"

He put down the book he was reading and opened the door. Shinohara's face was as smooth as a hard-boiled egg. "You hungry?" he asked, and handed him an enamel pot decorated with a flower design. "I made some chicken stew. Help yourself. It'd be great if you could wash the pot when you're done." He was wearing a coat and a backpack, and Tateno asked him where he was going. "To the shrine in the woods," Shinohara said, without looking back. Probably to catch ants and other bugs, Tateno realized. "Would it be all right if I came up there later?" he called after him. "Sure," the other said, turning the corner in the corridor and disappearing from view.

When Tateno stepped back into the room, Hino was beginning to stir on the upper bunk. "Morning," Hino said, and he returned the greeting. It was nearly noon, but Hino always slept twelve hours or more. He was from Nagoya. When he was six, his salaryman father had bought a new house in a suburban development there. His mother had adjusted badly to the move, complaining of the house's synthetic building materials, and suffered a breakdown. She became convinced that poison had been mixed into the wall paint, and what with one thing and another she ended up blinding her husband by spraying undiluted disinfectant in his face, then stabbing him eighteen times with a knife. Before she cut her own throat she tried to kill seven-year-old Hino as well, but he escaped with only a stab wound to the shoulder. Having been repeatedly told of the danger lurking in painted walls and urged not to breathe near them, Hino always felt drowsy or lethargic indoors. He was placed in an orphanage, but when he was thirteen he poured gasoline on the floor and started a fire that resulted in the deaths of four people who worked there.

After that he was put in a juvenile detention center, from which he escaped twice. Using a fake ID he found jobs at various construction sites, mainly working on high-rises. He felt comfortable inside the unpainted concrete walls of the buildings-in-progress and chose to sleep wrapped in blankets on the bare concrete floors rather than in the workers' barracks. Hino loved skyscrapers. He thought of them as living things—the way they grew, gradually changing shape as they reached for the sky. Not as *if* they were living things; he believed they were literally alive. "Think about it," he'd once told Tateno. "If an alien from space looked at your average high-rise building, why wouldn't he think it was some sort of life form?"

According to Hino, a building's electrical wiring and plumbing and air ducts were exactly like the blood vessels and organs and nerves you have in the human body. It was particularly the "respiratory system"—vents, ductwork, and so on—that interested him, and his supervisors had often told him he should try for a license as an air-conditioning engineer or a pipe-fitter. He knew that if he did that, however, they'd find out he was lying about his age. At sixteen he was found out anyway, on a construction site in Shinagawa, and

69

sent back to the detention center. Unable to bear life confined within walls, Hino used a steel pipe to bludgeon a probation officer, and this time he was sent to a psychiatric institution. It was there that he met a young psychiatrist and social worker who had heard of Ishihara's group in Fukuoka and suggested he look them up after being released. Hino did so, bringing with him his prized collection of tools for pipe-fitting and ductwork—portable acetylene torches, cutters, saws, breakers, and whatnot. He'd stolen most of the tools from construction sites, and he kept them stashed somewhere in the room. "I'll show them to you sometime," he would say, beaming, whenever the subject of high-rise buildings or ventilation systems came up.

Tateno put the enamel pot on a propane burner and lit the fire. "Smells good," Hino said, rubbing the sleep from his eyes. Tateno told him what it was. Hino stretched elaborately, then fell back on the bed and began doing his ab crunches, muttering, "Chicken stew, chicken stew," to himself. The room they shared was in what had once been a warehouse. The place wasn't hooked up to city gas, but it did have water and electricity. The bathroom, shared by all, was down the corridor, across from Shinohara's room. There was no water heater, however, so when you wanted a shower you walked over to the building Ishihara lived in. The entire complex stood near the bay, on relatively old reclaimed ground in Fukuoka's Nishi Ward, an area crammed with warehouses, commercial buildings, and housing projects, most of which were now deserted thanks to the long economic slump and the decline in population, not to mention a big flood several years earlier. The place was like a ghost town now. Some buildings were only steel skeletons from the third floor up, their developers having gone bust, and there were dozens of poured-cement foundations on which houses had never been built.

Tateno didn't know when Ishihara had first come to live in this area. Shinohara said it was about ten years ago, but others thought it was more like fifteen, and the Satanists—five guys named Orihara, Sato, Kondo, Miyazaki, and Shibata—claimed it was twenty. The

Satanists were all from the same town in Kumamoto. When Orihara was thirteen, Sato eleven, and the other three twelve, they'd told their teachers and subsequently the police that they'd met the Devil and been forced to become members of a secret religious organization called the Temple of Satan. As proof, they showed them sketches they'd made of the Devil, messages from the Devil they'd taken down in automatic writing, dead pets the Devil had dispatched in their neighborhood, and scars from burns and cuts on their own arms and backs and stomachs that they claimed he was responsible for. The descriptions of Satan given by all five were consistent and had a real ring of truth to them, and since the scars on the boys' bodies were clearly genuine, the mass media had jumped on the story. Soon the kids were famous as leading characters in what came to be known as the Lucifer Incident. Even Tateno remembered it; the Lucifer Incident had been the lead story of every news weekly and tabloid TV show for weeks.

He remembered seeing the five of them on TV, guiding a cameraman and reporter to a vacant lot or the woods behind their middle school or the neighborhood park and showing them the charred carcasses of dogs and cats, as well as fragments of metal arranged in peculiar patterns and a sort of altar covered with a thick black cloth. He also remembered the overexcited reporter shouting, "Is this the final proof that Lucifer—the Devil!—really exists?" The public— fed up to the back teeth with political and economic news about banks not letting you withdraw your own money, the government not letting you change your dollars for yen, and big corporations and financial institutions going bankrupt—became obsessed with the Lucifer Incident. In the end, according to police investigators, no actual proof of the Devil's involvement was discovered, but it had become evident that all five of the children had suffered severe physical abuse at the hands of their respective parents. Eventually a local resident testified that he'd seen the boys themselves tormenting dogs and cats. It was typical, the experts said, for abused children to do to pets what their own parents were doing to them. After undergoing psychological testing, they were all put in an institution,

71

but two years later they escaped, fled to Fukuoka, and joined the Ishihara group.

Hino dropped down from the upper bunk, threaded his way between the wall and the table and chairs and shelves, and brushed against Tateno as he swept out of the room, saying, "Toilet." This room the two of them shared had once been a rental storage space and was about the length of three shipping containers lined up end to end. The bunk bed was at the far end from the entrance, and the only other appointments were small bookshelves, Hino's laptop, a table, and a couple of chairs, but the space was so narrow that they had to walk crabwise and couldn't pass each other without making contact. There was a rarely used radio, but no TV and no windows. Ishihara instructed everyone not to watch TV. According to him, television had a way of artificially suppressing the sorrow and rage and weirdness that are natural to us all. He recommended reading instead, and all the boys here seemed to read a lot. Tateno too was getting through more books than he ever would have thought possible.

He'd been here three months now. For the first month he and Hino had spoken very little. Hino had the round and expressionless face of a stone Jizo statue, and when he was in the room during the day he was either lying in bed reading or doing exercises to strengthen the muscles in his stomach, shoulders, arms, and back. It was only after Tateno demonstrated his boomerang skills in an empty field that the two of them had begun to talk a bit more. Their first night as roommates he'd asked Hino if he really liked reading, and all he got was a clipped "Whatever." But Tateno hadn't been offended; he didn't mind that sort of curt reaction. There was an unspoken understanding here that it didn't matter if you weren't sociable, or if you didn't talk much or greet people properly or agree with everyone, and Tateno liked that.

When the chicken stew was warmed up, he put half of it aside on a separate plate for Hino and ate the rest, along with some bread and margarine. After washing the pot, he decided to go and look for Shinohara at the shrine in the woods. He had a feeling he'd be warm enough in just a shirt, but with no windows in the room he wasn't sure. He opted to wear a jacket just in case. One thing you learn when you live with homeless people or travel long distances hopping trains is that aside from human violence the thing to be dreaded most is the cold. When it's hot, you can always take off more clothes, but if it gets cold enough you can die. Last winter in Ryokuchi Park, Tateno had seen people freeze to death before his very eyes. He shouldered his boomerang case and walked out of the room, and was just passing the bathroom when Hino came out. Tateno told him that he was off to the woods and that there was a plate of stew waiting for him in the room. Hino had washed up in the bathroom and was still toweling his hair as he walked back down the corridor.

Plastered on the door to Shinohara's room, across from the loo, were handwritten signs in English, Japanese, and Chinese saying THIS DOOR TO REMAIN CLOSED AT ALL TIMES. The room he slept in was of the same long and narrow design as Tateno's, but he had a total of six other rooms at his disposal, which were exclusively for his frogs, scorpions, spiders, centipedes, cockroaches, and other assorted leapers and creepers. Shinohara claimed that the rooms provided an ideal environment for raising his pets. The lack of windows reduced the danger of their escaping and facilitated temperature and humidity control, and there was just enough space for two rows of cases and an aisle down the center—a perfectly efficient arrangement for attending to the needs of his frogs and bugs. Just once, Shinohara had given Tateno a tour of some of these rooms. Inside one was a sort of greenhouse, made of large panes of plate glass, that served as a breeding environment for poison-dart frogs. There were any number of varieties, some small enough to sit on the tip of your finger, others as big as the palm of your hand, but they were all decorated with astonishing colors and gleamed with a sort of flawless, metallic sheen, like the bodies of Ferraris or Lamborghinis. According to Shinohara, dart frogs lost their poison when bred in captivity, but at home in the jungles of Central and South America they were many times more poisonous than the king cobra. "They don't make much noise normally," Shinohara had said, "but in the mating season, when several different species are singing at the same time, it's really beautiful—like crystal bells."

In another room, he was raising cockroaches that grew to be almost as thick and long as a baby's arm. The mere sight of one of these monsters, with jointed, sectioned abdomens like those of snakes, was enough to make Tateno feel queasy. Known as Madagascan Giants, they were wingless, but there was no mistaking them for anything but roaches. Shinohara said he could sell their plentiful offspring at high prices, as feed for arowana and other large tropical fish. Tateno was perhaps most impressed by the centipedes, the majority of which were varieties he'd never seen before. One, a toxic-looking, dark-red native of Haiti, was described by Shinohara as a "ferociously aggressive little sucker." He said it would literally leap into the air to attack anything that moved. There was also a woodlouse the size of a tennis ball that uncurled to expose legs like thorns. Tateno gasped as he watched the armor-like sections of its dark-brown body move, each bristling with fine, busy little hairs. Shinohara casually picked the bug up and put it on the palm of his hand, then whispered to it as if cooing to a baby: "Let me see you curl into a ball… Good boy! Now stre-e-e-tch…" Tateno felt every hair on his own body stand on end. He vowed never to cross Shinohara.

The bedrooms were on the third floor, and Tateno had to use the stairs to get to the first floor and outside. There was a freight elevator, but it was broken. On the landing between the second and ground floors he ran into Yamada and Mori. They were both carrying plastic bags from a convenience store. "Hey," Tateno said, and Yamada responded with a grunt. Mori said even less—he was silently eyeing Tateno's boomerang case. Yamada and Mori had tattoos respectively of Mickey Mouse and Minnie Mouse on their shoulders. Yamada had been born in Tokyo, but when he was twelve his father lost his office job and moved the family to a remote mountain village in the Tohoku region, in north-eastern Honshu, to pursue some dream he had of becoming a farmer. They rented a thatched farmhouse three kilometers from the nearest bus stop, four from the nearest

74

neighbor, five from the nearest elementary school, and eight from the nearest store. His father hung a scroll of his own calligraphy on the wall—IN PRAISE OF POVERTY—and began cultivating a field. He declared that they'd all have to live on a thousand yen a day. This was just as inflation was beginning really to take off, and in order to stay within this budget the family had to get by mainly on corn and wheat dumplings, rice being too expensive.

Once every three days a dried fish or fish sausage would make an appearance on the Yamada family table, and once every five days the father would allow himself a single glass of the local sake. The man had dreams of farming but no actual knowledge or skill: the tomatoes and cucumbers were consumed by insects, the taro patch was decimated by a flock of crows, and in winter the house, with no heat apart from the cooking pit, was so cold that they all had to sleep huddled together, teeth chattering. The cold and hunger robbed the entire family of any strength or vitality, no one cleaned up or did the laundry, the kitchen and backyard filled up with garbage, and the outhouse overflowed with their waste. Malnutrition and lack of hygiene resulted in Yamada's skin breaking out, and even the smallest cut would fester and refuse to heal. If you looked closely you could see that he had cute, rather rabbit-like features, but in middle school—thanks to the pimples that covered not only his face but his entire body, together with the sores on his arms and legs and the cheap, soiled, smelly clothing he wore—he'd been bullied mercilessly.

The following spring, his mother left. His father went to Tokyo to find her and bring her back, but days went by and he still hadn't returned. There was no food in the house, and one morning Yamada collapsed on the dirt path to school. He was taken to the hospital in the nearest town, where they found that as a result of chronic malnutrition he was developing tuberculosis. His parents couldn't be contacted and no money was available to pay for treatment, so he was moved to a prefectural facility. During his three weeks there, he never once saw his father, let alone his mother. When he was released he went back to the thatched house, and there, above the packed-dirt floor of the living room, he found his father hanging by the neck. Yamada tore the IN PRAISE OF POVERTY scroll from the wall and stuffed it in his pocket, then stayed with his father's corpse until the police showed up. No one was able to get hold of his mother, and Yamada was put in welfare, where he met Mori. The two of them were exactly the same age.

Mori had ended up there after his brother, four years older, had bought a knife in order to commit suicide but chickened out, murdered his parents instead, and seriously injured his little brother as well, stabbing him in the stomach, the scars of which Mori still bore. Yamada and Mori had similar personalities and a similar air about them, but whereas Yamada resembled a rabbit, Mori looked more like an owl. Both were tight-lipped, uncomplaining, and incredibly gentle and even-tempered. From the welfare facility, the two of them commuted to the same middle school, but they were so self-effacing that it was as if they weren't even there, and since they didn't react in any way when teased or bullied or beaten, eventually everyone—students and teachers alike—learned to ignore them.

They got the tattoos when they were fourteen, at Mori's suggestion. Mori had been obsessed with the story of a serial killer in a book he'd read. The hero was a man who'd grown up bullied and abused, a complete loser and weakling, until he got a dragon tattooed on his back that gave him the power to kill one person after another. Yamada had heard the story many times, and one day during the summer vacation of their second year in middle school Mori took him to a tattoo shop in Shibuya. The place was run by a man named Kan-chan, a flamboyant tattoo artist they'd read about in a magazine. His work didn't come cheap, but Mori, who'd received a portion of the inheritance from his parents in cash, paid for both of them. Kan-chan had a hundred and forty-eight piercings, from his temples to his ankles, and was cradling a French doll with one burned, melted eye and needles sticking out all over its body. The boys had planned to get a tiger and a dragon tattoo respectively, but Kan-chan convinced them that tigers and dragons were old-fashioned. Besides, he explained, they could be dangerous for people who couldn't handle the powers they summoned. Trusting in Kan-chan's advice, they'd gone with Mickey and Minnie, and not on their backs but on opposite deltoids. When they stood shoulder to shoulder, it looked as if Mickey and Minnie were holding hands.

Believing they were now ready to become killers, they decided to murder a stranger as a trial run before going after Yamada's runaway mother and Mori's parricidal brother. They bought two knives apiece at a hardware store, but the clerk got suspicious and notified the police, who promptly arrested them. They were still on probation when they planned an attack on Mori's paternal grandmother. Yamada's mother had vanished and Mori's brother was in a hospital, so they'd decided on Granny, who was now the executor of the parents' estate. But on their way to her house with new metal baseball bats they were arrested once again. This time they were put in a psychiatric institution. It was there that they came across one of Ishihara's poems, reprinted in a tattoo magazine. They didn't understand the poem very well, but there was also a photo of Ishihara. Something about his face spoke to them, and they decided to go to Fukuoka and check things out. Even now Yamada kept a worn, crumpled sheet of paper on the wall of his room that read IN PRAISE OF POVERTY.

The stairway down was a long one and made a right turn every five or six steps, so even though Tateno descended two steps at a time it seemed to take for ever. The ground floor had been used to store furniture and had a high ceiling. When he opened the heavy steel door at the bottom, he felt a gust of fresh air on his face. The automatic doors at the entrance had been made of plate glass, but the glass was no longer there. The large floor space was home to mounds of ruined furniture that no one had ever bothered to claim. Any usable pieces had been carted off long ago, and what was left were things like tables with one leg, sofas with foam rubber popping out of the seams, quilts and comforters that had been reduced to rags, or rusty and bent metal shelves. Tateno stepped outside through the glassless door frame. The infrared sensor, supposedly long since dead, would trigger occasionally, opening and closing the doors as if in remembrance of days gone by. Whenever this happened, it gave Tateno the feeling that maybe Hino was right—maybe buildings really were alive.

Outside, he turned and looked up. Only the ground floor had a few small windows; from here you couldn't tell how many stories there were. A big H was painted near the top of the white outer wall that loomed over him like the hull of a tanker. No one casually passing by would ever imagine anyone was living there, much less kids like himself or Shinohara or Yamada. The cluster of warehouses covered four blocks, which met at a crossroads. There were sixteen in all, from Building A to Building P, and they'd been built about forty years earlier. A couple of decades ago the company that owned them had gone belly-up, thanks partially to just-in-time distribution systems by which warehouse inventories were being reduced. An auction was held, but there were no takers for the buildings, and since it would cost money to tear them down they were left as they were. Ishihara lived in Building C. Several of the other buildings housed a few members of the group that had formed around him. There were about twenty guys in all, and Tateno had met each of them individually, though he'd never seen them all together in one place at the same time.

Ishihara wasn't living there illegally. When he'd first come to Fukuoka, he and Nobue had rented an apartment near Hakata Station. Nobue eventually opened a shop selling vintage jeans and Hawaiian shirts, and when it became fairly popular with local youngsters he opened another selling imported motorcycles. Development in Nishi Ward had collapsed in the late 1990s, and an organization called the Young Entrepreneurs Group spearheaded an attempt to turn the abandoned warehouse district into a "fashion town." Nobue rented Building C for very little money and opened a new shop, but the whole project soon floundered. New land had been reclaimed everywhere, resulting in a glut of condominiums, hotels, and shopping malls. Tenants failed to materialize, and so did shoppers. Nobue's store, all by itself among the vacant buildings, continued to do a trickle of business; and in time, youths who'd been abandoned by parents, relatives, and even welfare institutions began drifting in from various parts of the country. Tateno once asked how the first kids had heard about Ishihara and Nobue, and Ishihara had said simply, "Hell if I know."

Ando, one of the first members to have joined the group, said he'd come to Fukuoka after hearing rumors about these two legendary and very strange old dudes who had once committed murders and even blown up a section of Tokyo with a bomb of mind-boggling proportions, just for fun. At the age of thirteen, in a housing development in Yokohama, Ando himself had killed a girl from his class and cut up her body with a handsaw. Fukuda, who'd come to Fukuoka shortly after Ando, said that Ishihara and Nobue simply had an aura about them that attracted boys with no home in the world, the way a magnet attracts iron filings. Fukuda claimed to be the only child of two members of a cult that had carried out coordinated terrorist attacks. He wasn't listed in a family register and hadn't even attended elementary school.

For some years, the informal group had struggled to get by on the trickle of income from Nobue's shop, but a major turnaround in their financial situation occurred with the arrival of a man named Takei. Takei was in his forties, not a kid like the others. After the departure of Nobue, he became the only older man in the group aside from Ishihara himself. He'd once worked in the foreign exchange department of a major bank but was laid off when he was thirty-one, after which he attempted suicide by slitting his wrists. Recovering in a hospital bed, he happened to read a book that explained the rewards Islamic martyrs received when they reached Paradise. After doing some research on the Internet he traveled to Yemen to join a training camp for militant Islamic guerrillas. He didn't know anything else about Islam but was very taken with the bit about the seventy virgins.

Takei underwent training for some six months, but he'd been sickly as a child and had grown into a frail and extremely nearsighted man who was only a hundred and fifty-eight centimeters tall, weighed a mere forty-six kilos, and couldn't register more than eighteen with

79

either hand on a grip dynamometer. Unable to run the fifty meters in under eleven seconds, drive a car, or even ride a bicycle, he was judged unsuitable for guerrilla operations and advised to go back to Japan. Nevertheless, the fact that he'd traveled all the way to Yemen to join the group had impressed the leaders and the other recruits, and he'd gained their trust. During his stay in the camp, he instructed the leadership in the basics of financial investment and foreign exchange—explaining to them, for example, why investing capital in a hedge fund was safer than trying to hide it in bank accounts, or how the dollar would react in the event of unrest in a politically unstable nation like, say, Bahrain. The organization actually profited from his advice, and this of course boosted his standing with them.

After returning to Japan, Takei heard rumors and legends about Ishihara and Nobue that compelled him to seek them out. He was still in contact with the guerrilla group at this time, and soon after his arrival he received information from them that an anti-government organization in Iran was going to attack the island of Abu Musa, on the western side of the Strait of Hormuz. He advised Ishihara to short the stocks of American oil companies operating in the Persian Gulf, and took the same position himself. Between this and speculation on oil futures, they cleared nearly a hundred million yen. He continued with his investments, relying on information from Yemen, and provided Ishihara and Nobue with very substantial funds. He was also given, by a Syrian guerrilla, the exclusive Far Eastern distribution rights to a soap made of olive and laurel oils, advertised as "The Soap Cleopatra Loved." Takei formed a company and made an obscene profit as the exclusive importer. This was before the big boom in "nutritious" soaps and shampoos containing wood vinegar, herbs, seaweed, and so on, but at one point, after the Cleopatra soap was discovered by women's magazines, sales reached into the hundreds of millions.

When Ishihara won the Kyushu Public Literary Prize for Poetry a decade ago, the city of Fukuoka took the opportunity to recognize his contribution to child welfare. The kids he was known to have taken under his wing were apparently no longer involved in illegal activities, and the city tacitly considered the Ishihara-Nobue operation a convenient way of shifting responsibility for these problem children. In fact, of course, the boys hadn't changed or been "rehabilitated"; they were only catching their breath, allowing themselves a period of rest and recuperation. The city didn't know, for example, that Shinohara was raising poisonous insects. No one knew how many youngsters were involved or what they were up to in those warehouses, and no one could review their backgrounds or personal histories since most of them had no resident-register codes.

Takei was an admirable financial manager for the group. But his real purpose in financing Ishihara was to start a revolution in Japan, and he seriously intended to employ the youths as soldiers in his struggle. When Tateno first met him, Takei had spoken at great length about these plans. Through his connections with the armed militants in Yemen, he'd been purchasing weapons and explosives, little by little, from such places as Russia, the Philippines, and China. Containers addressed to Takei's company arrived about once a month at the port of Hakata. Most of the containers were full of soap, but now and then weapons and explosives were mixed in with this cargo. According to him, about eight hundred thousand assorted containers reached the port each year. That made for more than two thousand a day, and it was impossible for Customs to inspect them all. To do so would mean clogging up the distribution system and forcing Hakata to lose out to rival ports such as Busan and Shanghai. Tateno hadn't seen any of the weapons yet, but Hino told him they included side arms, automatic rifles, and hand grenades, as well as high explosives.

Shinohara and Yamada had told him that Takei's arrival and all this talk of revolution were what triggered Nobue's departure. Nobue didn't like Takei. And he became completely disillusioned and left for good when young Kaneshiro joined the group. Kaneshiro was a guy who was interested in nothing but terrorism and devising different schemes for large-scale attacks, and several of the other kids had fallen under his sway. He seemed to hole up in his room every day, revising his plans, and Tateno had only met him twice.

81

But after seeing what he could do with a boomerang, Kaneshiro had been enthusiastic, saying, "We can use this!" He seemed a thoroughly serious person, genuine and sincere and not motivated by self-interest. But because he spent all his time thinking up ever bigger projects, he'd never actually done anything. Ishihara seemed neither to like nor to dislike Takei or Kaneshiro, or anyone else for that matter. He continued writing his poems, aloof from the minutiae of everyday life and growing increasingly sage-like and mystical. Terror, murder, revolution—whether such things occurred or not was of no real interest to him.

Ishihara often explained to the group that the important thing was to live apart from the majority. When he spoke about things that excited him he emitted a powerful aura, as if he were illuminated from behind, and his shining eyes, set adrift in their sockets, made you wonder what he was staring at. At times he seemed all-seeing, at others half-blind. His hands fluttered about as he talked, his fingers tugged at his hair, which stood straight up as a result, and he pumped and jiggled first one leg and then the other. He had an overwhelming presence. Once, while he was talking, Shinohara had leaned over and whispered in Tateno's ear, "There's a millipede called the Ethiopian Giant that I've only seen pictures of, but it's forty centimeters long and looks like something from outer space. It's so trippy that the Ethiopians think it's a messenger from God, but I'd say it's got nothing on Ishihara-san."

The man would begin speaking suddenly, as if struck by a revelation.

"I and I stopped masturbating. Or so we thought. But then I and I awoke this morning pulling the old pud. It's the plain Truth. Terrorism is awesome, violence is awesome, and even murder is awesome, but war sucks. War is for the mojority. Not *ma*jority but *mo*jority. The little people are always the ones who lose. That's why the only ones who want war are the majority. They either bully the little people or ignore them altogether. I and I hate pain and would rather not see things like terror and violence and murder in the world, but sometimes the little people have no other choice. The only thing I and I hate more than pain is the mojority. Whether on the level of village or city or country, their interests always come first. It was the need to protect the mojority that created the nation state, and in a country like this, it's no easy thing to live apart from all that. I and I and Nobue-chin were always ignored by the mojority, which left three-hundred-mile-long scars on our hearts, but now I and I realize that we were fortunate never to be accepted by them. *Fortunate*, not fartunate. I and I will repeat this over and over again many times and say it only this once because it's so important: you must never join the mojority. Even killing people would be *más mejor* than doing that."

The crossroads that separated the sixteen buildings pointed in all four directions. The road north ended at Hakata Bay, and going south took you straight to downtown Fukuoka. To the east was the shrine in the forest where Shinohara collected insects, and the road to the west dead-ended at a ghost town that was once meant to be a housing development. In the yards of the few houses that were still inhabited were the inevitable vegetable patches and chicken coops. Once Japan's foreign reserves were exhausted, oil became scarce and food distribution faltered to the point where some politicians said the country would soon face starvation. But neither Tateno nor anyone else in the Ishihara group was afraid of going hungry. They had all experienced things much worse than that.

The sea was some two kilometers away, but Tateno could smell it as he walked up the road, bordered on both sides by thick tangles of weeds. Down at the far end of the reclaimed land, looking out over the bay, was a girls' high school that had been abandoned and relocated when crime began to spread in the area. Tateno was from landlocked Yamanashi, so any view of the sea was something new and amazing to him, and since joining the group he'd discovered any number of spectacular lookout points. Next to the old girls' school were a sandy beach and a small, narrow park. There was a broken slide in the park, and by climbing its ladder you could see all of Hakata Bay. Dead ahead was an island, with a small ferryboat always either going or coming.

Having never seen ships dock or set sail before, he had also once spent a day on an old wooden bench in the ferry-service waiting room, just to watch. He found it all pretty exciting. Vessels entering the harbor blew their whistles, ropes were thrown from boats easing into their berths, and anchors plummeted from bows with a splash and a clanking of chains. The island the ferry went to was called Nokonoshima. In the waiting room were posters featuring the island, as well as pamphlets that Tateno had read so many times that he now knew them by heart. Nokonoshima Island was famous in Japan for its beaches and fishing spots. In the pamphlets, the white beaches seemed to stretch for ever. A lot of fruit was grown on the island, and the pamphlets mentioned a seedless papaya. Tateno was fascinated by this. If the papaya didn't have any seeds, what was in the core of the fruit? He was determined one of these days to go to Nokonoshima, eat a seedless papaya, and sail his boomerangs over that pure white sand.

As he was making his way up the road to the shrine, a rumbling that came from beyond a curve just ahead quickly became a roar, and he felt the earth tremble beneath his feet. The next moment, a pack of about fifteen bikers blasted past him, heading downhill. Several of them waved as they blew by. The Speed Tribes were all but extinct in Tokyo or Osaka, but they remained in Fukuoka like some sort of protected species. Members of this particular Tribe had been regulars at Nobue's shop, and they still visited Ishihara frequently. They'd been aficionados of Nobue's jeans and Hawaiian shirts and among his best clients, of course, for the big imported motorcycles. Well aware of the rumors that the pair had been responsible for some sort of massive explosion in Tokyo and were now lying low here in Fukuoka, the leaders and members of the Tribe all but worshiped Ishihara and Nobue. For them, perhaps the two older men represented a more exotic kind of rebel, quite distinct from the yakuza or the right-wingers they were generally in thrall to. "Ishihara-san, we'll help you out anytime," the Tribal Chief used to say. "When we gonna have another shop like Nobue-san used to run?" It was clear that the Chief hoped to form some sort of alliance with Ishihara's group, but Ishihara would always just mumble a vague reply, more or less ignoring any such suggestion. And yet the Tribe still dropped by from time to time to pay their respects. "If there's ever anything we can do, just say the word," the Chief always assured them.

Beyond the curve the road dipped briefly, but Hakata Bay was still just visible through the crumbling walls of the ruined school building. The sun was already on its way down. From up at the shrine he'd be able to watch it set over Nokonoshima. On the opposite side of the road was a shuttered nursery school. The windows were broken, the painted animals on the walls were flaking away, and the playground, with its see-saws and sandboxes and monkey bars, was now a refuge for the homeless. There were rows of cardboard huts and vinyl tarps. The people here had been shouting at one another, but when they saw Tateno they fell silent and shuffled into their huts. The Speed Tribe had probably just done something to them—thrown stones or bottles, or thundered through the grounds on their bikes, shouting threats. Maybe they thought Tateno was one of the Tribe, returning to dish out more punishment. Ryokuchi Park had been run by yakuza, and there were thousands of other occupants, so no one ever bothered them. But elsewhere around the country the homeless were being harassed and even murdered daily. It was said that their numbers were growing at an almost exponential rate. On his journey from Tokyo to Fukuoka, Tateno had noticed them hunkered down at almost every train station, highway overpass, riverbank, public park, and sheltered bus stop. When vagrants were attacked or murdered nowadays, it no longer even made the news.

For some reason, the sight of a man peering fearfully out from the shadows of his cardboard shanty enraged him. If this had happened before he met Nobue or came to live in Ishihara's compound, he'd probably have tried to kill something with his boomerang right now. He'd killed crows at Ryokuchi Park, and in Yamanashi he'd put down stray dogs. He probably would have killed a person eventually. And the homeless are the easiest people in the world to kill. Kids are scared of becoming failures themselves in later life, and the media reinforce that fear by depicting the homeless as shameful losers in a winner-take-all society, people who'll never get back on their feet and will have to scrounge for leftover food, wearing dirty rags, smelling to high heaven, and living in cardboard boxes till the day they die. After bank accounts were frozen and inflation had set in, the poor came to be scorned even more openly. Some kids probably reasoned that if it was all right to look down on the destitute, it must be all right to knock them around as well.

The sun was slanting toward the west. Ahead, he could see the top of the shrine's tall red torii gate protruding from the dense woods that covered the final gentle slope. Ants and other insects had built whole civilizations in the moist ground behind the shrine. On Tateno's right was what had once been a shopping street, now a ghost town, and he stopped to look it over. A sign with the words MEINOHAMA SMILE TOWN arched over the entrance to the street. The cord for the sign's decorative illumination had been severed and hung flapping in the wind. A headless mannequin leaned out toward the street, impaled on the broken glass of a clothing-store window. Some sort of white powder had spilled from the innards of an industrial freezer that lay on its side at the entrance to a butcher's shop. A pile of smashed energy-drink bottles had collected at the foot of a pharmacy's broken steel shutter; a rusty compact station wagon sat decomposing in front of the greengrocer's; and a small swing hung from the eaves of a stationery store. It was a portable swing, built for infants, and it waggled in the wind from time to time, causing the chains by which it dangled to creak and groan. Tateno stared at it. There had been one just like it in the garden of the house he grew up in.

Tateno was the only child of a Yamanashi-based building contractor. When he was small, his family had been very well off and employed some twenty workers, who were housed on the grounds in a sort of prefab tenement building. His grandparents lived with the family, and every year they all traveled to Australia or New Zealand together and went boating, skiing, or skin-diving. When Tateno was twelve, his dad bought him a wooden boomerang, an

Aborigine hunting tool, at Sydney Airport. On their return, they practiced throwing it together over a meadow on a nearby hill. His father had been a baseball player in high school, and he could throw the boomerang a tremendous distance. Tateno's dream was to make it fly the way his father did, in a long, graceful arc, and he began practicing each day after school. Having been at it till dark one day, about a year and a half after he started these sessions, he was taking a short cut home when he spotted the familiar silhouette of his father in the wood ahead. He was about to call out to him but froze when he sensed that he was witnessing something he shouldn't. It occurred to him to run away, but his body wouldn't move. In a place well hidden from the road, his father was digging a shallow trench. When he finished digging, he put down his shovel and with the heel of his boot pushed a long, heavy bundle over the edge. Tateno could clearly make out a human foot protruding from the bundle as it fell into the trench, and he had to clap a hand over his mouth to suppress a scream. An electric torch flashed its light for a moment, and his father's face showed clearly against the dark trees. It was a terrifying face. A face he scarcely recognized.

The fact that he couldn't tell anyone about this was a real source of anguish for Tateno. He had seen his father burying someone, but even more frightening was the expression he'd seen on his face in that brief flash of the electric torch. It was as if his father had become someone else—that face didn't belong to the man Tateno knew. He ditched school from that day on and went to the hillside to throw the boomerang over and over again. He threw it in order to stave off the fear he felt, focusing his mind only on trying to recreate the beautiful arc the thing described when his dad threw it. He had just reached the point where he could consistently make it go where he aimed it, when his father was arrested. Because of the depression, construction jobs had dwindled and the company had been on the verge of bankruptcy. Some of the workers had complained of back wages they were owed, and his father murdered six of them, one at a time. After the arrest, Tateno's mother returned to her family home in Fukushima, taking his sister with her, but Tateno refused to budge. His grandparents were against his staying behind and dragged him to Fukushima several times, but he always escaped and came back to Yamanashi. His sessions with the boomerang continued, and by the time he could throw it even farther than his father had, he'd also found a way of overcoming his fear—the horror of that transformation he'd witnessed in the wood. He had to acquire the ability to become the same sort of person his father had been at that moment, to prove to himself that it could happen to anyone. He began making boomerangs of sharpened steel, and when eventually he set out for Tokyo, he was capable of decapitating a stray dog at a distance of fifty meters.

"You looking for Shinohara?"

It was Kaneshiro, descending the path from the shrine. Behind him were Matsuyama, Takeguchi, Toyohara, Felix, and Okubo, and they were all drenched with sweat. That meant they'd been practicing some martial arts up here. Tateno had been invited to join them but hadn't taken them up on it yet. According to Hino, the wristbands Kaneshiro wore on both arms were there to hide the scars of multiple suicide attempts he'd made before discovering and devoting himself to terrorism. Matsuyama, behind him, had become convinced as a child that his mind was being controlled by the TV, and at the age of fourteen had burst into a regional NHK studio and shot two people dead with a homemade pistol. Young Takeguchi, whose face was as pretty as any female teen idol's, was a bomb-making specialist. When he was ten, his father had walked into the offices of the company where he'd just been laid off, with sticks of dynamite strapped to his chest. He succeeded only in blowing himself up, and the footage from a security camera that had captured the entire scene was shown on television dozens of times. Watching the footage, Takeguchi was forced to conclude that his father had failed simply because he was ignorant about explosives, and he took it upon himself to compensate for this disgrace. He did so by learning to make and detonate an astonishing variety of bombs. The short, hulking boy named Toyohara had once stolen his grandfather's samurai sword and used it to hijack a bullet train, taking the life of a conductor in the process. Felix was Japanese, in spite of the name. His father, a civil engineer, had been killed along with his mother by a street thief in Colombia, where they had lived since before Felix's birth. The orphaned boy was placed in an institution, where he was effectively raised by a homosexual Brazilian hacker eight years his senior. The nickname Felix, given him by the Brazilian, became his handle when he himself began hacking. Okubo was a native of northern Japan who'd once been a rather famous child actor, appearing frequently in television commercials and dramas. As a small boy he'd possessed the face of an angel, and by the time he reached elementary school he was something of a superstar. But as he grew, his face became more and more like anyone else's, and by his middle-school years the offers had stopped coming in. It was at that point that he started using the name Kamimoto for a separate email address to which he sent himself letters. Over time, he began to suffer the delusion that the only people who deserved to live in this world were himself and Kamimoto. Everyone else ought to die. By the time he was arrested, back in his hometown of Iwate, he had committed forty-six acts of arson.

"Tateno, we're training again the day after tomorrow. Why don't you join us?"

Kaneshiro's invitation was delivered in the tones of a student-council president gathering support for a pep rally. "I'll come if I have time," Tateno said, which made Kaneshiro light up and say, "Really?" Kaneshiro had been noticeably more respectful ever since seeing his boomerang skills in the vacant lot behind the warehouse, but in fact he was polite to everyone. Nonetheless, Tateno considered him the most dangerous of all the people around Ishihara. Kaneshiro never smiled, but he never looked gloomy or worried either, and unlike most of the others he never spoke about his past. His face was thin but healthy-looking, his eyes clear and piercing. There was never anything hesitant or unfocused about him. And you sensed that when he actually did get around to carrying out some sort of terrorist attack, that icy expression on his face wouldn't change at all.

89

After parting from Kaneshiro and the others, Tateno hurried up to the shrine to join Shinohara. The narrow stone steps were bordered on either side by thick woods, and the cold, moist air seeping out from under the trees reminded Tateno of home. Had he changed since his Yamanashi days? He had people to hang out with here, and he was calmer, but he didn't really think he'd changed. He'd figured out that he wasn't going to get anywhere killing dogs and crows, and he no longer saw much point in beating up homeless people, but aside from that... He still felt that weird energy boiling up from deep inside, and he didn't think it was going to be kept under just because he had friends to talk to now. And this was probably true, to one degree or another, of every member of the Ishihara group.

He began to sweat slightly as he climbed the stairs. The sun descending over Nokonoshima was huge, and it made the entire sea sparkle. His spirits rose at the thought of searching for insects with Shinohara and watching the sun sink into Hakata Bay.

PHASE ONE

1

# NINE COMMANDOS

*April 1, 2011*

H AN SEUNG JIN and the eight members of the Special Operations
Forces under his command boarded their ship and, once the
sun had gone down, set sail, accompanied by twenty other vessels
intended as decoys. The stern bore a Japanese name: *Atago-Yamashiro
Maru*. To all appearances, it was an ordinary trawler, but the hull,
with a camouflaged twenty-millimeter machine gun installed, was
of reinforced steel. The engine room had false walls, conceal-
ing weapons, explosives and two rubber boats, and contained an
eight-hundred-horsepower engine. Kang Deok Sang, the training
supervisor, had told his charges that over the past couple of years
some two thousand decoys had been mobilized in support of the
mission. Kang was an instructor in the General Political Bureau;
Han Seung Jin was a political officer in the SOF Light Infantry
Guidance Bureau.

Kang hadn't spoken extensively about the decoys, but apparently
the National Security Agency, the Military Affairs Mobilization
Bureau of the People's Army and its reconnaissance division, the
West Sea Fleet command headquarters, and even the Coast Guard
had been called on to provide ships. Each day over the past two
weeks, a large number of vessels had set out simultaneously from

various ports, heading for Japanese waters. Sometimes there would be seventy of them for several days running; then the number would drop to ten. The strategy was to throw Japan's Maritime Safety Agency and the Self-Defense Force off their guard by setting off a series of false alarms. "They won't pay you the slightest attention," Kang had said when he saw them off, his shiny cheeks bulging in a big smile.

The ship's captain stood at the helm, keeping one eye on the radar. Han Seung Jin reckoned that the man was in his late forties, but he knew neither his name nor his rank. In the pilothouse with them, in a floor space no larger than two ping-pong tables put side by side, were the first officer and Kim Hak Su. Han marveled at the sight of the sea, spread out in the darkness like a grand hall, the ceiling and floor painted black, the walls hung with thick satin of the same raven shade. Dense clouds covered the sky, and from the receding shoreline no light could be seen. The vessels accompanying them were likewise invisible. There was just a light breeze, with the gentlest of waves, so that even as the ship chugged through the open sea, he could scarcely sense that they were moving. Han wondered for a moment whether these calm waters were a good omen but then quickly dismissed the thought. Emotions could only get in the way of the job. Though he'd been assigned to numerous clandestine missions, including security work at nuclear facilities and sabotage in the demilitarized zone, this was to be the first time he had infiltrated enemy territory. And yet his mind was as calm as the glassy surface of the dark water, devoid of both tension and excitement. Those under his command were the most able and courageous operatives in the Republic. They'd been thoroughly trained and were ready for anything.

His deputy, Kim Hak Su, had been two years Han's junior at college. During the recent training period, Kim had celebrated his thirty-seventh birthday and received gifts from the Dear Leader himself: a fountain pen and some sweets. Han had always been as tough as they come, ever since primary school, and was deservedly confident in his boxing and *gyeoksul* skills; but even so he would not have wanted Kim as an opponent. *Gyeoksul*, the art of the hard punch, was all about killing, and Kim was a past master. Strikingly tall, he had a direct and steady gaze, and while his thin nose hinted at sensitivity, his square jaw counteracted that impression, as did a deep bayonet scar running from the corner of one eye to the temple above. His father had been a political officer with the Air Force Command in Pyongyang, his mother a professor of piano at the Mangyongdae Children's Palace. As Han's second-in-command, Kim was well qualified: clear-headed, brave, unquestionably loyal to their Comrade General and the Republic, and fluent in Japanese. If he had a flaw, it was perhaps a perfectionism that made him unforgiving of any failure or breach of etiquette on the part of others. He had a short fuse and could be relied on to punish any offender both physically and mentally.

The captain was looking at the clock: they would be entering South Korean territorial waters in three more hours, Japanese waters in six. From there it was another ninety minutes to Fukuoka, their destination. It was nearly time for the meeting; the rest of the team were waiting below. Afterwards, they would have to inspect their weapons and go over specific details of the operation. "Let's go," Han said, and Kim responded with a nod. As they were leaving the pilothouse, the captain and first officer stood at attention and saluted. About the mission Han and his subordinates had been entrusted with, they knew nothing, but respect for the Special Operations Forces was unequivocal, not only in the military but throughout the country. During food crises, the commandos alone were supplied with rice and meat broth. Everyone knew this, but no one complained. Dissatisfaction was focused on corrupt local Party officials and their secretaries, some of whom had been set upon by mobs and burned out of house and home, while others had been purged. The commandos, however, were special. The masses knew of their severe, sometimes even fatal, training, and of the extremely dangerous nature of their missions. There was also general awareness that they were a key factor in upholding the revolutionary cause on which the fate of the Republic hinged.

*

Han Seung Jin and Kim Hak Su descended the steep, narrow stairs. Kim stopped halfway down and lifted one foot to inspect the sole of his shoe. "I have the odd feeling of walking barefoot," he said. Han was experiencing the same sensation. They weren't wearing lace-up commando boots but rather rubber-soled cloth shoes made in the South. These were extremely light, the rubber absorbing the impact of their steps on steel stairs and producing scarcely a sound. "I've never worn things like this before," remarked Han. He found himself thinking of the two sons he'd left behind. They were now in primary school and were exactly as he had been in his own childhood: brawny and unmanageable. Their favorite sport was soccer, and every day they came home caked in mud. Their mother was forever scolding them, telling them to settle down or to study, but they rarely listened to her. Now, for a few wistful moments, Han imagined presenting his sons with feather-light footwear like this and seeing the surprise and delight on their faces. He knew, however, that he would never see those faces again. He was prepared to give his life for the Republic, and this mission could very well demand that sacrifice. But even if he were lucky enough to survive, he could never again return to his homeland.

The rumble of the diesel engine reverberated through the cabin; along with the smell of oil came a regular and soothing vibration, its very steadiness an assurance that they were indeed moving toward their destination. Those in the cabin were looking out of the portholes, reading by the dim emergency lights, or sitting on the wall bunks, but when Han and Kim came in, they sprang to their feet, stood at attention, and saluted. Kim automatically returned the salute, but Han quietly ordered them to stand at ease, saying that as the mission had already begun, such formalities were no longer called for. The cabin, measuring just over twelve square meters, consisted of berths on opposite walls with a small wooden table anchored to the floor and a sofa that could accommodate four, though out of deference to Han, who stood next to the table, his subordinates sat down side by side on the narrow bunks. Their faces were all in dead earnest as they waited, legs pressed together, hands on thighs, backs straight, eyes straining forward. To the right were those from the 907th Battalion of the Eighth Corps, to the left those from the State Security Department.

"Talk to each other in Japanese," said Han, speaking himself in that language. They responded with frowns and confused expressions. To the right nearest him was thirty-two-year-old Choi Hyo Il from Tongchon in Kangwon Province. He was wearing a bright-green T-shirt, a denim jacket, and jeans—an outfit ill-matched to his appearance. On one cheek he had a long, thin knife scar, and his shoulder muscles bulged from long years of *gyeoksul* training. The denim he was wearing for the first time in his life made him look like a bear in a suit.

Choi raised his hand and asked in imperfect Japanese why they should be speaking that language now. Han could sense that Choi's grammar was off, but he wasn't sure just what the problem was or how to correct it. After being assigned to the mission, he had tried to improve his own command of Japanese by reading some contemporary novels lent him by Professor Pak Yong Su of Kim Jong Il Political-Military University. But neither he nor any of the others had been able to brush up their speaking skills. Their compatriots in the General Association of Korean Residents in Japan, the Chongryon, had not been included in the undertaking, and there was hardly anyone in the Republic familiar with the vocabulary and speech patterns of younger Japanese. Moreover, concern for absolute secrecy had meant that Han hadn't been informed about particular details until just before the ship's departure. At the beginning of their training, he was given the barest outline of their task: to infiltrate a city on the island of Kyushu and take armed control of a particular sector.

According to the plan now made known to him, up to the time they actually seized the area, they were to act as though they were among the apparently numerous travelers from South Korea. In establishing and maintaining control, however, they would have to be able to issue orders to their hostages in Japanese. Han had learned to read and write Japanese, but it was of the formal variety, complete with honorific expressions. He had no command of the casual speech one needed for conveying one's message quickly and accurately or for delivering simple but important commands and instructions.

"Very well, then," he said. "You may speak Korean if you like." There was something else that had been nagging him ever since the final briefing, an issue that went beyond speaking Japanese, though he didn't know how to resolve it. He and those under his command had been brought together soon after the mission was authorized and had immediately begun their training. In addition to taking refresher courses in Japanese, they had practiced firing revolvers, rifles, and RPG-7s, honed their *gyeoksul* skills, and learned how to operate Japanese Self-Defense Force weaponry. They had also pored over detailed maps of Fukuoka City, studied the geography of Kyushu, Shikoku, and western Honshu, rehearsed the speech patterns of Korean tourists from the South, familiarized themselves with Japanese coins and currency and public and mobile telephones, learned how to check into a hotel and to take taxis, buses, and trains, and even practiced manipulating the shorter, lighter chopsticks used by the Japanese. And yet they had not learned how to engage in the joking banter of South Korean tourists. Time had not allowed for that, and such instruction was unavailable in any case. There was no shortage of instructors in the art of killing people or blowing up facilities, but no one in the Republic could teach you how to behave like a traveler from the puppet regime.

"What's wrong? It doesn't matter what you talk about, just say something! After all, you're supposed to be good friends from the South."

All eight assumed the same perplexed expression. They were already sitting erect, but now they stiffened further, their faces looking even more earnest. There were a few twitching lips and brows as well. This was a serious problem, thought Han. Commandos had no concept of friendship. It wasn't that they had never experienced it but rather that they'd forgotten what it was like. And so, sitting here now, they were incapable of engaging in casual conversation or banter. In order to pass as tourists from the South, they were wearing fancy sweaters, shirts, and jackets, but they were all experts in the martial arts and tremendously fit, and the clothing couldn't conceal their physiques. They might be taken for professional athletes, except for the knife or bayonet scars that Kim Hak Su, Choi Hyo Il, and Jang Bong Su bore in various places—the temple, the cheek, the neck—and that sharp, watchful look in their eyes.

Above all, they never smiled. In the three months that he'd trained with them, Han hadn't seen so much as a quick grin. Though they themselves were unaware of it, all eight conveyed an impression of brute force. You wouldn't have to be Japanese to be suspicious of a group like this standing around or walking down the street. They might as well be wearing sandwich boards declaring: DEADLY COMMANDOS.

The Great Leader had himself established the tradition that fellow soldiers should not form close attachments. The methods for ensuring this fell into two distinct categories. Firstly, there was the rigor of their training, of a severity unimaginable to the ordinary person; it left them with neither the time nor the psychological leeway for close ties. Secondly, to prevent any sort of attempt at a *coup d'état*, a system of mutual monitoring was firmly in place. Not knowing who might be an informer, a soldier was naturally loath to confide in anyone. Another influential factor was the ending, as of the early 1990s, of opportunities for study abroad. At the time of Han's graduation and entry into the Light Infantry Guidance Bureau, the Republic was still sending students to the Soviet Union and the Eastern bloc countries. Han had spent a year and a half in the Ukraine, but he was among the last to be granted permission, and with Gorbachev establishing diplomatic relations with the puppet regime and the subsequent demise of the USSR, the door was permanently closed. Experience abroad had facilitated friendships; nowadays perhaps the only way to form strong relations was in juvenile gangs.

"What's wrong?" asked Han by way of provoking a reaction. "You can't even talk to each other?" Sitting at the far end to his right, Pak Myeong exhaled heavily. The twenty-nine-year-old was from

Pyonggang in Kangwon Province. Appropriately for one whose family belonged to the Party elite, he had distinguished himself at Kim Il Sung University. His talent for languages having been recognized, he was sent after graduation to Kim Jong Il Political-Military University, where he studied Japanese and English in addition to the full spectrum of sabotage and subversion strategy. At present he was wearing a brown-green sweater and cream-colored cotton slacks. His entire outfit, including the shirt and brown duck-bill shoes, was made in Japan. Pak had an appealing face, with a broad forehead and large eyes, and the expensive clothes suited him. Yet perspiration was trickling down that same forehead. Jo Su Ryeon, sitting next to him, was likewise breathing hard, with beads of sweat forming on the bridge of his nose. The air was in fact warmer, as the ship was moving southward at a steady forty knots and would soon be entering waters claimed by the puppet regime. But it wasn't the temperature that was making them uncomfortable.

Thirty-three-year-old Jo was a native of Pyongyang. His father was a renowned professor of languages and literature at Kim Il Sung University, his mother a leading journalist for the Central News Agency. He had joined the SOF Eighth Corps on graduating from the Writers' Academy, but after three years of basic training he had gone as a cadet to the Kim Hyong Jik University of Education, named after the Great Leader's father. From there, having demonstrated extraordinary talent, he was enrolled in Kim Jong Il Political-Military University, where he excelled in languages and sharpshooting, along with poetry and novel writing. Han remembered having thought when he first met Jo Su Ryeon that the man would have been a sensation as a people's actor. He was tall and slim with a deep, resonant voice and eyes with extended slits that curved upward at the outer corners.

Word had it that when Jo walked through the halls of the university, there were audible sighs from the women he passed. In the gray jacket and jeans he was now wearing, no Japanese would have dreamed that he was from the Republic. And yet though his looks might inspire admiring murmurs from women, this didn't make him any less an SOF officer. His three years of basic training and his graduation from the Political-Military University meant that he'd mastered the full range of sabotage techniques and martial-art skills. Of course, that was true of his comrades as well; all were capable of ripping into the intestines of an enemy with their bare hands.

"If there's anything you want to say, speak up," said Han softly, glancing around the room at each of them. Pak Myeong and Jo Su Ryeon were not the only ones who were ill at ease. To Han's surprise, even Jang Bong Su's forehead was damp. Jang had been the youngest person ever admitted to Kim Jong Il Political-Military University. He had a flair for sabotage operations, as though he'd been born to the task. A narrow nose, thin lips, and a calm and steady gaze went with a personality that wasn't so much cool as cold-blooded. He'd led many a clandestine operation against would-be defectors and brought back a number of political criminals who had fled across the border to Jilin. Among escapees he was known for carrying out the cruelest of orders without hesitation, sparing neither the very young nor the very old. And yet this same man, thought Han, was now sitting here stiff-backed with tension.

The only exceptions appeared to be the two women, Kim Hyang Mok and Ri Gwi Hui, who sat nearest the far wall on the left. Kim came from a village near Ranam in North Hamgyong Province; Ri from Chongjin in the same province. Their faces were as intense and serious as the men's, but they occasionally exchanged glances and seemed to be generally more relaxed. There was an air of innocence about them. Kim, who'd just turned twenty-seven, had worked in the Railway Security and the Capital Air Defense Corps before entering Kim Jong Il Political-Military University. From there she'd gone to the State Security Department's reconnaissance division. At university she had studied Japanese and English, as well as finance and business, while also undergoing the usual combat training. She had a small build, with sloping shoulders and large, round eyes. She wore her hair in bangs and was winsome enough to have been in the drum-and-fife corps of the Revolutionary Opera Company. She could move with surprising speed and agility. Having grown up in a harsh mountainous region, where she had trapped rabbits, hunted deer, and dug holes in the ice to catch catfish, Kim had certain advantages over city dwellers. Indeed, when it came to training for mountain warfare, in treetops or in the snow, she was more than a match for any male soldier.

Raising her hand, Ri Gwi Hui asked in Japanese for permission to speak. Ri was twenty-eight. On graduating from secondary school in Chongjin, she'd been assigned to the Ministry of People's Security. There she had done so well that she too was sent to Kim Jong Il Political-Military University, where she studied Japanese and Chinese, together with electronic communications and all there was to know about sabotage and subversion. After that, like Kim Hyang Mok, she'd joined the Agency for State Security and Reconnaissance. Ri was of medium height, lithe and athletic, her even features suggesting intelligence. Her task was of major importance: gaining access to the Basic Resident-Register Network in order to gather, sort, and analyze demographic data for the Fukuoka area.

"Yes? What is it? You needn't raise your hand."

"Even if told to say what one wants to say, it can be hard to think of anything."

Ri had risen and was standing at attention as she spoke. Han was of two minds. On reflection, he realized the absurdity of ordering members of the SOF to speak freely, when it had been relentlessly instilled in them—not verbally but rather in the way that salt and pepper are worked into raw chicken—that they were to have neither their own will nor any personal feelings. Absolute submission to orders was all that mattered. For no other reason, new recruits were tied to posts and whipped for hours on end with cow intestines lined with copper wire. Their senior comrades would punch them, sometimes wearing boxing gloves, sometimes not. There was also the practice of stretching a strip of inner-tube rubber with a sort of giant slingshot, then releasing it right in a recruit's face.

All recruits were subjected to two particular forms of hazing. The Motorcycle required them to stand with legs apart, knees bent, and arms raised, as though they were straddling a motorbike.

They had to remain motionless, sitting on invisible saddles, for as long as an hour, even though within five minutes the strain on legs and loins caused the muscles to scream. The order would finally come—"Go!"—whereupon they had to run full tilt into a cement wall. If they were thought to have cushioned the impact in any way, they were forced to repeat the action. With the Helicopter, recruits were obliged to maintain a rigid posture, arms outstretched, as they were swung horizontally around. Once sufficiently dizzy, they were released and dropped onto the concrete floor. No bending of the body was permitted.

After being transferred from the Guidance Bureau to an active SOF unit, Han had been repeatedly subjected to the Helicopter. He had suffered a broken nose, cracked teeth, and numerous concussions. Sometimes the pain had been so intense he'd considered pretending to be unconscious; but to test this, recruits would have ice-cold water poured over them or have their eyelids pricked with pins, and if found to be faking they were hazed all the more brutally. The effectiveness of all this was unrivaled in terms of suppressing individual volition and emotion. Numerous methods had been developed in the Republic to control human behavior through pain, humiliation, and fear, and they were used on everyone, from the elite SOF down to the common criminals, ideological offenders, and counter-revolutionary elements who languished in concentration camps, no better off than farm animals.

Han now recognized that it had been a mistake to ask his subordinates to open up. Though able to endure extreme duress, they were quite incapable of ordinary chitchat among acquaintances. Besides, friendship was more than a simple exchange of views, surely. He tried to remember what he'd talked about with childhood friends and how he'd managed to get on good terms with Russians and Hungarians at the Kiev Polytechnic Institute. From his primary-school days in the small town of Tanchon, South Hamgyong Province, he had been known as a confirmed ruffian. After school he and his pals would gather to discuss, for example, which antagonist of theirs needed a thrashing. Boxing was particularly popular in those days. Han and some of the others idolized Choi Cheol Su, the Olympic flyweight gold-medal winner, and had begun training at the town's only gym. On their way home they used to talk endlessly about Choi.

When he thought of Kiev, his first memory had to do with a singer. Having kept up his boxing, Han often sparred with an Angolan student, who one day asked him whether he knew anything about Madonna. Yes, it was a popular subject in Western paintings, he'd replied. The Angolan had doubled up with laughter and then shown him a magazine photo of the blonde American pop star. The story got around to other foreign students, giving Han a sort of identity among them and allowing him, little by little, to make friends. What friendship required was simply a common topic of interest. A boxer, an American singer, who to beat up next—it didn't really matter what the topic was.

"You all know the folk tale about Hong Gil Dong, don't you?" Here, thought Han, was a legend known to all Koreans, North and South, that he could use as just such a focus of interest. Hong Gil Dong, the son of a provincial nobleman and a servant girl, becomes a sort of Robin Hood. From an early age, he shows a talent for *chukjippeop*, a special form of the martial arts akin to Japanese ninja techniques. This enables him to fly, to disappear, to shape-shift, to leap over mountains, and to run faster than the wind, and he uses his powers to take various politicians, and finally even the king, to task. He forms an eight-man squad, breathing life into seven straw figures to turn them into animate replicas of himself. Once he has extracted a promise from the king to rule justly, he and his seven companions disappear, and there the first story ends. According to a sequel, however, he later returns and gathers the kingdom's countless poor onto a fleet of ships and leads them across the sea to a hitherto unknown land, where they create a new nation in which everyone can live a life of dreamlike happiness.

"When explaining this operation to me, Comrade Kang said that I should think of the eight of you as the modern embodiment of Hong Gil Dong."

Kang Deok Sang had indeed made a reference to the legendary hero. "The mission you'll be leading is of enormous importance to the Republic," he'd told Han. "Its conduct is left entirely to your discretion, but I'd like to discuss certain crucial aspects. Your team is to pose as a group of insurgents who have fled the Republic after a failed coup. The Party will denounce you as such to the world at large. Two hours after the nine of you have gained control of the target, four companies from the SOF's Eighth Corps, with a troop strength of over five hundred, will arrive in Fukuoka by air. You will assume command of this combined force. They too will, of course, be named as insurgents. You will be described as an officer of a hardline faction who, stubbornly opposed to the peaceful reunification of the Fatherland, has been forced to leave the Republic at the head of fellow rebels. Nine days after the four companies have secured the city, one hundred and twenty thousand troops from the Eighth Corps will arrive by ship in Hakata Port—all of them supposedly as insurgents. But remember. Even when the Party denounces you as such, it will, in fact, be fully recognizing you as national heroes, as the modern equivalent of Hong Gil Dong. I'm not exaggerating when I say that you are leaving the Peninsula to transform Kyushu—where potters and other craftsmen and laborers were once forcibly taken from the Kingdom of Chosun—into an ideal state."

Han asked whether, in the event of an attack from the Japanese police, the Self-Defense Force, or the American military stationed in Japan, a counterattack would be authorized.

"Yes, of course," Kang had replied, but then added that none of that was likely. "Just two hours after you seize control of a vital urban sector, four companies land and immediately expand the area under control. This will take place on a Saturday when, according to our sources, their top Cabinet ministers will be at meetings in various parts of the country to explain government policies. The Prime Minister himself may not be in Tokyo on that day. It won't be possible for them to put together an effective crisis-management team in a mere two hours. All you have to do once you've established control is to inform the Japanese government politely but repeatedly that you cannot guarantee the lives of the hostages you've taken. This should ensure that the four companies coming by plane—all elite troops under the age of thirty—are immune to attack. If the SDF threaten to take action, they can be dissuaded with a simple announcement that the hostages will be the first to die.

"Fukuoka is a large city, with a population of more than a million. Sacrificing civilian lives is simply not an acceptable option for the Japanese government, and unless it issues an appeal for help, the Americans will likewise be unable to act. According to Professor Pak Yong Su, Japan as a nation has never survived a crisis by strategically allowing for casualties and will therefore refrain from sacrificing the few for the benefit of the many. The Battle of Okinawa doesn't contradict this; in that case the Japanese simply blundered their way into helpless slaughter. You will explain that you have left the Peninsula in order to establish a new, free state in Fukuoka and, by extension, Kyushu—much as Hong Gil Dong is said to have done. And that should be enough. You will be liberating the entire region from the oppression of Japanese imperialism, bringing it freedom and justice. It is the same claim made by Muhammad when conquering Mecca, the Crusaders marching on Jerusalem, Imperial Japan invading mainland Asia, Adolf Hitler launching his blitzkrieg, the Allies defeating the Nazis, and the United States invading Afghanistan and Iraq. Hong Gil Dong is still relevant today."

To get control of all Fukuoka before the main body of troops from the Eighth Corps arrived, they would need to seal off the city themselves. That would be impossible, suggested Han, with only four companies of men. Kang had replied, "When those companies land, you must see to it that a rumor is spread to the effect that commandos from the Republic, speaking Japanese and dressed like Japanese, have already secretly left Fukuoka and are heading for Tokyo, where they intend to attack the Imperial Palace and the National Diet. The government is sure to respond by closing all airports, seaports, and roads around the city. The area will be sealed off without your using a single soldier. The main islands of Japan have never been invaded, so the Japanese have no practical experience of this sort of crisis. The government and news agencies will immediately start thinking of missiles being launched from the Republic or terror operations aimed at their nuclear facilities. Of course, it would be madness for us to do anything that risky. We may be forced for purely defensive purposes to occupy one of Japan's many coastal islands, but that will be the extent of it. Merely by shooting a few policemen and taking some of the civilian population hostage, you'll have the Japanese government on its knees. Is Japan the sort of country that's prepared to resolve the issue by annihilating its citizens along with the enemy? No, it is not."

Listening to these words, Han hadn't been able to conceal a tremor of excitement. This operation would go down in history. The thought that they would be proclaiming themselves insurgents and that they would be branded by the Fatherland as rebels didn't bother him. Kang had assured him that the families of all the SOF officers involved would be given special privileges, and in fact once the operation had been authorized and training had begun, Han's family had been moved from Kumhwa in Kangwon Province to guest quarters in Pyongyang. In due course they would be given a high-class apartment on Kwangbok Avenue and his sons would be enrolled in one of the capital's schools. It was likely that every soldier involved would be assured of similar treatment for their immediate families. Would the promises be kept? In any case, there was no alternative: they could remain at home disgraced, or leave the Peninsula as heroes.

Prior to the launch of the mission, a letter of encouragement had arrived from Kim Gweon Cheol, Deputy Director of the Fourth Section of the Organization and Guidance Department. Kang had read it aloud in ringing tones to the nine commandos.

"Greetings, comrade soldiers, loyal warriors. A warm glow of pride must rise in your breasts as you prepare to embark on your mission, sailing into the very jaws of death for the sake of a united Fatherland, that cause for which our Great Leader burned with zeal, and for which our Dear Leader now tirelessly devotes himself every hour of every day. For that same cause we know your own hearts too are beating, your wills like molten steel. You who go now to fulfill our people's most cherished hopes, forsaking the joys and comforts of home for a distant land, will never be forgotten. Your orders come down from our glorious leader himself; failure is inconceivable. His august command ensures success and, holding us in its firm embrace, helps us to stand as steadfast protectors of socialism, the Fatherland, and our pioneering spirit."

"What do you think? Can you see yourselves as Hong Gil Dong?"

Han sat down on the sofa. The very sound of the legendary name, with the image it conjured up of a healthy, energetic, rosy-cheeked youth, seemed to have a good effect on him. Choi Hyo Il and Cho Seong Rae got up from their seats and began slowly pacing the cabin.

"But Hong Gil Dong was just a boy," muttered Cho, looking at the ceiling. "I think of myself as an adult, a soldier pure and simple."

Cho was from Yongdan in North Hwanghae Province. Both he and Choi were exceptions in that neither was from the upper ranks of society. Ri Gwi Hui's father was a prominent engineer; Jang Bong Su was the second son of a captain in the Capital Air Defense Corps; and Kim Hyang Mok's father was a physician trained in Moscow, her mother the daughter of a revolutionary hero who was, in turn, a distant relative of Kang Pan Sok, mother of the Great Leader. Choi, by way of contrast, had been born into a poor farming family, and Cho was the son of the cook at a restaurant-and-sauna place. Their political pedigrees were impeccable, but they were certainly not from elite backgrounds. Tall, gentle-looking, thirty-year-old Cho was known as a gallant soldier—gallant in both senses of the word. On the one hand, he had achieved perfect scores in mountain-and-snow training; on the other, he had also landed in the brig a number of times for fooling around with women in the mountains outside Pyongyang.

"No one is saying you *are* Hong Gil Dong," said Kim Hyang Mok. "The commander is speaking metaphorically." She was sitting in a more relaxed position, hugging her knees.

"Right," Choi grunted. "You never hear of Hong Gil Dong going off into the bushes with a girl."

Cho's face instantly flushed, and Han thought things might turn nasty. But then Cho just sighed and scratched his head like a kid caught in some kind of mischief, and the others burst out laughing.

"Well," he said, "I can't claim to be innocent of things like that. But it's not my fault. It's the ratio of women to men in the Republic. There are just a lot more women, right? And all the brightest and best-looking ones flock to the capital, so it's even worse there. They say about eighty per cent of female workers in the Pyongyang Spinning Mill and the Pyongyang Textile Plant are single. They're starving for love and sex. It's not as if I took advantage of them. Sure, I invited them on a picnic sometimes—brought along some rice, kimchi, bean paste, meat, that sort of thing, and food was really scarce back then, so some of them were grateful and wanted to pay me back in the only way they could. I never forced myself on them."

Cho's grandfather was said to have fought in the liberation struggle as a common soldier and died throwing himself on a grenade to save his commanding officer. That placed the family solidly within the inner circle of patriots. His father, in turn, had been a soldier in the SOF, assigned to the 91st Battalion of the First Corps. The brigade was a clandestine unit, directly attached to the National Defense Committee that guarded the guesthouses used by their Comrade General, while also carrying out overseas sabotage and espionage operations. This gave him access to the Ministry of Culture's special guesthouses on the outskirts of Pyongyang, where one could spend a month with beautiful young women gathered from all over the country. Outside of that time limit, however, it was strictly forbidden to associate with them on a private basis. For violating that prohibition, Cho's father had been stripped of his rank and made a cook. In the Republic, adulterous relationships were outlawed, and only fools and those who couldn't control their sexual impulses engaged in them. Cho, like the others, had received a top-notch education, and he was clearly no fool.

His lighthearted self-deprecation had a loosening effect on the group, and gradually they began to talk more freely. Kim Hyang Mok remarked that their mission made her think more of *The Tale of the Fifteen Youths* than of Hong Gil Dong, and the others agreed. The Great Leader himself had told this story to children during the Anti-Japanese Imperialist Movement, and later it had been turned into a novel. Fifteen boys and girls borrow a boat from some adults for a day of sailing. On their way back, they're caught in a storm and driven far off course, finally running aground on an uninhabited island not far from the Arctic Circle. There they survive only by heroically overcoming many hardships and obstacles. They build a house, domesticate reindeer, and hunt seals, which provide them not only with food but with clothing and lamp oil. From time to time they trap a migrant bird, tie a message to its leg, and send it off in the hope of being rescued. They gather herbs to make medicine, learn to fashion pottery from red clay, and extract salt from seawater, which they use to preserve food. During their long exile, divisions arise, but their leader patiently reunites them. In the end, they manage to build a boat, sail out into the frozen sea, and head for home.

It was true, Han thought: the characters in *Fifteen Youths*, who struggled to survive on an uninhabited island, came closer to symbolizing this mission than did that other hero. The members of his team had now broken up into smaller groups, chatting about various things: the tale they'd just been reminded of, sexual misconduct, the South, Japan...

"You can soon start taking turns napping," Han told them. They all answered him together, but no one saluted. At last, thought Han, they're getting into character as South Koreans.

2

# SEEDLESS PAPAYAS

*April 2, 2011*

J ANG BONG SU awoke five minutes before the morning call.
Outside the porthole it was still pitch black. In the immediate
vicinity, there were several large fishing vessels the size of the *Atago-
Yamashiro Maru*, and many more still in the distance. It was not yet four
o'clock, with two hours to go to daybreak, but they had all slept, and
everyone was now awake. An accurate internal clock was required of
all those belonging to the Special Operations Forces. In the course
of their training they'd learned, when ordered to sleep for exactly
five hours, to do just that. While on the march, you had to be able
to grab all the sleep you needed during infrequent thirty-minute rest
stops, whether in sweltering heat or freezing cold or mosquito-ridden
marsh dankness. They were even capable of sleeping in increments
as short as ten seconds. During winter training in the mountains,
taking a ten-second doze while tramping through the snow meant
the difference between keeping up and falling behind. If you slept
beyond ten seconds, however, you keeled over. Deprived of regular
intervals of sleep, the body couldn't continue to function. Mere
physical exhaustion could be alleviated simply by lying down, but
real sleep was essential to rest the brain; without it, mental fatigue
accumulated, with a proportionate loss of concentration.

After splashing his face with fresh water from a basin in the head, Jang checked his operational clothing and equipment: a T-shirt with an American cartoon character printed on the front, a pink cotton shirt, a light green windbreaker, jeans—known as "American trousers" in the Republic, where they sold for unbelievable prices on the free market—a leather belt with a brass buckle, cotton socks with a strange little smoking-pipe logo at the top, Nike basketball shoes, and finally snug-fitting cotton briefs. There were also two extra changes of T-shirt, underwear, and socks. These went into a blue South Korean backpack, in a separate compartment from the Belgian pistol, the Czech light machine gun, and the four hand grenades. He and each of the others had been supplied with these, as well as a canteen, sunglasses, compact binoculars, a floral-patterned handkerchief, a Chinese counterfeit Seiko watch, a leather wallet containing both Japanese yen and US dollars, a forged South Korean passport, five packs of Japanese cigarettes, a disposable lighter, and a Japanese mobile phone. Female agents Kim Hyang Mok and Ri Gwi Hui were applying make-up with the aid of hand mirrors and sample photographs, but apparently imitating the way South Korean women used cosmetics was no easy task. Kim Hak Su, the second-in-command, came below to announce that they'd entered Japanese territorial waters and would be reaching their destination in a quarter of an hour.

Jang left the cabin and went up on deck, where several commandos, their preparations completed, were already waiting. Choi Hyo Il was among them, smoking a cigarette. He tried to say something to Jang, but it was drowned out by the engine noise, so he gestured for him to follow. The two of them walked around the bridge to the other side. The view quite took Jang's breath away. There, stretching out before them at an oblique angle in the pre-dawn darkness, were the lights of Fukuoka, shrouded in what appeared to be a thin mist. He was reminded of the Milky Way as he had seen it as a boy in the countryside, when the sky seemed to descend to earth. Later he had often gone to Chinese border towns in pursuit of political criminals on the run, and there too he had been astonished at the illumination. This, however, outshone them all. He had never seen such an expanse of brightness. The array of buildings, nearly all of them glowing, stretched across his entire field of vision. From on top of the tallest of them came orange flashes; in fact, the entire row of high-rises along the coastline emitted a subdued, pulsating light. Jang's heart was pounding, and his throat went dry; it was like being drawn into the embrace of a luminous giant.

"There it is."

Kim Hyang Mok had materialized beside him, and was staring at the sight with defiance in her eyes. Next to her was Ri Gwi Hui. Their hair blew about in the breeze that came off the bow, and Jang caught the sweet smell of their perfume. It was a scent not encountered in the Republic, the sort of fragrance that softened strained nerves. Ri was gazing at the coastline dispassionately, but Kim stared with a smoldering hatred. Her grandfather had joined the anti-Japanese guerrillas in Manchuria as a young man; captured at the Battle of Pochonbo, he'd been tortured and killed. Her father had taught her to regard the Japanese as a race of monsters, and there, reflected in her eyes, was a great city that belonged to them. I too, thought Jang, must try to feel like her. This, after all, was the haunt of people who had brought about the division of the Fatherland and even now might be plotting to invade it. Was it because of the mild climate that those lights, glimmering in the haze, seemed unthreatening? They were intangible, ambiguous, illusory, and Jang couldn't shake off the feeling that he was dreaming. Visible from the port side was an island that was linked to Fukuoka by a long bridge. Though it was still four in the morning, both lanes were filled with cars, the beams of their headlights colliding.

The ship passed between the island with the bridge and another island to starboard, then slowed as it headed directly for a third. Here, at what was apparently a well-known tourist site, they would disembark. On the far side of this island was a dock from which ferries left every hour during the daytime, taking passengers across Hakata Bay in just fifteen minutes. Jang and his eight companions would be

113

posing as South Korean tourists who had spent the night in one of the island's inns and were now heading back to the city. The ship entered a sheltered cove and maneuvered toward a bare landing pier nestled within an L-shaped breakwater. It was apparently intended for pleasure boats. Now in the shadow of the promontory, they could no longer see the radiant buildings of Fukuoka, their field of vision filled instead by a thickly wooded slope. The island that lay before them was unlit. As they had learned in training, there were about a thousand inhabitants, with one elementary and one middle school, three inns, five public restrooms, and one taxi. Autumn, when the cosmos were all in bloom, brought the largest number of tourists, and in the summer there was a big outdoor music festival. Spring was a time for fishing, and so Jang was carrying a pole, as were Cho Seong Rae, Jo Su Ryeon, and Ri Gwi Hui. Kim Hyang Mok had a plastic creel hanging by a strap from her shoulder, while Han Seung Jin, his second-in-command, Kim Hak Su, and Choi Hyo Il dangled long cylindrical cases for carrying multiple rods, though in fact each contained a rocket launcher.

There was barely any movement of wind or waves, and the air on the island was neither hot nor cold. They docked and quickly disembarked, Jang jumping up onto the pier with the ease of a child hopping over a puddle. The thought that he was for the first time stepping onto Japanese soil did not occur to him. From the forest ahead came the cry of a bird. He quickly adjusted his eyes to the darkness. The wooden pier was narrow and the boards uneven, but the use of flashlights was out of the question. Han took the lead, moving gingerly. Making his way along the pier, Jang heard the sound of the ship's engine. He looked back to see the white wake as it slowly pulled away, and was suddenly seized by a strange dizziness, as though his feet did not belong to him. His heartbeat was erratic, slowing down and then speeding up again. He pressed his hand to his chest through his outer clothing, concerned that his companions might notice. He wasn't particularly worried—it was surely just some sort of arrhythmia—but it made him feel like a toy robot whose batteries had run down. The sensation was quite new to him, and he wondered about the canned cod he'd eaten on the ship the night before.

He was debating whether to tell Han about his condition, when he noticed that the legs of the soldier ahead of him were a bit shaky, too. It was Choi Hyo Il. Jang gave him another careful look, thinking he might have been mistaken. But no, there was indeed a slight tremor in his step. It was said of Choi that once, during the joint exercises held by the 907th Battalion at Pyongsan, he had slipped out of the barracks with a few friends after lights out and headed for a hostelry some twenty kilometers away. There they stuffed themselves with meat and drink and raised such hell that three passing patrolmen had come in to reprimand them, at which Choi, enraged by the interference, beat them to death with his bare hands and then escaped back to the barracks. SOF operatives were required to harden their fingers and hands by thrusting them unbent into buckets filled with raw adzuki beans—left-right, left-right—for up to an hour at a time, until their fingers were raw and bloody. The pain was enough to make some of them faint, and within a week their fingernails would fall off. But they accustomed themselves to it, and when the nails grew back, they would switch to sand. The sand wedging under the nails caused a different kind of pain, but this time they didn't fall off. The one-hour-a-day practice went on for a year, at which point the buckets were filled with pebbles, this now requiring special care to avoid breaking bones in their fingers. Within two years, the tips of the fingers became as deadly a weapon as any knife. Choi was said to still train every day with his bucketful of pebbles. Tough as they come—and yet his legs were now wobbly. Was he afraid? In Jang's case, he thought he'd lost his capacity for fear since joining the State Security Department, but it must still have been lurking somewhere inside him. The sight of the departing ship, his last link to the Republic, had apparently brought it to the fore, but in this he clearly wasn't alone. The reassurance that even Choi Hyo Il was not immune helped steady him. The vessel was now well on its way, lost among the other fishing boats. Whether he liked it or not, there was no turning back.

115

Beyond the pier lay a narrow game trail leading up a dark, wooded hill. They trudged single-file, Jang sweating slightly as he went, not knowing how long the climb would be. The slope was steep, with thick vegetation on both sides of the path. The cries of birds grew shriller with the dull approach of dawn. They were struggling over slippery red clay, contending as well with scattered rocks and protruding roots. A moment's inattention could result in entangling one's fishing pole in the branches, stumbling over a root, or slipping on a rock and crashing into the comrade behind. Still, this was a pleasant hike when compared with cross-country training in the winter months back home. With that thought in mind as he continued to climb, Jang felt a wave of energy welling up in him. Earlier he had slept for nearly two hours, whereas once, while tracking down a South Korean Christian pastor who was aiding would-be defectors, he had gone without any sleep at all for a full three days.

On board the ship the night before, they had had rice and kimchi with their codfish, but the energy he now felt seemed to come less from the food than from the clothes he was wearing. Above all, he felt a lightness in his feet, almost as though he were barefoot. Unlike the standard-issue lace-up boots, these shoes gave a good grip on the ground too. His T-shirt had an agreeable, well-aerated feel to it. He had never worn such comfortable clothing before, and at first he couldn't get used to the idea that it belonged to him. In the Republic, the undergarments worn by both soldiers in the People's Army and ordinary workers were not private possessions but shared. They were all identical, with only slight variations in size, and one simply selected what one needed from a huge pile of laundry in the common changing room. The rationed underwear was heavily starched and did little to absorb sweat, making one vulnerable to chills in the winter months.

During their training for the current operation, when underwear was passed out with the information that this was to be treated as personal property, Ri Gwi Hui and Kim Hyang Mok were each handed the tiny, semi-transparent snippet of cloth that constituted a pair of underpants, along with a brassiere of the same color. They both asked an instructor why they needed to wear these things, when no one could see them from the outside. They were told that the sort of underwear worn in the Republic was unknown in Japan and that as all Japanese women wore bras, they would raise suspicion if they didn't do likewise. Fingering their new panties, which looked no bigger than a camellia when bunched in the hand, Ri Gwi Hui and Kim Hyang Mok stood for some time staring at what apparently struck them as symbols of decadence.

As the darkness gradually lifted, Jang could see the two women walking ahead of him, with Han Seung Jin in the lead and then Pak Myeong. Ri was wearing a light purple windbreaker, white trousers that came to just above her ankles, and a baseball cap with the letter Y superimposed on the letter N. Kim had on gray jeans and a denim jacket. Both were carrying backpacks, Ri's marked with a cartoon cat. Jang found himself imagining the underwear they must be wearing but quickly suppressed the thought.

By the time they reached the end of the trail, light was glowing on the eastern horizon; to the west, except for a few scattered clouds, the windless sky was clear. They were now on a wide gravel path, and the going was easier. The illustrated tourist map suggested that it was a scenic trail. They stopped to get their bearings. On the right was a meadow of tall, lush grass, and through the thicket to their left was the sea. From here they would pass a coffee plantation and make their way down to the ferry landing. Han had said that if they met any Japanese along the way, they were to greet them with smiles. They had been climbing the steep game trail for over an hour but were sweating only slightly. Cho Seong Rae took a single swig from his canteen. They checked one another's clothing and equipment. Ri and Kim took scarves out of their backpacks and tied them around their necks. From primary-school girls to grandmothers, women in the Republic were all very fond of scarves. Han peered at those his subordinates had just put on. "What's wrong?" asked Kim, but Han said he was only concerned that there might be telltale DPRK stars on them. She tweaked the edge of her scarf and told him solemnly that it was a Chinese copy of a famous French product: Louis Vuitton.

117

They passed several fields of cultivated flowers. Ri pointed out some pretty white ones with golden centers, identifying them as a type of narcissus. Other fields were full of yellow flowers bursting with countless delicate little petals. Here and there were cherry trees, whose pink buds were on the verge of opening. The gravel under their sneakers crunched in the crisp morning air. Han had instructed them to walk each at his own pace, to avoid looking too military, and Jang, who was used to working alone in his role as an intelligence officer, had no difficulty in following that order. He took great pride in being a secret agent. Gathering information was his calling, and it took precedence over anything else. At heart, he disliked taking part in team operations and felt he was not cut out for them. Behind him, Choi Hyo Il was making small talk with Ri Gwi Hui, telling her that the scarf suited her and asking whether she knew that the insignia on her cap was that of an American baseball team. Choi was basically nothing more than a killing machine; Jang saw himself differently. Han was still in front, walking alongside his second-in-command, Kim Hak Su. Jo Su Ryeon and Pak Myeong were talking about fishing. Outside Pyongyang, on a branch of the Taedong River, there had been a well-known fish farm, and both men had often gone there as children to fish. But then, famously, the river had overflowed its banks, and tens of thousands of fish were swept away. Those that got stranded on land were scooped up by nearby inhabitants and sold on the free market. It was said that with the softening of America's stance toward the DPRK, the worst of the crisis was over. Yet while food and medicine were more available than before, there was still starvation in the provinces, with deep-rooted corruption among cadres in both the Party and the military. The secret naval base from which their ship had departed was in an appalling state of disrepair. Most of the boat shelters that had been carved into the cliffs had caved in, the drainage system had rusted into uselessness, and there wasn't a drop of fuel in the storage tanks. Diesel fuel for their vessel had apparently been brought in from Seongheung, taking an entire day to arrive.

Jang found himself wondering what the future would hold, after the "insurgency." Once the Dear Leader had carved his name in history by uniting the Fatherland, he might well, as had been rumored, retire to China. It was no doubt true that with America less hostile and China offering its guidance, reunification was no longer just a dream. Yet there were countless obstacles still to be cleared. Merely mixing the two populations, North and South, would lead to chaos. The economy too would be thrown into disarray, and the hardliners in the People's Army would probably refuse to lay down their arms. In maintaining their support of the Comrade General, the United States, China, and the South hoped to minimize the turmoil that would accompany any steps toward reunification. The present operation, introducing troops into Fukuoka, was intended to eliminate several of the main obstacles, while at the same time forcing Japan to play a losing role. Japan was increasingly seen as a nuisance not only in East Asia but in the world at large. Its economy would not recover, which in turn was stimulating a resurgence of militarism. Many of the big corporations had moved overseas, and there were reputedly over a million homeless people in the large cities.

Jang was impressed by the meticulousness of this operation. Surely it was too well scripted to be the work of the Republic alone. Even if the great powers had not been directly involved, they must at the very least be aware of the operation and preparing to turn a blind eye to it. In the end, more than a hundred thousand hardcore DPRK troops, together with UN troops—mostly American and Chinese—would probably wind up being stationed as occupying forces in Kyushu, the US and China having forged an alliance. The island would become a buffer zone, preventing any direct clash between the two superpowers. As the military presence would be maintaining public order in Kyushu and ensuring the security of its inhabitants, it would fall to Japan to pay for the costs. The situation would also provide an opportunity to construct a new Kyeongui railway line across the Peninsula, helping connect Europe and the Far East, as well as pipelines carrying natural gas from the shores of the Caspian Sea and petroleum from the oil fields all the way to Busan. The disruption would be confined entirely to Fukuoka and Kyushu. The focus of any military alliance between the US and China would be some distance away from the borders of either country, and the joint Sino-American task of providing peacekeeping troops would allow the Americans to put the lid on their own anti-Chinese hardliners. Meanwhile, those Japanese calling for an expanded military would find their hopes stymied, as any attempt to beef up the nation's military capabilities would be predicated on a retaking of Kyushu. And Japan had neither the strength nor the will to take on both the United States and China there. Their southern island thus lost, the Japanese would be totally isolated: economically, militarily, and politically.

"We'll eat here," said Han, as they reached a rest area beside the trail. Through the trees, they could see the ferry landing below. Rows of camellia bushes grew amidst the well-trimmed grass; beneath wisteria trellises stood three sets of concrete tables and seats. Nearby were also a drinking fountain and a public toilet, along with a platform structure made of brick, perhaps used for grilling meat or fish. It was still early in the morning, with no sign of any tourists. Jang Bong Su sat down at one of the short, rectangular tables and shrugged off his backpack. Jo Su Ryeon came over and took the seat across from him, and from behind came the voices of Ri Gwi Hui and Kim Hyang Mok. Jang turned to see them standing there bashfully, like girls at a picnic. He guessed that they wanted to be at the same table as Jo. Han and Kim Hak Su sat facing each other at one of the others, with Choi Hyo Il now joining them. At the third table, Pak Myeong sat across from Cho Seong Rae. Cho called to the women to join them, but they demurely declined, saying they had a favor to ask of Jo Su Ryeon. "Would that be all right?" Ri inquired, whereupon Jo stood up and invited them to sit. Yes, indeed, just like a college outing, thought Jang.

A slight breeze arose, carrying a sweet, fruit-like fragrance toward them. Their illustrated map showed some greenhouses on the coffee plantation. It seemed likely that tropical fruit was being grown. The scent was quite strong, and the two women and Jo Su Ryeon were sniffing the air. "I wonder whether it's some sort of flower," said Kim Hyang Mok. True daughters of the Republic that they were, she and Ri now unscrewed their canteens and poured out some water for the men. Cho Seong Rae looked on with envy. "Aren't you going to do the same for us?" he said teasingly, but the women ignored him. "It smells more like fruit to me," Jo remarked, opening his lunchbox. Then, looking across the table, he added: "But perhaps Comrade Jang would be a better judge of that." The lunches, packed in aluminum boxes, consisted of rice, mackerel in hot pepper paste, and cucumber kimchi. There was already something nostalgic about the smell of spicy bean paste and garlic, as though a last farewell had been packed into those small gray boxes. "Why do you think that?" Jang asked in the deferential tone that Jo's status called for. Four years Jo's junior, he would never have thought of touching his food until the other had already begun to eat. Moreover, he liked Jo Su Ryeon. The man's chiseled features made him look like a people's actor, and his deep voice was soothing. "You've often been to China, haven't you?" came the reply. "I imagine you've seen lots of things in your travels."

"Well, I also think that it's some sort of tropical fruit, but I can't tell you what the name of it might be." Jo was sitting next to Kim, Jang next to Ri. The concrete seats were close together, so that every time Jang turned or changed position his elbow or knee would graze hers. It occurred to him that it was the first time he'd ever been in such a position. He had been an only child, with neither friends nor sweetheart. As a small boy, he had wanted an older brother and had been jealous of a classmate next door who had one. Those feelings had long been forgotten, for though his solitariness had remained the same over the years that followed, there was no point in brooding about it. So why remember this now? Smiling a bit, Jo began to recite a poem in his beautiful voice. At the next table, Cho Seong Rae and Pak Myeong looked up from their lunchboxes and turned to listen. This was the favor that the two women had asked of him:

to recite the revolutionary verse he was said to have composed as
a university student.

> *I walk the road to a united land,*
> *Guided by the Guards' red arrow...*
> *For fifty years and more*
> *We have done without milk and bread,*
> *All for one precious goal:*
> *To forge tanks and cannon*
> *In the holy war*
> *That will make us whole again...*

Jang was struck by how peaceful the setting was. The handsome
profile of Ri Gwi Hui sitting beside him, the sweet scent in the air,
the warm sunlight through the wisteria forming complex shadows on
the tables, the flat, mirror-like sea below, the ships passing leisurely
to and fro... And yet something wasn't right; some signal told him
to be wary. Now the others noticed it as well. It was the scent, which
had grown stronger and nearer. The branches of some camellia
bushes swayed, and from out of their shadows stepped two Japanese
men carrying cardboard boxes filled with reddish, oval-shaped fruit.
"*Ohayo gozaimasu,*" said the younger of the two as he approached.
The other, a man in late middle age, was apparently his father. The
two were both wearing work overalls and baseball caps, with towels
around their necks. "Might you folks be wantin' to buy some of
these here papayas?" the younger man asked. "Much cheaper than
over at the coffee plantation." It was clear that they were peddling
their fruit, but their way of speaking was unfamiliar. Jang tensed,
not knowing what to do, but realized that what they were hearing
must be the local dialect. Han returned the greeting, as did his eight
subordinates. Jang assumed that their linguistic performance would
pass muster, but the two men now seemed wary. They sniffed at a
lunchbox on the table, then exchanged glances. "Real good papayas,"
said the younger man, perhaps in his mid-twenties, holding out a
box for Han's inspection. "They're seedless, so the eatin's easy." Both

he and his father looked nervously around them. Perhaps selling the fruit privately was not permitted. "Sorry, we are not interested," was Han's formal reply. The faces of the two men abruptly showed suspicion. "Where're ya from?" the older one asked Han in a thick voice, as he stared down at him. Perhaps mistaking the tension in the air for alarm on the part of the nine strangers, he put down his box, took out a cigarette, and lit it, eyeing them all the while. He then leaned toward his son's ear and spoke in a low voice, though perhaps he meant everyone to hear.

"Ya smell that garlic?"

"Where're they from?"

"China, I'd guess, or Korea."

"Just a while back some Chinese swiped a bike right in front the post office."

"We better call a police officer an' have him come up here."

"*Hae-bwa!*" ordered Han. Choi took one step forward and drove the fingertips of his right hand into the son's face, his index and middle fingers sinking deep into the eye sockets. A sound like the whistle of cold wind came from his victim's throat. It was not a scream; more as if the nerves themselves were crying out in fear and pain. The father stood there uncomprehending, his mouth agape and all the color draining from his face. Seeing Choi's fingers buried to the hilt in his son's eyes, he opened his mouth to scream, only to have Kim Hak Su seize him by the shoulder and crush his jaw with the heel of his hand. There was a cracking sound like that of a dead branch breaking. The force of the blow spun the man's head halfway around, his body collapsing in the arms of his assailant, who dragged him into the trees behind them. The farmer's open mouth had been twisted into a smiling yawn. His son was still standing, impaled on Choi Hyo Il's fingers, his entire body shaking. "You fool," murmured Han disapprovingly. "Why go for the eyes? You've got blood on your jacket." Choi extracted his fingers and, with the same hand, now covered with blood and yellowish slime, grabbed the young man by the back of the head and snapped his neck, the cervical vertebrae cracking like sticks of chalk. Pak Myeong and Cho Seong

Rae picked up this second corpse and carried it off into the trees. Jang Bong Su and Jo Su Ryeon made it their business to ensure that there were no witnesses, scanning the area slowly before giving their leader the all-clear. Han ordered everyone to clean up and move out. Ri Gwi Hui had taken Choi's jacket, soaked the right sleeve with water from the faucet, and was pounding it against a rock to remove the blood. With the heel of her shoe, Kim Hyang Mok dug a hole for the eyeballs, covering the remaining gore with earth. Back from disposing of the father's body, Kim Hak Su asked how soon the police would be out looking for the missing men. Han looked at his watch. "It'll take time. Anyway, there's no one on this island capable of arresting us." There was a general feeling of relief, of getting back to normal. "What about the fruit?" asked Kim Hyang Mok, and Han said: "Toss it into the shrubbery."

"Nine adult tickets please." Ri paid for them with three one-thousand-yen notes that she took from her brown vinyl wallet, and collected the change. It would be twenty minutes or so until the ferry's departure. Jang Bong Su was with the others, standing against the far wall of the waiting room. About twenty other prospective passengers were in the small room, which was equipped with only eight chairs. There were two school kids in uniform, a young mother with her baby and a female friend, a middle-aged couple, a tourist group of seven or eight, three construction workers in hard hats, a gray-haired man in a suit, and three Westerners—a young man and two young women, carrying huge backpacks. Jang's first impression on seeing Japanese people of so many different ages in one place was that there was no sign of any vitality in their eyes. Were these the same people who had occupied and ruled the Peninsula through military superiority? Kim Hak Su and Choi Hyo Il were sitting side by side on two of the chairs, but the Japanese were keeping their distance. One of the helmeted workers, a bearded man, noticed the scar on Jang's neck and quickly looked away. While no one was staring at them or showed any sign of unease, it was clear to Han that they were hardly blending in, so he indicated to Jang that they should go and have a look at the souvenir shop. Jo Su Ryeon, Ri Gwi Hui, and Pak Myeong went along with them.

The shop, situated across the dock from the waiting room, was stocked with a variety of noodles that were presumably a local specialty, tropical fruit grown in the greenhouses of the coffee plantation, citrus wine, coffee beans and sweets, dried fruit, postcards, and books about the island. Jo picked out a small bag of mixed dried fruit and paid eight hundred yen, plus another hundred and forty yen in sales tax. "Don't know what this money's equivalent to," he remarked, to which Pak Myeong, having done a rough calculation, replied that eight hundred yen was approximately what the commandos earned in a month. "Couldn't very well stretch out a bag of fruit that long," said Jo with a wry smile. "How about trying our wine?" the middle-aged saleswoman asked Jang. On a table were some small cups. "Do you speak Japanese?" she asked. "Yes, we do," replied Jo, which made the woman smile. "This is blueberry wine," she said, holding out four cups on a tray. Jo glanced out the window toward the waiting room. Han was standing outside, his back to them as he smoked. Kim Hak Su was talking to the two Western girls, relying as much on hand gestures as on words. "One small cup can't hurt," said Pak Myeong, and asked the woman whether the wine was strong. "Not at all," she replied, shaking her head. "It's like fruit juice." Jang took a cup and sniffed at it. He could detect no alcohol, but there was something old and familiar about the smell. Jo also took a cup and then a sip, and his face instantly lit up. "It's just like..." Pak completed the thought: "*Tuljjuksul!*" Jang too had a taste, remembering that it was a Japanese herbalist who in the early twentieth century had discovered blueberries growing at the foot of Mount Paektu, analyzed their medicinal properties, and then developed and marketed blueberry-based drinks and syrups. "Good, isn't it?" said the saleswoman. The three men nodded.

Inside the souvenir shop was a corner where customers could watch coffee beans being ground, with the beverage then served in handmade ceramic cups for three hundred yen. With time still remaining before the ferry left, Jang and his companions decided to try some. There were milk and sugar containers. Not knowing how much of each to put in, they asked the clerk behind the counter, a young woman who was wearing a scarf and no make-up. "About a spoonful, I'd say," she replied, "but some people like it black." Jo muttered that "black" must mean without either milk or sugar, then sampled the brew and declared it delicious. Jang could find nothing the least bit delicious about it; to him, it just tasted bitter. Ri, who had bought a bookmark in the form of a crimson pressed tropical flower, was looking out the window. Her friend Kim Hyang Mok had left the waiting room and was standing just outside. It was said that Hyang Mok had once been married, back in her native town, and had borne a child that later died. Perhaps it was painful for her to be around the young Japanese mother and her baby.

Seen closer up, the cityscape of Fukuoka looked like part of an absurdly immense machine. Jang stood leaning out over the ferry's railing and gazed at the imposing buildings before him. Next to him stood Pak and Ri. The ship was plowing through the waves, dousing their faces and clothes with spray, but none of them minded it. As the city with which they'd grown familiar during their training got larger, they found themselves focusing on one strangely shaped, round-roofed structure they had often seen photos and diagrams of. "You'll get soaked standin' there!" a passing crewman called out to them. Ri pointed at the large structure and asked him what it was.

"Fukuoka Dome," he replied, adding that a baseball game was to be played there that day—the "season opener." Would they be going to see it?

"Perhaps we will," Ri replied vaguely. Yes, Jang said under his breath, we'll be going there all right. But not to watch baseball.

# 3

# A HERD OF ZOMBIES

*April 2, 2011*

W E *ought to be occupying this hotel rather than the baseball stadium.*
Kim Hak Su was in his room, adjusting the sheath of his
combat knife, when the thought occurred to him. They had been
prepared for a skirmish with the Coast Guard or the Self-Defense
Force, but except for the two farmers they'd been obliged to eliminate
on the island, everything had gone off without a hitch. He'd even
had a conversation with two Australian girls on the ferry. They told
him they were going on to Seoul and asked if he knew of a cheap
hotel there, and Kim told them he was from the countryside and
didn't know Seoul well. The talk had then shifted to Korean arts
and taekwondo. When the ferry landed, he and his eight comrades
had split up into three groups to take cabs to their hotel. Strangely,
even disconcertingly, it had an English name: Sea Hawk. On the
way there from the landing he had also seen from the cab English
lettering on restaurants and signs, including LIQUOR SHOP and RICE
SHOP. He asked the driver whether this was an American residential
area. "Nah," the elderly driver had said with a deprecating chuckle.
"But nowadays ya see English just about everywhere."

In a corner of their minds, the educated classes in the Republic
all combined a deep-seated hatred of the Japanese with an

uncomfortable sort of respect for a country that had once fought so fiercely against the West. The same sentiment was probably shared by people in China, South Korea, Vietnam, and Indonesia as well. In the Republic the most prominent factories, roads, bridges, and tunnels had all been built by the Japanese during the occupation. The Chongjin Steel Company, the chemical-fertilizer company in Kamhung, and the bridge linking Korea and China on the Tumen River were also largely constructed by the Japanese. Yet even if this mixture of animosity and grudging respect was common in East Asia as a whole, what did it matter anymore? Japan had degenerated into a country that was little more than America's servile, tail-wagging lapdog. While Han was checking them in, Kim and his comrades took in their surroundings. The lobby's ceilings, walls, and floors were all made of marble, as if it were a palace. People were coming and going in every direction, while others sat conversing idly in the coffee bar. Many of the men and women looked vulgar, with hair dyed in the manner of Westerners, absorbing the effluence of decadent Western music, and consuming Western food and drink. There was even a man with an earring, as though he were a woman.

Heeding Han's warning that they should be prepared to fight if the police were summoned because of any problems concerning registration, Kim had his hand on the pistol inside his backpack. The hotel staff, however, merely bowed and grinned. Han later noted wryly that they weren't even asked for their passports. A bellhop came to take Kim's baggage; though Japanese, he was dressed as an African. Kim was tempted to punch the man. He seemed to have stepped out of some sort of comedy film or come directly from a costume party. Kim had once visited several Eastern European countries when they were still part of the Soviet bloc. In the first-class hotels there, the bellhops had worn simple tuxedos or high-collared uniforms, with bow ties. He glared at the "African" until the poor man started profusely apologizing for what he took to have been some breach of courtesy on his part. When Han later asked his second-in-command what had happened, Kim told him that the bellhop had been dressed in an African costume. "Wasn't that insulting?" Han explained that the Sea Hawk was known for having international themes to its various levels, and that the floor the nine of them were on was supposed to represent Africa. Any disrespect was unintentional, he said.

The decor did indeed smack of something African. The bedcovers were of a tie-dyed fabric, the chair backrests shaped like horns, and the walls decorated with native spears and shields. As Kim unpacked his knife, pistol, and machine gun, he complained to Pak Myeong, his roommate, asking why a Japanese luxury hotel would give itself an African flavor. "Does it matter?" asked Pak, checking the safety catch and magazine of his own gun and then slipping the first hand grenade into his hip belt. "Africa, Mars, Hades—what difference does it make?" He went on calmly inspecting his equipment. This, thought Kim, is a very cool-headed young man. There were few people in the SOF who would say anything to Kim when his temper was up, and even the most stalwart did so with some trepidation. The only exception was Han Seung Jin, a man Kim trusted and respected more than any other officer. But here Kim was turning red with rage, and this youngster Pak Myeong didn't seem intimidated and didn't try to mollify him. At the age of twenty-three, Pak had made quite a name for himself with the 907th Battalion when, while serving for six months as a propaganda broadcaster in the demilitarized zone, he managed to persuade no fewer than three officers from the South to defect.

On reflection, Kim could see that Pak was right. They had taken rooms in the hotel so they could check their equipment and go over operational plans prior to carrying out the mission, and the decor was nothing to get worked up about. Nodding slightly at the boy, he raised the cuff of his trousers and began to attach the knife sheath to his ankle. But deep down he still thought they should be taking over the hotel. He would have liked to slit the throats of those Japanese baggage carriers dressed as Africans. The sight of those buffoons bowing and scraping before foreign tourists was mind-boggling. Where was the Japan, he grumbled aloud as he finished securing

129

RYU MURAKAMI

his knife, that once shook not only Asia but the entire world? His whole perception of the country was being warped.

As he tucked a fourth grenade into his belt, Pak reassured his superior that he quite understood his feelings. It was the Japanese, he said, whose perceptions had become warped. His eyes turned toward the television set, which the bellhop had left on after explaining its various functions. A man in a yellow wool sweater, his fingernails painted and his face daubed with make-up, appeared on the screen along with a small dog. The dog had long hair, a pointed muzzle, and extraordinarily large eyes; and around its torso was a sweater just like its master's. In response to the emcee's question about the dog's favorite food, the man grinningly replied that it was a meat broth delivered by a specialty restaurant for pets. Pak looked away from the screen. "After losing the war," he said, "Japan became America's mistress and managed to become rich in a hurry. Now that the economy's in a shambles, it's starting to feel bitter about a lot of things. That's on top of its usual sense of inferiority and guilt. The Japanese have nothing to look forward to and no plan of action. A country that knows what it wants, and knows what it needs to do to achieve that, wouldn't dress up its workers as Africans." Kim thought admiringly that he was quite right about this. His respect for Han's choice of men grew all the more. Looking again at the dog on the screen, Pak remarked quite seriously: "Much too scrawny to go into a *tan'gogi* soup." Kim had to agree.

The attack on the baseball stadium was to begin at 19:00. Kim and Pak joined the other members of the team in Han's room for a final cross-check. Designed for two people, it was crowded with nine. Han sat in a chair by the window. Next to the table beside him stood Jo Su Ryeon. Kim sat in a chair on the other side of the table, the remaining six on the bed and floor. This was the final run-through; they had already gone over all the details ad nauseam. The first team, consisting of Han and Jo, would enter the stadium from Gate 3, immediately occupy the broadcasting booth, announce the military seizure of the area, and simultaneously convey the KEF's demands to the Japanese government. The remaining seven would be divided into three teams. Second-in-command Kim Hak Su and Ri Gwi Hui would enter from Gate 2 and seize the first-base infield seats; Jang Bong Su and Kim Hyang Mok would enter from Gate 4 and cover the third-base infield seats; and Choi Hyo Il, Cho Seong Rae, and Pak Myeong would enter from Gate 8 and take control of all the outfield seats. The stadium had a total of thirty-two exits, and obviously they couldn't cover them all. Therefore, anyone attempting to leave despite orders to the contrary would be warned with a show of small arms. Anyone disregarding that warning would be shot. Han handed out a transceiver to each of them. It seemed there was some danger of the cellular networks overloading if everyone in the Dome tried to use their phones at once.

The sun was beginning to set. From their rooms they could see the streets of Fukuoka and the sea. Beyond the city, as far as the hills, stretched row upon row of private homes and office buildings. Han was saying that he would signal the withdrawal from the stadium by transceiver. The hostages would then all be released. Were there any questions? Choi was the first to put up his hand: What should be done in the case of mass resistance? Tonight's Pacific League opening game would attract more than thirty thousand fans. If they took the risk of fighting back, weapons would be useless against them. The scenario was improbable, Han explained, but if this happened, they should retreat and join up with the first team in the broadcasting booth, temporarily holding back the crowds with random machine-gun fire.

Ri asked the next question: Was it to be announced from the beginning that they weren't regular troops from the Republic but rather a rebel army faction? "Of course," Han replied. "To do otherwise would be to open the Republic to possible attack. We will say that we are fighting against the dictatorial regime of Kim Jong Il, that we desire peace for the Republic, the happiness of the people, and the unification of Korea, and that we are here to advance those demands." Hearing this, Ri bit her lip and pressed a handkerchief to her eyes, and Kim Hyang Mok put an arm around her shoulders.

The others, too, looked solemn. Seeing this, Han rose to his feet and said gently: "Come on now. Buck up." Looking from face to face, he continued: "In 1853, a peasant named Ha Nil Ga from North Hamgyong Province crossed the Tumen River into Russia. Ha was the first emigrant-pioneer, enduring the harsh Russian climate and many hardships to develop the land. Thanks to his revolutionary efforts, more Koreans followed in large numbers, and eventually the Korean Autonomous Region was created. After that, many patriots made their way there, some voluntarily, others fleeing oppression from the Japanese imperialists. Never losing heart, though accused of being renegades, traitors to the Fatherland, and spies, they remained steadfast in their aims. Those patriots are now wholeheartedly revered in the Republic as forebears of the Revolution. For the sake of bringing peace and security to the Republic, we too must endure the humiliation of being temporarily branded rebels, but let us keep in mind the honor that will accrue to our families. We should have no regrets. Only through loyalty and sacrifice can the nation's happiness be won. And only through loyalty and sacrifice can ordinary people be transformed into heroes."

Ri Gwi Hui dabbed at her eyes, nodding, then bowed deeply to Han, who brushed off her emotion by remarking that energy expended on tears and apologies should be refocused on the task at hand. Kim Hak Su thought to himself that as long as they had Han as their leader, their spirits wouldn't waver. He now asked a question himself about the transceiver channels; and Ri, who had regained her composure, replied as the team's communications expert. Then Cho Seong Rae wanted to know under what circumstances the rocket-propelled grenades could be used. Han had a ready answer: if the police launched a massive counterattack, or if it became necessary to put on a show of force during the process of securing the stadium.

The sun was lower on the horizon, its slanting rays casting orange patterns on the sea. The townscape of Fukuoka, for all its massive size, had something unreal about it. Even the vehicles on the streets below had the appearance of toys, and the urban scene as a whole resembled a well-constructed model. From the moment they entered the hotel rooms and looked from the windows on the upper floors, they had been dazzled by the sheer scale of it all. And yet within five minutes the wonder had worn off. As Kim Hak Su gazed at the view, he wondered whether he should bring up something that had been on his mind since their encounter with the fruit sellers. It was still troubling him now, though he couldn't quite define what it was. He was brooding over this at the window when he found Han standing beside him. "What are you thinking about, Comrade Kim?" he said, clapping his second-in-command on the shoulder. "You look worried, and that's not like you." Kim shook his head. "I'm not exactly worried," he said. "It's just a nagging thought." Han grinned at him and said, "Well, you'd better get it off your chest now. There won't be time for discussions once we've moved in and are on our transceivers."

"I was thinking," Kim said, "about the two fruit sellers. I'm not good with words, so I don't know if I can explain it, but when Choi poked his fingers in the one man's eyes, the other one didn't try to make a run for it. And then when I got angry with that baggage carrier, he reacted like a dog hit on the head with a hammer. He just stood there and apologized." Han suggested that when people are truly frightened, they become incapable of understanding what's happening to them, and Kim seemed to accept this explanation. In any case, they had more pressing things to do, such as checking the message Jo Su Ryeon was to broadcast. And yet… the moment Choi punctured the eyes of the young man, something in the father's body seemed to cave in, leaving him as empty as a straw doll. In the next instant Kim himself had grabbed the father's shoulder and crushed his jaw with the heel of his hand, and he remembered how little resistance the blow had met with. It wasn't that the older man's jaw was fragile, but rather that all the life had gone out of him: he had already accepted death.

Kim had previously killed two people using *gyeoksul*. The first was a political criminal in a concentration camp. The second was a caged special-forces infiltrator from the South, already half-dead after torture and interrogation. Yet neither of the victims had simply given in. The last one, in fact, had resisted like a frenzied animal. To Kim, the death of the fruit seller was mystifying.

"Esteemed ladies and gentlemen," Jo Su Ryeon had written, in stiff but polite Japanese. "To everyone gathered here in Fukuoka Dome, a very good day to you. My name is Han Seung Jin, commander of the rebel army faction of the Special Operations Forces of the Democratic People's Republic of Korea…" Choi pointed out that "day" should be changed to "evening"; Jo agreed and started over. Everyone enjoyed listening to him read. Kim, though fluent in Japanese, had no gift for words and so continued to stare out the window. The sun was setting, and a golden haze now enveloped the hills. As a boy, he had thought that every evening when the sun went down, it was extinguished, and that what rose the next morning was a new sun, born in the night. It was in this endless dying and renewal, he thought, that the notion of constancy must originate. Almost as constant, back in the Republic, was the image of the Japanese as complete monsters. But was that, in fact, the case? When he hit the fruit seller, it didn't even feel as if he'd punched the jaw of a living being. That lack of any sort of resistance continued to puzzle him.

"This way for guests heading to Fukuoka Dome to see the season's opening game between the Fukuoka Softbank Hawks and the Chiba Lotte Marines…" A female staff member stood at the entrance of a passage next to the hotel reception counter repeating this message. As the nine walked past her, with Han Seung Jin in the lead, she smiled and bowed deeply to them. Kim Hak Su had hanging from his shoulder the fishing-rod case containing the RPG. In his backpack was an Uzi sub-machine gun, hand grenades, and anti-tank rockets; a pistol was hidden under his windbreaker. He was the last to enter the passageway, both sides of which were lined with shops selling clothing, souvenirs, and shoulder bags. Groups heading toward the stadium were walking briskly. Many of the people were wearing caps and windbreakers emblazoned with a cartoon-hawk emblem. One group began to sing what sounded like a fight song and looked over at Han and his companions, as though urging them to join in. Han smiled at them, nodding with feigned enthusiasm.

Emerging from the passage, they saw Fukuoka Dome stretching out before them, like an immense spaceship in a piece of science fiction. The game had already begun; from beyond the soaring steel wall came the roar of the fans. Breaking into their four teams, they headed for their assigned entrances. Choi Hyo Il, Cho Seong Rae, and Pak Myeong followed the wall to the left; the others went right. Kim Hak Su and Ri Gwi Hui had the farthest to go and so quickened their pace, Kim striding off and Ri trotting in his wake.

The distinctive, awe-inspiring form of the Dome, gleaming silver in the reflection of streetlamps and car headlights, seemed to bear down upon them. We don't have any buildings like this in the Republic, thought Kim. Pyongyang's Arch of Triumph and the bronze statue of the Great Leader were certainly imposing, but they weren't modern like this and had a very different feeling. Pairs of spectators called to each other to hurry up as they trotted toward the entrance. The local baseball team, the Hawks, seemed to have quite a following, with tickets for the opening game being difficult to procure. Without being informed of their purpose, a collaborator in Japan had been asked to buy them, along with mobile phones, transceivers, and maps, but had failed to get any tickets. Since their weaponry wouldn't pass unnoticed through the metal detectors at the gates anyway, however, Operations Command had concluded that it wouldn't matter if they had tickets or not.

They passed Gate 4 and came to Gate 3. Han's team would be entering here, but there was no time to wait and see if they arrived safely. Jang Bong Su and Kim Hyang Mok were presumably already inside the stadium, and the absence of gunfire, explosions, or any hue and cry suggested that they hadn't met with resistance. They had been authorized to open fire if necessary; if initial warning shots went unheeded, they were to aim at arms and legs. To the left was a children's recreation room. According to the building plan that had been drummed into their heads, Gate 2 should soon be in view, and now there it was, marked in huge letters. A sole ticket-taker, wearing an orange windbreaker with the team logo on the back, was leaning against a pillar next to the entrance. Kim had Ri go ahead. She gestured to indicate that her companion had the tickets, but before the man in orange could say anything, Kim had a pistol pointed at his forehead: "Not a word. Keep your mouth shut. We are Special Operations Forces from North Korea." The man just looked at him, dumbfounded. Kim lowered his pistol. "Do you understand? Don't move," he said, and walked on.

"Wait!" the man cried in a quavering voice. "Wait a minute!"

Kim turned back to see him standing motionless, his face sheet-white. "That's not allowed!" He didn't seem to know how to react, as if unsure whether "North Korea" and the pointed pistol were for real or just a prank. Kim feared things were going to end as they had on the island with the fruit sellers. When he ignored him and pressed on, the man shouted after him, "Stop!" Up ahead at the metal detector, Ri Gwi Hui was pointing her pistol at a security guard. The man was dressed in a navy-blue uniform and armed only with a nightstick. Next to him was a female guard. Ri, gripping her pistol with both hands, kept it right at the man's nose, but to her consternation he reacted with no more than a faint smile of embarrassment, intermittently glancing at his female colleague, as though nervously trying to communicate something to her. If they lost any more time, Han's announcement might begin before they were in position. Stepping ahead of Ri, Kim took the guard's shoulder with his left hand, pushed him down, and smashed his right knee into his chest. The man fell to his knees with a rasping groan, holding himself and writhing in pain, while the woman covered her mouth with her hands and gave a muffled scream.

"*Tallyeora!*" Kim barked at Ri, and the two began running. Now inside the stadium, they sprinted down a long corridor, passing another security guard. "No running, please," was all he said, but suddenly two more guards were coming toward them from the opposite direction. With the other teams presumably already in the stadium, they must have been alerted that there were intruders. Kim and Ri turned left and ran up a flight of stairs leading toward the stands and then into a tunnel-like corridor, where three female ushers asked to see their tickets. Brushing past them, they ran on until they came out into the open air.

The sight that met Kim's eyes was overwhelming: a field of dazzling green artificial grass and a lofty gray ceiling composed of a massive steel framework in complex patterns. He had never seen such a huge sports arena. Nor, for that matter, had he ever seen a baseball game. The whoops and shouts of the spectators shook the air. He was astonished most of all by the gigantic electronic scoreboard directly in front of him. The sheer scale of it prevented him at first from grasping what it was, and for a moment he just stood staring at it. A cartoon hawk was running across a display that had to be a thousand times larger than any movie screen in the Republic. The entire stadium reverberated with the sound it emitted, as colorful swashes of light pulsated and swirled. Ri ran up one of the flights of concrete steps that divided the spectator seats into various sections, and Kim followed. They needed to get to the top so as to have the whole array of infield seats before them and the wall at their backs. With every step Kim took, the RPG banged against the inside of the fishing-rod case. Now he heard the shrill sound of a whistle and looked back to see three guards pointing at him and ordering him to stop. Ahead of him, Ri was still bounding up the steps. The security service would have already notified the police. Han's announcement had to be made before they surrounded the stadium.

As they passed a young drinks vendor with an ice chest suspended from a strap around his neck, the kid caught sight of the pistols, as did some of the spectators. They heard voices behind them saying things like, *What's going on? Was that a gun?* Looking back, Kim saw people staring at him with looks of disbelief. At this stage, the spectators could still have left the stadium easily enough, and yet none of them had done so even after seeing two figures dash up the steps with pistols drawn. Again Kim felt the same dread premonition, but he couldn't let it distract him from the task at hand. At the top of the stairs, he handed his backpack and fishing-rod case to Ri. Still holding his pistol, he stood guard, scanning the crowd below while Ri unzipped the various pouches and removed the two Uzi sub-machine guns. She handed one to Kim, together with a spare magazine, and strapped the other to her shoulder. Next came the eight hand grenades, four to hang on Kim's belt, the other four for herself. Finally, having removed the RPG from the rod case, she again slipped the backpack on, leaving one of the pouches half-open so as to have immediate access to the rockets. A few spectators nearby began to raise a fuss—*What are they doing? Is this for real? Are they filming a movie or something?*—but no one was attempting to escape.

There was a lull in the game, while the batters and fielders switched over. A commercial for beer appeared on the giant scoreboard, accompanied by an ear-splitting jingle. The crowd around Kim were showing signs of agitation, and members of the cheering section below were looking up this way with puzzled expressions. The cheering section was split into three contingents of about a hundred people each, gathered in three separate spots along the third-base line. The members stood out because of their headbands and strange white getup, not to mention the huge banner bearing the hawk emblem that each contingent was gathered around. Some had painted their faces like primitive savages. Six minutes had gone by, and still the announcement had not begun. The guards assembled at the foot of the stairs all had wireless handsets to their ears, no doubt waiting for instructions. "Team One, Team One. Colonel Han. Comrade Jo Su Ryeon. This is Team Two. Can you hear me?" Ri got no response from the broadcasting booth, but Jang Bong Su of Team Three and Cho Seong Rae of Team Four checked in to ask if she had heard from their commander. "Not yet," she replied and they reported the same. The situation was similar for all three teams: the crowds around them were growing restless and the guards were closing in.

A video advertisement for Toyota now flashed on the enormous screen, and Kim found himself irresistibly drawn in by the size and brilliance of the images. A dark-purple car driving on a seaside road was suddenly seen soaring into the air, the next instant racing through a red desert, then plunging into the sand, and finally barreling around a caldera lake that looked quite like the summit of Mount Paektu. Ri nudged him in the side: there were six more guards by the gate, pointing in their direction, talking into their transceivers, and attempting to calm the spectators. Standing at the top of the stairs, Kim kept his eyes to the right while Ri looked left. One of the spectators nearby, a man in his thirties with two primary-school-age children in tow, spoke to them: "Excuse me." Kim glared at him. "Can we go to the restroom?" When the man repeated the question, Kim motioned with his chin for them to go. The man thanked him, got up, and, together with the children, slowly walked down to the end of the stairs, where the guards called him over for questioning, their eyes still on the intruders.

A woman sitting to the left of Ri said to her, "Where are you from?" just as a transmission came in from Team One. "This is Jo Su Ryeon. Can all of you hear me?" Ri replied: "This is Team Two, over." The sound emanating from the billboard and the din of the spectators' voices drowned out Jo's voice. Ri pressed the receiver tightly to her ear and repeated his message for Kim: "The broadcasting booth has been secured. Light resistance. No casualties. Our message will be read in one minute. Over." Ri responded: "Team Two reporting. Our position is secure. No resistance; no casualties. Over." The transmission ended with Jang Bong Su and Cho Seong Rae providing much the same information. Ri had spoken loudly, in a clear voice, and now people in the crowd nearby were saying, *Hangul! They're speaking Hangul!* The clock on the scoreboard read 19:13. In two minutes the Airborne Squadron would be taking off with the four companies of the 907th Battalion on board. Kim was concerned about the situation in the broadcasting booth but told himself that with a man like Han Seung Jin in command, there would be no indecision, no confusion, and no mistakes in judgment. Han had covered for Kim when he went AWOL from the 907th Battalion to attend his mother's funeral, as a result of which his superiors had subjected Han to a brutal punishment involving a blowtorch, which left a keloidal clump where his ear had been. In tears, Kim had gone down on his knees to apologize to his benefactor, who laughed it off, saying that it only meant he'd not be able to wear reading glasses when old age caught up with him.

The youngish woman to Ri's left spoke again. "Excuse me. Are you Korean?" She clearly assumed they were from the South. She was wearing a cap with the Hawks emblem and eating noodles from a polystyrene cup. "No," replied Ri. "Guess not," said the woman to the man next to her, apparently her husband. She was still munching her noodles. "Don't talk to the spectators," Kim admonished his partner. "Don't answer their questions." The woman's chopsticks were in constant motion as she stared at the two of them, her gaze shifting from their faces to their weapons and then back again.

"Esteemed ladies and gentlemen." Han's voice came over the loudspeakers. "To everyone gathered here in Fukuoka Dome," he continued, "a very good evening to you. My name is Han Seung Jin, commander of the rebel army faction of the Special Operations Forces of the Democratic People's Republic of Korea. We are interrupting the festivities here today in opposition to the dictatorship of Kim Jong Il, for the sake of peace in our Republic, the happiness of our people, and the fulfillment of their dearest wish—the unification of our Fatherland. In view of this development, tonight's game is now terminated. I repeat: the game is now terminated."

The response to the announcement was muted. No one seemed particularly surprised or frightened. Most had blank, uncomprehending expressions on their faces.

"My troops are all in position. We are well trained and armed with automatic weapons. For the time being, you must stay where you are. Do not leave your seats until you are told to. Under duress, we will open fire. If you engage in any sort of misconduct, we will shoot to kill."

The players at bat came out on the field and stared up at the broadcasting booth. The umpires walked toward the booth, stopped—perhaps able to see for themselves the men or the weapons in there—then motioned to the players to return to the bench. The three infield and two outfield umps came trotting back as well. The batboys likewise disappeared, and soon the field was empty. The screen on the scoreboard continued to pulsate with the animated bird and the message GO, GO, GO HAWKS, but the sound was off and the spectators had fallen silent. A message came over Ri's transceiver. She listened and repeated for Kim's sake, "This is Team One. Have heard from the Japanese Cabinet Secretariat and passed on our demands. Waiting for a reply. The airborne forces are on course. Repeat. Airborne forces have been launched. All teams, report your situation." The clock on the scoreboard now read 17:19. The aircraft transporting the four companies would be arriving in two hours, bypassing southern airspace. Tense-looking security guards in the Dome were still gathering at the gates. As part of the demands made to the Japanese government, the airborne troops were to be allowed to land safely; in addition, no police personnel or vehicles were to enter within a five-kilometer radius of the Dome. Any sign of police activity inside that area would result in the execution of spectators. Team Four reported to Jo Su Ryeon that the spectators were getting restless. Kim Hak Su too could hear murmuring from the first-base infield seats. Everyone was now aware of the armed intruders and understood that the game had been cancelled, but no one among the thirty thousand spectators had the faintest idea how to deal with the situation. Ri looked at Kim and pointed down toward the home-team dugout. The three cheering-section contingents were merging there, each group flying their big Hawks banner. A large, bearded man in front of the largest group, carrying the biggest banner, appeared to be their leader.

"What the hell?" he shouted into his megaphone, looking up at Kim Hak Su. The words prompted scattered laughter and cries of, "You tell 'em!"

"You really from North Korea?" the bearded man shouted. "Your girlfriend up there—she in one of the Dear Leader's Joy Brigades?" In response to this, a roar of laughter came from as far away as the outfield bleachers. The guards joined in too. It wasn't that the man's remark had struck anyone as genuinely funny. Kim recognized this laughter as an attempt to release tension and suppress fear. The series of advertising messages on the enormous screen continued automatically, and the voice of the man with the megaphone reverberated around the stadium. Handing his banner to a fellow member of the cheering section, he began walking slowly toward Kim and Ri, dangling and swinging his megaphone. Over the transceiver came Han's voice saying: "Team Two, can you hear me? Stop those people in white!" Ri asked Kim what they should do. "If they come any closer," he said, "we'll order them to stop. If they don't obey, we'll fire warning shots in the air. Don't fire at their feet. The bullets might ricochet." The groups in white had converged and were filing into the aisle behind their bearded leader. "How many do you think there are?" he asked Ri. "Two hundred fifty to three hundred." There were no heroes here, thought Kim. This fool may think he can shout into a megaphone and swagger up to armed soldiers, but that's only because he doesn't know danger when he sees it. He's an idiot, like that clown in the hotel. The bearded man reached the bottom of the stairs, where a guard tried to restrain him, only to be sent flying. "Hell!" the man shouted at him. "Why don't *you* lot go up there? North Korea, my ass! Nobody messes with Fukuoka!" Again the stadium erupted in laughter. Players came out of the dugouts to watch. With his retinue in tow, the bearded man began to mount the stairs one by one. "Stop! If you come any closer, I'll shoot," Kim shouted. People in the crowd moved out like widening ripples on water. "Go ahead and shoot!" the man yelled, thumping his chest and taking another step as though to call Kim's bluff. Again there were cheers.

If he fired warning shots, fools like these would probably just keep coming. Inside, they were terrified, but extreme fear can drive people over the edge. If he shot him in the legs, he might ignite that fear and cause a stampede. If they all rushed them at once, he'd have to use the machine gun, but killing several dozen of them would make negotiations with the government more difficult. These people were like kids throwing a tantrum—or worse, zombies who'd lost touch with their real souls. At moments of crisis, people who just couldn't deal with the stress often did things that were suicidal. A child you could just take in hand, but how do you get people like this in touch with their souls? They had to be shocked back to their senses, but how do you do that? How do you get a herd of zombies to go back into their graves?

"Take cover, down there!"

So saying, Kim picked up the RPG that lay at his feet. To avoid the back-blast, he stepped away from the wall and ordered Ri to load the weapon. "What's the target?" she asked. "Never mind. Just load it!" He raised the muzzle to an elevated position, knowing the outer limit of the weapon's range. "Loaded!" said Ri, and Kim pulled the trigger. An explosive blast ripped through the stadium, followed by a powerful shock wave as the rocket soared above the playing field toward the huge electronic scoreboard. A second later, half the scoreboard was reduced to shreds of plastic and glass, as gray smoke poured from what remained and sparks shot toward the roof. The crowd was hushed, all faces frozen. Now at last they knew where they stood. Kim put aside his RPG and, descending the steps, approached the cheerleader. "Well? Shall I shoot you?" he asked, pressing the muzzle of his pistol against the bearded man's pale forehead. The man only moaned, a damp stain spreading on his white trousers. "Now go back to your seat!" Kim commanded him. Bobbing his head liked a chastened child, he did as he was told.

# 4

# ANTONOV AN-2S

*April 2, 2011*

K AWAI HIDEAKI'S immediate thought on hearing about the occupation of Fukuoka Dome by North Korean guerrillas was, "Why does it have to be Saturday evening, of all times?" There were always a few people at work on weekends and holidays in CIRO to cover in case of emergencies. Kawai wasn't on the emergency shift, but he'd been bothered by reports of the Korean People's Navy amassing a range of vessels at the Nakwon and Mayangdo bases over the past day or two and had come in this afternoon to check his email. Satellite images from the US Department of Defense showed that most were transport ships, not warships. North Korea had few large battleships, and those they did have were mainly used for maneuvers off the coast.

According to one email from the Korean Intelligence Division, around a hundred ships had assembled and were preparing to sail. It was the first time anything like this had happened. Kawai had hastily contacted informed sources in Korea, China, and the US, but was still none the wiser and had been just about to go home when NHK broadcast the newsflash. Reports were coming in that Fukuoka Dome had been occupied by an armed group right in the middle of the opening game of the season, but it was not known whether they were Japanese extremists, an organized crime syndicate, or foreign terrorists. Other TV stations also soon began interrupting their programs to relay events in the Dome. The game was not being shown live, but all the stations had cameras set up there that were capable of live broadcasts.

As soon as the guerrillas began their statement with the phrase "Esteemed ladies and gentlemen," Kawai's heart sank. As head of the Korean Affairs Section of CIRO's International Division, it was immediately obvious to him that this was a North Korean group. Many members of their Special Forces and State Security Department's Reconnaissance Bureau had learned Japanese, but they were unfamiliar with contemporary Japan and tended to use old-fashioned words and phrases rarely heard these days. "Esteemed ladies and gentlemen" was followed incongruously by "To everyone gathered here in Fukuoka Dome, a very good evening to you," which brought sniggers from a few of the assembled CIRO staff who'd gathered in front of the TVs. But then the announcer identified himself. "My name is Han Seung Jin, commander of the rebel army faction of the Special Operations Forces of the Democratic People's Republic of Korea." A momentary hush fell over the room, and then everyone rushed back to the phones and computers on their desks, keeping one eye on the TV. No one was taking it lightly, but the reality had not yet sunk in and the atmosphere was largely one of sheer astonishment. Kawai grabbed his own phone and called a contact in the South Korean intelligence bureau. The office at the other end of the line was already in uproar. As soon as the contact came on, he wanted to know what the Japanese government intended to do about the situation. Kawai had been hoping to find out what was meant by "rebel army faction" and who Han Seung Jin was, but here the Koreans were already wondering what his own government's response was going to be! "Have they made demands of our government?" Kawai asked back.

There was a stunned silence before the contact read out the guerrillas' list of demands. No police within a radius of five kilometers from Fukuoka Dome. Disable all air-defense systems around Kyushu and ban all activity by the Air Self-Defense Force for two hours, beginning now. If these demands are not met, fifty people at a time will be executed in Fukuoka Dome. Who on earth in the government would be dealing with this, wondered Kawai. The Chief Cabinet Secretary was back in his provincial constituency for the early summer elections. All three deputies were in Tokyo, but he didn't know whether they were at work right now. He asked his contact about the "rebel army faction" and their commanding officer. The man told him that the North's Committee of State Security had already issued a statement through their embassy in Beijing, saying this armed group of rebel officers was acting independently and without the sanction of either the North Korean government or the Korean People's Army. And Han Seung Jin, he added, was a political officer in the Eighth Corps. Kawai's head reeled. Things were moving too fast. Any official statement from the DPRK about unidentified or spy ships would usually come a few days after the start of an incident, if not several weeks later, so why had it been so quick this time? "You mustn't give in to the guerrillas' demands!" insisted the contact angrily. "Even if it means sacrificing some of the people in Fukuoka Dome, demands from the North must not be met!"

Nobody higher up had yet contacted Kawai, which must mean that the Cabinet's crisis-management room was not yet functional. He hung up and turned again to the TV, which was repeating the guerrillas' statement over and over again. "We are interrupting the festivities here today in opposition to the dictatorship of Kim Jong Il, for the sake of peace in our Republic, the happiness of our people, and the fulfillment of their dearest wish—the unification of our Fatherland…" As Kawai listened to each phrase enunciated in strangely imperfect Japanese, the reality of the situation began to sink in, removing any last remaining doubts that this could actually be happening. He reviewed the list of demands. He could understand their not wanting to allow police access, but what to make of the other condition regarding the air-defense system? Were they planning to launch a missile? But surely a rebel faction wouldn't be capable of that—if they could lay their hands on a missile launcher, then they couldn't possibly just be insurgents. So what on earth *was* their objective? Money? An aircraft to make their getaway?

Just then, the room resounded with cries of shock and horror. The guerrillas had demolished the ballpark's giant electronic scoreboard with a weapon of some kind. The NHK anchor reported shrilly that Fukuoka Dome had been destroyed by a missile, and there must be casualties! To the left of the centerfield screen, a plume of black smoke was rising amidst a shower of tiny sparks. Some of the spectators, women and crying children among them, could be seen staring in stupefaction at the charred remains. The explosion was shown again, and someone commented that it looked just like an action movie. On TV, the explosion wasn't as loud or as spectacular as it would be in a movie, but because this was real, the effect was devastating. And it had come just as everyone, the news anchor and guest commentator included, had been puzzling over what the motive for the occupation of the Dome could be. The guerrillas had announced their nationality and status, and that the stadium was now effectively under their control, but their aims were as yet unstated.

People all over Japan were watching the live broadcast. The entire Cabinet—from the Prime Minister and Chief Cabinet Secretary down to all the ministers—must be scrambling to get here. But how long would it take to get a task force up and running? In the event of a major disaster or terrorist attack, the initial response would involve first collating information in the Cabinet's crisis-management room before anything was handed up. The Deputy Chief Cabinet Secretary for Crisis Management would summon an emergency team of related agencies at director-general level, and a planning room would be set up in the Prime Minister's official residence. Then the PM would call an emergency meeting of the Cabinet ministers in order to come up with a plan of action, and if integrated action was deemed necessary, a task force would be set up. Typically the response to, say, an unidentified ship would take about twenty hours from initial discovery to convocation of the Security Council of Japan.

\*

147

A few minutes after the rocket explosion, Kawai's mobile phone and desk phone rang simultaneously. He picked up the desk phone, and heard Iwata, the head of CIRO's Domestic Division, summoning him at once to the Cabinet's crisis-management room. An order had also been put out in the Chief Cabinet Secretary's name for all CIRO staff to report to work. Kawai went to the bathroom, combed his hair and adjusted his tie, then picked up all the data he thought might be useful. The crisis-management room was located in the Cabinet Office, which had moved two levels underground a couple of years ago. It was built to withstand even a terrorist bomb attack—although what terrorist these days would bother to go after the Cabinet? Only the government and the media still believed that North Korea would attack high-profile targets like the Imperial Palace, the Prime Minister's official residence, the Cabinet Office, nuclear power stations, the bullet train, or Tokyo Harbor. They were stuck in the template of all-out war between nations.

Two years ago, some of the brightest young minds in the Intelligence HQ of the Defense Agency had submitted a report saying that if North Korea ever did organize an attack on Japan, it would be on an outlying island—but they had essentially been ignored. There were some seven thousand islands around Japan, and four hundred and twenty-three of these had people living on them. There was nothing to stop a North Korean commando unit from occupying an inhabited island. All they needed to do was kill the local police, take the residents hostage, contact the mass media, and present their demands to the Japanese government. They didn't need major population centers or key installations, just a small squad armed with automatic rifles and hand grenades. It was a nightmare scenario, but short of bringing back the draft it was impossible to guard all the islands with populations of four hundred or fewer with trained soldiers. The government therefore decided that this sort of thing could never happen, and dismissed the report.

Kawai was walking along the dim linoleum-floored corridor when a call came from the General Affairs Section Deputy Leader, Suzuki, who was on his way in by taxi. He lived out in Tachikawa on the

Chuo Line, so it would take him at least an hour. Kawai lived near Musashi-Sakai on the same line, and was well aware that it was one of the most popular for suicides, which meant frequent interruptions. The train was the fastest way to get to work, but in an emergency a taxi was the safer bet. "I'm counting on you to back up Iwata till I get there," Suzuki told him, and then asked what his view of the situation was. Kawai replied that there was so little information as yet that he couldn't really say much, but several things just didn't add up. Suzuki grunted agreement and said, "One thing I don't get is this 'rebel army faction' stuff. What's that all about?" Kawai was just about to answer, when Suzuki said, "Hold on a minute," and spoke with the taxi driver. He heard the driver say that the Chuo Expressway was closed—there must have been an accident or something, or maybe it had to do with the attack on Fukuoka Dome—and they'd have to take surface streets. That meant that Suzuki was going to be even later. Kawai wondered if the expressway was closed because some Cabinet minister was heading along it to get here.

"I find it hard to believe that members of the People's Army would rebel," he said.

"So who the hell are they, then?" asked Suzuki.

"I don't know." He really *didn't* know.

A press officer from the Cabinet's crisis-management room reported that an SDF helicopter was bringing the PM in. He had apparently been in Morioka attending a rally of the local prefectural party. The Chief Cabinet Secretary had been in his constituency in Okayama, and since there wasn't a helicopter available for him there, he was on a bullet train to Osaka, where he would be able to board one. The Minister for Foreign Affairs had been at a "Dialogue with Citizens" event in Nara, where a private helicopter pilot offered to help; but the helicopter had a limited flight range and had to stop off in Nagoya to refuel. The Minister for Home Affairs had been in Ibaraki at the opening ceremony for a digital museum, but since the expressways were jammed by day-trippers on their way home from Disneyland, he'd caught a train back to Tokyo. The Minister of State for Defense had been at home in Sagamihara, and was being driven in with a police escort. The superintendent general of the Metropolitan Police had given a talk at a career-training workshop in Saitama, after which he'd gone to watch the opening game of the season between the Lions and the Fighters. The whereabouts of the head of the National Public Safety Commission was unknown, and no one had managed to contact him.

The highest-ranking bureaucrat currently present in the room was Deputy Chief Cabinet Secretary Yamagiwa. Yamagiwa was sixty-seven, and had come to the Diet from the Bank of Japan. He had no ministerial experience, having served innocuously as a Diet member in what used to be the biggest faction of the Liberal Democratic Party, managing to avoid making any enemies. Feeling the pressure of imminent retirement and wishing to make a name for himself, however, he had taken up the post of deputy chief cabinet secretary. When the LDP had split four years earlier over the issue of the freeze on bank deposits and consequent inflation, the younger reformist faction joined forces with the leading faction of the Democratic Party to form a new party called Japan Green. To begin with it was ridiculed as the Green Tea Party, but it gained support amongst independent voters, prompting several core Diet members of the LDP and DPJ to join, one after another. Eventually Japan Green had taken power from the LDP-Komeito coalition that had won the previous general election by a narrow margin. And Yamagiwa was the grandee of Japan Green.

The other leading members present were Iwata, chief of CIRO's Domestic Division; Kondo, the Cabinet Crisis-Management Center's Systems Maintenance section leader; Yoshizaki, from the Intelligence and Analysis Service's First Division at the Ministry for Foreign Affairs; Korenaga from the Second Investigation Department at the Public Security Investigation Agency; Tsuboi from the Foreign Affairs Division of the Foreign Affairs and Intelligence Department at the National Police Agency's Security Bureau; Katsurayama from the Security Division of the NPA's Security Bureau; Yonashiro from the Documentation Division of the Defense Agency's Intelligence HQ; his colleague Sakuragawa, from the Research Division; and Hida, from the Regional Support Bureau of the Home Affairs Ministry. Other than Hida, they were all from intelligence-related services, although none of them from sections dealing directly with terrorism. Iwata's team gathered intelligence on national political parties and labor unions, while Kondo's dealt mainly with computer data. Yoshizaki's division primarily analyzed intelligence from the US State Department and CIA. Korenaga's department investigated extremists and religious cults in Japan, while Tsuboi's mostly gathered intelligence on foreigners in the country, and Katsurayama's provided protection for VIPs abroad. Yonashiro's division, as its name suggested, classified and circulated documentation, while the main function of Sakuragawa's was to investigate hostile nations and their military, equipment, and current status. Everyone present was considerably higher ranked than Kawai. None of them even knew who he was, other than Iwata, who was just winding up his briefing when Kawai entered the room.

"NHK and commercial broadcasters have as many as ten television cameras between them in Fukuoka Dome. Also, the surveillance cameras are still intact, and the control room is reporting that as things stand there are between ten and twenty armed guerrillas. This tallies with the numbers captured on the various TV cameras. There are two or three in the Dome's broadcasting booth, between three and six in the infield stands, and five to ten in the bleachers. Of course, there may be more hidden in the stadium's passageways, restrooms, restaurants, and so on—a possibility that rather ties the hands of security personnel. We've ascertained that the guerrillas are armed with pistols, sub-machine guns, and rocket-propelled grenades, but, again, we can't discount the possibility that they might have other firearms and explosive devices."

As thirty-one-year-old Kawai walked in, the senior people around the doughnut-shaped table all looked at him as if wondering who the hell he might be. There was no space at the table, and since Iwata indicated a row of stacking chairs without armrests by the wall, he took a seat there. These were intended for young aides from the secretariat's office, the Foreign Ministry, the Police Agency, and the Defense Agency. Whenever documents pertaining to statistics, guidelines, agreements, and so forth were needed, the aides would discreetly approach the round table like the black-clad stage assistants in kabuki and hand them to their superiors. The large, square room had maps of Japan and the world on the walls, computers with access to top-secret data, several dozen hotline telephones, and a number of television monitors with inbuilt IP video phones, and was built to withstand even being at the epicenter of a major earthquake.

The television monitors at the center of the table were showing images from the NHK broadcast. Smoke was still spewing from the wrecked scoreboard, but there had been no major developments since. It was unknown whether there were any casualties. The demands made by the North Korean rebels were periodically repeated: *No police within a radius of five kilometers from Fukuoka Dome. Disable all air-defense systems around Kyushu and ban all activity by the Air Self-Defense Force for two hours, beginning now.* The Prime Minister and Chief Cabinet Secretary had both indicated that the demands should be met. There had been three telephone contacts with the guerrillas, who apparently hadn't requested anyone in particular to negotiate with. Yamagiwa had spoken to them on the first phone call, Korenaga on the next, and then Tsuboi—but the exchanges could hardly be called negotiations. The rebels had made their demands, and the moment Korenaga and Tsuboi said they "understood," the line had gone dead.

Yonashiro rose to his feet. "Surely we can't shut down the air-defense system?"

"We had to say we would, to prevent anyone getting killed. That's all," Yamagiwa replied.

After some discussion, it was decided to ignore the instruction to disable the air-defense system for two hours. SDF radar was monitoring airspace as usual from the Kyushu bases at Ashiya and Kasuga, and the Unijima substation in the northern tip of Tsushima Island. The order hadn't referred specifically to radar, and in any case it wasn't possible to tell from outside whether the radar system was functioning or not. The Western Air Defense Force's Nyutabaru and

Tsuiki bases, and the South-Western Air Defense Force's Naha base, were all on twenty-four-hour alert against airspace violations, and had fighter planes ready to scramble at a moment's notice.

"If an unidentified aircraft comes within the flight-identification zone and fails to respond," said Sakuragawa, "then we give the order to scramble, right?" Yamagiwa brushed the question off, merely saying that in such a contingency, they'd consider the situation and give instructions accordingly. Sakuragawa and Yonashiro seemed stunned by this reply and immediately started phoning the various bases. "Scrambling means emergency interception," muttered a young aide from the SDF's Intelligence HQ sitting next to Kawai in the outer ring of chairs. "Saying we'll consider the situation when it happens is tantamount to admitting we won't be able to intercept." The rebels' demand to close down the warning system had raised the specter of the Taepodong ballistic missile in many people's minds. And now Yamagiwa was asking, "If a Taepodong is launched, will the ASDF be able to shoot it down?"

"I've already answered that question dozens of times in the Diet and in Cabinet meetings," Yonashiro told him. "Without an effective missile defense system, once a missile has been launched, shooting it down with fighter planes or ground-to-air missiles would be like catching an arrow with your bare hands. Impossible."

"How did that bunch get into Japan so easily in the first place?" Yamagiwa growled. He clearly didn't like having his ignorance exposed.

"I've put in dozens of requests for more P-3Cs, to no avail," Yonashiro said matter-of-factly. "The condition of our fleet of surveillance planes has deteriorated and the number on regular patrol has actually decreased. We don't even have our own spy-satellite system but rely on US military satellites to watch what's going on around the North Korean coast. You have to understand that with our current number of surveillance planes, detecting a suspicious North Korean ship is like looking for a contact lens in a public swimming pool."

The room's phones were ringing off the hook with calls from Diet members and other bigwigs, including the Fukuoka prefectural governor and the mayor of Fukuoka City. The mayor was agonizing over whether they should evacuate residents. And what about the Dome complex? Customers in the shopping mall and hotel had been urged to leave as quickly as possible. They couldn't tell the room guests to leave, however, with the risk of further terrorist attacks on the station or airport. A bigger problem, though, was the fact that issuing an evacuation order was likely to cause panic. Worse still, right opposite the Dome was the National Kyushu Medical Center. This hospital provided the highest quality care in the whole region, with many terminal cancer patients, almost four thousand operations carried out yearly, and a large number of emergency patients. If they evacuated the area around the Dome, how would they handle the hospital?

The callers raised all kinds of concerns. What should they do about any casualties in the Dome? Could the Self-Defense Force deal with those? What about contacting the International Red Cross? Were missiles likely to be used? Could they please be given any relevant information as soon as possible? Was it possible to clarify which things they could decide for themselves, and when they should await government instructions? These were matters for which the local authorities needed urgent answers, but all they got was, "We're keeping an eye on the situation, and will let you know in due course."

"So just what is this rebel army faction?" Yamagiwa asked those seated at the round table. Yoshizaki of the Foreign Ministry quoted the statement from the North Korean embassy in Beijing. "That much is already in here," Yamagiwa told him irritably, shaking the dossier in front of him. Just then a call came for Yamagiwa from the Prime Minister and Chief Cabinet Secretary with directions to convene a Cabinet meeting to discuss the application of emergency legislation. A young aide from the Cabinet Secretariat leaped up from his chair by the wall and started making phone calls. Would the emergency legislation improve matters? Kawai didn't think so.

Just who would make the decision to evacuate residents in the vicinity of Fukuoka Dome? Under the Emergency Acts of 2004, the chain of command was vague at best. In principle, in the event of a terrorist or other attack, a government task force would give directions to prefectural governors, but under certain circumstances the local authorities might be obliged to use their own judgment if the matter was urgent. However, the precise circumstances were left unspecified. Nor was there anything in the Emergency Acts that dealt with the possibility of terrorists blending in with the general population, or of residents getting caught up in street fighting. It bandied about words like "aggression," "terrorism," "weapons of mass destruction," and so forth, but had nothing to say about dealing with a real, live enemy at close quarters.

One hour after the initial occupation, the crisis-management room issued the order for all police to remain outside the stipulated area, but there was nothing to stop curious onlookers from gathering near the Dome. Local TV stations had sent out mobile broadcasting vans that showed an ever-growing crowd there. To contain this problem, the Fukuoka city council decided to set up a police cordon at a radius of seven kilometers from the stadium, but it took another fifteen minutes to obtain government approval. Blocks were to be set up on the expressways and highways first, although it would be impossible to monitor the city's maze of narrow side streets. To prepare for further terrorist attacks, reinforcements from other prefectural police forces were brought in, and riot police were deployed at Fukuoka Airport, the Hakata bullet-train terminus, the government district, and the port facilities.

Contact with US military personnel stationed in Japan revealed that by now the US army was on the relatively high alert of DEFCON 3. The commander of US forces in Japan and the American ambassador had both confirmed that they would respect the Japanese government's wishes and instructions, and would not take any action without contacting the Japanese government in advance. Nevertheless, they had already closed the consulate in Fukuoka and evacuated all personnel to the base at Yokota. And anyone would have thought civil war had broken out from the sobering

TV coverage of the American embassy in Tokyo, where heavily armed soldiers with night-vision scopes were stationed all around the grounds, and snipers armed with rifles and light machine guns were installed on the roof. A young Foreign Ministry aide sitting in the outer ring told Kawai that there had been a tenfold increase in the number of US marines on guard.

The Prime Minister and Foreign Minister had apparently been trying to phone Washington, but it was early Saturday morning there, and they hadn't been able to get hold of a single senior official, let alone the Secretary of State or his deputy. Maybe it had something to do with the anti-American mood prevalent in Japan lately, Yamagiwa suggested to Yoshizaki from the Foreign Ministry, but the latter was on the phone and couldn't answer. After a while Yoshizaki hung up and reported that he'd finally managed to get through to someone from their Bureau of East Asian and Pacific Affairs on his home number, only to be told that it was basically an internal problem for Japan. "What about the damned Security Treaty?" demanded Yamagiwa angrily. Yoshizaki said that it was only the opinion of that particular employee and not an official response from the State Department, before taking another call.

Most of the key members around the table were working the phones—landlines or mobiles or both at once. All the landlines were in use, and as soon as someone hung up on one call, the phone would start ringing again. Typescripts of all calls were supposedly circulated to everyone present, although there weren't enough typists to keep up, let alone anyone to edit the information. Kawai sat in his stacking chair reading the printouts constantly being handed to him. All this random information was just confusing, he thought. Instead of trying to get hold of the US top brass and the State Department, they should first be considering how to guarantee the safety of those thirty thousand people in Fukuoka Dome, and second, analyzing the demands made by the North Korean guerrillas and what to do about them.

\*

How long before Suzuki got here? Kawai checked his watch. It was past nine in the evening. Kawai had been in the room for an hour, and an hour and forty minutes had already passed since the start of the crisis. Suzuki's arrival was unlikely to change anything anyway. Even if the Prime Minister and Chief Cabinet Secretary turned up it was doubtful any action could be taken quickly, since they hadn't yet discussed, much less decided, their priorities. And without priorities, they weren't going anywhere. Here everything was ad hoc—the question of whether ASDF planes could be scrambled or not was just one example of the simultaneous discussions going on amid the clamor of ringing telephones, shrill TV anchors, and keyboard clatter. None of the people at the table were in any way stupid; it was just that they were completely unaccustomed to this type of situation, and knew practically nothing about North Korea. They all had their own specializations, so this was only to be expected, but the fact that they didn't ask the advice of people who did know about such things was a major problem.

There were plenty of things that Kawai was itching to say. He wanted to discuss the likelihood of rebellion in the North Korean People's Army, for instance, and the nature of the particular branch of it that the guerrilla leader belonged to, not to mention the need to contact people in Beijing and Seoul. Yet he was seated with the other low-ranking bureaucrats on the fringe of things, where you weren't allowed to say anything unless you were asked for an opinion. There were around thirty other staffers seated near him, but they were simply making internal calls and distributing memorandums. Occasionally they might be called up to the round table to whisper some information into their boss's ear. They were all experts in something or other, but they couldn't offer an opinion openly from these seats. They would have to wait until they returned to their ministry or agency or department, prefacing their comments even then with some phrase such as, "I hope I'm not intruding, but…" or "I apologize for speaking out of turn, but…"

One young bureaucrat came into the meeting room on the verge of tears to say that the Cabinet Secretariat was being hounded by the media demanding to know why there hadn't yet been any official statement. An NHK anchor and his studio guest, a military analyst, had just expressed their dissatisfaction and concern over the lack of any comment from the Prime Minister, while commercial broadcasters had been less circumspect in their calls for the PM to address the nation. But the consensus here was that it would be inexpedient for any top politician to face the media when there was still too little information to take any firm countermeasures. Furthermore, the PM was currently in a helicopter and it was physically impossible for him to comment.

Of course, the fact that he was in a helicopter was also top secret. And in the meantime, Yamagiwa was unable to make any official statement since he wasn't authorized to act as a government spokesman. "Tell the media that even after 9/11, the US President didn't make any statement until the next day," he roared. The Prime Minister had had to make his way to the nearest SDF base in Morioka, from where it was at least two hours by helicopter to his official residence in Tokyo. "Two hours," muttered Kawai, pulling a map of the Korean Peninsula out of the papers he had prepared. Why had the people occupying the Dome insisted on the air-defense warning system being closed down for two hours? This had already been bothering him, but now he was beginning to feel a real sense of foreboding.

The crisis-management room was noisier than ever. Katsurayama from the National Police Agency was yelling at Yoshizaki, "How the hell can we confirm the North Korean statement that it's a rebel army faction? Get on the phone to Beijing, or Pyongyang!" Whenever there was an international incident, Foreign Ministry officials always took the blame; in peacetime they were considered an incompetent elite, in an emergency they were gutless wimps. There was some truth in the criticism, even though the ministry did have a number of talented young analysts and negotiators; and when a country's diplomats were no good, the risk of war was heightened. "We've been constantly on the phone to the North Korean embassy in Beijing, as it's not possible to call Pyongyang directly," Yoshizaki quietly replied.

"What about getting some information from the Korean Residents Association?" Katsurayama, a bit calmer now, said, "They seem to be just as surprised as we are." The General Association of Korean Residents in Japan, commonly seen as the de facto DPRK embassy, had already denounced the event as "an outrageous terrorist attack carried out by a section of treacherous officers of the People's Army intent on destabilizing the Republic." Katsurayama was from the Security Division of the NPA and presumably was kept informed by their sources in the association. Then again, while North Korea might say publicly that the "Chongryon" was important as a source of funds and information, it was clear that they didn't really trust the association.

After talks between the NPA's Tsuboi and the Prime Minister in his helicopter, it was decided the Osaka police would send an SAT, or Special Assault Team, to Fukuoka that night. Kawai wondered how much the government or the NPA knew about North Korean Special Operations Forces. The People's Army as a whole was hobbled by a lack of resources and fuel, but its SOF units were still extremely well equipped. It wasn't possible to get exact numbers, but they were said to be a hundred thousand or even a hundred and fifty thousand strong, while America's Green Berets, for example, numbered only about fifty thousand. The Eighth Corps was the army's flagship SOF, but all twelve corps were specially trained. Also, the North Korean secret police boasted its own special operations unit, as did the intelligence agencies known as the Operations Department and the United Front, and indeed there were several under the direct control of the Party brass. Other branches of the military that had similar crack units included the Capital Air Defense Corps and the Third Engineers Brigade responsible for nuclear power installations, not to mention Kim Jong Il's own private army and bodyguards, the enigmatic Twenty-Second and Thirty-Ninth Units.

All these outfits were made up of people selected for their ability and courage. In other countries, young men and women from solid backgrounds with good brains and physical fitness could be expected to get ahead in various fields, but in North Korea they went into special ops. Training was extremely tough, lasting from three to six years, after which recruits had become super-fit soldiers who were themselves dangerous weapons in one-on-one combat. There was an anecdote about an SOF soldier, the only one of twenty-two men to make it back to the North after the 1996 submarine infiltration of the South at Gangneung on the east coast, who crossed the border holding his guts in place with his own hands after having been shot in the belly. Recruits were the children of the core elite, and in addition to clothing, food, and accommodation, they received better medical care and education, all of which helped establish an unwavering loyalty to Kim Jong Il.

Listening to the conversation between Yoshizaki and Katsurayama, Kawai couldn't help feeling that the story of the rebel army faction simply didn't add up. In the transition period from Kim Il Sung to his son, the People's Army had been restructured any number of times—not so much in order to adapt it to the post-Cold War world as to stamp out any possibility of rebellion or *coup d'état*. Its complex organizational structure was nigh on impossible for outsiders to understand—even the Korean Intelligence Division hadn't really grasped it. The priority of their national defense systems was less to protect the country than to ensure that the military remained under the control of Kim Jong Il and the Workers' Party. Kim himself had made conspicuous efforts to secure his position with the army even before coming to power, and would probably try to destroy the country himself at the first hint of sedition. It was just inconceivable that the armed guerrillas were a rebel army faction; Kawai was becoming increasingly convinced of it. Staring at the map of the Korean Peninsula, he tried to think what those two hours could mean. Why did they want the air-defense system shut down for that amount of time and not, say, twenty-two hours, or two days, or two weeks, or two months?

Kawai felt someone tap him on the shoulder and looked up to see Suzuki's rather flushed face. He'd probably had a beer before he was summoned. "Looks like a slow Saturday night for Tokyo's fun spots," he said as he took a seat. "There are rumors of a Taepodong on its way, and all the bars are deserted." He glanced at his watch. "Still took nearly two hours to get here," he muttered.

Everyone seemed worried about a Taepodong, but there was no way that North Korea would fire a missile at Japan, for the simple reason that it would mean the end of Kim Jong Il's regime if they did. Any missile fired at Tokyo would spark all-out warfare in the area, and Kim was not so stupid as to start a war against the South Korean army and the US forces based in Korea. A war would mean that America's plan to recognize the regime in exchange for their abolishing nuclear warheads and nuclear-fuel-processing facilities, as well as continuing face-saving talks on unification, would all come to nothing. If a missile were ever to be fired at Japan, it would be because Kim Jong Il had himself decided that the country called North Korea should cease to exist.

"What's going on?" Suzuki asked, as he scanned the room. "It's a mess," said Kawai, the map of the Korean Peninsula still spread out on his knees. "Is that your verdict, or that of everyone here?" Suzuki was already running his eyes over the thick pile of briefing papers. "Both," said Kawai wryly. "I missed it," Suzuki sighed, mechanically turning the pages. "How many times did you wonder about those North Korean warships setting sail? That was all probably leading up to this—a blind for this operation."

"Quiet, please! Everyone be quiet!" Hida, of the Home Affairs Ministry, rose to his feet, still holding the telephone receiver. "I'm on the phone to the security guards' room at Fukuoka Dome. They have a couple of water cannon for subduing rioters and drunks, and are asking whether they can use them on the guerrillas. What does everyone think?" he asked excitedly. Yonashiro and Sakuragawa looked uncertain, while Yamagiwa, Korenaga, and Tsuboi started firing questions: What's the water pressure? Who'll operate them? Do they know for sure how many guerrillas there are in the Dome, and where they're located? Hida repeated the questions into the phone.

161

"Gimme a break," an aide seated next to Kawai muttered incredulously. He was from the SDF Intelligence HQ. "They want to throw a bit of water at guys armed with rocket grenades? It's not like they're dealing with some student demo!"

"The two hours are almost up," Suzuki said. "No Taepodong yet—so what was the guerrillas' demand about? The SDF radar hasn't picked up any missiles or unidentified aircraft or anything."

*The radar hasn't picked up anything.* Something clicked with those words, and Kawai's ominous premonition suddenly took concrete shape. The North Koreans had the Soviet-made transport plane, the Antonov An-2. It was a biplane, an antique of the sort you only saw in museums nowadays. Constructed almost entirely of wood and flying at low altitude, it was hard to detect on radar. North Korea had something like four hundred of these planes, which they used for special operations. Kawai started calculating the distance from their main airbases to Fukuoka, avoiding South Korean airspace. At the Antonov An-2's cruising speed, it would take between two and two and a half hours for them to arrive. If the planes had taken off before the guerrillas announced their demands, they could be there within two hours.

Kawai looked at his watch. It was 9:17 p.m. At the round table, Hida and Sakuragawa were bickering. "Whose responsibility will it be if the guerrillas retaliate by executing hostages?" demanded Sakuragawa, to which Hida shot back: "It's our duty to consider every means possible!" A call came from the Chief Cabinet Secretary saying that it would take too long to get to the helipad from Osaka Station, so he was coming by bullet train. Yoshizaki informed Yamagiwa that he should be able to talk to the US deputy secretary of state in about three hours' time. Yonashiro was offering the use of one of the SDF's large transport helicopters to transfer the SAT unit from Osaka. Tsuboi expressed gratitude for the offer but told him it wouldn't be necessary: the Osaka police would soon have all their own helicopters available. Katsurayama was working on how to coordinate the Fukuoka prefectural police, the SAT unit, and other prefectural police forces. Suddenly laughter was heard at the door to the room. A Cabinet member had at last arrived. It was Nomiyama, Minister for the Environment, dressed in a morning suit, having apparently come from a wedding party in his constituency. The relief at a minister finally turning up was palpable, and there was another round of laughter when he quipped, "Are there any movies where the hero fights terrorists in tails?" Nomiyama had been a founding member of Japan Green after working for a major trading company. "Thank you for holding the fort," he said, turning to Yamagiwa and shaking his hand.

As Nomiyama took his seat at the round table, there were cries of "What the hell is *that?*" All eyes turned to the TV screens, which now showed a formation of aircraft like migrating birds flying lower than the surrounding buildings, captured by a camera that had been filming onlookers outside the hotel next to Fukuoka Dome.

"What *are* they?" asked Suzuki.

"Antonov An-2 transport planes," said Kawai.

The camera zoomed in, filling the screen with a single plane. "Looks like it's for training or something," muttered Yonashiro, rising to his feet. They were beautiful, like something out of an old documentary, thought Kawai. There were no identifying marks on them—they must have painted over the stars. The leading plane dropped even lower and prepared for landing. "What's it doing? There isn't any airport around there!" cried Yamagiwa. Hida, phone in hand, pointed out that it was the site of the old Gannosu Air Station, with three landing strips for small aircraft running alongside the JR rail tracks, and lit by streetlights in the area. The Antonov An-2s began to land one after another. One, two, three, four, five, six, seven, eight… someone was counting them off. They could already make out about twenty of them on the screen, and still more were coming in.

"How many personnel can each of those things carry?" Suzuki asked, the color draining from his face.

"Ten to fifteen apiece," Kawai told him. He seemed to remember that Suzuki was from somewhere up north—Fukushima, or was it

Akita? Kawai himself was from Tokyo, his wife from Nagano. He was glad he didn't have any family in Kyushu.

The first plane pulled up at the end of the landing strip, the door opened, and out poured soldiers in camouflage fatigues. All were heavily armed with AK assault rifles and rocket-propelled grenades. Once on the ground, the soldiers stayed low, looked around them, and fanned out at speed to cover the planes still coming in to land.

# 5

# DECLARATION OF WAR

*April 2, 2011*

NOTIFIED BY TELEPHONE to report immediately to Ishihara's room, Yamada and Mori ran to Building C. It was only two hundred meters or so, but neither of them was much of a runner, and they had to stop twice to catch their breath, as a precaution against passing out. Building C, where Ishihara, Ando, Fukuda, and the forty-something Takei lived, was the same shape and size as their own building, but Ishihara's room wasn't like anyone else's. It had once been a motorcycle shop, run by an old friend of his whom Yamada and Mori had never met. It was about the size of a basketball court—at least ten times the size of the other rooms—and the ceiling was two stories high. But Ishihara had turned it into a communal living room, which he called the "Living" for short. He had sectioned off one corner of the room with a handmade plywood screen and dubbed this triangular space his study. It had a small desk and a rocking chair, where he'd sit to think deep thoughts or pick the guitar or write poetry.

Yamada knocked at the door to the Living, but no one came to open it. They could hear people cheering. "It's probably open," Mori said, and he turned the knob. Inside, they found the entire group assembled—a very rare event. They were all watching television.

The TV was a fifty-one-inch plasma-screen model, a discarded relic that Felix had repaired. The floor of the Living was concrete, covered with random patches of linoleum, wooden pallets, and a large carpet where shoes were banned. In the center of the room was a long, flower-patterned sofa and a table. Kaneshiro, Fukuda, Takeguchi, and Shinohara sat side by side on the sofa, with five or six others leaning against it or sitting on its arms. Yamada and Mori slipped out of their shoes and plopped down among the group seated on the carpet.

Ishihara had dragged out his rocking chair, a battered specimen that cried out for a shawl-knitting old lady. This chair, along with the sofa, had been reclaimed from a garbage dump and restored by Fukuda, Takeguchi, and Ando, who were good at that sort of thing. Ishihara sat facing the television. To his left were the big bookcases that held his library, and rising behind the bookcases was the long steel stairway that led from this, the first or ground floor, straight up to the third. On the opposite side, next to the entrance, was a large accordion curtain, behind which was the old boiler room, now subdivided and refurbished as a narrow kitchen, a toilet, and a shower. Building C had been a warehouse for furniture and musical instruments and was equipped with an enormous climate-control unit, so it was comfortable in both summer and winter. Building H—where Mori and Yamada stayed, along with Tateno, Hino, and Shinohara—had no air conditioning and only a few small windows, which made it hellishly hot in summer.

When they sat down, no one greeted them or asked what had taken them so long. No one here said things like *How you doing?* or *What's going on?* or *Sorry I'm late!* or *Everything all right?* Mori liked this and thought it made life a lot easier, but Yamada missed that sort of small talk. Not that he imagined he'd have any answer for greetings like the ubiquitous "*Genki?*" In fact, he didn't really have a clear sense of what being *genki*, or "in good spirits," was supposed to mean. On the TV were some guys holding military weapons, and each time one of them was shown in close-up the group cheered. Yamada turned to Sato, next to him, and asked if it was a movie. Sato was one of the Satanists. He had big eyes and a sweet face.

"No," he said. "It's real. And it's live. Those guys are guerrillas from North Korea."

Yamada and Mori looked at each other. The screen switched briefly to the TV studio, where a news anchor peered into the camera and said, "It's not clear what the armed guerrillas want!" Okubo said, "What's this guy, an idiot?"—and several voices replied in the affirmative. Someone shouted, "They want to kill and destroy, that's what they want!" Mori smiled and murmured, "Real guerrillas. Fantastic!" Yamada wondered how long it had been since he'd last seen Mori smile, then realized he'd *never* seen him smile. "Where's this happening?" he asked Sato. "Fukuoka Dome," Sato said, his big eyes never leaving the screen. The baseball stadium? Yamada secretly loved sports. He'd never actually participated in any, outside of phys-ed classes in school, but he liked to watch people run and jump and throw or kick balls around. He didn't like Fukuoka Dome, however. He was creeped out by Warm Hands Plaza, with its ghastly bronze replicas of the outstretched hands of Michael Jackson and other famous people, and he was even more creeped out by the official Hawks cheering section, who all wore matching white tunics. He'd also once had a very unpleasant experience at the food court in the shopping mall next to the Dome. He'd ordered pork-bone ramen at a noodle place there before noticing that all the other customers had discount coupons that entitled them to a free plate of gyoza dumplings. The man at the next table told him the coupons were being handed out at the entrance to the food court. Yamada had only eaten half his ramen, and since he hadn't paid yet he figured he still had time and went to get one of the coupons. When he returned, he found that his unfinished bowl of noodles had been taken away. He wanted to burn down the shop and watch the guilty waitress blaze from hairdo to pubes, but he had no lighter and no gasoline. Worse, the waitress was a sexy-looking thing, if a bit chubby, so he was unable even to speak to her and left the shop with tears of rage welling up. Yamada hoped the guerrillas would blow Fukuoka Dome to smithereens.

Matsuyama pointed at the TV and said, "Who are the people wearing those ridiculous outfits?"

Yamada was able to answer that. The Hawks cheering section were making their way up the aisle toward a pair of guerrillas. Their leader, a man with a long beard, shouted at them through a hand-held megaphone: "What the hell?" The anchorman, speaking from the studio, said with some anxiety, "It's no time to be playing the hero! That's dangerous!" Fukuda said, "Hero? It's just some dickhead with a beard!" A security guard tried to stop the cheering section, but their leader pushed him aside with his megaphone and shouted "What the hell?" again. Takei muttered, "Is that all this asshole can say?" The camera now zoomed in on the guerrilla at whom the man was pointing his megaphone. He was holding a pistol, with a machine gun slung over his shoulder. "Check out the muscles on that guy," said the Satanist Kondo. "Think *he's* been working out?"

Yamada looked over at Kaneshiro, whose eyes were glued to the screen. Just about everyone else was shouting *Kick ass!* or *Shoot him!* or *How cool is this?* but the aspiring terrorist hadn't said a word. He looked like a mountain climber surveying the final approach to the summit. Yamada admired Kaneshiro's combination of intensity and detachment. It called to mind something Shinohara had once said about a certain snake, the black mamba. "It's the simplest, most amazing creature on the planet," Shinohara had told him, his eyes shining. "Its neurotoxin is ten times as powerful as the king cobra's, and it'll attack anything that comes within six meters—elephants, lions, rhinos, whatever. Most of the poisonous reptiles have a special electric signal in their brains that triggers the attack mode, but black mambas are *always* in attack mode—there's no off switch. That's why they look so miserable when they don't have anything to strike at." Hearing this, Yamada had imagined a snake with eyes like Kaneshiro's.

The guerrilla pointed his pistol at the man and said something. He was too far away from any microphones to be audible, but Mori translated. Mori had gone through a long period, after his brother killed their parents and botched his own suicide, when he didn't speak and refused to hear. During that time, he got in the habit of reading people's lips instead of listening to their voices. *Stop! If you come any closer, I'll shoot.* He held his hand like a pistol as he transmitted the words, then lowered it and smiled bashfully. The five Satanists shouted at the TV in near unison: "Shoot him!" Felix asked why the cheerleaders were dressed like "gay bikers." Having grown up in South America, he wasn't familiar with much of Japanese pop culture. The question was aimed at Matsuyama, next to him, but Matsuyama had joined the *Shoot him!* chorus. Tateno, the new kid, answered instead, saying, "People like that, they just get off on dressing alike."

When Yamada was in sixth grade, his father had lost his job and decided to take up farming. The family moved to a mountain village in Fukushima Prefecture, a place where wild monkeys greatly outnumbered the people. A group dance called the *Soran-odori* was a big deal with all the villagers, and everyone was supposed to join in. Yamada had hated doing it, and he'd been chewed out viciously when he refused to take part. The Soran dancers had headbands too, and long, billowy tunics like something the ancient shaman queen Himiko might have worn. He felt sick just thinking about it again.

From the TV speakers there suddenly came a sound like someone opening a well-shaken can of soda. A puff of smoke issued from the top row of seats on the first-base line. Takei leaped to his feet and shouted "RPG! RPG!"—a throwback to his guerrilla training in Yemen. The rocket spat short orange flames behind it and left a white vapor trail as it raced in an almost perfectly straight line toward the back screen in centerfield. It was beautiful, Yamada thought—a home-run ball for the ages. And then the right half of the enormous electronic scoreboard exploded with a thunderous roar and the brittle, crackling sound of glass shattering into a billion pieces. Sparks flew out in every direction, like luminous butterflies bursting from their cocoons. The crowd seemed to have frozen solid. Even the anchorman was speechless. A stunned silence reigned briefly in the Living as well. Yamada sat there with his mouth hanging open, astonished at the RPG's destructive power. Mori too looked stunned, like an owl caught in the beam of a flashlight.

After launching the rocket, the guerrillas had complete control over Fukuoka Dome. The spectators sat in their seats as still as mannequins. There were no more announcements over the PA system, and the entire stadium was bizarrely quiet. This made a deep impression on Yamada: there was a certain strange power in watching thirty thousand people sit in absolute silence. It was especially satisfying to see the cheering section, in their stupid costumes, looking utterly defeated. Everyone in Ishihara's living room was pumped. Tateno was bobbing his head affirmatively, and the five Satanists were beaming like a boys' choir about to break into song. Takeguchi and Toyohara had actual tears of joy in their eyes. Felix was pumping both fists, Matsuyama was all dimples, and Okubo leaned back and gazed heavenward, as if thanking God for this gift. Hino, a soft-spoken kid from Building H, was pretending to hold an RPG on his shoulder and quietly imitating the sound the rocket had made: *Pashoop! Pashoop!* Shinohara, as shiny-eyed as one of his frogs, was slapping Tateno on the back. All of them were exhilarated to see a crowd of that size subdued by just a handful of people, to see power stripped from the same general public that had treated them like dirt all their lives.

After some time, when nothing further happened, the TV broadcast switched back to the studio. A military analyst and a university professor, an expert on North Korea, had joined the anchorman to speculate on the guerrillas' intentions. "They describe themselves as a rebel army faction opposed to the Kim regime, but it seems doubtful," the professor was saying. He explained that the influence of the Party permeated every nook and cranny of the North Korean military. Mutual surveillance was the norm at all levels, so that even though tiny buds of resistance might appear now and then, they had very little chance of ever blossoming. The anchor asked how the North Koreans could have infiltrated Fukuoka. "We've heard so many news reports about suspicious vessels," the military analyst said, "that we tend to think that none of North Korea's armed spy ships ever escape our notice, but it's impossible for our surveillance planes to keep an eye on all the seas around Japan." He pointed to a map that had been set up in the studio. "We have an incredible number of fishing vessels operating in the waters around Kyushu, especially at this time of year, and it would be easy to disguise a North Korean spy boat as one of them. As you know, our defense budget has been slashed each of the last several years. The SDF have no surveillance satellites of their own and have to rely on the Americans for much of their intelligence. But it isn't possible to monitor every vessel that leaves every port on both the east and west coasts of North Korea. Most of the spy boats spotted thus far have been identified by reconnaissance flights of the P-3C Orion surveillance aircraft, but that's probably something like two or three boats for every fifty that are out there. The old cliché about looking for needles in a haystack just about sums it up."

On a different channel, displayed in a small rectangular inset in the corner of the screen, they were still showing Fukuoka Dome. Kaneshiro used the remote to switch over. Inside the Dome, a sea of spectators sat there staring straight ahead, but the guerrillas were no longer visible anywhere. Perhaps those in the broadcasting booth, where there would be monitors, had ordered the others to move to locations where the cameras wouldn't pick them up. The spectators sat in their seats like children being punished. No one was whispering to the person next to them, and no one tried to stand up. A mother stopped her child rustling a paper bag full of sweets. The white-clad cheering section looked as if they'd been sentenced to mass execution. They sat slumped over, feet together, hands on knees.

A little while ago, reporters in the press box above the infield seats had been furiously typing copy on their laptops, but they had stopped abruptly when the rocket was fired and were now just sitting quietly like everyone else. Had the guerrillas told them to cease all communications, or was it simply that nothing was happening? The players for the Hawks and the Marines were still in their respective dugouts, along with the coaches and batboys and umpires. They presumably could have left the stadium through the locker-room exits, unless guerrillas were stationed there too.

A soft-drink vendor was sitting on the steps of one of the aisles, his tray beside him. The camera zoomed in on the empty paper cups, then the cylindrical drink dispenser, the nozzle of which was dripping slowly. The stadium security guards sat together primly in a row of folding seats, facing the field. They weren't using their walkie-talkies now. On one of the seats were piled all their handsets and riot batons. Had they elected to disarm themselves? It seemed unlikely that the guerrillas would go to the trouble of ordering them to lay down their meager weapons and equipment; they themselves must have decided to surrender their only means of communication and self-defense. "It would appear that there are people who need to go to the restroom but can't," a reporter said in an anguished tone of voice, implying that this proved how heartless the terrorists were. But since the rocket launching, the guerrillas hadn't made any public announcements over the PA, which meant they hadn't said that no one could go to the restroom, any more than they'd told the security guards to lay down their batons. Yamada wondered if the spectators hadn't just assumed that they were to stay where they were and make no sudden movements. Earlier, one of the guerrillas had been speaking Japanese. Why didn't people just raise their hands and ask if they could use the toilet? Not to ask and to wet yourself, then blame the nasty guerrillas, seemed ludicrous.

Yamada wondered what he would do if he were in that position. There was no way you could stand up to pistols and machine guns, and he would hate to get shot, so he'd never have done what the bearded guy did. That was sheer lunacy. But what if he couldn't hold his pee any longer? To pee in your pants in front of thirty thousand people—not to mention on TV—would be too humiliating. He'd probably raise a white handkerchief, the international sign of surrender, and ask if he could use the restroom. Of course, he probably wouldn't actually *have* a white handkerchief, but maybe he could borrow one from somebody. In any case, he'd definitely do everything he could to keep from pissing his pants. He might also look for a chance to escape. One thing he wouldn't do was just sit there like a Zen monk, the way all those people in the Dome were doing.

No one in the Ishihara group would have marched toward people who had guns, yelling at them through megaphones, but neither were any of them the sort who would suddenly curl up like condemned prisoners. They'd been treated since earliest childhood the way these spectators in the Dome were being treated now, and they were used to dealing with it. They'd been under constraint and pressure from the moment they first became aware of their surroundings, threatened with punishment if they didn't follow orders. And they'd had it engraved on their minds, with the edged tools of fear and pain, that they were powerless. Everyone in this world was a hostage to some form of violence; it was just that most people never realized it. That's why when the people in the Dome suddenly found themselves at the mercy of armed guerrillas and face to face with the raw reality of power, they became so disoriented that their brains ceased to function properly. You wouldn't challenge a gun with a megaphone if you were capable of thinking, but neither would you slump in your seat afterwards like someone under arrest.

The cameras switched to a view outside the Dome, where rubberneckers had begun to congregate. Guests from the hotel next door, taxi and truck drivers, and groups of cyclists and pedestrians had gathered on the street and in the parking lot to gape at the stadium. Many were taking photos or talking on mobile phones. Most had begun their vigil after seeing the rocket explode on TV, and since nothing more had happened they appeared to be getting bored. Neither the police nor the fire department had shown up, but the crowd nonetheless kept its distance. The Dome and the high-rise hotel were aligned parallel to the coastline. On the opposite side of the Dome was the big shopping mall, and across its vast parking lot was the Kyushu Medical Center. It seemed that most of the shops in the mall were closed. Few cars were plying the nearby streets, and on TV the anchor said that traffic on Fukushima Expressway Route 1 and other main arteries in the area was being strictly regulated.

"Let's go down there and cheer them on," Okubo said, and the five Satanists all expressed approval of the idea. Felix suggested they make a banner saying: "A hearty welcome to our friends from North Korea! Congratulations on a successful terrorist operation!" and Fukuda, Hino, and a few others literally applauded.

Kaneshiro was studying Ishihara's face. "What do you think, Ishihara-san?" he said. "Should we try to help the guerrillas, join up with them?" When Ishihara replied "Do as you please," the entire group cheered. Yamada too thrust both fists in the air, thrilled to think that the battle had begun at last. He'd once read somewhere that North Korean soldiers were unrivaled when it came to combat. If the Ishihara group could join them as a support force, they could help keep the thirty thousand sheeple in Fukuoka Dome under control. Neither Yamada nor Mori had ever been in a fight in their lives, but they shared an abnormally high tolerance for pain. The tattooing, for example, hadn't hurt in the least, and Mori had once stepped on a nail that became embedded in his foot, but didn't even notice until one of the attendants at the institution heard an odd clicking sound, discovered the nail, and pulled it out with a pair of pliers. Yamada had had similar experiences and learned from a doctor that this sort of thing wasn't unusual in survivors of severe trauma. From the time Kaneshiro had mentioned assisting the guerrillas, Mori had been hyperventilating, making an owl-like *Phoo! Phoo!* sound and showing his oddly round, puckered dimples in a big smile. Seeing Mori like this made Yamada happy, and he exposed his rabbit-like front teeth in a grin of his own. It would be fun to ally themselves with the guerrillas, to be on the winning side for once. Like leaping on the back of an anesthetized whale or elephant, beating your chest, and howling.

"We'll need to take weapons, right?" Takei said, and Kaneshiro, rising to his feet, said that of course they would. Takei had a habit of speaking and gesturing like the host of a variety show. He clapped his palms together and said, "All right! We'll have to dig what we need out of storage. Probably best to take weapons we'll be able to exchange with the North Koreans. The Browning and the Uzi might prove valuable. And the Vz 61 Scorpion, of course—it's good for close range, and pretty much the last word in urban terror. Will we need the AKs? Trouble is, it's difficult to choose our weapons until we know whether the Self-Defense Force is going to show up, and in what sort of numbers."

"Shouldn't we have explosives too?" Takeguchi suggested, and Fukuda seconded the motion. These two were bomb-making special-ists. Takeguchi had been indirectly inspired to start making bombs by his father, who in protest against getting fired from his job had strapped dynamite to his waist, burst into the offices of his old company, and succeeded only in blowing himself to bits. Takeguchi wasn't capable of respecting a man who'd died that way, but he wasn't capable of looking down on his own father either. What he'd decided after much deliberation was that it wasn't about the old man being bright or dim, admirable or laughable, winner or loser, but that he'd simply lacked sufficient knowledge about explosives. From the age of ten, Takeguchi had begun making bombs out of everyday household materials. On the Internet it was easy to find recipes for homemade bombs, but even with the simplest of recipes the actual construction was difficult. You needed a delicate touch, steady nerves, concentration, and a solid grasp of chemistry. Bomb-making basically came down to inducing the crystallization of an oxidizing agent and a combustible agent by mixing them together. The mixing and drying procedures were the hard part.

Takeguchi had made his first bomb at the age of ten years and seven months. There wasn't much to it—he merely crammed dry ice and nails into a small energy-drink bottle and replaced the cap—but it was a spectacular success. He later made grenades with aluminum powder he obtained by shaving down one-yen coins, bazooka bombs with homemade black gunpowder and PVC pipes, and simple incendiary bombs containing a mixture of tar and sawdust.

In time, Takeguchi learned that all combustion, all explosions, depended upon the molecular arrangements of the materials used. The high explosive trinitrotoluene, or TNT, was an organic com-pound composed of carbon, hydrogen, nitrogen, and oxygen, and there were countless other compounds that contained these four elements. The fearsome destructive power resulted from a nitro group and a methyl group bonding uniformly to a ring of carbon and hydrogen; explosions happened when an unstable material attempted to stabilize itself all at once through the exchange of protons and electrons. An explosion wasn't a material throwing itself apart, it was a massive amount of energy released in a specific chemical resolution.

Takeguchi liked the concept of an extremely unstable material trying to stabilize itself. He became more and more fascinated with bombs, and at thirteen he used iron oxide and aluminum powder to create an incendiary grenade, with which he burned down one wing of his school. Several students failed to escape in time and died in the fire. He was sent to a reformatory, and there he met Fukuda, who later introduced him to the Ishihara group. Fukuda's parents were members of a cult that had committed large-scale terrorist attacks. He'd been moved from one school to another, but it was in middle school that he got to know about both explosives and morality. He came to the conclusion that sex was what was messing up the world, and that the most evil manifestation of sex was commercial prostitution. At the age of fifteen he used a simple bomb he'd made out of chloric acid and sugar to blow up a newly opened "fashion & health" massage parlor in Akihabara.

Takeguchi made full use of the reformatory library to deepen his knowledge of chemistry and electricity. After Takei joined the Ishihara group, they were able to obtain high explosives and electric detonators, and their bombs took a great leap forward in terms of precision and size. From talking with these two, Yamada had learned that we live our daily lives surrounded by materials that are potential bomb components. Not only had they made bombs from sugar and aluminum but detergents, yarn, cow shit, egg whites, and even blood.

"You talk about helping them, but…" Ishihara turned away from the muted TV to address the group. His eyes looked sleepy. "Won't you just be seen as meddling?" The last word had a big impact

176

on everyone. It was a word rarely pronounced here, and one that represented a hated concept. Yamada hadn't even heard it in years and couldn't remember at first exactly what it meant, but it had a slimy and nauseating vibe to it. Ando grimaced and repeated the word under his breath: *meddling*.

Ando was eighteen and had a handsome face, with remarkably regular features. Yamada could only dream of looking like that— lean and sculpted. Like himself, Ando enjoyed watching sports and reading, and the two of them sometimes exchanged books or discussed soccer or the marathon. When Ando was thirteen and living in the suburbs of Yokohama, he murdered a classmate and used a handsaw to cut her corpse into eighteen pieces. He had subsequently been placed in a mental institution under strict surveillance, but a handful of websites popped up treating him as a hero. A male nurse had once shown him printouts of some of the sites, and Ando still despised the man for meddling like that, sticking his nose in where it wasn't wanted. Ando had come straight to Fukuoka after being released and hadn't yet had an opportunity to punish the guy but often said that if he ever did meet up with him, he was going to murder him on the spot. He told Yamada that being treated as a hero was repulsive to him. "All I wanted was to prove to myself that if you killed even the best sort of person and chopped them up, they'd just be plain old slabs of meat, so I did it to the girl I liked and admired most in my class."

Kaneshiro was looking at Ishihara in a wounded way. "You think?" he said. "Meddling?" He probably saw this as his long-awaited opportunity to wreak havoc. And Yamada had to admit he felt much the same way, if not, perhaps, to the same intense degree. To tear things down, to lay waste, to slaughter everyone, and turn this world into piles of rubble in the wilderness, was a vision that surely all the boys who'd gathered around Ishihara shared. The fixed belief that this dream would one day come true was all that allowed Yamada and the others to maintain a certain precarious mental balance. "But, Ishihara-san," Kaneshiro said, "didn't you just tell us to go ahead and assist them?"

177

"Yeah, but I and I was faaar faaar away just then." Yamada loved the musical way Ishihara spoke sometimes. It seemed to open the door to a vast new universe. "But, hey, you're all free to do as you like. I and I don't care one way or the other." As he said this, he got up from the rocking chair, took the remote from Kaneshiro, switched the channel from NHK to TV Asahi, leaving the sound off, and watched the female news anchor baring her gums. "I and I have tried and tried to forget," he said, "but there's one thing we just can't remember. These guys are lying through their teats. They're not a rebel faction. If they were rebels, they'd rebel in their own country, right? Normally. Even I and I think taking thirty thousand hostages is pretty cool, but there's something fishy going on here. Did you know that this newsbabe's knowledge is as wide-ranging as her vagina but not as deep? I know a guy who dated her for three months and said that in order to make her come—stop me if you've heard this before—he had to pump her wide-ranging knowledgina for so long he ended up with a slipped disk. However. Be that as it may. Kaneshiro, you want to fight the Self-Defense Force, right? But that's nut banana happen. The SDF will stand down because of the hostages. So who do you fight? You gonna kill all those average citizens sitting there watching no baseball game?"

Ishihara was right, of course, but he'd already won the argument the moment he used the word "meddling." A poet can conquer armies with a single word, Yamada thought. Just as Kaneshiro sank to a sitting position on the floor, deflated, the anchorwoman began gesticulating excitedly. Ishihara chuckled. "As an anteater probed at her hole," he intoned, "the newsbabe was shouting out 'Goal!'" Kaneshiro reclaimed the remote and turned up the volume.

"...have been sighted, according to information we've just received. We're cutting now to our harbor cam."

It was a dark, grainy picture of the night sky that slowly resolved itself into things you could see were clouds, with waves below. *What* had been sighted? As Yamada peered intently at the screen, a small point appeared, like a pixel of light. It grew larger and fuzzier, and then two more points of light appeared behind it, then three behind those two, and five behind those. "Birds, migrating?" someone wondered aloud. The growing shapes did indeed resemble birds, but they didn't *feel* like birds. It was as if a many-eyed beast of indeterminate shape was slowly emerging from the darkness.

Yamada had experienced starvation once, as a child. When you don't have anything to eat, and gnawing hunger gradually becomes the horror of starvation, everything you see around you begins to look like food. Your visual acuity becomes incredibly sharp, but hunger interferes with the brain's analysis of the data. Toward the end of his ordeal, Yamada was sitting slumped in a chair, too weak to stand, when he noticed a mosquito coil. It took what seemed like hours to convince himself that the familiar but strange-shaped object wasn't food. He kept staring at it, and as he did so, tiny specks of light began to dance around in his field of vision, like fireflies filling the room. They were quite beautiful, Yamada thought. Like colored molecules.

The specks of light on the TV screen looked a lot like those starvation molecules. They were coming in low over the sea. Finally, when they were caught in the glow of the city itself, their shapes became discernible. They were biplanes, flying in formation. The lead plane made a wide, sweeping turn parallel to the coastline, simultaneously lowering its landing gear. "Is there anywhere to land in that area?" the anchorwoman wondered. The camera was panning, following the plane. You could see the narrow, bridge-like sandbar called Umi-no-nakamichi, which connected the tip of Kashii to Shikanoshima Island, and along which ran a Japanese Railways line. Next, a regularly spaced row of lights came into view. They were the lights beside the tracks, Yamada realized just as the first biplane was touching down.

It landed on a long, straight stretch of concrete partially overgrown with weeds. "It's the old Gannosu Air Station," Fukuda said. As the second and third planes were preparing to land, the first came to a stop at the end of the runway, a hatch on one side opened up, and a stream of soldiers poured out. "Who are these guys?" Takei

179

said. "They've got trench mortars!" Mori was counting the soldiers as they jumped to the ground. A total of sixteen emerged from the first plane. Eight of them spread out to secure the runway, and the rest began offloading the baggage—big camouflage-patterned duffel bags and wooden crates and metal boxes, which they carried over to a vacant lot next to the JR station and piled up there. "I couldn't see very well, but I thought I saw AGS-17s too," Takei said, and was about to expound further when Kaneshiro interrupted. "Let's watch quietly for a minute, all right?" Takei clammed up and began taking notes on the soldiers' weapons and equipment.

Once it was unloaded, the first plane taxied off the runway and came to rest in front of a large public park with soccer and athletic fields. The second and third planes landed and went through the same procedure, and now there were dozens of soldiers scattered around the old airfield. Ten or so split off from the main group and ran across the park toward Gannosu railway station. They were holding handguns and crouching as they ran, as if attacking an enemy stronghold. "Can I say something?" Takei said. Kaneshiro nodded, and without stopping his note-taking Takei offered his opinion. "This is an operation they've rehearsed dozens of times. Unless they constructed an airfield with the same dimensions as this one and went over the operation again and again, getting the timing down, they couldn't possibly do this so efficiently."

The planes were lining up facing the park. Two pilots emerged from each, and some of them were waving signal lights to guide the next wave of planes while others picked up their weapons and joined the soldiers. By now the unloaded boxes and crates were piled as high as freight containers. A clearer picture came on the screen, a close-up of some of the men who had just deplaned. They had hooded camouflage jackets, lace-up boots, AK-74s slung from shoulder straps, and soft camouflage caps rather than helmets. They were hollow-cheeked and not very big, but with a steely intensity in their eyes. The soldiers you saw in movies or on CNN were usually American; the sight of narrow-eyed Asian troops in this sort of gear had a strangely powerful impact.

Men were shouldering boxes from the planes and carrying them to the growing stacks of cargo. Not a single soldier was just standing around watching. Some stood guard with their weapons at the ready, some unloaded cargo, and others raced off to help guide planes, direct the newly arrived troops, or establish communications via radio, walkie-talkies, or mobile phones. They all seemed to know exactly what to do. Takei was right: it had been meticulously planned.

"An NHK mobile broadcasting unit has apparently arrived near the scene," the anchorwoman said. "We are presenting this in cooperation with NHK." Her voice was trembling slightly. She must be scared, Yamada thought. Well, he was scared too. "These guys are from North Korea or whatever, right?" Fukuda said. "And Japan and North Korea are enemies, yeah? So if these guys are rebels, that means they're enemies of the North Korean government, or at least of Kim Jong Il, which makes them our allies, right? So why aren't they acting like allies? If they had to get out of their country after a failed coup, the first thing they would do here is lay down their arms, no? This looks more like the way an occupying army would behave." The program switched back to the studio, where the anchor, who looked noticeably paler, said, "We've just received word that reporters are questioning the Chief Cabinet Secretary."

Shigemitsu Takashi had been a core member of the conservative faction of the former Democratic Party of Japan and served as a liaison with LDP members who jumped over to Japan Green at its inception. Having arrived from Okayama by bullet train to a rainy Tokyo Station, he'd been spotted and surrounded by the media swarm. At first he tried to wave the cameras away, saying he had yet to discuss the situation with the Prime Minister, but the reporters weren't having it. Many of them were angry. "You're not dodging us!" they shouted. "Say something! Think of the hostages' families! Speak!" Hemmed in and jostled by the crowd of reporters, Shigemitsu banged his forehead against the lens casing of a camera; and when he finally made a statement, blood was mixed with the rain trickling down his face. "Our first and foremost concern is the safety of the people of Fukuoka. I am on my way to the Cabinet crisis-management room to discuss how best to deal with the situation." Ringed with security guards, he then climbed into a waiting car and was whisked away.

That statement was too lame even for a fucking politician, Yamada thought. The worst part was the guy's face. Not the rain and blood, but the shame that was written all over it. Yamada's father had looked like that not long before hanging himself—so ashamed of his own failure that he wanted to die. He'd tried to hide his shame from everybody, but there was too much of it inside him, and it oozed out on his face. A face like that is unnerving to look at. It would have been better if Shigemitsu had just burst into tears and sobbed, *I'm as scared as you are!*

"That was Chief Cabinet Minister Secretary Shigemitsu speaking with the press," the anchorwoman announced as the screen switched back to Gannosu Air Station. Ishihara sprang to his feet again. "Interesting!" he said, and began moving his hips in a lilting rhythm. "Verrry interesting!" Yamada didn't understand what he meant and asked Mori and Sato, but nobody seemed to know. The scene switched from the airfield to the street in front of Gannosu railway station, identifiable by a large black-on-white sign. The station had been unmanned until a few years earlier, when the neighborhood was redeveloped on a major scale. Outside the exit was a small roundabout where nine or ten taxis were parked. It was a scene you might find in any provincial city in Japan, except for the North Korean soldiers combing the streets, commandeering vehicles at gunpoint.

They took control of every taxi, truck, bus, and passenger car in the vicinity. Everyone but the drivers was ordered out of the vehicles. Trucks' cargoes were quickly unloaded and left by the side of the road, with a soldier in the passenger seat then directing the driver toward the landing strip. Troops were standing on the highway that ran alongside the railroad tracks. Several tractor trailers and dump trucks that had just delivered materials for repairs at Umi-no-nakamichi Seaside Park were also commandeered. No one resisted. Everyone was overwhelmed by the sight of the army fatigues, the no-nonsense weapons, and the intensity in the soldiers' eyes, to say nothing of their sheer numbers. "*What's* interesting?" Kaneshiro asked Ishihara, who didn't reply but continued shaking his hips, interjecting a rhythmic but unenlightening "Hoi! Hoi!" as he did so. Yamada couldn't see anything funny about North Korean soldiers carjacking Japanese citizens. But if Ishihara was amused, there had to be a reason.

The stacks of cargo were transferred piece by piece to the vehicles. A soldier or two joined the driver in each truck or car, and larger squads filled the buses. The camera zoomed in on a soldier in the passenger seat of a taxi, telling the driver where to go. "*Fu-ku-o-ka Do'*," Mori said, reading the man's lips. The driver shook his head and tried to explain that the road to the Dome was barricaded. Apparently the troops who'd arrived on the planes didn't speak much Japanese. Rather than repeat his command to the driver, the battle-ready soldier simply punched him in the side of the head. He did this mechanically and without hesitation—just part of procedure. Other drivers were clobbered not with fists but with gun butts or knife handles.

The soldiers' expressions never changed—not even when hitting a man, or watching him bleed or scream. An air of ruthlessness had been unleashed, and it was an atmosphere that Yamada knew all too well. There had been attendants with violent tendencies at his institution, and whenever one of the kids got beaten an electric tension would pass through all the others, cowing them into submission and compliance. That sort of atmosphere didn't come suddenly into being; nor was it introduced from somewhere else. It was always there; you just didn't always notice it. It appeared as if out of a lifting fog, conjured into existence by a momentary action and reaction. The drivers—even those with blood or tears running down their faces—put their engines in gear and drove. From the landing strip, the procession of vehicles cut across the park to the highway and headed west.

All the biplanes had landed and were now parked in one long, straight row. The anchorwoman said in a shaky voice that there were a total of either thirty-one or thirty-two of them. Ishihara, still swaying his hips, raised his index finger in front of his face and ticked it back and forth, going, *Tsk, tsk, tsk!* It was clear that he disapproved of something, but it wasn't clear what it was. "Don't tell me you still don't get it?" Ishihara spun to the right so that he was facing everyone and blocking the TV. "Everything that nincompoop just said is poppycock," he said. "Which nincompoop?" Kaneshiro asked, and Ishihara snatched the remote from his hand and cracked him on the side of the head with it, hard. The blow resounded sharply, and two triple-A batteries flew out and clattered to the floor.

Kaneshiro held his head and moaned. "Why'd you do that?" he said, with an accusing sort of pout. "Sorry," Ishihara said. "When I and I saw those dudes hitting the drivers, we got all itchy inside with the desire to do like as they did. But you're partly to blame. Asking us which nincompoop... What other nincompoop could it be? Kiddies! Who remembers what the nincompoop said? That the safety of the citizens of Fukuoka is the government's highest priority. Which means they can't offer any resistance, yo! They have no counterstrategy—no nothing, yo! It's what you call an *antinomy*, yo! Interesting, no?"

On the TV screen, half hidden by Ishihara, riot police were reopening the expressway at the Kashii on-ramp. They were dismantling their own barricade of thick, pointed timber posts, behind which were parked a pair of windowless duralumin-surfaced armored vans, which other cops were now beginning to move. They must have received word that a convoy of vehicles filled with North Korean soldiers was approaching. "Ishihara-san, we can't see the TV," Kaneshiro said, standing and taking a step back, preparing to duck. Ishihara moved to one side petulantly, stamping his feet but still wriggling his hips. "Nooooo!" he said. "No, no, no, yo! Why keep watching this?" A voice off-camera—a male anchor this time—said, "The North Korean rebel troops who are holding the crowd at Fukuoka Dome hostage have announced that any helicopters approaching the area, including those belonging to news organizations, will be targeted with surface-to-air missiles!"

The armored vans backed slowly down the on-ramp and no sooner had they cleared the lanes than the first taxi roared up and squealed to a stop just short of the tollbooth. The passenger and rear doors opened, and two soldiers emerged, the first armed with a pistol and an automatic rifle, the other a pistol and an RPG. One of the vans was still slowly backing up, and a lone riot policeman, clearing away the last timber post, froze in his tracks. The weapons were trained on him. Even on TV, you could see that the RPG was aimed at his chest and the pistol at his forehead. The driver of the van must have noticed what was happening; the van hiccuped violently and stalled. But by now the convoy was arriving, and the two soldiers lowered their weapons, keeping their eyes fixed on the riot cop, and got back in the taxi, which sped off up the ramp onto Route 1.

"You can piss in a shitter," Ishihara said, "but you can't shit in a pisser." On the screen behind him, a succession of taxis, trucks, passenger cars, and buses was moving at speed up the on-ramp. Solemnly he announced that "The nincompoop is dropping into a shithole of epic profundity." He then raised the remote over his head and said, "Takei! Who is this nincompoop of whom we speak?" Takei cowered and said, "The newsbabe?" Realizing he'd guessed wrong, he turned to scramble away but was too late. He caught the remote on the back of his head and curled up, cradling his skull. "It's the politician," Kaneshiro told him. "That's right," said Ishihara, and cracked Kaneshiro on the head again. "You're *right*, I'm *left*, she's *da-a-ancin'* away!" He swiped at the heads of Tateno, Shinohara, and Hino as he chanted this, but they were too fast for him, and he missed all three. "You can't shit in a pisser," he intoned again and pointed toward the ceiling. Everyone gazed upward, but there was nothing to see but dusty pipework and stained cement. "Made you look," Ishihara said, and began literally roaring with laughter—laughing so loudly that it drowned out the TV. He writhed and twisted as he did so, thrusting his hands this way and that, hopping about, and yanking at his hair. This was Yamada's first experience of the full-blown Ishihara laugh. It was a laugh that made you feel that nothing was impossible, and that nothing really mattered—that even if everything were destroyed and the planet reverted to a primeval wilderness, it wouldn't really be such a big deal.

The laughter stopped as abruptly as it had started, and Ishihara spoke. "A nation state is something that always protects the mojority by sacrificing the few," he said. "If the safety of citizens is really their first and foremost concern, then they can't put up a fight against these North Koreans. If they *are* going to fight them, then putting the citizens' safety first is just impossibullshit. The North Koreans know this as well as the smell of their own poop, and they're one plop ahead. Roaches never dream they're going to die in a puff of KO Pest Spray. The real question is, what's important to protect? That's the question, and the guerrillas know this down to the marrow of their bones, down to the last pimple on their throbbing knobs, but the nincompoop standing out in the lonely neon rain at Tokyo Station doesn't have a foreskin-lint hint of a clue. If you want to destroy the invaders, you have to sacrifice some of the little people. This battle will prove that everyone runs the clitorisk of becoming the minority sometimes. And that, kiddies, is taboo knowledge that nobody dares let escape their lips, not even in a stifled yawn or a squelched belch. I and I alone get it. Why? Because, because, because I and I have always lived as a minority of one who might be eliminated at any given moment, while the nincompoop's been claiming his place in the mojority since he was in his mummy's tummy and wouldn't understand what I and I'm talking about if he was reborn five trillion times."

The convoy of commandeered vehicles sped past Hakozaki Pier. All eight on-ramps around the city had been barricaded, so there was no other traffic on the expressway. It was reported that the convoy was heading west. All lights had been turned off in the city and prefectural government offices in Tenjin, and large numbers of shield-bearing riot police surrounded the buildings. According to a reporter on TV, the governor and the mayor were in an undisclosed, secure location, where they were holding meetings to formulate a plan. Everyone had apparently fled the government district shortly after the guerrillas took control of Fukuoka Dome. "But neither the prefecture nor the city has advised the public to evacuate," the reporter said as the screen showed the darkened streets. Yamada didn't think it likely that the North Koreans would attack or occupy any government buildings. No one but the soldiers themselves knew what they were planning, but surely they didn't intend to take over the whole city. There were thirty-one or thirty-two transport planes. If the planes held an average of fifteen or sixteen soldiers, that made a total of about five hundred. There was no way five hundred troops could control a city of a million people.

This is surreal, Yamada thought as he watched the screen. Soldiers from North Korea, the country Japan had considered its greatest threat for over a decade, commandeering a slew of cars, buses, and trucks owned by Japanese citizens and then racing unchallenged down an empty highway. Riot police dismantling a barricade and waving them through as if they were visiting VIPs. Thirty thousand people held hostage in Fukuoka Dome. And it had all happened in what seemed like the blink of an eye—less than three hours had passed since a rocket-propelled grenade destroyed the scoreboard. Wasn't there something the government could do? Couldn't some public official—the Prime Minister, say, or the governor—go to the Dome and listen to the guerrillas' demands? Why had nothing like that been done before letting these foreign troops take to the empty highway? Put a couple of white motorcycles in front of that convoy, and they might have been state guests.

The convoy exited at the Momochi ramp, to approach the Dome. There were eleven taxis, eight semis, seven smaller trucks, six buses, and twelve passenger cars. The crowd outside the stadium had disappeared soon after the TV showed footage of taxi and bus drivers being knocked on the head with gun butts, and most of the guests and workers at the hotel had gone. The lights were still on at the Kyushu Medical Center, however. On the roof and in front of the entrance hung large Red Cross flags. "There are hundreds of patients who can't be moved, and others in the process of being operated on," the reporter said in a grim voice. "Words fail me when I think of the poor families of these patients." Yamada thought the man talked a lot for someone words were failing. The convoy pulled up in front of the main entrance to Fukuoka Dome. About thirty soldiers emerged at a low crouch with weapons drawn and ran to establish two widely spaced columns between the vehicles and the main entrance to the stadium. Once in position, the men dropped to one knee, facing outward to protect the corridor they'd created. Most of the remaining soldiers ran down this corridor toward the Dome, while a smaller contingent directed vehicles to the vacant expanse of land between the hotel and the Kyushu Medical Center and began unloading equipment there.

"Ladies and gentlemen, thank you for your patience." The voice came over the PA system inside the Dome, breaking the long silence. "Forces friendly to our cause have just arrived from the DPRK. Like us, these troops are dedicated to bringing down the government of Kim Jong Il. Together with you we want to turn Fukuoka into a haven of peace. We have brought you some simple tokens of our friendship, and we ask that you accept them in the spirit in which they are offered." Soldiers were now fanning out through the aisles, taking from cloth shoulder bags cheap-looking pink nylon scarves and small sprigs of artificial cherry blossoms and handing them out to people in the seats around them. There could scarcely have been enough of these gifts for all thirty thousand, but the spectators who received them did so with smiles, and some even shook hands with the soldiers. None of the soldiers were smiling, however.

More troops continued to pour in, and many of them began to trade clothing with spectators. Some took off their camo jackets and swapped them for windbreakers or sport jackets or sweaters. The people who were approached weren't really in a position to refuse. Some of them put their new army jackets on, and others held them tucked under their arms. The voice came over the PA system again: "Ladies and gentlemen, we are sorry to have kept you waiting. Please do not run, but make your way slowly and in an orderly fashion to the exits." Everyone stood up and headed for the aisles and corridors. At first the exodus was calm and orderly, but eventually a few people started running, and this led to a general stampede for the exits that was only exacerbated by the fact that it was hard to distinguish between spectators and soldiers.

On the open land outside the Dome, troops were driving stakes into the ground and setting up big tents and canopies. "Take a close look." Ishihara pointed at the soldiers on the TV screen. "Nobody in dear old Nippon is saying this yet, which is weird, but I and I am declaring it right here and now. *That*," he said, "is the enemy."

# PHASE TWO

PHASE TWO

1

# BLOCKADE

*April 3, 2011*

T HE FLAG of the Koryo Expeditionary Force was hoisted outside
the banquet hall they'd designated their provisional headquarters. The name had apparently been chosen by Professor Pak
Yong Su. The Republic, Professor Pak explained, had retained the
ancient name Chosun for the country, but now they were to use
another. "Koryo" could be understood as "high mountains" and
"shining water." The name of the Koryo Dynasty was a contrac-
tion of Koguryo, the northern kingdom that had preceded it by
a millennium. The design of the flag, a red tower against a white
background, with "Koryo" written in Hangul, was meant to represent
in simplified form the famous five-storied Koguryo pagoda.

   Though he hadn't slept for more than thirty hours, First Lieutenant
Pak Myeong of the Operations Section was brimming with energy.
The four sections of the 907th Battalion had been merged into one
effective unit, and now that this first important assignment had been
accomplished, he was in high spirits, confident that he had been a
credit to the Special Operations Forces of the Republic. The four
hundred and eighty-four combat troops, plus the nine members of
the advance team, had come through so far without a single death,
injury, or defection. They had proceeded with preparations for

setting up a camp and completed the work in less than three days. The encampment was one that needed no trenches, minefields, or barbed wire; the only requirements were tents, field rations, sentries, and checkpoints on the roads around the hotel, the Dome, the shopping mall, and the hospital. For the young shock troops of the 907th Battalion, it had been child's play.

Twenty or so key officers, including Pak, had stayed up all night planning the governance of Fukuoka and the delegation of authority. Colonel Han Seung Jin had been officially installed as commander of the Koryo Expeditionary Force, and this hall, on the third floor of the Sea Hawk Hotel just across from Fukuoka Dome, had become their HQ. Pak Myeong had been put in charge of day-to-day business but was subordinate to Staff Major Ri Hui Cheol, commander of the First Company of the 907th Battalion. Born and bred in Kusong, Phyongan Province, Ri was a specialist in international law.

Second Lieutenant Ri Gwi Hui had secured the hotel's electronic generator and communication circuits, allowing them to set up an intelligence section in the command center. Together with Second Lieutenant Pak Chun O of the Second Company and Warrant Officer Kim Sun I of the Third Company, she had created a multipurpose database of personal information drawn from resident codes in Fukuoka and outlying areas. Her most important task was to uncover politically hostile and criminal elements. With the collaboration of officials at Fukuoka City Hall and those in charge of the Kyushu public Internet databank, as managed by NTT Data and Fujitsu, complete access had already been gained to the general administrative network and the Basic Resident-Register Network. Major Ri Hui Cheol had made it known that if the necessary information was not made available, Japanese nationals held currently in confinement would be executed. All of the codes had been provided. Surprisingly, they had also readily handed over all personal data held by banks and various loan-shark corporations regarding the credit history of individuals and by health-care institutions regarding medical history. "Japanese nationals held currently in confinement"

FROM THE FATHERLAND, WITH LOVE

referred to the drivers, remaining hotel guests, and employees now being kept hostage.

At six o'clock on the morning of April 3, the governor of Fukuoka Prefecture, the mayor of Fukuoka City, and the chief of the prefectural police were sent electronic summonses in the name of the KEF's commanding officer to appear at KEF headquarters. They were to arrive at nine o'clock unaccompanied, without even an interpreter. They were told that should they be late or otherwise fail to comply with instructions, those persons detained at the Sea Hawk Hotel would be subject to immediate execution, for which the dignitaries themselves would of course bear responsibility. At the time the 907th Battalion troops had linked up with the nine members of the advance party, they had taken hostage any hotel guests and employees who hadn't escaped in time, along with two hotel physicians and six security guards. These "detained" individuals included: nine tourists from Australia, Taiwan, Malaysia, and Canada, and eighteen who were Koreans from the southern half of the country; fourteen hotel workers from the Philippines; forty-five resident Japanese, a number of whom were elderly or disabled; and a further thirty Japanese employees working at the reception desk and dining facilities. The hotel being a high-rise building, all that was needed to convert it into a detention facility was to stop the elevators and lock the emergency exits. Once the governor and the other two had provided certain intelligence data and signed a joint declaration, the foreign visitors, including the southern Koreans and the Philippine workers, would be released. All Japanese tourists and employees, with the exception of senior citizens, the infirm, and minors fourteen years and younger, would remain in KEF custody.

The proximity of a hospital, with a large number of patients whose condition made transfer impossible—people in need of emergency surgery and patients dying of cancer—meant that US troops and the Self-Defense Force were effectively prevented from attacking the nearby KEF encampment, even with precision-guided weapons.

*

195

At a little after seven in the morning on April 3, Pak Myeong was absorbed in documents pertaining to plans for the new government when a steaming cup was placed in front of him. Looking up, he saw a female officer standing at attention and saluting. Dressed in a uniform that was slightly too big for her, she had large, almond-shaped eyes, a charmingly small nose, lips that suggested a strong will, and still girlishly plump cheeks. He saw from her insignia that she was a warrant officer, but he guessed that she wasn't yet twenty-five. "I'm sure I'll enjoy this," he said, thanking her and then asking her name. The soldier introduced herself as Ri Gyu Yeong and gazed at him until shyness got the better of her and she lowered her eyes. Pak picked up the cup, took a sip, and let out a shout that reverberated through the silent hall. Second Lieutenant Ri Gwi Hui, sitting at a computer on a nearby table, had been looking his way and burst out laughing. Eyes still lowered, Ri Gyu Yeong bit her lip. "Damn!" Pak muttered. He was reaching for his handkerchief to wipe up the spilled tea, when the young warrant officer handed him a packet containing the soft sheets of paper called "tissues."

"Was it too hot?" she asked with an apologetic expression. Pak nodded. "I used what I thought were black tea leaves," she continued, "but I didn't know how hot the water should be." According to her file, if Pak remembered correctly, Ri Gyu Yeong was an army doctor. There were altogether eighteen women soldiers who had arrived in Fukuoka with the Fourth Company of the 907th Battalion, twenty if Ri Gwi Hui and Kim Hyang Mok of the advance party were included. All-female platoons within the 907th Battalion's light-infantry, aerial infiltration, and reconnaissance brigades, under the direct control of the Political Bureau, had been established in 1990.

Not yet having begun her medical work here, she was helping out at headquarters for the time being, no doubt assisting in the preparation of food when Fukuoka officials such as the mayor were expected. Pak cautiously put his lips to the cup and sipped at the tea. It was so thick that it numbed his tongue and the inside of his mouth. And there was no sugar in it. "Is it bad?" Ri asked uneasily. "You might have sweetened it," Pak replied. Ri apologetically told him that she hadn't been able to find a sugar jar. Pak thought of telling her that the Japanese use small single-serving paper packets but then saw that her eyes were glued to the large flat-paneled television set that had been left on and was showing policemen setting up barriers on an expressway. Colonel Han, his hand on the remote control, turned up the volume, and everyone turned to look. First Lieutenant Jo Su Ryeon and Second Lieutenant Cho Seong Rae nodded with an air of satisfaction. "I'm sorry," said Ri Gyu Yeong, "I don't understand Japanese very well. What's happening?"

"The government is blocking off Fukuoka," Pak explained.

The previous evening, when 907th Battalion troops had entered Fukuoka Dome and exchanged clothes with their hostages, those able to speak Japanese had let it be known that a dozen or so Japanese-speaking SOF soldiers dressed as ordinary Japanese would be heading toward Tokyo. The story was that, as North Korean rebels, they were intent on coexistence with the Japanese and thus felt obliged to make their way to the capital, wearing civilian clothes, to pay their respects at the Imperial Palace and the Diet. The drivers of commandeered vehicles near Gannosu Air Station had been given the same line. Some of the SOF troops spreading the rumor were seen with maps of Tokyo. Fukuoka Dome hostages and various drivers had passed it on when interviewed by television and newspaper reporters, and had probably repeated it when questioned by the police. The idea of North Korean commandos, fluent in the language and dressed in ordinary clothes, appearing in the heart of Tokyo scared the government stiff. In the minds of the public, too, the idea of national institutions being targeted by trench mortars and rocket-propelled grenades was terrifying. Just as Colonel Han had predicted, this unprecedented situation for both the people and the government had led the authorities to order the police and the Self-Defense Force to seal off Fukuoka in an attempt to contain the occupying KEF.

Television announcers kept repeating that this action, applying to the whole of northern Kyushu, was in accordance with the provisions of Emergency Acts designed to protect civilians. Appearing at a press conference, the Chief Cabinet Secretary was asked whether they were in effect abandoning the people of Fukuoka but rebuffed the question, saying, red-faced and tearful, that this was absolutely not the case. In fact, however, Fukuoka had become a landlocked island. First, the SDF had closed the Fukuoka, New Kitakyushu, and Saga airports before dawn on April 3. It hadn't yet been decided whether the blockade would extend to other Kyushu airports, including those in Nagasaki, Kumamoto, Miyazaki, and Kagoshima, but domestic airlines had voluntarily canceled all flights in and out of the island on the grounds that safety could not be assured. Citing the threat of terrorism, international airlines had likewise announced an indefinite suspension of flights. Hakata Station had also been closed. The high-speed bullet train of which the country was so proud was still running between Tokyo and Okayama, but most of the Kyushu rail network had been shut down. The ferry routes linking Moji with Kobe and Osaka, and Miyazaki, Hyuga, and Oita-Saganoseki with Honshu, were no longer operating. Hakozaki Wharf, which handled container cargo, and Higashihama Wharf had also, for all practical purposes, ceased to function.

As for vehicle traffic, the Kanmon Tunnel had been barricaded, and parts of the Kyushu Highway and the national routes were now off-limits. Caught up in the crisis were overnight express buses that had left Fukuoka on the evening of April 2 headed for Tokyo, Nagoya, Kyoto, Osaka, and other cities on the mainland. Pursued by police helicopters on the Sanyo and Meishin Expressways, they were stopped and boarded by armed officers who subjected the passengers to a thorough interrogation. Lined up on the runways of Fukuoka Airport were armored vehicles along with armed SDF personnel, and at the adjoining army base an SDF battalion and US-made attack helicopters were standing by. The SDF had also closed the Shimonoseki Tunnel, with armored vehicles and tanks guarding the northern end. The government was using the army to isolate Fukuoka and the police for security checks in Tokyo and other major cities. Haneda Airport, the Imperial Palace periphery, and government buildings were teeming with the navy-blue uniforms of the riot police. The present state of affairs, newscasters reported, clearly smacked of martial law.

"Why? What for?" murmured Ri, as she looked at the TV images. Pak could well understand her reaction. Why, instead of engaging the KEF in combat, was the Japanese government sealing off Fukuoka and going to such extraordinary lengths to monitor activity in Tokyo? It had been completely taken in by the rumors. A moment's thought would have made it obvious that the KEF was in no position to turn the entire nation into an intransigent enemy, inviting an all-out counterattack. No, the government had simply panicked at the prospect of terrorist strikes in the capital and reacted in a manner that was doubly counterproductive. First, it was wastefully expending men, equipment, and money on these cordoning operations. Tens of thousands of SDF and police personnel must be involved, which alone would cost a fortune. Secondly, the blockade meant stopping the flow of both people and products between Kyushu and the rest of the country. The economic fallout would be colossal.

Ri Gyu Yeong went on looking at the television screen with the same puzzled expression. Pak knew what she was thinking. Why weren't Japan's military forces on the attack? If the costs of defense were already ruinous, why not go on the offensive? If the Republic were in a comparable situation, the Dear Leader wouldn't hesitate to order a counterattack. Eliminating the KEF would undoubtedly mean a lot of civilian casualties, but the financial cost and the physical damage would be relatively small. On joining the operation, Pak had asked Colonel Han if it were true that the Japanese government wouldn't engage in any sort of military action that might affect civilians. "Is that just for humane reasons?" he ventured. Han had responded with a laugh. "A humane politician," he said, "is like a bellicose pacifist—a contradiction in terms. Politicians are obliged to accept the fact that their job involves sacrificing the minority for the majority. The Japanese government's primary concern won't be the lives of Fukuoka's citizens but the nationwide fury the government itself would incur, and the loss of support it would suffer, if it ordered the SDF to attack and many died as a result."

Ri now excused herself, saluting and saying that she was on hand should Lieutenant Pak need her assistance. The packet of "tissues" she'd handed him after he had spilled the tea still lay on the table. They were neatly folded, so that each one could be removed separately from the open slit in the plastic wrapper, on which the name of a taxi company was printed. Pak wondered why a taxi company would be in the business of producing these things. He took out a sheet to feel the texture. Never before had his fingers touched such thin, soft paper. He put it to his mouth and then wiped his cheek. It felt to him like silk. The thought occurred to him that the whole nation of Japan was much the same: soft. The air at daybreak on Nokonoshima Island had been tepid and soft, like the evening air at Fukuoka Dome—and like that young farmer's eyes. Choi Hyo Il had described the sensation of gouging out his eyes as being "like poking through bean curd."

The Japanese underwear distributed at the training camp was so soft and smooth that it seemed hardly made of real material. The hotel beds and sofas too had a feathery touch. Pak waved the tissue paper in front of his eyes. The slightest breath was enough to make it flutter like a butterfly. Ri Gyu Yeong had told him that she'd acquired them from a taxi driver forced into service at Gannosu Air Station. They were apparently given away without charge. It wasn't something limited to certain privileged customers, but rather an abundant and inexpensive commodity distributed free to quite ordinary people. The level of technology required to produce it was beyond Pak's imagination. And yet far more baffling was how a country capable of such know-how could also be so politically inept. Wasn't anyone thinking of the consequences of shutting off Fukuoka from the flow of goods and services? He himself came from a world of frequent food and fuel shortages, even for the privileged, and he knew that the social consequences could be hellish.

The meeting with the governor and mayor would be held in a separate banquet hall adjoining this one. Thirty minutes beforehand, Pak Myeong went in to make sure everything was ready. Side by side on the front wall were the flags of both Japan and the KEF. On a large sheet of paper decorated with artificial cherry blossoms were written the words CELEBRATING FRIENDSHIP, in both languages. Hung from the ceiling against the surrounding walls were radial braids of red and white, and in the middle of the room was a long, narrow table on which a cloth embroidered in the Korean manner had been laid out. Depicted on it was a sage teaching virtue to a tiger emerging from a bamboo grove. Jo Su Ryeon had deliberately chosen this and brought it from the Republic as a symbol of the relationship between Fukuoka and the Koryo Expeditionary Force.

Laid out on the center table and on several smaller ones along the walls, filling the room with their fragrance, were yellow, white, and purple tulips, primroses, daffodils, rape and cherry blossoms, azaleas, and camellias. Second Lieutenant Kim Hyang Mok and her female subordinates had begun preparing the arrangements early that morning.

Food and drink were already in place. The ample beverage selection included Pyongyang *soju* and purplish-pink Kamhongno, Japanese whiskey and beer, coffee and a variety of teas (including ginseng), as well as water and soda. The food was nothing short of a sumptuous feast, one worthy of May Day or the Great and Dear Leaders' birthdays. Most striking was the basket in the middle of the main table, filled with apples, tangerines, melons, and other kinds of fruit that Pak Myeong had never before seen, though he could guess that they were South Sea rarities: one was green, egg-shaped, and covered with downy fibers; another was yellowish and shaped like a sweet potato. Next to the basket was a bowl piled high with chestnuts, deep-fried jujubes, sesame cookies, and various Korean candies. And all of this was surrounded by various meat dishes, including deep-fried beef, pork and kimchi on skewers, minced chicken patties, and, most fragrant of all, the deep-fried slices of pork known as *cheyukjon*. There were also deep-fried mackerel and stir-fried green pepper and octopus. A bowl of chilled seaweed-and-cucumber soup sat at each place setting.

For Pak Myeong the aroma was nostalgic, abruptly recalling his own village, as his mother sometimes cooked *cheyukjon*. Pak had been brought up and raised in a hamlet near Pyonggang in Kangwon Province. There, pork was something for special occasions, being normally reserved for members of the Party. His paternal grandfather had been killed in action during the Great Liberation War, but though this gave the family a perfect pedigree, they all lived in straitened circumstances, and from an early age he'd been obliged to work in the family orchard. When he was five, a younger brother was born, and as part of the celebration he found himself eating *cheyukjon* for the first time. He remembered his father boasting that for consistently producing first-rate apples and peaches, the regional head of the Party had given the family some pork. Making *cheyukjon* first involved mixing bean curd—after the water had been wrung out with a towel—with kimchi (also strained), ground pork, salt, black pepper, garlic, and sesame oil. Then egg yolk was added before it was all deep-fried. The aroma it produced was one of a kind.

After tasting *cheyukjon* that first time, the five-year-old Pak asked his parents if they had made it when he was born too. "Yes, of course," his mother replied. "But I don't remember eating it!" he said, and the assembled relatives and neighbors all laughed. After that, his mother had cooked *cheyukjon* for him on various special occasions: when he joined the Party, for example, and when he received permission to go to university. On the day he left for Pyongyang, his mother told him with a sad face that there was no pork with which to make his favorite dish. At the time, there was not even enough rice or maize to eat, let alone meat. She said that the older men who worked in the orchard had spent three full days scouring for rice. He went outside and looked at the rice paddy he had played near as a child. It was now winter, and he could see high-school girls with red mufflers, members of an ice-skating team, gliding on its thickly frozen surface. Beyond were the hills where he had gone to pick acorns, nuts, and berries. Weeping, his mother told him again and again that when he returned, she would make some *cheyukjon*, but Pak just gazed fixedly past her at the girls and their red mufflers.

Later, whenever he went home, he found that conditions were worse than ever. His parents looked more and more emaciated, and his father's neuralgia got so painful that he couldn't work. Each time Pak returned he could see that the orchard, like the hills themselves, had been further whittled away. Unable to bear the cold and the famine, the villagers had cut down the apple trees as well as the trees on the slope, where they planted maize instead. And even when the paddy field froze over in winter, there were no longer any skaters. Once, on furlough, he brought some pork with him, but there was no sesame oil, garlic, eggs, or bean curd. There was not even any kimchi. His mother said she couldn't make *cheyukjon*. Not knowing what went into it, Pak had somehow thought that all that was needed was the meat. Here, in a room made ready for a banquet, Pak felt oddly drawn back into the past. In the monochrome of memory, amidst winter snow against somber hills, the only hint of color was in the image of those skaters. At the back of his mind he could still clearly see them, their mufflers flying in the wind, alongside the sad, gaunt face of his mother. *Why are you remembering all this?* he asked himself. The mayor of Fukuoka and his entourage were about to arrive. *Pull yourself together.*

"In the name of the Koryo Expeditionary Force, I hereby welcome His Honor the Mayor of Fukuoka City and His Excellency the Governor of Fukuoka Prefecture." Han Seung Jin had worded his greeting to take account of the fact that the mayor was older than the governor. The mayor was of slight build, whereas the governor was a fleshily imposing figure, with a paunch and a bright complexion that indicated ample nourishment. On entering the room, the two men looked at the feast prepared for them in wide-eyed surprise, clearly not having expected such treatment. They were shown to the table in the middle of the room, across from Colonel Han. On his right was his second-in-command, Major Ri Hui Cheol, who due to his limited Japanese was relying on Second Lieutenant Ri Gwi Hui, next to him, to be his interpreter. At the far end was Pak Myeong, who in his administrative capacity was recording the meeting's proceedings. Still standing behind their seats, the mayor and the governor glanced warily at Ri Gwi Hui with her laptop; they had already been given reason to fear her investigative skills.

Accompanied by two NHK Fukuoka cameramen as designated media representatives, along with a man identifying himself as the chief of the prefectural police, the pair had arrived in a large black Toyota at Checkpoint A. The occupied zone was bordered by the Hii River to the west, the coastal expressway and beach to the north, the Komo River to the east, and Yokatopia Avenue to the south; and the KEF had set up five checkpoints—one at each of the four corners and one more midway along Yokatopia Avenue. Checkpoint A was near the hotel, at the foot of the big bridge over the Hii. Ri Gwi Hui was waiting there to confirm the men's identities before they got out of the car. As she later said with a laugh, it was no doubt the first time they'd had an AK-74 pointed at them.

The identification check showed that while the men purporting to be the mayor and the governor were indeed who they said they were, their companion, Okiyama Hiroto, was not the prefectural chief of police but rather the head of the National Police Agency's Kyushu bureau. In an instant, Ri had access to a fund of information about him. Drawing on resident-register data, she indicated that she knew his place of birth, the university he had attended, and his work record in the foreign-affairs section, noting as well the operation he had undergone for a herniated disk four years before, his wife's pen name as a haiku poet, and the fact that their second grandchild had started at a prestigious kindergarten in Tokyo. With three protruding front teeth, the bespectacled, late-fiftyish bureaucrat looked very like a squirrel. At the mention of his wife and grandchild, he paled.

It had been Major Kim Hak Su who'd gone to meet the three at Checkpoint A as the KEF representative. He was so angry that Ri Gwi Hui thought for a moment he was going to shoot Okiyama on the spot. SOF troops under his command had often quailed at his rebukes, and now the 1.85-meter-tall Kim towered menacingly over Okiyama like a soccer referee chewing out an errant player. "You are not the prefectural chief of police!" he shouted, pointing a pistol at the man's temple and threatening him with public execution.

Okiyama broke down, quietly begging that his family be left out of this. The mayor, whose name was Tenzan, despite being short, thin, and stoop-backed, pleaded Okiyama's case with Kim, pointing out that he was guilty of nothing more than following government orders.

Instructions finally came from Han saying that Okiyama was to have his papers confiscated, that he was to formally acknowledge having misrepresented himself, and that he was to be arrested and detained in the hotel. Okiyama submitted to the humiliation of confessing: "I, Okiyama Hiroto, have committed identity fraud in a deliberate attempt to disrupt the Koryo Expeditionary Force as well as the stability of Fukuoka and its citizens." Ri Gwi Hui then presided over a simple impromptu trial, reading aloud the charges, pronouncing the accused guilty, and ordering him to be taken away. Okiyama thus became the first "criminal" arrested by the KEF. His hands bound behind him, he was frogmarched away by two soldiers, with the entire event recorded by NHK Fukuoka.

After being led into the banquet room by Han, the mayor and the governor handed slips of hard paper to each of the KEF officers present, introducing themselves: "*Tenzan de gozaimasu.*" "*Yoshioka de gozaimasu.*" In the center of the little rectangular cards were their names in thick Chinese characters—Tenzan Toshiyuki, Yoshioka Masaru—and in the upper-right-hand corner their titles. These slips of paper, Jo Su Ryeon quietly explained, were business cards, known as *meishi*. They appeared to be made of a unique sort of paper, as though of translucent fiber. Pak felt the bumpy surface, wondering what technique had been used for the embossed lettering. He had never seen such things before and wondered what their purpose was. Wasn't it enough simply to jot down a new acquaintance's name, position, and contact information?

"Well, thank you very much," said Han politely, holding up the cards. "In the Republic, we do not use these convenient '*meishi*' of yours, though from now on I suppose we will be obliged to! In the meantime, we will introduce ourselves verbally." He gave a resounding laugh, from the pit of his stomach, at his own little joke. The governor feigned a smile; the mayor did not. "Again welcome!

Please sit down." When they were seated, Han reached across the table to shake hands with both of them. The short Tenzan leaned forward, taking care not to let his suit brush against the food, while Han, still clasping both men's hands, smiled into the NHK camera. As this was the only part of the meeting that the media would be allowed to film, the cameramen would now withdraw, returning only for the joint news conference that would follow. Although the KEF's seizure of Fukuoka was of worldwide interest, the blockade imposed by the Japanese government precluded representatives of the foreign media from being present. Lieutenant Jo Su Ryeon, director of propaganda and guidance, had granted NHK exclusive coverage for the beginning of the meeting; they would be joined at the press conference by reporters from four newspapers—the *Asahi*, *Mainichi*, *Yomiuri*, and *Nishi Nippon*. All participants had been required to provide their resident-register information.

"When we in the Republic entertain important guests," said Han, pointing to the display of food, "we tend to go somewhat overboard. Our purpose today, however, is less to entertain than to form a friendship. First, I wish to propose a toast to His Honor the Mayor and His Excellency the Governor." At this point, two women soldiers, Kim Sun I and Ri Gyu Yeong, entered the room, now dressed not in khaki but in navy-blue skirts and white blouses, with orange scarves around their necks. Kim had clear, pale skin, a broad forehead, a small mouth and nose, and eyes whose corners slanted slightly downward. She was tall, with the well-balanced body of a gymnast. The two women each took a bottle of liquor from the table, went to stand behind Tenzan and Yoshioka, and prepared to pour some Kamhongno into their glasses. "*Sake?*" Yoshioka asked in surprise, covering his glass with his hand. Kim stood holding the bottle at the ready, looking disconcerted. Ri too appeared uncertain whether to pour anything into Tenzan's glass.

"Why are we being served alcohol at a time like this?" Yoshioka whispered into Tenzan's ear. Han Seung Jin smiled, silently fixing his gaze on the two men. "Why not?" said Tenzan, holding out his glass. "I'll have a drink." The liquid flowed in, making a sound like a

gurgling infant. "I'm not much of a drinker," Yoshioka said, gesturing
with his hand to stop Kim Sun I when she had filled the glass halfway.
"This is a special brand of *soju* made in Pyongyang," Han explained.
"We brought it from the Republic for the sole purpose of drinking
it with Your Honor and Your Excellency." When everyone's glass
had been filled, Han rose to his feet and exclaimed, *"Kanpai!"* Pak
Myeong had never tried Kamhongno before and found it delicious.
As though sensing his reaction, Jo glanced at him from several chairs
away and gave him a look that said: *Don't overdo it.*

"His Excellency has just asked why we should be drinking under
these circumstances. My reply is that this special Pyongyang product,
like the feast you see before you, is intended to inaugurate a mutually
beneficial relationship." So saying, he emptied his brimming glass in
a single gulp, then motioned with his chin toward the NHK cameramen as a signal to Jo to have them leave. The lieutenant announced
that coverage of the day's events was over for the moment and that
the media representatives should wait in the lobby until the press
conference. "We will now discuss that relationship," Han resumed,
once the people had left. "The necessary basis for any such association is mutual trust." He then took a big bite of the skewered pork
and kimchi he had in his right hand and a sip from the bowl of cold
seaweed-and-cucumber soup in his left. Jo also began eating with
gusto, while Ri Hui Cheol gnawed on some deep-fried mackerel,
crunching every bone. Ri Gwi Hui had for the moment put her
laptop to one side and was working on some minced chicken and
kimchi in a bowl piled with rice. The sound of her chewing was
rather pleasant, as suggested by the Korean proverb that the crunch
of kimchi sounds better than birdsong. Pak Myeong, remembering
this, thought that it must refer to the pleasure of seeing and hearing
a beautiful woman eating, and this blended with the nostalgia he
felt as he savored his *cheyukjon*. The taste wasn't quite the same as
the dish his mother had cooked. Presumably there were subtle differences in the recipe between regions, and even between families.

Tenzan and Yoshioka looked on in amazement as their hosts put
away meat, fish, cabbage, and rice with the speed of hungry wolves,

not knowing that the SOF were trained to do most things as quickly as possible and that the officers had, in fact, scarcely eaten since taking over Fukuoka Dome. Even as he was making alarmingly short work of the food, Han brought up the subject of *Juche* as a simple illustration of what he meant by "a mutually beneficial relationship." Representatives of the Republic who were engaged in negotiations habitually mentioned this practical, home-grown ideology. It was not set policy to do so, but it was nonetheless uniform practice. With the gradual introduction of liberalization, however, the Dear Leader had himself expressed the unprecedented view that when dealing with foreigners a long-winded exposition of the national ideology was unnecessary. His decision in this regard had arisen after the American representative at the non-aggression pact talks displayed impatience when being treated to a two-hour lecture on the subject. Han was now saying: "We stand firmly by the belief that by focusing on our common humanity, and striving to further that humanity through scientific progress, we can overcome our differences in social organization and culture. Your Honor, Your Excellency, working hand in hand, we can start building a new society here. I dare say that half the battle is having confidence that this is worth doing—and can be done."

From deeply ingrained habit, he was on the verge of expanding on the philosophy behind this, but Major Ri raised a hand to gently dissuade him. Curtailing his remarks, he went on: "The principles of *Juche*, with their emphasis on independence and self-reliance, are something we in the Republic grow up with and frequently have recourse to; but we are by no means dogmatic about them. After all, at the heart of everything are human beings, and the fact that everything changes and evolves is reassuring. It is again our common humanity that enables us to coexist." He then told Pak Myeong to distribute copies of the Master Plan for Harmonious Government. Pak had spent the entire night grappling with the draft and had completed it forty minutes before the meeting. There were three basic points for agreement, along with two concrete policies and demands, and one announcement. The points were:

(1) the peaceful coexistence of the Koryo Expeditionary Force and the residents of Fukuoka; (2) the joint effort of the KEF and Fukuoka's representatives to work out the particulars concerning that relationship; and (3) the ultimate independence of the KEF and Fukuoka from Japan.

Han paused and asked whether there were any questions. Tenzan looked up from the document, removed his reading glasses, and asked calmly, "You spoke just now of *Juche*, but aren't you rebels?" Tenzan was bright red in the face from only half a glass of Kamhongno, but his speech remained clear. "We are," replied Han with a nod and a smile. "But if you staged an attempted coup in the Democratic People's Republic of Korea and then fled to Fukuoka, why don't you lay down your weapons and seek asylum?" Han remained unruffled: "We are neither asylum seekers nor aggressors. Rather we have abandoned our country and come here to pursue a cause—true justice." He then looked at Major Ri. In faltering Japanese, Ri apologized for having to use an interpreter and then began speaking in Korean, with Jo translating for him.

"There are many examples in history of insurgent troops allying themselves, even while still armed, with people of other countries and fighting with them for a cause. Such partnerships have been well received, from ancient times to the present day—from the empires of Alexander the Great, Rome, Genghis Khan, and the Ming, to what we're now seeing in Central Asia and Russia. It wasn't so long ago, during World War II, that armored brigades in Finland rebelled against their Soviet-allied government and joined forces with the German army. And there were Polish soldiers who, defying the puppet regime that was reconciled to the Nazi occupation, threw in their lot with the Soviet army. South Korean soldiers rejecting the Syngman Rhee regime went over to the side of the DPRK-Chinese alliance. During the Vietnam War, many South Vietnamese and Cambodian soldiers coexisted, in common opposition to their governments and in the common desire to fight the Americans. We hope you will see us as forces offering a helping hand to Fukuoka and other democratic elements among the Japanese people."

"All the examples you've given," replied Tenzan, "involve wartime conditions. Fukuoka is not at war. Neither do we want this 'mutually beneficial relationship' you refer to." Hearing Tenzan say this, the governor looked at him with a mixture of anxiety and reproach, as though to warn him that they might all be killed for talking like that. And yet, as Pak Myeong noticed, the hand with which Tenzan was holding his glass of Korean liquor was trembling, an obvious sign that he was scared as well. Han replied to Tenzan's objection: "For sixty years the Republic has merely been observing a truce. War is just another aspect of diplomacy and politics; it is a great mistake to think that peace and war are polar opposites. We are not asking you, your Honor, your Excellency, to agree with the Master Plan for Harmonious Government. We are merely giving you notice of it. Should you oppose it, you will be arrested for taking a stand against harmonious coexistence. That unfortunate development will further result in making impossible the release of the foreigners now being confined in this hotel, something the governments of Canada, Australia, Taiwan, Malaysia, and South Korea will hardly welcome. Responsibility for that will rest entirely on your shoulders, and once you are locked up with the others, you will be in no position to argue further. Would you care to take a look at what has become of Mr. Okiyama, while being held for false impersonation?" Without waiting for a reply, the commander took out his mobile phone and ordered his subordinates to fetch the man in question, though discreetly out of range of NHK's cameras.

It wasn't long before two KEF soldiers dragged Okiyama into the banquet room, holding him by both arms. The sight made Yoshioka squeal, and Tenzan gagged, and gagged, clutching a handkerchief to his mouth. Okiyama was half-naked, and his right shoulder was covered in blood, the flesh split and flapping open, with a bit of white bone exposed. His face was badly scratched and contorted, a yellowish liquid was dripping from one eye, and his left hip looked out of joint and incapable of supporting his weight. Barely conscious, he revived just long enough to grimace and give a groan that sounded like air leaking from a balloon. This was too much for Yoshioka: he had turned pale, and his plump body was shaking. His eyes wandered about in a daze, he knocked his glass over, and the muscles in his cheeks began to twitch as if he were laughing, or choking. Tenzan was trying hard to maintain his composure, still holding his handkerchief over his mouth. "Various questions were put to him concerning the movements of the Special Assault Team, the regular police, and the Self-Defense Force, but he declined to answer," Han said, taking a sesame cookie from a plate and putting it in his mouth. Ri Gwi Hui was eating a deep-fried jujube; and Jo Su Ryeon asked Kim Sun I if she would hand him an apple.

Yoshioka and Tenzan tried not to look. The governor was on the verge of panic, as though he might at any moment stand up and scream. Pak had never seen people react like this. In the Republic, it wasn't uncommon to see someone who'd had the stuffing beaten out of them. Everyone knew what happened to political offenders and ordinary criminals, and in the military, the sort of punishment that Okiyama had been subjected to was something one learned to expect. Any KEF soldier could have identified the treatment he had undergone simply by looking at him. He had probably been made to do the Motorcycle several times, which would account for the hip injury, perhaps with renewed damage to his herniated disk. In reaction to the excruciating pain, he might inadvertently have scratched his face and damaged an eyeball. After that, the subject would have been made to sit cross-legged, then beaten on the bare right shoulder with a wooden staff. This too caused great pain, and it wouldn't have taken many blows to tear away the flesh and expose the bone. Okiyama probably didn't know anything about any joint plans drawn up by the police and the SDF. If he had known, he would readily have spilled his guts. There was no reason to expect a Japanese to stand up to the sort of torture the SOF were familiar with.

Okiyama's raucous breathing blended with the sound of Ri Hui Cheol chewing his kimchi. Yoshioka's eyes were wide with fear, and Tenzan was struggling to speak. His face, flushed with Kamhongno moments ago, had now lost its color. He had closed his eyes and was

biting his lip. To Pak it seemed he was trying to regain his composure and get his thoughts in order, but it was probably impossible.
These Japanese simply weren't used to violence; they lived in a soft,
tissue-paper world. Tenzan looked up and glanced again at the poor
Okiyama. "I understand," he said. "What do you understand?"
asked Han. Tenzan replied with a distracted expression and in an
almost inaudible voice: "I accept the Master Plan."

Prior to the news conference held at 10:30 that morning, a total of
fifty-nine foreigners at the hotel were released from their various
rooms, along with eighteen Japanese. The released Japanese were
children under the age of fourteen, the ill, and the handicapped,
and included both tourists and hotel employees. All had been well
treated and were in good spirits. The fifty-nine former hostages
were to be taken in a bus provided by the KEF from the hotel to
Checkpoint B at Momochihama Bridge. From there they could walk
to the downtown area. The South Korean tourists, mostly students,
spoke freely with the soldiers, asking Pak and Jo whether there really
had been a *coup d'état* in the DPRK. Would Kim Jong Il's regime
continue? Would the KEF now be attacking Busan from Fukuoka?
What kind of relationship did they intend to build with the South?
"Unfortunately," said Pak, "we can make no comment at this time.
We'll be informing the world at large of our situation, thoughts, and
plans when the appropriate time comes."

The press conference began in the hotel lobby, but Yoshioka had
excused himself, saying he was feeling ill. Terrified by the sight of
Okiyama, he'd been reduced to a nervous wreck. He'd stood in a
corner of the room, leaning against the wall and weeping like a child,
refusing to reply to anything the mayor said to him. As if comforting a child, Warrant Officer Ri Gyu Yeong put an arm around his
shoulders and led him into another room, where she would gave
him a tranquilizer and let him rest. Representing the KEF at the
press conference, in addition to Pak, were Colonel Han and his
second-in-command, Ri Hui Cheol, with propaganda director Jo
Su Ryeon officiating. "First," said Jo, "our commanding officer,

Colonel Han Seung Jin, will receive a report from His Honor, Mayor Tenzan, concerning the basic agreement." Tenzan's voice wavered as he outlined the three main points. When he finished reading out the third item concerning the independence of Fukuoka, there was commotion among the members of the press corps.

The reporters rose to ask what the hell this meant, but Jo told them that questions would have to wait until the end. Next Pak Myeong presented the two concrete policies for the new joint government. These two administrative mainstays were: (1) the issuance by the KEF of yen-convertible notes, and (2) the arrest of both politically dangerous elements and serious criminal offenders. A list of offenders had already been compiled but would not be announced out of concern that the guilty might attempt to flee. The task of rounding them up would be carried out with the cooperation of the Fukuoka police. Though a meeting with the prefectural chief of police had been cancelled, His Excellency Governor Yoshioka along with His Honor Mayor Tenzan had pledged their support. The KEF, Pak added, was a military organization without police functions. Thus, the assistance of the prefectural police was essential.

Yen-convertible notes would be backed by the financial resources of the KEF, but in practice paper money would not be issued. Payments for food, drink, clothing, medicine, sanitation, and residential-building construction would be made electronically; KEF officers would make payments with the memory cards they carried. Pak did not explain what he meant by "financial resources," but the reporters present didn't seem to be interested in this aspect. He had prepared an answer: gold bullion brought from the DPRK. In reality, however, funding would come from assets confiscated from politically danger-ous elements and serious criminal offenders. After their arrest, their bank accounts would be transferred to the KEF, while information concerning overseas capital, stocks, and securities, along with savings concealed in the name of third parties, would be extracted under interrogation and these resources subsequently appropriated.

Politically dangerous elements and serious criminal offenders—corrupt politicians and power-brokers, corporate extortionists,

213

and those who'd racked up fortunes through gambling, loan-sharking, prostitution, and drugs—were to be attacked root and branch. Included on Lieutenant Ri Gwi Hui's list were members of Chongryon, the General Association of Korean Residents of Japan. Their home and business addresses were known, and as Fukuoka was already sealed off, they had nowhere to run even if they got wind of their impending arrest. The yen-convertible note had been planned by Major Ra Jae Gong, a product of the National Security Agency and commander of the 907th Battalion's Third Company. Ra was rumored to have been involved in the transfer of the Comrade General's personal assets to a Swiss bank account. A monetary and economic expert, he had been put in charge of managing the financial operation in Fukuoka. From his straightforward and unequivocal point of view, no one could object to taking money from crooks.

Finally, Han had an announcement: ships carrying a hundred and twenty thousand rebel troops from the People's Army would be docking in Fukuoka in eight days' time. Tenzan, who had already been told this at the banquet, lowered his eyes and bit his lip; the assembled journalists, for their part, were momentarily stunned. They stopped writing, exchanged glances, and conferred in undertones: *Did we hear that correctly? A hundred and twenty thousand troops on their way here?* Lieutenant Jo explained the plan. "As soon as these troops arrive at Hakata Port, they will be integrated into the KEF. They will then construct living quarters on vacant land in Hakata Ward, Chuo Ward, Sawara Ward, Nishi Ward, and the Gannosu area of Higashi Ward and thereby become fellow Fukuokans. In due course they will form a fine workforce in this new land, advancing the 'lightning progress strategy' developed in the Republic, and devoting themselves fully to peace and prosperity in East Asia. That is the substance of our announcement. Now if you have any questions, we'll be happy to answer them."

"Yokogawa of the *Nishi Nippon Shinbun*. I must say I find myself speechless with shock, and I'm sure my fellow journalists feel the same way hearing this. I have several questions. First, when will these reinforcements leave the DPRK by ship?"

Yokogawa was the oldest of the four reporters, with the thinnest hair, but though he claimed to have been rendered speechless, he spoke out purposefully in his booming tenor. "I cannot tell you when exactly the ships will leave port," said Jo, "but, as I'm sure you all know, it should take about fifty hours for naval vessels to reach Fukuoka from the east coast of the Republic."

Yokogawa nodded and scribbled a note. "Has General Secretary Kim Jong Il authorized their dispatch? This morning the Korean Central News Agency expressed the opinion that you are indeed a rebel group and have nothing to do with either the Democratic People's Republic or the Korean Workers Party. As such, the response of other countries to your actions is of no direct relevance to the DPRK, even if the Japanese or American governments attack you. As these governments are already denouncing the DPRK over this incident, there is some question as to whether the General Secretary will permit the departure of ships carrying rebels. What do you say to that?"

Yokogawa scratched his head with his pen as he posed the question. His outward appearance suggested a weary, middle-aged man, but Pak could see that here was a professional and tenacious journalist. This press conference was being broadcast worldwide, but that didn't seem to bother Yokogawa in the least. Nor was he intimidated by the presence of KEF sentries armed with AKs or by the fact that all Han's subordinates were packing pistols.

"Strictly speaking," Jo replied, "we have not launched a rebellion against the Comrade General. We have raised our banner against the ultra-liberalizers in his entourage and those generals and bureaucrats who have become the puppets of foreign interests. Our Republic is presently being led astray by the honeyed words of American imperialists and bowing to outside intimidation. As a remedy, we have left the Fatherland, prepared to endure the humiliation of being named as rebels for the sake of establishing a new homeland, together with Japan's democratic forces. The Comrade General is surely not indifferent to our fate, and any statements he may have made to the contrary only reflect the prevailing domestic situation. It was precisely in response to our national crisis that we, the Koryo Expeditionary Force, have abandoned our own country. Consequently, we will not yield to intimidation, whether from Japan's SDF or from US forces stationed here. If we are attacked, we will counterattack. The KEF is currently comprised of four companies from the Special Operations Forces' 907th Battalion. These are elite troops armed with the latest weaponry and highly trained in street combat. No matter whose army is sent against us, we will not be easily defeated. Moreover, if hostile elements should gain control of the Party and attack our comrades waiting to leave the shores of the Republic, or if any other nation should attack them once they have departed, we will retaliate. Such measures may include executing politically dangerous elements we have already taken into custody and ordering special-operations personnel who have already infiltrated other urban areas of this country to carry out acts of retribution."

Behind his glasses, the reporter Yokogawa opened his eyes wide as he listened to this, then nodded and took some notes, muttering to himself. Of course, the reference to SOF infiltrators in other Japanese cities was a piece of disinformation. Yet it wouldn't be difficult for the KEF, in fact, to send agents into Osaka or Tokyo on sabotage operations—and no doubt they would do so if necessary. An *Asahi Shinbun* reporter named Ito raised his hand and stood up to ask, "What do you intend to do now?" Taking advantage of the ambiguity of this, Han replied, "I have not slept for more than a quarter of an hour since yesterday morning, so I am planning to take a nap." A *Yomiuri* reporter named Moriwaki asked what "independence from Japan" was supposed to mean. "Surely you know what the term 'independence' means?" he was asked. Moriwaki replied that of course he did. "Then please confine your questions to those you do not already know the answer to." Yokogawa burst out laughing, but when Moriwaki glared at him, he stopped and nodded an apology. A member of the NHK crew asked what was to become of those Japanese tourists and hotel employees who were still being detained. Pak answered this one, saying that some would be released once certain politically dangerous elements and criminals had been arrested, and Yokogawa spoke up again. "On what legal grounds," he said, "will you carry out those arrests? In other words, which country's laws will you be applying?"

Jo and Han looked at each other, as if confirming that they needed to keep an eye on this journalist. "As a general rule," Han answered, "Japanese law will be applied in the case of ordinary criminals. As for political offenders, ethical principles accepted internationally will take precedence over strictly legal considerations." Pak explained further: "We anticipate establishing bylaws for the governance of Fukuoka, as well as revising some existing laws, but it would be a mistake to think that we have come to Fukuoka in order to inflict unreasonable punishments and penalties on any of its citizens. The Koryo Expeditionary Force intends to follow the path of coexistence. We believe that the long-standing historical ties between the people of our Peninsula and the people of Kyushu will make for a positive common influence. We the Koryo Expeditionary Force aim to foster well-being and order, creating in Fukuoka and all of Kyushu a land of mutual respect and prosperity. We the Koryo Expeditionary Force have no intention of attacking either the Self-Defense Force or the US troops based in Japan, much less the local citizenry. As long as no military action is launched against us and there is no violent resistance or hostile propaganda, we the Koryo Expeditionary Force will live in our enclave as peacefully as doves. Since the time of our arrival here in Fukuoka, we have not fired a single shot. It is true that in the course of securing Fukuoka Dome we were forced to launch a rocket-propelled grenade, but even then there were no fatalities or injuries. For its part, the Japanese government has set up a blockade, cutting off Fukuoka from the mainland. You, the citizens of Fukuoka, should reflect on the significance of that act. Is it not your destiny and ours to live together in one harmonious community?"

"A last question," said Yokogawa. "Do you think the Japanese government will ever allow Fukuoka to become independent?"

Colonel Han Seung Jin replied: "We do not intend to ask for permission."

217

# 2

# KNIGHTS OF
# THE ROUND TABLE

*April 3, 2011*

J UST BEFORE DAWN on April 3, Yamagiwa Kiyotaka was relieved
of his duties as deputy chief cabinet secretary. Officially he was
to resign due to poor health, but in fact he'd been given the axe.
Prime Minister Kido and Chief Cabinet Secretary Shigemitsu had
both been hopping mad when told of the arrival of another five
hundred or so North Korean commandos in Fukuoka. Shigemitsu,
who had a Band-Aid on his forehead after a run-in with a TV camera
at Tokyo Station, bitterly accused Yamagiwa of being incompetent,
and Kido had started yelling at him the moment he strode into the
crisis-management room.

Kido Masaaki had not always been involved in Japanese politics,
having spent much of his career as head of an NGO providing
refugee assistance and humanitarian aid in places like Cyprus,
Cambodia, and Palestine. He had been propelled into the limelight
six years ago, when he was named as a possible candidate for the
Nobel Peace Prize because of his work as part of the committee
overseeing the EU-led Palestinian peace process. Despite an exposé
in the British tabloid press about him having spread the Nobel Prize
rumors himself, he stood as the former Democratic Party candidate

for prime minister at the general election and was voted in. Kido had just turned fifty at that time. When the Liberal Party split over the freeze on bank deposits and spiraling inflation, and its young reformist faction merged with the main Democratic Party faction to form Japan Green, they were unable to agree on which camp should provide the new party's leader. It was thought that someone untainted by party politics was needed, and Kido seemed the ideal candidate.

Yamagiwa had disliked Kido from the start. Kido's professional experience was the opposite of his own. A graduate of a Christian university, Kido had been licensed as a lawyer on the East Coast of the US before passing up the high-paying corporate world for a career in international environmental NPOs. He was better known abroad than in Japan for his work in conflict zones. Yamagiwa, on the other hand, had taken the conventional route of graduating from the School of Law at Tokyo University and then working for the Bank of Japan, only becoming a Diet member on retirement. Kido was also tall and handsome, still in his early fifties, fluent in English, and often featured in men's magazines even after becoming prime minister. Yamagiwa's dislike of him stemmed not from envy of his position or appearance, however, but from the man's underhanded-ness—although this was a defect that all politicians shared to some extent. Kido's behavior and way of speaking changed according to whom he was dealing with: faced with someone powerful he would be courtesy itself, and if a good impression was needed he was all smiles, but with someone who didn't matter he'd not bother to conceal his impatience.

He was good at remembering people's names and backgrounds after only meeting them once, and the press loved him for his outspokenness, but the fact remained that everything he said and did was calculated. Few politicians or bureaucrats had seen the real Kido. As deputy chief cabinet secretary, Yamagiwa had often had occasion to work under him and had inevitably noticed this side of his character. Despite a successful career, Yamagiwa lacked strong connections, money, and presence, and was little more than a convenient punchbag for the brash Prime Minister, who often humiliated him in front of his own staff. Yamagiwa was in his late sixties, and had come across any number of men of this type. All of them, without exception, had grown up in modest circumstances, had had bad relationships with their fathers, and were both insecure and intensely ambitious. They studied and worked hard but were excessively concerned about other people's opinions of them, and to compensate could be unduly high-handed with those weaker than themselves. Ironically, this youngish international figure, considered an outsider in respect to Japanese politics, was in fact a classic example of the Japanese politician.

Shigemitsu Takashi, a mid-level Diet member of the old Democratic Party at the time, was the one who had persuaded Kido to stand for PM. The Chief Cabinet Secretary was of course a lawyer by training, and for almost ten years, beginning in his late thirties, he had served as governor of Okayama Prefecture. He had revitalized Okayama City and its surroundings, creating a special economic zone comprising medical care, education, agriculture and fishing, and implementing wide-ranging tax cuts. Okayama was said to have developed by leaps and bounds with Shigemitsu as governor, although some economists pointed out that all he had really done was to create an irreversible gap between rich and poor. Shigemitsu had studied at Stanford after graduating from a good university in Tokyo. He was four years older than Kido, but still in his fifties.

Kido and Shigemitsu had returned by helicopter and bullet train from Morioka and Okayama respectively, and by the time they reached the Cabinet Office it was already around eleven at night. Kido would have arrived earlier had he flown directly to the heliport at his official residence, but after his intention to do so was broadcast on the TV news, he'd been forced for security reasons to change his plans. On entering the crisis-management room, he had pointed a finger at Yamagiwa and bellowed, "Have you any idea what's going on? What the hell have you been doing all this time?" He slammed the pile of documents he was holding onto the table, and swore in English.

From Yamagiwa's point of view, it was outrageous that he should take the blame. It was not his fault that a lot more terrorists had just flown in. Apart from anything else, he had been the first Cabinet member to arrive, followed later by the Environment Minister. None of the other ministers had shown up yet, while the head of the National Public Safety Commission had gone fishing without leaving an emergency contact number and wasn't even aware of what was going on. Still, he couldn't deny that his response to the crisis had been less than stellar, particularly since his mishandling of the media had resulted in the leak about the Prime Minister's helicopter. But he couldn't very well have told a nation in shock that the PM's whereabouts were unknown.

"Sorry, but I'll have to ask you to leave the crisis team," Kido told him as he took his seat at the round table. This amounted to being fired from his post as deputy chief cabinet secretary. Yamagiwa's face flushed with outrage, and his heart beat so violently he thought it would fly out of his mouth. There were almost thirty staffers in the room at the time, and he had been dismissed in front of all of them. He was about to protest, but quickly realized he was being made a scapegoat. Someone had to take responsibility for the unprecedented occupation of Japanese territory by North Korean guerrillas, and Yamagiwa was the obvious choice for fall guy.

He rose to his feet, but Shigemitsu stopped him. "Hold on. Until this meeting is over, you are still deputy chief cabinet secretary. You have a duty to report on developments so far." Yamagiwa fought back tears of frustration and an urge to punch them both as hard as he could. *Nobody* could have done anything in the circumstances! In just two hours? Did they think that if they'd both been here, those North Koreans wouldn't have flown in? In any case, they *hadn't* been here. They'd been off swanning around the countryside!

But all he said was, "I see," and, head still bowed, he sat down again at the table. Protesting the unfairness of it all would be seen as an attempt to shift the blame, and would only cement his fate as the sacrificial lamb. Shortly afterwards, Itagaki, the deputy chief cabinet secretary for crisis management, arrived. "Other ministers

will be turning up soon, so would you mind moving to another seat?"
someone whispered in Yamagiwa's ear. He got up and walked to a
chair as far away from the Prime Minister as possible. As he did so,
he was watched sympathetically and also apprehensively by Iwata
of CIRO, Yoshizaki of the Foreign Ministry, Korenaga of the Public
Security Investigation Agency, Katsurayama of the National Police
Agency, and Yonashiro of the Defense Agency—all of whom were
clearly aware that the same treatment could be meted out to them
at any time. They had already moved from the central table to the
chairs along the wall. The lower-ranked aides had given up their
seats and were either leaning against the wall or had left the room.

Ministers of state and various bureau chiefs were arriving one
after another in the crisis-management room. Foreign Minister
Ohashi; Motoki from the Asian and Oceanian Affairs Bureau;
the female Foreign Ministry official Tsunemura Taki; Togo from
the North American Affairs Bureau; Finance Minister Takahashi;
Justice Minister Nagano; Minister of State for Economic and Fiscal
Policy Atoda; the commissioner of the Financial Services Agency
Moriyama Kazue; Arita from the Inspection Bureau, and Misaki
from the Supervisory Bureau, of the Financial Services Agency;
Minister for Economy, Trade, and Industry Umezu; Koganei of
the Manufacturing Industries Bureau; the female Minister for
Information and Communications, Matsuoka Kusuko; the Minister
for Health, Labor, and Welfare Minami; the female Home Affairs
Minister Araki Yukie; Minister of State for Defense Shimada; the
Senior Vice Minister for Defense Takamura; Chief of Staff for
the Ground Self-Defense Force Shinomiya; Chief of Staff for the
Maritime Self-Defense Force Kanno; Chief of Staff for the Air
Self-Defense Force Godai; Commissioner General Oikawa of the
National Police Agency; Superintendent General Nanbara of the
Metropolitan Police; Kosaka of the Info-Communications Bureau;
and others. The Minister of Land, Infrastructure and Transport was
being flown back from a meeting in Hokkaido by the SDF, and was
due to arrive at one o'clock in the morning. Word had come from

the family of the head of the National Public Safety Commission, Kurusu, that he had returned from his fishing trip blind drunk, so a member of the Commission named Sadakata was called upon to substitute for him. The Chief Cabinet Secretary told them that they would establish the Crisis HQ in the Cabinet as well as a National Safety Committee in the official residence.

The room was becoming increasingly claustrophobic with the arrival of more and more people. The TVs were all on, showing the non-stop coverage and special broadcasts from NHK and other stations; the phones and faxes were ringing continuously; computer keyboards were clattering; and a heavy aroma of coffee and green tea hung over everything. Umezu, the Minister for Economy, Trade, and Industry, turned to Shigemitsu and said, "The Crisis HQ is supposed to be set up in the event of a missile or terrorist WMD attack, isn't it?" Umezu was a veteran Diet member on the right of the old Liberal Democratic Party, and didn't get on at all well with Shigemitsu.

"With all due respect, isn't having part of your country occupied by North Korean terrorists a good enough case for a Crisis HQ?" Shigemitsu didn't bother to hide his exasperation. What an idiot, thought Yamagiwa. Umezu had just been winding him up, and he'd have done better to let it pass. "That's not what I meant," Umezu said bluntly. Shigemitsu was younger, and he wasn't about to defer to him. "These people call themselves a rebel army faction, but what do we, as the government, call them? An invading army? Terrorists? Spies? Illegal-arms smugglers? We can't very well call them our guests, can we?" This last quip roused laughter from Matsuoka, Minister for Information and Communications, as well as the bureau chiefs of the Ministry of Economy, Trade, and Industry—all of them anti-Shigemitsu.

This wasn't to say that Shigemitsu had many enemies. He'd had sufficient flair and public support to get Kido installed as prime minister. Nevertheless, the pair of them had yet to produce any substantial results. There had been a slight improvement in the level of inflation, and the slumped yen and government bonds seemed set to bottom out—but now this had happened. It was unclear how it would impact on Kido and Shigemitsu. No, even if things turned out well, the Cabinet would probably not survive. Umezu would no doubt force responsibility for the incident onto Kido and Shigemitsu, and was probably already thinking that once things were under control he could aim for the premiership himself.

"Obviously they are terrorists, and in my opinion that's what we should call them," said Shigemitsu. Just then, a call came from the Fukuoka prefectural police for Oikawa, head of the National Police Agency. After a brief exchange the latter, looking pale, stood up, phone still in hand. Everybody looked at him. "I've just been informed that some of the terrorists are headed for the Diet and the Imperial Palace," he said sheepishly. There was an audible gasp around the table, and the room fell silent as ministers and bureau chiefs stopped speaking mid-sentence, the aides seated in the chairs by the wall stopped talking on their cellphones, and even the clatter of clerical workers' keyboards ceased.

As the sound of voices died, noises from fax machines and the coffee maker echoed through the room. A new mood seemed to have taken over. It wasn't that people looked startled, or gloomy, or anxious, or even furious or frantic. They looked deflated, Yamagiwa thought, as if the life had drained from their faces. It was the sort of expression worn by someone meeting a prospective marriage partner for the first time and finding that they were far uglier than they had looked in their photo. Everyone felt disheartened and inadequate in the face of this new complication.

"What do you mean?" Kido asked Oikawa. He was always asking people what they meant, thought Yamagiwa, stifling a laugh. What a stupid question. How much room for interpretation did the news leave? "Were we informed by the terrorists themselves?" asked Shigemitsu. "No. It's what we've been told by hostages released from the Dome, and by drivers of some of the commandeered buses and taxis," Oikawa replied. "They're bluffing," said Kido. "If they really meant it, they wouldn't go spilling the beans to their hostages," he added, but then buried his face in his hands. It was ninety-nine per cent likely to be false information, but what if it was true? You couldn't very well ask the terrorists themselves to confirm or deny it. Yamagiwa was beginning to feel he was probably lucky to have been fired. This was just about the worst possible development, and it was hardly surprising that everybody looked so discouraged. It wasn't the sort of problem that you could solve and get brownie points for; whatever action they took would have a price, and a terrorist attack on Tokyo would mean the collapse of the Cabinet and the end of Kido's and Shigemitsu's political careers.

Visually, it was difficult to distinguish between Japanese and North Koreans, and the people occupying Fukuoka Dome could also speak Japanese. Dressed in civilian clothes, it wouldn't be at all difficult for them to carry concealed weapons on a plane or bullet train, or even drive to Tokyo. They could also get a ferry to Osaka or Shikoku and continue by train from there. Japanese airports didn't have the infrared or magnetic machines used in the US for searching hand luggage. The terrorists could even send their weapons by courier and travel unarmed—it would be impossible to search all the courier services operating there. Bullet-train passengers were not subject to any security check. Japanese people were not in the habit of carrying around their passports or other ID, so checking their identity on domestic flights and at train stations would be an enormous undertaking. Even if they issued an order for everyone to carry some kind of ID, the terrorists might already have arrived in Tokyo. The light transport planes had arrived just after 9:00 p.m., but there was no telling how long the advance team had been in the country. Even if they had landed at Hakata Airport just that morning, some of them could have flown straight on to Tokyo. It was a nightmare scenario.

"Shouldn't we be considering the option of attacking North Korea?" inquired Umezu. Seven years ago Umezu and his cronies from the right-wing faction of the old LDP had managed to get a bill passed revising part of the foreign-exchange law, prohibiting the transfer of funds to North Korea. It had taken effect from April the following year, but ultimately there were any number of third countries through which funds could be transferred, so it wasn't much use as a bargaining chip. "What exactly do you mean, attacking North Korea?" demanded Shigemitsu, again unable to hide his irritation. Umezu loosened his necktie and then thumped both hands down on the table. "What I'm trying to say is that while all this is going on, there's a rogue state there quietly watching. Behind this rebel army faction, or whatever the hell it is, it's got to be the little Generalissimo himself pulling the strings. That's why we mustn't take the option of attacking them off the table. At the very least, the threat of attack would give us leverage."

Sitting next to Umezu, Matsuoka Kusuko nodded dutifully at everything he said. She had made a name for herself when, as CEO of the Japan branch of a foreign-owned telecommunications group big in Europe, she had tried to buy out NTT Data Corporation. She wasn't so much a telecommunications expert as a hard-nosed Western-style businesswoman who, prior to being invited by Kido and Shigemitsu to join the Cabinet, had overseen the buyout of around twenty corporations with the backing of an American investment bank. She had a round, full-moon face, and wore a short red dress cut low in the back. At fifty-four, she was the epitome of an aggressive Thatcher type.

"Well, Article 9 of the Constitution is still in force, you know," Shigemitsu pointed out. "Good grief, are you still banging on about that?" Umezu shot back, shaking his head, then continued in a quieter voice: "Look, there's basically no difference between self-defense and attack. The vital issue is whether circumstances force a country to it or whether they just see an opportunity. I say assemble the Maritime SDF in the Japan Sea and give the Generalissimo a bloody nose. Let's drive it home to them that there's nothing to be gained by winding Japan up. That's a more realistic solution, wouldn't you agree, Ohashi?" Foreign Minister Ohashi said, "The Korean Central News Agency has already stated that North Korea considers these soldiers to be a rebel faction and has offered to dispatch a force to deal with them. But we've informed North Korea via diplomatic channels that they should keep out of it. The last thing we want is the ridiculous situation of a North Korean civil war starting on our territory." Ohashi had started his political career in the Asian and Oceanian Affairs Bureau, but having also worked at the consulate in New York and frequently visited Beijing in his diplomatic capacity, he had strong connections in both America and China. With relations with these two big powers worsening over recent years, Kido and Shigemitsu had contrived to get Ohashi, still in his early fifties, appointed as Foreign Minister. He hadn't had any striking successes in that position, however.

"What's more, I doubt whether America and China would welcome any retaliation on our part," Ohashi added. Umezu turned red in the face. "What the hell has it got to do with America and China?" he bellowed, leaning forward. "We don't owe them anything! Can't we do anything without worrying about their reaction? And all those American troops here in Japan, why aren't they doing anything? The whole point of the Security Treaty was in case something like this happened, wasn't it? So what has America got to say for itself? I heard that we couldn't even contact them!" The Prime Minister raised both hands. "Calm down, Umezu. This is a matter of the utmost importance, so let's keep our wits about us." Umezu nodded, closed his eyes, and took a deep breath. Pathetic, thought Yamagiwa. He could understand how Umezu felt, but the man had just gone and contradicted himself, lamenting the need to consider America and China's reaction, while objecting to the lack of action by US troops based in Japan.

It had been under Umezu's leadership all those years ago that the fundamentally anti-US right-wing faction of the old LDP had sent SDF troops to Iraq to demonstrate their allegiance to the Bush administration. Japan could not afford to offend the US, still a great power, and needed its support in order to stand up to its neighbors. But in just a few years circumstances had changed. With the dollar's collapse, the US had been toppled from its position of supremacy. There was even a theory that it had deliberately ceded the number-one spot; once a leader was weakened, it cost too much to maintain preeminence. Of course the US was still militarily strong, but the euro was on the rise as settlement currency, especially for oil. And then the US had announced its appeasement policy toward North Korea without even consulting Japan. America didn't give a damn about North Korea, of course, but it did take relations with China seriously. America was like a philandering big shot, with Japan the kept woman unceremoniously dumped when the money ran out. Being kept by a big shot wasn't necessarily bad or unreasonable. As long as the woman had chosen to stand by the man for her own reasons, she shouldn't have any real regrets even when dumped. If she'd stayed with him out of some romantic notion of wanting to make him happy, however, she would end up hating him.

The right-wing faction of the old LDP and indeed the majority of Japanese people considered the US disloyal and resented them for it. They were equally unhappy about the US-North Korean détente. Umezu wasn't a hardline militarist, but he was a classic example of a Japanese man whose pride had been wounded by America. To condemn politicians like Umezu as foolish was perhaps overdoing it. From now on Japan was bound to take an increasingly hard line in diplomacy. If public opinion tended to the hard line, then diplomats seeking to compromise would be seen as letting the country down, making negotiations more difficult. There were already moves to revise the Constitution, and politicians were increasingly vocal about changing Article 9 to allow for a large-scale military build-up, including nuclear capability. Yet this would obviously attract hostility in East Asia and lead to Japan's further isolation in the region. If Japan broke away from the US, isolated itself in East Asia, and antagonized China, how could it keep body and soul together? This was the quandary, as Yamagiwa saw it.

"There's nothing else for it," said Kido gloomily. "We'll have to blockade Fukuoka."

A groan came from several of the ministers and bureau chiefs. Umezu pressed his lips into a thin line, folded his arms, and stared up at the ceiling. Matsuoka's shoulders slumped as she looked down at the documents in front of her, while Oikawa removed his glasses and started polishing the lenses. Moriyama Kazue smoothed out the creases in her skirt, and Nagano massaged his temples. It was hard to tell whether Ohashi was nodding or shaking his head. Takahashi fiddled with the strap on his cellphone, and Atoda alternately removed and replaced the cap of his silver fountain pen. Minami took out his handkerchief, perhaps to wipe the beads of sweat on his forehead, but he just stared at it for a few moments and then put it back in his pocket. Everyone fidgeted aimlessly, and sighed sporadically—even the aides in the chairs along the wall. So it's come to this, thought Yamagiwa, feeling the energy drain from his body. The PM looked vacant, his eyes glazed. Of course, he was from Oita, Yamagiwa remembered. How many other people in the room were from Kyushu? Shigemitsu covered his face with both hands. It felt as though the room itself was heaving a mournful sigh. "Hasn't the Transport Minister arrived yet?" Shigemitsu asked a staffer, who looked at his watch and said, "He's due to arrive in a few minutes."

Shigemitsu began making a list of all the ministries and agencies, and their respective bureau chiefs and section heads, that would have to be involved in implementing the blockade. Oikawa asked whether it should apply to Fukuoka alone, but Kido responded that in practice it would have to include the whole of Kyushu. There was no point sealing off only Fukuoka Airport when it would be just as easy to drive to Saga or Nagasaki and catch a plane from there. A staffer brought in a large map of western Japan and mounted it on a display panel. Nagano asked which law would give them the grounds to set up a blockade, and Shigemitsu responded that the Emergency Acts would cover it, adding that this legislation also enabled them to dispense with the approval of the Diet. Kido called Shimada and Oikawa over to where he was seated, no doubt to discuss a possible role for the SDF in this. There was practically no precedent for the SDF and police to work together, but the North Koreans were so heavily armed the police alone would probably not be able to cope, and the understanding and cooperation of both would be vital.

After a short consultation, it was agreed that the SDF would take charge of sealing off the airports, stations, ports, bus terminals, and roads in Kyushu, while the police would set up checkpoints on the mainland. This would be the first public security deployment of the SDF since their establishment in the post-war period. It was decided that engagement with the terrorists would be avoided as far as possible. This didn't mean that the SDF would retreat if attacked, only that they would not be the ones to initiate contact. If the terrorists resisted and it was impossible to avoid a confrontation, then the appropriate response would be left to the judgment of the commanding officer on the ground. "What about international flights to and from airports in Kyushu?" asked Ohashi. "We'll have to suspend them," Kido said. Motoki of the Asian and Oceanian Affairs Bureau and Imaizumi of the Trade Policy Bureau started speed-dialing their counterparts in China, Taiwan, South Korea, and the United States.

On arrival, Doihara, the Minister for Land, Infrastructure and Transport, was left speechless by the news of the blockade of Kyushu. He hadn't yet been informed that the terrorists were headed for Tokyo, and had not summoned the chiefs of the respective bureaus for road, rail, and civil aviation. There wasn't time now, he said, so they would just have to contact each individual airport, station, and port, and each airline, railway, and ferry operator to order the suspension of all services. He also summoned all his ministry's section heads on standby to the crisis-management room. Minami, the Minister for Health, Labor, and Welfare, asked Shigemitsu what the duration of the blockade was likely to be. Shigemitsu, who was in the middle of phoning around Kyushu's prefectural governors, said, "How the hell should I know?"

Minami was clearly miffed. "You realize what you're doing, don't you?" he said. He had originally worked for a labor union and had been prominent in the former Democratic Party, but being a realist familiar with economics he had announced that the age of labor unions was over and had promptly become a neoconservative, retaining his political base with the support of the Japan Federation of Economic Organizations. He was initially branded a traitor by his allies, but later gained points for crossing swords with the medical association and succeeding in semi-privatizing the hospitals. Shigemitsu interrupted a conversation with the mayor of Fukuoka, putting his hand over the mouthpiece to respond to Minami. "And just what do you mean by that?" he said.

"The blockade won't only stop all traffic out but all traffic entering Kyushu as well, is that correct?" Minami asked. "Naturally," said Shigemitsu. Kido, Umezu, and other ministers were listening intently to this exchange. "I suppose you do realize that you are also preventing the delivery of goods?" Minami's voice was low and carried well, and at over 1.8 meters tall, he was an imposing figure. Many said it was his smooth, authoritative presence that had won out against the medical association. Even the aides in the chairs by the wall were now hanging on every word. "Medical supplies will soon run out, you know," he continued. Shigemitsu's eyes glazed over as he sat with the phone receiver still in his left hand. "Hospital supplies of dialysis fluid and blood, especially for operations, are particularly vulnerable. And that's not all. If the blockade drags on, food and fuel will run low. I can't give any details without consulting the people on the ground, but distribution systems have changed, you know, regardless of whether you're dealing with things like medical supplies, food, fuel, and raw materials. Especially in retailing, the trend has been toward drastically reducing stock, so any disruption to transportation routes will have considerable repercussions." Looking grim, Minami dabbed at the sweat on his face as he spoke. Shigemitsu thanked him, then told the mayor of Fukuoka at the other end of the line to check up on hospital supplies, warning him also to watch out for stockpiling and unscrupulous traders withholding goods. "No, I'm afraid I don't know," he repeated a number of times. The mayor was probably asking him how long the blockade was to continue.

The atmosphere around the table was even gloomier after Minami's warning. Minister of State for Defense Shimada and Shinomiya, chief of staff for the Ground SDF, were on the phone to the GSDF Western Army and the GSDF 4th Division HQ, consulting the map as they discussed the blockade points and allocation of men. Doihara proposed closing the Kanmon undersea tunnel connecting Kyushu to the mainland, and the PM agreed to the immediate deployment of the 40th Infantry Regiment, based at Kokura, to the tunnel entrance at Moji. The other end of the tunnel, at Shimonoseki on the mainland, was to be closed by the Yamaguchi prefectural police. Oikawa of the Police Agency wondered whether it was wise to station troops at transport hubs within Fukuoka City, such as Hakata Station, Nishitetsu–Fukuoka Station, and Hakata Port, and on the city's thoroughfares. Their presence in the area around the terrorists' main camp might unnecessarily raise tensions and even provoke a clash. After consulting the head of the Defense Agency, Shigemitsu decided to put the police in charge of blockading Hakata Station and other locations in the city, although the SDF were to go to their aid if they came under attack. Oikawa agreed that the SDF should take care of Fukuoka Airport, an obviously important hub.

Kido meanwhile was discussing the details of an emergency press conference with an aide. Blockading Fukuoka was such an extraordinary measure that the Prime Minister would have to appear on TV and explain it in person to prevent panic. Yamagiwa wondered what on earth he intended to say. Apart from anything else, did it really make sense to seal off Kyushu when the terrorists were already headed for Tokyo? The measure was being taken under the legal framework of the Emergency Acts, yet in this case it wasn't to safeguard the entire nation; if anything, it was to protect important places and people in Tokyo. What would the people of Fukuoka and Kyushu think about being cut off from the nation under a law that was originally designed to protect them?

All the room's occupants were now clutching phones and issuing instructions, focused on getting the blockade in place. "I *know* it's impossible to seal all the roads off," someone yelled. Foreign Ministry personnel from the minister down were busy explaining the suspension of all flights in and out of Kyushu to the air travel authorities in the US, China, South Korea, and Taiwan. The American response to the suspension of flights from Hawaii was apparently rather curt. Meanwhile, telegrams expressing both regret and encouragement were coming in from the US President and Secretary of State, and from top officials in China and South Korea. All said more or less the same thing: they expressed shock at this deplorable act and offered to help in whatever way they could; they pleaded for calm in any response to North Korea, given that this was a rebel faction; and they hoped for a quick resolution and for the safety of Japanese citizens. Yamagiwa wondered doubtfully why the US President hadn't called in person. And why wasn't the US ambassador present, or any representative of the US forces in Japan? Was the Foreign Ministry even consulting with the Chinese and Korean ambassadors?

Yamagiwa remained in the seat farthest from the Prime Minister and was ignored throughout. He alone had nothing to do amidst the whirling chaos of loud voices, endlessly ringing phones, and staffers running around. In all of his long years at the Bank of Japan or even as a politician he had never felt so humiliated. But he had discovered something unexpected. As a non-participant, he could clearly see how bizarre this typically Japanese decision-making process actually was. All the ministers, bureau chiefs, and their respective underlings were entirely focused on the blockade of Fukuoka. There was no denying that stopping all traffic in and out of Kyushu was an enormous undertaking, but in the meantime the basic approach to dealing with the terrorist incident hadn't been decided—it hadn't even been discussed. In other words, no overarching priorities had been established. The highest priority should probably be to disarm the terrorists, in which case shouldn't Kido, as Prime Minister, be laying the groundwork for negotiations to that end?

An emergency call came in from Osaka police prompting another flutter of agitation around the table. An express bus that had left Fukuoka in the middle of the night was now on the mainland speeding along the Sanyo Expressway. Other buses had also since departed, so it was decided to track them all by helicopter, stop them on the expressway, and run ID checks on all the passengers. If any terrorists were on board and put up armed resistance, they should respond by shooting to kill—Kido, Shigemitsu, and Oikawa all okayed this. "What if they take hostages?" Oikawa had asked, but it was agreed to defer dealing with that until the situation arose. Listening to this exchange, Yamagiwa's sense of unease grew. Still, if he'd been part of the proceedings himself, he realized, he probably wouldn't have had any doubts about it.

It was one o'clock in the morning, and the most powerful people in Japan were still ensconced in the Cabinet Office. The PM's eyes were bloodshot, and the Chief Cabinet Secretary's voice was increasingly hoarse as he spoke on the phone with the governor of Kyushu. The other ministers and bureau chiefs loosened their ties, undid a few buttons, rolled up their shirtsleeves, chewed on their pens, or tugged at their hair as they took notes. Even the women among them had no thought to spare for their appearance as they immersed themselves in the task at hand. An impartial observer would certainly have had the impression that they were all working flat out. And indeed they were, issuing tough, complex instructions that would result in the mobilization of tens or even hundreds of thousands of people.

Yamagiwa felt a sense of hopelessness wash over him. On turning fifty, he had gone through a midlife crisis and had been on anti-depressants for a couple of years. Here in the crisis-management room, watching these people frantically at work, he got the same sour taste of futility that sometimes made him feel like saying to hell with it all. At first he thought it was because he'd been left out in the cold, but he was beginning to feel it was more than that. Being outside the frenzy of the round table, he had become painfully aware of the Japanese government's inability to see the big picture—and if *he* could see it, no doubt other outsiders could see it too.

The crisis room was two floors underground and windowless, but the TV screens were showing the sky lightening over the seaside city of Fukuoka. NHK and various independent broadcasters had been covering the incident through the night. The NHK footage of the neighborhood around Fukuoka Dome was probably taken from the roof of the TV station. The terrorists had banned all helicopter flights over the Dome, and made it clear they would shoot down any aircraft infringing this ban. The scene being broadcast showed an expanse of green military tents in the area between the Dome, the high-rise hotel, and the hospital, with plumes of smoke from cooking fires rising here and there.

Periodically an ultra telephoto lens closed in on the terrorists' flag. It wasn't the North Korean flag, naturally, since they were a rebel army, but bore a cryptic design on a white background with something written in Hangul below. Yamagiwa was thinking that they couldn't have chosen a more preposterous place for their camp, but he was also impressed. While the government had spent the night organizing the blockade, the terrorists had constructed a full-blown base camp, with tents, strategically positioned vehicles, sentry posts, and what looked like several checkpoints. A few ministers at the round table suggested attacking it with American precision-guided missiles like those used in the Gulf War, Iraq, and Afghanistan, but an SDF expert explained that it was too close to a large hospital for this to be feasible. Even if they used a bomb with a limited lethal blast range, those who survived would likely take cover in the hospital or other buildings in the area and further complicate the situation. As things stood now, according to telephone interviews broadcast on TV, the terrorists hadn't yet entered the hospital. The Kyushu Medical Center was a huge, maze-like building complex with numerous blocks connected by corridors. It probably would have been safer for them to occupy it from the start, but they had chosen instead to set up camp on the vacant, park-like ground outside.

The Chinese and South Korean consulates were inside the area now under the terrorists' control, and the US consulate was not far away. These, however, had been evacuated as soon as the Dome was occupied. The US consular personnel had been flown to the Yokota base near Tokyo, while the staff of the other consulates appeared to have gone to the mainland by bullet train or car. A small research institute and school for the handicapped east of the Dome had also been vacated. Nevertheless, most of the residents of the adjacent districts had been left behind. In the event of a natural disaster, the city authorities, the police, and the fire department knew how to go about evacuating residents. In this case, however, any evacuation would risk causing panic, and they didn't have the facilities to transport and accommodate huge numbers of people.

Doihara had put his head down on the table and was fast asleep. The PM looked refreshed, having showered and shaved following an hour's nap in another room. After a night of issuing orders, most of the ministers and bureau chiefs were now taking a brief rest in the rooms provided. For reasons of confidentiality the admin staff couldn't be relieved; they had spread blankets over their knees and were dozing sitting upright. All this time, Yamagiwa had been completely ignored. Shigemitsu had told him to stay until the end of the meeting, but he couldn't say whether the meeting was over or not. He'd dozed off several times in his large and comfortable leather-upholstered chair—and why not, he thought defiantly; after all, he *had* been relieved of his post. Now, as he drafted his letter of resignation, he kept one eye on a TV special about the Fukuoka occupation, but there hadn't been any new developments since the release of the hostages in the Dome and the installation of the rebel army base camp, and the guest commentators seemed to have run out of ideas.

Yamagiwa basically agreed with what the experts on North Korean affairs were saying. One university professor insisted that there couldn't be any such rebel faction within the People's Army, and a Japan-based Korean journalist agreed that while it wasn't impossible for an insurgent movement to emerge, it could never have become as organized as this. If the troops controlling part of Fukuoka weren't a rebel army, therefore, shouldn't they be disarmed—or even eliminated? Nevertheless, none of the experts had any idea how to get them to lay down their arms, or how to respond when no demands had been made. Neither did any of them have an answer when the anchor asked, "If they're not a rebel army, then just what are they?"

The TV cameras were still showing the terrorists' camp. Along one edge, ten portable toilets had been erected—not the tall, thin, fiberglass boxes you saw on construction sites, but simple canvas-covered structures. A hole they had been digging must have been for a septic tank, and two sewage disposal trucks with CITY OF FUKUOKA emblazoned on their sides were already lined up in the parking area. The camp had been set up in just one night, entirely by hand. The TV had shown several hundred soldiers putting up tents and digging holes in the dark, most of them young, and all working flat out. Not a single one was shirking or looking as though he didn't know what to do.

As she watched the North Koreans at work, now and then wiping the sweat from their faces with the sleeves of their army fatigues or exchanging a joke and laughing, one female anchor on an independent TV station marveled: "They don't look much like terrorists, I must say." Yamagiwa couldn't help agreeing. Whoever heard of a group of terrorists coming to a foreign country, brazenly erecting tents, and digging a septic tank, all with smiles on their faces and in full view of television cameras? Terrorists usually kept themselves out of sight. That's how the commentators were still referring to them, however—as "the North Korean terrorists." They probably didn't know what else to call them.

The screen image switched from the camp to the studio, where the anchor reported that the mayor of Fukuoka, the prefectural governor, and the chief of the prefectural police had been summoned by the terrorists to a meeting. Shigemitsu had been informed of this only a few minutes earlier by the mayor of Fukuoka, but all the ministers had already been called back into the room, and the round table was once again buzzing with activity. Stowing his half-written letter of resignation away in his briefcase, Yamagiwa wondered if he'd ever be able to go home. Apparently, the North Koreans were now calling themselves the Koryo Expeditionary Force. Umezu's pronunciation of "Koryo" was corrected by someone from the Foreign Ministry, at which Umezu, irritable from having his sleep interrupted, barked, "Who the hell cares?" There was some confusion over whether they should call them by this new name or keep referring to them as terrorists. Several of those present insisted that calling them the Koryo Expeditionary Force would amount to official recognition, while others maintained nevertheless that they couldn't go on calling them terrorists for ever. Eventually it became clear that anchors and commentators on CNN, NBC, and the BBC, as well as TV stations in France, Germany, and China, had all started using the name Koryo Expeditionary Force, or KEF for short. For the moment, the PM said, the official Japanese line should be to refer to them as "the North Korean terrorist group calling itself the Koryo Expeditionary Force." This was agreed to and adopted, which meant that TV stations and newspapers in Japan would be obliged to follow suit.

Hearing that the prefectural police chief had been summoned along with the mayor and the governor, Sadakata of the National Public Safety Commission, a man in his late seventies, spoke up for the first time. Apparently unable to get his head around the new designation, he kept referring to "this Koryo gang." His proposal was to substitute his own subordinate, the Kyushu regional police bureau chief Okiyama, for the head of the prefectural police. Sending someone with close ties to central government would be a good way to get direct information, and this Koryo gang wouldn't know the difference anyway, he said smugly.

No one was terribly impressed with the plan, but most agreed that the KEF was unlikely to know the difference. And all of them, including Kido, were exasperated with having to get information secondhand from the mayor's office and the press. It was therefore decided to implement Sadakata's proposal, and someone phoned the mayor and the governor to inform them. If they wanted inside information, wondered Yamagiwa, why didn't the PM go to Fukuoka himself? He probably wasn't the only one there thinking this, but nobody was about to say it. If Kido were to go, there was always the danger of him being taken hostage. There was no shortage of politicians ready to take his place, of course, but that wasn't something you could say out loud.

Just after seven in the morning Kido, clean-shaven and wearing a fresh shirt and tie, appeared before the TV cameras in the Prime Minister's office to announce the blockade of Fukuoka. "Fellow

238

citizens, it is my painful duty today to ask for your cooperation and understanding during these trying times. As you will all have seen on television by now, Fukuoka Dome was occupied last night by a North Korean terrorist group calling itself the Koryo Expeditionary Force, and a further five hundred or so terrorists have since illegally landed in Fukuoka. This is an impermissible intrusion, showing absolute disregard for our country's sovereignty and for international law. As the representative of Japan's government, I have made a stern protest to North Korea—the Democratic People's Republic of Korea—and am quite determined that with the cooperation of our allies we shall bring this matter to an early conclusion. Unfortunately, we have further been informed that this North Korean terrorist group calling itself the Koryo Expeditionary Force may not have confined itself to Kyushu; it has been reported that some of its agents are now traveling in the guise of Japanese citizens to infiltrate other big cities, including Tokyo. In order to safeguard the lives and property of all our citizens, I have no choice but to temporarily suspend traffic to and from not only Fukuoka but all of Kyushu. This measure is being implemented under our Emergency Acts and, although temporary, will cause considerable hardship for the people of Fukuoka and Kyushu. However, we cannot allow the terrorists to encroach any further on our country, and so I must ask for your understanding and forbearance for a time. The government will make every effort to ensure that there is no shortage of medical supplies, food, fuel, and other necessities of daily life, so I ask you to please remain calm in spite of the trying circumstances. Anyone seeking to profit from this emergency by stockpiling or hoarding any of these necessary goods will be firmly dealt with." Repeating his plea for people to remain calm and patient, Kido then bowed solemnly to the camera.

After the speech had been broadcast, Shigemitsu took questions from reporters in the Official Residence press room. The issue of greatest concern to the Japanese press was how long these restrictions would last. Shigemitsu insisted that they would only remain in force until the danger of the terrorists' incursion into other areas had passed. With regard to mobilizing the SDF without the prior approval of the Diet, he insisted that in the case of an emergency it was permissible to get *ex post facto* approval. When a reporter from Kyodo News Service asked whether the use of this measure meant they were in effect abandoning Fukuoka and Kyushu, Shigemitsu raised his voice to say: "Absolutely not!" The Prime Minister himself was from Oita, and many other government officials were also from Kyushu, he stressed, his eyes brimming with tears.

The foreign press were less circumspect in their questions. One reporter from the *Washington Post* asked whether they were considering retaliation against North Korea. When Shigemitsu responded that at present they were not, the reporter pressed him to specify under what circumstances this would be considered. Shigemitsu avoided the question by asserting that it was classified information. A BBC reporter asked whether it would be an option for the SDF to attack the Koryo Expeditionary Force. "Given that some of the residents of Fukuoka are still being held hostage, I can't answer that question," replied Shigemitsu. All the reporters referred to the KEF by name, without any mention of the word "terrorists."

What do you think the Koryo Expeditionary Force wants? How can you take countermeasures without knowing what the demands are? Have you requested backup from the US forces based in Japan? If not, why not? Have you started negotiating with the KEF? Who's in charge of the negotiations? Is there any plan for the Prime Minister or Chief Cabinet Secretary to go to Fukuoka to talk to their commander? Are you in contact with the KEF? Do you intend to contact them? Shigemitsu evaded all these questions, saying only that he was unable to answer at this point in time. Asked when he would be able to answer, he replied that he didn't know. The reporter from the Chinese Xinhua News Agency was particularly persistent. "Does Japan consider the Koryo Expeditionary Force an enemy that has to be eliminated?" Shigemitsu wiped his forehead and said, "We are gathering information to ascertain the true identity of the terrorists," which didn't really amount to an answer. If he declared them to be an enemy force, it would mean that they had to be driven out; yet as a sovereign nation, Japan could hardly regard a horde of armed illegals as anything *but* an enemy force. "Please understand that as long as the residents of Fukuoka are in effect being held hostage, I have to be discreet," he said, bringing the press conference to an end.

In its wake, reports in the US, British, and Chinese media were critical of Japan. FOX TV featured a former CIA chief who suggested that Japan's recent military build-up was behind this incident. "Anyone would agree that North Korea is a failed state," he said, "but it's a small one and therefore easy to control. However, once a major power begins to slip, it can become a real liability"—a blatant dig at Japan. The BBC rolled out an expert on international law who maintained that a blockade was, broadly speaking, an act of war, and a former Territorial Army general commented that instead of defending itself against what amounted to an invasion, the Japanese government was responding by sacrificing its own territory. A major Hong Kong network came out with the nonsensical view that if the KEF really was a North Korean rebel army faction, then it was difficult to say whether its occupation of Fukuoka constituted an act of aggression or of self-defense, citing the example of the former Imperial Japanese Army defying the will of their own headquarters and advancing into Manchuria on the noble-sounding pretext of saving Japan from Russia. Listening to all this made Yamagiwa bristle. Not that he felt any sympathy for Kido and Shigemitsu—it was good to see them with their backs against the wall. But he couldn't bear to see Japan and its government criticized and sneered at by the media of other countries—and allies at that—in the midst of this crisis.

Within Japan, however, the blockade seemed to be accepted with relative calm. The TV was showing interviews with mayors, factory managers, store owners, and residents all over Kyushu, most of whom seemed resigned to the situation. When a doctor from the Kyushu Medical Center right next to the KEF camp was interviewed, everyone in the crisis-management room was watching. Dr. Kuroda Genji looked tired, and told the interviewer that he'd just returned home from the hospital. "The soldiers haven't come into the hospital, and the examination and treatment of patients is proceeding normally. Sick patients can't wait, so we're just getting on with what

241

has to be done. We doctors, nurses, and other hospital staff have been allowed to come and go as usual, and to return to our homes when off duty. Last night we saw a rise in the number of cases of stress-related bronchitis and asthma attacks. By the end of the night I really needed a break. The soldiers have set up checkpoints on all the roads out, but when I showed them my ID card I was let right through. They had a computer at the checkpoint, and they appear to have all our personal details on their database. All of us working at the hospital, as long as we show them some ID, can pass any time we want. That's what I was told."

Everyone at the round table had relaxed somewhat following Kido's speech to the nation and Shigemitsu's press conference, but now the doctor's comments about the database caused a new stir. "What's that all about?" demanded Kido and Shigemitsu, getting to their feet and turning to Araki Yukie, Minister for Home Affairs. She immediately got on the phone to Kai Tomonori, head of the Local Government Wide Area Network (LGWAN) and told him to come right away. Kai was a former private university professor who had supported the creation of the national database of Japanese citizens commonly known as the Juki Net. Shigemitsu, meanwhile, had called up the mayor of Fukuoka to check whether the Juki Net had been leaked. The mayor confirmed that the people in charge had been threatened with the execution of hostages, and had handed over all the resident-register codes to the KEF. They hadn't been hiding this fact, he said apologetically, but there were just so many things to do that they hadn't yet had time to report it. "The resident codes?" muttered Kido, a baffled look on his face. "But how come the terrorists have access to *all* their personal details?"

"Can we say something?" The head of the National Police Agency raised his hand and indicated the man seated next to him, who was dressed not in uniform but in a smart gray suit. The man got to his feet and introduced himself as Kosaka, head of the police Info-Communications Bureau. "Prime Minister, I'm sure you and the other ministers are aware that under the amendment of the tax system it was made possible for people to use their resident-register code as their tax-registration number." Kosaka glanced at Kido and Shigemitsu, both of whom nodded. "When the tax-registration number was originally established, it seemed practical to link it to the basic pension number. However, there were two major problems with this. To begin with, there were legal issues involved in linking two numbers administered by different ministries. Even if these could be resolved, a further problem was that not everybody was registered for a pension and some would have had to apply separately for the tax number. This meant that it was more convenient to link it to the resident-register code. Nevertheless, the ban against private use of resident codes was a major obstacle to this, and accordingly the law was amended to make this permissible on condition that it was supervised by the requisite authority."

"I have no idea what you're talking about," said the PM, shaking his head. "What does revoking the ban on the personal use of the resident-register code have to do with the terrorists being able to get their hands on personal information?" Few of the politicians at the round table were computer savvy. Some were frowning and whispering amongst themselves: *Did* you *understand that?* Yamagiwa himself hadn't realized that personal information could be so easily leaked from the resident codes, either. In reality, the main reason for linking the resident code and the tax number and allowing its private use was that local councils just prior to the collapse of regional finances had been unable to afford to run the Juki Net. The fact that there had not been any serious problems with the Juki Net up until then had also been a factor in the decision.

"Are you saying that anyone who has access to the resident codes can steal personal information?" asked Kido. Just then, however, the director general of LGWAN arrived, and Kosaka let him take over. Kai Tomonori had apparently been nicknamed Tom while studying in America, and he liked this pet name to be used even at work. With the appearance of Tom Kai, the atmosphere there instantly felt lighter. At forty-three, with a dark, lean face and trim body, he was a lot younger than anyone else at the round table. Kai was about to take the empty seat next to Araki Yukie, but she objected, telling him that its occupant had just popped out to the restroom. "Oh, I'm sorry. Well then," he said, remaining standing as he started his explanation.

Kai was dressed in a dark-blue suit of a well-cut, light wool fabric, a pale-blue shirt with a white collar, and a pink-and-yellow-striped tie. He looked like a young Wall Street financier, thought Yamagiwa. A few strands of his oiled hair hung down over his forehead. But his looks were betrayed by a slight reticence in his speech. When Umezu told him to speak up, he looked wounded and apologized with unnecessary deference. Kai came from a wealthy family and had studied electronics at Tokyo University and in the US, although no one could accuse him of being a career academic. It was said that he had wept tears of joy when his appointment to the Home Affairs Ministry was announced. He had the high-handed air common among the elite who had studied in America, but also gave the impression—perhaps because of his dark eyes and long eyelashes—of being somewhat spineless.

According to Kai, as long as you had the resident-register codes, it wasn't hard to get hold of the corresponding personal information. The codes themselves were extremely secure, but if they were leaked, then it would be possible to acquire all the personal data associated with them via the government Internet database or various private sources. "Even I could do it," said Kai regretfully, as though he were somehow to blame. Nobody had ever imagined a scenario where the codes might actually be handed over to a bunch of terrorists by the authorities themselves. "Hold on a minute," someone interrupted. "You're not saying that private information on everyone in Japan has been leaked, are you?" Kai's reply was barely audible. "No," he said. "Just everyone in Fukuoka."

A little before nine in the morning, the mayor of Fukuoka and his two colleagues arrived at one of the KEF checkpoints. They had an NHK TV crew in tow, and although the sound was poor, for the first time the KEF soldiers were shown in close-up on TV screens. The Chief of Staff of the Ground SDF, Shinomiya, had summoned a subordinate from his seat by the wall and instructed him to make a note of all the KEF equipment and weapons. The checkpoint had been set up on the Jigyohama side of the Yokatopia Bridge, and consisted of a sandbag bunker mounted with a machine gun. "That's a PKM general-purpose machine gun," muttered the aide, noting it down. One of the commandeered small trucks was parked alongside the checkpoint, and inside the sandbag boundary was a small wooden hut about the size of two telephone booths shoved together.

Visible inside the hut were a cellphone, a radio set, and a laptop computer. A tall, sturdily built officer came out to meet the visitors. "*Ohayo gozaimasu*," he greeted them in Japanese, looking them up and down without even the trace of a smile. The three were asked to show some identification, but when they put their hands inside the breast pockets of their suits, the two soldiers behind the officer instinctively leveled their rifles at them. Yamagiwa was impressed by the speed and fluidity with which the soldiers reacted. With guns pointed at them from both sides, the mayor and his colleagues tensed, and the image shown on TV wavered as the cameraman took a step backwards.

"I hope they're okay," muttered Oikawa, his eyes glued to the TV. "Why shouldn't they be?" asked Shigemitsu. "Because that third man isn't really the prefectural police chief," Oikawa said, glancing over at Sadakata of the National Public Safety Commission, who was snoring in his chair and in danger of slipping from the armrest at any moment. Oikawa may have been the only minister there who remembered Sadakata's suggestion to send his subordinate in place of the prefectural police chief. It hadn't been much of a plan in the first place, but what difference would a cop's affiliation make to the KEF? "You sent someone else?" asked Kai, but nobody answered him. After the brief glimpse inside the shed, the TV cameraman had been ordered not to film there, and now the TV screen was filled with the nervous faces of the mayor, the governor, and Okiyama.

Suddenly the officer shouted, and a pistol was leveled at Okiyama's head. "A Browning FN Hi-Power pistol," noted Shinomiya's aide.

"It'll splatter his brains all over the place if he's shot at such close range." The women ministers, and some of the men, averted their eyes. "You are not the prefectural chief of police! You shall be publicly executed!" came the voice. "They might really shoot him," said Shigemitsu matter-of-factly. A female KEF officer was saying something, but the mike was too far away for them to hear. All the voices sounded muffled, in fact, and the lone camera was aimed into the sunlight to focus on Okiyama's profile and the pistol, both in dark silhouette.

What he was seeing on the screen seemed unreal to Yamagiwa—not quite like a movie, but not like plain news footage either. With no commentary or narration, it might have been one of those shows that pulled hidden-camera pranks. Okiyama had ill-assorted features—puffy eyelids, flat nose, protruding front teeth. His mouth hung open and his jaw was trembling. "He's following government orders," the mayor was heard explaining. "Idiot!" exclaimed Shigemitsu, and Umezu groaned: "What a thing to say!" But the mayor had told the truth. What if Okiyama was actually shot? Even this probably wouldn't seem quite real in these peculiar circumstances.

It reminded Yamagiwa of an almost identical scene from the Vietnam War—the famous footage of a senior South Vietnamese official executing a Vietcong prisoner. Yamagiwa remembered that the prisoner had had his hands tied behind his back and looked as though he'd already given up hope, but when the pistol was thrust against his temple his face had contorted in fear. The bullet was discharged with a puff of smoke, and the barrel jerked upward as a black hole opened up in the side of the man's head. A stream of blood spurted out and the POW, face still twisted, toppled over sideways and out of frame. On the TV screen now, the KEF officer shouted at Okiyama: "You're a criminal!" He withdrew the pistol from Okiyama's head, and the camera pulled back for a wider shot as he added: "You are under arrest for the serious crime of identity theft." The mayor and the governor stood rooted to the spot. Two soldiers approached Okiyama and tied his hands behind his back with what looked like wire. Okiyama screwed up his face and pleaded with the officer that he had a wife and children.

As they watched the man being taken toward the Sea Hawk Hotel, Moriyama Kazue told Umezu that she'd heard that when North Korean police catch defectors at the border with China, "they put wire through their noses to lead them away." Umezu looked shocked. "Are they really that nasty?" he said. "Oh, yes. Japanese NGO workers always say they'd rather kill themselves than be caught by the North Koreans." Okiyama disappeared into the underground passage leading to the hotel. The mayor and the governor were ushered into a waiting car. The TV cameraman was put into another car, and there was a brief shot of the KEF camp before the picture went dead and the screen cut back to the NHK studio.

"The police chief appears to have been arrested by the Koryo Expeditionary Force. But what on earth for?" the anchor asked a commentator. "Get the name right!" Shigemitsu barked angrily at the screen. "The North Korean terrorist group calling itself the Koryo Expeditionary Force!" Justice Minister Nagano concurred: "As our national TV station, they ought to be toeing the line." Finance Minister Takahashi nodded agreement with a wry smile. They could hear the puzzled-looking commentator wondering what they'd meant by "government orders." Shigemitsu leaned toward the PM to whisper hoarsely, "The calls from the press'll be coming in soon," and Kido, looking pained, said, "I know, I know."

The KEF officer had said the charge was identity theft. But Okiyama was only there under false pretenses because Sadakata had suggested he go. Relegated to the provinces, Okiyama's career had been undistinguished. He had no particular investigatory skills, and had never been likely to accomplish much by pretending to be the prefectural police chief—no one at the round table had had any illusions about that. Okiyama was in this fix basically because a few muckety-mucks had been irked by having to depend on secondhand information from the media and local government in Fukuoka. They had also been unwilling to offend an old man by refusing his proposal, and had assumed that a bunch of North Koreans wouldn't be able to distinguish between one branch of the police and another anyway. Sadakata, meanwhile, was still fast asleep, dribbling. Kido and Shigemitsu beckoned Oikawa over, no doubt to discuss the issue of responsibility for the arrest.

Oikawa kept glancing at Sadakata. All NHK had to do to find out about the circumstances behind the event was to phone the Fukuoka city council. The Home Affairs Minister had been the one to issue the order to send Okiyama to the meeting, and the decision to do so had been made at the highest level of the government. It hadn't occurred to anyone that he might be caught out. Kido and Shigemitsu were probably putting pressure on Oikawa, as commissioner general of the National Police Agency, to ask Sadakata to assume responsibility for this fiasco and resign. Sadakata was of an age where it wouldn't be at all strange for him to retire from public service, and he had little to lose by resigning. Of course, there were plenty of others who could take the rap in his place. The PM and Cabinet Secretary themselves were scarcely blameless—they had taken up Sadakata's proposal after practically no discussion. Until a few hours ago, thought Yamagiwa, he too had been part of that same world. If he hadn't been relieved of his post, he probably would have recommended making Sadakata take responsibility. Now he wasn't so sure.

More people arrived at the crisis-management room. From the Ministry for Land, Infrastructure and Transport were Kamamoto, director general of the Policy Bureau, along with his colleagues Shibayama of Freight Distribution Facilities and Kobayashi of the Freight Forwarders Division; Kanaya of the Roads Bureau; Aisaka of the Ports and Harbors Bureau; Gonda of the Railways Bureau; Maeyama of the Maritime Bureau; and Sagara Yumiko, director general of the Civil Aviation Bureau, along with Sakakibara of the Flight Standards Division and Susaki of the Air Traffic Services Department. Representing the Ministry of Health, Labor, and Welfare was Enami of the Health Policy Bureau and his colleague from the National Hospitals Division, Takigawa; Unno of the

Pharmaceutical and Food Safety Bureau; and Yamamoto of the Health Insurance Bureau. They were followed by Tokoi of the General Food Policy Bureau in the Ministry of Agriculture, Forestry, and Fisheries, and Masuyama Yukiko, director general of the Local Administration Bureau of the Ministry of Home Affairs. Clutching thick dossiers, they gathered behind their respective ministers to discuss the practicalities of the blockade of Kyushu and guaranteeing supplies of foodstuffs, medical supplies, and fuel.

Yamagiwa periodically nodded off in his seat at the far end of the round table. Trays of sandwiches and rice balls kept circulating, and every time he ate something he tended to doze off. He still had not been told whether he should leave or stay. Kido and Shigemitsu had probably even forgotten that they'd dismissed him from his post. The matter of Sadakata's resignation had been more or less forgotten in the furore caused by a statement made earlier by the mayor of Fukuoka at a joint press conference with the KEF. The mayor had appeared on his own, prompting some people to wonder whether the governor had been arrested too, but according to information received by NHK from a KEF spokesman he was feeling unwell and was resting in another room.

The press conference was held in a screened-off section of the lobby of the Sea Hawk Hotel, and the figure of an armed guard could be glimpsed through a gap in the screen. The only press to have been invited were an NHK TV crew and four newspaper reporters, each with their own photographer, who were seated on sofas in the lobby. With such a small media presence and the mike stand decorated with artificial flowers, it didn't feel much like a press conference at all. The diminutive mayor, wearing a pained expression and repeatedly adjusting the frames of his reading glasses, read out the basic points of agreement reached between the city of Fukuoka and the KEF. Beside him stood the KEF commanding officer, calmly observing. Firstly, the mayor said, they had agreed that Fukuoka City and surrounding areas should endeavor to coexist peacefully and prosperously with the Koryo Expeditionary Force; secondly, that the specific details of this coexistence would be decided thereafter by consultation between Fukuoka City and the Koryo Expeditionary Force; and lastly, that Fukuoka City and the Koryo Expeditionary Force would ultimately seek independence from Japan.

There was a moment of stunned silence at the word "independence," and then the crisis-management room erupted in fury. "He must have been coerced," Shigemitsu protested, but Umezu said that casually mentioning secession like that was not something the head of a local government should do even under the threat of death. "But remember, there are civilian hostages," Ohashi reminded him, his tone conveying less sympathy for Mayor Tenzan than rage against the KEF. The mayor had clearly been threatened; everyone in the room understood this. Even so, the very mention of independence from Japan was anathema to the government. It was like seeing your wife embraced by another man, Yamagiwa thought—you'd be enraged even if you knew it was done under threat of violence and against her will. And your anger would be directed not only at the aggressor, but at the one succumbing to him.

The mayor and the KEF commander kept repeating the words "peace" and "coexistence." It was to coexist with the citizens of Fukuoka, and to bring true peace and prosperity to the city, that they had come from North Korea. They had not invaded Fukuoka and intended no harm to its citizens, but any individuals or organizations hostile to the project, or carrying out any military attack or violent protest or pernicious propaganda activity, would be punished. It was a transparently contrived rationale, which Yamagiwa felt he'd heard before. It wasn't all that different from what the Americans had said after invading Afghanistan and Iraq, and in fact Saddam Hussein had made similar announcements after invading Kuwait. The Japanese military had probably said something of the sort while establishing their rule over Manchuria. The French in Algeria, the British in India, the Israelis in Palestine, and even Hitler in Eastern Europe—hadn't they all claimed something similar? Anyone invading another country by force of arms justified it in much the same way. For the side being oppressed, however, it was an absurd line of reasoning—apart from anything else, it wasn't as if they'd invited their oppressors over or wanted to coexist with them.

It was decided to appeal formally to the UN Security Council; but when the Foreign Ministry contacted the office of the UN delegation, they were informed that the KEF's status as a rebel army appeared to be an obstacle. Both the Korean Central News Agency and the North Korean embassy in Beijing had repeatedly announced that the invasion was the work of a rebel faction of the People's Army. The DPRK had no objection to Japan disposing of the rebels, and was even willing to dispatch a sufficient military force to deal with them. According to the UN delegation in Japan, it would therefore be difficult for the Security Council to justify imposing sanctions against North Korea.

After the mayor's statement, the KEF announced that they would be issuing a new currency, and would also be arresting certain people for political and other serious crimes. The new currency would apparently be linked to the yen, but it would be electronic rather than paper money. "Is that possible?" Shigemitsu asked Atoda, Minister of State for Economic and Fiscal Policy. Atoda replied that as long as suitable capital, whether in dollars or yen, was accepted by stipulated banks as funds, it wasn't difficult to have an independent settlement currency. The KEF was at pains to indicate they had no intention of depriving Fukuoka City or its people of their assets. If they needed, say, food or clothing, then they would pay for it. "I wonder if they *have* dollars or yen," put in Moriyama Kazue of the Financial Services Agency. Tsunemura of the Foreign Ministry explained that the North Korean army had accumulated a lot of dollars via trading firms and the like, and Motoki of the Asian and Oceanian Affairs Bureau reminded them that North Korea wasn't "a nation that possesses an army, but an army that possesses a nation." With regard to the arrests for political and other crimes, the KEF said they would refrain from announcing any names for the present to avoid the possibility of the culprits fleeing.

When the KEF commander announced next that a further hundred and twenty thousand troops of the rebel army would arrive in Hakata

Port eight days later, not a sound was heard in the crisis-management room. Such troops would be massing on the east coast of North Korea, but it wasn't known which ports they would be leaving from or on which day. A reporter asked whether rebel troops would be permitted to leave port. The commander answered that not only would they leave, but should any of the boats in which they were traveling be attacked, by whatever country, there would be reprisals. The implication was that either Japanese nationals arrested for political or other crimes would be executed, or terrorist attacks would be carried out by the Special Operations Forces already embedded in various cities around Japan. After that, the commander responded to all questions from reporters by repeating that they had come to Fukuoka not as invaders, but as new partners.

The more Yamagiwa heard the words "coexistence" and "mutual prosperity," the more meaningless they sounded, and eventually he found them so abhorrent they literally made him shiver. "Next he's going to tell us that a million refugees are on their way too!" someone said, trying unsuccessfully to lighten the atmosphere. A sense of resignation descended over the table. It felt suffocating, as if the air had grown twice as heavy. Kido and Shigemitsu had their heads in their hands. Yamagiwa hadn't forgiven them for making him a scapegoat, but he couldn't help sympathizing with them somewhat. Neither had so much as touched the plates of rice balls and sandwiches. Working through the night at their age was exhausting, and made worse by the knowledge that whatever decisions they took would have a direct effect on people's lives. And their initial response to the events in Fukuoka had been wrong—mainly because they hadn't decided on their priorities. Ultimately, the two of them were probably just incompetent clowns—but even clowns got burned out. Kido turned his bloodshot eyes to Shimada, Minister of State for Defense, and asked what the options were for attack. Shigemitsu abruptly stopped cleaning his glasses, and everyone at the table tensed up.

"Do you mean our options for attacking the ships carrying reinforcements?" asked Shimada. Kido shook his head. "No, the camp in Fukuoka." Shimada called over an SDF official in his early forties who had been sitting on a chair by the wall, and introduced him as Horiuchi. Horiuchi was a colonel in the Intelligence HQ of the Joint Staff Council, and a specialist in the war against terror. He was lean, wore rimless glasses, and had a rather gloomy face. After an underling brought him a diagram of the area under KEF control, he spread it out on the table. The area was bordered to the east and west by rivers, to the north was the Hakata Bay coastline, and to the south Chuo Ward, which was residential. "It's a fairly large area," said Horiuchi, indicating the zone marked in red with a telescopic pointer. "Ideally we'd have a cloudy night. First we send in a commando unit from the sea. While they're freeing the hostages in the hotel, we create a line of defense on this road between the hotel and the camp, cutting the terrorists off. At the same time as the infiltration by sea, we land a second commando unit from the Hii River just here, to the west of the Kyushu Medical Center. This unit would stake out a line of defense along *here*, to prevent the terrorists from entering the hospital, and to attack and neutralize the five checkpoints and nine sentry posts, thus surrounding their camp. From the south we spring a surprise attack with helicopters to coincide with the raid on the hotel. This is pretty much our only option."

Umezu and Doihara looked at each other with some enthusiasm. "Not bad! We might be onto something here." The colonel's somewhat downbeat air and cool delivery had apparently made the use of armed force sound like a realistic possibility, and it was as though a faint ray of light had broken through. The PM asked a female staff member to bring him a damp hand towel, and, loosening his tie, he slowly wiped his face and neck. He appeared to be trying to strengthen his resolve to become the first prime minister ever to issue the order for the SDF to attack. Looking over at him, Shigemitsu took a couple of gulps of his now lukewarm coffee. Someone pointed out that the SDF must have gained some experience overseas, which should help.

But Horiuchi himself just sat lightly tapping the diagram with the tip of the pointer and working his lips. The Defense Minister and the chiefs of staff of the Ground, Maritime, and Air SDF sat with their arms folded, fidgeting restlessly and shaking their heads. Eventually Horiuchi spoke up, explaining apologetically that he hadn't quite finished. Kido leaned forward, and Shigemitsu frowned and ran his fingers irritably through his hair. Horiuchi let out a deep breath and continued, "The problem is that we lack information, so this plan entails a number of risks. First of all, it's possible that some of their people have been deployed to locations other than the camp, the hotel main entrance, checkpoints, and sentry posts. For example, the hotel's two west side entrances, an underground parking lot accessible from the north, and the shopping mall to the south of the Dome. If this is the case, there's a risk of our men being surrounded. Likewise, it's possible that the checkpoints and sentry posts shown on TV are meant to distract attention from, say, camouflaged monitoring devices, snipers, or patrols in the area. According to what little information we do have, practically all of the terrorists are from the Special Operations Forces, which means that they'll be well up on such tactics. If they are using things like that then we'll be in trouble from the start.

"It's also possible that the terrorists have a surveillance team equipped with night-vision goggles on the hotel's helipad. They may have set antipersonnel mines at strategic points, and they may even have biological or chemical weapons at their disposal. In any of these cases, we will fail and can expect major losses. If we decide to go ahead with this operation, it will be bigger than anything we've ever undertaken before, and the collaboration of our counter-terrorism forces will be vital. By this I mean a police Special Assault Team, a Special Security Team from the Coast Guard, the MSDF's Special Guard Team, and the LSDF's Ranger Corps. The unit landing from the seaboard will consist of one squad to free the hostages in the hotel, one to create the line of defense cutting off the camp, and one to attack the terrorists in the hotel—for which we'll need a minimum of a hundred and twenty men with diving skills, ideally two hundred.

"At present, though, we can only guarantee the immediate dispatch of eighty men from the Special Security Team and Special Guard Team combined. For the helicopter attack, we can send the

Ranger Corps from the bases at Metabaru in Saga and Takayubaru in Kumamoto, but unlike the American ones, our CH-47 Chinook and UH-60 Black Hawk transport helicopters are not sufficiently armored. Even bullets from the RPK light machine guns and PKM machine guns at the checkpoints can penetrate them, and an RPG is guaranteed to bring them down. In other words, we could lose the helicopters before even landing the Ranger Corps. As I said before, if the operation fails in the first phase, our men will be surrounded and wiped out.

"But even if the first phase is successful, it will be extremely difficult to prevent the terrorists from breaking through our defenses to the residential quarters of Chuo Ward or to the Medical Center. If we evacuate Chuo Ward in advance they'll get wind of the plan, and in any case it will be nigh on impossible to prevent major casualties among civilians or hospital patients and doctors. And there's one more factor that needs to be considered. Less than three kilometers from their camp, on the Higashihama Pier right next to the Fukuoka prefectural government office, there is a storage facility for lique-fied natural gas. If these storage tanks get hit by, say, an anti-tank rocket, start to leak, and are then detonated with another rocket or even a hand grenade, the result could be catastrophic. We've done a simulation showing how the blast could travel throughout the city's gas pipes, sending the whole of Fukuoka up in flames."

By this stage, his listeners' reservations had turned to open disap-pointment. The prevailing mood seemed to be that if the plan had that many holes in it, he should have said so in the first place instead of getting their hopes up. Sensing this, Horiuchi added rather loudly, "In modern warfare, including the war on terror, what matters most is information. For example, we don't know which floors of the hotel the hostages are being held on. However well trained the anti-terrorist units are, in these circumstances—" He stopped abruptly as Kido held up his hand. "What would be the expected casualties?" the PM asked. Horiuchi glanced over at Shimada questioningly. Shimada jerked his chin at Kido and Shigemitsu as if to say he should give it to them straight.

"If, by some miracle, the operation was successful, the casualties would be in the region of five hundred; if it failed, there could be several tens of thousands, and a lot more if they have biological or chemical weapons, depending on the wind direction, temperature, and population density." Kido asked what the likelihood of success was. "Two per cent," Horiuchi said bluntly, almost defiantly. Umezu cleared his throat and muttered, "Holy shit!" Doihara kneaded his temples with both hands, while Minami stared at the ceiling with folded arms. All three women ministers smiled wryly and sighed. Horiuchi began to say that perhaps they'd forgotten about the possibility of terrorist cells having been set up in other cities in Japan, but Shimada interrupted and told him they'd heard enough. The diagram was cleared away and Horiuchi went back to his chair by the wall.

"What about the US forces based here?" asked Shigemitsu, but Kido shook his head. Umezu, applying eye drops, said, "The Americans can't even tell the difference between the Korean and Japanese languages, let alone between North Korean terrorists and Japanese citizens." It was a typically anti-American comment from him, thought Yamagiwa, but also probably true. For a hostage situation what was needed was the anti-terrorist strategies of the police and special forces. The US military here didn't have any unit with special training in anti-terrorism, and it would take too long to get one dispatched from the US—if they ever agreed to send one. Also, he couldn't believe that simply because the Americans were in the forefront of the war against terror, they'd be able to come up with anything better than the strategy outlined by Horiuchi.

In the oppressive silence that prevailed, Nagano began coughing furiously, as though the sandwich he'd been eating had stuck in his throat. Umezu stood up and patted him on the back. Exhaustion showed in everyone at the round table. Kido had been sitting with his eyes closed; now he wondered aloud if they could get the terrorists to the negotiating table. "But that would be tantamount to recognizing them as a legitimate partner for negotiations!" said Shigemitsu. Kido muttered, "I guess so," and sank back into silence.

The KEF commander reappeared on the TV screen. Yamagiwa noticed for the first time that his right ear was flattened and covered in what seemed to be scar tissue. The skin looked as if it had melted, and the earhole was just a crack. It looked too unnatural for a scar from an accident or combat wound. Yamagiwa wondered if it was a burn—he remembered seeing a torture scene in a movie where someone's ear had been seared with a blowtorch.

"How about sending in an undercover SAT team to capture some of the terrorists when they start making those arrests?" suggested Oikawa. "It'd be dangerous, but if we can catch even one, we'd be able to get information out of them." A number of ministers voiced approval—none of them from Defense—and an enervated Kido weakly agreed to add that to the agenda. Though staff members were still issuing instructions, the ministers and bureau chiefs had lapsed into silence. They were already showing signs of giving up, thought Yamagiwa. And Kido and Shigemitsu had already deceived the nation by carrying out the blockade of Fukushima under emergency laws designed to protect all citizens.

The image of the KEF commander's ear had arisen again in Yamagiwa's mind, when he heard someone at his side say, "Yamagiwa-sensei, you must be tired too." It was Masuyama Yukiko, from the Home Affairs Ministry. "No, I'm all right," he said, realizing that she hadn't yet arrived when Kido fired him. Still, it was odd. She must have heard about his dismissal by now, and no bureaucrat ever went out of their way to be nice to someone who'd been dismissed, not from meanness but rather to avoid rubbing salt into the wound. Perhaps Kido and Shigemitsu had changed their minds? A faint hope began to well up in him. If there was any possibility at all of that, then perhaps he should be considering his next move.

In any case, he hadn't yet handed in his resignation, and the situation had completely changed since last night. Even Sadakata hadn't really been held to account for sending in a substitute. Presumably this meeting would continue without a break until they had decided on a basic course of action, making do with the occasional nap until then. What if he were actively to support Kido and Shigemitsu, he wondered, but then immediately told himself it was pointless, just wishful thinking. Once notice of a dismissal had been given, even verbally, it was never revoked. But why hadn't he been sent home? Either way, he would probably be well advised to consider which direction the discussion at the round table might take from here on.

He knew intuitively that they would indeed consider the option of accepting Fukuoka's independence. There had been little public backlash over the blockade. What would independence entail? It didn't necessarily mean that the movement of people or goods would cease. Anybody with relatives in Kyushu would probably be allowed to move relatively freely between there and the mainland. And it wasn't as if the local people were being killed in terrorist attacks, or even caught up in any fighting. Approving the independence of Fukuoka had to be an option. If that was the direction the discussion took, then it might be advisable to make his opinion clear from the start.

Someone like Moriyama Kazue, commissioner of the Financial Services Agency and originally from northern Japan, would probably argue that if Kyushu had its own currency then Fukuoka might actually profit commercially. The Defense Agency had warned that any attack on the KEF might cost tens of thousands of lives. And how many more would it be once the rebel reinforcements arrived? Japan had never been invaded in all its history, and it was inconceivable that people in Fukuoka would engage the North Koreans in guerrilla warfare or carry out suicide bombings and what have you. It would be better to negotiate to preserve the human rights, lives, and assets of local residents. Umezu and Doihara were bound to protest that approving Fukuoka's independence was an outrage. Shigemitsu and his ilk would no doubt say that politics should aim for the greatest benefit of the greatest number of people, and that sometimes it was necessary to sacrifice the minority for the majority's sake. Attacking the handful of terrorists in Fukuoka Dome would have settled things with a minimum of collateral damage, but it was too late now.

Now that the situation had become so serious, they should be thinking about how to minimize casualties—at least, that was bound to be the dominant opinion. It wasn't as if the KEF would meekly agree to disarm. They couldn't go back to North Korea, they had nowhere else to go, and surely they knew better than anyone that their safety depended on their military strength. Yamagiwa was convinced that most of those present would consider the maintenance of peace to be paramount.

Way back in the early 1970s, one prime minister had responded to a hijacker's demands by issuing a statement that the lives of hostages were more important than anything on earth. The West furiously criticized him for giving in to terrorism, but Japan had defended its own value system and dug its heels in for a peaceful resolution. The independence of Fukuoka would render both nuclear weapons and a military build-up meaningless, which meant that the moderate factions and the opposition could well support that option. Apart from anything, the government had not yet declared the KEF to be an enemy force. Once they did so, they would presumably be obliged to fight them by whatever means available; not fighting would amount to accepting that they weren't adversaries.

Resignation was gradually spreading around the table, like a bad smell. Resignation meant submitting to greater power, and abandoning any idea of resistance. Power was built and maintained with violence. A population accustomed to peace had no taste for either meting out or being subjected to brutality, and couldn't even imagine what it would involve. People unable to imagine violence were incapable of using it. Like that officer's ear: nobody wanted to think about how it had been burned. They didn't even want to think about ears being burned. They didn't want to burn anyone, and they didn't want to be burned. But the reality bearing down on everyone at the table right now would entail one or the other, or possibly both. There was only one way to avoid it—and that was willingly to sever part of their territory from the rest of Japan.

# 3

# BEFORE DAWN

*April 4, 2011*

Yokogawa shigeto hadn't been asleep long when he felt his wife Naeko shaking his shoulder. Woken from a nightmare in which his newspaper office had run out of paper and printed the daily edition on stone instead, he bawled out like a child, "Gimme paper!" Naeko pressed a cellphone into his hand and smiled. "You were dreaming," she said. Dazed, Yokogawa threw back the blanket, slowly sat up, and gazed vacantly at the hanging scroll on the wall in front of him. The ink painting of a tiger and dragon battling a vast army from ancient China had been a gift from a Korean artist he'd known when working at the Seoul office. Somehow he always found it soothing to see this scroll in the morning. He wasn't especially interested in either art or tradition, he just liked that particular painting. He glanced at the clock and saw that it was three in the morning. From the kitchen came the sound of the coffee maker and the aroma of Kilimanjaro. "Not up yet?" Naeko poked her head around the door. She had a cardigan slung over her nightdress.

"Hello? Yokogawa-san, are you there?" It was Matsuoka, from the city-news desk. Yokogawa had scarcely had any sleep since the first reports of North Korean guerrillas occupying Fukuoka Dome. He'd been inundated with requests for information from domestic and foreign media following the joint press conference given by the commander of the Koryo Expeditionary Force and the city mayor yesterday morning. The *Asahi* and *Yomiuri* newspapers had sent their top reporters from Tokyo to the press conference, but they hadn't been able to get any proper answers from the KEF commander. Japanese reporters were good at summarizing events, but hopeless at quizzing subjects, especially foreign ones. Yokogawa had learned the importance of incisive questioning from his time in Seoul, where he'd seen how all the foreign journalists would go for the very questions most likely to fluster politicians and industrialists—the sort of things that required consistent answers, ensuring that the gloves were always off at press conferences. Reporters in Japan were only trained to root around for information.

Yokogawa had really stood out from the other journalists at the hotel in Fukuoka. His face had been broadcast the world over, and his Fukuoka-based newspaper had been besieged by TV crews including CNN and the BBC ever since. When his boss at the paper had finally ordered him to go home and get some sleep, he'd had to sneak out the back door like a thief, or a corrupt Diet member, to grab a taxi. Naeko held up a tray with a cup of steaming coffee and pointed alternately to the kitchen and the bedroom—did he want it in bed or out here? He jerked his chin in the direction of the kitchen and said hello to Matsuoka as he got up. "Did you manage to get some rest, Yokogawa-san?" He could hear people answering the phone in the background—"*Nishi Nippon Shinbun*, city-news desk"—and someone yelling, "Then get it confirmed by the KEF commander, dammit!" He sat down at the kitchen table and raised the coffee cup to his lips, feeling himself return to reality with the familiar din of the newspaper office in his ear.

It seemed that the KEF was about to start the round of arrests. *Nishi Nippon Shinbun* was just one of three news outlets including NHK and the *Asahi Shinbun* to have been given permission to go along, and they wanted Yokogawa on hand. So *that* was what it was about. He shook his head and took another sip of coffee. As a veteran reporter in his late fifties, it would come as no surprise if his paper urged him to take early retirement. He had spent practically all of his thirties in the Seoul office, and seven years of his forties writing editorials. His tough, outspoken style had won him a lot of fans, but he had always felt the heat from politicians and public officials. After his stint as an editorial writer he was offered the position of chief editor, but he turned it down and went back to reporting instead. He liked this sort of work—and you had to be at the center of the action to do it. He now ostensibly belonged to the city-news desk, but he also sometimes wrote copy for the politics and business-news desks. Being *Nishi Nippon Shinbun*'s star reporter sounded good, but Yokogawa thought of himself rather as a handyman who could write fast and had good contacts. "Matsuoka, are you telling an old man of fifty-seven to get back to work after two hours' sleep?" he said, his resonant voice rising in pitch. "I'm afraid so," Matsuoka laughed.

Naeko brought him a freshly ironed shirt with a suit and necktie. "You'll eat before going, won't you?" she asked. "I made some rice balls, and I can warm up some miso soup with clams." Yokogawa wasn't hungry, but it would probably be a long session. "Okay, thanks," he said. Naeko put the rice balls on the table, and the soup on the burner. The kitchen walls were covered with photos of the two of them around the time they'd first started dating. When their only daughter, Yoshiko, married and left home, she had searched out pictures of her parents as a young couple, had them framed, and hung them on the walls. "It's gonna be just the two of you from now on," she'd told them. "These'll help you remember how to be lovey-dovey." A fresh, salty fragrance rose from the miso soup as Naeko placed it on the table, a little pile of thinly sliced green onion floating on top. Yokogawa looked away from the photos. Yoshiko had married a lawyer five years her senior, and now lived in Yokohama with two children of her own. In recent years it had become an annual event to go to Yokohama in the spring to see the grandchildren and have dinner in China Town. When Yoshiko brought the kids home with her in the summer, they would take them to the beach at Karatsu in Saga Prefecture. Little by little, the grandchildren had become the main focus in their life. Naeko was looking at the newspaper on the table. It was the evening edition of yesterday's *Nishi Nippon Shinbun*, and the front-page story had been written by Yokogawa. The bold headline in white lettering on a black background read: BLOCKADE TO CONTINUE, SAYS PM.

"Yoshiko called several times yesterday. She said you appeared a lot on TV."

"Oh, really?" said Yokogawa, putting his arm into a shirtsleeve and telling himself not to be jittery. *Just speak and act as usual.*

"I wonder when we'll be able to see her again," Naeko muttered, as if to herself. It was a difficult question. All of Fukuoka's residents must be feeling similarly anxious. Would the Prime Minister or Chief Cabinet Secretary be able to reassure them? They'd probably hide behind some vague answer: "The government is doing its utmost to find a solution to the problem." But such fudging wouldn't fool Naeko, who had lived almost thirty years with a no-bullshit journalist. "I don't suppose we'll see her for some time," said Yokogawa. "But nobody knows what the future holds, so there's no point fretting about it. That North Korean bunch I met yesterday were more civilized than I'd expected. They probably won't do anything too terrible."

"It's scary to think about what might happen," Naeko said with a faint smile. "But I'll be fine as long as I can hear your voice."

As he went out the front door, Yokogawa told her to take some sleeping pills if she needed to, but to make sure she got some rest. Getting into a taxi, he thought, *My voice?* He and Naeko had met in the choir club at college. Yokogawa had been a tenor, Naeko an alto. It was the defeat of the student movement when he was in high school, and then, at Kyushu University, the vicious infighting among left-wing radicals, that had clinched the matter for him and he'd taken refuge in the choir club, singing Beethoven's Ninth and Mozart's Requiem and the like. For better or worse, the collapse of the student movement had left in its wake a pervasive sense of political demoralization. Even after returning to Kyushu from Seoul, Yokogawa's frequent contact with politicians had convinced him more than ever that politics was a waste of time.

Yesterday, though, he realized he'd been wrong. Conflict was essential to politics. During Yokogawa's time as a newspaper reporter, the dichotomies in Japanese society—rich-poor, conservative-reformist, business-labor unions, and so forth—had all become less obvious. No doubt they were just suppressed, but you couldn't blame the politicians, the bureaucrats, or the media for that. Society as a whole had suppressed opposition because it was less bother that way. Yokogawa had been given a jolt by the North Korean officers he'd met at the press conference yesterday. They must have grown up in a world where struggle was a fact of life, the only thing they could be certain of. In that sort of environment, politics became necessary. Politics was basically about distributing resources amongst people with very different interests—and it was when a conflict of interest became apparent that the concept of negotiation arose. The politicians Yokogawa knew were not really engaged in politics as such. He'd go so far as to say that the reason nobody was trying to negotiate with the KEF was because it hadn't even occurred to anyone to do so.

The taxi driver had the radio tuned to NHK, but there was no new information. Apparently it had not yet been made public that the KEF was starting to make arrests. That didn't necessarily mean that NHK was being restrained or was coming under any government pressure; the information probably just hadn't been confirmed yet. Four years earlier, when the government had proposed revisions to the Foreign Exchange Law and a freeze on bank accounts, it had imposed restrictions on the media. Interest rates were skyrocketing, and it was said to be only a matter of time before the economy went into meltdown; and when rumors of a media gag spread on the Internet, banks nationwide had been attacked by mobs smashing windows and beating up bank clerks. The riot police had been deployed, and there had been casualties. The last time cities like Tokyo and Osaka had been blanketed with the smell of tear gas had been over the amendment of the Japan-US Security Treaty four decades earlier. The government had tried to justify itself, but ironically the riots only subsided once the legal measures were officially announced. Politicians had learned their lesson and had made no attempt since to regulate, manipulate, or suppress information.

Up ahead was Fukuoka Airport, normally brightly lit up at this time of day with preparations for the first arrivals and departures, but today still sunk in darkness. There were no lights on the runway or in the terminals or control tower. Most of the troops sent to enforce the blockade had already withdrawn since passengers had stopped demanding to be allowed to fly, and there were now just two SDF trucks on the tarmac. Yesterday media helicopters had been circling around all day, but they'd all disappeared once night fell. The silhouette of the airport, shrouded in darkness, reminded Yokogawa of a coffin. It was as if the pulse of some giant creature had stopped. "The cops are stopping cars near the airport, and it's best to avoid the expressway. How about taking side roads?" asked the driver, and Yokogawa agreed.

He lived just east of the airport in a district called Shimemachi, about a twenty-minute taxi ride from the *Nishi Nippon Shinbun* office in the city center. Taking the expressway would normally shave five minutes or so off the journey, but not with the blockade. The roads around the airport were deserted, with no sign of the usual lines of trucks. The area around Shimemachi was a major distribution center for medical supplies, clothing, and fuel, and was full of factories and industrial parks. The noise and vibrations from the endless convoys of trucks every morning often brought complaints from residents of the neighborhood. This morning, however, Yokogawa only saw two or three trucks. Supplies from the mainland would have been interrupted, of course, but goods in the warehouses couldn't have been depleted that much in just one day. He asked the taxi driver about it. "It's because of the police roadblocks," the driver told him.

These had been set up on all the main through roads in Fukuoka, including the Kyushu Expressway, which was the major artery running from Moji through Fukuoka all the way down to Kagoshima and linked to all the island's main cities via national trunk roads.

There were twenty-six roadblocks altogether, and the entire Kyushu police force had been deployed to man them. Cars and trucks were being exhaustively searched one by one, with the exception only of special vehicles like tankers, and so traffic was of course backed up. Unable to do their job, most trucking companies seemed to have given up and weren't bothering to send out any vehicles.

"I don't get it," said the taxi driver suddenly. "If any of these North Koreans want to go to Tokyo, they can easily get around them roadblocks. All they have to do is go east and take their pick of the little side roads, and once they hit the coast they can grab a boat and nip across to the mainland where they can jump on a train. The police must know that much!"

The driver was only saying what everyone in Fukuoka already knew. All the police and SDF in Kyushu wouldn't be able to stop the KEF commandos from sneaking over to the mainland if they wanted to. Yet the government had still opted for the blockade. In other words, this was all purely for appearances' sake, a charade intended to reassure citizens that the government was taking the security of the nation seriously. And everyone knew it. They hadn't contained the guerrillas in Fukuoka, they'd cut the people of Kyushu off from the rest of Japan. The Prime Minister and Chief Cabinet Secretary had wept when they announced the blockade. Were those really tears of compassion for the people they were sacrificing? Toward the end of the Pacific War, commanding officers had wept as they sent off kamikaze pilots to die. It seemed that Japan's leaders always shed a tear or two when some poor bastards had to take it in the neck. Afterwards, of course, they forgot all about them.

"How's the taxi business? Has there been a drop in custom?" asked Yokogawa. "About forty per cent," answered the driver. "Everyone's afraid of going out, especially with more of 'em on the way over from North Korea." He told Yokogawa that he'd been dispatched to take an elderly patient to the Kyushu Medical Center for dialysis treatment, but the old man's niece, who was to accompany him, made a fuss about going there. "Do you want me to die?" the old man had said angrily, and the niece had snapped back, "Why can't

266

you go to another hospital?" A furious row broke out between them, and both had asked the taxi driver his opinion. The driver, thinking of those armed North Koreans, had been unable to offer much comfort. In the end, the niece refused to go, and the driver had taken the sick man alone to the Medical Center. It was the first time he'd been to the area since the start of the crisis, and he'd almost pissed himself when they were stopped by the rebels at a checkpoint. A woman soldier asked for their resident cards and put them into the card reader. When they came up clean, she gave the passenger a concerned look and told him in Japanese to get well soon before waving the cab through. "She had bright-red cheeks," said the driver, smiling. "These days you don't often see such bright-red cheeks here, even out in the country. She was like the women I knew when I was a boy."

He looked in the rear-view mirror. "Say, aren't you that reporter from the *Nishi Nippon Shinbun*?" he asked. "I guess I am," Yokogawa replied, thinking to himself that he really had become famous. "All them college professors and whatnot on TV are making the North Koreans out to be cold-blooded killers. That woman soldier I met didn't look like one to me, though. But then, she's along for the ride, so... I dunno, maybe they *are* all a bunch of killers. What do you think?" The question gave Yokogawa pause. Asked whether the Hawks could win the championship this season, he'd have no problem answering, "Yes, definitely," or, "No, they haven't got a hope," even though it was obvious that nobody could possibly know the outcome yet. Everyone seemed to want the future to be black or white, and predictable. With baseball it didn't matter what you said, but deciding whether the KEF was dangerous or not was rather different. Depending on the circumstances, the rebels might well kill Fukuokans without so much as a second thought. They were probably capable of slitting the throats of old men, women, children—even infants—with no more feeling than if they were swatting flies.

The young officers he'd seen yesterday were unlike anyone you saw in contemporary Japan. Both physically and mentally they were sharp as knives—and not the kitchen variety, either. That commander and his aide were doubtless as well trained in using a combat knife as they were in preparing documents and speaking at press conferences. Along with the spread of education and culture in advanced democracies like Japan, the very idea of killing or hurting other people had become anathema. Yet though the KEF pair may have received the very best education available to the elite in a socialist country, they would also have been exposed to a harsher reality, where life was cheap and death a constant shadow.

The taxi driver's question only left room for two answers, black or white: they're good guys, no need to worry; or they're depraved and we're all doomed—but Yokogawa couldn't give either. He fudged by saying he really didn't know and changing the subject to his own business and the effect the blockade was having on it. A million copies of a forty-page newspaper required a huge amount of paper, and the printer's stock wouldn't last two days. It was normally brought in by land from Yatsushiro in Kumamoto Prefecture and by ship from Ehime in Shikoku, but with the blockade in place nobody knew whether it would continue to get through. At yesterday's editorial meeting it had been decided for the time being to publish a six-page edition in place of the morning issue, cutting all the usual home, culture, sports, and entertainment sections, and all ads, and to suspend the evening issue altogether. The driver didn't show much interest in paper-supply problems, however, and before long was talking again about the woman soldier's rosy cheeks.

They headed as usual up Sumiyoshi Avenue toward Hakata Station, but the big black building looming out of the dark before them wasn't immediately recognizable. The only people to be seen in the station area were the riot police. The bright lights and neon of this normally lively district had all been turned off, leaving what looked to Yokogawa like an Eastern European town he'd seen in a spy movie long ago. The shutters were down at the station entrance, and the glass door of Hakata Post Office was boarded up and secured with chains. The usual line of taxis waiting for passengers was gone. Only a white banner outside the Izutsuya department store announcing a sales campaign for Chinese products fluttered in the breeze.

Trains could usually be seen stopped at platforms on the elevated tracks, but since yesterday they had all been transferred to Shimonoseki to prevent them being hijacked by the KEF. The taxi driver had just been describing Hakata in the late Fifties and what the Tenjin district and the sumo arena were like at that time, but at the sight of the darkened station he fell silent. The sight of the closed, empty station would have weighed on anyone; it was a powerful symbol of the blockade. Economic activity in Fukuoka hadn't completely ceased, and at the press conference yesterday the mayor had said that the city buses would begin running again this morning. Today was Monday, and most people in the areas not directly affected would no doubt be going to work. At the talks between the KEF and the mayor, it had been decided to keep the schools open. Eventually, though, the already rattled residents would begin to feel trapped in their own city, and that could only lead to serious levels of fear and anxiety.

His office was at the heart of the government district in Tenjin 1-Chome, alongside City Hall and the central police station. The newspaper occupied the top five floors of their own fourteen-story building, Nishi Nippon Shinbun Kaikan, and leased the lower nine floors to a department store. Until the day before yesterday there had been two security guards at the entrance; now there were six. They were civilian guards armed only with nightsticks and stun guns, and given the KEF's firepower were clearly only there to provide some peace of mind. But it was low-paid employment, and with the increased demand for guards from many local businesses, security firms had suddenly found themselves short-staffed. The sound of a rotor starting up came from the helipad on the roof. It would be daylight in two hours. No doubt the helicopter would be flying throughout the day again.

Yokogawa first went to the international-news desk to learn more about the reaction abroad to the KEF occupation and the government blockade. He was surprised to find the office thick with cigarette smoke—the smoking ban had evidently been abandoned. With their nerves shot to pieces since the occupation of the Dome, even those who'd given up had probably started again. Kodama sat at the desk, slurping down some instant noodles, with his shirtsleeves rolled up above his elbows and his eyes a bright bloodshot red. When he saw Yokogawa come in, he cleared a huge pile of papers off a chair for him. Real-time reports from news agencies were constantly feeding in on his computer screen: the US government had called for restraint on the part of both the KEF and the Japanese government; the Department of Defense and the commander of the US forces stationed in Japan confirmed that public order was being maintained and that US troops would not get involved in the situation; an undersecretary of state claimed that the Japanese government had absolutely no measures in place for protecting the US consulate in Fukuoka; the Chinese government stated that they had once again obtained confirmation from North Korea that the force occupying Fukuoka was a rebel army faction; and the South Korean government feared that the blockade of Fukuoka and Kyushu would be a major obstacle for the East Asian economy. It was clear that South Korea and China were avoiding saying anything that might provoke the North. With no change in the situation, there was nothing new to report.

"Have a look at this." Smirking, Kodama put his cup of noodles on the desk and scrolled down to an article from a British tabloid, sent in by Reuters, suggesting that the Japanese government had funded the KEF to overthrow the Kim regime but that the *coup d'état* had failed and they had fled to Fukuoka. "There are a few other interesting theories too." He took a pack of Hi-Lites out of his shirt pocket and lit one up. AFP had sent an article from a Moroccan daily claiming that Kyushu aimed to gain independence from Japan and become the fifty-first state of the USA, while a Hong Kong paper wondered what the exchange rate of the Kyushu yen against the Japanese yen would be in the event that Kyushu did become independent. "Folks abroad don't seem to have grasped what the blockade actually means," Yokogawa commented. "Can't say I understand it myself," said Kodama, shaking his head, the cigarette still in his mouth. "Weren't you a Seven Stars man?" Yokogawa asked. "They've sold out all of a sudden—can you believe that?" Having spent seven years in the North American office of the paper, three and a half of those years as bureau chief, Kodama had many friends in the American media. When the Japanese government had announced the blockade yesterday, he had flown into a rage and slammed his fist on the desk. Why didn't the SDF attack? The small team of commandos that had initially occupied Fukuoka Dome may have been terrorists, but the five hundred uniformed troops were clearly an invading army.

After the press conference, Kodama had said angrily, "Who gives a damn whether they're a rebel army or not? They have to be stopped now! They occupy the Dome, we call it a terrorist attack, they get a foothold, and there goes our national sovereignty. And instead of fighting the invaders, our government goes and imposes a blockade. Isn't that just conceding defeat? If the SDF had attacked, there'd have been civilian casualties, sure, including a lot of patients at the Medical Center, but who knows how many we'll end up with anyway? If another hundred and twenty thousand troops arrive from North Korea, that'll be the end. That's in seven days, right? Maybe it's already too late." The lounge was packed with reporters grabbing some shut-eye, while several others lay on sofas around the office or rested their heads on their desks, fast asleep. The final checking of the morning edition had just been completed. It must have been a tough choice for the editors to decide which articles to include in the six-page edition. Yokogawa thanked Kodama for showing him the news-agency reports, and was just leaving when Kodama stopped him. "You're going along with the KEF on the round of arrests, aren't you?" Yokogawa nodded. "You'd better borrow a bulletproof vest from the police." Apparently he'd received information from Germany that someone in the Police Agency had unofficially contacted the crack GSG-9 counter-terrorism unit. "If the government's dumb enough to send in an SAT team, there could be one hell of a shoot-out."

271

Making his way to the city-news desk, Yokogawa tried to think of reasons why Japan *hadn't* attacked the KEF. True, the combination of the terrorist attack and invasion by combat units made any response difficult. Thirty thousand spectators had been held hostage in Fukuoka Dome, while there were a large number of patients in the adjacent Medical Center, some of whom were too ill to be moved. The KEF had arrived barely two hours after the occupation of the Dome, when the surrounding area hadn't yet been evacuated. Supposing the SDF had attacked them? Had there been the will to do so, they could immediately have sent in fighter jets and attack helicopters from the Kasuga base right next door. The terrorists would probably have been caught ill-prepared, although there could have been a horrendous number of civilian casualties.

Then again, it might all be down to a simple lack of experience, he thought. The only occasions in recorded history that any foreign force had tried to invade Japan were the Mongolian expeditions in the thirteenth century. The Americans in Japan at the end of World War II had been an occupying force, not an invading army. If the Mongol army had succeeded all those centuries ago, Japan's history and culture would have taken a totally different course. There probably wouldn't have been kabuki, or the tea ceremony, or ukiyo-e woodblock prints, or haiku poetry. What would have happened if in August 1945 Japan hadn't surrendered unconditionally and there had been prolonged fighting on the mainland? Not only America, but the Soviet Union and China almost certainly would have invaded, and Japan would probably have been partitioned off much like Germany had been and the Korean Peninsula still was. Invasion and occupation by a foreign army was the worst thing that could possibly happen to a nation and its people, and of course it was better not to have experienced it. Without that experience, however, the country had no means of deciding whether to capitulate or attack. "I dunno," Yokogawa muttered to himself. Should the SDF attack the invaders? He just didn't know.

\*

272

The city-news desk was buzzing. A major disaster never failed to bring a newspaper office to life and the phones were ringing off the hook, with some reporters speaking into several phones at once. There was the constant clatter of keyboards; news reports from CNN, BBC, and other stations were being shown on five TV monitors; and the fax machine was beeping continuously as more and more stuff came in. A tall female reporter by the name of Saeki Yoshiko was sitting with her feet up on her desk drinking a can of beer, dark rings under her eyes. She had just swigged down the last of the can when she noticed Yokogawa come in. She got up and clapped him on the shoulder. "Good luck going with that bunch today. I'm off home to shag my man and get some sleep," she said as she walked out of the office. Yesterday Saeki had gone to a KEF checkpoint to get information, and her report had been printed as a boxed article on page two. She was probably still high on the adrenalin. The office was more chaotic than usual, with memo pads, copy materials, food wrappings, and paper coffee cups scattered about the floor, and the recycling bins piled high with cans and plastic bottles.

Nabeshima from the business-news desk and Karita, chief of the regional-news center, were also there, seated on a sofa facing Matsuoka's desk. The regional-news center corresponded to the political-news desk in other newspapers, and mainly covered local politics, government, and elections in Kyushu. As Yokogawa approached, the three of them stood up to greet him and made space for him on the sofa. Matsuoka looked especially happy to see him, and said they'd arranged for him to meet the KEF at four-thirty. The reason Yokogawa was popular with local reporters, according to the person who toasted him at some party or other, was his freewheeling but common-sense approach, and his cool head. What that meant, Saeki had explained later, was that he was able to see through to the reality in a given incident. "Let's say a drug-addict mother strangles her child—it's awful, but it's a reality. If you get all moralistic and let it upset you, there's no way you can produce a balanced report. You've got to have the skin of a rhinoceros."

Once Yokogawa was seated, the three started talking about the
challenges presented by the six-page format, but after a bit they
lowered their voices and drew closer until their knees were almost
touching. Nabeshima looked around cautiously. "It appears they've
got bank accounts," he whispered to Yokogawa. "At the Fukushima
Ajisai Bank and the Shin Kyushu Bank, I'm guessing, and maybe
the Seiwa Bank too, but we can't confirm it because the banks themselves refuse to discuss the matter on the record." Yokogawa asked
if the accounts were in the KEF's name, but the other three smiled
wryly and shook their heads. "No, and keep your voice down, will
you?" According to information leaked to Nabeshima by one bank
employee, the KEF had secretly taken over the account of an existing
company. "The mediator for the account was apparently someone
high up in City Hall," said Karita, frowning. "In the end the KEF
managed to get a huge amount of money together, somewhere in
the order of several billion or tens of billions of yen. City Hall was
feeling the pinch and the banks had one foot in the grave—they
must have jumped at the chance, even if it meant they'd be branded
as collaborators."

"Yokogawa-san," said Matsuoka, his hair tousled and lank, "I heard
that the mayor wants to see you, but don't go telling him about this
bank account stuff, okay? There are factional splits in City Hall over
the KEF, you know. The mayor probably has no idea these accounts
exist." Yokogawa replied that once the KEF started buying things,
everyone would know about them. The other three exchanged a
glance. "It's only conjecture based on the bank leak," explained
Nabeshima, keeping his voice low, "but if the government gets wind
of the KEF accounts they'll try to freeze their assets, right? Obviously
they can't do that without the bank's cooperation, however. And
the bank can hardly go to the KEF and tell them, sorry, but your
account's been frozen on government orders. If you've got a gun
to your head, you do as you're told. You'll do whatever you can to
cover up for them—secret accounts, fictitious account names, whatever. And what if the government excludes the Kyushu banks from
Japan's financial market? They'll have to freeze every single account

on the island, won't they? Of course, if it comes to that, it's like the government announcing that all the cash and bonds held in banks here aren't worth the paper they're printed on. So even if Fukuoka and the rest of Kyushu don't deliberately seek independence from Japan, we might find ourselves effectively cut off anyway."

"Wow," said Yokogawa. He had mixed feelings listening to the three of them. It probably was true that the KEF had bank accounts, and that top people in the banks and in City Hall had helped them along. Karita had used the word "collaborators," and no doubt that's what they'd be labeled for dealing with an invading army. But then, who could blame them? When the rocket destroyed the electronic scoreboard in Fukuoka Dome, it was as if the spectators had been frozen and seemed to lose the ability even to react. They did as the commandos told them. Even now, nobody knew how to respond to the KEF. Nabeshima was probably right when he said the government was leaning toward separation from Japan—but that didn't mean they were happy about it. They probably didn't know what they should sacrifice and what they should try to save, and therefore couldn't make any decisions. They hadn't issued any order to fight the KEF, but neither had they told people to cooperate with them; and all the measures they had taken, including the blockade, had been ad hoc, not part of any overall policy. Given the circumstances, what could anyone do when threatened by guns but obey?

The other three began discussing what would happen with mail and courier services between Kyushu and the rest of the world if the blockade continued. Airmail might be difficult, but surface mail would only need permission from the ministry to allow trucks through. The ban on exports of cars, machinery, electrical appliances and so forth from Hakata Port was a problem, but, as Nabeshima said, they were bound to be resumed at some point. None of the three had had any sleep that night, but they were all pumped up and eager to talk. "I ordered one of those dirty photo collections from Amazon," Karita said, "and I'd just been notified that it'd been dispatched when that lot went and occupied the Dome. I'm a bit nervous that it might slip through somehow and get into my wife's hands." Matsuoka and Nabeshima laughed, puffing away on their cigarettes. Matsuoka was smoking Hi-Lites and Nabeshima Mild Larks, although both of them normally preferred Seven Stars. Kodama had said that Seven Stars had sold out—a result of supplies not getting through? Matsuoka mentioned that the clubs in Nakasu would probably still be open, and Karita, laughing, said, "That Korean pub by Haruyoshi Bridge—the one called the Pleasure Brigade—might have to think about changing its name now, though!"

Yokogawa had been instructed to go to the camp's Checkpoint D at four-thirty that morning, so he had just enough time to drop by City Hall. His boss had called to say the mayor wanted to see him, and that he should keep the meeting a company secret. Matsuoka, Nabeshima, and Karita saw him off from the city-news desk with various bits of advice: we don't know how long electric power will last, so take an ordinary camera instead of digital; you'd better change those leather shoes for sneakers in case you have to run for it; don't go trying to speak your pidgin Korean to the KEF, and so on. They wanted to accompany him as far as the elevator, but he waved them away. "No need to overdo it, you know," he told them.

To be honest, he did feel nervous about the upcoming session with the KEF. Just the thought of going back to that camp made his heart beat faster. But that didn't merit seeing him off with so much fuss. He'd always tried to avoid overblown send-offs when going to cover conflicts overseas—the more normal the departure, the better. Farewell parties or dramatic partings from your friends and loved ones were just unhealthy. For journalists and photographers habitu-ally reporting in war zones, the more dangerous the mission the more they tried to maintain a semblance of normality, as if they were just going for a walk in the park. Yokogawa went out through the back entrance and got into a chauffeur-driven car. City Hall was right up ahead, and in the deserted streets it stood out more than usual.

All the floors of the building were brightly lit. There hadn't been any rest for civil servants since the KEF occupation and the blockade.

Yokogawa went to the main entrance and showed his business card to the guard, telling him that he had an appointment with the mayor. The guard directed him to the Environment Bureau on the thirteenth floor, not to the mayor's office, but when he stepped out of the elevator nobody was waiting for him. There was a row of meeting rooms down one side of the corridor, with numbers starting from 1301, but he had no idea which one to go to. They were partitioned off by frosted glass, and continued down the corridor to double doors that opened onto a large meeting room at the end. He could hear voices coming from several of the rooms, but he couldn't just barge in to see who was there. Just as he'd decided to go back and ask the guard for the room number, he heard his name called from behind. He turned to see Mayor Tenzan, whom he'd met many times before in his role as a reporter, peeping out of one of the rooms.

"Sorry to drag you out at this hour." Tenzan looked even more exhausted than the previous day. He was clean-shaven, but his necktie was crooked and his shirt crumpled, his thinning hair tousled, and his stoop more pronounced than usual. The room was about twelve square meters in size, with a rectangular plywood desk and a few old easy chairs with broken springs. By the window was a leafy potted plant that clearly needed watering, and on a table in the corner was a thick pile of leaflets on environmental health and the disposal of industrial waste. The desk was littered with empty drinks bottles, a teapot and cups, and an aluminum ashtray overflowing with cigarette stubs. The wall clock hung at an angle, and the silver lettering that read DONATED BY TANAKAMARU CLOCKS was discolored.

"I apologize for not coming out to meet you." Tenzan didn't have a Kyushu accent, having been born and raised in Tokyo. It was only after a successful career as a management consultant that he'd run for the mayoral elections in his mother's hometown as a candidate for the old Democratic Party, and won. He had appealed to the electorate by saying that although he'd never lived in Fukuoka, its blood ran through his veins, and that he believed the regeneration of the city depended on not being swayed by outside opinion. He had drawn on his experience in his previous job to streamline the administration through the use of NPOs, in a bid to restore public finances, and he'd achieved some results by exploiting connections with East Asian businesses and the special deregulation zone. But he was said to have made many enemies within the establishment.

Tenzan looked around the small, shabby meeting room. "My reason for seeing you in a place like this is that I wanted to update you on the present circumstances without being overheard by other staff." When Yokogawa gave him a dubious look, he said, "Let me explain," but launched into a long preamble about his efforts not only to rationalize and deregulate government operations but to change the mindset of city employees. The best way to do that, he'd decided, was to unite them in a common goal, and the first goal he'd set was to improve interdepartmental communication. As at yesterday's press conference, Tenzan spoke in a muffled, somewhat husky voice—a voice that irritated some and impressed others, who felt it indicated an artless sort of honesty. Yokogawa felt neither way; he just wanted him to get to the point.

"Well, just as we were beginning to make real progress with our communication issues, this goes and happens. The fact is, after the press conference yesterday, I wondered about the garbage and the, well, the sewage and whatnot from their, what's it called, their encampment in Jigyohama, and so I put out feelers to the KEF commander about having our staff deal with it." Every time he shifted in his seat, the springs groaned. "These days we outsource everything, including garbage and sewage collection, so anyone less than mid-level management, people capable of talking business with contractors, wouldn't do, of course. There has to be smooth cooperation, otherwise—well, as you know, the KEF aren't exactly tolerant, so anything could happen. I really had to steel myself to ask senior staff for their help with this—after all, they all have families too. But five hundred people produce an awful lot of garbage and sewage, and if you don't dispose of it properly there's the danger of an epidemic. And now we've got to accommodate the reinforcements said to be on their way. We don't want them just appropriating

278

whatever land and buildings they choose, and we certainly don't want them spread throughout the city, so I came up with the idea of getting them to base themselves on a stretch of reclaimed land in Odo—that depopulated area around the old elementary school that closed down? But we're going to need the very best personnel from the public works and building equipment divisions to get it ready for habitation. The first one I approached was a female senior staff member named Onoe Chikako, who was originally in the Port Authority. She's extremely good at her job, and she also speaks a bit of Korean. She was rather shocked, of course, but I managed to convince her. And having a woman agree to the assignment made it a lot easier to persuade others.

"But then what should go and happen? A total of eight city employees have been at the KEF camp since yesterday afternoon, and from what I hear they've been falling over backwards to please the North Koreans, going way beyond the call of duty. Now, what's that all about?" Tenzan put a hand to his chin and sat up straighter, unhunching his shoulders. Yokogawa had already heard that some of the City Hall staff had set off for the KEF camp as if heading for the lions' den, but before long had been pitching in with big smiles on their faces, as though they were all old friends. He thought the psychology involved was probably something along the lines of the Stockholm syndrome, but he didn't have time to get into that now and looked meaningfully at his wristwatch. Tenzan didn't seem to be in any hurry, however. From one corner of the room came a buzzing sound, probably a fly. The whole room smelled like the butt-filled ashtray, and water was dripping from the air conditioner, which looked as though it hadn't been repaired for years. From outside, City Hall looked like a palace, but once you were inside you saw the effects of the budgetary crisis. It was neither hot nor cold in the room, but beads of sweat glistened on the mayor's forehead. Yokogawa noticed that something black was mixed in with the sweat—hair dye, probably. Tenzan looked increasingly uncomfortable. The hands resting on his knees were trembling, and he blinked rapidly, as if his eyes were sore. Yokogawa finally realized that he wasn't just griping; he had something important to communicate, and was making every effort to get it across, in spite of being exhausted to the point of collapse.

"The problem," said Tenzan, his voice even huskier now, "is that discipline in City Hall is breaking down. The whole place seems to be disintegrating. The assembly isn't functioning, and some workers seem to be at the beck and call of the KEF, as I told you. Those that are close to them are actively following their instructions and working on their behalf even inside City Hall. Some of our people have already started searching for a suitable piece of land for them—for the extra hundred and twenty thousand on the way, that is. On the other hand, a lot of staffers don't take at all kindly to this. Maybe there's an element of jealousy there, although I don't know if you can really call it that. But there seems to be this mistaken idea that the safety of those in favor with the KEF is somehow guaranteed. In a time of emergency, what's most to be feared is a schism among those of us entrusted with governance of the city, and that's exactly what seems to be happening. But what worries me most is the possibility of something similar happening in the central government."

Tenzan glanced at the wall clock. He kept licking his lips and clearing his throat. After taking a deep breath, he said, "The day before yesterday, two SAT units were sent over by Osaka City police. SAT stands for Special Assault Team," he began to explain, but Yokogawa cut him short, saying he knew what SAT was. "Combined, the units from Fukuoka prefectural police and Osaka City number almost sixty men. And the combined squad appears to be under the command of the leader of the Osaka SAT, who's a captain in rank. The prefectural police are hopping mad because their chief, who's an inspector and should be in command, is being left out of the loop. It's a real mess. Osaka sent in the SAT units, but the order apparently came from the National Police Agency with the backing of a number of Cabinet ministers. This was leaked to me by someone in the Cabinet crisis-management room who's worried about it. He didn't specify which ministers were involved.

"The problem is, they're not here officially on government orders, which means the government won't be held responsible for whatever happens as a result. And apparently they're considering trying to capture KEF personnel. The prefectural SAT has just under twenty men, and their equipment and training are completely different from the Osaka SAT units. Some of the latter were trained in the US and Europe and have the latest weapons and equipment, and they tend to look down on the prefectural SAT. I've only just heard about their arrival and have no idea what exactly they're planning. But if they really do try to capture some KEF soldiers, it'll entail a huge risk to residents, and I can't take responsibility for that. And it's not at all clear who the hell *will* be taking responsibility."

So that's what this is all about, thought Yokogawa. They certainly wouldn't spring an attack on the Jigyohama camp in order to capture a few KEF men. The anti-terrorist police were basically trained to arrest criminals and save lives, not fight; they weren't capable of taking on Special Operations Forces armed with rocket launchers and machine guns. So they must be planning to ambush separate individuals as they went on their round of arrests. "Is there anything I can do?" asked Yokogawa. "Please keep us informed about how the KEF arrests are going," said Tenzan gratefully. "Fine," said Yokogawa. "But I might not have a chance to contact you if things get dicey." Yokogawa envisioned getting caught up in a shoot-out, and decided that it really would be better to borrow a bulletproof vest.

Dawn had not yet broken. The black silhouettes of buildings loomed up along Route 202, where some twenty riot police were washing down the road and sweeping up shards of broken glass outside the blockaded Nishitetsu–Fukuoka Station. Late last night, a mob of about a hundred youths had hurled bottles, stones, and plastic bags filled with excrement and paint at the riot police. More than a few had been arrested, and some were seriously injured after being beaten with batons or shoved to the ground with duralumin riot shields. Some of the riot police had been injured too. Nishitetsu–Fukuoka Station was only three kilometers from the KEF camp, but it was a small station on a privately run local railway, and considerably fewer police had been sent to guard it than at JR Hakata Station or Hakata Port. They were right under the noses of the heavily armed North Korean soldiers but were equipped only with the standard batons, shields, and water cannon used to deal with demonstrations. The squad must have been very edgy when the crowd, many of whom had lost their jobs and now felt physically trapped in the city, yelled at them to get the trains moving again and started throwing stones. And there had been other incidents. It was only the first day of the blockade and supplies of food and fuel had not yet bottomed out, but panic buying had already begun at convenience stores and gas stations. Stones had been thrown at the office of the Association of Korean Residents in Japan, fires had been set at pachinko parlors run by people connected with the Association, and a clash between a cult group trying to flee Fukuoka and police at a roadblock had produced a number of casualties.

Some of the riot police peered into Yokogawa's car as it drove slowly past. They looked like they didn't want to be there. There had been few demonstrations in recent years, and most of them had probably never confronted an aggressive mob. Asked by a television reporter what he would do if the Koryo Expeditionary Force came along, one of them had answered that he didn't want to think about that. Yokogawa fought an urge to roll down the window and tell these boys that if the KEF did show up, they should run like hell.

At this time of night, it took less than ten minutes to get from Tenjin to Jigyohama, and there was still plenty of time. Yokogawa asked the driver to go slowly while he searched media reports related to SAT units on the in-car PDA.

Special Assault Team, abbreviated as SAT. Made up of specially selected young police officers equipped with high-performance sniper rifles, sub-machine guns, night-vision goggles, etc., and trained to deal with incidents such as hijackings and hostage situations. Started in secret by Tokyo and Osaka police following the 1977 Dhaka Incident when the Japanese Red Army hijacked a

Japan Airlines flight. Their existence was first made public by the National Police Agency in 1996, when it had five branches in the prefectural police departments of Hokkaido, Chiba, Kanagawa, Aichi, and Fukuoka, with approximately two hundred personnel. They will respond to an emergency request for assistance outside their prefectural boundary. In 1979 they resolved a hostage situation at a Mitsubishi bank in Osaka's Sumiyoshi Ward by shooting dead the hostage taker.

Kyodo News Agency, May 2000

SAT units from Osaka police 2nd Mobile Unit and Fukuoka police 1st Mobile Unit were dispatched to aid Hiroshima police in the hijacking of a Nishitetsu Express bus. Hiroshima prefectural police stormed the bus at the Kodani service area, and the SAT units provided specialist assistance.

*Asahi Shinbun*, May 2000

It has been decided to deploy a National Police Agency anti-terrorist Special Assault Team (SAT) in Okinawa from 2005. The area is considered at high risk of terrorist attack due to the presence of US military bases, and dispatching a unit after a request for assistance from the prefectural police would currently take too long. SAT units have been expanded since their formal establishment in 1996, and there are now ten units with three hundred members in all, located in Tokyo and Osaka MPDs, Hokkaido, Chiba, Kanagawa, Aichi, and Fukuoka.

Kyodo News Agency, February 2002

Following last month's suicide bombing outside the National Diet, the government has established an anti-terrorism task force (under the deputy chief cabinet secretary for crisis management) with a budget of 5 billion yen. A spokesman said this would be mostly used to cover the costs of equipping the police anti-terrorist special assault team (SAT) and training them abroad. SAT members will be sent to train in Germany, the US, and Britain.

The SAT units were apparently initially trained by Germany's counter-terrorism unit GSG-9 (the Grenzschutzgruppe 9, or Border Guard Group 9).

*Mainichi Shinbun*, September 2008

The joint anti-terrorism conference held by the National Police Agency and the Self-Defense Agency to tackle terrorism by Islamic fundamentalists and North Korea is under way, and confirms mutual cooperation between these two organizations. It appears that in the case of terrorist attacks such as the suicide bombing outside the Diet building in August this year, not only police SAT teams but also the SDF's Rangers will be deployed. However, the NPA expressed misgivings about the SDF being in charge of anti-terrorist strategy in urban areas.

Kyodo News Agency, November 2008

Yokogawa had a nasty presentiment. The decision to dispatch the Osaka SAT units to Fukuoka had been taken when it became known that a small group of North Korean terrorists had occupied the Dome, but the situation had completely changed with the arrival of four entire companies in light transport planes. The SAT units were not trained to deal with an armed force five hundred strong, and were no longer appropriate for the current situation. Nevertheless, some police officials and politicians might well get it into their heads that now they'd been dispatched, they had to be used. It was unclear who had proposed it, or who had the right to decide, or where the responsibility lay, but it seemed that a plan that no longer made any sense was going to be carried out. In the past Yokogawa had often told himself that however uninformed or incompetent bureaucrats or politicians were, surely they couldn't be *that* dumb, only to have them prove him wrong again and again. At the time of the controversy over using the same number for the Basic Resident-Register Network code as for the tax records, he'd written an editorial saying that surely they couldn't be stupid enough to do that, but then they had actually gone and done it. When he investigated further, he'd been shocked to find that the Diet had approved it only because the decision had been made some time earlier and couldn't be changed.

The car was passing Ohori Park. The park's perimeter was outlined with blue plastic sheets covering the shacks of homeless people. Their numbers had been steadily increasing over the past few years, and just about all the parks in the city were inhabited. Either they hadn't yet gone to sleep or else they were up early, for some of the shacks were dimly lit. Stealing electricity from power cables was common. Through the plastic sheeting faint silhouettes could be seen holding what looked like glasses, as if a party were in progress. Smoke from cooking fires rose from other shacks. Were the homeless unaware of the North Korean army camp next door? And what would the KEF soldiers make of the people living in the park?

Beyond, the Sea Hawk Hotel rose up before them like a gigantic sword. For Yokogawa, that tall, blade-like building was turning into a symbol of the KEF. When the baseball Dome and the hotel were completed twenty years ago, the entire city had seen them as symbols of a new Fukuoka with a bright future ahead of it. Yet with the decline of Daiei, the major retail chain and former owner of the Hawks baseball team, and the economic demise of both the city and Japan as a whole, they had become symbols of lost hope.

Yokogawa wondered why Tenzan had made a point of calling him in to tell him about the Special Assault Teams. The forthcoming arrests were bound to take place in different locations, so any information he could provide from accompanying them would be of little use. And Tenzan must have access to the names and contact numbers of prefectural police officers going with them. Knowing what kind of KEF squadron was in charge of the arrests and how they were being carried out wouldn't help. Could it be that the mayor was quietly suggesting he leak the information about the SAT units to the KEF? If the KEF was alerted to the danger, the SAT teams might be dissuaded from carrying out their plan or otherwise fail in their operation, thus protecting residents and police officers. If that really had been Tenzan's intention, then what should he do? Could leaking the information protect people from the irresponsible tactics of idiot politicians and bureaucrats? Gazing up at the Sea Hawk Hotel slicing into a sky that was just beginning to glow faintly with the approaching dawn, Yokogawa felt his heartbeat quicken.

Checkpoint C, at the junction of Yokatopia Avenue and the road around the Dome, came into sight as Yokogawa's car emerged from the residential area to the south. Night-lights were on in practically all the houses, or otherwise in the gardens. The KEF camp was just a short walk away, but the residents had not been evacuated. They couldn't leave the city because of the roadblocks, but they hadn't been given any guidance at all; no one was telling them to seek shelter elsewhere, but neither was anyone reassuring them that they were safe staying put. What went through the minds of the residents of this neighborhood as they watched news reports about the KEF on TV? If you had relatives or friends in the area, what kind of advice would you give them? If Kodama on the international-news desk were to see the lights on in this neighborhood, would he still insist on the SDF attacking? Would Kodama feel the same way if his own home was here, with his wife and children inside? Yokogawa realized it was really quite simple: the way you reacted to the KEF depended on where you lived. How many people in Tokyo could fully appreciate the anxiety and fear the locals here were feeling?

Checkpoint D was also just off Yokatopia Avenue, on the road that ran between the Hawks Town shopping mall and a school for children with disabilities. Twenty meters before it was a stop line, and Yokogawa's driver slowed to a halt. A machine gun protruded through a gap in the sandbags ahead, and two soldiers stepped out in front of the car and leveled weapons at them. One was a sub-machine gun and the other a Kalashnikov assault rifle. Well, no one would ignore an order to stop from these guys, thought Yokogawa. It was the first time his driver had been to the camp, and he was extremely nervous. "They don't shoot people by mistake, do they?" he asked in a tense voice as he fiddled with his glasses.

"They haven't fired a single shot since they got here," Yokogawa reassured him. "Relax. These guys are pros. They don't shoot needlessly." The real danger would be if the driver freaked out and tried to speed away.

The soldier signaled to them to move forward slowly. Having a gun aimed right at you caused a fear that was like something wriggling in the pit of your stomach. The driver was rigid with tension, and somehow his foot slipped and tapped the accelerator. The car jumped forward, the driver screeched and stepped hard on the brake, and Yokogawa bumped his head against the upholstered ceiling. One of the soldiers ran toward them, his sub-machine gun still poised at the hip. The other raised his Kalashnikov to his shoulder and pressed the stock against his cheek. Left foot in front, both knees slightly bent, he leaned forward, prepared to fire. The driver was close to panicking. He was holding the frame of his glasses with both hands, his face quivering. Trust me to pick this guy, thought Yokogawa as he opened the car window and called out loudly in Korean, "I'm sorry, there's a problem with our car."

The soldier running toward them looked at Yokogawa incredulously: had he really spoken in Korean? Another man came out of the checkpoint and slowly approached them. "Who are you? Name, please!" he said in halting Japanese. This soldier was not wearing green camouflage fatigues, but a bluish uniform of denim-type fabric and a cap with a hard visor like those worn by the police, with a badge reading "Guard" in Hangul. Yokogawa gave his name and affiliation, asked the driver for his license, and handed it together with his own ID through the window. The guard took them, told them to wait, and slowly walked back to the checkpoint. "It's all right, don't worry. Calm down and take deep breaths," Yokogawa urged the driver, who kept apologizing in an unnaturally high-pitched voice and was on the verge of tears. Several soldiers were in and around a small shed behind the sandbags. The guard who had taken their ID went inside it, and after a while returned. He had an almost boyish face. "I am Tak Cheol Hwan of the KEF Special Police. Mr. Yokogawa, come this way, please. Your driver can wait in the car park." Yokogawa was uneasy about leaving this spineless driver alone in the camp, and asked in Korean if he could send him back to the newspaper and have him pick him up later. "That's fine," Tak replied.

Two mobile armored vehicles belonging to Fukuoka prefectural police were parked right next to the checkpoint. The MAVs had a flattened shape, as if designed to slink over the terrain, but sported wheels with big, heavy-duty tires rather than caterpillar tracks. They were apparently American armored personnel carriers that had been converted by a Japanese automobile manufacturer, with the machine-gun emplacements removed. In the four sides of the turret were armored shields and gun ports designed to fire tear gas and rubber bullets for use in riot control. Right next to the front gun port was a loudspeaker and a wide-beam searchlight. Inside, the driver's cab was separated from the passenger compartment by a thick steel plate, with a small hatch for access. An officer from the prefectural police was already in the driver's seat, and riding shotgun was a KEF soldier wearing the same bluish uniform as the soldier named Tak Cheol Hwan. Tak had said that he was from the KEF Special Police. Perhaps it was their equivalent of the military police. As they climbed into the passenger seats of the first vehicle, Yokogawa tried asking Tak whether this was the case. He replied almost apologetically that he didn't have his superior's permission to answer questions about military matters.

They entered the passenger compartment through double doors at the back. There was no step or handhold, so Yokogawa put one foot on the floor of the compartment, about seventy centimeters off the ground, grabbed hold of the door hinge, and tried unsuccessfully to pull himself up. Not only was it too high but the hinge was difficult to get a grip on, and he just couldn't manage it. After watching him try a few times, Tak helped push him up from behind. Then, in the time it took Yokogawa to thank him in Korean, Tak placed one foot inside the compartment, leaned forward, and lightly kicked off from the ground to step aboard. Yokogawa was impressed.

The interior of the MAV was surprisingly big, with a row of narrow seats along either side, facing each other. It was rather like one of those old buses you used to get in rural areas, and looked as if it could seat up to twenty people at a squeeze. In the center were a few steps leading up to the turret. Eventually five uniformed officers from the prefectural police arrived and helped each other up into the compartment. They were all in their early thirties or so, prob- ably the best age in terms of fitness and experience—accompanying the North Koreans on the round of arrests was going to be no easy task. Yokogawa greeted them cheerily, but they merely glanced at him without replying or even nodding an acknowledgment. What a rude lot, he thought, but then realized that they were probably just rather cowed by the KEF. Aside from the seats and the leather straps that hung down above them, the interior was completely bare. There were horizontal slits in the walls—gun ports, about three centimeters wide—but no windows. The small steel seats were hard and cold, with just a thin cloth covering, and the steel interior wall of the vehicle was the only backrest. It'd be tough if you suffered from piles or lumbago. Through the gun slits Yokogawa saw an NHK cameraman and reporter rush past.

A tall figure appeared outside the rear door. Silhouetted against the light, he was not clearly visible but appeared to be an officer. Tak was now visibly tense. The officer leaped nimbly into the MAV, and looked around at everyone seated there. Seeing his eyes for the first time in the dim interior, Yokogawa was seized with an irrational urge to get the hell out of there. His skin crawled, as if bugs were making their way up his lower body. The man's shoulders bulged with muscles, and there was a long, thin scar on his cheek. But it wasn't because of these that Yokogawa felt afraid. The officer took a seat directly facing him, and asked Tak whether everybody was there. Just as Tak replied that one newspaper reporter hadn't yet arrived, the *Asahi Shinbun*'s Ito poked his head through the back door and said, "Sorry I'm late!" Four-thirty had come and gone a couple of minutes ago. He was about to climb in, but the tall officer told him in Japanese, "We will not permit your lateness." The man's phrasing was a bit odd, but his pronunciation was spot on. Ito apologized again, saying that it had taken a while to check his documents, probably because his address was in Tokyo. "We will not allow it," the officer said again and stared at him, expressionless. Ito stood frozen for a moment, then swallowed hard and said, "I see." The officer reached out to pull the metal doors shut, right in Ito's face, and in a voice that seemed to rattle the steel walls, ordered the driver to "Go!" What a set of pipes, thought Yokogawa—he makes my tenor sound like a choirboy's.

The MAV rode high off the ground, and it was a rough ride. Yokogawa sat opposite the officer, with the steps up to the gun turret between them. As soon as they set off, the man unsmilingly introduced himself: "I am Choi Hyo Il, captain of the Special Police." The prefectural police officers also introduced themselves by name, company, and rank, but Yokogawa didn't take any of it in, being aware only of the Korean, who sat with his legs spread wide, hands on knees, back straight, now and then clearing his throat. Yokogawa had come across many distinctive characters in his ten or so years on the city-news desk before being transferred to Seoul. He had been in close contact with right-wingers and left-wingers, violent thugs, hoodlums, racketeers, politicians, and detectives, but he had never encountered anyone like Choi Hyo Il before. He'd once gone to interview a gangster whose daughter had just been sent to juvenile prison, and when he asked about this he'd been threatened with a sword. "So a kid follows in her father's footsteps—what the fuck's it got to do with you?" the thug had roared, before stripping off his shirt to reveal his tattoos, whipping out a razor-sharp antique sword, and lunging at him. Thinking he was about to die, Yokogawa had pissed himself. But the fear this Choi instilled in him was something else altogether.

Tak sat toward the front, while Choi was next to the rear door. Choi wore an armband with "Police" written on it in Japanese, but instead of the blue of the Special Police his uniform was the dark green of the army, with a field cap of the same color. Maybe the uniform was different because he was a captain, or perhaps since he was unusually tall for a Korean there hadn't been a police uniform to fit him. A Kalashnikov hung from his shoulder, an exceptionally small sub-machine gun was in a holder at his hip, and a number of hand grenades hung from his belt. Yokogawa had never heard of police carrying hand grenades. The difference between the battle-ready Choi and the prefectural police, armed with just revolvers and batons, was stark. There were six Japanese cops in this vehicle, including the driver, and three KEF people. Assuming the same was true of the MAV following them, that meant twelve Japanese cops in all. The ones seated alongside Choi seemed to have gone beyond nervous, to emotional shutdown. Choi, Tak, and the North Korean up front didn't talk to each other; they simply stared absently at the floor or walls, letting their bodies move loosely with the bouncing and swaying. This was the second outing to make arrests, and the Japanese police were probably working in shifts. It was clearly the first time the five in the passenger compartment with Yokogawa had come in contact with the KEF.

A printout of a memo about the person to be arrested was passed around. His name was Maezono Yoshio, of Daimyo 1-Chome in Chuo Ward. Yokogawa plucked up the courage to say to Choi in Korean, "May I ask you something?" The Japanese police looked at him dully, as if to warn him not to make unnecessary trouble. Choi held his eye for a while before answering—gazing at him so steadily and directly that it made his stomach hurt. "What is it?" said Choi in Japanese. Though his voice was slightly hoarse, it carried well, and his speech was polite enough—but that in itself was slightly unnerving. "Do you have an arrest warrant for this Maezono?" asked Yokogawa. "Yes," replied Choi shortly, still staring him in the face. "Who issued the warrant? From which organization? Under which law?" Choi shook his head. "I cannot give details. Please ask the propaganda and guidance section." When Yokogawa replied, "All right," his voice felt unnaturally loud. And he noticed that his armpits were damp, though it wasn't at all hot in there.

Without any windows, it was impossible to see what was going on outside. Yokogawa couldn't even make out the usual city landmarks through the gun slits. From Checkpoint D to Daimyo 1-Chome usually took about ten minutes, but they were taking side roads in order to avoid the blockaded highways. Choi stood up and climbed the turret steps. Tak was looking at Yokogawa curiously, but when their eyes met he looked away. The object of his interest was the Canon digital camera hanging around Yokogawa's neck. Come to think of it, he hadn't yet taken a single photo. Conscious of the guy in the turret, he quietly asked Tak if he could take his picture. Tak shook his head regretfully. "No photo. Special Police," he said in broken Japanese. "I understand," said Yokogawa, wondering how old the kid was. He might even still be in his teens, but there was something about him that was mature beyond his years. His face was young, but his eyes were intense, and though he seemed simple and unaffected, there was nothing placid about him. Tak now got up and looked into the driver's cab. The MAV was slowing down. Choi was still standing in the turret, his legs right in Yokogawa's line of sight. The bottom of his trouser leg was slightly hitched up, allowing a glimpse of a large combat knife sheathed in a case on his ankle. Cord was wound tightly around the knife's handle, and the dully gleaming case was made not of leather but of metal.

He wasn't sure the mayor had really been suggesting he inform the KEF about the SAT units, but in any case there was no way he could leak the information to these guys. If he tried, he might find himself hauled in for interrogation. The thought of having to face a man like Choi alone terrified him. Besides, he didn't want to pass anything on to the very intruders who were trampling all over his town and depriving people of their freedom. Confronted with aggressors capable of great violence, it was tempting to cozy up to them. Feeling constantly on edge was exhausting, and it was easy to give in to wishful thinking—"Maybe the KEF aren't so bad after all." The prefectural cops were still sitting there looking completely out of their element. They'd been ordered to take part in this procedure because there was no question of not complying with the KEF; effectively the whole city was being held hostage and had no choice but to obey them. But these police officers were performing the job with their faculties of thought and judgment on hold. Too scared to think about the circumstances in which they found themselves, they had become like lifeless puppets. Yokogawa wanted somehow to preserve his awareness of people like Tak and Choi as violent invaders. And whatever the mayor wanted, there was no way he personally was going to play along with people who had robbed him of his own freedom.

The MAV came to a halt. Choi opened the rear door and motioned to the Japanese police to get out first. As Yokogawa was getting up from his seat, the vehicle lurched forward and he almost fell. Tak caught his arm and helped support him. "I must be getting old!" said Yokogawa wryly, nodding his thanks before jumping out. They were a few hundred meters up a side street heading from Taisho Avenue toward Tenjin. He was shocked to see a few dozen onlookers gathered on the street. The KEF hadn't announced who they were going to arrest, so how had they known where to come? Practically all of them were young men. Some were on bicycles. A few were talking on cellphones, and others were surreptitiously taking photographs. A load *clack* came from somewhere near the turret and the searchlight came on, lighting up the front entrance of a large estate between two towering apartment blocks. The NHK cameraman and reporter he'd seen earlier had arrived as well. Yokogawa knew the reporter by sight and asked him about the crowd. "Someone must have spotted the armored vehicles and followed them, spreading the word by cellphone," came the reply.

Dawn was just breaking. An officer from the prefectural police said Maezono's name into an intercom at the gate, and ordered him to come out. It was a grand gate with a roof, like those you often saw in period dramas on TV. To its left was what looked like a small service entrance, while beneath the main gate a security camera moved up and down and side to side, apparently operated by remote control from inside the house. A dog was barking on the other side of the gate—a big dog by the sound of it. Ten uniformed police fanned out haphazardly around the one in charge of the intercom, while the six KEF men formed three neat pairs, one in front of the gate and one at either end of the fan. All held their guns at the ready, with one of each pair in a low crouch and the other standing. The pair in the middle, one of whom was young Tak Cheol Hwan, had their guns trained on the gate, while the other two pairs covered the road and the apartment blocks on either side. Choi was on the road to the right.

The onlookers stood at a distance of about thirty or forty meters, quietly watching the proceedings. It seemed their numbers were gradually growing. Nobody bothered to tell them to go away. The prefectural police were far too preoccupied to do anything about them, and the KEF people merely ignored them. Yokogawa stood with the NHK cameraman outside the cordon of police, taking pictures without the flash. Tak made no objection. Apparently it was okay to take photos as long as he didn't zoom in on any faces. He had the strange sensation of being shielded from the scene by some kind of transparent film. It didn't feel real. At first he thought perhaps it was because of the searchlight that turned the gate and its immediate surroundings as bright as day. Apart from the dog barking, the setting was unnaturally quiet. The police officer at the gate kept repeating into the intercom, "Maezono Yoshio, open up," while the others stood in silence. None of the onlookers said anything either. Even the NHK reporter, who had just whispered for the audience of his live broadcast that he was outside the house of Maezono Yoshio, said nothing more. Yokogawa felt as though he were stuck in a paused video.

The house was a traditional single-story Japanese residence, in grounds occupying perhaps a thousand square meters. People stood on the balconies of the surrounding condos, looking down nervously at what was happening. The NHK camera was alternately filming the police officer speaking into the intercom, the three pairs of Special Police, and people watching, and the images were being sent out live on their satellite and Internet channels. "Please wait a moment," came a voice through the intercom, followed by the sound of footsteps on the other side of the gate. A buzz ran through the onlookers. The NHK cameraman tried to get close, but Tak held up his hands to stop him. Behind the gate a voice said, "Quiet!" and the dog stopped barking. The gate creaked open and a small man appeared, holding up a hand to shield his eyes from the dazzling light. His long hair was slicked back, and he wore tight-fitting trousers and a sweater with a loud pattern. He also had a light-green scarf wrapped around his neck, and when Yokogawa saw this he remembered who the man was. The scarf was something of a trademark. Maezono had twice been arrested on suspicion of forcing Chinese women into prostitution—charges that didn't stick—and he'd been wearing a similar scarf both times.

"Maezono Yoshio, I am arresting you on charges of immorality, financial misconduct, and illicit personal enrichment," the police officer said, reading out the arrest warrant. As the officer took him by the arm and was about to handcuff him, a man with a shaved head clattered up behind them. He was dressed in a running shirt, pajama bottoms, and sandals with white socks, and he was carrying a shotgun over his shoulder. Bowing his head and repeatedly apologizing, he squeezed between the policemen to reach Maezono. Seeing the shotgun, the cops stepped back to make way for him. Maezono and the skinhead exchanged a glance, and Maezono spoke to the officer with the handcuffs. "We'll go with you, but could you call those guys off?" he said, indicating the Special Police. The shotgun-toting skinhead kept bowing and apologizing obsequiously, but he was sweating and seemed thoroughly wired, as though he'd been taking stimulants. Maezono drew closer to the cop, presumably to shield himself from the guns leveled at him.

The NHK cameraman took a couple of steps forward, trying to get a shot of Maezono's face. Seeing this, the skinhead shouted, "Hey, back off, willya!" He unshouldered the shotgun and aimed it at the cameraman. Instantly Tak, who was standing diagonally to the left behind Maezono, raised his Kalashnikov and fired two shots. Orange flames spouted from the barrel, and Yokogawa felt he'd actually seen the slugs drill into the side of the man's head. A gaping hole appeared there and the skull exploded, spattering brains, bits of which stuck to Yokogawa's face. Some of the brain matter got on the TV camera lens as well. The cameraman lowered the camera to clean it, then froze when he looked down and saw what was left of the man. A chorus of garbled cries came from the police cordon. The man had lost the upper part of his head, but he didn't die right away. He was still holding the shotgun, his fingers twitching, and the remaining half of his face shook from side to side, wobbling the roe-like remnants of his brain as blood flowed onto the ground. Yokogawa was trying to get rid of the stuff on his cheek, then suddenly sank to his haunches to puke. At the edge of his vision he saw the KEF escort Maezono to the MAV, but he couldn't stop throwing up.

4

# IN OHORI PARK

*April 5, 2011*

C HOI HYO IL returned to the Sea Hawk Hotel with a sixth
felon in custody. As he entered the reception area, he found
to his surprise that the artificial temperature produced by the air
conditioning no longer bothered him. Previously, from the time of
his arrival with the advance party, he'd felt uneasy whenever he set
foot in the place, as though it made him unable to feel the contours
of his own body. He was better adapted to the bracingly chill air of
the Republic. If the hotel air didn't seem to trouble him now, it was
mainly because he was feeling proud of the way he'd performed as
captain in the newly established Special Police.

The arrest of the felons had begun at 2:00 a.m., and Choi had
brought in half-a-dozen culprits by the end of the morning. After
the first few arrests, the Special Police had split into two squadrons,
with Choi leading one and Pak Il Su, who had already detained
four people, the other. The KEF's reconnaissance section had
compiled a list of 169 prime targets; half of these were to be taken
into custody within the seven days before the last reinforcements
arrived. The current pace—ten arrests over a half-day period—was
a little slow. Most of those on the primary list lived in neighbor-
hoods fairly close to the camp, the command center having decided

that unfamiliarity with more remote areas made efforts there too hazardous.

Inside Choi's MAV, the felon Omura Kikuo, apparently a frequent visitor to the hotel, boasted to his prefectural police escort that two years before he had held a party for eight hundred guests in the reception hall. "That's really something," the policeman said, frowning uncomfortably. Along with his colleagues, the officer knew just where Omura was heading—the detention center—and just how he would be treated there. Omura was a socialite and one of the richest men in Fukuoka. He was wearing a three-piece suit of plain but clearly expensive material, a red silk necktie, carefully polished leather shoes, and tortoiseshell glasses. The prefectural police may have felt a measure of pity for him, but they must also have derived some satisfaction from knowing what lay in store for someone whose earnings exceeded theirs several thousandfold. A fat and sixtyish physician, Omura had been the first in Fukuoka to incorporate his hospital, along with an affiliated nursing home. He had subsequently racked up huge profits and had been a major financial contributor to both the Democratic Party and the now defunct Liberal Democratic Party. As was noted in the arrest warrant, he was suspected of padding insurance claims, evading taxes, bribing politicians, and charging illegally high fees for the treatment of such rare diseases as asymptomatic HIV infection and distinctive lymphangioma.

The two KEF officers responsible for rooting out offenders had used the resident-register codes and supplementary information to identify the top taxpayers in Fukuoka: owners of upscale condos and villas in prime locations; purchasers of gold coins and bullion; high-level clients of securities companies; individuals with substantial insurance policies of various kinds; holders of private overseas bank accounts; major contributors to charitable organizations and NPOs; heavy financial backers of political parties; travelers to overseas destinations flying first-class or using individually chartered planes; big-spending credit-card users; owners of imported luxury cars, large motorboats, yachts, and light aircraft; members of upscale golf, tennis, and yacht clubs; and high-paying patients of medical facilities outside the insurance system. The occupational and financial backgrounds of these people were then investigated, and with the help of the municipal and prefectural police a roster was drawn up of those suspected of tax evasion, bribery, or illegal transactions. For two reasons, the provisional headquarters had prioritized the arrest of ordinary criminals over political ones: firstly, because it was imperative to seize their assets; secondly, because any effort to ferret out ideological opponents was considered premature.

Choi first took Omura into a small room inside the banquet hall and had him put his seal to a document stating: "I, Omura Kikuo, Felon #10, willingly submit to interrogation by the Koryo Expeditionary Force." Next came a rudimentary medical examination—temperature, blood pressure, pulse, gastrointestinal, and cardiac condition—to see how well he would stand up to grilling. It was important not to allow detainees to die of shock before they had provided needed information. The prefectural police officers had left the room once the assent form was completed. Now alone with the Koreans, Omura for the first time looked uneasy and asked whether an interpreter was needed. Choi gave a curt reply, saying in faulty Japanese that being able to conduct the interrogation necessarily meant knowing the language. Omura smiled in relief at this. Here's a rich man who's never known a hungry day in his life, thought Choi, and he's the only one with a grin on his face. But he'll soon forget that he ever knew how to smile.

They went down to the parking area in the lower basement, taking the emergency stairs. The air was cold in the dimly lit stairwell and filled with the dusty smell of concrete. From behind the wall separating them from the parking area came faint, disjointed groans and whimpers, and whenever Omura caught the sound, he would stop and look inquiringly at the men accompanying him. Choi caught a whiff of a jasmine-like scent. Here was a man who on the verge of being arrested and taken away had put on a womanly perfume. His gray hair was parted in the middle and smoothed down on both sides. His forehead and cheeks were ruddy, belying his age. The surface of his gray jacket was as smooth as satin, without a single wrinkle, his cufflinks were made of pearl, and on his ring finger, its short, plump shape resembling a bananito from India or Australia, was a broad wedding band. The rim of his wristwatch, its black dial softly glowing, was encrusted with jewels.

In the Republic, bribes were paid in the form of watches among corrupt Party members and bureaucrats. Seiko products were on sale in foreign-exchange shops for dizzyingly high prices, but Choi had never seen the likes of this timepiece and could well imagine the amazement that it would cause back home. Omura's living room had seemed like something out of a royal palace. The carpet was so thick that it seemed to swallow Choi's boots, and in the display cabinets were brands of whiskey and cognac quite unknown to him, along with rows of glasses of various sizes and shapes. From the ceiling hung an apparently antique chandelier of frosted glass. This man, thought Choi, knows nothing of the sort of punishment that causes you to scream involuntarily—pain so intense that you don't even know you're screaming.

Warrant Officer Ra Yong Hak led the way, running down the stairs before knocking on a steel emergency-exit door and announcing that they had brought in Felon #10. The door opened, and Ra motioned Omura to enter. Once inside, he froze. What was once a parking lot with spaces for sixty vehicles had been turned into a detention center, with grille partitions made of timber or galvanized iron. The cells were barely two meters square, and each was equipped with a waste bucket and a single blanket. At present only nine were occupied. The whimpering that Omura had heard came from a cell at the back; reverberating off the concrete floor and walls, it was like the distant yelping of a dog. A guard was beating the back of an inmate's hands with a whip made of pig intestines lined with copper wire. Inmates were not permitted to move. Except when sleeping, eating, or relieving themselves, they had to sit cross-legged, hands on knees. After an hour in this position on the hard floor, a man felt pressure on his lower back and pain in his leg joints, but if he relaxed his posture, a guard would give a whistled warning;

after two repetitions of this offense, the aforementioned punishment would be imposed. The skin would crack from the whipping, and as the nerves in one's hands are just above the bones, the pain thus inflicted was excruciating. Frequently the lashes resulted in carpal fractures.

Five separate cell blocks ran parallel to one another, separated by passageways about a meter wide. Each contained fifteen to twenty cells with shoulder-high partitions made of sheet iron obtained from scrap merchants. They were open at the top. Grounded in cement to support the cells were wooden braces, against which thick plywood was nailed to form the back wall. A door in the front turned on a hinge and was opened with a key releasing a bolt lock. The blankets were half their normal size, having been cut in two, and there were no pillows. The prisoners wore only thin cotton bathrobes and rubber sandals.

A man could be seen tottering along a corridor, dangling a waste bucket from his hand. This was Felon #9, a lawyer in his late sixties by the name of Otsuka Seiji. He had worked in a broad range of organized-crime syndicates, instigating and supervising money-laundering as well as tax evasion and had made quite a fortune for himself. Arrested by Pak Il Su of the second squadron, he now found it his duty to collect all nine buckets and take them one by one to the toilet next to the elevator. But after many hours in the cross-legged position, his right knee and ankle were swollen purple; unable to walk properly, he was dragging one leg and making very slow progress. The stench from the bucket drifted across the entire parking lot, and a guard thundered at him that if he allowed even a little of the contents to spill, he would have to clean it up with his own robe. Like a boy who's been scolded, the man began sobbing as he trudged on. His shoulders were shaking, his head waggling back and forth as he wiped the tears with his free hand.

Next to the emergency exit stood a large shuttle bus, with all the seats removed, converted into an induction station. Its windows afforded a view of the cells and their abject inmates, showing how unlikely they were to make an escape. Two guards stood rigidly at attention and saluted Choi. Omura had gone pale but was still struggling to maintain his dignity. Inside the bus he was ordered to undress. Next his hair was inspected, then his mouth, and finally his rectum. His three-piece suit, pearl cufflinks, gold wedding ring, jewel-encrusted wristwatch, and tortoiseshell glasses were all confiscated. He was told that failure to obey any and all directives would result in a beating, with blows from guards trained in taekwondo and *gyeoksul* inflicting bone-penetrating pain, and that recurring disobedience would result in more drastic punishment. Finally, Omura was handed his prisoner's clothing—an unwashed hotel bathrobe, reeking of sweat and other body odors. Deprived of his glasses, Omura had difficulty getting his arms through the sleeves. Within a day, all trace of his "dignity" would be gone.

Choi sent Ra back to the campground to continue preparations for the arrests to be made that afternoon. He then made his way over to the interrogation room next to the parking-area elevator, eager to know the results of the questioning. The room, which had once been an administration office, was about three meters by four. Ropes and wires dangled from the walls, and in the middle was a small table, onto which a metalsmith's anvil and a vice were bolted. Next to these lay a blood-smeared pair of pliers and a hammer. A blue vinyl tarp covered much of the linoleum floor, and against the wall stood two soldiers holding staves with blackened points.

Only felons were being held here on B2, the building's lowest level. The hostages—all able-bodied males aged fifteen or older—including hotel employees, guests, and some of the drivers commandeered by the 907th Battalion—were confined to the guest rooms on the twenty-second floor. KEF soldiers had emptied the B2 parking lot, breaking into all the vehicles, hot-wiring them, and driving them to the campground, leaving only the shuttle bus behind for its intended purpose. The prison-guard squad, in the language and spirit of the Republic, had soon begun to refer to the facilities for the hostages as *chodaeso* ("guesthouses") and the space on B2 as the *kwanliso* ("administrative center"—the official name for prison camps).

Instead of his camouflage battledress, Choi was in regular army green, with a band on his right arm identifying him as a member of the Special Police. At the sight of him, the guards sprang like taut strings to attention. His accomplishments were well known among members of the 907th Battalion. He had been promoted to captain after his role in the occupation of Fukuoka Dome. As one who, unlike most in the KEF, had actually been involved in military action, he was regarded with a certain awe. In 1995, he and his comrades had crossed into the South and there killed a number of puppet regime soldiers and civilians. And in 1998, he had participated in an exchange of gunfire with enemy troops on an uninhabited island in Kyonggi Bay.

And yet the determining factor for Choi was not the extent of one's first-hand experience but rather one's training in rapid response. Such training involved marching in formation and responding instantly to the instructor's commands: dive to the ground, fire from a prone position, reload, jump to your feet, shift direction and march, now hit the dirt again... Sometimes the training sessions went on for two days, with only a two-hour rest in the middle. Accumulated fatigue could play havoc with your ability to react to a changing situation. You neglected to adjust the sights on your weapon, forgot how much reserve ammunition you had, lost sight of the enemy, or failed to confirm your location and shot at your own comrades. As the very essence of combat preparation for the Special Operations Forces, rapid-response training meant rehearsing a string of actions until they became so deeply ingrained that the body was able to perform them automatically. And you had to perform them to perfection, like a precision instrument, whether it was day or night, in any environment and all extremes of weather.

When Choi came into the room, he asked Lieutenant Ri Su Il, the officer in charge of police interrogation, whether Felon #6 had provided the names of the asset managers and bank-account holders. Ri was a native of Sepon, Kangwon Province, near the Demilitarized Zone. In 2008 he had been transferred from Defense Headquarters to the 907th Battalion. With his rimless glasses, the twenty-seven-year-old had the air of a scholar, but his résumé included an eighteen-month stint as the leader of a sniper platoon on the DMZ. He was an expert in interrogating and indoctrinating enemy spies and political criminals. He informed Choi that they were finished with Felon #6 and that Felon #7 was now cooperating with the confiscation of his assets. He pointed to a powerfully built figure sitting on a chair, putting a thumbprint to a form. The purpose of referring to the inmates by number rather than by name was to deprive them of their identity as well as their property and thereby to nip in the bud any form of resistance.

Felon #7 was the boss of an organization dealing in illegal waste disposal. He was indeed a giant of a man, but since being brought to the administrative center, forced to wear a filthy hotel robe, and subjected to half a day with the guards, he was now as meek as a wether. He had tried to sign the document, but since the skin on both his hands was split open, he found it difficult to hold the pen. The assets he was forfeiting were scattered in numerous accounts (more than ninety million yen in one, thirty million dollars in another), along with nearly a billion yen in stocks and bank debentures and a collection of antiques that included swords, porcelain, and scrolls.

Ri Hui Cheol, the deputy commander, had decided that owing to the complex legal procedures involved, real estate would be exempt from confiscation. Furthermore, given Japanese public opinion in this regard, the family members of the felons would not be held culpable. This had rankled with Choi, for when a crime, whether political or not, was committed in the Republic, the punitive net was spread over three generations. Both Colonel Han and his deputy insisted that as the Japanese wouldn't understand such a practice, regarding it as retrograde, it would cause needless hostility to apply it. Choi and his fellow commando Kim Hak Su had both expressed contrary opinions, but they were overruled. The purpose of the three-generation principle was not simply to inflict collective punishment and to reinforce the ruling system through fear, but to encourage people to respect and understand the importance of their ancestral lines. The idea that the occupiers, the KEF, should give any consideration to the feelings of the occupied was incomprehensible to Choi.

Felon #6 was being given a bandage for his finger, which had been crushed in a vice. A Korean resident of Japan, he had served as an official in the Republic-affiliated Chongryon, the General Association of Korean Residents in Japan, while running a string of pinball arcades and companies producing and selling fake European designer handbags. Having speculated in the Republic's currency before revaluation, he was now suspected of tax evasion. At the time of his arrest at a swank condominium, he had invoked the name of a high-level member of the DPRK Worker's Party and said in a threatening tone: "Do you know what'll happen to you for this?" Since the party official's name was quite well known, the other Special Police officers had hesitated for a moment. Choi Hyo Il, however, walked straight up to him and slammed his fist into his shoulder, breaking his collarbone. This resulted in Choi's being reprimanded by the deputy commander, Ri Hui Cheol. It was the Fukuoka police who were responsible for arrests, with the collaboration of the KEF; the exercise of force other than in self-defense was to be avoided. The Fukuoka police had provided a total of eight mobile armored vehicles and were supplying drivers and ten uniformed officers to participate in the arrests.

Choi could understand why physical force should be kept to a minimum but objected to the very idea of working with the Japanese police. His maternal grandfather, he'd protested, was murdered by the Japanese during the occupation. This kind of cooperation made no sense to him. Lieutenant Pak Myeong of the operations section had explained that by involving Fukuoka police personnel they were heading off any attack by the Japanese Self-Defense Force or the local US military, and further pointed out that by making the Japanese authorities primarily responsible for arrests, they were demonstrating to the Japanese public that the KEF was serious about establishing "a mutually beneficial relationship." Choi apologized to the deputy commander for having resorted to violence while making the arrest, but in his heart he was still unhappy about the matter.

Once Fukuoka was subdued, the Japanese police should have been disbanded and all its members punished. As a child, he had often heard his grandmother describe the events of August 15, 1945. The first thing liberated patriots did was attack police stations and kill the Japanese officers. She said that the entire village had stormed the local police outpost with farming implements, singing Korean songs as they went. The police were seen as the frontline agents of imperialism and the direct oppressors of the people. Choi had been taught since infancy that the Japanese police chiefs were worse than even the inhabitants of the puppet regime and the Americans who ruled them. For him, the police were emblematic of Japan. Why should he be cooperating with them?

Having ascertained how the interrogations were going, he left the parking lot and ran up the emergency stairs. In twenty minutes, at 13:00, he was due to lead the KEF's afternoon operations. He heard a scream from the detention center below and thought: *Fool. Screaming won't make the pain go away.* He remembered the first stages of *gyeoksul* training, back when he was a recruit in the 907th Battalion. The other recruits would whimper in their beds every night after the ordeal of plunging their hands again and again into bean-filled buckets. His own way had been to silently endure it all, in the belief that suffering would ultimately be transformed into strength. He'd been born in a farming village near Tongchon, Kangwon Province, where his parents grew vegetables on a plot of land that overlooked the sea. His paternal grandfather had been a hero in the Great Liberation War, serving as a member of the Anti-Aircraft Corps in defense of the capital. His parents had also been well respected and had been granted by the Party a house where Japanese had been billeted during the occupation. It was the sole building in the entire village that had a tiled roof.

But near the river on the outskirts of the village, in a place where the sun barely reached, was a settlement of undesirables. These people, some three hundred of them, lived crammed together in a collection of dilapidated tin-roofed buildings that reeked like animal cages. They received the scantiest of food rations and no medicine or medical care. Both adults and children were virtually naked, and would lean against the back wall of their dark, doorless shacks, staring outside. Though the young people were timid and quite listless, they were known for thievery and other crimes. One day when he was twelve, Choi had seen a few of them cutting and stealing some telephone wire. The ringleader, afraid that Choi would report them to the authorities, hit him on the head with a hand tool of some kind, nearly killing him. In due course, the culprit and a crony of his were arrested and executed by firing squad in the town square. Choi found this public event exhilarating. Fired at close range, the bullets from the automatic rifles tore the heads of the condemned right off, sending bits and pieces of their faces flying. He was impressed by the sheer power of the steel bullets, in contrast to the softness of the human body. Once the shooting was over, the officer in charge told the spectators to stone the corpses. The adults drew back from the sight of the pulverized heads and body parts, but Choi came eagerly to the fore. The head of one corpse shook as though it were still alive when a fist-sized stone he threw struck what was left of the face.

Choi graduated from secondary school and joined the army, where, having proved more than usually competent, he was selected for the 907th Battalion. At the age of sixteen, he was already over 1.8 meters tall and was learning taekwondo from his father. Basic training presented few problems for him, as he had hardened his body in high school through long-distance swimming. Both his parents and the Party leaders taught him that pain is a blessing, not something to be avoided but rather faced and accepted. When his nails first fell off as the result of *gyeoksul* training, the softest breath on his fingers made him wince, and when the bandages were taken off, it was all he could do to keep from fainting. And yet there came a time when, as though by magic, the pain eased. After being sent by the army to the Kim Jong Il Political-Military University for Japanese-language instruction and sabotage training, he asked a doctor there about it and was told that when part of the body is repeatedly injured, substances are dispatched in massive amounts to block the pain-transmitting nerves.

The People's Army taught that when an enemy grenade landed in a trench, one's first reaction should be to pick it up and throw it back, the next best thing being to kick it into a drainage ditch. If neither move was possible, the nearest soldier was to throw himself on top of it, the aim being to minimize casualties. Training exercises included learning to fall full-length on dummy grenades. Choi had often heard stories about how during incursions in the South, platoon leaders had sacrificed their lives to save their men by acting as human shields. Into the left breast pocket on his uniform was sewn a teabag-like pouch, containing gunpowder. All he needed to do to ignite the tiny fuse was to tear off the button, and the explosion directly above the heart would cause instantaneous death. The device had been handed out to participants in the Kyonggi Bay operation, and there were only a few officers who carried it now, even among those of the 907th Battalion. To Choi, it meant that even at the moment when a man had to end his life, pain could be transformed into strength.

Choi went to see Lieutenant Jang Bong Su at the provisional command center; he needed the list of felons, as well as other relevant materials and arrest warrants. The offices were dense with cigarette smoke. Most of Han's subordinate officers were smokers. It occurred to him that a tobacco supply must have arrived. In the Republic, a man couldn't get by without cigarettes. They were even used as currency in the provinces. It had been just two days since the KEF, with the cooperation of local officials, had opened accounts in the city's three regional banks, in the name of certain philanthropic groups and dummy corporations. The stocks and bonds of the five who had already agreed to the confiscation of their property had been converted into liquid assets totaling seven hundred million yen. The day before, this had been made available in yen notes. The complex task of transferring the confiscated wealth to KEF accounts was in the hands of Ra Jae Gong, whose experience in managing part of the Comrade General's secret funds and in dealing with overseas financial institutions was most useful. The impounded assets were first sent to foreign banks, where they were turned into various forms of securities before being funneled through other banks and finally reappearing as yen deposits.

One of the first purchases made, apparently, was a truckload of Seven Star cigarettes. When the stacks of boxes were unloaded, there were shouts of excitement from the troops—including the women, none of whom smoked. In the Republic, the Japanese brand had a special aura about it. There was hardly a man in the entire KEF who had ever smoked the genuine article. Chinese counterfeits were in circulation, but outside the hard-currency shops in the major cities, they were unavailable. Moreover, a single pack cost what a buck private earned in six months. On seeing Choi, Jang tossed him a carton containing ten packs, as though throwing a dog a bone. "I can't pay for them," said Choi. Jang handed him a lighted cigarette and said with a laugh: "You can owe me, then."

The soldiers of the KEF were to receive a monthly salary in yen now, the amount varying according to rank. Food and clothing, along with Japanese-language materials, notebooks, and other writing things, were free of charge. Except on special occasions, the consumption of alcohol was forbidden. Neither were KEF personnel allowed to leave the occupied areas or to enter adjoining hospitals and places selling consumer goods. Thus, almost the only item on which they could spend their money was cigarettes. The women would no doubt save their entire earnings.

On one side of the banquet hall that was now serving as provisional headquarters, Choi could hear Japanese being spoken. Figures in suits of gray or navy blue were on the telephone, perusing and stamping documents as they spoke. These were officials on loan from the Fukuoka City Hall. The eight of them, including one woman, had arrived forty-eight hours before, at the direction of the mayor. Their job was to arrange for necessary transport; negotiate with banks; purchase food, cigarettes, clothing, and medical supplies; and secure reliable sources of fuel for MAVs and other Special Police vehicles. They were all astonishingly cooperative. They had bargained for price reductions on bulk sales of cigarettes and searched out inexpensive rice supplies. Rice harvested two years before was found to have been stored in the warehouse of a distributor who was then persuaded to sell it for next to nothing. In keeping with the recently issued joint declaration, municipal officials had given KEF officers and enlisted personnel Fukuoka local resident-register numbers, making them de facto citizens and thereby authorizing them to open bank accounts and sell stocks and bonds. There had not been the slightest bureaucratic opposition to this; on the contrary, in their dealings with the young KEF leadership, the Japanese had shown themselves to be both honest and efficient. At the moment, in fact, one official was speaking with a local disposal company. "There's nothin' dangerous about it!" he was saying in the local dialect. "I'm sittin' here with the Koryo folks right now. And I guarantee you, all fees will be paid prompt and proper." More significantly, these city officials had covertly played a major role in exposing criminal activity, using their authority, the city's financial clout, and human network connections to provide ongoing information regarding persons rumored to have squirreled away ill-gotten gains. Some of the officials argued that building living quarters for one hundred and twenty thousand newcomers would spur the local economy, and that using these funds to pay the labor force would be putting dirty money to good use.

Yet why were Japanese civil servants in general so eager to cooperate with the occupying forces? This had been a topic of discussion at breakfast today. Jang had suggested that playing up to those in power was part of the national character. Choi declared that the Japanese put on a submissive front to lull their adversaries into a feeling of trust, only to turn the tables on them later. Jo Su Ryeon had a different opinion, arguing that such meek behavior, however strange, was not peculiarly Japanese. Hostages, for example, come to sympathize with their captors; those held captive during bank robberies wind up falling in love with the robbers and even wanting to marry them. It was all, he claimed, part of the same phenomenon. When human beings are forced into life-and-death situations, they instinctively try to curry favor with those who control their fate and, in turn, cultivate positive feelings of their own toward their masters. "What about soldiers?" asked Jang. "Soldiers are of a different breed, set apart by military rules and regulations." Choi couldn't remember ever having had a discussion like this, and he felt strange as he ate his *jumuk bap*—rice balls stuffed with tinned sardines. His face was flushed and his pulse a bit fast, but it wasn't anxiety. It was not unlike the ticklish feeling one has on seeing a newborn baby. "I feel funny," he had frankly admitted. "Liberated, maybe?" said Jo with a smile. "We can't talk like this in the Republic, can we?" At home, pro forma, morale-boosting discussions took place in which the nation's leaders and the Comrade General were praised, and questions about how to advance their causes were raised, but free, wide-ranging debate on specific topics was unthinkable. That was because of the ever-present possibility of being denounced. "Liberated?" Choi scratched his head. "I don't know. I don't really understand it yet," he said. Jo and Jang had both laughed and said they didn't either.

"This is the man you'll be taking charge of today," Jang said. He handed over documents providing a name, address, occupation, and photograph, together with a printed map and an arrest warrant signed by their commander. The target was Kuzuta Shinsaku, a sixty-three-year-old resident of an upscale apartment building and a former member of the prefectural assembly. He now owned dozens of affiliated shops selling fishing and camping gear, but behind the scenes, through connections with Chinese gangs, he dealt in unauthorized drugs, rare animals banned from import, and transplant organs. Kuzuta had already been notified, with the warning that if he attempted to flee or go into hiding, criminal responsibility would fall on his family. As of that morning, the KEF had taken ten people into custody, but despite being told that the police were on their way, none of them had gone on the run. The fatal shooting of the henchman of Maezono Yoshio, Felon #2, had had a sobering effect, along with the threat of retribution against family members. Word had also been put out that anyone who aided or hid a would-be fugitive would be taken to the detention center, and this too had been persuasive.

Kuzuta, Choi was informed, was not at home but at a restaurant called the Hanazono—"Flower Garden"—situated in Ohori Park. The second floor, it seemed, had private rooms that were named after flowers, and in one of these, the "Pansy," Kuzuta would be waiting. Kuzuta was apparently concerned that his ailing mother, who was close to ninety, might die of shock if the police or the KEF came to his own place. His resident code revealed that his mother, who was being treated for a circulatory disease, was indeed living with him. The restaurant was located only a couple of minutes from his apartment. "His mother, is it?" Choi muttered, accepting the inevitable but not at all happy that they wouldn't arrest Kuzuta at home as planned. There was no particular reason for this, except that from ingrained habit he tended to be wary of any unexpected change. But regarding the elderly woman's condition, he felt sympathetic, as did Jang Bong Su. For men of the Republic, one's mother was a central figure, and an undutiful son was held in contempt.

Choi looked up at the sky as he left the hotel. Early in the morning there had been some drizzle, but now the sky was cloudless as far as the horizon, and the air was fresh. The shortest way from the hotel to the camp was through the group exit and across a broad four-lane highway. There were, however, next to no vehicles entering or leaving the area occupied by the KEF, so that the road was as quiet and deserted as the streets of Pyongyang at night. He knew there was little danger of a sniper attack, but the prospect of crossing the empty thirty-meter-wide thoroughfare in the open was still sufficiently unpleasant to make him take a detour through the front gate of Fukuoka Dome. From the banquet hall that served as the temporary command headquarters, he'd gone to the lobby, passed through the row of shops, and walked out. As he walked along the perimeter of the Dome, he could see well-aligned rows of green tents, between which drainage ditches had been dug to prevent them getting rained out, giving the entire camp area the appearance of a regularly patterned garment, or an elaborate wiring diagram.

The tents were arranged in a horseshoe shape, in the center of which was a large pavilion, the camp command station, along with an open assembly space. Here and there were places equipped with cooking stoves and simple chairs where soldiers could eat and intermingle. At the foot of the stairs leading down from the Dome was a sentry. There were twelve more guards inside the Dome itself, with sentries lurking at strategic points in the shopping area. It was hard to believe that only nine commandos had managed to infiltrate and occupy the stadium, but the sight of smoke drifting into the clear sky from various sites provided Choi with a vivid reminder of their accomplishment.

The empty land the KEF were camped on had originally been a park, and there were still three drinking-water facilities where the supply not been turned off, since the pipes through which the water was pumped were shared by the hospital, the hotel, and the Dome as well. Fukuoka's water was not only easy on the palate but there was no need to boil it—it was ready to drink from the spigot. To Choi this was an indication of sheer economic power. In his home village there had been a river in which killifish, eels, and soft-shell turtles swam. The water was so clear that, as a child, he could see the moss at the bottom, and it had tasted as sweet as nectar. But at about the time he graduated from People's School, a zinc factory was constructed in the middle reaches of the river. Then, with the collapse of the Republic's economy, electric-power shortages, and the lack of replacement parts for deteriorated machinery, the sewage-disposal equipment broke down. Eventually, poisonous effluents seeped into the river, and crooked-backed, ghastly looking fish, along with headless eels, began to appear. People living downstream went on eating the fish and drinking the water, and soon they too had crooked backs. Afflicted with nerve damage and other strange and alarming symptoms, they dropped like flies. On his return visits, Choi would listen as his mother tearfully told him of the horrible end of these local people, their faces twisted, foaming at the mouth, howling things that made no sense.

The campground was filled with the smell of kimchi, red peppers, and dried fish, as numerous columns of smoke rose into the air. The KEF troops had apparently just finished lunch. Scattered here and there, half buried in stone-lined holes, were stoves made from lidless oilcans, punctured for ventilation, on which perched canteens, cooking pots, or wire mesh for roasting meat and fish. Now, on the third day since the camp was established, the puffs of smoke and steam attested to the growing stability of life here. The young soldiers were in a jaunty mood. "Hey," someone called out to Choi, a broad smile on his face, "how about letting me help you nab those criminals?" This was Captain Heo Jip, commander of Squadron 4 of the 907th Battalion, an army doctor and chemical-warfare expert. It wasn't known whether Heo's special squadron was equipped with chemical weapons brought from the Peninsula. "You want to put me out of a job?" Choi called back, and the men around him laughed.

He crossed the campground, heading toward the Special Police tent halfway between Checkpoints A and B. The tents were flapping loudly in the sea wind gusting through the open space between the hotel and the Dome. Behind the tents was the hospital, a huge building that resembled the Pyongyang Children's Palace. In both scale and equipment, it laid claim to being the best appointed in Kyushu. Blank-faced patients were staring out of the windows, leaning on crutches, sitting in wheelchairs, or clinging to mobile IV stands. They seemed to be dressed in thick, padded robes that resembled the Russian *telogreika* jackets in the Republic. By contrast, the soldiers in the field down below were in T-shirts, and those washing their uniforms at the laundry site were bare to the waist. To these men, who back in their homeland had broken ice on wintry streams and lakes to wash their clothes, Fukuoka in April was like a southern health resort. The soldiers had all received new T-shirts this morning, along with two pairs of underwear and socks, from Kim Hyang Mok,

314

the female lieutenant assigned to the logistics and supplies section. It had apparently been no easy task to acquire one thousand plain white cotton T-shirts, but with the assistance of City Hall, she had placed an order with a proprietor in the shopping area adjacent to the Dome. Each of the American-made Gap products was wrapped in plastic, the shape of the T-shirt and pants indicated by means of a simple picture. In the Republic, only Olympic athletes wore such things, as the men must surely have known.

And yet they made no move to break open the wrapping to extract the contents. They merely stared at the pictures and letters, their expressions suggesting they had no idea what to do with it all. It took some time for them to grasp that this was now their own personal property. When Kim Hyang Mok had repeatedly informed them that they were to keep what she had distributed, one soldier at last poked open the plastic, took out his T-shirt, stripped to the waist, and gingerly pulled the garment over his head. Surprised at how comfortable it felt, he kept fingering the texture with both hands, a childlike grin spreading on his face. The man next to him did the same, and gradually the circle grew, like milk spreading through tea. From out of this T-shirted ring came the voice of someone saying that the soft, snug fit was like a mother's embrace.

At the regularly scheduled meeting, the question was raised whether, after the surprisingly inexpensive T-shirts, underpants, and socks had been acquired, there were any other clothing items that could be made available, such as "American trousers," long- and short-sleeved shirts, training wear, jackets, and sneakers. Kim Hak Su, however, was strongly opposed. Yes, the KEF uniforms were crude in both feel and design, and they neither absorbed sweat well nor provided adequate protection against the cold. Yes, there were uniforms that were more than twenty years old, constantly resewn and patched on the outside, while falling apart on the inside. And though the lace-up boots were solidly put together, their hard and heavy leather made them unsuitable for everyday use. But he insisted that more than a matter of comfort was involved; uniforms embodied the discipline those wearing them were subject to.

Kim went on to describe the unprecedented situation in which the People's Army had found itself over the past decade. Perhaps some of those present, he said, as privileged members of the Special Forces, were unaware that discipline throughout the 1990s had fallen remarkably. The cause was the extreme shortage of food, the changes in the rank and promotion system, and the substantial increase in the time soldiers were expected to spend in agricultural tasks. The Comrade General had decreed that the armed forces should be self-sufficient in non-staple food, and so every infantry company had its own farm and was raising livestock. From generals to NCOs, all were obliged to spend most of their off-duty hours tending to fields and fodder. And as they carried out this work, they dispensed with their uniforms, thereby blurring rank distinctions. When the corporals passed by generals, they failed to salute, and this became habitual. Uniforms were essential to discipline; the wearing of jeans and jackets by KEF troops would undermine and destroy order. Colonel Han Seung Jin had no alternative but to concede this point. It was decided that for the time being only T-shirts, socks, and underpants would be acquired, but it was also agreed that with the arrival of the Eighth Corps troops a local company would be asked to produce new uniforms and boots.

An incoming garbage truck was at Checkpoint A. In the morning there had been another round of negotiations between the City Hall representatives and the disposal company, and perhaps they had come to an agreement on the collection fee. The five hundred troops were producing a huge amount of waste, which was being buried in unused land between the hotel and the Hii River. Already the smell of rotting vegetables and fish had been leaking out, and if nothing was done, a breeding ground for contagious disease would result. The guard demanded identification and looked over the body of the vehicle, but none too closely: what potential attackers would risk coming disguised as sanitation workers to take on the entire camp? The men slept in four six-hour shifts, so that at any time of the day there were more than three hundred and fifty of them ready to repel a surprise attack. Nearby was the hospital, and to the south was a residential area, making the use of missiles, trench mortars, or aerial bombardment impossible. Assault helicopters were also out of the question, as the KEF had a dozen shoulder-launched surface-to-air missiles.

No matter what sort of attack it might be, rooftop spotters would detect it, instantly warning the troops to prepare to respond, with some then moving to the hospital grounds and others farther south. The content of official talks between the US Armed Forces Command Headquarters in Japan and the US Secretary of Defense had been released the previous night, noting that there had been no hostile action in Fukuoka, no civilian casualties, no looting or rape, and no reports of a breakdown of order. The Japanese government had expressed displeasure at the assessment that conditions were not such as to require or justify American military intervention, but no one there was advocating that the Japanese Self-Defense Force engage with the KEF; nor was that at the present time the opinion even of right-wing pundits in the media.

Choi was now next to the camp's command station, approaching a group of seven engineers who sat in a circle on the ground. When they noticed him, they all leapt to their feet and stood stiffly at attention, the blood draining from their faces. On the ground three magazines lay fluttering in the breeze. They were Japanese magazines with photographs of girls, some in swimsuits, some naked. Choi picked up the magazines and asked the men where they had obtained them. It seemed they'd come from the drivers of the buses and taxis that had been commandeered to transport the troops after their arrival at Gannosu. Knowing Choi's reputation in the battalion, the men stood there cringing, biting their lips.

Soldiers from other sections gathered around. Choi leafed through the magazines. All three had photographs, articles, and cartoon drawings, and two featured nudity. On a page entitled "Big-Boobed College Girls Series 5," a smiling young woman was shown standing on the street with her sweater pulled up and her breasts exposed. The caption read: "Ms. W.T., a second-year student at the same

317

university that produced Prof. S., last year's winner of the Nobel Prize for chemistry, has bravely bared herself for us… Sorry about that, Professor S.!" In the Republic, not even a prostitute would expose herself like this. One of the other magazines showed a girl with a caption reading: "Bomb-Boob Idol." She was on the sandy beach of what appeared to be a South Sea island, splashing about in the waves as naked as the day she was born. What could the caption mean? The combination of the two Chinese characters made no sense to him: how could "bomb" and "breast" go together? Choi pondered the question but found no answer, though he supposed that the implied comparison was to hand grenades. He looked up and saw dozens of soldiers standing around him.

What punishment should be meted out? Choi was at a loss. Back at home, the men would be sent to a *kwanliso* simply for being in possession of such things. He wanted to ask Jo Su Ryeon for advice, but it wouldn't look right. If he just laid into the men, he'd put them out of action for at least a week, and every able-bodied soldier was needed at a time like this. On the other hand, if he overlooked the offense, it would weaken discipline and might have political consequences. He spotted Choi Rak Gi of the logistics and supplies section in the crowd, and called out to him. The warrant officer approached, came to rigid attention, and saluted.

"Tear out seven of these obscene photographs and have these idiots hold them up in front of their eyes!" The NCO did as he was told, with a look of incomprehension on his face. The culprits, who had quickly formed a line in front of him, took the torn photos and, in obedience to a bellowed command, held them up with outstretched hands, as though in an ideological session. Curious to know what was happening, more soldiers came to watch. The seven engineers looked as if they might be reading poetry extolling the Comrade General. "For the next two hours," Choi ordered, "they are to stand there without budging, eyes glued to those photographs."

He then turned to the troops that had gathered and threw what was left of the magazines at them, one at a time, shouting: "Look!" The men recoiled and turned away. "Pick them up and look!"

Choi shouted again in a voice that seemed to shake every tent in the camp. He seized one of men by the neck and pulled him to the ground. "Pick it up!" The terrified soldier obeyed. Two of his companions scooped up the other pair of magazines and gazed at the pictures.

"This is a cesspool you've stepped into," Choi said softly, looking at the men with their eyes on the magazines. "Filth like this will always be lying in wait for you, ready to trap and corrupt you. You've had a glance. If you want more, you can do as these fools are doing. You understand? Don't forget! It's as addictive as any drug. Lots of you were given truth drugs as part of your training in ways to endure interrogation. Well, what you see here is just like scopolamine! If you're weak, it'll seep into the cracks in your brain no matter how hard you resist. Take one step outside the campground and you'll find yourselves up to your necks in smut. You can't escape it. It's there to test your strength. But we are here as part of a grand endeavor to create a new country, and there is no room for weakness! When you find photographs like these, or other such examples of soul-corrupting sludge, don't keep them hidden, and don't turn away. I want you to fix your eyes on them and know: *this* is Japan. It's the evil that runs in this nation's veins. We are soldiers of the proud 907th. We don't run from evil. We stand up to it." So saying, Choi glared at the engineers once again, then left them to the warrant officer.

Between Checkpoints A and B was a narrow pedestrian bridge, at the foot of which was a guard post—a one-man, sandbagged bunker covered with camouflage. Ten meters beyond was the Special Police tent. Choi paused here for a moment and looked back at the scene he'd left. The crowd of onlookers had shrunk, and no one was jeering or laughing. The engineers still stood in a row, with the warrant officer, staff in hand, slowly circling them. Choi couldn't shake off a sense of gloom. Incidents like this were bound to reoccur, and it wasn't just a question of dirty pictures. The T-shirts under the men's uniforms had a different feel from anything they'd worn in the Republic. The water didn't taste the same; neither did the rice.

319

The world beyond the control zone was awash in everything the photographs symbolized, a world that the men of the KEF, including himself, had never encountered. What effect it would have on them was something he couldn't predict.

In front of the tent, Choi's aide for the day, Warrant Officer Tak Cheol Hwan, had already lined up his men prior to setting out on their round of arrests. Tak was from Kapsan, Ryanggang Province, and had just turned twenty-four. He and four others would be accompanying Choi. Twenty-two-year-old Warrant Officer Ra Yong Hak, a crack shot, was from Kanggye, Jagang Province. The other three were first sergeants. Song Pa Ui, reared in a village at the foot of Mount Myohyang and trained in the chemical-warfare corps, and Kim Kyeong Gu, a Pyongyang native who had been slated to compete as a boxer in the Olympics, were both twenty-one; while Kim Han Yeol from Kaesong, North Hwanghae Province, who'd been transferred to the 907th Battalion from the Air Force, was twenty-two. These men were embarking on their eighth raid, but Choi never allowed his people to let down their guard. Whatever their previous experience, the operation involved serious risks.

Two MAVs next to Checkpoint A had already started their engines and were waiting to move. On first seeing one of these, Choi had been struck by the tires, with their rows of little rubber spikes and deep grooves. The People's Army too had armored personnel carriers, but all their treads were well worn. Of the eight MAVs that the prefectural police had provided, four were being used by the Special Police; the rest had been redesigned by the KEF to replace loudspeakers and searchlights with double-barreled 14.5-mm machine guns, 30-mm autocannon, AGS-17 infantry-support automatic grenade launchers, and AT-4 anti-tank launchers. Diesel fuel for the MAVs was secured at a gasoline station to the south of Checkpoint C. The station, with its seashell logo, was located near the puppet regime's consulate. Its proximity to the control zone having effectively cut off sales, the managers had been on the verge of abandoning the area when City Hall workers prevailed on them to provide fuel for the KEF.

Tak Cheol Hwan was informing his people and the prefectural police officers that there had been a change in the arrest site. The Japanese cops reacted to the announcement with little more than puzzled looks. With each sortie there were new faces among them, and on their first encounter with the KEF they were invariably on edge. Tak added that the procedures and points to note remained the same, then confirmed who the MAV drivers were and checked the map of the Ohori Park area. In his off-duty time he'd been boning up on his Japanese, mostly in the dim lamplight at the camp command station, and he hadn't slept more than three hours during the last three days. The prefectural police boarded the vehicles. Their faces all looked the same. None of them had any distinguishing features or facial expressions, and they didn't talk or do anything. An accompanying *Asahi Shinbun* reporter stood next to one of the MAVs, bowing in greeting to Choi Hyo Il. This reporter had arrived late for yesterday morning's mission and as a result had been denied permission to cover the story. Acknowledging a request filed the evening before, however, the propaganda and guidance section had reinstated him, taking into consideration the fact that he represented one of Japan's biggest newspapers.

The MAVs left Checkpoint A and slowly rolled through the control zone, with Fukuoka Dome to their left. Guards stationed on the campground's perimeter waved as they passed. Seeing the Special Police springing into action lifted the morale of their fellow soldiers. To the right of the MAVs lay the already full outpatient parking lot for the five-story, steel-frame hospital. Jo Su Ryeon had twice visited the hospital, with a municipal worker as his go-between, and met with its representatives to offer assurances: the KEF would not be a hindrance to their usual routine and would provide all possible cooperation and assistance. The issue of ID checks on ambulances was resolved when the hospital spokesmen declared convincingly that they would never condone any undercover plot involving emergency vehicles. "Our duty," he explained, "is to cure illness and save lives, not to carry out acts of aggression against you."

Across from the hospital was a major shopping center. Choi had never been there, but he'd been told by the logistics and supply section that it consisted of endless rows of shops in multiple, interconnected halls. In the middle, there was supposedly a toy store as spacious as a gymnasium. Kim Hyang Mok of the logistics and supplies section had said that the sheer number of items in it made her head spin. "You could gather all the toys in the Republic and still not match it," she'd added with a wry smile. Until the day before yesterday the shutters had been down, but now, except for restaurants and pubs, all the shops had been open since noon. Since hearing of the big purchase of T-shirts, other traders and shopkeepers were eager to establish contact with the KEF. On the right, beyond the shopping complex, was Checkpoint C. There the MAVs made a brief stop for verification of their orders. Around the checkpoint were piles of sandbags with machine guns poking through. The guardhouse of the southern puppet regime's consulate had simply been commandeered, as had that of China's consulate at Checkpoint B.

They were now entering a residential area. They passed a Buddhist temple, a small park, houses, low-rise dormitory-like apartment buildings, a hardware store, a pharmacy, and the kind of shop known as a "convenience store," operating into the wee hours, and when they finally came to the end of the street they turned left at a traffic light into a boulevard as broad as a small aircraft runway. Running below it was a subway line that apparently went as far as the airport, and they passed subway access points at regular intervals. Both the subway and bus systems were operating, and pedestrian and vehicular traffic was heavy here. But all traffic parted with the appearance of the MAVs. No sirens were wailing, and yet cars and buses in both lanes slowed, pulled over to the curb, and stopped. Pedestrians too came to a standstill, staring. Choi saw people spilling out of the shops, and cyclists following the MAVs, some even taking photographs. And now suddenly a media helicopter was hovering above them. Whenever he saw films about the Great Liberation War, Choi was particularly drawn to the scenes showing officers of the Liberation Army riding through the cities of the South in jeeps.

And at university he had admired Nazi German documentaries that depicted members of the SS and the Gestapo parading in Kübelwagen and tanks down the streets of countries they'd come to occupy. The mere presence of an invading force was enough to alter the whole landscape.

"Are you of the opinion that the local citizenry understand and are sympathetic to the series of arrests you've been making?" The question came from the *Asahi* reporter, and Choi thought it a foolish one. Did he think the KEF was some sort of peace delegation? A humanitarian service? Conquerors don't think about whether the conquered have "understanding" or "sympathy with" the actions they take. Their only concern is the means whereby control can be achieved most efficiently. If preserving life is more efficient than annihilating it, then that is the policy; if annihilation is more efficient, then so be it. The only reason this dolt with his half-assed questions was still alive and along for the ride was that a massacre would undoubtedly cause international disapproval and retaliation from the US forces stationed in Japan. Choi wanted to bellow this at him in just this way and then break his jaw, but he managed to keep his temper and responded with a question of his own. "What do *you* think of what we're doing?" he said. "I think those being arrested are all *kyoaku*," the reporter replied. Choi didn't know the word but gathered that it was a compound written with the characters for "giant" and "evil," suggesting great power in the hands of wicked men. The man seemed to be saying that, as those being taken into custody all met that description, many Fukuokans applauded their arrest.

Choi turned to his aide Ra to review how to use their mobile phones, and the reporter ended his questioning. Even though Choi had not replied to his question, he was busy scribbling away in his notebook. Incredibly, he looked quite excited, like a schoolboy going on a picnic. He now put his notebook aside and, holding onto an overhead strap and pushing a lock of hair out of the way, peered out through the gun port, a faint smile on his face. He was tall and lanky, with the blank look of a moron. If, as Choi had heard, the *Asahi* was Japan's most influential newspaper, why had they sent this fool along? He spoke no Korean, for one thing. The older reporter from the *Nishi Nippon Shinbun* had quite a good command of the language, and though he looked like a rural postman, he posed the stickiest of questions: the legal justification for the arrests, for example. Once the additional troops had arrived, the KEF would have the personnel to establish a full-fledged occupation government. In the meantime, questions about the legal basis for the various measures being taken were to be avoided.

The *Nishi Nippon* reporter had gone along for the arrest of Felon #2, a local gang boss named Maezono Yoshio whose sidekick had created a tense scene by brandishing a shotgun at the NHK cameraman covering the story. Tak Cheol Hwan had responded instantly by blowing the top of the man's head off. The newspaper journalist had written a story arguing that it was a case of justifiable homicide, intended to ensure the safety of the cameraman. This had been taken by the KEF as useful propaganda, and yet at the same time it represented a potential danger. At the end of the article he mentioned the view held in some quarters that while those detained had undoubtedly broken the law, attention must also be given to what laws were being applied in their arrests and how they were being treated thereafter, and that the public should refrain from giving uncritical approval simply because malefactors had been brought to justice. Although the writer had cleverly hedged that this was not his own opinion but rather of others unnamed, it was felt at headquarters that if he didn't voluntarily submit to re-education at the hands of the propaganda and guidance section, he should be placed on the list of those to be arrested as political subversives once the main force arrived.

Ohori Park was full of people enjoying the weather. The sky was cloudless, with a pleasant breeze bearing the scent of flowers from shrubs growing here and there, and the sounds of birds. The parking lot too was full, with four large tourist buses lined up end to end. The peanut-shaped lake was so big that, standing on the shore, one couldn't see the other side; on its surface, the radiant sun had formed a broad band of light, and there were bevies of ducks and swans, and rowboats bobbing about. Around the lake were a walking and jogging course, a children's park, an art museum, and a garden. At the water's edge, the sunlight was particularly dazzling, and many of the visitors were using parasols. A number of people, perhaps members of a hobby club, were hunched over pads and easels as they sketched or painted the lake and the bridge. Instead of entering the parking lot, the MAVs headed toward the restaurant where Kuzuta said he would be and came to a stop there. Several dozen gawkers remained on their bicycles some twenty meters behind. A helicopter was overhead, the word MEDIA painted on its fuselage in large letters.

The park visitors were startled by the sight of the MAVs. Through the broad windows on the first floor, diners in the unreserved section of the restaurant looked out and gasped, some rising from their seats. Women pulled their babies and children closer to them. Restaurant employees too were pressed up against the windows. Strollers and joggers came to a stop, and those absorbed a moment ago in their easels and sketchpads paused in their work. They all knew that inside the gray MAVs were members of the KEF, and that their job was to carry out the arrest of major criminals. Thanks to dramatic, repeatedly broadcast television footage, it was widely known that an arrest the previous day had been accompanied by a fatal shooting. This was not to Choi's liking. Panic could easily have unexpected consequences.

He first communicated by radio telephone to Tak in the other MAV to tell him to stay put for the time being, and to have him inform NHK via headquarters that the helicopter must leave the area immediately. Choi then stepped out of the rear door of his own MAV, taking only his aide, Ra Yong Hak, with him. The two were immediately met with excited murmuring and stares from the crowd of onlookers, who showed no sign of withdrawing. Choi had a good look around, then squinted up at the sun as he stretched his back, waiting for the helicopter to move off. In due course, it headed away from the lake in the opposite direction. When the sound of the rotor blades had grown faint, he turned to the crowd and greeted them in Korean: "*Annyeong hashimnikka!*" A few of them awkwardly returned his greeting. Clasping his hands behind his back, he approached the group of sketchers and painters. There were about a dozen of them, mostly senior citizens. The person who appeared to be their leader was a bearded man wearing a brown leather vest and a beret.

"Nice weather," Choi remarked, looking up at the sky. He reminded himself not to smile, knowing it might only frighten the man. "I also like to draw and to paint," he said solemnly. "This is such a pretty place. We have something similar in my country. There we also have a zoo and a botanical garden. On holidays many, many children and families visit there." The man in the beret told him that this place was called Ohori Park. "Ah, yes," Choi nodded gravely, then pointed toward the middle of the lake. "Quite a long bridge, isn't it?" he said. The elderly woman next to him looked away from her easel and replied, paintbrush in hand: "It isn't just one bridge, y'know—it's four little ones connected to three little islands." She then proceeded to give him the name of each bridge and island. She had to use her hand to shield her eyes from the sun as she looked up at him, but she maintained a calm and dignified expression all the while. She was wearing a floppy, broad-brimmed hat and a thin, brownish-gray cardigan. On her canvas she had painted waterbirds resting on the surface of the lake. "I understand. Thank you," said Choi with a bow. "You will excuse me now," he added, bowing to the others as well, and took his leave. They followed him with their eyes as he returned to the MAV but soon went back to their pencils and paintbrushes. People in the park and even the restaurant had been watching nervously, but when the exchange ended in a peaceful way they all seemed to relax and resumed whatever they'd been doing.

Choi quietly opened the door of the MAV and told the men to get out. He then called Tak again and ordered him to wait there in the second vehicle. He was quite sure that his team could handle the job alone. Putting the five Japanese policemen in the lead, he and

Ra slowly proceeded toward the restaurant. Kuzuta had deliberately chosen to be arrested at this public spot, out of consideration for his mother, and was probably waiting alone. The people in the park seemed to have accepted the KEF's presence and the fact that an arrest was about to take place. The *Asahi Shinbun* reporter had asked if he could go with them to Kuzuta's room, but Choi refused. The rear door of the second MAV opened, and Tak leaned out, looking his way. The gawkers had been edging forward, pushing their bicycles, but the MAVS blocked their view of the restaurant, and they began migrating to a better vantage point next to the parking lot.

The building containing the restaurant was quite big, with shops on both sides for souvenirs, presents, noodles, ice cream. To the left of the building stood a boat-rental outlet, where there was a small dock and paddleboats rocking in the breeze. The helicopter was circling some distance away. Choi looked back and sensed something in his line of vision that bothered him. He saw Tak peering out of the rear door of his MAV; the pouting *Asahi* reporter next to the first MAV with a camera in his hand; the vehicles in the parking lot to his left; the onlookers, whose numbers had now grown to more than a hundred... Something wasn't right, but he couldn't put his finger on it. He used his phone to call Tak and reminded him to stay on alert. The passageway leading to the second floor was in the back, to the left. Choi opened the door and sent the Japanese cops in first.

The private rooms were rather exclusive, it seemed. A notice attached to the side of the entrance politely stated that only customers with reservations were to proceed. Inside was what appeared to be a waiting room. A heavy chandelier, the electric lights of which were in the form of candles, hung by a thick chain from the ceiling. There was a leather sofa, and farther inside was a small bar, closed until dinnertime. "This way," came a sudden voice from upstairs. Choi and Ra looked up to see a waiter dressed in black. "Mr. Kuzuta is expecting you," he said in a weedy voice. The Japanese cops went ahead up the stairs. The wooden stairway was brilliantly polished, the handrail elaborately carved. On the walls were framed photographs of VIPs and celebrities who had dined here. Choi's eye lingered on the most prominent of these, showing a formally dressed Caucasian couple with glasses raised in a toast, the caption indicating that it was the United States Consul General and his wife. To the west of the park was an upscale area with rows of luxury condominiums. The US consulate stood on a plot of land just to the south of it, though the building was now empty, the diplomats and their marine guards having all been evacuated to Tokyo.

They reached the top of the stairs and entered a fan-shaped, second-floor hall with a wide balcony looking out on the lake. The balcony had a scattering of chairs and tables shaded by colorful parasols. Clearly this was a favored location for the rich to enjoy a meal with a full view of the water. Choi had not noticed the balcony before, but of course he'd entered the place from the opposite side. The floor of the hall was covered in thick carpeting, and in the middle was an enormous, black, sectional sofa arranged around a glass table. On the walls were built-in mirrors that seemed to double the dimensions of the place, and potted tropical plants were everywhere. The rooms themselves had been so arranged that each offered a view of the lake. The waiter pointed to the "Pansy" room, its name inscribed on a golden plaque. One of the policemen knocked. "Just a moment," came the reply, and shortly the door opened. A small man in a brown jacket appeared. Comparing his face with the photograph, Ra confirmed his identity.

Kuzuta's forehead was beaded with sweat, and he kept nervously licking his lips. One of the Japanese cops made a small show of extracting an arrest warrant from his pocket. The waiter had already disappeared. Choi motioned to Kuzuta to move back as he stepped in, followed by the others. Kuzuta was clearly terrified of him and avoided eye contact. The room was perhaps forty meters square. In the middle was a long dining table made of thick oak, with chairs placed around it, and in the corner was a brick stove. The sheet-glass windows faced the balcony and, beyond, the lake. The blinds had been raised, so that the entire room was filled with the dazzling reflection of the sun on the water, and the balcony appeared to be suspended in a white haze. As Choi came in, Kuzuta seemed to lose whatever was left of his composure and sank into one of the chairs. "Get up!" snapped the cop, and immediately began reading from the arrest warrant: "Kuzuta Shinsaku, you are under arrest on suspicion of illegal drug sales and the illicit sale of human organs." He hauled Kuzuta to his feet and took out a pair of handcuffs.

Why, wondered Choi suspiciously, were the blinds not lowered against this dazzling light? And at that instant, the glass burst inward and air poured in. He spun in a crouch to face the broken window and saw a metal cylinder, like a soft-drink can, rolling over the floor toward him. *Grenade.* He threw himself down on the object without a moment's hesitation, just as it exploded. His body formed the shape of an inverted V, and the room reverberated with the deafening roar. He felt as if sirens were screaming in his head. On his retinas the reflection of the lake appeared as a million suns that expanded until they formed a field of brilliant white, and he could see nothing more. His vision was gone. He couldn't feel his own body, and didn't know if he was face down or flat on his back. Where was his head? Where were his hands and feet? Which way was the window? The door?

He was about to lose consciousness and tried to bite his tongue to prevent that but couldn't tell his tongue from his teeth. He felt like a shapeless blob of flesh. *This is the room Kuzuta was in. There's been an attack.* He tried to tell Ra to call for backup but couldn't remember how to form words. Was Ra even there? He heard something, faintly. Like people trying to talk over the noise at a construction site. They were speaking Japanese, saying "Get down! Get down!" But who were they? And why was he still conscious, and not splattered all over the place? Choi Hyo Il wasn't dead. He smelled burning sulfur. The percussive blast, the flash of light—they'd attacked with a stun grenade. Why? Why not use a real one? Gunfire resounded in the room. The dry, staccato sound of a sub-machine gun. Volleys of bullets ripping through the air in every direction. Ra must be shooting it out with the enemy. Now the voices were shouting again: "Don't shoot! We need them alive!"

It was the buses, of course, those four tour buses with their curtains closed! He'd known something was wrong back there. The enemy had been hiding inside them. Special Forces from the SDF? Would the SDF use stun grenades? He could hear screams and groans. Voices were shouting: "Don't shoot! Don't shoot!" But why? Why not shoot? Weren't they the enemy? He felt people touching him. Then gunfire again, but farther away, outside the building. Rifle shots. Sub-machine guns. Bullets ricocheting off concrete and metal. The screams of many, merging into one. What was happening? Had Tak called in reinforcements? It would be impossible to take on four busloads without more people. The gunfire outside continued, and he could hear it more clearly now. Sounds of desperate wailing, and of breaking glass. A whirring sound that grew gradually louder: a helicopter?

He heard a voice close to his ear. "Grab him by the armpits. Stand him up. Hurry." He could tell that his body was being manipulated, and then, suddenly, he was aware only of acute and terrible pain. It entered from the surface of his body and seeped inward, until it reached the core of his being, which reacted with rippling convulsions. The pain ran through every part of him and then came to concentrate in one particular spot. This spot narrowed to a point, and then it exploded once again into a million suns radiating outward and ending in that brilliant, glittering expanse of white light. The pain gradually defined for him the outlines of his body. It was as if this blob of flesh were trying to create a shape for itself, with tapering spurs emerging and differentiating as head, body, limbs. The way a lizard regenerates a severed tail, he acquired an arm, then a wrist, a hand, and finally fingers. He tested those fingers, forming a clenched fist, and tried to move his arm. Below his waist he now had thighs, knees, feet. From out of the white light a shadow appeared—a tremulous, oscillating sunspot.

He tried to move his right hand. It was slimy, as though he were covered in oil. Shadows appeared in the sparkling whiteness that filled his eyes. They were moving about, their number increasing. Like sediment settling in a glass, images began to take shape at the lower edges of his field of vision. He moved his fingers to see whether he still had his AK and Scorpion, but both were gone. Jagged streaks of lightning slashed through his head. He could see nothing with his right eye, and what he saw with his left looked as though it were filtered through a night-vision scope, but even coarser and more distorted. Outside, the shooting and screaming continued. Who was firing, and who was getting hit? He was lifted off the floor and turned over on his back. It felt like the skin of his abdomen was being peeled off with sharpened sticks. Again he convulsed. An oval shadow appeared before his eyes; something within the oval was reaching toward him. He opened his eyes wide, first the right, then the left. With one, he saw nothing; with the other, the same watery darkness, with flashes of lightning that delivered bursts of intense pain. He was brought to his feet, and now he could see his stomach, bare of both clothing and skin, the burned, reddish-black muscles exposed. A body was lying in front of him, its torso torn to shreds, and there was blood, as though dumped from a bucket. He could just make out what appeared to be a blue uniform. Was it Ra? Others were lying there, but whether they were his team or the enemy, he didn't know.

He was dragged out of the room. All around him were dark, shadowy figures: in the hall and at the head of the stairs. Dozens of them. Before him was a large mirror, which seemed to contain a different world. He saw a man held up by two dark figures. The man's clothing was in tatters, and his raw, reddish-black belly and burned genitals were in full view. Who the hell was that? Choi had once gone to a concentration camp in mountainous South Hamgyong Province in the company of a member of the Politburo, at whose request he killed a political criminal with a blow to the chest. "You have a reputation for your *gyeoksul* skills," Choi was told. "Let's see if you can really stab somebody with those hands of yours." The prisoner who was brought before them was wearing rags that left him virtually naked, his genitals drooping down beneath lice-ridden pubic hair. To refuse or hesitate to carry out the act would have been an offense in itself. "This creature's been condemned as a traitor to

331

our Comrade General," the Politburo member told him, his face red with drink. "It's subhuman scum, and deserves no more sympathy than a maggot." He laughed and added: "Or do you sympathize with maggots?" It was the first time Choi had ever plunged his fingers inside a human being. He was surprised how hot it felt.

That subhuman was there in the mirror now. It was the same man. The image of that criminal scum was looking back at him and laughing: "You and I are just alike now. Look at you. Your smashed eye, your skinned belly and genitals..." The dark figures were dragging him toward the stairs, and the man in the mirror was slipping away. "No!" Choi shouted, forming a blade with his right hand and trying to twist away from those holding him. "I'm not like you!" he bellowed. The shadowy figure on his right let go, and the one on the left said, "Hey! What's going on?" Just below what appeared to be the head of the speaker was a narrow pale spot that must be the throat. With all his remaining strength, Choi drove his fingertips into that spot. He heard a strangled howl, as though from a dying dog. He had missed the larynx but scored a hit nonetheless: the tips of his fingers were warm and sticky. The shadow staggered back, still howling. "Son of a bitch!" someone shouted, and another shadow stretched out an arm and shot Choi in the knee.

He started to fall but was again held up by his armpits, and then his legs were being hoisted up in front of him. "Get him out of here! Out!" His right leg was bloody and bent at an odd angle, but he couldn't feel it. He wondered what damage he'd inflicted: it wouldn't have been fatal, but the bastard's windpipe was surely crushed. *I'm a man*, he told himself. *I'm not scum.* The whirling ceiling shifted to clear sky. He was outside. The gunfire ceased as if on cue. He could feel the wind from the blades of the helicopter directly overhead, and he heard a thin, weeping wail, like a mournful Western hymn. The first-floor windows of the restaurant had all been destroyed; bodies were strewn about in front of the place and along the paths. Torn scraps of canvas and sketch paper danced around in the wind. The four buses began rolling this way, with more shadowy figures walking alongside them. Peering past the parking lot, he could see that another MAV was coming. So Tak had indeed managed to call in reinforcements. The backup MAV was armed with thirty-millimeter autocannon. It rolled over fallen bicycles as it approached, crushing them like bugs. Why had the shooting stopped? Why wasn't the MAV turning its guns on the buses? It was toward those buses that he was now being carried, on the shoulders of the shadow people. *Hostage*, he thought. *They're taking me hostage.* Could he move his right hand? The left-side pocket of his uniform was still there. A dead hostage wouldn't do them any good. With a groan he reached toward his chest, looking for the button on the pocket. He found it and wrapped the thread around his index finger. He was about to pull it, when a strange image floated up in his mind. It was of the dog inside the gate at the house of the felon Maezono. A black dog with shiny fur and an elegant, slender face, its legs and body sleek and supple. Why was he thinking of it now? Such a beautiful animal. Choi pulled on the thread with all his might.

# 5

# SPIRIT GUIDES

*April 6, 2011*

M ORI LOOKED AT HIS WATCH. What was keeping them? It
was six minutes past noon. He and Toyohara had left their
bicycles in front of a convenience store on a corner in Odo, just at
the west end of Atago Bridge. They were lurking in the shadow of
a fat concrete pillar that supported the overhead Route 1, peering
east across the river and down Yokatopia Avenue. Felix had been
monitoring the police band and said that the Koryos were heading
for Odo and would be arriving at the *danchi*—the old public-housing
apartment blocks—at noon. They should be passing through here
any minute now. Mori had elected to do some surveillance these past
few days, having both the time and a bicycle, but no one showed
much interest in his reports. Toyohara went along because he had a
bike too, not to mention a pair of binoculars, which he was holding
now in such a stranglehold that his hands were trembling and the
tips of his fingers had turned white.

The North Korean troops were camped out near the high-rise hotel
and the Dome. They called themselves the Koryo Expeditionary
Force, but everyone in the Ishihara group referred to them as the
"Koryos"—an abbreviation Ando had first used and everyone liked:
it had a satisfyingly mocking feel. The Koryos had begun airing a

daily thirty-minute public-relations program on NHK Fukuoka TV, featuring a female news anchor interviewing the "propaganda and guidance officer" Jo Su Ryeon. On today's show Jo had announced that barracks for the incoming reinforcements would be erected on vacant reclaimed land in Odo and other sections of Nishi Ward. "Bidding has already been completed, and construction will begin immediately," Jo said with a smile, adding that the project would help stimulate the economy of Fukuoka. He also politely emphasized that any aggression toward the new arrivals would result in retaliatory measures being taken in Tokyo and other cities throughout Japan. The program began at eight-thirty in the morning, and NHK affiliates throughout Kyushu carried it live. Those outside Kyushu, however, regarded the show as propaganda and simply provided summaries of the content during their regular news programs.

Jo also laid out specific charges against the "criminals" who had been arrested, explained the shooting at Daimyo 1-Chome and the incident at Ohori Park from the Koryo point of view, and spelled out their vision for the immediate future. He guaranteed free economic activity but insisted that ordinary working people would be given special consideration; he censured the Japanese government's continued blockade of Hakata Bay as a hindrance to crucial trade with China, South Korea, and Taiwan; he announced a willingness to admit UN inspectors to the occupied zone in Fukuoka as soon as the time was right to do so; and he promised that the South Korean, Chinese, American, and other consulates would be reopened soon with extraterritorial rights according to international law. Jo's TV appearances made him the best-known of the Koryos. He was particularly popular among Japanese women for his handsome features, cogent explanations, and smooth speaking voice. Even the NHK anchor selected to interview him blushed whenever he looked directly at her.

When Mori had first seen Jo, he'd wondered how someone of the same species could be so different from himself. Mori was round all over and resembled an owl. His face was as soft and puffy as freshly baked bread, and his eyes, nose, and mouth were like half-buried

raisins. Jo's cheekbones wouldn't have looked out of place on a
Grecian statue; the skin covering his facial bones and muscles was so
taut and smooth that it might have been flesh-colored plastic wrap.
And whereas Mori's eyes were like pebbles embedded in wet sand, Jo's
were as sharp and clear as mountain pools beneath a cloudless sky.

For the time being, the additional hundred and twenty thousand
troops were to be billeted in the Odo *danchi*, as well as in abandoned
houses and a shut-down elementary school in the neighborhood. The
north side of Odo had once been heavily populated, but residents
had moved away as the recession dragged on, and a typhoon a few
years ago had pretty much finished the place off. Now it was a virtual
ghost town. The Koryos had purchased the entire neighborhood
from the City of Fukuoka and accepted bids from private contractors to reconnect and repair the water, sewage, electricity, and gas.
The work was to begin this afternoon, and Mori and Toyohara were
awaiting the arrival of the Koryo engineering corps.

Toyohara trained his binoculars on the far side of Atago Bridge. He
was a beefy lad with short limbs and a shaved head, and wasn't the
sort of person you'd expect to own precision optical equipment. He
looked as if he were trying to extract a pair of dark tubes from the
center of his face. The German-made binoculars were the oversized
type you saw dangling from the necks of generals in old war movies.
The metallic parts had a dull, dark patina, the surface of the leather
case was cracked in places, and the strap had been repaired more
than once with leather of slightly different hues. Mori wanted to peer
through the glasses but didn't know how to go about making that
happen. He wasn't familiar with the notion of "sharing." The only
thing his older brother had ever shared with him was the wrong end
of a knife, after using it on their parents when Mori was in middle
school. Neither had there been any sharing at the orphanage he'd
been placed in later. The stronger kids, and the ones whom the
nurses and attendants liked, monopolized all the toys and books.

Just before falling asleep, or whenever he closed his eyes to block out
the world, Mori always saw one of two scenes: the common room at

the orphanage, or the playground there. The interior scene consisted of children playing with blocks or engrossed in video games while he himself sat alone at the window, looking out. In the playground scene, he sat alone beneath a poplar tree while the other children tossed Frisbees, kicked balls about, and skipped rope. Something had always separated Mori from objects of amusement like blocks, video games, Frisbees, or soccer balls—something much more difficult to overcome than mere distance—and the concept of lending or borrowing possessions was one he couldn't even begin to grasp.

Toyohara pried the binoculars from his eyes. Whether because of nervous tension or because he didn't know his own strength, he always seemed to use more force than necessary when holding things—his fingers turned chalk-white when he gripped the handlebars of his bike as well. He now noticed that Mori was staring at the binoculars, and he looked from them to him and back again. "These were made in Germany," he said. Mori nodded and said, "I know"—this being the fourth time Toyohara had told him.

He thought there must be some sort of story connected with the binoculars. He was interested in old things and liked reading books about history and bygone cultures. He wanted to quiz Toyohara about them but didn't know exactly how to go about it. They're so cool—did someone give them to you? They look old. When were they made? How close does, like, the Sea Hawk Hotel look from here? Questions like these occurred to him one after the other, but they quickly got all mashed up in his head. He sensed that the moment he said anything aloud his enthusiasm would get all tangled with self-doubt, and he wouldn't know how to continue. So he said nothing.

He'd never had an actual conversation with Toyohara. Together they had chased after the Special Police on each of the two previous days, but in spite of all they'd witnessed they had scarcely spoken. Big things had happened—especially yesterday. A lot of people died, the Koryo officer blew himself up, and the MAVs' autocannon shredded four buses, right before their eyes. And yet the pair had barely exchanged three words all day. Of course, there had been a lot of excitement and confusion—not to mention bullets whizzing through the air—but he and Toyohara hadn't discussed it even after returning.

Toyohara stared at the binoculars in his hands, then peered at Mori for some time, and then at the binoculars again. Finally he looked up at Mori with a troubled face. Mori thought he probably wanted to let him look through the things but didn't know how to make the offer. Toyohara was half a head shorter than Mori, who was only 1.65 meters tall, but the muscles bulged on his broad shoulders and barrel chest, and his arms and legs, while short, were as thick and sturdy as logs. Ishihara often called Toyohara "Hulk," after the Incredible one. He was also extraordinarily hairy. Long black hair sprouted from his shoulders and the nape of his neck, he had a solid unibrow, and he was furry down to the second knuckles of his fingers and toes. On closer inspection, you discovered that he also had the face of a baby, but what you noticed first and remembered always was the physique and the body hair.

Toyohara had been a sickly child who'd suffered from infantile tuberculosis. His parents lived in Tokyo, but he was raised at the home of his paternal grandfather in Saga Prefecture, to the south-west of Fukuoka. His grandfather was descended from the ruling family of the old fiefdom of Nabeshima and served as the postmaster in a small country town. He was a proud man with a feudalistic outlook, and Toyohara was given the strictest of upbringings. The boy was forced to learn kendo and once had his head cracked open with a wooden sword. As a sixth-grader, he saw the animated series *Cuore: Three Thousand Leagues in Search of Mother* and decided it was normal for a child to want to track down his own mom, so he bought a platform pass and sneaked aboard a bullet train for Tokyo, but was soon caught and booted off. The next day he again boarded a bullet train, this time carrying one of his grandfather's antique samurai swords, in what essentially became a hijacking. The first conductor who tried to subdue him was run through with the blade. Toyohara extracted it with some difficulty, then attempted to behead the corpse. After defeating an enemy, one was obliged to remove his head, hold it up for all to see, and proclaim victory—at least according to the samurai code his grandfather had always instilled in him. Toyohara both respected and hated his grandfather, whom he called "Pop-Pop." He thought the old man would praise him for cutting down the offending conductor, but in fact he never so much as spoke to him again. It hadn't occurred to Toyohara to wonder whether his grandfather's tales of the Warring States were still applicable today. And he still couldn't understand how something that was good five hundred years ago could be bad now, or why the same behavior that made you a hero in war could make you a criminal in society. But then, those things didn't make sense to Mori either. Toyohara had arrived on Ishihara's doorstep bearing one of the very finest swords in Pop-Pop's collection.

The sky was cloudy over Yokatopia Avenue. The weather forecast had said the wind would be unusually chilly even for early April, but Toyohara was wearing a garish Hawaiian shirt, cotton shorts, and flip-flops. The shirt had red, yellow, and green skulls on it and was big enough to accommodate his broad shoulders but hung down to his knees, hiding the shorts, so that it looked more like a muumuu. Toyohara dressed like this even in midwinter, his body temperature being warmer than most people's. Mori was wearing a size XL blue shirt, jeans with a forty-inch waist, and a black nylon jacket that was much too small for him. He'd bought the jacket at an outlet in Kashii for exactly three thousand yen, including tax. Medium was the largest size they had, and he couldn't even zip it up, but he'd bought it anyway because the clerk said it looked good on him. He couldn't help noticing that people entering and leaving the convenience store nearby gave him and Toyohara a wide berth.

The sound of distant rotors grew louder, and a helicopter appeared above the Sea Hawk Hotel. Painted large on either side was the legend NHK FUKUOKA. The Koryos had announced that they would shoot down any helicopters flying over the hotel or encampment other than ones belonging to NHK or the Fukuoka-based newspaper *Nishi Nippon Shinbun*. "Here they come," Toyohara said and put the binoculars back in their case. The cars on Yokatopia Avenue all pulled over to the shoulder to make way, and the traffic lanes, which had been jammed with vehicles of all sizes and colors, were suddenly clear in both directions. Whenever the Koryos' armored vehicles appeared, an electric tension seemed to charge the air. Mori loved that moment. An MAV mounted with two machine guns materialized around a gentle curve in the road. Behind it was a microbus, and beyond that you could just make out another MAV. The NHK helicopter was hovering at a considerable distance behind the vehicles.

Toyohara pushed his bicycle out of the parking lot and got on it. It was the type popular with housewives, with a basket on the front and no crossbar, but the seat was too high for his short legs, so he had to pedal standing up. Gaining speed, the bike leaned left-right-left as his bottom swayed right-left-right. Mori straddled his bike as well. He would have liked to get a closer look at the MAVs, but it would probably be best to get back indoors before the Koryos reached the *danchi* complex. The Odo *danchi* weren't far from the warehouses occupied by the Ishihara group, and it was no time to be drawing attention to themselves. Today Takei was going to distribute the firearms. They'd been told to report to the Living first thing in the afternoon. Mori couldn't wait to get his hands on his own weapon, and wondered what kind it would be.

Takei had kept the weapons hidden in the basement of Building G, and in order to avoid being seen, he'd transferred them all to Building C under cover of night, with four helpers to do the actual carrying—Kaneshiro, Hino, Yamada, and Mori. Takei was nearsighted, farsighted, and astigmatic, and since he wasn't wearing glasses and there was no light above the door it took him for ever to open the various locks. At no point did it seem to occur to him to hand the keys to someone else, however. The interior of Building G, which had originally been a clothing warehouse, was thick with dust and smelled of mildew. Filaments of cottony stuff billowed up in little clouds at their feet, and after only a few steps Hino stopped and doubled over, wheezing, from some sort of allergic reaction.

The weapons were stored in the innermost room in the basement, an area of about thirty square meters. It was pitch dark until Kaneshiro switched on a flashlight. Against the far wall were stacks of cheap suitcases. Mori and Yamada pulled one down and set it on the floor, and Takei bent over to open it, wriggling in anticipation. "Look!" he said. "Look!" Inside were three long, flat metal cases and five oilpaper-wrapped packages about the size of hardcover books. Takei lifted one of the metal cases, put it on his knee, and opened the lid. "It still blows me away!" he said. The stock and barrel of the rifle were silvery in color, while the trigger and other movable parts were made of black steel. Mori swallowed his breath. It was the first time he'd ever seen a real gun close up. Yamada said "Whoa!" and bared his big rabbit teeth. "It's beautiful," Hino breathed, and reached out to touch the barrel, but Takei slapped his hand away. Kaneshiro said, "Let's start hauling the stuff," but Takei just took the weapon out of its case and stared at it dreamily. He then looked up at Kaneshiro, Yamada, Hino, and Mori in turn, with a Cheshire Cat smile. It looked like a recumbent crescent moon in the wavering beam of the flashlight.

"This," he announced without losing the smile, "is the legendary Dragunov." Takei had dyed his hair brown to look younger, but everyone said he was forty-eight this year. He had a vacant sort of face—one that was difficult to focus on. When he was standing beside a wall, regardless of the color of the paint, he seemed to melt into it and disappear. He wasn't particularly ugly, but the outlines of his face and body were somehow fuzzy and indistinct. He was about to attach the magazine and scope to the Dragunov right then and there, but Kaneshiro put his foot down, saying there was no time for that. Takei, Kaneshiro, and Mori carried the three flat metal cases on that first trip, and Hino and Yamada the oilpaper bundles.

Mori rode his bike up the sidewalk beside Marina Avenue, then through the shabby residential district of Toyohama. To his left, across the street, was an elementary school. It was the middle of the lunch hour, but the school bells suddenly rang out with that nostalgic *bing bong bang bong* melody and a voice came over the loudspeakers: *Attention all students. Return to your classrooms at once.* The lulling sound of the chimes seemed out of place amid the agitation caused by the approaching MAVs. Most of the students obediently migrated toward their classrooms, but some ran in the opposite direction, toward the front gate, where they'd have a good view of the street. People were getting used to the vehicles and their peculiar diesel rumble, and no one ran away when they approached now.

A lot of people had died at Ohori Park the day before, and NHK had run endless repeats of the shoot-out footage. It was a bird's-eye view, shot from a helicopter, and though it showed several deaths, many of the more gruesome things Mori had seen on the ground were omitted—like heads and limbs being blown off and bullets turning a child's body to bloody hamburger. Nonetheless, it had had an enormous impact. No one had ever seen footage of Japanese citizens being mowed down, other than in war documentaries of more than half a century ago. But the city government had yet to issue any instructions or notices. They didn't even warn people to stay away from the armored vehicles but merely kept advising that it was best to exercise caution when encountering "any potentially dangerous situations." Nor had the schoolyard announcement a moment earlier stated why everyone should return to their classrooms. Telling people not to go near the MAVs might seem adversarial, and apparently that was to be avoided at all costs.

Clerks and customers alike were pouring out of the convenience store, the post office, and the neighborhood shops to get a closer look at the MAVs. Some smoked, some drank cans of fruit juice, and some chattered excitedly with friends, lining the roadside as if for a parade or a marathon. If the citizens of Fukuoka weren't afraid, in spite of the tragedy at Ohori Park just the day before, it was because they had watched that tragedy unfold on TV and knew exactly what had happened and who was really to blame.

Just after one o'clock in the afternoon of the previous day, two officers of the KEF Special Police and five Fukuoka prefectural policemen had entered a building together to make an arrest. Some minutes later there was a loud explosion on the second floor. When four Koryo police from a separate squadron ran toward the building, a volley of gunfire erupted from four tour buses in the parking lot. It was all filmed from the NHK helicopter and witnessed by a large number of bystanders, and it was clear that the first shots came from the buses, which had been Trojan-horsed with members of the Osaka Prefectural Special Assault Team. One Koryo took a bullet in the neck and went down like a puppet with cut strings, all but decapitated by the shot. The remaining three took cover and returned fire with rifles and machine guns. Visitors to the park panicked and scattered in all directions. A ricocheting bullet shattered the glass of a restaurant window, and customers dashed outside, some running directly into the line of fire. If they had simply hit the dirt and stayed put, they might have been all right, but there was no such thing as a Japanese civilian who knew what to do in the midst of a sudden firefight.

The Koryos had promptly issued an official statement about the incident, to the effect that they were lodging a formal complaint against the Japanese government, protesting "this inexcusable act of naked aggression, which has resulted in serious injuries to civilians and members of the Fukuoka police as well as to our own personnel," adding that this time, and this time only, they would refrain from taking retaliatory measures. Koryo reinforcements had destroyed the four buses with autocannon fire, annihilating virtually the entire Special Assault Team. Many of the people in the park—Mori among them—had instinctively run toward the Koryos for cover, since the SAT had been the first to open fire, apparently with little concern about collateral damage. The entire incident only served to enhance the Koryos' image, increase the number of kids chasing the MAVs, and swell the crowds watching the public arrests. The Koryos had announced at their press conference that they would not interfere in any way with citizens who weren't hostile toward them. Now, ironically enough, thanks to the "pre-emptive" actions of the ultimately decimated SAT, they had gained credibility with the people.

Osaka prefectural police, for their part, issued a tortured statement explaining that their intention had been to detain KEF officers in order to extract information, that evacuating the park beforehand would have alerted the KEF to the plan, that the unexpected arrival of a second KEF squadron had endangered their men on the ground, and that they had lost control of the situation when the public panicked. The statement did little to stem the criticism from Fukuoka City, the mass media, and pundits who viewed the operation as "ill-considered." The chief of the Osaka prefectural police and a further dozen or more top officials accepted responsibility for the fiasco and resigned. The Japanese government announced that the operation had been planned by the Osaka police alone. The Chief Cabinet Secretary implied that while the idea of taking prisoners for interrogation was a reasonable one, the tactics employed were reprehensible.

But it was hard to believe that the prefectural police agency had acted on its own. The media and most of the populace suspected that the government had known about the operation in advance but forced the Osaka police to take the rap. Forty-six civilians had died, including six children under the age of thirteen. Only four survivors were listed as "injured." Ambulances had been late in responding, so even people with treatable wounds had bled to death or died of shock. Neither Fukuoka City nor the Japanese government had said a word about compensation for the victims.

Toyohara was heading home at full speed, his unseated bottom ticking left and right as he pedaled, with Mori following along behind. Mori's was a child's bike, but its five gears made it fairly fast. It had been rust-covered, with a broken chain and no tires when he found it, but Fukuda, Ando, and Felix, who were all mechanically inclined, had picked up spare parts here and there and helped restore it. There were lots of abandoned bikes around. Mori had once brought one home as a present for Yamada, only to find that he didn't know how to ride it.

In fact, about half of the Ishihara group had never ridden bicycles. Mori had stolen a bike from a parking lot and taught himself to ride the year before his brother freaked out, whereas Yamada had never even ridden one and hadn't even realized it was something you needed to learn. Most adults forgot how they learned to do it. Generally your parents or grandparents bought you a bike around the time you entered kindergarten, and you practiced on it with the help of others. Your friend or older brother or father held the back of the seat, and you kept trying, falling off again and again before you finally got it. Yamada was raised by parents who had no interest in him whatsoever, and he'd had no siblings or friends. But no one in the group had had an idyllic childhood; none of them had been taught cycling or swimming or other wholesome sports by their parents. Most had never even played soccer or catch.

Almost all of the houses Mori passed now lay vacant. Toyohama had been one of the earliest tracts of land to be reclaimed from the sea, and had fallen out of favor as newer developments sprung up. After its huge shopping mall went out of business, the neighborhood had quickly gone to hell. Row upon row of identical houses were squeezed together here like stones on a *go* board. He passed a toppled plaster statue of the Virgin Mary in a weed-choked garden; an old woman in bra and panties hanging clothes on a line to dry; a pile of empty liquor bottles spilling out of an alley; an empty bamboo birdcage swinging from a crooked eave; a family altar in a dark room with a big broken window; a concrete-block wall with torn and curling graffiti-covered campaign posters; a propane gas cylinder lying on the ground like a giant condom; a skinny dog attached to a short chain; a trampled carton of milk on somebody's doorstep, crawling with ants; a buckled, listing postbox decorated with a crude spray-painted vagina; children on a porch poring over a couple of comic books; children playing tag with someone's cap as a young mother in yellow sandals scolded them... These sights registered on his eyes as he pedaled past, but in his mind's eye he saw only the buses from yesterday, the ones that held the Special Assault Team, being shot to pieces with machine guns. He thought how awesome it would be if everything around here were blown to bits like that. The machine guns had made a sound that punctured the air and punched you in the pit of your stomach. He mimicked the sound and imagined the liquor bottles, the dog, the children, and the young mother all getting ripped to shreds by bullets.

Toyohara took a series of rights and lefts in an attempt at a short cut. Mori, bringing up the rear, continued straight on and lost sight of him from time to time. Since the streets were all more or less at right angles, there was really no such thing as a short cut, and shortly after Mori finally did turn, Toyohara reappeared right in front of him. Mori wondered where the MAVs would be now. The Koryos never ran them at full speed—he had followed every outing of the vehicles and was always able to overtake them on his bicycle. Presumably they were trying to learn the layout of the city and taking care not to cause any accidents.

The Koryos seemed to have given a lot of consideration to public relations, to avoid being disliked by the local people. It wasn't that they visited orphanages or helped old ladies across the street or weeded the parks, but they kept their encampment clean and sanitary and were invariably polite, so as to maintain the moral high ground. Jo Su Ryeon always bowed deeply to the camera at the beginning and end of each TV appearance. The criminals arrested by the Koryos were all figures of wealth and influence, for whom there was little general sympathy. And it was the Koryos who had transported the injured from Ohori Park to the Kyushu Medical Center, before the ambulances ever arrived. They also gathered up the victims' remains, wrapping them in thick vinyl sheets, and cleaned up the blood and gore. And that same evening, their commanding officer visited the hospital rooms of the wounded, with a bouquet of flowers for each.

Even before the explosion, a small incident in Ohori Park had made a big impression on Mori. A Koryo officer with a hard, scarred face had spoken to a group of old people who were in the park sketching. The interaction between the elderly citizens and the North Korean officer had been both unlikely and heart-warming. But, oddly enough, Mori couldn't remember it visually. He remembered that there had been some interaction, but he couldn't picture it in his mind. His memories of the events in the park were fragmentary and fleeting, like the brief glimpses he'd had of Toyohara pedaling along a parallel street.

The boarded-up shopping mall was visible ahead on the right. To the left, on the forested slope of a big hill, were a few scattered Shinto shrines. Shinohara, who raised frogs and centipedes and spiders in his rooms, collected ants to feed his creatures on the damp grounds of one of those shrines. Between the medical clinic and the elementary school was a convenience store where Mori often went with Yamada. Sometimes they'd buy a sandwich and a soda, then walk north to the water's edge, to eat looking out at the sea. On the way was a middle school and a McDonald's where members of the local Speed Tribe gathered, and farther along you came to a spot where the horizon opened up and the sea filled your entire field of vision.

Mori knew this area well and was able to picture all the streets. But his memories of yesterday in Ohori Park were piecemeal and disconnected, consisting of images that would leap suddenly into focus, like flashbacks. One of them was of an old man hit by a stray bullet, whose body seemed to swell up and burst. He'd been sketching, but squatted down on the ground the moment the shooting started, burying his head in his hands and wailing like a child. One of the Koryos ran right past him toward a ditch in which to take cover, and a bullet whizzed past the soldier and pierced the old man's back. Before he toppled over, the man's belly inflated for a split second and then burst in a shower of blood and intestines. When Mori talked about this, back at the hideout, Takei had said that SAT snipers sometimes used bullets with soft tips to make sure of a kill. The tip came apart on impact and sent a shock wave through the body, rupturing vital organs and leaving a gaping exit wound. The old man had been wearing a green vest of thick yarn. The bullet entered his back on a downward trajectory and exited at his groin. Internal organs, shredded by the shock wave and looking like dark red clumps of excrement, spilled from the hole beneath his belly.

\*

Toyohara left his bike next to the entrance to Building C, then ran inside and straight up the stairs. Mori followed close behind. They didn't lock their bikes; bicycle thieves wouldn't waste their time in a deserted warehouse district. Mori was completely out of breath, but the sensation wasn't unpleasant. He hadn't felt any pain when forced to run a marathon at the orphanage, either. Even when his legs began to cramp, he experienced only a vague sort of discomfort, and eventually both he and Yamada, running alongside him, passed out from oxygen deprivation. The doctor at the orphanage said that, astonishingly, they seemed to share a deficiency of the substance that stimulates the nerves to register pain. Mori and Yamada had subsequently tested this by choking each other, poking each other with safety pins, pinching each other's flesh, and so on, but the attendants and doctors found out and made them stop. Mori could feel heat and cold, and something close to pain in certain parts of his body—sometimes his head hurt, or his stomach ached, and when he went without sleep for a long time he'd feel a dull throbbing behind his eyeballs, but that was about it. It wasn't a question of faulty genes, the doctors said, but a psychological issue, which meant that at some point something might happen that would trigger the production of the proper metabolites. He was warned that unless and until that happened, however, he needed to take particular care of any flesh wounds, to make sure they didn't get infected.

Everyone had already assembled in the Living. They were all excited that the weapons were about to be distributed. Ishihara was in the rocking chair just outside his study, and Kaneshiro, Fukuda, and Takeguchi were standing in the center of the room. Fukuda and Takeguchi had apparently just finished making a batch of a new type of explosives they called "cookies." Ishihara, looking sleepy, leafed languidly through the vintage nude-photo book of a one-time porn actress. When he saw Mori enter the room, Yamada looked up through his black-rimmed glasses and said, "Welcome back." He had removed his black leather boots and was sitting on the carpet in cream cotton trousers, a pink shirt, and a beige jacket.

Yamada sometimes took part-time jobs. As bad as the economy was, whenever there was an opening at a sauna or massage parlor or love hotel, Yamada had no trouble landing it, for some reason. Mori had once gone to a massage parlor he worked at, lured by the promise of free entry. It was ten minutes before closing time, but Yamada wasn't at the reception desk. When a middle-aged Chinese lady came out, he told her he was Yamada's friend, and she led him back to a narrow, dimly lit room—scarcely more than a bed surrounded by curtains. Yamada, slathered in oil, was lying naked on the bed. His back shone crimson in the light of a bare red bulb. When he realized that Mori was standing there, the oil-sleek Yamada said, "Hey! You made it!" and gave him a rabbit-like grin. Yamada owned three suits he'd bought with money from his part-time jobs, and all three of them were beige. He claimed that one of the suits was from Italy, but Mori knew it was actually made in Honduras. Mori took part-time jobs as well sometimes—packing things into cardboard boxes or walking through the streets of the entertainment district in a sandwich board. Sometimes he got temporary work at a local bookstore. That was the best, because it gave him access to cheap books.

Toyohara gave his report: "Two mobile armored vehicles, each mounted with machine guns and autocannon, are about to arrive at the *danchi* in Odo."

As it happened, the plasma TV in the Living was showing a live shot of the two MAVs. They were already there on the *danchi* grounds.

"So you and Mori were poking around again?" Ishihara said.

"Yes."

The others all looked at them as if to say, "Oh yeah? You went again, eh?" No one had shown much interest in what the two of them had seen the previous day. None of them asked what it had been like in person. Not even Yamada had reacted much to Mori's accounts of all he'd witnessed these past two days. True, Mori wasn't very good at telling stories and, besides, the TV had shown nonstop coverage of the incidents. But he realized something from

349

Yamada's non-reaction, something that was true of himself as well. Neither of them had ever shared an emotion with someone else. When children experience happiness or sadness or are moved by a video or a picture book or something beautiful, they want to tell their family or friends about it. By telling others of our experiences and listening to others speak of theirs, we learn to share emotions—at least, according to a book Mori had found in the orphanage. He didn't know exactly what it meant to "share emotions," but he was pretty sure it had never happened to him.

Mori had grown up in a new housing development on the border of Tokyo and Saitama prefectures. His father had been a salesman for a real-estate company with headquarters in Tokyo, but the year after Mori was born the company went bust. What with the mortgage and tuition for Mori's older brother's private nursery school, the father was forced, when his unemployment insurance ran out, to take a job at a woodworking shop owned by an acquaintance in the neighborhood, and one day he lost the index and middle fingers of his left hand to a lathe. He had always been the silent type, but after the accident he barely ever spoke at all and eventually stopped leaving the house. Following treatment at a psychiatric clinic, he began working part-time at a neighborhood butcher shop, frying meat cakes and croquettes. Apparently the hourly wage for that was six hundred and eighty yen. Ever since Mori was a toddler his mother had repeated these words to him thousands of times: "Your father makes six hundred and eighty yen an hour." The family couldn't get by on what the old man was bringing home, so Mori's mother got a job at Mos Burger, and for a long time all the family ever had for dinner was meat cakes or chiliburgers. Both Mori and his brother grew up constantly hearing their mother remind them that she worked her ass off just so she could send them to private schools. Behind this ambition of hers was the fact that she herself had been tormented by her classmates in public schools. When Mori failed to be accepted at any of the private middle schools he applied to, his mother spent an entire night weeping and wailing that all her hard work and sacrifice had been for nothing, while his father, as always, sat silently drinking whiskey and staring at the wall.

At least Mori was aware of the fact that the concept of sharing was beyond him. But could a group of people who didn't know how to share really unite to fight a common enemy? When Ishihara named that enemy, the fighting spirit had been roused in all of them, but because there was no hierarchy in the group they lacked a proper chain of command. Boys like Mori and Yamada had ended up here precisely because it was a place where no one was forced to follow orders. They had all decided to fight the Koryos, but that was as far as it went. None of them had any experience of coming up with a plan and carrying it out by cooperating with others and delegating responsibilities. Not even the five Satanists had ever had a leader, or any particular plan; they had simply invented a story together and stuck to it, lying to the adults at every turn.

Mori wondered if this warehouse would be used as a base of operations for attacks on the new barracks in Odo once the reinforcements arrived. Set horizontally in one wall of Ishihara's room was a long, narrow window from which you could see part of the *danchi* grounds where construction was to begin. There were more than thirty apartment buildings, most of them abandoned. The only residents remaining were people too indigent or too old to leave, and their deaths often went unnoticed if they had no one to look out for them. But it was said that when the Koryo commanding officer came to look the buildings over, he was impressed and declared the apartments as good as those inhabited by high-level functionaries in Pyongyang. Most of them consisted of three small rooms and a kitchen-cum-dining area, and would apparently house ten soldiers each.

Mori felt that the idea of attacking the Koryos' own base was unrealistic. There was no way they could go head to head with these people. According to a military analyst on TV, the buses had been blown to bits by thirty-millimeter rounds fired from what were called autocannon—basically giant machine guns. You could see SAT guys staggering about inside, engulfed in flames. It was like a

351

special effects scene in a Hollywood movie. The buses shuddered and bounced as the rounds slammed into them, and in under a minute they were turned into skeletons of glass and steel.

Takei, who had spent half a year at a guerrilla-training camp in Yemen, had suggested a few different strategies. One was to attack the Koryo encampment with mortars, although there were no mortars on the list of items in his arsenal. He also suggested they use anti-tank missiles against the MAVs, but there were no anti-tank missiles on the list either. When Kaneshiro pointed out that it was no good thinking up strategies involving weapons they didn't have, Takei replied that real guerrillas captured the enemy's weapons to use against them. No one could see that happening, however. Fukuda and Takeguchi were preparing explosives, and Takei would distribute his stockpiled weapons to the group—only that much had been vaguely settled.

"Takei-san," Kaneshiro said, "just pass out the damn weapons, all right?" He was sitting on the big sofa, scowling impatiently. It seemed that Takei was determined to make some sort of stage show of the whole thing. Toyohara, Ando, and the five Satanists had been cast in it and were up on the third floor getting ready. Mori sat down on the carpet, along with Yamada and three others. The rest were sitting on the sofa or in armchairs. "Will someone go tell them to hurry up?" Kaneshiro said, and Ishihara glanced up from the photo book to say, "Don't get your knickers in a twist." He didn't seem at all curious about the forthcoming performance. But then, Ishihara could appear to be bored to death one moment and apoplectically excited the next. He was, to Mori at least, a complete mystery.

Kaneshiro, who was peering impatiently toward the top of the stairs, was about the same height as Mori but extremely thin, probably less than half his weight. He had a narrow little face, with small eyes, nose, and mouth. It was the sort of face Mori wished he himself had. You wouldn't call it handsome, but all the features were neatly arranged. There was something plant-like about him, and so self-contained that he was never tiring to be around. He didn't eat much, either. Once in a while you'd see him reluctantly nibbling on a protein bar. Mori, on the other hand, had always taken a lot of grief for his owl-shaped body and his doughy face. His father had been a bit overweight, but his mother and brother were both thin. After walking or running even short distances, Mori would have to stop awhile, wobbling and breathing hard. His wheezing was so loud that a teacher in elementary school had given him the nickname Steamwhistle.

"I want my weapon *now*," Hino was muttering. Matsuyama said, "I wonder what sort of gun I'll get," and Felix said, "I want one that doesn't weigh too much." Fukuda and Takeguchi were explaining their new explosives, the "cookies," to a small group gathered around them and saying that between these babies and the firearms, they could do something spectacular. The various little bombs were circular, oval, triangular, or star-shaped, and small enough to fit in the palm of your hand: they really did look like cookies. Takeguchi explained that they were made of a high-yield explosive called RDX mixed with wheat flour, baking powder, salt, lard, and water. He said that RDX wouldn't explode when exposed to an open flame, so that you could actually brown these cookies in an oven. "And eat 'em?" Tateno joked. "Definitely not," Takeguchi said. "They're extremely toxic and can induce epileptic-type seizures." The RDX in them had once belonged to the Iraqi military. It had been sold on the black market, and Takei's connections in Yemen had repackaged it as olive soap and shipped it to Japan. Takeguchi and Fukuda's laboratory was in the basement of Building E and was off limits to everyone else for obvious reasons—not that anyone wanted to go near the place.

Even Yamada seemed excited for once. "I've never even shot a *water* pistol!" he said, baring his big front teeth and laughing along with the others. He looked like a rabbit who'd just discovered a carrot and a female in heat at the same time. Hino and Tateno were laughing as well. Hino had a face like a stone-bodhisattva statue and rarely said anything at all, and though he sometimes flashed an embarrassed grin, Mori had never heard him laugh out loud before. The general excitement had a strange effect on Mori: it gave him a familiar feeling, but one he'd forgotten about since coming to Fukuoka—the sense of being left out. All the others were slapping one another's backs and talking about the weapons and laughing together, and though he wanted to join in he couldn't.

He was still having vivid flashbacks of Ohori Park. The iridescent windows of burning buses; the earthshaking booms of the autocannon; the *shoop* of a hot shell casing as it hit the surface of the pond; bullets pelting the ground like rain; the severed arm of a child, launched into the air by an explosion... Disconnected images bubbled up one after another in his brain. When one of the Koryo soldiers was hit in the right shoulder, leaving his arm hanging limply, he had quickly grabbed his pistol with his left hand and shot down a SAT guy coming in for the kill. The Koryos didn't grit their teeth or scowl or cry out but fought with the calm and dispassionate look of people working in a factory—or packing crates at Mori's part-time job. The speed with which they switched the magazines of their automatic pistols, the precision and efficiency with which they picked out some cover and ran for it—you'd have to have been there to believe it, Mori thought. You couldn't get the full effect just watching it on TV.

As he watched Yamada and the others whooping it up, his sense of discomfort only increased. Any crowd of people united in excitement scared him, but until now he had never felt this separation from Yamada and the other members of the group. Then again, the group had never felt this united before. Normally, if some of them got turned on watching a war movie or horror film, say, others would be indifferent or bored. Of course, there was something special about the focus of attention this time—actual weapons. The rifles Mori had carried from Building G had been heavier than the giant watermelons he'd unloaded at his job a couple of weeks earlier. Takei had unwrapped a pistol and allowed him to hold it. It weighed more than a laptop, and he couldn't hold it out at arm's length for longer than a second or two.

A gun was a hard, heavy, unfamiliar tool that Mori felt he would never be able to master. The Koryo soldiers, on the other hand, wielded their weapons freely and effortlessly, as if they were extensions of their own bodies. Once the battle was over, Mori had picked a spent rifle bullet out of the earth. The bullet had been flattened on impact into a compressed cone of hard metal. Mori pressed the cone firmly against the skin of his left forearm a number of times, but all it did was leave a small, reddish indentation. He was unable to imagine this little piece of metal bursting through the flesh, shredding muscle and bone, and creating a shock wave capable of rupturing internal organs.

At Ohori Park, Mori had learned that it was only in the movies that shooting someone would send them flying backward through a window or whatever. Bullets didn't lift people off their feet and send them through the air, they bored through the body at unimaginable speed. One of the four members of the Koryo police who ran to the building as backup was killed instantly when a bullet ripped through his chest and out his back. The one who'd been shot in the right shoulder had dived into a canal ditch to take cover, aimed left-handed at the SAT member who came running to finish him off, and shot him twice in the head at close range. This exchange took place just several meters in front of Mori, who was watching from the shadow of an MAV. The two shots were fired so rapidly as to sound almost simultaneous: *ba-bang!* The first one blew away part of the SAT guy's forehead and the second lodged in the center of his face. He stood there for some moments with his head partially pared away, moving his mouth as if trying to speak while blood and brain matter overflowed the wound and slid down his face, obscuring his features. He finally crumpled to the ground, but it seemed for ever before he stopped twitching.

Yamada was telling Shinohara about the handguns and rifles Takei had let him handle. "They're sooo cool," he said, his eyes shining and his front teeth on full display. It wasn't that Mori resented the others for whooping it up; he simply had the sense of being apart from something important. This wasn't a feeling he could consciously

355

dispel. When he was small, a sort of transparent barrier would suddenly descend around him, wedging him in so that he couldn't move. The first time it happened was on the bus to kindergarten. Riding the bus with the other children, he was seized with the distressing sense that he alone was separate from his surroundings and began to wonder if he was really even there. That doubt, once it had occurred, clicked with something ingrained in him as securely as one Lego piece connects with another.

It seemed to Mori the kindergartener that the doubt wasn't anything new, that it had always been lurking inside him, as a vague foreboding, before coming into full view, the way the scenery beyond a tree is revealed after an autumn storm. He knew it was ridiculous to doubt that he was actually there, on the bus with the other children. But then he remembered what happened at night, when he went to the bathroom. There was a mirror next to the toilet, and whenever he finished peeing and turned off the light, the Mori in the mirror disappeared. There must be some kind of switch that that could be flicked to make him disappear from the bus as well. What couldn't be denied, in any case, was that an invisible barrier now separated him from the others, and the barrier itself was impervious to the reality beyond it. It was terrifying. *Am I really sitting here on this bus with you? Can you really see me and hear my voice, or are you only pretending to?* He wanted to put these questions to the kid next to him but hated the thought of being taken for a nutcase.

Mori's heart was really pounding now. He hadn't experienced this feeling since becoming friends with Yamada and coming with him to Fukuoka. Why did it have to show up at a time like this? He believed that meeting Yamada had been ordained by destiny. Yamada was easy to be around—he seemed somehow less physically substantial than other people. Mori was pretty sure that if you cloned human beings in test tubes, they'd come out with faces and bodies and a general vibe a lot like Yamada's. His skin and muscles were spongy soft, and he had almost no hair on his body. He remembered seeing Yamada lying on the bed in the massage parlor, his naked back glistening in the red ceiling light. If he were to lose this guy, he'd probably never find another friend. Having someone else tattoo Mickey Mouse on their shoulder just wouldn't be the same.

"Hey, Mori." Ishihara was looking straight at him. "Hey, Mori the Ewok." He was sitting in his rocking chair in a pair of comfortable-looking linen pajamas. His pet name for Mori derived of course from the tribe of little owl-like beings in *Star Wars*. He held up a two-page spread from the vintage porn actress's photo book, raised his eyebrows, burbled an inscrutable "Blind blind blind blind blind," and burst out laughing. The photo was of the actress on all fours, with her ass high in the air and an eggplant half-buried in her vagina. Ishihara kept tapping at the photo, inviting him to inspect it closely. When Mori just gaped at him, uncomprehending, Ishihara pointed at the woman's anus and pouted. "Piles piles piles piles piles," he explained. Apparently he was indicating that the woman had hemorrhoids. This was so stupid that Mori, without thinking, let out a little laugh of his own. And the instant he did so, incredibly, the barrier disappeared. Ishihara couldn't have read his mind, surely; he'd just chosen him because he was nearby. But he wouldn't have shared his silly joke with an absent Mori, and that realization made the barrier dissolve.

"Here we go! Music, please," Takei called down from the top of the stairs. "Just push the switch on the MD player there." Shinohara was standing next to the old boombox and did as instructed. A soaring classical piece came on, and Felix, next to Mori, muttered "Wagner." Takei slowly made his way down the stairs in a dark-blue commando uniform. He was wearing leather gloves of the same color; a bulletproof vest, from which dangled a triangular groin protector; and lace-up boots. The elbows and knees of the uniform had flexible rubber guards, a sheathed combat knife was strapped to one shin, and on top of a woolen ski mask he wore a helmet, complete with radio headset. The jacket was too large and the pants too baggy, however, so that in fact he looked more like a construction worker than a commando.

357

He was holding a strangely shaped rifle in both hands—a futuristic-looking contraption, like something out of a sci-fi movie. It seemed to be just a flat, rectangular metal case turned on its side. Attached to the bottom was a pistol grip and to the top a scope. There was no discernible barrel, and it was hard to make out where the muzzle might be. It looked less like a weapon than a new kind of electronic musical instrument. Takei descended the final stairs with a look of reverent humility, timing his steps to the Wagner. When he reached the bottom, he turned to face the group, stood at attention, and bowed. "This," he said, indicating the apparel with a wave of his hand, "is the uniform of the German GSG-9, or Border Guard Group 9, and we've chosen, as appropriate accompaniment, the work of a composer said to have been loved by Hitler himself, the great Richard Wagner. Thank you so much. And now allow me to draw your attention to this beauty. This is the future of assault rifles, the much-talked-about Heckler & Koch G11. It fires 4.73-millimeter rounds with no casings to eject, allowing three-round bursts at up to an incredible two thousand rounds per minute.

"Shinohara, skip to the next piece, please. That's right, just hit fast forward." Takei took off his helmet and cap and gloves as Shinohara cued up the music. It was classical again, and this time Felix muttered "Tchaikovsky." Takei swept his right arm toward the top of the stairs, like an emcee introducing a singer to the stage, put on a big smile, and said, "Kondo, come on down... It's Spetsnaz! Yay!" Kondo the Satanist walked down the stairs dressed in a bulgy, shiny white, jumpsuit-style uniform and carrying three guns. Attached to the hooded jumpsuit, at spots corresponding to the wrists, elbows, shoulders, chest, and hips, were straps with attachments to cinch the material in. "He looks like the Michelin Man," Okubo said, and others grinned and nodded. Kondo had a rifle slung from each shoulder and one more in his hands. The two on his shoulders were both AKs, like the one the Koryo soldier had used the other day to drill those holes in the yakuza's head. The rifle in his hands was longer. Kondo wasn't small by any means, but he was thin and weedy, and it was clearly a lot of work for him to carry all three guns.

"Look here, everyone," Takei said, indicating the handgun in a holster on Kondo's hip. "You guessed it—it's a Tokarev! Thank you. And the uniform, here, as you can see, is what's known as a snow camo suit, very hard to come by, used by the former Soviet Union's Spetsnaz 'special purpose' forces. And this here—oh, baby—is the Dragunov SVD sniper rifle. That's right, the Snayperskaya Vintovka Dragunova. It spits out 7.62-by-54-millimeter rimmed cartridges at an unbelievable speed. Thank you so much. And this one, well, pretty ordinary, just an AK-74—that's Avtomat Kalashnikova 74. And over here, the AKM, or Avtomat Kalashnikova Modernizirovanniy. There were a lot of complaints about the AK-74 failing to bring down an enemy with a single 5.45-millimeter round, so they remodeled it to fire the 7.62-by-39 rounds used two generations earlier. Yo, Kondo! Don't just stand there with your mouth hanging open! Draw the Tokarev and hold it in the firing position." But Kondo shook his head and groaned, "Can't. These guns weigh a ton. My arms are about to fall off." He let the sniper rifle slide down until he was holding the end of the barrel, with the butt resting on the floor.

"Kondo! Stand up straight and hoist that weapon! Do you have any idea what a magnificent firearm you've got there? It's not a walking stick!" But in response to this outburst, Kondo just curled his lip. "Why is it only me who's carrying three rifles?" he said, and shrugged the two AK straps off his shoulders. He handed the guns to Hino, who was standing right in front of him. "No, no, no! We've only got one Spetsnaz uniform, so you've got to be the one carrying the AKs," Takei shouted as he relieved Hino of the rifles and gave them back. Kondo leaned the sniper rifle against his leg and took one AK barrel in each hand, propping the butts on the floor. The snow camo suit was completely waterproof, and his face was dripping with sweat. "Hot?" asked Shinohara, and Kondo wiped his forehead with his sleeve, letting the AK in that hand slip and clatter to the floor, and said it was like being in a sauna suit. "What the hell are you doing?" Takei bellowed. "If this was a battlefield, you'd be dead already!" Ishihara looked up from his photo book. "You don't even know you're already dead," he said, quoting a famous line from *Fist of the North Star*, then laughed and said, "Let it go, Takei. Get on with your little fashion show."

"Next tune, please," Takei said curtly. He was clearly miffed that Ishihara had called it a fashion show. Shinohara pressed a button on the boombox, and 'Santa Lucia' came on. "Oh! Italy!" Ishihara cried as Shibata, dressed in black combat gear, appeared feet-first from the top of the stairs. He too was wearing a bulletproof vest, as well as a helmet and goggles. The vest had a plethora of pockets to hold extra magazines, binoculars, a walkie-talkie, grenades, and what have you, but filled for now with styrofoam. Shibata was short and chubby, and the cuffs of his trousers dragged on the floor as he walked. In his left hand was a pistol and in his right a shotgun with a fat barrel and a stock like a gaff hook. Takei pointed at the shotgun.

"All right! This right here is your Franchi SPAS-12, considered the best shotgun of our time. SPAS-12—that's Special Purpose Automatic Shotgun, model number 12. Thank you. Now please take a close look at the pistol. You've all heard of Berettas, of course. This is the Beretta M92F. The Italian Special Forces uniforms are pretty tame, so I got one from elsewhere in Europe—the Special Operations Forces of the Spanish national police. Thank you very much."

"Next," Ishihara said. "Let's go. Next!" He got up from his rocking chair and approached Kondo and Shibata, inspecting their gear with sudden interest. Kaneshiro put a hand to his chin and peered at the guns in a pensive way, perhaps already imagining the coming battle. Hino was gesticulating wildly as he tried to convey his excitement at holding the AKs in his hands. Takei signaled to Shinohara, and the music changed again, this time to a spirited march that not even Felix—a walking encyclopedia of music—could identify.

"I thought that maybe Ishihara-san, being about the same age as me, might recognize this tune," Takei said, and Ishihara shouted "COMMMBAT!" and began loudly humming along. Apparently it was the theme song of an old American TV series about World War II. Sato was now descending the stairs in an outfit of dappled-brown camo. The transparent visor of his helmet was down. On the back of his bulletproof vest were four pockets, each about big enough to hold a slim can of soda. Fukuda explained to everyone that this was the uniform worn in desert conditions by Delta Force counter-terrorism units, and that it was designed so that the man behind could reach into one of the pockets of the man in front and take out a stun grenade (or "flashbang") and toss it into a roomful of terrorists. It seemed there were no stun grenades to be had, however, so these pockets too were packed with cylindrical sections of styrofoam. The helmet had a headset attached, but since there was no radio it amounted to mere decoration.

Sato had an automatic pistol in his right hand, a sub-machine gun in his left, a strange gun on a shoulder strap with a barrel even thicker than that of the Franchi, a holstered revolver on his hip, and hand grenades hanging from clips at his chest. Sato had a sweet face but was powerful and well proportioned and taller than everyone else except Shinohara. Even holding the two automatic weapons, his hands were steady. His face was painted with black stripes, and when he reached his spot in front of everyone he held the guns out and swept the room with them left and right, going *DADADADADADA* and jerking with imaginary recoil.

"Everyone, please," Takei said, and pointed at the sub-machine gun. "This is the legendary Thompson, as used by Sergeant Saunders. It fires seven hundred 11.25-millimeter rounds per minute. And this one here is the M16, the most famous of all automatic rifles, along with the AK. The cartridge is only 5.56 millimeters, but the high velocity makes it totally lethal. Now then. Please direct your attention to the weapon hanging from Sato's shoulder. It's the US M79 grenade launcher. Unfortunately, this isn't the original but the KM79—manufactured under license by the South Korean firm Daewoo. Works perfectly, though. And this is the famous wide-bore pistol, the Smith & Wesson model 1006 A1, with a ten-millimeter cartridge. Outstanding offensive weapon. All right! Turning now to the uniform... I thought of using the uniforms of SWAT, the SEALs, and the Green Berets, but finally decided on the Delta Force desert camo. The hand grenades are M67s, the newest model used by the

US army, and they explode on impact—your average terrorist can only dream about a grenade as cool as this."

At some point Ishihara had started punctuating Takei's explanations with more or less meaningless refrains from old Japanese folk songs while writhing around and waving the photo book as if it were a fan. There was no underlying rhythm to his movements—he wasn't doing a dance, or an exercise, or a martial-arts routine. His gyrations lacked any grace or equilibrium, and they definitely weren't symbolic of anything. Erratic and random though they seemed, however, they had quite an effect on people and always lifted Mori's spirits. They made you feel that nothing was forbidden, that you could do pretty much whatever you pleased as long as you could get away with it. Whenever Ishihara started squirming like this, it meant that something major—good or bad—was brewing.

Kondo had now propped his rifles on the floor in a tripod configuration. Yamada reached out to touch them, one by one, then turned and said, "They're cold!" He put his hand over his mouth and giggled. Tateno seemed more interested in the bayonet Takei wore in a sheath attached to his belt. He asked Takei if he'd show it to him, but was told to wait until afterwards. Hino, who had already held the AKs briefly, was muttering to himself, "The real thing is awesome. It's got real, you know, *heft*..." Long-haired Matsuyama and skinheaded Felix were pointing at the grenades hanging from Sato's belt and laughing about how if one of those went off right now they'd all be blown to bits. Matsuyama had a long face to go with his hair; and Felix, who always wore a blue cotton shirt and jeans, was built like a silverback gorilla. Okubo, who had been a popular child actor and later an arsonist with a total of forty-six fires to his name, seemed quite taken with Sato's uniform and asked if he could try it on later. Mori tried to picture the skeletal, skull-faced Okubo in the Delta Force desert camo.

Takei gave the signal again, and the music changed to a woman singing a sad song to the accompaniment of a violin and accordion. He raised his arm diagonally, and in a high-pitched voice called, "Orihara, *s'il vous plaît!*" Matsuyama said, "What? What did he just say?" and Felix told him it was French for something like "please." Felix spoke English and Spanish fluently and also had some French and Italian, but he couldn't read much Japanese. Orihara, who though only eighteen had the face of a seventy-year-old, came shuffling down slowly to the Frenchwoman's dirge wearing an olive-brown beret and a beige uniform and carrying a strange weapon rather like a wind instrument in silhouette.

Orihara was the one who'd first come up with the Satanism idea and researched how to conduct actual Satanic rituals. When Mori asked what these were like, he was told that they involved painting strange-looking symbols on the untanned hide of a goat with a mixture of rat blood, pig urine, and powdered bat carcasses, then hanging the hide out of a window. Mori wondered if it was because of doing things like this that Orihara's face had aged so drastically, but apparently he'd been born that way. Orihara took his place alongside Sato, Kondo, and Shibata. Holding the odd-looking weapon in his left hand, he struck an elaborate pose, dropping to one knee, extending his right arm, and pointing his index finger at the ceiling. "*Sous le ciel de Paris coule la Seine*," Takei intoned, and with arms outspread he walked around him. "This is the uniform of the French 11th Parachute Brigade, the crack squadron that distinguished itself in the Algerian War of Independence, becoming as feared as a quiver of cobras. The song's a *chanson*; and this—are you ready?—this is the famous FAMAS, the service rifle of the French army, nicknamed the Trumpet, capable of firing 5.56-millimeter NATO rounds at the incredible rate of nine hundred per minute. I don't mind telling you that this Trumpet here, along with the paratrooper uniform, was the most difficult item to get my hands on. Thank you, everyone. Thank you so much." Takei bowed with a flourish, tucking his right arm in at the waist like a crooner after nailing a song.

Kaneshiro seemed particularly impressed by the FAMAS and began clapping, whereupon all the others joined in, with Matsuyama and Felix using their fingers to deliver ear-piercing whistles. Orihara seemed to enjoy the applause. He leaped into the air, raising both fists and smiling like a boxer who'd just knocked out his opponent. When he smiled, you could see that all his teeth were dark brown. Apparently this was the result of another Satanic ritual, the details of which Mori had yet to hear.

"Where did Takei-san get these things?" muttered Okubo, who was sitting behind Mori. "Lots of different places, I guess," Mori said. He had heard that Takei bought most of his weapons from Russia and the Philippines, and that it wasn't as difficult as you might think. Rumor had it that if you went to the Otaru Canal in Hokkaido, even in daytime, you could see Russian sailors selling Tokarevs to high-school students, but Mori had never heard of machine guns or sniper rifles being readily available. Through his connection with the Islamist guerrillas in Yemen, Takei had dealings with professional arms smugglers in Russia and the Philippines, who paid off crew members of cargo ships to bring stuff in to the Port of Hakata, Kure Harbor, and Kobe. The ships flew under the flags of various nations—largely places like the Philippines, Myanmar, Malaysia, and Indonesia, but sometimes South American countries like Panama, Chile, or Argentina. Weapons from the former Eastern Bloc were apparently easiest to get because of loose regulations over serial numbers. You could get an AK on the black market for under a hundred US dollars.

Kondo's face was still dripping sweat, and in a croaking voice he asked for something to drink. With a laugh, Ishihara wriggled up to him, touched the snow camo uniform, and said, "Which direction were you facing when you had that snowball fight with the polar bear?" He wriggled and squirmed and laughed again. Nobody could predict what he would find interesting or funny, but there always seemed to be something behind his laughter, something he alone could see. He never revealed it in so many words, so you just had to wait and see what developed. "What do you want to drink?" Shinohara asked, and when Kondo said a Pocari Sweat, a number of voices called out, "Me too!" Tateno and Hino helped Shinohara in the kitchen, and they came back with trays laden with paper cups, soft drinks, bottles of mineral water, and a carton of milk. Ishihara asked for a tall can of beer, which he chugged at thirstily. Kaneshiro was sipping from a paper cup filled precisely halfway with mineral water. Tateno and Hino drank oolong tea, Shinohara and Felix milk, Kondo and the other Satanists Pocari Sweat, and Mori and Yamada Java tea. No one but Ishihara drank alcohol. Alcohol gave Mori a headache, and Yamada claimed to have immediately puked after once sneaking a cup of his father's sake and finding the taste repulsive. In fact, none of the boys in Ishihara's group had any use for alcohol or its effects.

Alcohol, it was said, liberated people. But nobody here wanted liberation, or would have known what to do with it. Alcohol was usually drunk in an intimate atmosphere, and an intimate atmosphere was one fraught with problems. You were compelled to conform, to respect the spreading sense of closeness in a group. If you didn't, you were punished. If you sat by yourself thinking in a room full of the fug of intimacy, people asked you what was wrong or if you were bored, and from there it would escalate until you were being blamed as an energy-suck and a gloomy bastard. When drinking, if someone made even the dumbest joke, you had to laugh. Everyone here felt that the sort of people who gathered in bars to drink and roar with laughter should be wiped out. And most of these kids had already acted on impulses like that.

"Gentlemen. Your attention, please," Takei said. "Next we have a duet." The music changed to something by a children's choir. Now Ando, who had once chopped up a female classmate, and Miyazaki, said to be the most violent of the Satanists, started down the stairs hand in hand. Both were wearing dark-blue uniforms and camo-pattern helmets with yellowish, translucent visors covering their faces. Ando carried an automatic pistol, and Miyazaki held a compact sub-machine gun just like the one carried by the Koryo officer who'd died in the explosion at Ohori Park. Miyazaki's cheekbones were long and angular, his nose as small as a wad of chewing gum, and his eyes and lips like mere wrinkles in a face as expressionless as a Moai statue or a Haniwa clay figure. Even when he thought he was smiling, to others it looked more like a spasm in his cheek muscles, or as if he was trying to dislodge something stuck between his teeth. Back when the morning tabloid shows were reporting heavily on the Satanists, the cameras had always closed in on Miyazaki's face—the very picture of a youth possessed by the Devil.

Ando looked almost Latin with his dark skin and sculpted features, and was the handsomest of all the boys. Felix had nice features too, but the long, single-fold eyelids and small mouth and nose gave him an almost comically classical Japanese look. Ando was more striking and exotic-looking. Takei claimed that when he first met him he assumed he was part Arab. After killing his classmate and cutting her into pieces just to prove that anyone can be turned into nothing more than bloody chunks of meat and bone, Ando had lost his sex drive. It was rumored that he'd had sex with the lower half of the girl's dismembered corpse, but Ando denied this and said he was still a virgin. He didn't turn religious, or homo, but ceased even to masturbate. The prodigious amount of sperm produced by an eighteen-year-old body accumulated and stagnated inside him and seemed to infuse his skin, giving him a peculiar sort of polluted vacuity. Strikingly handsome though he was, girls weren't attracted to him and gays never looked at him twice. Mori had once gone with Ando to rent some videos and noticed that all females, from toddlers to grandmothers, instinctively shrank away from him.

This hollow reservoir of stagnant sperm descended the staircase hand in hand with the expressionless Miyazaki. When they reached the bottom, they lined up facing the assembly alongside Sato, Shibata, Orihara, and Kondo. It was a tad creepy that they were holding hands, but worse was the fact that they were singing along with the recorded choir. "What was this song again?" Tateno asked, if only to distract himself from the hand-holding, and Takeguchi, juggling three cookie bombs as he joined in, said, "'Ah, Lovely Meadows.'" Yamada commented that it was originally a Czech folk song and the first tune ever sung on NHK's *Everyone's Songs*. Tateno asked him how come he knew something like that, and he explained that he'd watched a lot of reruns of old NHK shows from the Fifties and Sixties late at night with his dad. His father, who had aspired to and extolled poverty, only allowed the TV to be turned on late at night because he believed electricity was cheaper then.

"Here we go! Miyazaki is carrying the Vz 61, also known as the Scorpion, a sub-machine gun developed in the former Czechoslovakia. It fires 7.65-millimeter rounds at a rate of nine hundred and fifty per minute. Thank you! And over here, the gun Ando is holding is a high-powered military pistol from the Belgian firm Fabrique Nationale. I don't know any Belgian songs, and it's no good playing two tunes at once anyway, so I chose, as some of you seem to have recognized, a Bohemian folk song. As for the uniforms, neither the Czech Republic nor Belgium has any special forces worth mentioning, so I went for those of the Gendarmerie Einsatz Kommando of nearby Austria, known commonly as the Cobra Unit. *Dankeschön!*" Somebody asked Miyazaki and Ando if they were going to hold hands for ever, and they looked at each other and let go. Ando's cheeks turned bright red, but Miyazaki remained unreadable.

"Our final number will be Toyohara, but we need to set things up for him, so we'll take about a three-minute break. Thank you!" Takei ran up the stairs to the third floor. Ishihara had drained his beer and told someone to fetch him another, then sat down in his rocking chair and looked at the muted TV. On the screen, officials from the Fukuoka Department of Waterworks were surveying the grounds of the abandoned *danchi*, while members of the Koryo engineering corps went over diagrams with representatives of gas and electric companies. Two MAVs loomed behind the Koryos, and some company vehicles were parked on either side of the road that cut through the *danchi*, where workers had already begun digging. A big red subtitle flashed on the screen as the picture switched back to the studio: SOME 120,000 NORTH KOREAN REBEL TROOPS ARE MASSED AT FOUR PORTS ON THE EAST COAST OF NORTH KOREA, PREPARING TO SAIL TO FUKUOKA. Matsuyama, sitting in front of the TV, muttered, "I wonder if they'll really come." Ishihara turned up the volume.

"Why doesn't the Generalissimo arrest 'em all?" Fukuda asked, and Ishihara snapped at him to shut up and watch. The NHK announcer was standing beside a three-dimensional diorama-style map. He spoke gravely. "Let me summarize the responses of the Japanese and North Korean governments so far to this new development. The government of North Korea, through their official newspaper and a national television broadcast, as well as their embassy in Beijing, have issued the following statement: 'One hundred and twenty thousand troops are seeking political asylum overseas. Any attempt on our part to attack or arrest them would likely result in the so-called Koryo Expeditionary Force retaliating with strikes inside the nation of Japan. We have therefore determined that it is in the best interests of all concerned to refrain from any rash action.' Our own government, meanwhile, has been unwilling to take a stand on whether the North Koreans should or shouldn't attempt to stop and detain the rebels, who could be here within fifty hours of leaving port." The announcer now introduced an authority on the geopolitics of the Korean Peninsula, standing behind the diorama. The expert, whose thin hair was plastered over his pate, used a long pointer to indicate ports on the eastern side of the peninsula as he spoke.

"It appears that the majority of the rebel troops are from the Eighth Corps, which is led by a few hardline anti-American generals. We have reports that the Fourth Corps is involved as well, but in any case there seems no doubt that an intense anti-Americanism is predominant among the rebels, making them an obstacle to the official policy of improving relations with the US. The Eighth Corps is officially called the Special Eighth, so these are probably what we call special-ops forces. So far North Korea has refrained from clarifying whether they have been disarmed, and we can't tell from the satellite photos. But, personally, I believe they are indeed still armed."

"What are you, a moron?" Ishihara said to the man on TV. "Why don't you suck cold noodles through your nose?" It did seem unlikely that invaders would go to the trouble of discarding their weapons before invading. The dominant opinion among the media was that

North Korea would probably do nothing to stop the ships from sailing. Kim Jong Il didn't want to attack or jail the rebels; he just wanted them out of his country. The Japanese Maritime Self-Defense Force had deployed some fifty vessels in Japanese waters, while all the Air SDF bases on the west coast were on alert to scramble fighter jets. The SDF hadn't said they'd attack if the North Korean ships entered Japanese waters, but they hadn't ruled it out either. To say they would take action would amount to a declaration of war against the KEF. And Jo Su Ryeon, on the NHK Fukuoka propaganda program, had made it clear that retaliatory measures would be taken if the reinforcements were attacked.

The hundred and twenty thousand troops were apparently to board some four hundred transport and naval vessels, large and small. For the past three days, security had been beefed up at the Prime Minister's official residence, the Diet, the Cabinet Office, and the Imperial Palace, as well as airports and major train stations, to prevent any KEF attacks. What NHK wouldn't say is that if the troops were to take over the government offices of a few small cities or occupy some of the outlying islands, there would be nothing the central government could do about it. The day before, an article in one of the weeklies had stated that there was a movement within the government to restrict the Koryos to Fukuoka, or at least the island of Kyushu, so as to prevent the damage spreading to the mainland. A certain politician was quoted as saying that, after all, what the rebel troops wanted was Fukuoka, not the entire country.

"In any case we must closely watch the movements of these additional troops." With this *duh!*-inducing comment the expert wrapped things up, never expanding on the vital question of whether Fukuoka would have to be sacrificed. Mori thought it was a sure bet that the government would turn its back on Fukuoka. When you're preparing to turn your back on someone, you don't go around advertising it.

"All right! Ready? Is everyone ready? Thank you. And now, last but not least…" Takei spread his arms wide, the pitch of his voice rising as he tried to manufacture excitement for his finale. "Toyohara, come on down!" Shinohara hit the MD player, and the familiar theme song of a well-known movie began to play. Mori had seen it but couldn't remember the title until he heard Felix say "*Indiana Jones.*" There was a clank, and then another clank, as Toyohara began descending the iron staircase from the third floor. A murmur swept through the Living. Even Ando and the five Satanists let out a collective "Whoa," and Ishihara turned his gaze from the TV back to the show, then stood up from his rocking chair, his jaw dropping. *Clank... clank.* Toyohara paused after each step.

The calf-high lace-up boots were much too big for him, and because his legs were so short they came to just below his kneecaps. They must have had steel soles, too, judging by the metallic sound echoing through the Living. The hem of the black uniform jacket reached the tops of the boots, and over the jacket he wore a camo-patterned cape. His helmet, green and too small for his shaved head, looked like a turtle drying its shell on a sandbar. Much of his face was hidden by a gas mask, the type with a rubber nozzle protruding from the mouth to filter poison gas, but the mask was too small as well, and the rubber dug into the flesh of his cheeks and chin. Strange-looking optical instruments hung from straps around his neck, and beneath the jacket he wore a triangular bulletproof vest, to which was attached a rappelling harness covered with attachments of various sizes that clattered as he walked. He had a gun in each hand and a pistol in a belt holster.

Toyohara's oversized boots and limited visibility left him no choice but to ease down one step at a time. His silhouette was nearly circular. He didn't look like a soldier; in fact, he didn't look like anything human—more like a robot out of *Star Wars* or *Star Trek*. But everyone knew that Toyohara was a serious and sensitive lad in his own way, and he'd only made it down six steps so far, so no one laughed. As he got nearer the bottom you could hear his breathing, even over the *Indiana Jones* theme.

Mori himself was such a wheezer that he'd been given the nickname Steamwhistle at school, but even at its worst his breathing was nothing like this. After his older brother killed their parents, Mori had been put in a welfare facility near his father's family home. Early in his stay there he'd gone on a field trip to a cattle farm, where he was unfortunate enough to hear the bellowing of cows being slaughtered—killed by blows to the skull with a long spike attached to the end of an iron bar. It had been an unearthly sound that made Mori squat down on the floor with his hands over his ears, wailing and feeling that his very life was being squeezed out of him. The sound Toyohara was making reminded him of those cows. Ishihara had lost his usual aplomb the moment Toyohara came into view, and had turned toward the door, as if preparing to flee the room. Others were watching Toyohara slack-jawed, instinctively backing up as he descended.

Up to this point, Kaneshiro had stared hard at each of the uniforms and guns being modeled, but when Toyohara appeared he frowned as if in pain and turned away. Takeguchi and Fukuda began putting the cookie bombs back in their special case. Yamada spilled Java tea from his paper cup and stained his beige made-in-Honduras jacket but didn't even notice. Matsuyama and Felix didn't stand up and applaud as they had for the others but sat with bowed heads, hugging their knees. The five uniformed Satanists stood stock-still, and Ando, his pretty mouth still open, tried to hide behind Miyazaki.

"Whoa! Toyohara! Talk about intense!" Takei alone was in high spirits, seemingly oblivious to the weirdness. Mori remembered those war photographers he'd read about, who even in the midst of heavy shelling were too busy peering through their viewfinders to feel much fear. Toyohara's breathing grated not only on the ears but on the chest and brain. His boots hit the floor at the bottom of the stairs with a bludgeon-like *whomp, whomp*, and the eeriness was only magnified by his proximity: the harness and bulletproof vest made an unpleasant noise as they rubbed together, the camo cape fluttered in a draft from the open window, and the pleated filtration nozzle swung slowly back and forth. The nozzle was a strangely in-between length—too short to resemble an elephant's trunk and too long to be a pig's snout.

It was impossible to make out Toyohara's expression behind the gas mask. He stopped, raised both guns above his head, and tried to let out a rebel yell. The mask had a grip on his lips, however, and all he was able to produce was a high-pitched, screechy exhalation. Stumbling in boots twice the size of his feet, he lined up next to Ando and the five Satanists. The rubber of the mask was stretched to the breaking point to accommodate his soccer-ball-size head, and the goggle lenses were pulled so far apart that it looked as if his eyes were on either side of his head.

"All right, Toyohara, thank you!" Takei, still in the same high spirits, gave a flourish with his right hand and began introducing the equipment. Mori was starting to feel ill. "Look at this here. See it? It's the Israeli Uzi, the sub-machine gun of all sub-machine guns. It fires six hundred nine-millimeter rounds a minute, gentlemen. Thank you so much. And how about this? This is the pride of Israel Military Industries, the Galil sniper rifle. IMI's Galil attack rifle uses 5.56-by-45-millimeter NATO rounds, but this one fires the 7.62-by-51, which gives it a longer range. Thank you. Hanging from his neck is an Israeli night-vision scope with the latest in infrared thermography, capable of detecting targets even through concrete. You're all with me, right? Now allow me to draw your attention to the uniform our friend Toyohara is modeling so nicely. It comes straight from the Yamas undercover counter-terrorism unit of the Israeli Border Police, and it's not a replica but the real thing. The Yamas wear this during operations on the borders with Palestine and Lebanon and so on. Thank you." Takei gave another flourish with his right arm and wriggled like the emcee of a quiz show when a contestant has just won a small fortune or a Hawaiian vacation. "I'm sure you all recognize the music. I don't know any Israeli folk songs, so I chose a tune from a film by the Jewish director Spielberg-san. Thank you. Oh, and this pistol isn't from Israel but the USA—it's the Colt .45 Government, a monster that fires 11.43-millimeter rounds. I chose it for the ensemble because America and Israel are as close as Siamese twins. Thank you all so very much. That completes our show for this evening."

Takei was expecting another round of applause, but the final model's appearance had cast a pall over everything. Toyohara couldn't speak because of the gas mask, and Mori could hardly bear to watch anymore. It was like watching a friend be publicly humiliated, or an elderly aunt perform a striptease. But he also saw himself in Toyohara. The others probably felt the same way. Though scarcely able to breathe after clomping down one step at a time, Toyohara had held the guns aloft and tried to yell. The more earnestly he tried to fulfill his duties, however, the creepier and more comical he looked. But Mori was aware that he himself had been creeping people out since childhood.

The show had ended, but no one clapped. Everybody was hunched over, staring at the floor. The enthusiasm of only moments before was gone. The participants put their various rifles on the floor and detached the handguns and holsters from their belts, laying them in a row on the table. Kondo took off his snow camo and started wiping the sweat off his face and chest. Fukuda and Takeguchi, their faces twitching, quickly locked the cookie explosives in their duralumin case. An unusually stern and disgruntled-looking Ishihara told Tateno and Shinohara to take off Toyohara's mask and uniform for him. "Right here?" Tateno hesitated, foreseeing the result. "No." Ishihara gestured toward the corner kitchen. "Over there." The kitchen was separated from the Living by an accordion curtain. No one wanted to see Toyohara's sweaty, rubber-smelling face as the mask was peeled off.

"What's wrong?" Takei said, smiling and all but oblivious to the general mood. Ishihara was gazing at the rifles on the floor, and now bent down to pick up an AK. "What do you think, Ishihara-san? You like that one? If so, it's yours to use." Takei ran his fingers through his brown-dyed hair as he spoke, his pale face vacant and wraithlike. You could tell by his tone that he expected him to be delighted. "This is the only one, right?" Ishihara said, tapping the barrel of the gun on the floor. Takei, misunderstanding the question, said, "Oh, no. This is the AKM, but there's also an AK-74, and other assault rifles—we've got the M16 and a FAMAS, like

373

I said." Ishihara tilted his head to one side and then the other and said, "What I and I mean is, you only have one each of all these rifles?" Takei greeted this with a puzzled look and glanced around the room for support. He couldn't see what he was getting at, and neither could Mori. Just then, Toyohara walked back into the room supported on either side by Tateno and Shinohara. He was wearing only boxer shorts and a T-shirt, and steam was rising from his entire body. The smell of sweat-soaked rubber wafted around him, and he was still breathing heavily, looking at everyone with a mixture of anticipation and uncertainty, anxious to know if he'd done okay. Ishihara reached out to pat him reassuringly on the shoulder, but pulled back when he saw the imprints of the gas mask on his head and face. The goggles had left off-center circular marks around his eyes, and you could see where the taut rubber had dug into his forehead and chin. Most disturbing of all was the round red groove on his shaved, snow-white pate, engraved there by the band of the too-small helmet. His skull bulged out above and below this depression, giving his head the appearance of an unshelled peanut.

Ishihara stood over the handguns on the table and said, "And you have only one of each of these pistols, right?" Takei pushed out his lips sulkily, as if being unjustly accused, and told him, "I think this is an adequate number of weapons. What with the handguns, the assault rifles, the sniper rifles, the sub-machine guns, and the grenade launcher, we've got seventeen pieces here, not to mention the hand grenades and our explosives team. Since there's only twenty of us, and since we don't have access to a firing range for practice anyway, this is more than enough, don't you think?" Some of them were nodding in agreement. Takei's tone had grown rather testy, and Ishihara was still looking disgruntled, so that everyone there began feeling the tension. "And how much ammunition do you have?" Ishihara demanded. "About a hundred rounds per handgun," Takei said, "two hundred per assault rifle, a hundred per sniper rifle, three hundred per sub-machine gun, and fifty rounds for the grenade launcher—that's plenty of ammunition for a battle of this scale."

"I and I say *Ay ay ay*! This isn't weaponry for any battle. More like a geek hobby collection." The color drained from Takei's face. "Hobby" was one of the words they all loathed. It made Mori think of old men and women playing croquet. He'd never had anything like a hobby, and neither had the others. People who needed only to be working at their hobby to be happy didn't butcher a classmate or set random fires or cut down a train conductor with a samurai sword or blow up a massage parlor or make up stories about being abducted by the Devil. Shinohara raised creepy insects, but to him it was a job and a calling, not a hobby. A hobby requires time, money, and psychological stability, and these were things that no one here possessed. The insinuation that Takei was a mere hobby geek hit him like a body blow. "Not weaponry for any battle?" he said, his cheeks flushing red now. "What do you mean? These are all authentic weapons from around the world! Do you know what I had to go through to slip these past the authorities?"

"I and I noticed that all the guns you described were of different calibers," Ishihara said. "Which means they all take different ammo. Correct? That gun you're holding that looks like a salted salmon, what caliber is it again?" Takei looked down at the assault rifle in his hands. "This Heckler & Koch G11? It's 4.73-by-33 millimeters." Ishihara sighed. "Well, either I and I can't remember for trying to forget or can't forget for trying to remember, but run through all those calibers again, will you?" Takei, pointing affectionately at each gun in turn, said, "The M16 is 5.56-by-45 millimeters, the AKM is 7.62-by-39, the AK-74 next to it is 5.45-by-39, the FAMAS is the same as the M16, 5.56-by-45, and the handguns, let's see, the FN and the Beretta are 9-by-19, the Tokarev 7.62-by-25, the Colt Government 11.43-by-23, the Smith & Wesson 10-by-23, and as for the sub-machine guns, well, the Uzi is 9-by-19, Sergeant Saunders' Thompson is 11.25-by-23, the Scorpion is 7.65-by-17, and the Dragunov and Galil are both 7.62, but the case lengths are slightly different."

"See?" Ishihara shook his head. "What a loser. Takei, twenty years ago, I and I would have pulled down my PJs, bared my snow-white ass, and sprayed you with projectile diarrhea." He spread his arms to address the rows of guns on the floor and table before him. "O you pitiful stingers, you lonely insects, companionless, weepin' weapons. Sad stingers, come: let me hold you lovingly, yea, and squeeze you till the pips squeak. But listen to me: here you will find no mates, and no happiness. And there's no one to blame but that old fool Takei." Ishihara slowly looked upward, then folded his hands against his breast and closed his eyes as if in prayer. Listening to this impromptu poem, or whatever it was, Mori thought he finally understood what he was driving at. The others did too and began hashing it out with one another. Tateno said to Hino, "The Koryos all have AKs and Scorpions, right?" Matsuyama said to Fukuda, "Now I get it—if the calibers are different, you can't share ammo during a firefight." Felix told Yamada that NATO cartridges were standardized at 5.56 millimeters, and Takeguchi told Shinohara that was why, even though the guns of the German, French, Italian, and Belgian armies were different, they could exchange ammo. Ando told Takeguchi that when Europe was divided into East and West, the two sides used different calibers, to make their own ammunition useless to the enemy. Fukuda said to Ando, "Most of us have never fired a real gun, so we'll need to train and practice." Yamada asked Mori, "How can we train as a group, or hold drills, if the guns are all different?" and Hino said to Kaneshiro, "It's amazing that he found so many different kinds of guns, though," and Kaneshiro said to no one in particular, "Why couldn't he get weapons of the same caliber?" Shibata wondered what good uniforms were if they were all different; Sato said that this wasn't a high-school military-history club, after all; Miyazaki said it wasn't a fashion competition either; and Orihara muttered, "Fighting isn't about looking good anyway." Kondo wiped the sweat from under his arms and mumbled, "I mean, snow camo? In Fukuoka? In springtime?"

They weren't addressing their remarks directly to Takei, if only because none of them desired or were accustomed to confrontation of any kind. When someone made curry and it was delicious, they would all nod to themselves and mutter under their breath that it wasn't bad, but no one ever turned to the cook and said, for example, "Hey, Mori, this is great!" If a dish didn't turn out well, on the other hand, everyone would try a few bites and leave the rest but not say anything. Whoever made it realized that it wasn't any good, but his feelings weren't hurt. No one was used to offering criticism of any kind, so when they didn't like something they just kept quiet. This was the wisdom of children who'd grown up in dangerous surroundings, unable to trust anyone.

When Mori had first arrived at the welfare facility, he was scarcely able to speak to people. Having recently witnessed his brother's murderous rampage, he was terrified of any contact or interaction with others. A clinical psychologist there had tried an unusual method with him. He'd placed a doll between Mori and himself and used it as a medium of communication. The doll was named Suzy. "Hey, Suzy," the psychologist would say, looking at the doll. "Hey, Suzy, I'd sure like to talk to Mori-kun for a minute. I wonder what I should do?" Somewhat reassured because the man wasn't speaking directly to him, Mori had begun little by little to reply through Suzy.

The negative comments about Takei's guns-and-uniforms show were, Mori thought, mainly blowback from having had such high expectations. Everyone was focused on the coming offensive; a clear target for their destructive urges had finally appeared in the form of the Koryos. Mori didn't know what gave people the urge to destroy, but everyone here had it, and they all knew it. When there was no clear external focus for that drive, you turned it against yourself, or those close to you, or society. You cut yourself or killed yourself or stabbed your parents or murdered strangers or started fires or set off bombs, and of course society dealt severely with such behavior. Since coming to Fukuoka and meeting so many other kids from similar circumstances, Mori had managed to dial his own destructiveness down a few notches, but it had never completely disappeared. And now that a suitable object for it had come along, it was time to dial it back up.

Everyone here was a bit mental, but none of them lacked intelligence. They understood only too well that the Koryos were well-trained professional soldiers and virtually unbeatable as a fighting force. Since their sudden appearance at the Dome, the Ishihara group had been studying their every move, the way small children intently watch their parents. They knew that they didn't stand a chance without weapons, but Takei's armory, while impressive, had turned out to be less than practical. Mori didn't feel that the muttered criticisms were based on any actual ill feeling toward the man, however, but rather a general and sudden disillusionment. It was obvious that you weren't going to defeat the Koryos with the private collection of an eccentric gun enthusiast.

"Wait a minute." It was hard to tell unless you looked closely, but Takei was furious. There were tiny bubbles of foam at the corners of his mouth, and his shoulders were trembling. "Takei, pwease don't be angwy," Ishihara said, as if trying to comfort a child. Kaneshiro stood up and said, "Weapons are weapons, after all." Matsuyama turned to Felix and said, "That's right. If you pull the trigger, bullets come out. We can still fight," and Ando and Takeguchi and Fukuda nodded in agreement. Takei had been standing there in his GSG-9 uniform with his head bowed, biting his lip as though enduring an unendurable humiliation, but now he looked up. "Trigger? Bullets?" he said, then turned to peer over his left shoulder and point a coy finger at Matsuyama—a pose a pop star might have employed a decade earlier.

"What did you just say? 'If you pull the trigger, bullets come out'?" Scowling, he called Toyohara's name. Still in his T-shirt and shorts, Toyohara stepped stiffly forward, as if expecting to be yelled at, rigid with such tension that it filled the air of the room and made it hard to breathe. This was a genuinely serious lad. "Bring me that pistol you were wearing just now," Takei said. With an obsequious "*Hai!*" Toyohara picked up the Tokarev from the row of pistols on the table. "That's not it," Takei said, and Toyohara's cheeks flushed so red against his pale skin that they looked like ripe tomatoes. Fukuda said, "Here," and handed him a larger, silvery gun—the Colt Government.

"Look at this, everyone." Takei took the Colt and displayed it for all to see, like a magician holding up a top hat. Mori almost expected him to say, *Nothing up my sleeve*... "Look right here, this is the safety," he said, pointing to a little lever on the side of the gun. Mori was too far away to make it out. Kaneshiro, Fukuda, and Takeguchi were in the front row, but apparently they couldn't see it properly either: they looked at one another, shaking their heads and shrugging. Kaneshiro, looking thoroughly bored, muttered, "What you're saying is that if you don't release the safety, no bullets will come out, right?" Ishihara, seated in his rocking chair, released a beery belch. Perhaps he was a tad drunk; he was watching Takei's performance with sleepy eyes and not much apparent interest.

"That's right. The safety keeps the gun from going off accidentally. Now watch this. See? I'm pushing the catch forward, so the safety is off. Now we're set, right? Hey, Matsuyama, we're set now, right? If I pull the trigger now, a bullet will come out, right?" Takei was aiming a finger at Matsuyama again. "I guess so," Matsuyama said, looking perplexed. "Takei's just upset right now," Felix assured him. "He's just blowing off steam."

On the floor below the stairway was a square, beige-colored tin container about the size of an unabridged dictionary. Takei levered it open and extracted a square paper package, approximately half the size of a carton of cigarettes. Something was printed on the package in English, but Mori was too far back to read it. Takei slid the empty magazine out of the Colt, opened the package, plucked out a single cartridge, and held it up for all to see. "This is what you call a Hydra-Shok," he said. "Velocity is a bit on the slow side, but the kill power is exceptional." The bullet was about as long as the first joint of his index finger. In the center of the rounded, dull-gold tip was a small hole.

Takei loaded the magazine, counting out loud as he did so. "One round. Two rounds. Three rounds..." He loaded seven in all, slid the magazine into the butt end of the grip, and slapped it home. "Here," he said, handing the gun to Toyohara. He had him stand in front of the staircase, several meters away from the others and with his back to them. Taking up position beside him, Takei pointed at the big bookcase against the wall they were facing, clapped him on the back, and

379

said, "Shoot at the bookcase." Toyohara took aim. Ishihara sat up in
his rocker and was about to protest, when Takei turned and showed
him both palms. "It's all right," he said, then turned to Toyohara
beside him and shouted: "READYYYYY…" Toyohara opened his
stance and held the Colt Government straight out, supporting his
right wrist with his left hand. "AIMMMMM…" Ishihara's enormous
bookcase, which housed Rimbaud and Takuboku alongside *S&M
Sniper* and *Scatolo: The Complete Young Babes Pooping*, was about twice
Toyohara's height.

"FIRE!" Takei yelled, and Toyohara squeezed the trigger. His
index finger turned bone-white, but nothing happened. "What's
wrong? I said 'FIRE'!" Takei screeched. Toyohara's shoulder was
trembling, and his face turned scarlet as he tried unsuccessfully to pull
the trigger. "What's going on?" Yamada wondered, and Kaneshiro
snapped his fingers and said, "I get it. There's a grip safety." He
explained that the gun was equipped with another, internal safety
catch, and that you had to squeeze hard on the grip itself to release
it. Toyohara was on the balls of his feet, leaning slightly forward,
holding the pistol straight out in front of him, left hand cradling
his wrist—a stance that Takei must have taught him in rehearsals
upstairs. He was grimacing now as he continued to squeeze the
immovable trigger. Thick veins popped into relief at his temples.
His mouth was open, and a raspy moan leaked out: *Uuuurrrgh!* Mori
wondered if Toyohara himself wasn't going to explode.

His eyes were closed. His mouth was twisted and his hands and
arms, as well as his shoulders and knees, were shaking visibly. He
was blaming himself for the gun not firing. "What's the matter,
Toyohara? Shoot!" The anguished moan died, and Toyohara tried
to speak. No sound came out, but Mori could read his lips easily
enough: *I'm sorry!* There was a harsh chill in the air of the Living.
Toyohara was being deliberately tormented in front of everyone.
Perhaps Takei blamed him for destroying the party atmosphere of
his show. "That's enough," Ishihara said, and Takei spread his arms
and turned to the group, smiling, as if to say: *You see? Only we pros know
the real score.* And it was then that Toyohara's arms jerked upward

and a short flame spat out of the barrel of the gun. There was a percussive *pop*, like a car backfiring, and the steel staircase rang like a bell as the bullet ricocheted off it—the recoil being so powerful that Toyohara had missed the bookcase altogether. Kaneshiro, Fukuda, and Takeguchi dived to the floor, followed immediately by Tateno, Hino, Shinohara, Matsuyama, Felix, and the five Satanists. Mori, Yamada, Ando, and Okubo were equally startled but didn't move; they were still sitting upright on the carpet, mouths agape. Ishihara's eyes shone. "Woo-hoo!" he remarked from his rocking chair. "The little bug flew straight and true! Good work, Hulk!"

Mori's ears were ringing. He had heard more gunshots in Ohori Park than he could possibly count, but indoors the sound was very different, and he began to worry that the Koryos in the *danchi* had heard it. Toyohara was nearly in tears, mouthing the words *I'm sorry*, again and again. His hand was dangling at a strange angle. "He must've dislocated his wrist," someone said—apparently the recoil had pushed the joint out of its socket. But he was still holding the gun, presumably too focused on blaming himself to feel the pain. He didn't even seem to realize he'd actually fired the thing. Ishihara rose from his rocking chair. "It's all right, Toyo. That's enough!" he shouted, but Toyohara wasn't hearing anything. "Weird," Takei muttered, shaking his head. "The kid must be crazy strong." He stepped toward him and held out his hand. "That's enough," he said. "Give me the gun." But his words weren't reaching Toyohara, whose ears seemed as tightly shut as his eyes. He gave another grunt and clenched his limp-wristed hand again, and this time when his arms jerked upward the muzzle was pointed to the right, directly at Takei, no more than half a meter away. A brief spark pierced the right breast of Takei's jacket, accompanied by another dry *pop*.

Takei reeled back as if body-punched and looked at Toyohara as if to say: *Huh?* And then he crumpled, buckling at the knees before falling face downward. Under his right shoulder blade was a blackish-red hole the size of an apple, and both of his legs were twitching. The atmosphere in the room seemed to turn to chilled jelly. Mori could neither speak nor move. After some moments Ishihara bellowed:

381

"Kaneshiro, Tateno—get the gun!" Kaneshiro ran up and bear-hugged Toyohara from behind and Tateno lunged forward to grab the Colt, but no sooner had he taken it away than he cried out and let it fall clattering to the floor. "The barrel is red-hot!" he said. With Kaneshiro shaking him by the shoulders, Toyohara finally opened his eyes; and then, seeing smoke issuing from the barrel of the gun, he said, "Did I shoot it?" and started to smile until he noticed Takei lying on the floor beyond the wisp of smoke.

He squatted down and lightly touched Takei's bleeding wound, then looked up at Kaneshiro. "Did I do that?" he asked. Kaneshiro was having difficulty catching his breath and didn't reply. Ishihara came forward. "It wasn't you, Toyo," he said. "He walked right into the line of fire. He always was an unlucky bugger." Takei was still breathing, his legs still twitching. Blood had already pooled in a circle about a meter across. "What do you want to do?" Kaneshiro asked Ishihara. Everyone else stood or sat frozen—Yamada with his mouth open and his arms oddly akimbo—but Mori moved unsteadily to the window and peered out toward the *danchi*. Tateno asked what he was doing, and he said he was just checking to see if the Koryos heard the gunshots. The room went electric with tension.

"Can you see anything?" Fukuda whispered. "I see a bunch of people," Mori reported, "but they're too far away to tell what they're doing." Toyohara got to his feet, ran to the hat tree next to the kitchen, and brought back his binoculars. "Made in Germany," he said as he handed them over. Mori nodded: "I know." The binoculars were aligned to Toyohara's remarkably close-set eyes. Mori adjusted them, steadied them on the windowsill, and pointed them at the *danchi*. Work projects were under way at various spots on the *danchi* grounds, with large machinery tearing up asphalt and moving dirt around. He could hear crashing and clanking sounds, and could see the blue sparks of welding torches. Crews of workers were checking electrical wiring and testing the valves on water lines and so forth. The MAVs in the background weren't moving. But when he scanned to the right of the MAVs, his heart leaped into his throat. "Oops!" he said. He had focused on a Koryo soldier who stood near the entrance to the *danchi*, talking to a city official, and the soldier had seemed to look up and stare right into the lenses. Mori pulled back and ducked, the blood draining from his face.

Someone asked what was wrong, and he said, "I think we've been spotted." Everybody in the room, including Ishihara, hit the deck. It wasn't actually possible to see into the Living from the *danchi*, so they weren't really in any danger of being shot, but for a moment there was panic. The five Satanists, on the floor beside the gun table, all reached for weapons before realizing they didn't know how to use them. And who knew how to use the hand grenades? "Should we run?" Tateno said to Ishihara. Ishihara asked Fukuda and Takeguchi if those cookies of theirs were operative. Clutching their duralumin cases, they shook their heads—they hadn't brought any detonators. "Well, then, what are we waiting for?" Ishihara said. "Let's get out of here." He pointed at the Colt Government on the floor. "Somebody put the gun in Takei's hand," he said, already crawling toward the door, "so we can say he topped himself."

Hino picked up the Colt, but as he got closer to the blood-splattered body his nerve failed. "Give it to me," Kaneshiro said, squatting down next to Takei and holding out an open hand. Hino gave him the gun. Kaneshiro took hold of Takei's right wrist, but the moment he did so Takei's torso twitched and a faint *Oooh* escaped his lips. Kaneshiro rocked back on his heels and sat abruptly on the floor, saying, "What the hell? He's still alive!" Hino gave a sharp, rasping gasp, Tateno shivered, and Yamada stood with both hands clamped over his gaping mouth. "Shouldn't we take him to a hospital?" Shinohara said quietly. "Don't be stupid," said Ishihara. "They'd find out we have weapons here." Kaneshiro climbed to his feet. He stared at the Colt in his hand, then pointed it at Takei's head. "If we're going to claim it was suicide," he said, "shouldn't we make sure he's dead?" His eyes looked weird. They seemed to be out of focus, or focused on something a long way off. Ishihara slowly approached and took the gun from his hand. "It's all right," he murmured. "He'll be dead in a minute. You don't have to shoot him."

*

Everyone in the Living learned first-hand what it was like to watch someone slowly bleed to death. A certain quantity of blood was necessary to maintain life, and when the gauge went below that level, you expired. It was almost like a car running out of gas, Mori thought. They decided to wait until after midnight to take the body away and dispose of it. They'd have to wrap it up in the meantime. A jumbo garbage bag was brought out, but they could see immediately that the corpse wouldn't fit inside. "Shall we cut him in half?" Ishihara suggested. It was impossible to tell if he was joking or serious. Either way, Mori was shocked, but Orihara displayed his brown teeth and said, "Good idea!" Ando shook his head. "Forget it," he said. "Without an electric saw, it'd take for ever." Most of the group were in a state of shock and weren't thinking clearly, but Ando was calm and collected. They decided to wrap Takei like a mummy in a whole roll of garbage bags and secure the bundle with rope. Ando took charge of the operation and was soon telling everyone to hurry up: rigor mortis was setting in and making the body harder to manipulate.

They had to strip off Takei's clothes first, to make it more difficult to trace his identity if the body was found. Ando had his team strip down to their shorts as well, so as to avoid getting blood on their clothing. "Hey, Ando, were you in your undies when you chopped up your classmate too?" Ishihara asked from his rocking chair. Mori wondered why he had to ask a question like that at a time like this. But Ando, with no change of expression, just said, "Yes, I was." Takei's arms and legs were already rigid, and Ando had to slice through his clothing with a knife, tearing it away section by section. The trousers and boxers were surprisingly easy to remove, but the GSG-9 uniform jacket was a challenge. The blood it was soaked in was coagulating, and the material clung to the wounds in his chest and back. The gore-covered fragments of material Ando removed from the exit wound also contained hard little white specks and a pale, net-like membrane. "What's that white stuff?" Takeguchi asked. "Fragments of ribs," said Ando. "And lung tissue."

Three of them lifted Takei up while another three spread the big black garbage bags on the floor underneath. They stuffed the holes in his back and chest with wadded-up toilet paper, then turned him face up before laying him down on the plastic. "Maybe we should say a prayer or something," somebody suggested, but Ando said, "Later." Apparently they had to finish wrapping Takei quickly or he'd begin to decay. Ando explained that all the parasites and germs inside him had already begun an exodus of the body. "Well, I never!" said Ishihara to the dead man. "Takei! You've got a hard-on!" Mori decided not to look. Seeing the dead always connected him directly to the memory of his parents. "He really looks at peace, though, doesn't he?" said Ishihara, and Shinohara said, "Maybe it was a dream come true for a weapons geek like him to go out like that." At peace? Mori decided against his better judgment to take a peek. Takei's skin had turned the ochre color of curried rice, his lips and mouth were twisted grotesquely, and his eyeballs seemed to be drooping out from beneath the lids. He remembered his parents' dead faces and ran to the toilet, gagging.

As time went by, they all gradually regained some composure. Under Ando's direction, they constructed a stretcher from two long iron pipes and reams of duct tape. Fukuda went to borrow a Speed Tribe friend's minivan, and Miyazaki went with him. Ando and Fukuda were the only licensed drivers in the group. Orihara began folding little "spirit guide vessels" from sheets of newspaper. This was a custom he'd been initiated into as a little boy when his family visited Nagasaki, his mother's hometown, for a funeral. Mori joined in to help make the palm-size boats, along with Yamada and Toyohara and Orihara's fellow Satanists Kondo, Sato, Miyazaki, and Shibata. They reinforced the floors of the vessels with cardboard and coated the bottoms and sides with wax. Doing delicate work like this with their hands helped to calm them down. "I killed Takei-san, didn't I?" Toyohara said again, as if to confirm his worst suspicions. Sato shook his head. "It was an accident," he said. "It wasn't your fault," Yamada said, and Toyohara gazed at his bandaged hand and muttered, "It felt unbelievable, though." According to Orihara, they needed candles and flowers and fruit for the spirit guides, so Shibata set out for a convenience store.

Kaneshiro's strange excitement hadn't diminished. Ishihara took him aside and spoke to him about madness. "Madness isn't something you can suppress," he began, "but you can't give it free rein either. You've spent your life dreaming of murder and mayhem, and now that this has happened right before your eyes you're getting all excited, and there's nothing abnormal about that in itself, but what happened didn't happen because of anything you did or anything under your control. It's only natural if it makes you go a bit mental, but just remember that if you try to suppress madness, it condenses into a little ball, and one day the ball will explode. Normal and mad aren't really that clearly distinguishable. And 'normal' has nothing to do with the missionary position. Madness lies within, but what we might call the essence of fellowship—the something that symbolizes normality—is always floating around somewhere outside. I and I made this happy discovery after a solid century of research and experience."

"But you're not even fifty yet, are you?" Kaneshiro said, and Ishihara slapped him on the forehead and said, "Shut up and listen." Kaneshiro said, "Ouch," and sulked a bit, but his eyes were a little less weird now. "As I and I was saying, the essence of fellowship that's floating around somewhere is a fragile thing, hard to pin down, very elusive and ephemeral. The sense of being connected with others, or being needed by others—that's something that requires faith, because it can never be proven. Just look," he said, taking Kaneshiro's pointed chin in his hand and pushing his head up and down and to either side. "Can you see the essence of fellowship floating there?" he said. "All I see is the ceiling and the walls and the floor," Kaneshiro mumbled, and Ishihara burst out laughing. "Exactly," he said. "You only get to actually see it maybe two or three times in a lifetime."

Mori was walking with Yamada and Toyohara through the residential section of Atagohama. If the group had all gone together, they'd have drawn attention to themselves, so they were heading for their destination—the breakwater at the north-eastern edge of Atagohama—in twos and threes. They had carried Takei's vinyl-wrapped corpse to the van on the makeshift stretcher and slid it into the back, along with some concrete blocks, chains, ropes, and Orihara's spirit guide vessels. After Ishihara told them to wear black since it was a funeral of sorts, Mori and Yamada had gone back to Building H to change into black shirts and jackets. Neither of them had black trousers, so Mori put on a pair of midnight-blue sweatpants and Yamada made do with gray jeans. Toyohara was wearing a navy-blue, skintight running shirt and a pair of dark-green shorts. On the back of the running shirt was the distinctive M of the University of Michigan.

"I couldn't believe how much blood there was," Toyohara said as they walked along. It had taken a long time to clean it all up. Takeguchi had fetched some chlorine from his bomb lab to use on the concrete floor, but a dark stain still remained. Mori turned to Toyohara and asked if his hand didn't hurt. Since no one in the group had a certificate of residence, they naturally had no health insurance either, which complicated things if they got sick or hurt. When Shibata developed appendicitis about six months ago, Ishihara had managed to arrange an appendectomy for him through an acquaintance at the Junior Chamber of Commerce. For stomachaches and colds they bought over-the-counter medicines and rested, and for serious cuts or infections they sometimes used dubious extracts that Shinohara had harvested from his frogs and centipedes. Toyohara said he didn't know why but it didn't hurt much at all. Maybe he was still numb with shock. "I really feel bad about Takei-san, though... When I was a kid and cut down that guy on the bullet train, I was amazed how easy it is to kill a person if you have a good weapon, and I feel the same way now. Most people don't think they'd die that easy. It's a huge thing to realize."

The road through the residential area was dotted with potholes filled with gravel that crunched beneath their shoes. The typhoon several years before had done a lot of damage here. Many homes had been gutted, but people had patched the roofs and walls of others and were still living in them. When the hundred and twenty thousand reinforcements arrived, they'd be staying right near here. It was one in the morning, but they could hear the earth-movers and generators still running at the *danchi*. It seemed the Koryos were going to work twenty-four hours a day.

The Koryos hadn't heard the gunshots or shown up at Building C after all; Mori had been mistaken when he thought he saw the soldier staring back at him. The noise they were making at the construction site must have drowned out the gunshots. Mori's relief was tinged with a certain sense of powerlessness; it was as if they were beneath the Koryos' notice. They had decided to fight, but no one had any idea how to go about it. They had weapons, but the weapons were all of different types and nobody had any experience operating them. Before they'd inflicted so much as a scratch on the enemy, one of their own was already dead because of a boneheaded accident. And the enemy still didn't even know they existed.

A cold onshore wind was blowing. The sky was cloudy, with no moon or stars. A baby cried somewhere in the distance but soon stopped. Where the residential district ended, they came to a wide street, and when they had crossed it, sea smells rose to meet them. The dark expanse of the bay was to their right. To their left, in silhouette, was a row of abandoned, half-built condominium towers; and in the distance, beyond these skeletons, they could make out the Dome and the Sea Hawk Hotel.

The minivan had already arrived at the breakwater. Matsuyama, Ando, and Felix were in the back of the van, attaching the concrete blocks to Takei's body with the ropes and chains. The breakwater stuck out into the bay in the shape of an F. Near the middle it dipped down to nearly water level, and the van was parked in that depression. Ando and the others had pulled the stretcher partway out of the van, so that one end rested on the breakwater's edge. They were going to slide Takei down it and into the water. Shibata lit up the operation with a hooded flashlight. Four of them crouched on the breakwater, holding the stretcher tight, while six others each lifted a concrete block. Inside the van, Miyazaki held the head of the bundle

388

that was Takei while Ando, standing outside, took the feet. "Here we go," Ando said quietly and pulled hard while Miyazaki pushed. As Takei began to slide over the edge, Matsuyama and the others hurled their concrete blocks. They splashed into the water in rapid succession and disappeared, followed immediately by Takei's body.

They concealed the minivan amid the condo ruins, then each of them put some candles, flowers, and fruit in their pockets and carried two of the spirit guide vessels—one in either hand—down the steps on the sheltered side of the breakwater. There were only the gentlest of rolling waves here. No one spoke. They gathered around Orihara, who showed them how to prepare the little boats. He peeled a tangerine and placed half of the peel in each of his two vessels. Everyone else did the same, and the scent of sweet citrus wafted in the air. Orihara then placed several small, daisy-like flowers in each boat, dripped wax from a lit candle onto the cardboard floor, and set the candle in it like a mast. He climbed carefully across the rocks at the water's edge and launched his two vessels. Everyone then proceeded to do the same. Ever so slowly, the tide pulled the little boats out toward the open sea. They squatted on the rocks and silently watched as the candles gradually spread out, the flames reflecting off the dark water like stars in a morphing constellation. With each gust of wind, the fragile flames flickered and threatened to go out, and as soon as the boats left the protection of the breakwater they'd undoubtedly tip right over. They were the feeblest, most unreliable lights Mori had ever seen. But they were also the most beautiful. He was surprised to find that tears were rolling down his cheeks. Not wanting anyone to see, he quickly wiped them away and bowed his head. But when he glanced up, Yamada too was wiping his eyes. Mori looked around him. Tateno and Matsuyama and Sato and Shinohara, Felix and Fukuda and Takeguchi—all were wiping away tears as they watched the spirit guides float away. *We're all sad*—the moment he realized that, he remembered what Ishihara had said to Kaneshiro: *The essence of fellowship is floating around somewhere.* It was something very frail, very fragile, very indistinct. Like those spirit guide vessels, maybe. Mori experienced a mysterious sensation of warmth radiating out from his core. The sense of fellowship was a quiet thing, he thought. It wasn't about believing that they were inseparable, or about acting in concert or joining hands. It was about gazing together at those weak, indistinct, and soon-to-be-extinguished flames.

"But, I mean, what was that geezer's life all about?" Ishihara wondered aloud. They were back up on the breakwater, and he was staring down at the spot where Takei had sunk. "He gets downsized at his job, fails to kill himself, heads off to Yemen or wherever, gets downsized there too, swears off alcohol and massage parlors, and puts all his money into accumulating weapons, and dies on the day he finally unveils his prized collection." There were no traces left of Takei on the breakwater or in the water below. He'd been so well sealed in the vinyl that not a drop of blood had escaped. There was nothing to see but the gray concrete and the dark sea. They began plodding back to the warehouse. "On the other hand," Shinohara said, "today, with the show, may have been the high point of his life." Ando muttered, "Everybody has to die when their time comes." Ishihara raised his head and looked at the Sea Hawk Hotel in the distance. This high-rise building was meant to be shaped like a ship, but from here it looked more like a knife. It pierced the low-lying layer of clouds, the red light at its tip winking on and off. That light was the exact opposite of the now-vanished lights of the spirit guides. It seemed to be mocking them all as they straggled homeward. And it seemed to symbolize, and flaunt, the power of the Koryos. Everyone must have been feeling it—they all kept their heads turned away from the winking red light as they walked along.

Except Ishihara, that is. He continued to gaze at it. "The Koryos have their camp next to that hotel," he said, and laughed with a clucking *ku-ku-ku* sound. Mori stopped in his tracks. *Please don't start with that laugh at a time like this*, he thought. But Ishihara had already started—now doubling over, now bending over backwards as he cackled. His performance didn't have the same edge it normally

390

had, however—it was a desperate, fuck-it-all sort of laugh. "If we could just knock down that hotel," he gurgled, "we could kill 'em all!" Nobody laughed along with him. Why make such stupid cracks, Mori wondered, when everyone was feeling so crushed and hopeless? But now Takeguchi drew to a halt. "What did you just say, Ishihara-san?" Ishihara stopped laughing abruptly and scowled. "Takeguchi, don't make us say the same crappy joke twice. This isn't pleasant for anybody. What I and I said was, if we could just knock down that hotel, we could kill all the Koryos."

"Hang on a minute," Takeguchi said, with a serious frown, and glanced at Fukuda. The two of them exchanged a few words in undertones and nodded back and forth. Mori heard fragments here and there—"RDX," "cookie," "LSC." Finally Takeguchi turned back to Ishihara, then ran his eyes over the rest of the group and pointed at the Sea Hawk Hotel.

"It wouldn't be easy to bring down a building like that," he said. "But it's not impossible."

6

# NIGHT IN TOKYO

*April 7, 2011*

K AI TOMONORI, known in the Home Affairs Ministry as "Tom,"
at last finished writing up his report on the leak of the resident
codes in Fukuoka. He had spent the past four days and nights working
on it after being specifically instructed not to delegate the task to
anyone else, presumably to ensure that the media didn't get their
hands on it. This was the first time he'd ever had to write a ministry
report without any assistance. It was exhausting work, and essentially
meaningless, simply about covering his own ass. By the time he left
the office, passing a dozen or so armed SDF soldiers standing outside,
it was already past eleven at night. It would soon be April 8. Over
four hundred ships were in ports along the east coast of North Korea,
apparently due to set sail in the afternoon of April 9. Four ports
had been cited—Rajin, Chongjin, Kimchaek, and Wonsan—but
according to information from US military satellites, more ships
appeared to be gathering at Tanchon, Ranam, Kyongsong, Riwon,
Sinpo, Rason, and Sinhung. If what the terrorists calling themselves
the Koryo Expeditionary Force had said was true, these ships would
be on their way within the next thirty-odd hours. The fleet included
converted fishing boats that were small and slow, and skirting South
Korean territorial waters would further slow them down, but they

were likely to arrive some forty or so hours after leaving port. It was a major crisis, and all the government buildings were brightly lit up as politicians and civil servants alike worked around the clock. While one team was planning rescue operations in the event of a biological or chemical weapons attack in Fukuoka, another was examining ways to secure the communications networks in all the principal cities.

For the past four days, however, the government had been primarily occupied with preparing the legal basis for the Maritime Self-Defense Force to intercept the North Korean ships, and how to deal with the US government and Japan-based US forces, as well as the Chinese government and the UN Security Council. Even Kai's indirect involvement had left him feeling that the government didn't know what it was doing. It had taken hours of debate before the decision was taken to stretch interpretation of Clause 20 of the Japan Coast Guard Law, promulgated in the wake of the spy ship incident of March 1999, to allow the Maritime SDF to prevent the expected fleet from entering their territorial waters. The Foreign Ministry had also been pushing the US and other allies to stop the ships leaving North Korea on the basis that it would provoke military conflict in East Asia. However, a senior official in the US State Department had apparently responded off the record that the only threat of conflict came from Japan if it attacked the ships carrying the rebel army.

Outside it was exceptionally warm for April, but Kai soon realized the heat was due to the lighting used by the riot police. The entrances of all the government buildings and surrounding streets were as bright as day, and there was a constant tinnitus-like hum from the generators. He felt unsteady on his feet. He hadn't had any sleep to speak of for the past five days, and he smelled bad, having been unable to wash thoroughly in the cramped showers in the ministry. He didn't feel particularly stressed, but he was still too wired to be able to sleep right away. He decided to go for a drink, and called his mother to let her know that he wouldn't be home until late. Kai wasn't much of a drinker. A doctor had once told him his low tolerance of alcohol was probably psychological. His mother was a teetotaler, and this had probably affected him—whenever his mother disliked something, he tended to follow suit. But there was a bar in Akasaka that never had any loud karaoke or rowdy customers, and never put any pressure on you to drink more than you wanted. The proprietor, Sanjo Masahiro, had started the place after retiring from an undistinguished career in the Financial Services Agency. Its pleasant atmosphere was conducive to enjoying a quiet drink along with some good music and conversation.

For the last couple of days, TV broadcast vans had been banned from the Kasumigaseki government district, and the number of TV cameras and reporters allowed in had also been severely restricted. The only civilian vehicles circulating in the area were chauffeur-driven limos, taxis, and official cars. It wasn't that the area had been sealed off as such, but the riot police checkpoints were so stringent that ordinary traffic naturally avoided it. According to the National Police Agency, over fifty thousand riot police from all over eastern Japan had been mobilized. The number of SDF soldiers guarding the ministries and agencies had also been substantially increased. They had been kitted out with gas masks, and a chemical protection squad from Omiya had already arrived in Tokyo. Tanks and armored personnel carriers had become a familiar sight. Rows of riot police trucks lined the roads, and riot police were permanently deployed every few meters and in the local subway stations, on the alert for terrorist attacks. The whole area felt as if it were under martial law, and not many people were out on the street. As Kai walked past the riot police, he held up the photo ID hanging around his neck for them to see, and they double-checked his face against it.

When he'd declined an official car on the pretext of wanting some fresh air, he had been warned to be careful. Just the day before yesterday Doihara, Minister for Land, Infrastructure and Transport, had been attacked by a man wielding a wooden sword as he was about to get in his car after attending a meeting of top domestic and foreign airline executives in a central Tokyo hotel. His attacker had been an unemployed man in his late forties with no political background, his motive being simply that the blockade had prevented him from being at his mother's deathbed. He was easily overpowered by a bodyguard, but the media had shown widespread sympathy for the man, however. For the past six months, Doihara's attacker had been sending his entire unemployment benefit package to his elderly mother in Fukuoka, who had heart and lung problems, and he himself was severely undernourished. When her condition had taken a sudden turn for the worse and his relatives sent word for him to come immediately, there were no planes or trains in operation to Fukuoka, so he was unable to travel. Numerous other people had been similarly affected.

Kai flagged down a taxi and asked to be taken to Akasaka. The elderly driver kept glancing in the rear-view mirror at his face and ID. Kai felt uneasy. What if the man was from Fukuoka? He might get aggressive if he knew that his passenger was a government official. Until recently, Kai had never really bothered about what part of the country people were from. Now, though, ministry employees from Kyushu, especially those from Fukuoka, had acquired a particular aura, as though each was capable of sudden violence. According to a survey conducted in 2008 by the Statistics Bureau, there were about four hundred thousand people from Fukuoka and a million or so from Kyushu as a whole who were now living elsewhere in Japan. Given that there was a daily average in Fukuoka City of thirty-four weddings and twenty-nine deaths, with the corresponding figures for Kyushu as a whole at two hundred weddings and three hundred and twenty deaths, this made for an awful lot of people unable to attend the weddings and funerals of family, friends, and relatives. The combined monthly passenger figures for JAL and ANA flights to and from Fukuoka had approached a million, which translated into a daily average of sixteen thousand passengers arriving at Fukuoka Airport. The backlog was obviously enormous, with the accumulation of freight destined to leave Fukuoka for East Asian countries like Korea and China in the past four days alone said to amount to some ten thousand large containers.

There had been several other incidents, too. A spate of suicides among female high-school students had been sparked by the cancellation of the Kyushu leg of a tour by a popular rock band. The night the concerts had been called off, a high-school girl in Kumamoto jumped off a building, and subsequently girls in Fukuoka and Nagasaki had taken overdoses or slit their wrists, making a total of seven deaths in all. One psychologist interviewed on TV said that the cancellation of the tour wasn't entirely to blame, and that the sense of isolation caused by the blockade had also played a part. Then the day before yesterday, Umezu, the Minister for Economy, Trade, and Industry, had resigned over a related incident. Early in the morning of the seventh, a patient suffering from acute kidney failure died due to a lack of dialysis solution at a private hospital in Saga. Umezu was himself from Fukuoka, where his family was heavily involved in local industry, and he must have come under a fair amount of pressure from the local business community. People seemed to be divided in their attitude toward his resignation, with around fifty per cent voicing disapproval.

Public opinion on the blockade kept vacillating. Even within the government there were factions opposed to it, although there was also support from the opposition. The main media outlets daily overplayed the issue without taking a clear stand either way. And then all of a sudden a consensus arose that, should the blockade be lifted, major mainland cities like Tokyo and Osaka were bound to be attacked. There was a general sense of guilt at having imposed the blockade, so some kind of justification for it had to be found if the people of Fukuoka weren't to have been sacrificed in vain. It had to be accepted as inevitable. And it followed that any assault on the KEF or its ships would result in widespread terrorist attacks.

For the past couple of days, rumors had been spreading on Internet message boards that the North Koreans would target liquefied-natural-gas facilities, and before long the national media had picked up on it. One website run by an American couple, both scientists, attracted particular attention. They had long been warning that LNG installations were soft targets for terrorists in that an entire city could go up in flames if pipes or tanks were hit. Subsequently, the top story in one national paper detailed how Fukuoka would be engulfed in a sea of flames in the event of an attack on the Seibu Gas installation on Higashihama Pier. One expert pointed out that although underground LNG containers were protected against earthquakes and soil liquefaction, an anti-tank rocket could crack the upper surface and cause a leak that might well explode with the power of a small atomic bomb, which led to frenzied speculation that gas terminals and pipelines across the country could also come under attack.

Once the media had decided that if the blockade was lifted the whole country might explode, nobody—neither the politicians and media who had remained on the fence about the blockade, nor even human rights and antiwar advocates—was any longer able to voice opposition to it. Or rather, thought Kai, they were no longer under any pressure to take a side. For the same reason, conservatives and right-wingers were unable to push for an attack on either the North Korean terrorists' camp in Fukuoka or their backup fleet. The question of whether the KEF actually intended to carry out terrorist attacks around the country ceased even to be debated.

Yet even as public opinion fluctuated this way and that, cracks began appearing in the veneer of humanitarian concern to reveal glimpses of vested interests. Two days earlier, the Japan Federation of Economic Organizations had started criticizing the blockade on behalf of companies exporting parts for automobiles and electronic equipment from Fukuoka to China, and demanded that freight operations be resumed from Hakata Port to East Asian destinations. Since these were influential exporters, their opposition to the blockade had a major effect. There were also persistent rumors that unless deliveries were resumed, Chinese firms would start petitioning the Japanese government. The government couldn't afford *not* to consider lifting the blockade. The PM and his deputy weighed up numerous options, but kept running up against the unfortunate fact that Fukuoka City had handed over the resident codes to the North Koreans, and some private banks and firms were actively collaborating with them. For all they knew, the city might have issued them

Japanese passports. If this was the case, it would be impossible to contain them once air and rail travel was resumed.

A further concern was that if they allowed exports to go ahead, there was a risk that it would further consolidate the occupation. The possibility of Prime Minister Kido and Foreign Minister Ohashi going to Fukuoka to negotiate with the KEF leaders had also been discussed a number of times, but the principle of not negotiating with terrorists kept getting in the way. This point was of major importance for the government, though it probably made little difference to the people of Fukuoka. But there was criticism from abroad that in not going to Fukuoka or appointing a negotiator, the Japanese government was demonstrating its cowardice and incompetence.

Near the Kasumigaseki exit of the Tokyo Metropolitan Expressway, a group of people sat on the ground in a candlelit vigil. It was a peaceful demonstration by young and old alike, with a banner that read "LOVE AND PEACE TO ALL THE PEOPLE OF FUKUOKA." Someone was playing a guitar, and everyone sang along. Looking at the flickering candlelight, Kai suddenly felt sick to his stomach. He wanted to grab them by the collar and yell at them, "Just how the hell do you think all this love and peace will get there?" In Fukuoka people were actually dying. A yakuza carrying a shotgun had been shot at point-blank range by a member of the terrorists' police squadron. The man had fired two bullets in quick succession from a Kalashnikov into the victim's head. And then a whole crowd in Ohori Park had been caught up in a shoot-out. The streets of Fukuoka were already full of death.

Kai had the taxi drop him at the top of Hitotsugi Street, and removed his ID pass from his neck as he set off down the sidewalk. The tension prompted by the heightened police presence else-where was absent from Akasaka's entertainment district. Heavily guarded areas were around the Diet and the Imperial Palace, the Kasumigaseki government district and the Defense Agency, as well as Tokyo Station, Haneda Airport, the port facilities, the Metropolitan Government office, and the embassies of important countries. Outside the metropolitan area, places like nuclear power stations, dams, LNG and oil storage facilities, and SDF bases were also covered. Entertainment and shopping areas were not considered targets and so were left unguarded. It wasn't that nobody worried about it—what if sarin gas was released in, say, a cinema in Kabukicho? But without a tenfold increase in the number of police, SDF soldiers, firemen, and doctors, there was no way of preparing for such a scenario; and so the government had simply taken the optimistic view that these places were not in danger.

It was Kai's first visit to Akasaka in quite some time. The bustle and atmosphere was unchanged, but there were a lot of foreigners, especially Americans, around. Inflation and the recession were keeping Japanese customers away, and with the collapse of the yen overseas visitors found Japan a bargain and came in droves. A flashing neon sign drew attention to a famous Italian restaurant that had its main branch in Rome. The sign combined the restaurant's name with prawns, salami, and the tripe that the place was famous for. In the alley next to it, two homeless men were checking out a plastic bucket of raw garbage. They had removed the lid and were rummaging inside with their bare hands. One was stuffing macaroni and spaghetti leftovers into a plastic bag, while the other was chewing the last bits of meat from a bone—lamb, maybe, or chicken. Apparently missing some teeth and unable to bite properly, he scrunched up his mouth and used his tongue, gums, and remaining teeth in an effort to strip the meat off. He looked like a baby with its lips clamped around its mother's nipple.

The man stuffing pasta into a bag was at most in his late twenties, and the one sucking on the bone wasn't of an age at which you would normally lose your teeth. He'd probably had them smashed in by someone. Kai had read in a weekly magazine of a trend amongst juveniles to work over people like this. Both men were dressed in shirts, cotton pants, and sneakers, and both had their long hair pulled back in ponytails. Their clothes and shoes were grubby, though if they hadn't been scavenging in garbage bins they probably wouldn't have been noticeable. As Kai stood watching them, the bone-sucker

399

looked over at him. His eyes locked with Kai's, but his expression didn't change.

A group of people with ID passes from the nearby TBS TV station appeared. An anchor from the TBS evening news program had recently resigned in protest over the blockade. He was a former university professor from Fukuoka. His resignation had apparently been big news down there, but hardly even gained a mention in Tokyo. At the start of the blockade, the daily reality of those "sacrificed" in Fukuoka had been widely debated on news programs. In an appeal to viewers' sympathy, the media had been focusing on individuals affected by the blockade, from crying children at Fukuoka Airport unable to travel to Disneyland, to businessmen prevented from going on business trips, lawyers complaining that important documents weren't getting through because the mail had been stopped, journalists whose papers were limited to a six-page edition because of the shortage of paper and ink, and pharmaceutical companies and hospitals scrambling to secure supplies of disinfectants and blood agents. After the Ohori Park incident, however, such reports had abruptly ceased. The word "sacrifice" had an attractive ring to it, with its sense of noble self-denial—until, that is, the reality hit home with bodies shown being blown apart.

In the middle of the group of male TBS employees was a woman anchor in charge of the evening news. She was well known, with the intelligence and good looks typical of TBS. She was probably on her way out for a bite to eat with her crew, having finished the evening broadcast. Her long, slim legs were sheathed in flesh-colored stockings, and she wore a pale-green suit and a scarf around her neck. Her hair was tinted brown; her eyes slanted upward at the corners. As they walked, the men suddenly burst out laughing at something she'd said. Attracted by the sound, passers-by noticed her, and a group of students called out, "We love your program—keep up the good work!" Kai felt rage welling up inside him again: with Japan in such a serious fix, how could they be so lighthearted? The anchor ignored him as they passed each other—there was no reason why she should have noticed him, but Kai felt as though he'd been cold-shouldered. There were a lot of people in Kyushu who couldn't laugh right now even if they wanted to. Did these people really understand that? After they had gone, the scent of the woman's perfume seemed to linger in the air. The smell was odious to him.

Outside one building, a Japanese bar girl was locked in an embrace with a foreign customer wearing a soft gray suit that looked Italian-made. He had one arm around her waist as he kissed her repeatedly on her cheeks and forehead, murmuring to her in English, "I'll be right back to see you. Don't forget you promised to come to Kyoto with me…" East Coast accent, thought Kai. After Tokyo University, Kai had gone to study at a small college in Boston through a contact of his mother's. His homestay family was extremely strict, and he became fluent in English. Following the 9/11 attacks, it had become difficult to obtain a student visa for the US, so there were few foreign students around and hardly any other Asians. He had often felt hurt by the behavior of the East Coast rich kids toward him, but he'd stuck to them like a suckerfish and even made a few friends. His given name was Tomonori, so he told them to call him Tom. During those days, he often thought of returning to Japan, but his mother would never have allowed it.

Kai's father ran an import-export retail business dealing in luxury tableware and furniture; his mother was the daughter of a diplomat and had lived for many years in the US. Kai was their only child, and with his father often away from home on business, his mother's ambitions for him were a strong influence. The main reason Kai had given up the idea of becoming an academic in favor of the Home Affairs Ministry was his mother's urging him to "make something of himself." When he'd been promoted to director general of the LGWAN, newly formed to expand the Juki Net, she had been overjoyed. There wasn't much that Kai wouldn't do for her sake—making her happy and earning her praise made it all worthwhile. He sometimes thought it was probably because of her that he'd never married, even though he'd dated a number of women. But he had no regrets.

Kai entered the alley where the bar was located. He could see a woman asleep on a sofa in a closed-down ethnic food place, but he couldn't tell whether she was homeless or just drunk. A group of middle-school kids came out of a convenience store and, catching sight of a policeman in the distance, scuttled away. A young man was gathering skewers from the garbage can outside a yakitori restaurant: quite well dressed in suit and tie, he didn't look down-and-out. He tied the skewers with a rubber band and put them in a bag, possibly collecting them to sell. A woman yelled from the other side of the building. It sounded like an elderly person—probably a homeless woman being bullied by that gang of school kids he'd seen a moment ago. Many innocent elderly people had been "sacrificed" in Fukuoka. Yet strangely no one—not even the government—appeared to have caught the full impact of what had happened in Ohori Park.

Inside the bar, one customer sat at the counter, and a couple more were on a sofa. Jazz music was playing at low volume. Sanjo, the bar owner, always made his own selection from his collection of vinyl records, not CDs, for the nightly playlist. Resting on an easel marked "now playing" was an album by Stan Getz. It was an old bossa nova recording featuring a plump-cheeked female Brazilian vocalist. Kai thought its languorous mood suited the atmosphere and décor of the place. The sturdy oak counter had been meticulously polished, and the Spanish-made sofas along the wall were upholstered in paisley with comfortable arm- and backrests. On the walls papered in a simple design hung reproductions of works by the likes of Goya and Mondrian. Behind the counter, a Wedgewood tureen filled the place with a briny, buttery smell. Sanjo told his customers, "In *kaiseki* cuisine a broth is always served before the main dish," and urged them to have some of his traditional Boston clam chowder before starting to drink. Exhaustion washed over Kai as soon as he entered the bar, and instead of sitting at the counter he sank onto a sofa.

Sanjo came over with a tray on which he'd placed a bowl of soup and a straight vermouth in a Venetian glass with an elaborate gold-leaf pattern. "Let's get you warmed up first," he said, spreading a linen cloth on the table and placing the glass and soup bowl on it. "Talk to you in a bit," he said with a smile and went back behind the counter. He was always at pains to put his customers at ease by serving them some warm soup and a light aperitif right away. Kai had never much liked clam chowder when he was in Boston, but in this bar he only had to smell it to feel himself relax.

Seated in a black leather-upholstered chair at the counter was the owner of a French restaurant in Moto Azabu who was a regular here. Kai had often been to his restaurant. The chef there, who had trained at a three-star restaurant in Montpelier in the south of France, served a delicious bouillabaisse and dessert soufflé. On the other sofa were two women: an art dealer and her business partner, who mostly promoted young Mexican artists at their gallery in Minami Aoyama. The business partner, though still only about forty, was the widow of the CEO of a major paper manufacturer and had inherited a vast sum of money. Kai sipped his drink and nodded at them in greeting. He took a cracker from the demitasse saucer and broke it up into the clam chowder, then picked up the silver spoon engraved with the name of the bar and dipped it in. Smoke from the restaurant owner's cigar—a Cohiba Robusto—wafted over from the counter. I can't think of anywhere more relaxing than this place, thought Kai, exhaling deeply. The art dealer and the widow were deep in discussion over an etching by Goya on the wall. The piece depicted a scene from Napoleon's invasion of Spain, with soldiers shooting people against a backdrop of a mound of corpses. It reminded Kai of the images of Ohori Park shown repeatedly on TV.

The Osaka SAT team had laid an ambush for the North Koreans with the help of a certain Kuzuta Shinsaku, who was on the terrorists' list of people to be arrested. In line with the SAT plan, Kuzuta had asked for the arrest to be made at a restaurant in Ohori Park instead of at home, and the terrorists had agreed to his request. The Koreans had sent a squadron of only six Special Police, which meant they were heavily outnumbered. Where the SAT people miscalculated was in failing to anticipate the opposition dividing into two squadrons. The SAT captain and his team had hidden in the restaurant, while his deputy had waited in the buses with a backup squadron. On being informed that the Koreans had split into two groups, the SAT captain told his deputy to get instructions from Osaka. But just as this was being done, a squad member hiding on the restaurant terrace had detonated a stun grenade in the belief they'd been spotted by one of the terrorists. This was impossible to verify, but nobody blamed him. How else should he have responded to unforeseen circumstances? He couldn't have known that the decision to go ahead had not yet been cleared with those higher up.

The following day, the *Asahi Shinbun* reporter accompanying the terrorists on their round of arrests had published a detailed report in which he stated that the SAT had opened fire first, and worse, that they had fired from a position that was most likely to put bystanders at risk. When the terrorists' reinforcements started retaliating, the crowd of onlookers had cheered. Foreign governments and media held that the SAT's strategy had been unjustifiable, a senior official in the British government commenting that if they were prepared to sacrifice ordinary citizens, then why didn't the SDF just go ahead and attack the Koryo Expeditionary Force? The chairman of the UN Security Council took the unprecedented step of urging the Japanese government to show more restraint. Of the forty Osaka SAT members, twenty-four died, twelve were injured, and four surrendered and were now being held captive. Valuable personnel had been lost due to a strategic error.

"You're looking pretty glum, Tom." Sanjo had brought a drink over and sat on a stool facing Kai's sofa. 'Corcovado' started playing. Kai said he couldn't believe they'd fouled up so badly in Ohori Park. Sanjo nodded and smiled ruefully. He was drinking Famous Grouse Scotch. It was a cheap brand with a label bearing an illustration of the bird, but he liked its flavor. Kai himself had never acquired a taste for whiskey. He took a sip of vermouth, and even this burned his throat and stomach. Sanjo was of medium height and build, and always dressed in a white long-sleeved shirt, navy-blue pants, and dark-brown lace-up shoes. His hair was completely white, but perhaps because he was single and relatively free of worldly cares, he didn't give the impression of being that old. Now and then, to keep up his English, he would translate an old spy novel. On graduating from a private university in Tokyo, he had been employed by the Tokyo branch of a foreign financial institution and had subsequently spent almost twenty years working in its UK head office and in Barbados. Toward the end of the Eighties, he had gone to work for what used to be the Financial Services Agency on a temporary basis, and ended up being employed there until retirement four years ago, when he opened this bar. Kai had first been brought here by Matsuoka Kusuko, the Minister for Information and Communications, and had been a regular customer ever since.

"I suppose the Foreign Ministry has petitioned the Security Council?" asked Sanjo, then muttered, "But in any case it's a mess..." His slim neck rippled as he swallowed some whiskey. The occupation of Fukuoka was certainly an act of aggression as defined by the United Nations, but it wasn't clear that the aggressor was another nation as such. The foreign media referred to the Koryo Expeditionary Force by name, as a group of armed defectors. Furthermore, there hadn't been a battle, and the Japanese government hadn't formally demanded that the terrorists disarm. In other words, there hadn't yet been any real contact—they had simply imposed a blockade. And although they could blame North Korea as much as they liked, it wasn't as if they could expect the North Korean government to restore Fukuoka to its original state.

"They should have sent the Foreign Minister to the UN to explain our situation," said Sanjo, before asking what the government planned to do about the fleet preparing to sail from North Korea. "They don't seem to know yet," Kai replied, scooping up the last spoonful of clam chowder. With a pang of dismay, he remembered that the Foreign Ministry had assigned a task force to review international law in search of a solution. Over two hundred staff members had twenty-four hours to prepare a report on precedents such as Israel's invasion of Gaza, the issue of sovereignty in the Falklands War, and the UN resolution on the invasion of Kuwait by Iraq. But it was just like Sanjo said: they should have made Japan's position and wishes known to the whole world right from the start.

"Shall we all have some melon before we go home?" Sanjo pointed at a wooden box on the bar. "I got these fantastic melons from Miyazaki. Brought the last one along to share with everyone tonight." When Kai asked what he meant by the "last" one, Sanjo explained that he couldn't get any more due to the blockade. He glanced at the clock. "Right, I'll close the bar, then," he said, walking over to the door and switching off the neon sign. "We don't want a bunch of new customers coming in now. There won't be enough melon to go around." The art dealer laughed and said, "As if you ever get any new customers!" She was wearing a Chanel suit that looked good on her. Her friend wore a simple dress that had a slight sheen to it, set off with a necklace of evenly matched pearls. Sanjo cleared away the soup dish, changed the record from Stan Getz to Bill Evans, and came back with another whiskey, humming along to Evans's piano rendition of 'Willow Weep for Me.' "So how are these North Koreans laundering all that moola they've been stealing?" he asked Kai. Money-laundering was a subject Sanjo had specialized in. "But then they probably don't need to bother," he added, "since the ones they're arresting have already done it for them—all those drug dealers and yakuza and international con men. One of the regional banks must be collaborating with them—in which case, you can't call it money-laundering as such. The people they've been arresting have all been busy laundering their proceeds through unregistered credit or bank bonds, gold bullion, Swiss bank accounts, accounts under false names in Hong Kong, or offshore funds in places like Andorra or Lichtenstein, Monaco, the Cayman Islands, Nauru. Whatever way, the stuff must be normalized by now, so all they have to do is grab it."

"They can always invest in art," chimed in the widow. According to her, paintings were more popular than ever as investments, especially after the rise of international Internet auctions. "There was a time when wealthy Saudis were rumored to be using Netherlandish art to mobilize funds to support terrorism, so the FBI introduced a

406

system whereby any trade of over half a million dollars had to be registered, but basically it's like Sanjo-san says: it's just not possible without the cooperation of the banks. And of course the banks don't want to make enemies of the rich."

"Wine's a good investment too," put in the art dealer, raising her glass. The two women were drinking a Château Cheval Blanc Saint-Émilion. Kai's homestay family in Boston had had wine every evening with dinner, and although he himself hardly ever drank he had become quite familiar with the varieties and their fragrances and flavors. The Cheval Blanc had an almond aroma. "More and more people are buying vintage Bordeaux over the Internet. A dozen bottles of, say, a 1982 Le Pin will be worth tens of thousands of dollars. There are companies that specialize in buying on commission, as well as the management and storage of the wine. Depending on how you go about it, you can easily launder huge amounts that way."

"But those North Koreans don't know the first thing about Château Le Pin," the widow said cheerfully. "According to all the magazines, the Generalissimo drives a Benz, has a Rolex, and drinks Rémy Martin. But he's never been to the West, so he doesn't really know anything about the world. Just like Japan thirty or forty years ago. In our case it was Koenig Specials, Franck Mullers, and Grande Champagne Cognac, because we didn't know any better. Now, of course, people act as though they've been drinking Le Pin all their lives."

She swirled the wine around in her glass and brought it to her nose, savoring the aroma. "And just how long have *you* been drinking it?" teased her friend, and everyone laughed. The two women accompanied their wine with cluster raisins, and now and again one of them lit up a cigarette. The art dealer was from Yamanashi. The widow was Tokyo born, and lived within a stone's throw of the bar in a large house set in extensive grounds, with her secretary and two borzoi dogs. Once the laughter had died down the sound of Bill Evans's piano came through again with 'Someday My Prince Will Come.' The notes were like jewels dancing in the air.

407

Kai felt unburdened—the sort of feeling you get when a persistent fever has finally broken—but some nagging thoughts that hadn't bothered him while he was at work began to resurface in his mind. The biggest puzzle was why these terrorists were as effective as they were. They showed an astonishing skill in the way they ruled the city and dealt with public relations, not to mention their shooting and combat ability.

With an economy in tatters, widespread starvation, and several hundred thousand so-called political prisoners reportedly held in concentration camps, there was the possibility of the Kim Jong Il regime collapsing at any time. The level of international confidence in the regime was zero, and the only leverage they had for negotiating was the nuclear threat. And yet a group of just five hundred men and women from that country had not only taken control of Kyushu's capital—a city with a population of a million—but also appropriated the assets of Japanese nationals, and were using Japanese workers to build housing for them with that money. They had seized upon the Ohori Park incident to inform the world, via their own TV program, that it had been the Japanese government that attacked Fukuoka citizens; they had told the foreign media that they were willing to accept UN inspections; they had accurately read the moves of Japanese firms and foreign countries wanting the shipping of car parts and semiconductors to be resumed; and they had announced that they were willing to allow all countries to reopen their consulates at any time. China was apparently considering doing so soon, since once the export embargo was lifted, moving the backlog of cargo would be a priority. And if South Korea and the US followed suit, the legitimacy this would give the occupation would be disastrous.

"I hate to say this, but there's a possibility that Japan is already screwed," said Sanjo. "We're the only country that has anything to lose by an army of North Korean hardliners establishing a base in Fukuoka. I'm apolitical, not right-wing or left-wing or liberal or anything else, but this really smacks of a conspiracy. Not necessarily an international conspiracy—more likely it's a unilateral action by North Korea, although I do get the feeling that there's some kind of tacit agreement in the international community. Acts of aggression are prohibited by international law, in order to preserve peace. But there's no state of war in Fukuoka. Didn't a spokesman from the US State Department protest just the day before yesterday that the Japanese government had neglected its duty to protect their consulate in Fukuoka? If America can make a complaint like that in all seriousness, then you can see where things are headed, can't you? The government probably should be applying the provisions in the penal code for crimes related to an external threat. That's the law under which anyone who assists or offers any military benefit in the event of armed aggression by a foreign country can be sentenced to death or life imprisonment. But now that we've imposed a blockade, we can't very well start indicting people, can we?"

Sanjo had been a finance pro trained in offshore funds. He had been managing accounts of several hundred million yen by his late twenties. He modestly claimed that all he did was fiddle with them and move them around by computer, but if you understood where and how the world's money circulated, you could see the way the power games between countries played out. "Of course that gang of North Koreans in Fukuoka is tough," he said, taking his empty glass back to the bar, where he poured himself some more Scotch before returning to his stool. "In diplomatic terms, those guys are old pros at walking the tightrope between Russia and China, and playing chicken with America by using nuclear brinkmanship to force negotiations for a mutual non-aggression treaty. Being a diplomat there means knowing that if you fail, you'll be purged—and not just you but your whole family. Sent away for 'discipline.' It's the same with finance.

"For a country in which seventy per cent of the people are starving, they've somehow managed to run the place by manipulating information, eliminating anyone who protests, and pestering other countries for money. It makes me sick, but they've actually become really good at it. When it comes to propaganda, nobody can hold a candle to them. 'A matchless intellect, as bountiful as the sun, as indomitable as steel'—at one point there were thirty-eight such phrases glorifying Kim Il Sung. And it's not easy to come up with things like that, you know. They have to be subtle enough to take in a whole mass of people. And then, if the Generalissimo or one of his aides doesn't like what he comes up with, the guy in charge of propaganda will be sent packing, along with his family. It's a hard-ass society. The Special Operations Forces undergo fearsome training programs, and are well funded, too. The provincial officials in Kyushu don't stand a chance against them. But they'll end up their own worst enemies, you mark my words. They're not civilized enough. Even Pol Pot and the Nazis lost because of that."

The occupants of the bar listened to him, nodding. Bill Evans was playing 'My Foolish Heart' now, with Scott LaFaro's bass picking out the wistful melody. "Anyone ready for some melon?" Sanjo asked. "We are!" chorused the two women, raising their right hands like schoolgirls. The box was brought over and Sanjo, humming along to the music, opened the lid with a knife. The women drew closer, exclaiming, "You can already smell it!" As they watched the melon being lifted out, the restaurant owner muttered, "But you can't blame them for the blockade. It probably *was* a mistake, but it's easy enough to say that now. When you have to make big decisions, you don't always know how they'll turn out." Sanjo stopped humming to say that even a school kid could now see that the blockade was a mistake. "I don't understand politics," the widow admitted, spreading a handkerchief over her knees. "But the worst thing is when people are injured or killed. As long as that doesn't happen it doesn't make much difference whether there's a blockade or an occupation, does it?"

"The last melon from Miyazaki!"

Sanjo plunged the knife into the fruit. He had laid the table with some white Herend plates edged with a butterfly print, and a bottle of port. It had been the widow who had taught him to pour port on melon. "Well then, let's crack this open in honor of the people of Kyushu." It was a 1928 Taylor's. "That's a good vintage. Are you sure you don't mind opening it?" asked the art dealer, leaning forward. Sanjo slowly turned the corkscrew, taking care not to break the cork.

After pouring the wine, he split the melon in two to reveal its moist flesh. An intense fragrance spread as he removed the narrow seeds, and some of the juice dripped onto the plate. "Sorry to be greedy, but…" The widow reached out with her index finger, scooped some up, and licked it. Her red lips glistened with juice.

# 7

# DECADENCE DISCOVERED

*April 8, 2011*

JO SU RYEON was heading for the Fukuoka office of NHK. The thirty-minute KEF propaganda program ran at 8:30 every morning. On the first day it had been a live broadcast, but now it was being taped the afternoon before. This allowed for editing, which was of course to Jo's advantage. The recording session started at 16:00 but was preceded by a production meeting, so he left the command center at 14:00.

Senior officers had told him to get a civilian suit made at a nearby shop so as to avoid the sternly military look of a uniform, and he'd gone there to have his measurements taken. Until the suit was ready, he was making do with the gray jacket, polo shirt, and jeans that he'd worn on the day of the initial landing. "In a get-up like that, Comrade Jo," joked a colleague on seeing him in the hotel lobby, "you're going to have all the girls in Fukuoka after you." Since an army pistol made quite a bulge and ruined the casual effect, Jo had been issued a Soviet-era PSM, a small, thin handgun that slipped neatly into his jacket pocket.

This would be the fourth day of broadcasting. Until yesterday, for the sake of security, he had been escorted by three members of the Special Police, but today he was accompanied only by Warrant

Officer Ri Seong Su. Headquarters had decided that risks to his safety were minimal after the scathing criticism the government had been subjected to following the Ohori Park episode. The fact that NHK personnel would be riding with him precluded the possibility of an attack, and neither the SDF nor the police were likely to try anything once they were inside the television-network offices. The reduction in Jo's escort was also a welcome development for the Special Police, who were short of men to help with the arrests now that three, including Choi Hyo Il, had been lost and others wounded.

"*Ohayo gozaimasu!*" Ogawa, who supervised NHK Fukuoka's news-gathering section, wore a big smile as he opened the door of the long black car. Jo had learned that people in television exchanged "morning" greetings, no matter what time of day or night they met. "I see you're not in uniform," he added approvingly. "Good idea. It's vital in this business to project a friendly image." At fifty-six, Ogawa ranked fourth in the Fukuoka branch of the network. He was of larger than average build and always wore a black or navy-blue suit, with a necktie and matching pocket handkerchief. Jo had Ri get in first. Hanging from Ri's shoulder was a Scorpion sub-machine gun. The fact that Ri had made it into the SOF, despite having a relative who'd defected to the South, was a testimony to his own excellence and absolute loyalty as a soldier.

Ogawa looked back from the front seat and said cheerfully: "We couldn't be happier with the popularity of the program." The driver next to him smiled and nodded in agreement. It was always the same driver, whose face Jo was now quite familiar with. He wore white gloves and the sort of dark-blue cap that one saw on the heads of the Red Guards. He was a pleasant man in late middle age who never failed to offer a greeting and a smile. Jo knew that Ogawa's praise was half truth, half flattery. The man was currying favor in order to be in a better position when the extra troops arrived and the KEF took full control of the city, but that wasn't all there was to it. After the previous day's session, as they were having a chat over coffee, Ogawa had dropped hints of a certain hostility and anger toward Tokyo, and implied that the sentiment was shared by

413

many of the upper crust here. This may have reflected a sense of inferiority at being situated in the south-west corner of the country, far removed from the center of power. There was a parallel of sorts in the Republic, where those in rural areas felt a mixture of attraction and antagonism toward Pyongyang. Administering Fukuoka successfully would mean having a good understanding of public sentiment, and Jo made a mental note to look for an opportunity to press Ogawa for more details.

The NHK offices were located south of Ohori Park. Next to it on one side was a Shinto shrine, on the other a private middle school. When the park came into view, Ogawa, who had been reading out favorable letters and faxes from viewers, lowered his voice and finally fell silent. The ruined, charred buses had been removed, but the restaurant remained as before, with windows shattered and a portion of the second floor blown away. Except for two or three young people taking photos of the wreckage, the place was largely deserted despite the fine weather. There were no signs forbidding entry, but perhaps people were reluctant to set foot on the site of the bloody gun battle they'd seen replayed on TV again and again. More than seventy Japanese had been killed, including members of the Special Assault Team, the prefectural police, and many civilians. The three KEF members who died were First Lieutenant Choi Hyo Il; Warrant Officer Ra Yong Hak, a sharpshooter; and Sergeant First Class Kim Kyeong Gu, a welterweight Olympic-boxing contender. Three more had been severely injured: Warrant Officer Tak Cheol Hwan, who'd taken a bullet in the right shoulder; Sergeant First Class Song Pa Ui, who'd been shot in the left thigh and as the result of blood poisoning ended up having his leg amputated; and Sergeant First Class Kim Han Yeol, who was hovering between life and death after suffering brachial and abdominal wounds.

In the wake of the incident, an evaluative session was held in conjunction with the submission of a report by the wounded Warrant Officer Tak. He emphasized the fact that the large crowds in the park had made it virtually inconceivable that the Japanese police would attack. It had been assumed that if the Japanese government was willing to risk civilian casualties, they would have already ordered the SDF to strike at the encampment itself. According to Kim Hak Su, the operation had been a guerrilla-style attempt to seize KEF officers, and if the entire SP squad had entered the restaurant, they might all have wound up in the hands of the Japanese authorities. As it happened, Choi had ordered Tak to stand by with the other four men of the second team. When Tak was asked whether Choi might have had some sort of premonition, he could only say regretfully that he didn't know. Kim Hak Su warned everyone that the Japanese police could not be taken for granted. The operation had ultimately failed, but the plan itself had been carefully thought out, and the Special Assault Team had shown itself to be both brave and well trained. From now on, the policy would be to reject any and all requests from people scheduled to be taken into custody. For permitting the felon Kuzuta to dictate the location of his arrest, First Lieutenant Jang Bong Su was reprimanded and ordered to undergo self-criticism.

The issue then arose of the disposal of the three dead soldiers. In Japan, cremation was almost always the rule, with only the remaining bone fragments placed in the grave. Kim was adamant about following Korean custom and burying the soldiers but was opposed by Ri Hui Cheol and Ra Jae Gong, who argued that this might alienate the locals. Everyone was concerned about the potential effect on troop morale, however. Kim had correctly maintained all along that without continuous training, some soldiers would lose their fighting spirit and sense of discipline. Lack of space made drill impossible, and live-ammunition training was of course out of the question. Nor were the men allowed to spend hours and hours singing military songs, as they would be doing in the Republic, for fear that the citizenry and the media would interpret this as belligerence. The officers found opportunities to assemble the troops and give them pep talks, but this was hardly sufficient. Along with the level of discipline, the soldiers' sense of urgency was steadily slipping. They ran in formation every morning and did push-ups and sit-ups, but were idle most of the day. In the Republic, soldiers had no time off; here, fights were breaking out over card games, and new supplies—things like towels, toothbrushes, tooth powder, and sandals—were being pilfered.

As a representative of the propaganda and guidance section, Jo was asked for his opinion concerning the burial issue. He responded by saying that while they themselves had strong feelings about funeral rites, so did the Japanese, who apparently looked on inhumation as barbaric. Also to consider, he pointed out, was the sense of outrage over the death of Choi Hyo Il, a much-admired and popular officer. Rumor had it that he had been mowed down by the Osaka police, when in fact he had sacrificed his own life. The rumor had originated with members of the engineer corps, who were in contact with TV-viewing municipal workers, garbage collectors, and builders involved in the ongoing construction of temporary quarters for the troops yet to arrive. In anticipation of their arrival, these Japanese were trying to ingratiate themselves with the rank and file of the KEF by offering them various presents, from amenities such as lighters, ballpoint pens, shavers, scissors, and nail clippers to electrical goods such as portable radios, flashlights, and batteries; medicinal aids such as insect repellent, eye drops, ointment, and sticking plaster; and tools such as knives, pliers, and hammers. They also brought alcohol and Japanese magazines featuring indecent photographs.

"Tomorrow," Jo had proposed, "I'll approach people at NHK and ask them just how negatively they would view inhumation. In the meantime, I would suggest that we have the remains of these three heroes lie in repose and refrain from burying them." Despite an angry objection from Kim, who vehemently argued that as an occupying force they were not obliged to consider the feelings of the occupied, his proposal was adopted. Traditional funeral biers were to be constructed in the hotel lobby, where the three bodies would lie in state, bound in white cloth and resting on ice to delay putrefaction.

In front of the entrance to the NHK building, a dozen or so Japanese women were waiting for Jo's arrival. "You're dressed in civilian clothes!" exclaimed one, as she approached him with a bouquet of flowers. Her friends were trying to hand him a box. "*Ohayo gozaimasu*," he said with a bow, accepting the dozen roses but declining the box. "Why won't you accept our gift?" the woman asked with a look of disappointment on her face. She appeared to be in her early thirties. "I baked these cookies just this morning!" Jo put his nose to the box and remarked that they certainly smelled delicious. He spoke in the local dialect, which made them titter. "You see? Please take them," the woman said, looking at Jo with a rapt expression. "Ah, wait a minute," he replied, still smiling but stepping back a pace. "As an officer in the Koryo Expeditionary Force, I have to set an example. I think you all know that in my country we're still suffering from food shortages. Unfortunately, certain corrupt officials have used their power to obtain food strictly for themselves. We must never condone that sort of thing. And so, while I'm grateful, I can't accept your gift. But I can think of some children who would enjoy these cookies. How would that be?"

A high-school girl wearing glasses clapped in approval, and soon all the women joined in. Ogawa took the present, saying he would give it to a school for the physically and mentally handicapped he was to visit after the broadcast. A guard escorted them as far as the entrance. The cameras of the commercial television networks as well as those of NHK had caught the friendly give-and-take in its entirety. Amid the laughter and applause, Jo had shaken hands with each of the women. All the while, Ri Seong Su maintained his wary expression, holding his sub-machine gun to his chest and scanning the crowd.

Jo, Ri, and Ogawa crossed the lobby and got into the elevator. Jo's presence now caused little reaction. The first day he'd arrived at NHK with a Special Police escort, the lobby, until then full of bustling employees and loud voices, had ground to a halt, as though suddenly frozen in mid-reel. Few Japanese had ever been in the immediate vicinity of soldiers carrying AK rifles and sub-machine guns. Moreover, these men were from the Special Operations Forces and had a menacing look and way of moving. And yet people are capable of accustoming themselves to anything. It had been less than a week since the landing on Nokonoshima, and already Jo had become somewhat accustomed to Fukuoka, just as the NHK workers no longer grimaced at the sight of Ri's weaponry. Still, he reminded himself of what Professor Pak had told him: that when the Japanese and their ways ceased to seem strange, it was time to take extra precautions.

The advertising on a movie poster in the elevator caught his attention. Above the photograph of a man dressed in women's clothing, sitting in a chair and singing, it announced the tenth anniversary of NHK's satellite-television service with an uncut showing of Luchino Visconti's film trilogy, beginning with *The Damned*. What struck Jo about it was the caption: "The Operatic Aesthetics of Decadence." Ri glanced at the man in black fishnet stockings and red lipstick and scowled. Seeing Jo stare at the poster, Ogawa asked if he liked Visconti. In his job at the State Security Department, Jo had been allowed to read foreign literature and to watch foreign films as part of his background research, but he was unfamiliar with this director. "No," he replied. Under his breath he muttered the word "decadence" to himself. It gave him a strangely wistful feeling, reminding him of a time when he'd made a concerted effort to understand the meaning of that term.

In the corridor, a woman was waiting for him beside the door to the performers' lounge. Her name was Hosoda Sakiko, a twenty-six-year-old announcer assigned as his counterpart. She stood against the cream-colored wall with her hands behind her back. "*Ohayo gozaimasu*," she said. "You look younger in civilian clothes." She was slim and for a Japanese rather tall. Over her quietly elegant dress, gray with faint orange stripes, she wore a white cardigan. Unusually for a Japanese woman of her age, she did not dye her hair. Though intelligent and even-tempered, Hosoda could be quite feisty and uncompromising. When the broadcasts first began, Ogawa had told her not to deviate from the script, to which she'd replied that in that case perhaps he'd better find someone else for the job. Several possible replacements had been interviewed, but when no suitable candidate was found, it was she who ended up with the assignment, and after some discussion it was decided that questions and comments that were off script would be permitted. Looking at her made Jo think of early summer and an azalea-scented path in the park by the Potong River Amusement Park. "I see you've been given another bunch of flowers," she said, leaning down to sniff them. "Nice!"

During the planning session, Jo said that in the first half of the program he wanted to introduce a well-known Korean folk tale. The room they occupied had an oblong table with tubular chairs, and a make-up stand. Sandwiches and coffee had been laid out for them. Participating in the discussion were Hosoda, Ogawa, and the program director, a man in his late thirties named Shimoda. Jo gave them a synopsis of the tale: 'Samnyeon-koge,' or 'The Three-Year Mountain Pass.' According to legend, anyone who stumbled and fell on this pass would only have three more years to live. One day, an old man returning from selling cloth in a neighboring village is admiring the beautiful vista from the path when he trips on a pebble and falls. Feeling doomed, he takes to bed, refuses to eat, and becomes seriously ill. A quick-witted lad named Toldori, who works in the village watermill, tells him to go back to the mountain pass and stumble again, saying that each time he does so he will gain three years of life: twice will mean six years, ten times will mean thirty years. So the old man goes back and deliberately falls down again and again. Believing he will now live another two hundred years, he soon recovers and is happier and healthier than ever.

Hosoda gazed intently at Jo as he told the story. She had a high forehead, soft hair falling over her shoulders, and sparkling, mischievous eyes. Shimoda, parting his long hair with a pencil, asked what the moral of the story was. "I wouldn't worry about that," Jo replied, but Shimoda persisted. "You're just going to tell the story? No illustrations or anything?" he said, then looked down at the table. Jo turned to face the man. "I think you misunderstand. The purpose of this program is not to entertain but rather to provide

419

what we regard as necessary information. What the story hints at will be obvious even to children. Explaining it would only ruin it." Up to this point Jo had been speaking politely, but his voice now had an edge that chilled the room. In the Republic, this man would be sent to a *kwanliso* for re-education. He had no manners, and Jo had no use for people who couldn't watch their tongues.

"I understand," said Ogawa, then turned to Shimoda and told him to go and see how things were coming along in the studio. The man went out scratching his head, with Ri staring after him. Jo knew he had overreacted, but since leaving the Republic he felt his traditional values had come under threat, and it unnerved him. Ogawa apologized. He was well aware that, once the additional troops were in place, a process of dividing the cooperative from the uncooperative would begin. No matter what form it took, resistance to the KEF was inadvisable, as was noncompliance. "I'll have him dismissed," he said with a penitent look. "There's no need for that," Jo told him. "The problem is not that he's uncooperative but that he's incompetent. If children are instructed in what a story means even as it's being told to them, they won't think it out for themselves, and they'll lose interest in stories altogether."

In the Republic, there was only one "moral" to be garnered from any tale: unconditional reverence for the Great Leader and the Dear Leader. The obvious lesson of 'Three-Year Mountain Pass,' for example, was that in any age the old ways of thinking must make way for the new, and that in the present day the beloved Comrade General was the one putting everything right. But the truth was that within Jo himself, this absolute devotion to the two "Sons of Heaven" was in conflict with an analytical mind that regarded such devotion as unscientific and outmoded. To maintain his faith, he had over time constructed a formidable mental barrier. Since leaving the Republic, however, cracks had begun to appear in that barrier, offering glimpses of something he couldn't yet identify.

"I agree," said Hosoda quietly. Ogawa turned toward her with a supercilious frown that inquired what a young female announcer could have to say about it. She lowered her eyes, as though having read his message. "If I may be allowed to speak…" Ogawa turned his head aside, ignoring her, but Jo told her to go ahead. "I think Jo-san's point is a good one," she started to say, only to be interrupted by Ogawa and reminded that off-air she was to refer to her cohost by his military rank. Jo nodded, to indicate that she should humor the man. "I'm sorry," she said. "Lieutenant Jo. What I'm thinking is that this program is watched by a lot of mothers, and mothers care about how their kids learn things. And it's true that unless children enjoy the tales they read or hear, they soon lose interest. I remember in elementary school, we were constantly being told what the theme of a particular story was or what the writer wanted to convey. Kids don't like that."

Jo nodded and looked from Hosoda to Ogawa. The latter seemed miffed at what he must have interpreted as insubordination. He was frowning. It would be best to help the man save face, if only to avoid further discord. "Well, then," he said, turning to Ogawa and adopting the manner he would have used with his elders and superior officers in the Republic, "would you be willing to accept my proposal?" Ogawa visibly relaxed and said that of course he would. "And how would it be if, once I've finished the story, Hosoda-san asks me what the moral might be? I'll then say that it's important for children just to enjoy a story and to draw their own conclusions as to what it means." As he spoke, he looked at Hosoda as though to warn her not to say anything before Ogawa answered. "I think that's a splendid idea," Ogawa said, all signs of resentment gone from his face. It would be useless to ask a chameleon like this about the burial question.

Ri Seong Su was standing on guard near the entrance to the room. Ogawa urged him to join them for coffee and sandwiches, but he just shook his head without even looking their way. "Has he already eaten?" Ogawa asked Jo, who said: "He may not have had lunch yet, but he can't eat while on duty." Ogawa nodded but looked disgruntled. Refreshments had been prepared, and he'd gone out of his way to include the security guard, only to be rebuffed. He was probably incapable of understanding that for Ri this was enemy territory, a place where constant vigilance was required.

As they ate their sandwiches before recording the program, the three of them selected questions submitted by viewers. A bundle of postcards, emails, and faxes attested to the popularity of the program, and Ogawa selected several comments to read aloud. "Jo-san's clear-cut way of speaking is so refreshing… Please tell the government to lift the blockade… With the arrest of so many criminals, it's like a spring-cleaning… Watching this program, I feel I want to know and learn more about North Korea… The national and Osaka police who killed so many civilians look down on Fukuoka…" Jo knew that he was deliberately not being shown any messages critical of the KEF; at some point soon he would have to insist on seeing everything. Without a grasp of just how much anxiety and dissatisfaction there was out there, he couldn't properly perform his job.

There were questions both trivial and serious. What kind of music do you like? What do you eat every day? What is your ideal kind of woman? How come you speak Japanese so well? How does one join the Koryo Expeditionary Force? Will we ever be able to have baseball games again? Are we going to get newly released movies? My father went to Tokyo on business just before the occupation—when will he be able to return? Aren't you worried that Fukuoka might become a battleground? Will children here have to give up on going to school in Tokyo? When will this week's comics be available? Is the KEF really a rebel army? When the reinforcement troops arrive, will they all study Japanese? What kind of work will the KEF now undertake? Will Hakata Harbor be reopened for exports?

"This one's really onto something!" exclaimed Ogawa, showing Jo a postcard that asked why the program could not be broadcast nationwide. Outside of Kyushu, only segments were being shown as part of the news. Jo assumed it was a government decision not to allow KEF propaganda to be seen all over Japan. At first, however, he had been surprised that programming varied according to region; in the Republic, the idea of locally tailored content was unthinkable. "In TV programming, as with everything else in this country," Ogawa remarked with a certain bitterness, "Tokyo has the upper hand. Broadcasting is divided into sectors: prefectural, areal, and national. This is the Kyushu area block. If some elementary-school kids go on a study trip to visit an Arita porcelain kiln, there's a 'pupils see the potter's wheel' sort of story on prefectural TV. If, on the other hand, there's a food-poisoning outbreak at the same elementary school, it's reported throughout Kyushu. And if one elementary-school kid kills another, then it's nationwide news. But local news in the Tokyo area is automatically national news as well. When a weak typhoon is approaching somewhere south-east of the capital, the whole Kanto block is sure to get excited. And, of course, that then becomes national news, so we here in the most active typhoon corridor are subjected to endless coverage of some faraway fart of a storm." As he spoke, Ogawa had his face turned toward the bay window. The trees of nearby Gokoku Shrine tinted the frosted glass-green.

Ogawa sipped at the cup of coffee Hosoda had refilled for him. "I was in the economics section of NHK's Tokyo bureau more than thirty years ago, when the budget for the Kyushu super-express was settled. An auditor for the Ministry of Finance joked: 'Why should Tokyo taxpayers, squeezed and squashed during rush hour, have to cough up money for a train moving air around in Kyushu?' The implication was that there wouldn't be any passengers. Everyone laughed except me. I was annoyed, and shot back with: 'So are you telling people not to live in Kyushu or Shikoku or Hokkaido?' He just looked at me like, 'What's got *you* so riled up?' Of course, the man had a point: Tokyo-area residents pay high taxes and benefit from few public-works projects. But do they have nuclear power plants in and around the capital? No. Any industrial-waste treatment plants there? Nope. And Tokyo systematically sucks up young talent from the provinces, first for the universities and then for the bureaucracy, the financial institutions, and the corporations. Just between us, the fact is that the only people left in the provinces these days are either stupid or old."

Hosoda Sakiko puffed out her cheeks, as though to say "Does that apply to me as well?" but after glaring surreptitiously at Ogawa, she gave Jo a quick smile. Looking past her pale, soft cheeks to the wall beyond, he could see the same poster that had caught his eye in the elevator: "*The Damned*: The Operatic Aesthetics of Decadence." In the propaganda and guidance section back in the Republic, he had been told to write an essay explaining to farmers and workers the perils of decadence. He had read through Japanese novels describing bizarre sexual behavior and watched southern Korean films with overtly sexual themes, but he failed to grasp what the concept meant. He assumed there must be something alluring about it—otherwise, why would it exist? But pictures of nude women and descriptions of sexual intercourse did not in themselves have any special appeal. So what *was* it all about? It then occurred to him that instead of trying fully to understand the concept and explain the gravity of the threat in readily understandable terms, he would try to imagine how the upper echelons of the Party conceived it and write what would appeal to them, with frequent use of metaphor—demons and temptresses and spreading cancers, to which the only antidote was the study and practice of *Juche*.

For putting these thoughts to paper Jo had received the Winged Horse Badge of Honor and was given a ticket to the gigantic show known as the Arirang Festival Games. The games ostensibly commemorated the ninetieth birthday of Kim Il Sung, but in fact their purpose was to counter the soccer World Cup shared that same year between the puppet regime and Japan. Kim Jong Il himself had assumed command of the massively funded undertaking, which involved over a hundred thousand participants, including young children, secondary-school pupils, university students, People's Army soldiers, dance troupes, massed bands, gymnasts, and circus performers.

The games were unprecedented in scale, featuring human billboard mosaics, laser beams, people's artists performing elaborate dances, and sixty-meter-high trapezes—all beneath the colossal illuminated ceiling of the 150,000-seat May Day Stadium. It was undoubtedly the greatest show on earth, something that one would never see anywhere else. The army of performers practiced every day for six hours, receiving no pay and forbidden to engage in any other kind of activity. Jo thought of this huge endeavor as having everything—except decadence. It was beautiful, but it wasn't something that aroused more than admiration for the work and willpower that went into it. Decadence, he assumed, had a power that was hard to resist, and human beings were swept up in it even as they became aware of its dangers. It contained within it a sense of guilt, which led invariably to disillusionment and ennui. Decadence was only consumed; on its own, it produced nothing. It was thus utterly absent from the Arirang festival.

Hosoda was looking at him as though wondering what he was thinking about. The room was well heated, and she had taken off her cardigan. Seeing her white arms and shoulders quickened his pulse; he felt a tightness in his chest. It was the same sort of feeling he'd experienced among the sweet-smelling azaleas at home. There was a sense of guilt as well. He asked if they minded him smoking, and turned to look out of the window as he lit a cigarette. He could see vague, wavering green shadows. These were presumably the trees swaying in front of the shrine. Sometimes black shapes would flit past. He thought they might be swallows. No other birds flew so quickly. "Swallows… " Jo half-muttered the word to himself as he remembered the nests under the eaves of the apartment in his native Pyongyang. The building had originally been for groups of political advisers from the Soviet Union, and when they left, members of the judiciary, administrators, diplomats, and university professors had moved in. In spring it was nice to hear the sound the newly hatched chicks made. When Jo was small, he had seen his father pause in his work to watch the parent birds bringing them food. That was before his father had burned his entire collection of Pushkin and Gorky.

His father was a professor of languages and literature at Kim Il Sung University and one of the Republic's leading poets. In the 1960s, at the age of thirty-nine, he had written the lyrics for 'When My Life Ends,' the theme song of a tremendously popular movie called *The Rails of Blood*. Everyone learned to sing it, young and old; and it was even taught in schools. He had written countless other songs as well, and in any country with copyright laws he might have earned huge sums of money. Yet he never made the slightest complaint about this and was fond of saying that professors did not belong in the privileged class. The family led a modest life, but in the Republic intellectuals were nonetheless respected, as Koreans were still imbued with a Confucian outlook. The Great Leader, Marshal Kim Il Sung, had purged all of his political enemies and rewritten history, but he had been unable to eradicate traditional values. Jo's father was held in particular esteem, and in the family room was a Japanese television set. Such a costly item was beyond his professor's salary; it had been sent directly by Kim Jong Il himself in admiration of his revolutionary poetry collection, published in 1984. On the back of the set was an inscription declaring it to be a gift from the Leader of the Workers' Party Politburo's Standing Committee. On the side, in larger letters, his father had written: "For Su Ryeon, on his sixth birthday."

At the beginning of the 1990s, bad harvests and flooding, along with an extreme shortage of foreign capital, resulted in fuel shortages that in turn affected distribution. The Republic was gripped by famine. The residents of Pyongyang, unable to head for the Chinese border to buy things there, sold their electrical appliances and furniture just to obtain food. Even then, Jo's father refused to pander to the Party. Those with connections to the upper echelons had their salaries raised and were on the receiving end of foreign aid that was being siphoned off, but he consistently distanced himself from the apparatus of government and its functionaries, and so found himself ostracized. Members of the Party elite who had been his students would secretly come with presents of rice, pork, and sesame oil, but he stubbornly refused to accept them, saying that it made him a likely target for entrapment. He sold the Sony television set, his Montblanc fountain pen, his rosewood desk, the electric refrigerator his younger sister—a special diplomatic envoy—had sent from Africa, and finally chairs, curtains, dishes, and medical supplies, so that all that was left in the home were his books, pots and pans, and some basic tableware. Among the books were forbidden works that could not be sold.

In time, Jo's father lost his exemption from the Friday labor requirement imposed on office workers and intellectuals. He'd been excused previously in consideration of his age, but every Friday from then on he put on his laborer's clothes and headed off to help transport bricks or clean up after the floods. It was at about this time that he stopped eating at home, saying that he would take his meals at the university dining room. Later it became clear that he'd been ashamed of not being able to provide food for his family, and in reality was eating next to nothing; he had already resigned himself to death. Jo's mother often wept without saying why. One day when Jo was thirteen, his father took him to the vacant lot behind their apartment building, and there he burned all of his remaining books. Afterwards, turning his emaciated face toward the boy, he said: "I want you to become the sort of person who can write good poetry. You don't have to actually compose it; you need only have the capacity to do so whenever you want to. Good poets are those able to gaze into the darkness of their own hearts. A vivid or beautiful poem is not necessarily a good poem. Poetry that doesn't stand side by side with the reader has no real power. Do you understand, Su Ryeon? Write poems that stand side by side with the reader."

His father had ostensibly died of tuberculosis, but the underlying cause was starvation. In the months before his death he seemed to be longing for the end, but he wasn't at all the sort of person who would take his own life. In the Republic, suicide was a crime, in which the immediate survivors were deemed complicit and punished by being sent off to remote mountain areas. And yet it wasn't because of official prohibition that he opted not to commit suicide. Jo had heard him say repeatedly that, to his mind, suicide was worse than murder. But accepting death was different from choosing death. Jo's father had continued fighting for what he believed in even as he gradually resigned himself to his own demise.

Jo went on to Saman Secondary School, the capital's best after the one attended by the Dear Leader and the children of top officials, where he excelled in literature, languages, mathematics, and tae-kwondo. He entered the SOF Eighth Corps after graduating from the Writers' School. What his father had told him about poetry remained for him a mystery. Poems were subjective and autonomous. Poets didn't stand "side by side" with anyone; their poems arose, rather, from their own feelings and values, and were shaped by their own sense of language. Surely his dying father couldn't have been saying that the poet should compromise with his would-be reader. It was only later that Jo came to understand what he'd really meant...

Ogawa was still going on about Tokyo versus Kyushu. "More than twenty years ago," he said, "an avalanche of soil and rocks resulting from the volcanic eruption of Mount Unzen damaged the homes of a huge number of families in the area." He had his hands wrapped around his cup of coffee as though to keep it warm. "Mount Unzen is here in Kyushu, of course. At about the same time, there was an unusual increase in the water level of the Fuji Five Lakes, resulting in the flooding of some tourist bungalows along Lake Saiko. Well, which event do you think got more news coverage? And then there's the Minamata-disease calamity. Those of us born and raised in Kyushu still swear that if the water pollution that caused that disease had been discovered in Tokyo Bay instead of in this area, the govern-ment would have reacted very differently. Fukuoka has now become the hub of trade with China, so things are a bit different, but not so long ago the governor of Fukuoka Prefecture—population five million—would go hat in hand to petition the Finance Ministry's Budget Bureau, bowing and scraping like a grasshopper as he handed his calling card to the bimbo at the reception desk of the deputy director's office. Just pitiful! When Fukuoka was blockaded, I remem-bered that and thought: Wouldn't ya know it!" Ogawa looked at Jo and concluded with a comment that seemed intended to gauge his reaction: "The beginning's bound to be difficult, but for a long time I've felt that independence might not be such a bad option for us."

\*

"I'm sure all of our viewers found the tale of the 'Three-Year Mountain Pass' very interesting. And the narrator's comments were refreshing, weren't they? Thinking for yourself is essential, though that's easier said than done." Perhaps because of the intense lighting, there were hints of sweat on Hosoda's forehead and the tip of her nose. The surrounding area was in semi-darkness; only she and Jo were illuminated. Fanned out behind the cameras were the crew, with their lights and other equipment. Ogawa was looking on, arms folded. Shimoda wasn't there, a replacement director having been introduced to Jo just before taping.

"Let's take a five-minute break," said Ogawa. Asked whether he would like to go back to the performers' lounge, Jo replied that he was fine where he was. The make-up people came in and with soft tissues lightly dabbed away the sweat on the face first of Jo, then of Hosoda. As they sat drinking some cold water that a staff member had brought them, Jo said, "I'm sorry, I didn't do that very well." She reached over to tap him lightly on the thigh and said, "Don't be silly. It was fine." Her nails were short and unpainted, and she had lovely fingers, long and thin. Someone adjusted the microphone attached to her collar.

"No," Jo continued. "I know that speaking isn't my forte. When I remind myself of how many people are listening to what I'm saying, I begin to feel I'm not speaking completely from the heart." Hosoda was about to make a further comment but held back. When her microphone had been adjusted, it was Jo's turn, while she was given another touch of lipstick. The microphone was clipped to his jacket collar, and when the crew member—a thin young man with long hair—moved it, he must have realized that the bulge he felt was a pistol. He apologized sheepishly, and when he'd finished he said, "If you don't mind my saying so, you have a wonderful voice." Jo thanked him.

As the taping recommenced, he began responding to questions posed by viewers. Hosoda would first read out each of them. *What kind of music do you like?* "I listen mostly to classical music, but I also enjoy traditional Korean folk songs." *When will the latest comics be available?* "That's something for the Japanese government, not the KEF, to decide." *How come you speak Japanese so well?* "When I was a university student, I got by on four hours of sleep a night. I studied a lot." *Aren't you worried that Fukuoka will become a battleground?* "I understand that you may be thinking of the sad incident in Ohori Park, but I can promise you that the KEF will never instigate an attack." *Is the KEF really a rebel army?* "We, the Koryo Expeditionary Force, have never called ourselves such, but it is true that we have risen up against corrupt elements within our Republic's bureaucracy that are the cause of many problems, including inequalities under which the people languish. We have risen up to rectify the matter." *Will Hakata Harbor be reopened for exports?* "The KEF has received word that the Chinese government may call for the reopening of foreign consulates. If that should occur, the Japanese government will be obliged to lift its blockade."

Hosoda read the last question: *What is your ideal kind of woman?* "First, she should be well educated, with a good heart, enthusiasm, and a smiling face as gentle as the sea is wide." Looking at Hosoda, he added: "I also like large eyes." She gave him a happy smile: "Thank you for a most enjoyable talk."

With the taping completed, they returned to the performers' lounge, where Jo removed his make-up with a hot towel and put in a call to Ri Hui Cheol, the deputy commander, on his mobile phone. In order to get Hosoda's frank opinion about the burial question, he needed time to talk to her when Ogawa was not around, and rather than arrange this with Ogawa directly, he thought it better simply to have Ri tell him that this was what they wanted to happen. He started to explain this on the phone but was promptly interrupted by Ri telling him to speak louder. There was cheering in the background. Jo held the phone away from his ear and muttered, "What's going on over there?" Ri Seong Su, standing next to him, pointed to his left wrist.

Ah, the watches! This was the day the troops were going to have waterproof digital watches distributed to them. While trying to procure some vitamin supplements, Kim Hyang Mok had stumbled

430

on a huge supply of timepieces gathering dust in a company warehouse. These large watches, their faces enclosed in hard rubber, had apparently been popular a few years before but fell out of fashion and wound up in storage. Kim purchased some three thousand five hundred of them for less than three million yen, including new batteries. They were to be given first to members of the advance party as a reward for distinguished service, with officers in the main force also getting their share, and finally to those of the rank and file thought deserving of them.

Jo shouted his request into the cellphone again. Ri assured him, in an unnecessarily loud voice, that he'd take care of it. "I'll call Ogawa and tell him and say you need her for about an hour to go over some important new material. But, tell me," he said, "where will you take her? Where will First Lieutenant Jo Su Ryeon, the TV heart-throb, have his private talk with that beautiful announcer, that Ryu Hwa Mi lookalike? You can't very well use the NHK offices, with Ogawa there." Ryu Hwa Mi was the most popular people's actress in the Republic, appearing mostly in historical dramas, and there was indeed a strong resemblance. Jo said he'd talk to Hosoda in the car. To take her to headquarters was out of the question, as was, say, going for a stroll in the park. He would simply have the car circle the campground. The deputy commander granted permission, but told him to be sure to finish within an hour and get right back to camp.

Ri Seong Su, the guard, was now looking this way. Jo told him that they would question the woman in the car, on their way back to camp, and he responded with a click of his heels and a salute.

Orange sunlight streamed in from the car window, reflected off the lake in Ohori Park as the day waned. It seemed that a courteous call to Ogawa had inspired him immediately to agree to send Hosoda off, telling her with a smile that this sounded important and that her help was needed. The NHK car was a black Toyota. Flying on the front-left side was a red pennant with the NHK insignia. Whenever Jo saw it, he envisioned the KEF banners that would soon be fluttering from squadrons of vehicles in the streets of Fukuoka. Hosoda

Sakiko sat next to the driver, behind whom was Ri Seong Su. The car's interior was spacious, and in the middle of the back seat was a lace-covered retractable armrest, inside which was a telephone. To make a call, you put the little coiled receiver over your ear and pushed the buttons on the box.

Ri, still gripping his sub-machine gun, was keeping a watchful eye on the world outside the lace-curtained window, but occasionally his gaze would shift to the small liquid-crystal screen to the left of the driver. This electronic device utilized radio waves that bounced off a communications satellite to determine the vehicle's position, and it responded to the driver's verbal commands and questions. "How is traffic on the Kokutai Road?" he asked now, and a pleasant female voice answered: "Traffic is heavy, but moving." The device would also give spontaneous updates and suggest alternate routes. The first time Jo saw one of these, he recognized it as something that was going to alter special operations completely—allowing agents to disperse and still know one another's location, for example. On the roof was a twelve-inch liquid-crystal television, and next to the armrest was a remote control, no larger than a pack of cigarettes, for the CD and DVD player, the air conditioning, and the television.

Just after passing Ohori Park, Jo told Hosoda he wanted her opinion on a certain matter. "Sure!" she said, turning around in her seat to look at him. "I'd like you to see Nakasu. Shall we talk there?" And without pausing she told the driver to take them to Haruyoshi Bridge in Nakasu 1-Chome. Jo was taken aback. His idea had been to drive along the road that circled the Sea Hawk Hotel. "No, not Nakasu. Jigyohama," he said, sitting up and leaning forward. Hosoda half turned again, stared into his eyes, and said with a laugh: "No way!" For an instant he was unsure what she'd said, as though Japanese had suddenly become an unknown language to him. He ran it through his mind again. Yes, she had clearly refused his suggestion.

The car did not make a left turn toward Jigyohama but followed the Kokutai Road toward Tenjin and Nakasu. On their left the remnants of Fukuoka Castle could be seen. Together with Pak Myeong, Jo had spent several days studying the geography of Fukuoka as part of the preparations for administering the city. They would soon be crossing the Tenjin administrative and business area and come to a Nishitetsu–Fukuoka Station. On both sides of the wide three-lane road were high-rise apartments and commercial buildings, along with hotels and gasoline stations. They were steadily moving away from the campground. Jo could feel his pulse beating. They stopped at a traffic light; the drivers adjacent to them glanced in their direction and then looked away. All around them it was growing darker. It was unlikely that anyone would realize that KEF members were in the car. Ri Seong Su was in uniform, but the lace curtain on his window partially blocked him from view. He was still looking straight ahead as the light turned green, but now his face had a puzzled expression—the car hadn't turned at the usual corner.

Jo himself was in a state of confusion. He wasn't used to being defied by anyone, and wondered whether this was a trap. A felon had apparently colluded with the Japanese police to have the scene of arrest changed to Ohori Park. Was Hosoda now trying to waylay them, too? Surely not. The decision to consult her and not Ogawa had been made only minutes before, and she'd been with Jo the whole time since, with no opportunity to contact anyone else. Only Ogawa and a few people other people knew that she was with him in this official NHK car. It was inconceivable that the SDF or the Japanese police would be waiting for them in Nakasu. "Hosoda-san, please listen to me," he said. "Yes?" she replied, turning around once more. But words failed him. Something in his brain was not functioning. He wanted to explain that he couldn't go anywhere outside the encampment and the television station, but nothing in Japanese emerged. What was wrong? Why was he suddenly unable to put sentences together in her language? "We're almost there," she said and began to speak to the driver.

He didn't know how to respond to being contradicted, because it was something that simply never happened. In the Republic, whether in the military, in the workplace, at school, or at home, no subordinate—and Hosoda fitted that description—would oppose one's requests. This was not a tendency; it was an absolute. Subordinates,

433

children, or younger siblings would never directly contradict their superiors or elders. Only infants were permitted to be cantankerous. A willful woman like this would be purged from the military and the party and sent off with her family members to a remote work camp, and that would be the end of it. From the instant such defiance was expressed, all interaction would cease. "Hosoda-san," Jo said, leaning forward again, "we need to go to Jigyohama, not Nakasu." But his voice barely rose above a whisper. "I'm sorry," she said, turning toward him, "what did you say?"

Should he deal with the matter by shouting that they were going back? Call her a fool and hit her? That wouldn't solve anything. How would she react if he resorted to violence? Would she shrivel up? Angrily protest? In any case, he'd never be able to extract her candid opinion regarding the burial issue after any such outburst, and time was running out. But he knew there was another factor here as well: his attraction to her and the sense of guilt that this aroused. He didn't *want* to hit her or yell at her. Again he told her they must return to Jigyohama, but his voice was feeble—it reminded him of when he would beg for the hazing to stop when he first joined the Corps. Hosoda had never lived in a country in which the communication between superiors and subordinates consisted exclusively of commands, submission, and supplication. "Are you still on about that?" she asked peevishly, then made a more surprising statement: "Well, in that case, I'm getting out."

This woman has real character, thought Jo. She wasn't just playing some coy kind of game with him. If he refused to go to Nakasu, she'd undoubtedly ask to be let out of the car, just as she'd told Ogawa to go find someone else for the job if he didn't like how she did it. Already they were passing Nishitetsu–Fukuoka Station, dark and deserted now, the entrances cordoned off with chains and ropes. As the reality of the blockade had sunk in and become a fact of day-to-day life, traffic to the area had dwindled, and the riot police had withdrawn. Even with rush-hour congestion, they would be in Nakasu 1-Chome within five minutes. It occurred to Jo that though strictly speaking he required permission to go there, he had only said that he would be talking with Hosoda in the car. Ri Hui Cheol had given his authorization without their destination being specified. Looking outside through the lace curtain, the other Ri asked where they were going. To Nakasu, Jo answered quietly. The man still looked puzzled, presumably not knowing the place, but he nodded and continued to stare straight ahead.

Traffic had been slowing and finally ground to a halt at the Haruyoshi Bridge signal, where dozens of cars were backed up. The western sky was still faintly blue, and the buildings along the water appeared as black overlapping shadowgraphs. From the foot of the bridge they could see the reflections of colorful neon lights on the surface of the Naka River, and willow trees swaying in the breeze. To the left was a restaurant with a sign consisting of a huge crab, its claws slowly moving back and forth. Jo found himself staring at it. The river itself did not compare in scale with the Taedong, but the dense crowds of people and the buildings were amazing. The streets seemed to quiver with light and sound. It was like looking at a swarm of luminous insects. Motorbikes carrying takeaway noodles and pizza weaved their way between the car-choked streets and sidewalks overflowing with pedestrians. Steam rose from the street stalls on the riverbank, the lights of a pachinko parlor flashed, and women walked up and down the street in glittering dresses.

Nakasu, Jo had been told, had nearly twenty bridges. City Hall workers assigned to KEF headquarters had told him that on the small, dolphin-shaped island, less than a kilometer long and two hundred meters wide, there were hundreds of eateries and more than two thousand bars and pubs, not to mention amusement centers, cinemas, and stores. As an entertainment district, it was the largest in Japan, in both sales and overall size. Whenever the subject of Nakasu came up, the municipal workers would suggest to KEF personnel that they all go there for a drink sometime. "They must mistake us for officials from Tokyo, here on a junket," Colonel Han Seung Jin had said with a sour grin. Interestingly enough, the area had reportedly become even livelier since the arrival of the KEF.

More people, it seemed, were in an eat-drink-and-be-merry mood, as they faced an uncertain future and sought to forget about the blockade and the occupation.

But this was no place for the present three passengers to be walking around. Hosoda was tall and conspicuous, and Jo's face was one that a television audience would remember. Ri was armed, and dressed in a military uniform. If they were to get into a confrontation with drunks or find themselves surrounded by a crowd, there could be serious trouble. If Hosoda decided to leave them, Jo thought, he could ask the driver for his opinion regarding the burial issue. He had wanted a young and educated informant, but he might have no other choice. He'd been foolish to choose her. The car was moving again, at last. After crossing Haruyoshi Bridge, the driver signaled a right turn. In contrast to the dazzling neon signs and the multitude of people earlier, they were now in a dimly lit, one-way alley. The car slowed. There was a row of low buildings containing shops that in the darkness had an all the more dubious air, their signs, jutting out into the street, made it difficult for cars to pass. The entrances were half-illuminated in garish red and blue, with curtains preventing anyone from seeing inside.

Hosoda had been chatting with the driver, saying that at such-and-such a sushi shop the fish wasn't very fresh, or that the mother of such-and-such an NHK person was ill, or that this area was always a squeeze to get through; and occasionally turning to tell Jo that they were almost there. But now she had fallen silent. Ri was frowning as he observed the heavily made-up women out on the street, dressed in what was little more than underwear. They passed a shop with a small sign advertising electrical insect traps; Jo spotted the slippered foot of a woman through a gap in the shop's curtains. He wondered why Hosoda had brought them to such a place and again suspected a snare of some kind. And yet the shop entrances and the alley itself were extremely narrow, and the mostly wooden, two-storied buildings were too confining to allow troops to deploy. The twisting street likewise ruled out the possibility of a sniper attack. Most importantly, no large vehicle could get in. And armed policemen or SDF personnel couldn't show up in a district like this without causing a commotion and probably scaring everyone away—customers and shopkeepers alike.

The car had made several turns and was now deep inside yet another alley. The din of the main thoroughfare had quite faded away. They hadn't gone far, but already they were in a different world, as though they'd entered a cone of silence. They passed a rubble-strewn vacant lot and the remains of a parking lot, replete with abandoned cars. Middle-aged female touts were standing here and there, all dressed in woolen sweaters that reached to their hips. Several approached with folded arms and peered into the expensive car, obviously looking for men with money to spend. As the sun had only just gone down, there weren't many fun-seekers out and about yet.

At one corner of the alley was a small children's park, overgrown with weeds and surrounded by a plain ironwork fence. The park had one see-saw, a swing set with no swings, and a dilapidated bench, on which a boy wearing shorts and sneakers sat alongside an old woman wrapped in a blanket. The two were huddled in conversation while their red-haired dog circled the bench, sniffing the ground. From afar the blanket looked like a *turumagi*, the outer garment of traditional Korean dress. The fluorescent street light above the pair was dying, blinking out repeatedly only to flicker back to life, creating a sort of subdued strobe effect. The woman reached into a bag and gave the dog a treat. Jo was taken by the scene: it reminded him of something.

On completing his three years of basic training in the SOF Eighth Corps, he had been assigned to a course in propaganda. Granted a three-day leave, he had taken a short trip, first going to Sariwon and then, hitching rides on army trucks and tradesmen's vans, west to Cape Changsan. From there he could see the area the southern puppet state arbitrarily called the armistice line. Across the water lay Baeknyeong Island, where elite southern troops were stationed, with a watchful eye directed north. At the tip of the cape was a People's Army camp, and he'd been grilled by guards as to what he was doing there. He presented his ID and furlough papers and said that he'd wanted to see for himself the reality of national division here on the coastline, to get a first-hand sense of the tense and volatile conditions the Fatherland confronted. He wasn't pretending: he genuinely wanted to confirm for himself that the Republic that had killed his father was indeed in a state of crisis. His personal belongings were inspected, and he was asked to show his return ticket, but after three years of military training he could scarcely have been mistaken for anything but a special-forces officer. The soldiers respectfully sent him on his way, pointing him in the direction of the only inn in the area and wishing him a safe journey.

Cape Changsan was enveloped in fog, the immediate landscape was desolate, and it was easy to lose one's footing in the strong sea wind. Jo was caught in the rain and drenched to the skin, his boots covered with mud. Though it was summer, the beautiful shoreline was empty, the beach being blocked off by barbed wire. Here and there were signs warning of landmines. He walked along the red dirt road, now as boggy as a rice paddy, until he reached the inn. The sign advertising the restaurant was tilted, its paint was chipped. There were no other guests, and Jo was told that there hadn't been any in three weeks. The innkeeper poured him a cup of *soju* from a large crock, saying that it would do him good. While the bathwater was being heated, the rain eased off, and distantly, from somewhere outside, came a husky male voice singing a traditional *pansori*. The innkeeper told him that the singer had been imprisoned as a partisan in the South during the Liberation War and sent to a POW camp on Jeju Island, later opting to go north when prisoners were exchanged. He was out there in the empty field down the way, the innkeeper said, if Jo was interested in meeting him. *Pansori* had vanished in the Republic, having been banned long ago, and Jo had never heard anyone actually perform any of the famous old narrative-style songs.

He walked along the muddy, utterly deserted path, following the voice. Out in the open field formed from a flattened hill of reddish soil was what looked like a dilapidated construction shed, and beneath its rotting eaves an old man was sitting on a sofa, singing for a young boy who sat next to him. The old man was dressed in a ragged overcoat, and he twisted and turned as though doing a kind of dance as he chanted a passage from the well-known story of *Chun Hyang*. It was the sad scene in which Chun Hyang and Mong Ryong symbolically exchange a jeweled ring and a mirror as they part, vowing to meet again: "A pure man's heart shines like a mirror; a faithful woman's conviction shines like a jewel." It was said that performers of *pansori* trained their voices by singing directly into freezing winds, and the rough poignancy of the man's voice touched Jo to the quick and seemed to move even the clouds and the tide-scented air. And as he listened, the words of his dying father echoed in his mind, intertwined with the melody: "Write poems that stand side by side with the reader." At last Jo felt that he understood. *Find a way through!* That's what his father had meant. Analyze thoroughly how the reader will interpret what you write. Anticipate what those in power want. Find a way through!

A year later he had composed the revolutionary verse that everyone now knew:

> *I walk the road to a united land,*
> *Guided by the Guards' red arrow...*
> *For fifty years and more*
> *We have done without milk and bread...*

If he had written of rice and meat soup, he might well have been arrested by State Security agents. In order to make any reference to the food shortages he'd had to resort to items that were foreign to the Republic, so that he was only indirectly addressing the suffering of the Party and the people. And when he entered the State Security Department himself, poetry had, in various senses, provided a way through. Even now, when he wrote poetry, he remembered the desolate landscape of Cape Changsan and the voice of that *pansori* singer.

"Here we are," said Hosoda Sakiko. The car had stopped in front of a cheap eatery with a soiled *noren* curtain at the entrance.

It was situated behind the park where they'd seen the boy with the dog and the old woman. Across the way was an unsavory-looking establishment called Mademoiselle. "It's a bit of a dump, but the gyoza here are delicious," Hosoda said as she opened the car door and started to get out. "Wait!" said Jo. "I can't go in there. It's against regulations." Still gripping the door handle, the young woman cast her eyes down and was silent. The car was parked snugly against the entrance. Without turning, his hands still on the steering wheel, the middle-aged driver now spoke up, looking at Jo in in the rear-view mirror: "I think this place is all right, sir." His voice was soft and hesitant. "Forgive me. I know it's not my place to be putting in an opinion, but... This building is going to be torn down soon. I think Hosoda-san wanted you to see what the old part of town is really like. I won't move the car. If anything comes up, I'll let you know right away. And at this time of the day there aren't likely to be any other customers. It shouldn't be a problem."

"All right, but only for ten minutes," Jo said to Hosoda. "In ten minutes, no matter what, we're going back to the campground." She clapped her hands together and thanked him, her usual smile returning, then marched inside. Jo and Ri followed, after first making sure no one else was in the alley.

The place was small and cramped, and smelled of garlic and chives. There was a counter with eight or ten stools and a table for two in the corner. A woman with bleached-blonde hair was sitting at the middle of the counter, munching on gyoza and drinking beer. Next to the entrance was a steep, narrow set of stairs leading up to the second floor. A small, thin man behind the counter said, "Saki-chan! Bit early tonight, aren'tcha?" His face paled when he saw Jo come in behind her, followed by Ri; and the bleached blonde jumped to her feet, her mouth still full of food. A middle-aged woman standing beside the small man—his wife, presumably—turned to look, and when she saw Ri, with his sub-machine gun, she tottered and let out a muffled cry. The blonde covered her gaping mouth with her hands, as bits of fried dumpling dribbled out. Ri looked at the stairs, told Jo he'd check the second floor, and started up, still wearing his boots. "Wait!" said Jo, and turned to the proprietor: "Is anyone up there?"

"Nobody right now. Some regulars from a construction company may be here around seven-thirty, and there's another group with a reservation, but it wouldn't be any trouble to turn 'em away. I'll do it now, in fact. Just need to telephone. No problem at all." His face looked frozen with tension as he reached for the phone. "Don't worry about it!" Hosoda said, laughing. "We won't be staying long." She pulled out stools for Jo and Ri. Jo sat down; Ri didn't.

A number of shallow iron pans were stacked on a shelf behind the counter. Hosoda greeted the blonde woman, who in a daze was wiping up the mess she'd made. "Wasn't expectin' this," she said. "Ya scared the stuffin' outta me." She drained her beer and reached into her silver-colored handbag, removed a long, thin cigarette from a flat case, and tried to light it, a task made difficult by her trembling hands. Holding his sub-machine gun, Ri continued to peer outside, making no move to sit down. "I'm sorry," Hosoda said to the owner, "but would you mind closing up for about a quarter of an hour? If other customers were to come in now…" They'd be bound to collide with Ri, and any resulting commotion would attract onlookers—and possible trouble. The proprietor nodded at his wife, and she ducked under the counter, went outside, took down the *noren*, and pulled the plug next to the sign.

"What's the point of turnin' off the sign?" she grumbled, coming back. "We get no customers this early in the evenin' anyway." She looked toward Ri, who was standing in front of the curtain cord. He moved aside, realizing that she wanted to close the curtain, but she was apparently intimidated by the gun and remained motionless, so he closed it for her. She thanked him, and he bowed in return. "Could you make us six helpings right away?" Hosoda asked the proprietor. "And three more to take home to Granny." She beckoned to Ri to sit down, but he only nodded, remaining as vigilant as ever, staring out through the narrow gap he'd left in the curtains. The wife kneaded and stuffed the dough, while the husband began frying the morsels, which were no larger than an adult's little finger. He laid them in the skillet, then added a dash of water and covered it with a wooden lid. As the pork dumplings sizzled, the room filled with a mouth-watering aroma.

After first explaining to Hosoda how traditional funeral customs in Korea differ from those in Japan, Jo asked her how she thought Fukuokans would react to burial. Before offering her own opinion, she turned to the proprietor. Sweat was dripping off his forehead as he stood by the fire watching over the dumplings. "So," he said, "in Korea, ya bury 'em just like that, do ya?" Cooking oil had left brown stains on his white apron. "As long as ya take care with where ya do the buryin', I don't suppose it matters much." He then turned to his wife standing beside him: "What d'ya think?" She shook her head and didn't reply. It took her about two seconds to work the meat into the dough with a spoon and fold the little packet that would go into the pan. "I guess she don't know," her husband said. "That's right," she said. "I dunno nothin' about that. But it seems to me that if a body dies and isn't buried in keepin' with his country's ways, he can't very well get to heaven." Her hands did not stop moving as she spoke.

"You have your answer there, don't you?" Hosoda said. She took out three sets of wooden chopsticks from the stand, removed their paper wrappings, and broke them apart. One pair she gave to Jo. "I'm putting your chopsticks here," she said to Ri, and began mixing some sauce for the dumplings. Ri remained where he was but nodded, saying in Korean: "*Kamsa-hamnida.*" Even he couldn't help glancing at the fragrant steam that billowed from the skillet. "You say I have my answer," said Jo, "but what is it?" Hosoda was pouring a mixture of soy sauce, vinegar, and a reddish oil into three small bowls. "The issue may not be burial itself but rather where it's done," she said, still holding the bottle of oil. "There are a surprising number of shrines and temples in this town, and people probably wouldn't like the idea of your men being buried on sacred ground. But my guess is that anywhere else would be fine—except residential areas, of course. It might be a good idea to pay a courtesy call on the nearest shrine or temple before you do anything, though."

442

With a swooshing sound, a pan of gyoza was set before them. "It's very hot, so don't be touchin' it," said the proprietor, wiping his forehead. Hosoda ordered a bottle of Kirin beer, poured a glass for Jo, and urged Ri to join them, but he again shook his head. The bite-size dumplings were fried to a crisp. Jo had eaten dumplings before, steamed or in soup, but this was the first time he'd eaten them fried. "How is it?" Hosoda asked, as the proprietor and his wife looked on expectantly. "Very good," he replied. He drank some beer but stopped at half a glass. He was glad that he'd decided to pose his question to her. The municipal workers would only have said what they thought the KEF wanted to hear, and he'd never have been able to elicit the opinion that the temples and shrines in the vicinity should be advised. When he returned to headquarters tonight, he would have to prepare a report. He'd also need to decide on a burial site. As for talking to the local clergy, he thought he could handle that himself, without involving his superiors.

The proprietor turned a switch on a wall control panel, and the room was filled with music. Jo took it to be jazz. American music was banned at home, but he had often heard it as part of his research into enemy culture. To him it was sloppily arrhythmic. The combination of trumpet, saxophone, bass, and drums was turgid; and the voice of the singer on this tune had a rasping quality. He looked at Hosoda beside him, wondering whether she liked this kind of music, but her face was hidden by her hair, from which came a faint scent of fruit or flowers. "You'd be so nice to come home to," the vocalist sang. Performers in the Republic (he was thinking of the Pochonbo Electronic Ensemble, for example) invariably had clear voices. Could the huskiness of this jazz singer's voice be regarded as a bit decadent? There had been a similar quality to the voice of the *pansori* singer he'd heard on Cape Changsan. He could make out the words "Under an August moon burnin' above… " It was a love song. A possible line for a poem took shape in Jo's mind: *Her voice, like a hungry caress, leaves a sweet wound on my heart.* He immediately rejected it, however, as too direct and simple.

When the song ended and an instrumental piece came on, Jo happened to look up at the proprietor, who was staring at Hosoda with a puzzled frown. Her head was down, her shoulders quivering. Jo hadn't noticed because he was sitting right next to her. "Saki-chan," the proprietor said in a worried tone. She slowly stood up and turned to Jo. Tears were running down her pale cheeks. What could be wrong with her? She took a deep breath and then, astonishingly, sank to her knees on the wet concrete floor. The blonde woman had been applying lipstick but now froze; the proprietor and his wife too looked on dumbfounded; and even Ri gasped as he eyed the kneeling figure, her hands pressed together as if begging for mercy

"Please don't kill any more people in Fukuoka! I have no idea what's going to happen from now on, but, please... don't kill or hurt or torture anybody... People here are far from perfect, but there's a good side to them too. And they're terrified. Believe me, we're all scared to death! Please. Spare the lives of the people in Fukuoka—and Saga, Nagasaki, Kumamoto... Don't kill *anyone* in Kyushu. A lot of us hate Tokyo, but we don't want you to hurt anyone there either. Please don't kill us Japanese." The proprietor came out from behind the counter and, together with the blonde woman, helped her to her feet. Ri was still looking at her in bewilderment. Jo's immediate reaction was: *So that's why she brought me here.* He felt a mixture of anger and disappointment. At the same time, he couldn't help thinking that nobody else had dared to confront him or his comrades in this way. In the presence of armed soldiers, no Japanese official from either the central or local governments had ever said this sort of thing. Only her...

Ri motioned to Jo that it was time to leave. Hosoda was standing up now. Her knees and the hem of her dress were grubby, her face still wet with tears, as she attempted a broken apology. Jo didn't know how to react. He paid the bill, and the three left the restaurant. No one was on the street. The driver got out and started to open the front door on the passenger side, but Jo stopped him and performed the task himself, allowing Hosoda to get in. The proprietor, his wife, and the blonde woman came out, looking on anxiously. Suddenly remembering something, the man ducked back inside and reemerged holding a plastic bag, which he shoved through the open window: the dumplings Hosoda had ordered for her grandmother. Jo took the package and handed it to her. She tried to thank him, but all that came out was a garbled sob.

Once they'd left Nakasu and were heading west on the Kokutai Road, traffic thinned out and the car picked up speed. No one spoke. Hosoda sat with her head bowed. Jo was still contending with a mixture of resentment and exasperation. "How many Koreans did Japanese policemen and soldiers torture and kill during the colonial period?" he wanted to shout at her. "Don't you know what you Japanese did to us? Ask any Korean!" It was partly disappointment too, that she'd chosen this occasion to make a scene, just when he'd begun to enjoy the food and beer and light conversation. The proprietor had been friendly, and his wife might easily have been a Korean *omoni*, simple and straightforward. Hosoda had ruined it. *We're all scared to death of you and the KEF!* The only reason she'd taken them there was to tell him that.

They were now approaching Jigyohama. As Checkpoint C came into view, Hosoda said "Could you let me out here?" Jo checked with Ri before agreeing. When the car pulled up in front of a gasoline station, she slowly opened the door. "There's something I want to tell you," she said, and stepped outside. The driver looked at Jo in the rear-view mirror, waiting for further instructions. Should he have him drive off, or should he get out and talk to her? Reminding himself that he was still going to need her cooperation, he got out of the car. Hosoda was standing in the shadow of the large sign of a scallop shell. She had her back to the car, her hands clasped behind her holding the sack of dumplings and her handbag. At the sound of the door slamming shut, she turned around and came toward Jo, her eyes cast down. There was nobody else on the street, no other cars. The gasoline station had already closed and was now likewise deserted.

445

"I'm so sorry that I lost it like that," she said. Her large eyes were moist. The sea breeze was gently playing with her dark hair. Her white cheeks were stained with tears, and the bottom of her white dress was smudged. "I didn't intend to say what I did," she continued, dabbing at her cheeks with a handkerchief. "But when I think about what's in store for Fukuoka, for my family, I can't even sleep. I guess I let my feelings get the better of me. I suppose it was childish of me to turn to you, but who else could I talk to?" Jo didn't know what to say, though part of him felt that there were many things he wanted to tell her. His anger had vanished without a trace. In its place was a painful, choking feeling. If only he could keep this woman at his side for good...

"I have to ask you directly," she said, anxiety showing on her face. "Will we meet again tomorrow?"

She was staring earnestly at him. Her worried look and slender figure made her seem so helpless that he felt the urge to take her by the shoulders and embrace her. He could scarcely breathe; his throat was dry. All he could do was nod again and again. He coughed and was about to say "*Sayonara*," when Hosoda dropped her dumplings and handbag onto the pavement, put her hands around his neck, and kissed him. She then whispered in his ear: "I'm so glad." Her lips were cool and soft, the sensation was overwhelming. Jo thought for a moment that he would lose his head completely. Hosoda drew back and picked up her things. "Till tomorrow then," she said. With a wave of her hand she turned, her back now to the campground, and quickly walked away.

Jo lingered for a moment watching her go. Before returning to the car, he wiped his lips, but the sensation remained, as though it were seeping into him. He thought about her question: she hadn't said "Can I meet you?" or "Do you mind meeting me?" but "Will we—will you and I—meet?" It was a way of speaking he wasn't used to. Inside the car, he saw the driver staring at him in the mirror. He realized they weren't yet moving. "Take us to headquarters," he said, his voice unsteady. "Yes, sir," the driver replied and started up the engine. Jo's pulse was still erratic; the small pistol in his jacket pocket moved with every thump of his heart. As they passed Checkpoint C, Ri shifted his sub-machine gun and relaxed. Had he seen them kiss? Jo wondered about it but knew he could scarcely ask. Ri asked permission to smoke, then patted open his pack of Seven Stars, extracted a cigarette, and, after tapping the filter end against his left thumb, offered one to Jo. "She really looks like Ryu Hwa Mi, doesn't she?" he said, an impish grin on his face.

Ri was giving him a light when his phone rang. "What's going on there?" It was Ri Hui Cheol, speaking in a grim tone of voice. "We'll be with you shortly," Jo told him, exhaling smoke. There had been an incident, the deputy commander said, and quickly briefed him. When he hung up, Ri looked at him anxiously. Jo turned his eyes toward the campground. Engineers had set up two wooden posts next to the assembly area. When Ri saw this, he immediately stubbed out his cigarette, the color draining from his face. "An execution?" he asked. There could be no other explanation for the stakes; any soldier in the Republic would recognize their purpose.

Apparently, Corporal Song Jin Pal had beaten Sergeant Rim Cheong Gye at cards and won the watch that Rim had been issued. Rim then got himself drunk on some whiskey supplied by a Japanese retailer and tried to retrieve the watch by sneaking into Song's tent, together with an accomplice, Corporal Jo Chun Rae, also of the engineer corps. It seemed that Rim had wanted to make a present of the thing to his older brother, who was with the main force, the scheduled arrival of which happened to coincide with his birthday. Song had discovered the two rummaging about in his tent and threatened to go to the Special Police. They had then held him down and stabbed him with a bayonet that lay at hand. On the orders of an army doctor, the seriously wounded corporal had been taken to the Kyushu Medical Center. A summary court martial was convened, and the two culprits were sentenced to death by firing squad. The execution would serve to tighten army discipline and instill a certain fear in the local population. The men would be shot at sunset the next day.

Jo crushed his cigarette in the ashtray. A court-martial decision was irreversible. The sensation left by Hosoda Sakiko's kiss was fading away, and the severity of the Republic's rule was reasserting itself. This severity would become even more evident once the main troops arrived. The cracks in his defensive walls were widening, revealing the outline of something that couldn't be seen from within the Republic. The car was approaching the hotel entrance. As soon as he got back, he would probably have to prepare a written statement for the local television and newspaper media. This would be sent out only after the execution, to avoid the potential nuisance of civilian onlookers, and would explain that violations of military discipline must be met with swift and unyielding justice. The mood of the campground was noticeably subdued as they passed. Executions always brought home to the troops the sobering thought that they might be next.

Decadence, thought Jo, had nothing to do with desire for a woman. Decadence wasn't anything seductive. Long ago, his father had told him a Western story about two children who searched everywhere for the "bluebird of happiness" to no avail, only to find on their return that the feathers of the caged bird in their own home were blue. Jo had searched long and hard for the meaning of "decadence." But it now dawned on him that it was right here, in front of his nose. True decadence wasn't anything carnal; it was about sacrificing the powerless minority for the sake of the majority. He remembered the Arirang festival. It occurred to him that the games were nothing other than an immense celebration of the majority, and the legitimacy of power. The festival didn't lack decadence after all—it was decadence itself, on a colossal scale. In a mighty river, one searches in vain for pools or drops of water. An execution witnessed by the entire military assembly would be an unpleasant business, but it was almost certainly a necessity. The measures taken by headquarters were not mistaken. Political principle and administrative rule implicitly called for procedures and instruments for sacrificing the weak. As long as the masses, the military, and the nation were in a state of equilibrium, these instruments could remain dormant and inconspicuous. But in times of crisis, they were employed to the full; those in the minority were sacrificed, and everyone began scrambling desperately to avoid being included among them. And in that instant, decadence showed itself for what it was.

The car pulled up to the entrance. Jo erased the sensation of Hosoda Sakiko's tender kiss before making his way toward headquarters.

# 8

# THE EXECUTION

*April 9, 2011*

D R. KURODA GENJI had just finished the morning ward round. Stepping out into the linoleum-floored corridor, he felt a sudden craving for some Hawks Town ramen. He always ordered the noodles in a thick soup made from pork-bone stock, complete with lard floating on top and a dollop of garlic paste. The stuff didn't really taste all that great, but now and then he got an irrational craving for it. Now aged fifty, Kuroda worked in the department of respiratory medicine at the National Kyushu Medical Center. Many of the patients at this hospital suffered from intractable or terminal illnesses, and those with problems in their bronchial tubes and lungs, even when still quite young, were emaciated in appearance. Perhaps his taste for those thick, juicy noodles came from examining such patients day in day out.

In any case, it wasn't possible—the gaudy neon lights of Hawks Town were still off, and the ramen shop wasn't open. He hadn't been to the mall since the start of the occupation, but he'd heard that although some of the traders selling clothes, shoes, and medicine were doing business with the KEF, all the eateries there had closed down. They probably had little choice, since they were unlikely to get any customers: the soldiers cooked for themselves, and none of the locals would want to eat out in the occupied area. Late last night a Speed Tribe gang had driven their cars and bikes around the camp waving KEF flags and yelling in broken Korean that they wanted to enlist, and there had been a bit of a ruckus when KEF sentries fired warning shots. But nowadays it was only idiots like that who had the nerve to take any kind of action.

Kuroda shook his head, as if to banish all thoughts of ramen, and walked toward the elevator. He'd grab lunch in the cafeteria instead. Several people were in the elevator hall—a patient wheeling a drip stand, several members of his family, a nurse... and Dr. Seragi. Kuroda quickly turned and tried to retreat, but he'd already been spotted. "Hey, Kuroda! You had lunch?" the older man called out. Resigned to the inevitable, Kuroda walked over and got into the elevator with him. Seragi Katsuhiko was an honorary consultant at the hospital, and a national authority on clinical immunology. This year he would be eighty-three. He was something of a maverick, having distanced himself from the Medical Association, and being from Tokyo he wasn't part of the Kyushu University clique either. This made him popular with the younger doctors, and also with the residents and trainees. Under the healthcare reforms of recent years, the power of the Medical Association and the university department of medicine had clearly begun to wane. Also, all general hospitals, public and private, needed at least one well-known and respected figure in order to attract the best doctors. This was partly why Seragi was still working at his advanced age.

"How are the wife and daughters?" Seragi asked in the elevator. "I guess they're doing okay," Kuroda told him. Kuroda's wife had been a nurse, and was a close friend of Seragi's second daughter, an ophthalmologist. Three or four times a year, the latter's family would get together with the Kurodas for a Chinese meal at a hotel in Tenjin. Seragi himself hadn't joined them initially, but after his wife died a couple of years ago they'd invited him along, thinking he must be lonely. They had all been surprised by the alacrity with which he'd accepted. He ended up talking and eating more than anyone, and from then on he had dominated the gatherings. He acted as if it were all about him.

451

Seragi led the medical world in the field of autoimmune diseases. He'd been a champion of healthcare reform, and when public and private practices had been merged into the so-called dual healthcare system, he had held out for independent inspections of medical facilities, which in the end he obtained. Seragi was an excellent doctor, and Kuroda had a lot of respect for him, but he could be exhausting to be with. He was of average size and at first glance looked fairly mild-mannered—if you ignored that unsettling glint in his eye. There probably wasn't anyone in the Center capable of standing up to him, and when he lost his temper not even the CEO could cope. Kuroda followed him into the cafeteria, thinking ruefully that he'd just wanted to eat lunch alone and in peace. The ramen shop had been perfect for avoiding precisely this sort of situation. The cafeteria was divided into separate areas for staff and visitors, but the menu was the same. As Seragi walked in, a number of doctors and other staff rose to their feet to greet him, and he smiled and nodded, gesturing that they should sit down. Kuroda chose the set meal A, while Seragi placed on his own tray a dish of tofu and rice and a bowl of udon noodles with egg, and headed for a vacant table by the wall. To their right was a small atrium, built to allow in light, but today was cloudy and rather dark.

The tables and chairs were made of fragrant unvarnished wood, and the tablecloths were cotton, with yellow and white checks. Until four years ago, there had been cheap plywood tables and metal folding chairs. When the dual healthcare system was introduced, however, a budget was made available to improve the eating arrangements. Kuroda's set meal consisted of tuna salad, grilled chicken, some stewed vegetables, vegetable soup, and rice. "Is that the one for high blood pressure?" asked Seragi, and Kuroda nodded. The tuna was the type preserved in brine, not oil, and the grilled chicken was skinless breast meat, while the stewed vegetable dish contained sweet potato and apple, flavored with lemon. With a steadily aging society, the focus now was on comprehensive medical care aimed at improving lifestyle habits, including diet, and for the past few years, three dieticians had been assigned to the cafeteria. Various menus had been put together to protect people—patients and doctors alike—against high blood pressure, heart disease, and diabetes. Kuroda did wonder, though, whether it was really necessary to make even the young resident and trainee doctors eat things like tasteless, fat-free tofu burgers. Everyone was tempted by some fatty ramen now and then.

Seragi took a mouthful of tofu, his gaze fixed on one of the televisions placed in each corner of the room. The NHK lunchtime news broadcast had been extended and a news anchor, his hair neatly parted on one side, was saying that the ships were setting sail from North Korea. "Each of these dots represents a ship," he said, pointing at a US military satellite photograph. Anyone would have thought the world was about to end from the expression on his face. Still looking at the screen, Seragi rummaged in the pocket of his white coat and brought out a small Tupperware box. Using his chopsticks, he scooped out some green paste and added it to his noodles. "It's from Saga, made from the rind of fresh yuzu and green chilies. Want some?" Kuroda shook his head. Yuzu pepper paste didn't go well with tuna salad and grilled chicken.

Everyone was watching the report impassively as they ate their rather bland meals. According to the satellite picture, ships of varying sizes had first left the four major ports of Rajin, Chongjin, Kimchaek, and Wonsan, and it had been confirmed that others subsequently departed from Tanchon, Ranam, Kyongsong, Riwon, and Sinpo. It was a large fleet with well over four hundred vessels, and it would take some time to close ranks once all the ships had left their respective ports. There were antique-looking Soho- and Rajin-class frigates, Sariwon- and Tral-class corvettes, Taechong offshore-patrol vessels, plus assorted missile boats, all of which had their decks crammed with soldiers. Transport ships, freighters, and even large converted fishing boats also appeared to have been mobilized. In two days' time, on the morning of the eleventh, they would reach Japan's exclusive economic zone, and by midday they'd cross into Japanese territorial waters. As the news sank in, a hush fell over the cafeteria. There probably wasn't a single person in Fukuoka who wasn't apprehensive about what was going to happen now. Kuroda himself was relying more and more on sleeping pills. Once he started thinking about all those extra troops and what might happen to his two daughters and ailing mother, he just couldn't get to sleep. This wasn't the sort of issue about which you could pretend it would all work out somehow. The apparent calm here in the cafeteria wasn't the result of anxiety and fear shutting down the thought processes; but neither was it because these people were taking the crisis lightly, or thinking that as medical doctors they weren't likely to be arrested or shot.

Once the KEF had been reinforced with an additional hundred and twenty thousand armed troops, they would probably begin to crack down harder. Things might get very nasty indeed. But what could anyone here do? It wasn't even possible to escape, with the government blockade still in place. All they could do was get on with the job as usual. The patients couldn't wait. Yesterday there had been an incident in the KEF camp, and a soldier had been brought in with a serious stomach wound. A KEF army doctor and an officer with good spoken Japanese brought the man but didn't come inside the hospital; they pulled up to the guards' station near the entrance and asked to see someone in charge. It had been decided to send Kuroda, who just happened to be in the waiting area by the main reception.

He interacted with KEF guards every day when he came to work, and wasn't particularly nervous about this. Both the doctor and the officer translating for him were exceptionally polite. They asked if the wounded man could be operated on here, since they lacked proper facilities themselves. Kuroda immediately contacted the emergency room, and the soldier was put on a stretcher and taken straight into ER, just as any Japanese would be. Kuroda had seen the surgeon this morning, who told him matter-of-factly: "The damage to the kidneys was the worst part. He's in Recovery now, but he won't ever be a soldier again."

The TV was now showing a press conference with the Chief Cabinet Secretary, deputizing for the Prime Minister, who was

FROM THE FATHERLAND, WITH LOVE

apparently in an emergency Cabinet session and unable to appear before the media. Chief Cabinet Secretary Shigemitsu strongly censured North Korea for allowing the fleet to leave port, and kept repeating that the ships would not be allowed to enter Japanese territorial waters. "Does that mean they'll be attacked if they try?" asked a reporter, to which Shigemitsu replied in typically evasive fashion: "That would be a last resort." The coastguard and Maritime SDF had already dispatched ships to the boundary line, and fighter planes were ready to scramble at a moment's notice. Another journalist wanted to know whether the US forces in Japan would be asked to lend support. It was an odd question coming from a major newspaper known for being anti-American, but Shigemitsu ducked it by saying that this wasn't a simple act of aggression. "A hundred and twenty thousand foreign troops have set sail for Fukuoka, and you're saying that's not an act of aggression?" asked the reporter sharply. "The US State Department has described them as armed refugees," Shigemitsu replied in a much louder voice than usual. That meant that the US government didn't consider the KEF an invasion force.

A few days earlier, Kuroda had read up on the US-Japan security treaty. He'd never had much interest in international politics or economics, and aside from the occasional mystery novel when he was on an international flight, he never read anything other than specialist papers in his own field. He read the treaty carefully, all the while thinking he would never have done this if it weren't for these KEF characters showing up. The full title was "Treaty of Mutual Cooperation and Security between the United States and Japan," and he read it carefully. He also pored over the Japan-US defense cooperation guidelines, issued toward the end of the Nineties. Nowhere in either of these documents was it written that if Japan came under attack the US forces based here would automatically counterattack. He'd been surprised at first, but then realized that of course you couldn't just take military action on another country's sovereign territory unless that country asked you to, even if you were allies. The cooperation guidelines stated that in the event of Japan coming under armed attack and acting independently to resist it as quickly as possible, the US would lend appropriate assistance. Any sovereign nation in these circumstances would obviously take independent action—and yet the Japanese government still hadn't made any demands of the KEF, at least not publicly. In fact, all they had done was dispatch an SAT unit, resulting in almost a hundred casualties, most of them civilians.

There had been a cross-party call to allow the immediate transport of medical supplies to Kyushu after a patient at a private general hospital in Saga had died from urinary poisoning due to insufficient dialysis fluid. Even in Fukuoka they were running short of dialysis fluid, not to mention blood for transfusions, antibacterial drugs for surgery, disinfectant, insulin, anesthetics, and so on. But it was a medical NPO based in Kobe, not the government, that got things moving. The government recognized the need to get the distribution of medical supplies up and running again, but they refused to negotiate with the KEF. The NPO had therefore chartered seven trucks and filled them with medicines, intending to drive to Fukuoka and negotiate directly with the KEF, who issued a statement saying that they had no intention of obstructing or preventing any nongovernmental vehicles or airplanes distributing medical supplies—or any other goods, for that matter. However, the SDF soldiers manning the blockade at the entrance to the Kanmon undersea tunnel were shown on TV stopping the trucks from crossing into Kyushu. The resulting barrage of criticism at home and abroad eventually forced the government to allow the transportation of medical supplies there, but even after this incident they still had no means of directly negotiating with the KEF.

It probably wasn't just the government's fault, though. Nobody in Japan had any real idea of what independent diplomacy involved. Kuroda himself had taken it for granted that if Japan was attacked by North Korea or China, the US military would automatically step in. Everyone was under the illusion that Americans would basically do all the fighting for them, unreasonable though it was to expect any country to be that benevolent. What Kuroda wanted right now was for the Japanese government to come to Fukuoka and negotiate with the KEF—and virtually all the inhabitants of Fukuoka must have felt the same way. But the government just kept up their mantra of refusing to negotiate with terrorists. "Terrorist" was a useful word that had been sealed in the public's imagination by the 9/11 attacks. Government officials still called the KEF "the North Korean terrorist group calling itself the Koryo Expeditionary Force," and NHK followed suit. But the local residents couldn't care less what they were called. When the enemy were on your doorstep, the priority was to avoid getting yourself killed—even a child could understand that.

"If we attack the fleet, it'll mean war with the KEF, won't it?" said Kuroda. Seragi sucked up some noodles. "I don't think so," he muttered, shaking his head. "How can you go to war when the Prime Minister, the Cabinet, and even the public haven't got the will for it?" On TV, the anchor with the neat side parting was asking a military expert how Japan should respond to the situation. "According to clause twelve of the revised Japan Coast Guard Law, the SDF should first fire warning shots at the fleet," was his grave-faced answer. "Even I could have told you that much," said a surgeon sitting behind them, provoking titters around his table. "It's not easy to say how things might pan out after that," the expert went on, "given all the complex political considerations and possible options." But in fact the options were dead simple. Either they attacked despite the risk of KEF reprisals, or they decided the risk was too high and allowed the fleet to dock at Hakata Port; it was one or the other. But nobody was prepared to point out this hard reality—not the government, nor the media or the pundits. They didn't want a terrorist attack, but neither did they want the fleet to land—so they just dithered over what to do.

"Well then, let's have a look at what's going on in Fukuoka," the anchor said, as the scene cut to a middle-aged male reporter outside the Daimaru department store in Tenjin. "Yoshida-san, what do things look like from your end?" Yoshida was a familiar face, a middle-aged reporter for NHK Fukuoka. "I'm here in the busy

Tenjin district, where it's just business as usual," he said. He seemed
irritated by the question, and that prompted a smattering of applause
in the cafeteria. "Yoshida-san, it's been confirmed that the North
Korean fleet has set sail," said the anchor, but Yoshida just frowned
and fiddled with his earpiece. It was a cloudy day in Fukuoka, and
a strong wind was blowing. Rain was expected at any moment, and
many of the people outside Daimaru were carrying umbrellas. The
shops and department stores in that area were all open for business.
Buses were running, and people were at work or out shopping, just
as they would be in normal times. "Yoshida-san, the reinforcements
have already left North Korea," the anchor tried again, and again
Yoshida fiddled with his earphone and frowned, still gazing dumbly
at the camera. The anchor was clearly ruffled by this. "Wait 'im
out, Yoshida!" someone said, to chuckles and cheers in the cafeteria.
"Make that Tokyo bastard squirm!" said someone else, eliciting more
laughter. Seragi peered intently at the TV screen, his chopsticks
suspended in mid-air with a load of noodles on them. "That's not
it," he muttered. "He's not being contentious. He just doesn't know
how to answer—after all, it wasn't even a question, was it?"

"Yoshida-san," said the anchor, pulling himself together and trying
a new tack. "Can you describe the mood as people go about their
business in town today?" Yoshida waved a hand at his surroundings. "As I said before, things seem quite normal here," he reported.
"That anchor's missing the point," said Seragi. "It's not as if there's
a typhoon on the way. It's an army. He doesn't seem to get that, but
Yoshida does—everyone in Fukuoka knows it only too well. And he's
supposed to go around asking people how they *feel*? It's ridiculous."
Seragi looked away from the screen as though he'd had enough.

Kuroda had never been bothered much by TV reporting before
the KEF came along, but now it occurred to him that most viewers
didn't want facts from TV, they wanted reassurance. Just as they
wanted the player who hit the game-winning home run to tell
them he was happy about it, they wanted people in Fukuoka to say
they were scared. That way, they could commiserate while feeling
safe themselves. And TV broadcasters responded to that desire for

reassurance. The scene now switched to demonstrations around the country, where thousands of people formed circles around the LNG tanks in Hiroshima, Osaka, Miura, Kanagawa, and Chiba. It was surreal to see the huge, half-buried silver gas tanks ringed by people holding hands in a bid to prevent terrorist attacks and promote peace. There had been endless talk on the TV news and chat shows about the threat of the LNG tanks being blown up and engulfing entire cities in flames. Presumably the demonstrators thought the terrorists would be deterred by the human daisy chains they were forming around them.

An elderly lady came out of the kitchen with a remote control and turned the TV volume down. Nobody wanted to watch these smug love-ins. Having finished his meal, Seragi had already turned his gaze from the TV and was talking with a plastic surgeon at the table behind. They were discussing the fact that some patients had deteriorated from the shock of the occupation, while others had perked up, determined to leave hospital as quickly as possible. Kuroda had seen similar examples in his own department. There had been quite a few elderly patients brought in with pneumonia contracted partly as a result of stress, while several patients had been so keen not to remain hospitalized right next to the KEF camp that their symptoms actually improved. Perhaps the extra motivation helped rally their immune systems.

Seragi had launched into a raunchy story from his wartime days, not bothering to lower his voice, and the younger doctors at the tables around him pricked up their ears. He rarely talked about his army days, and was scornful of people who came out with war stories when they were drunk, but it was known that he had entered the army as a minor and was stationed in North Korea. Even now, the focus of the anecdote wasn't himself but an army doctor in his battalion who was an obvious homosexual. The army had been particularly concerned about recruits who suffered from phimosis, or non-retractile foreskin, since they were prone to infections that prevented them from fighting. In an attempt to address this problem, officers apparently gave instructions on how to stretch the skin manually. "They used to get everyone together in the large assembly hall, then say, 'All of you with phimosis, step forward!' It's hard to believe it now, but nobody tried to dodge it. After all, we were all naked, and things like phimosis and piles and whatnot had already been recorded in the medical for new recruits, so they already knew who had what. Well, in every company of five hundred men, there'd be thirty or forty with phimosis. They were made to stand in a row, stark naked, and when the order was given, they had to stroke their willies all together according to instructions from a medical officer, a sergeant. And all the while, that doctor I mentioned sat glued to his chair, just staring."

Seragi spoke dryly, without any change in his expression. Yoshizaki, the head of the cosmetic-surgery department, had asked him about his experience of North Koreans—if he didn't think there was a streak of cruelty in the national character—not about young recruits masturbating. Perhaps Seragi wanted to avoid the question. "Guys with phimosis tended to circle the hand around the shaft, like this," he continued, gesturing with his own right hand, "and stroke the whole thing, foreskin and all. The sergeant would see that and start bellowing in a voice that rattled the walls: 'Not like that, you fools!'"

Everybody at the nearby tables laughed, and someone from the obstetrics and gynecology department said, "But could they get it up, with hundreds of guys watching?" To this Seragi replied, "Sure they could—they were young and sex-starved, and where was a new recruit going to find a woman? No, they didn't have any problem getting it up. Well, the sergeant would then tell them how to proceed. 'The proper method for masturbation is as follows. You hold the penis in the left hand and peel back the foreskin with the right, exposing the head of the penis, which you then stimulate directly. If you find the friction painful, just rub a little spit on it.' You see, if boys with phimosis didn't pull back the foreskin first, it would stretch even more and just make the condition worse. Anyway, then the sergeant would get one particular soldier to come up on stage and demonstrate. This fellow was from Tohoku, had been in the army a couple of years already, and his cock was a monster—so big that even the guys in the back of the hall could see it clearly. He'd get up on stage and bawl out his own name and rank, then rip off his loincloth and start stroking it like a master, as if he was playing an instrument. And all the rookies with phimosis were made to get up there and perform alongside him. Thirty or forty boys up there pulling on their hard-ons—it was quite a spectacle. And when the spunk started flying, that doctor I told you about would get so carried away that he'd jump up out of his chair and yell '*Banzai!*'"

The cafeteria erupted in laughter. Even the kitchen ladies poked their heads out to see what was going on. Kuroda wondered whether the old man told stories like this at home too. After his wife died, he had moved in with his granddaughter. Seragi Yoko was a dermatologist here at the hospital, but she was a self-effacing, well-mannered woman. How on earth did she cope living with a loudmouthed grandfather who casually told stories about monster dicks?

After the laughter died down, Seragi turned serious. "Some of the junior officers I knew were fine men who'd studied science and engineering at technical schools and colleges around the country. They were talented, and decent, too. There are people who say that burying your nose in books is bad for you, but I don't agree— knowledge and skill make a person's character. Better to read even one book on the natural sciences or philosophy than do Zazen or stand under a waterfall, I say. Not all the Japanese troops in Korea or China were bastards, obviously, but... Do you see what I'm getting at, Yoshizaki?" Yoshizaki said he thought he did: "There's no such thing as 'cruelty' as a national character. Is that it?" Seragi said, "Something like that, I guess." He put the box of yuzu pepper paste back in his pocket and looked around at his audience.

Kuroda was just getting to his feet when his cellphone rang. At the same moment, his name was announced over the PA system: "Dr. Kuroda, please report immediately to the main entrance." On the phone was the head of security, Koshida, who informed him in a shaky voice that the KEF army doctor and officer who had brought in the injured soldier the day before were waiting for him there. Kuroda wondered why they'd asked for him, but then remembered that he'd given them his name card—they were so correct and well mannered that he'd automatically responded in kind. "Do you know what they want?" he asked, but was told, "They said they'll tell you when they see you. Please come quickly."

"What's up?" Seragi asked Kuroda, a mischievous expression on his face. When Kuroda told him, he looked amused. "Maybe they've found out about your crimes. Drop by the pharmacy and get yourself some Voltaren in case they arrest you," he called after him. "It might help a bit when you're being tortured."

"I'm sorry to put you to so much trouble," the KEF officer said to Kuroda, "but would you mind accompanying us to the command center?" They were waiting outside the front entrance, which was where they'd been yesterday, but this time he was surprised to see they had a car with them. It was a large gray Toyota sedan with a little KEF flag attached to the wing mirror. A junior officer, presumably the driver, had opened the rear passenger door and was standing at attention beside it. On the TV news, Kuroda had seen an officer—the one with a keloidal scar where his ear had once been—pull up to City Hall in the same car. At least he probably wasn't being arrested, since they used an MAV to transport detainees. But it was only a few minutes' walk from the Medical Center to the Sea Hawk Hotel—was the car because they were in a hurry, or was it out of respect for him? What would he do if they demanded that he become their official doctor, or help establish a military hospital or something?

"How long do you need me for?" Kuroda asked the officer. The doctor said something in Korean, which was translated as two hours. Two hours—well, he could probably manage that. Kuroda called up Takahashi, the director of the respiratory department, and explained the situation, asking him to change the afternoon shift of consultations. Takahashi had already heard from the head of security that the KEF had come to see Kuroda, but he was surprised to learn that he'd been summoned to their command center. "Are you sure it's all right?" he asked, the worry evident in his voice. "Well, they've gone to the trouble of sending a car for me, and they asked so politely, it's kind of hard to refuse," Kuroda told him. "I guess," said Takahashi. "But you take care, all right?" And just how am I supposed to do that, Kuroda wondered as he hung up. Before getting into the car, he asked the officer why, out of almost two hundred doctors in the hospital, they had chosen him. This was translated for the army doctor, who brought out the name card Kuroda had given him yesterday and said something. So that's all it was, thought Kuroda. But the officer interpreting pointed to the job title under Kuroda's name. Beneath "Deputy Director of Respiratory Medicine, National Kyushu Medical Center" was a second title that read "Lecturer in Virology, Faculty of Medicine, Kyushu University."

A few spots of rain appeared on the windshield. The army doctor in the front passenger seat had given his name as Heo Jip, while the interpreter sitting to Kuroda's right was Pak Myeong. Kuroda wondered why they needed a specialist in virology. Had something happened at the Sea Hawk Hotel? If there'd been an outbreak of some infectious disease, he couldn't deal with it alone; he would have to call in specialist staff from the public-health department. And all he taught at the university was basic virology for first-year students, nothing advanced or specialized. After graduating from university he'd worked, on the recommendation of his professor, as a technician in the graduate school virology lab at Kyoto University. Spending his days collating lab data on viral infections helped him realize he was more interested in clinical medicine, and he left Kyoto after two years and returned to Fukuoka, where he was soon invited to join the respiratory department at the Medical Center. Known for its advocacy of advanced comprehensive medical care, the hospital had many elderly or seriously ill patients, and there were frequent outbreaks of viral respiratory infections.

Perhaps he should warn them that they also ought to contact the public-health department, he thought as the car pulled slowly away from the entrance. The hospital building receded behind him. It was then that he noticed the distinctive smell in the car. It was a pungent odor, like spicy miso and kimchi mixed with sweat, and Kuroda suddenly found himself struggling for breath. He regretted complying with their request to accompany them. He should have realized that meeting just outside the hospital was one thing, but being taken to their HQ was quite another. In the hospital he was surrounded by friends and colleagues and felt safe. He should at least have found someone to go with him.

A revolver with a dull black hammer was at Pak's hip, and grenades shaped like baby pineapples hung from the driver's belt. The three North Koreans sat in oppressive silence. Enveloped in that oppressive smell, Kuroda's thoughts turned dark, and he began to revise his impression of the army doctor and his interpreter. He had thought there was a certain charm to Heo Jip's large eyes, but here in the car the man looked downright gloomy. Beneath a pointed nose were thin, bloodless lips, and now he could see cruelty in those round, deep-set eyes. He'd been thinking of trying to find out more about KEF medical issues, but he now realized this wasn't someone he could enjoy a conversation with. Pak Myeong, seated beside him, might have passed for nobility, but his refined features, seen up close, seemed cold and mask-like, and though young, he had no trace of youthfulness in him. He must be about the age of the trainee doctors at the Medical Center but was utterly unlike any of them. His strangely mature face was taut with discipline and wariness.

The road from the hospital to the Sea Hawk Hotel passed by the KEF camp, and to reach the hotel entrance on the Dome side you had to do a U-turn at Checkpoint A, just before Yokatopia Bridge. Kuroda had often been inside the hotel for a party or seminars in one of the banquet halls. He could see the camp on his left. It looked emptier than usual, probably because of the rain. One large tent in particular stood out, and in a clearing in front of it were two upright wooden posts about two meters high, though one was slightly shorter than the other. They were square-sided, perhaps a hand's width across, and blackish—probably scrap lumber taken from the nearby landfill. Sandbags had been piled up behind them. It looked like the setting for some kind of ritual or ceremony. Or perhaps the posts would be wrapped in wadding for use in bayonet training. No soldiers were in sight, but it all looked a little spooky. Noticing the direction of Kuroda's gaze, Heo said something to Pak. "That's for the execution this evening," Pak explained, but his pronunciation was a little odd, and to Kuroda it sounded like "eggs section." He assumed it was some kind of North Korean custom or celebration, and just nodded in reply.

"The corporal you so kindly treated yesterday was stabbed in the stomach by two men who were trying to kill him. They will be executed this evening," Pak added, jerking his chin at the two stakes. This time Kuroda clearly heard the word "executed." As it sank in, the image of blindfolded men bound to stakes floated into his mind. His heart started pounding. Now that he thought about it, the posts were just tall enough to accommodate a man's full height. The army doctor, Heo Jip, had twisted his body around in the front passenger seat and was watching him, as if to check his reaction. It had been a mistake to think he was immune to the KEF just because he passed through the checkpoint every day on his way to work, occasionally chatting in broken Japanese with the men on guard. It was similar to enjoying a conversation with a yakuza in a bar. Chatting with a gangster about women or golf in a public place was not the same as being summoned to his office because he had something he wanted to discuss with you. Pak was also staring at Kuroda, evidently keen to see how he reacted.

"By execution you mean—" The young officer answered the question before Kuroda finished it: "Firing squad." Kuroda had heard on a talk show several years earlier that executions in North Korea were made public in order to serve as warnings to others. And those two posts were right out in the open. The hospital's north-facing windows and balconies overlooked the KEF camp, and the upper floors, particularly from the fifth to the tenth, had wards for seriously and terminally ill patients. What effect would witnessing an execution have on patients with, say, a heart condition?

Kuroda was about to ask whether the execution was going to be made public, but stopped himself. He suddenly felt afraid that the question might cause offense and result in his being locked up, too. These guys were quite capable of it. Until you'd seen them at close quarters, there was no way you could understand the fear they inspired. He was already regretting having come along with them—but what if he'd refused? This, he supposed, was what it was like to be controlled by violence. When you're under threat of violence, there are no options; your own wishes and judgment are suspended. It's only when people lose something that they realize how important it was to them. Kuroda felt trapped. It was a feeling he'd never had before, as if his limbs and torso were slowly shrinking. He no longer cared whether the execution was in public or not.

At Checkpoint A, instead of making a U-turn, the car turned right and headed for the tour-party entrance. Heo said something to the driver, who pointed ahead and nodded. Pak put the documents he was carrying into an attaché case. It seemed they were about to arrive. But where the hell were they going? Kuroda had heard that the City Hall staff usually entered via the fourth-floor front lobby, on the Dome side. The entrance to the banquet halls was on the first floor on the opposite side, overlooking the sea, with an underground parking lot down below. It was there on level B2 that the arrested were apparently being held. Seragi had teased him that he'd be arrested himself, but maybe he really was being taken to the detention center.

It was rumored that people had been investigated online. This was a frequent topic among colleagues out drinking together: how the targets were the type who traveled first class on trips abroad and owned holiday homes, yachts, or cruisers, or who were members of exclusive fitness clubs, or owned expensive art objects, or kept secret assets—as well as those who led lifestyles of questionable social morality. Kuroda himself, come to think of it, had flown first class to Hawaii a couple of times, when a travel agent acquaintance had let him know about some special offers. And he co-owned with a couple of fellow doctors a small boat in a marina in Omura Bay. He was also member of a fairly expensive sports club. And he possessed several pieces of Arita porcelain from the Gen-emon and Kakiemon kilns. Then there was that bank account he kept secret from his wife, with a deposit of around 720,000 yen as an entertainment fund—and the hostess from a club in Nakasu he'd had an affair with some fifteen years ago. Kuroda's insides began to churn. His throat, chest, and belly felt constricted, and he could feel himself sweating at the temples and armpits. Pak peered at him and asked, "Is something the matter?" Heo also turned to look at him. The car passed the tour-group entrance, then the parking-lot entrance, and continued along the road around the hotel, finally pulling up outside the first-floor banquet halls.

The driver got out and opened the door for him, but Kuroda turned to Pak and in a trembling voice asked, "Am I under arrest?" The Korean gaped at him for a moment, then translated for Heo Jip, whereupon the two of them burst out laughing. "Why on earth would we be arresting you, Dr. Kuroda? Please, go ahead." Pak indicated the open door and shook his head, still chuckling. "But why didn't you use the main entrance?" asked Kuroda as he got out of the car. Pak translated this for his colleague, who looked down for a moment before apparently telling him to explain. "The front lobby is closed," said Pak. "And so are all the floors above it. We have moved our command center here, to the first floor. Three soldiers have fallen ill with a rash, fever, and nausea, and we want you to examine them. Also, we have been infested with insects. We are worried about the possibility of contagion."

As they passed through the door into the banquet lobby, a pungent odor of disinfectant made Kuroda's throat and eyes sting. It was probably isopropanol, which was said to be a skin irritant and was hardly ever used in Japan now. He asked Pak about it and was told that a local fumigation man had done the job for them. Apparently the fellow had a whole load of stuff in storage that he didn't know what to do with, and let them have it for virtually nothing.

The senior officer Kuroda had often seen on TV was there to meet him in the spacious lobby. He was smiling pleasantly, but with a solid build suited to rugby or judo and one ear reduced to a burn scar, his presence was intimidating. Taking Kuroda's hand in a strong grip, he greeted him in Japanese and gave his name as Han Seung Jin, commander of the Koryo Expeditionary Force. Together with Pak and Heo they sat down on comfortable chairs in one corner of the lobby, and a woman soldier brought them some tea. Kuroda began to calm down. As soon as they were seated, the three North Koreans lit up cigarettes. They didn't seem at all bothered by the disinfectant. Pak savored the smoke as he exhaled, and then said something to his commanding officer. Han roared with laughter, before saying, "Ah, Dr. Kuroda. Arresting you is the last thing on our mind!" He leaned forward and clapped him lightly on the shoulder with one hand. "We summoned you here because we need your expertise."

The commander's Japanese, including his choice of words, pronunciation, and intonation, was excellent. Kuroda gave an embarrassed laugh, shaking his head. But he knew he mustn't let his guard down with this lot, however friendly they might seem. Along with the tea there was a plate piled with some kind of Korean sweets. They were round and flat, with alternate swirls of white and black sesame. Pressed to try them, he took one to calm his nerves. It was delicious. Here he was, being cordially entertained—all but pampered—by the top leadership of the KEF, but that didn't mean anything had changed. He must remain alert. These people were treating him like this because he was useful to them, that was all. If he ceased to be useful, no more sweets; and if he ever posed any threat, they would simply eliminate him.

A red carpet led from the lobby, made a right-angled turn to the left, and continued along the grand foyer. At the corner was a series of rooms, each named after a tree: Katsura, Elm, Laurel, Maple, Oak. The double doors of the Oak Room were wide open, and Kuroda could see three bodies laid out inside, each covered with a yellowish-white cloth and tightly bound with a cord of the same color. Flowers had been laid around them. They were the KEF casualties from Ohori Park, he was told. Their burial had been scheduled for this evening, but it was now postponed until tomorrow morning, so as not to coincide with the execution.

On either side of the foyer was a large ballroom. KEF officers, armed soldiers, and some of the City Hall staff were coming and going between the two. These must constitute the command center that Pak had said was moved from the third floor. "Well, shall we get going? I'll show you around." Han, the commander, stubbed out his cigarette, straightened the collar of his khaki uniform, and stood up. Pak led the way, with Kuroda following and Heo and Han bringing up the rear. Pak was tall but slim, with narrow shoulders, while Heo was short and had a slight stoop. They got on the escalator by the cloakroom and went down to level B1. "The criminals are on the next floor down," the commander told Kuroda, again clapping him on the shoulder.

"When the main force arrives, they will be transferred to our new facilities," explained Pak, stopping before the glass door to the level B1 parking lot. "We recognize that they also have human rights, so—well, the level B2 facilities are not too bad, but sooner or later we'll probably have a visit from UN Security Council inspectors. It's quite possible they'll say it's inhumane to keep them locked up underground, or something of the sort." Kuroda wondered if a team of UN inspectors really would come to Fukuoka. And if they judged that the KEF posed no threat to the international community, would that legitimize the occupation? "Dr. Kuroda," said Han, resting a hand on his shoulder. Perhaps in North Korea body language like this was a way to put a visitor or a subordinate at ease. "China has already approached us independently."

Kuroda thought he'd never seen a military uniform so suit a man before. The visor of his khaki cap was topped with gold braid, the narrow collar of his starched white shirt was complemented by a narrow, deep red tie, and rows of medal ribbons lay across his left breast. His crisp, angular silhouette in the snugly fitting uniform made Kuroda feel quite inadequate in his own white coat. He had been about to take it off before getting into the car, but Pak had told him he was fine as he was. His ID was still hanging around his neck, too. The commander was a little taller than him. His tone was conversational, and he was smiling, his hand still on Kuroda's shoulder. Kuroda vaguely recalled seeing footage of Kim Il Sung at an award ceremony—or maybe it was Kim Jong Il—putting his hand on a child's shoulder and smiling benignly, in much the same way.

"You know, Dr. Kuroda, business in China has really been disrupted by your government's blockade. Korea has been affected too, but it's worse for China, and they want to resume trade as soon as possible. When the fleet arrives, we intend to hold talks with Fukuoka City about opening the port and airport. We believe that once our main force is here, China will reopen its consulate." Standing there nodding his fat head, with the commander's hand on his shoulder, Kuroda felt ashamed of himself. If the fleet was allowed to dock, and if trade with China was independently reopened and UN inspectors gave their stamp of approval, no matter what the government said and whether or not independence was declared, Kyushu might be irrevocably cut off from the rest of Japan.

Pak pushed the glass door open and gave a shout. Inside a small janitor's office beside the parking-lot elevator hall sat a woman medic, going over some documents. The lot itself contained a couple of abandoned buses and three or four cars that had probably belonged to tourists or fans attending the season opener. When Pak barked at her, the medic bounced up from her chair and hurried over, apologizing. She was wearing a white mask, and she handed all four of them masks of their own, as well as latex gloves and plastic shoe covers. Over her uniform she was wearing a white smock that was more like an apron, and though her face was barely visible beneath her cap and mask, her eyes and forehead suggested she was still in her late twenties—and a doctor, Kuroda decided. Women doctors and pharmacists had a distinctive air, probably because, much more than their male counterparts, they had to sacrifice their youth to intense study. She must have been fairly high-ranking to have been put in charge of this isolation facility, yet she stood at attention when answering questions from Heo, while the men acted almost as if she weren't there, not even introducing her to Kuroda.

Having put on the protective gear, they entered the parking lot. It was in semi-darkness, illuminated by just one strip of fluorescent lighting. Kuroda felt calmer in the knowledge that the medical examinations were about to begin and he would be able to concentrate on the patients. One of the buses had been turned into a sick bay. Its doors were sealed with plastic sheets and masking tape, and a stepladder stood alongside it. With Pak holding the ladder steady for him, Kuroda was invited to have a look through the window. Some of the seating had been removed and a row of cots set up in its place. The patients lay curled up in blankets, their arms and legs held in tightly, their breathing shallow. Kuroda couldn't tell their age through the glass. There was little in the way of medical equipment—not even any IV drips or catheters. What did they do to relieve themselves? There was a toilet in the corner of the parking lot, but were they made to walk that far? When he asked, the woman doctor answered directly in halting Japanese, "Me... I do it." Apparently they were using disposable diapers. The soiled items and any soiled clothing and sheets were placed in plastic bags and taken outside, where they were burned. For the moment it seemed they were focusing on isolation and hadn't yet given any positive consideration to treatment.

They opened the door of the bus and passed one by one under the thick plastic curtain. Pak remained outside. It was hot in there, the air heavy with fever. There was no ventilation, but he was told that now and then they turned on the engine to run the air conditioning. Six cots had been lined up in the small space at the center of the bus, and the seats that had been removed were piled up at the back. "We now have three here, but it will be more if... contagious," said the woman medic. The patient in the bed nearest them, a soldier with a shaven head in his mid to late twenties, was lying on his side. He wore a hotel bathrobe over his T-shirt and diapers, and his right arm had been covered in gauze and bandaged. Beside his cot was a long, narrow table spread with hotel bath towels on which had been laid out a kidney tray and stethoscope, tweezers and gauze, nursing diapers, a plastic washbowl, tissue paper, bandages, oilpaper, wooden spatulas, a flashlight, and some bottled water. There was also a thermometer and an ultrasonic sterilizer. The latter had been donated by a local home appliances company but was sitting there unused, for want of an electricity supply.

The medical supplies included Isodine antiseptic, alcohol disinfectant, a gray ointment labeled in Hangul, some antibiotic capsules—probably ampicillin—and a white powder in a bottle. The woman doctor told him the latter was hydrochloric acid ephedrine, a medicine mostly used in cases of bronchial asthma and administered to prevent airborne infection caused by coughing. Kuroda commented that it was dangerous to give it to patients with a fever because of its strong side effects, but Heo shouted through his mask, and the woman doctor translated: "Yes, we know that. It is only for emergency." Kuroda asked her to take the patient's temperature, while he himself checked his breathing: sixteen breaths in thirty seconds, and shallow. However, there was no discoloration of the hands and feet, and no typical indicators of a respiratory disease. The man's temperature was 39.4 degrees. When he asked whether the fever was constant or varied periodically, the woman took out her notes and answered that it had been high since the onset of the illness. On being questioned, Heo told him that the patient was bandaged due to an ulcerative rash. The man in the next cot down was bandaged from the ankles to the knees, and the one beyond him had gauze on his neck and chest, and both arms were bandaged.

Kuroda had the woman remove the bandages from the first patient's arm. The combination of a high fever and a rash made diagnosis difficult, the range of possibilities being almost unlimited, from the trivial to the life-threatening, but he had to consider the possibility of a viral or bacterial infection. The patient's arm was red and swollen from the wrist to the shoulder. Kuroda first shone the flashlight at it, but found the red spots easier to see in just the fluorescent light. The skin on the fingertips was swollen in a maculopapular rash, with blisters on the back of the elbows, and ulceration around the wrists and the back of the upper arm. He asked if the patient was in pain, and was told that the joints and muscles all over his body hurt. The conjunctiva was bloodshot and the lymph nodes on his neck were swollen. There was a red rash on the tongue. Kuroda pulled down the patient's pants and diaper to check his penis; the lack of discharge precluded a sexually transmitted disease. He asked whether there was any nausea or vomiting, taking a moment to explain the word "nausea" to Han, but the patient replied that no, he didn't feel sick.

With the patient still lying on his back, Kuroda palpated the space between the lungs and the liver, but didn't find anything out of the ordinary. When Heo and the woman doctor tried to raise him to a sitting position, he moaned in pain. Kuroda picked up the stethoscope. It was an ancient contraption of the sort not found even in the remotest parts of Japan these days, with spots of rust on the aluminum chest piece and rubber tubing that had stiffened and cracked. The man's pulse was rapid, and there was a slight murmur in the lower left atrium, although it was impossible to say just by listening to it whether this might indicate a faulty valve or a coronary aneurism. The commander asked whether it was a contagious disease, and Kuroda told him that it was very possible. Beads of perspiration showed on Han's forehead. Kuroda too was sweating, and the woman doctor dabbed at his forehead with a tissue as he worked. A small insect alighted on the window, an odd little thing, of a sort Kuroda had never seen before. Heo squashed it with the tip of a gloved finger. Once the examination was over, the patient lying on the cot asked the woman if Kuroda was a doctor, then raised his head and thanked him. He was so weakened that he must have found it comforting just to have someone check him over. Kuroda wanted to reassure him, but he didn't have any satisfactory medicines to offer, the man's nutrition was insufficient, and the environment was awful. Worse still, he couldn't identify the illness. All he could do was tell the patient to rest. The man nodded and did his best to smile.

The second patient was also in his late twenties, and had a birthmark covering his eye and forehead that was at first hard to distinguish from the rash. His symptoms appeared to be worse than the first man's. He was vomiting and had diarrhea, and was very emaciated. It seemed to be excruciating for him even to speak. Having complained of feeling cold he had been wrapped, shivering, in several layers of blankets, but Kuroda said they should remove some of them. Too many would make the fever worse and accelerate the wasting. His temperature was 39.5, and his breathing rate seventeen breaths per thirty seconds. The sheets were stained with yellow vomit, his diapers with blackish diarrhea. Asked if his legs itched, he tried to answer but almost passed out with the effort. Kuroda thought this was more likely to be from exhaustion than anything else, but just in case he checked the optic nerve. He didn't have a penlight so he used the flashlight to check the response of the pupil, and then checked the range of vision—hardly satisfactory, but enough to conclude that there was no nerve damage. The rash hadn't blistered, but there was some swelling.

The commander wiped his forehead, grimacing beneath his mask. Few people could remain undisturbed by the sight of an ulcerative rash like this, not to mention the stench of diarrhea, which with the lack of ventilation was enough to make anyone gag. He offered to switch on the engine so they could have some air conditioning, but Kuroda said the noise and vibration would interfere with his work. He noted bruising on the parts of the legs that weren't covered in the rash. As with the first patient, the conjunctiva was bloodshot, the lips cracked, and there was inflammation of the oral mucous membrane and a strawberry rash on the tongue. The lymph nodes in the neck were also swollen. Given his extreme emaciation and weakness, Kuroda decided against sitting him up for examination with the stethoscope.

"I wonder if it could be hemorrhagic fever," Kuroda said to Heo as they left the bus and put on some new gloves. With Pak translating, he replied, "I've heard this is a danger in South Korea, but is it here too?" Kuroda said that if he meant HFRS—hemorrhagic fever with renal syndrome—there hadn't been any cases of it in Japan. Contagion was through a hantavirus, carried by the wild striped field mouse, and there had been cases in South Korea and eastern China, though as far as he knew there had been no new outbreak in South Korea for twenty years. It had a two-week incubation period, which meant that if these patients had it, they must have contracted it before arriving.

Kuroda asked when their symptoms had first appeared. "About half a day ago," the commander replied. Checking the log, Heo added, "The first patient started complaining of the symptoms eleven hours ago, the second one ten hours ago, and the third eight hours ago." They had apparently isolated the patients and moved the command center this morning. When Kuroda asked whether hemorrhagic fever was known in North Korea, he was told rather hesitantly that they'd never heard of it there. Nevertheless, he thought, the place directly bordered China and probably did have the same species of field mouse, so the existence of the disease couldn't be ruled out. "Are you sure?" he asked again. The three quietly discussed this among themselves, before the commander said, with some difficulty, that medical intelligence in the Republic was not as well organized as it should be. "But if it's an infectious disease," he added, "would there not be more cases?"

"Humans are the end host for the hantavirus," Kuroda explained. "In other words, HFRS doesn't spread from person to person." He then asked Han if they inoculated against measles in North Korea. "Of course," the woman doctor answered for him. High fever, rash, bloodshot eyes, muscle pain, and so on were typical symptoms of measles, but it was a childhood disease and rarely seen in Japan since vaccination became widespread. However, in the US and elsewhere many cases had been reported among adults who had not received the booster shot, so perhaps it was the same in North Korea? When he put the question to them, the four looked at each other. "The vaccine is given between the ages of four and six. Those three would have been due to get it in the early Nineties, but it's possible they didn't," Han admitted. "At that time, there was a widespread shortage of food and other commodities. Do you think that's what it is?" Kuroda said he really couldn't say at this stage. "I'll have to take a blood sample and send it to the pathology lab for testing."

From the symptoms he thought it more likely to be something like Kawasaki disease or the bubonic plague, which featured edemas and swelling of the lymph nodes in the armpits. With measles, there was mostly swelling of the lymph nodes in the neck, and the rash spread from the head down to the lower body, whereas in these three patients there was no rash on the head. Kawasaki disease was a childhood disease, but its cause was as yet unknown. It was similar to scarlet fever, and a number of cocci had been suspected but ruled out after antibiotics proved ineffective, after which research had turned to *Yersinia pestis* and viral infections. Kuroda thought he should consult Seragi, who was familiar with cases of connective-tissue disorder, and had also written a paper on Kawasaki disease. He took out his cellphone, but it was out of range—not surprisingly, since they were underground. "Do you want to make a phone call?" asked Han. "I thought I'd talk to a colleague about it." Han frowned. "I must ask you not to do that," he said, putting his hand on Kuroda's shoulder again. "We don't want word of this getting out."

By taking the patients to the Medical Center they could determine right away whether it was measles, but it didn't look as if this was an option. "What treatment are you giving them?" Kuroda asked. "Antipyretics and antibiotics," the woman doctor replied, adding that the antibiotics were ampicillin tablets and chloramphenicol ointment. But antibiotics only stopped bacteria from propagating and weren't effective for viruses. The men should be hospitalized. "I'm afraid that in the circumstances we cannot do that," said Han, looking uncomfortable. "We shall treat them here. In any case, let's talk about that later."

Kuroda stopped himself from pointing out that this was no place to be treating any patients. Part of him thought it was their problem and he shouldn't get involved any more than he had to. But yesterday they'd brought in a soldier who'd been stabbed in the stomach, so why weren't they doing the same for these three? The doctor in him wanted to help them, but the fear he'd felt in the car on the way over was stronger than his sense of moral responsibility. Just think where you are, he told himself. Medical ethics is not an issue here in this parking lot. You're not just a doctor, you're a fifty-year-old resident of an occupied territory with a wife and two kids and an ailing mother dependent on you.

The parking lot was deathly quiet, without even the background hum of air conditioning. The conversation had come to an abrupt halt, and in the silence he could just make out a faint rustling sound by his feet. Looking down, he saw several small bugs wriggling around on Heo's shoe cover, scratching at the plastic. They looked like fruit flies. Heo yelped, shook the bugs off, and squashed them underfoot. Kuroda looked at his own feet and saw the same things crawling over them. He bent down to get a better look, but the woman stopped him and used the pencil in her hand to brush them off. As she did so, they hopped and scuttled away. They were the same insect he'd seen on the window inside the bus a short while ago. At first he thought they might be tiny flies, but these things didn't fly, they jumped. It was creepy. They were very like the drosophilidae he remembered from science textbooks, but much smaller.

Looking carefully at the concrete floor, he could see lots of them crawling and hopping all over the place. They had managed to survive the disinfectant. Maybe they were exceptionally strong breeders, or the temperature down here suited them. Heo began to scold the woman, apparently for not having managed to get rid of them. Han stopped him, then discussed something in Korean with the others for a few moments before turning to Kuroda and saying bleakly, "To tell the truth, we were suddenly infested with the things late last night."

At a distance of about twenty meters from the quarantine bus stood a cream-colored microbus with HIIRAGI TOURS painted in green on the side. This was where a collection of the bugs was being kept. The windows had been sealed with tape, and the passenger door at the back was welded shut. The central door was covered with a primitive shutter consisting of the blue plastic sheeting commonly used

477

on construction sites, which was tacked onto a wooden frame and weighted down with blocks. The three officers appeared reluctant to enter the bus, and told the medic to fetch a sample of the bugs in a container. Kuroda asked if they were dangerous. "We don't know," he was told, "but better not go near them, just in case."

They made no move to help as the woman shifted one of the heavy blocks holding the plastic sheeting down and ducked inside. She said something in a loud voice, and Heo and Pak immediately put one foot each on the trailing plastic to keep it closed. A few moments later she emerged carefully holding several bottles of different sizes tight to her chest. She slowly descended and gently placed these on the ground. As she repeated this process, a number of the bugs managed to escape. Pak quickly crushed them underfoot, but a couple got away and made for the far wall of the parking lot.

Watching the woman doctor, Kuroda asked what her name was, and was curtly informed that she was a warrant officer called Ri Gyu Yeong. The men kept glancing at their feet to check their shoe covers. Kuroda wondered why they had such an aversion to the insects, but when he took a closer look at the bottles, it became obvious enough. There were six bottles in all, each containing bugs of different species and sizes. After getting the go-ahead, he picked up the first container, about the size of a milk bottle—then almost dropped it again. The top was sealed with thin plastic and wire, and the bottom half was thick with the carcasses of dead insects that resembled crickets but, like the flies, were noticeably smaller, milky-white in color, and scarcely bigger than grains of rice, some with a semi-transparent shell and others with transparent innards. "Are they crickets?" asked Kuroda. "Probably," the commander said gloomily, "although we've never seen this type before." In another milk bottle were some of the tiny flies. It was so crammed with dead ones that it was hard to make out their shape, but they were clearly flies. Kuroda wondered if there were any live samples inside, and was told that there were, though it had been extremely difficult to catch them. Holding the bottle up to the light, he could see that they did indeed have wings. So why did they jump instead

478

of fly? "Some of them can fly," said Ri Gyu Yeong, coming back out from under the plastic sheeting. She picked up another bottle and put it on the roof of a Honda van parked under the fluorescent light fixture.

They all gathered around the van and peered into the bottle. "Are any infectious diseases carried by flies?" asked Han. "Sand flies are carriers," said Kuroda. "There are two types present in Japan but in such small numbers that they've never been a problem. However, they're known worldwide as an intermediate host of a parasitic worm called leishmania, and as a carrier or intermediate host of several viruses." The others drew closer, listening intently to his explanation. "Diseases caused by leishmania are broadly classified into those affecting the internal organs, skin, mucous membrane, and so on. One is a dermatological disease known as oriental sore, which produces swellings on the skin that become ulcerated and in rare cases form leprous growths. After an incubation period of two to four days, there is a sudden high fever, as well as mucosal congestion, and pain in the eyes, head, back, and limbs. Occasionally there can be gastrointestinal damage and reduced white-blood-cell count."

"Do sand flies bite?" asked Ri, pencil and notepad at the ready, at the same moment as the commander pointed at the bottle and asked, "Are those sand flies?" Kuroda said, "No, they don't suck blood. The virus is carried in their excrement and carcass, which then attaches to fine particles in the air that you breathe in or that stick to wounds, causing infection. But are these sand flies? I don't know." Heo had been intently following Pak's quick translation of his explanation, but complained loudly about the last bit, his voice echoing around the parking lot. The commander raised a hand to calm him down. "I've never seen a sand fly," Kuroda said. "These are too small to be sure, but they look like some type of fruit fly to me. However, I'm not an expert. Common fruit flies don't jump, they fly. The reason I said I don't know is that you can't be vague about details when you're dealing with an infectious disease. There's still a lot that we don't know about viruses. So to identify these things, I need to take a sample and ask the lab to investigate."

"There are other insects too," said Pak, pointing at a bottle about the size of a mayonnaise jar with two centipedes inside. "They're alive," said Ri, and Kuroda automatically stepped back. "They were caught just this morning," added the commander, poking the bottle with his finger. The centipedes were a vivid red with legs of almost a primary yellow, and they measured about four centimeters—not long, but their bodies were thicker than regular centipedes and their numerous legs were long and jointed, and scrabbled angrily against the glass bottom. "This insect attacks," said Pak. "And it really hurts if you're bitten." Ri told him that over twenty people had complained of intense pain after a bite, and the three in the bus were among them. Poison from a bite could indeed explain the rash, he thought. The others seemed to think so too. "But if there is any risk at all of an infectious disease, we have to be ready to respond accordingly," Heo told him. And he was right, of course.

But where on earth had this outbreak of rare insects originated? Had they come hidden in clothes from the cold North Korean climate and proliferated on arrival in warm Fukuoka? All four were agreed that no such centipede existed in the Republic. None of the several dozen officers at HQ, all from different parts of the country, had ever seen anything of the sort; nor, for that matter, had any of the City Hall staff. One of the centipedes twisted and struck the bottom of the bottle with its tail, then rubbed its head frantically against the glass. It was a predatory sort of movement. "It's feeding," said Ri. "There are some small insects in there." The fluorescent light reflecting off the glass made it hard to see properly, so she took her notebook and held the black cover up behind the bottle. Kuroda saw there were lots of tiny white things stuck to the glass that at first glance looked like specks of fluff. They were springtails, a pretty common insect in Japan, often found underneath stones in damp gardens. He asked her whether she was feeding them to the centipedes, but she shook her head. She spoke in Korean, with Pak interpreting: "When we found the centipedes, they were covered with these bugs."

Ri Gyu Yeong's voice was pleasant, even through the mask. It was slightly hoarse, but nice to listen to. Her eyes were long and slanted, and beneath her cap her short hair was a glossy black. Kuroda was so used to women with gray or dyed-brown hair that the natural black looked almost exotic. Through the interpreter, Heo now asked whether centipedes were pathogen carriers. Kuroda said he'd never heard that. Arthropods that caused infection were mainly mosquitoes, mites, fleas, and lice. Then again, he really didn't know much about centipedes at all, and had no idea how many species existed in Japan, let alone in the world. In fact, he didn't even know the difference between a centipede and a millipede. The only thing that came to mind was a news item he remembered about a large outbreak of millipedes somewhere in Japan that had caused the wheels of a train to slip when they crawled across the tracks. But he did know that centipedes had a histamine venom, like wasps. And of course there were viruses and bacteria in their bodies, and you couldn't rule out the possibility that a virus in the springtails the centipedes were eating might also undergo genetic changes and cross over.

Pak pointed at two other milk bottles. One was about a third full of dead springtails that looked just like instant-soup granules. In the second bottle, swarms of live ones clung to the glass or hopped about. "Late last night there were hundreds of thousands of these insects jumping around on the third and fourth floors. The crickets and flies seemed to be first. It wasn't as if they all turned up at once, just that by the time we noticed them they were already crawling all over the carpets and desks. We first saw them on the steps to the fourth-floor lobby in the middle of the night, but by morning their numbers had exploded."

In the last bottle was one insect of a type that Kuroda had definitely not seen before. It was about three or four centimeters long, with an orange head not unlike an ant's, and a body that was semi-transparent and divided into numerous segments. It had four pairs of legs that were transparent near the body but at the tips the same orange as its head. The legs were jointed and covered in fine downy hair. It reminded Kuroda of something out of the movie *Alien*. "What the hell?" he muttered. "Shall we go upstairs?" the commander said.

*

"There it is." The commander pointed at the enormous glass and steel-frame structure adjoining the lobby entrance on the fourth floor. The three officers led Kuroda, sheltered by the umbrella Pak held over him, along the open-air promenade. The rain slanted in off the sea, drenching the tails of his white coat as they walked past an area of white stone benches and trees to reach a huge cafe-restaurant. Seen from outside, it looked more like a sports hall or art museum, with its latticework of steel beams constructed in the spiral form of a conch shell. They stood gazing through the raindrops streaming down its glass walls at the tropical decor inside.

The restaurant was called Cafe Luggnagg, after the enchanted isle in *Gulliver's Travels*, and its ceiling must have been over forty meters high. There were about a hundred tables, a stage for performances, and on the south side a treehouse, accessible by elevator, which was used for wedding ceremonies. The entire space was enclosed in an artificial rainforest, with luxuriant palms, banana and rubber trees, aviaries housing parrots and other birds, and a waterfall. Kuroda had often been there with colleagues for cocktails, or to have some South Sea food with his family.

According to the commander, the air conditioning at Cafe Luggnagg had been turned off ever since the occupation, as nobody was using the space. With its airtight glass walls, it could get pretty hot in there, depending on the weather. The occupation had lasted almost a week now. Kuroda was asked whether the insects he'd just seen could have bred and multiplied in this huge hothouse. Although he wasn't a biologist or entomologist, he thought it possible. Even in homes left empty for some time you'd find insects hitherto unseen there on your return.

When the cafe had been open for business, someone must have been responsible for periodically watering the plants, spraying insecticide, pruning branches, and sweeping up fallen leaves. With neglect, along with the rise in temperature, weeds would have grown, bacteria would have propagated in stagnant water, and fallen leaves would have rotted. The caged birds had evidently been unattended, and were probably dying of starvation. It was conceivable that the carcasses of some had already started to decompose. Any closed artificial ecosystem would soon break down if it wasn't maintained.

"Has anyone been inside to check conditions there since the outbreak of insects?" he asked, but the commander shook his head as if this was out of the question. He added that the insects had got into the air ducts in the hotel, so the top floors had been made out of bounds; all the exits on the fourth-floor reception and third-floor banquet halls had been sealed off; and the Japanese hotel staff and tourists being held hostage had been moved to some of the lower-level banquet rooms. Kuroda could see that these people had no intention of disinfecting the cafe. Once the fleet arrived, they'd abandon the hotel and move to the temporary accommodation now under construction. If the hothouse insects proved to be the cause of the men's illness, they'd probably just torch the place without any more ado.

He'd never be able to like these people, he realized. They were polite and surprisingly well mannered, but that was just the other side of their insular nature. The elite that pledged loyalty to the group was taken good care of, but anyone who protested, or who had different values, or who was weak or handicapped, was simply stamped out, like an insect.

Kuroda and the officers, together with Ri Gyu Yeong, returned to the first-floor lobby for a final discussion. This was largely just a matter of summarizing the situation and making sure they understood each other. Kuroda decided simply to answer the questions put to him, and refrain from giving his opinion or advice. He confirmed four main points: he didn't know whether it was an infectious disease, but it was a possibility; he didn't know whether the insects were the source of infection, but it was a possibility; if it was about ten hours since the three men had fallen ill and nobody else had complained of symptoms, the disease had probably been contained; but in any case, it would be best to keep the contaminated area sealed off and continue to isolate the patients.

Tea and sesame cookies were served again, but Kuroda didn't have the energy to eat anything. Ri had removed her cap and mask to reveal rosy cheeks, and was helping herself to the cookies, looking pleased to be included in the discussion. Once they had gone over the main points, Han thanked Kuroda for his help that day and dismissed Ri and Pak. He then changed the subject. "Normally I'd ask you to treat those three men in your hospital," he started. "That would be the natural human response. However, reinforcements are due to reach Japanese territorial waters two days from now. Until then we have to avoid anything, however minor, that could be used against us by your government. As the commanding officer, I cannot entrust three sick soldiers to a Japanese hospital. We shall be collecting Corporal Son, who was admitted yesterday, before the fleet arrives.

"You must understand that the Republic was decimated by cholera in the Liberation War and the turbulent period that followed it. Later on, there were frequent major outbreaks of dysentery after flooding. We lacked sufficient medicines, so there were many deaths, especially of children and the elderly. Everybody in the Republic, without exception, has a deep dread of infectious diseases. Were those three men to be admitted to your hospital and diagnosed with such a disease, our soldiers' morale would plummet. I have to maintain morale as best I can until the main force arrives. And there is an even more important issue, which has to do with the leadership of the main force. Let us just say that they would not be pleased to find our soldiers receiving treatment in a Japanese hospital. I am in a very difficult position."

Who did he think he was kidding? This guy would say anything to get the effect he wanted. The fact of the matter was that he was capable of abandoning his own people, when they were sick with a life-threatening fever. And yet his account of the outbreaks of cholera and dysentery touched a chord. Kuroda had been in elementary school when one summer heavy rain in his hometown in northern Kyushu had flooded the sewers in the underground shopping mall, and due to administrative bungling there had been an outbreak of dysentery. Four of his classmates had died, including one who was a close friend. It was as they placed flowers on the boy's desk that Kuroda decided to become a doctor when he grew up. Children were the ones most vulnerable to infectious diseases. Sanitary conditions in North Korea must be pretty bad. He recalled TV images of malnourished children. Han must have seen an awful lot of kids die. And when he said that they all lived in fear of a possible epidemic, Kuroda had in spite of himself commiserated with him: "I can understand that."

Still, he wondered why the man was telling him all this. Heo was seated beside him, but he didn't understand Japanese, and Pak was some distance away, smoking, so it felt as though Han was secretly confiding in him. It made him feel trusted, and that feeling seeped comfortingly into the crack that had opened up in his psyche. His nerves were frayed from the anxiety he'd felt ever since leaving the Medical Center. "Dr. Kuroda, can you understand my position?" asked Han. "Of course," he said, nodding repeatedly as the two shook hands.

"Good. Well then, I'll see you to the car." The commander rose to his feet and called over to Pak. "Why don't you take some cookies, to share with your friends and family?" he suggested with a smile, and Kuroda gratefully accepted. He thought his colleagues might enjoy trying something unusual like this, and had a vision of himself producing the cookies and holding forth about what he'd seen in the hotel, adding that he couldn't reveal certain details. "I'm afraid we don't have anything better to put them in," the commander said, filling a paper bag provided by a woman soldier. "Be careful with them, they crumble easily," he added as he handed them over. "Thank you very much," said Kuroda, and bowed his head deeply.

The car was apparently parked by the B1 exit. The commander accompanied Kuroda onto the escalator, with Pak leading the way and Heo Jip following behind. "Do you know how those cookies are made?" Han asked, putting his hand on Kuroda's shoulder again. "They're called *keganjon*, which means literally 'sesame sweets.'" Kuroda tried saying the name out loud. He was told that the *ke* was pronounced with a sharp exhalation of breath. Pak demonstrated: "*Ke, ke*—it's like coughing up phlegm." The commander laughed and said, "But that sounds disgusting!" Kuroda laughed too. "How about teaching your wife to make them for your children's birthdays? All you need is some fresh white and black sesame, and some brown sugar melted in honey."

Down in the B1 parking lot, Kuroda began heading for the exit, but Pak and Heo moved in on either side of him and, hands on his shoulder blades, steered him toward a staircase in the corner. Why weren't they going outside? They passed by the glass door of the janitor's office, where Ri Gyu Yeong was already back at work. Catching sight of them, she stuck her masked face out and bowed. The commander, meanwhile, was continuing with his recipe. "You have to keep the white and black sesame seeds separate. That's important. You lightly fry them just long enough for them to swell up, like a flea after sucking blood."

Pak opened the door to the staircase, making the rusty hinges screech unnervingly. The walls glowed dully under a dim fluorescent lamp. The smell of disinfectant, along with another smell he couldn't identify, hung in the air. Kuroda's smile had frozen with uncertainty, his face muscles twitching, and his throat was dry. Yet he still hadn't quite grasped what was happening—or perhaps was refusing to take it in. This staircase connected to the B2 parking lot. And that was where the people arrested were being held. Had they always planned on bringing him here instead of back to the Medical Center? His mind went blank. The stairs were dotted here and there with dark stains. He knew immediately what it was, but he couldn't connect it with the word "blood." It was as though his brain had seized up.

"Put the black and white sesame, after frying, into separate bowls and add the melted sugar and honey. You call this 'syrup,' right? You've got to make sure that the sesame and syrup are both warm." From the bottom of the stairs came sounds like stone being crushed with a metal bar and of boards being ripped up. On the staircase landing, he caught sight of a single shoe—brown leather, a man's— lying upside down. There was gum or something stuck to the sole, with a white mold sprouting out of it. He really was being taken to the detention center. A bitter taste rose from his bowels, and he felt his lips trembling. What had happened to the owner of that brown shoe? Had he gone berserk? Had they then proceeded to beat him?

"Once you've properly mixed the still-warm sesame with warm syrup, you spread the mixtures out flat. If you like, you can use one of those small rolling pins, like pins used for making the skins of dumplings." As they descended the stairs, the smell of excrement grew stronger. Fear welled up in Kuroda, to the point where he could almost feel it oozing out. He looked up at the ceiling and turned around to protest, when Pak suddenly gripped his shoulder and twisted his arm up behind his back. It hurt, and he found himself immobilized. Pak was murmuring in his ear: "Dr. Kuroda, we are going to give you a tour of the detention center. Don't worry, we aren't arresting you, just giving you a tour."

Held firmly on either side, he was virtually carried into the parking lot. The floor was wet, with puddles here and there, judging from the sloshing of their footsteps. Kuroda could see a hundred or so detainees, people who'd been arrested for alleged serious crimes, lined up like a row of Buddhist statues at a temple, seated at regular intervals, cross-legged or kneeling, atop what looked like wooden pallets laid out on the floor. A soldier emerged from a large bus and, noticing the commander, stood at attention, saluting. Kuroda felt his field of vision warping. The scene before him was utterly unreal. Further inside, some prisoners lay wrapped in blankets, presumably very sick. The hem of one man's cotton hotel gown was raised to reveal a leg swollen to twice its normal size; another had purple bruising behind his knees. The whole place reeked of excrement. Soldiers wearing face masks were in the process of dismantling the place, ripping up the pallets and corrugated iron and stacking them on the floor. Some were even breaking up the cement on the pillars with pickaxes. That must be what he'd heard from the stairwell earlier. When the soldiers caught sight of Han, they all immediately stopped working and stood in rigid salute. Han waved a hand to indicate they should carry on.

The smell was like a cross between the smell of the homeless and that of the dying. Whether cross-legged or kneeling, they all sat with their hands on their knees and their backs hunched, like prawns, their heads drooping. Their hands were dark with grime, but he could see that the skin on some of them was split open, showing a thin white stringy stuff inside. Broken bones, perhaps. Some of them seemed to be suffering from cyanosis, with their fingers strangely twisted. And all the while, walking alongside Kuroda, Han continued his cooking instructions. "You spread out the mixture thin as paper on a flat board. You have to take care it doesn't stick to the rolling pin as the syrup cools." Ordinary houseflies were buzzing around one prisoner lying in a gown stained black around his buttocks. "Tell your wife it's a good idea to coat it with a little bit of sesame oil. That will stop the mixture from sticking to it. You want to end up with a paper-thin square."

Incongruously, the image of Ri's mouth as she was eating those cookies floated into his mind. Her lips had been chapped and were bare of lipstick or salve, and she used the pointed tip of her tongue to lick away some crumbs stuck to them. They passed a prisoner whose hair was matted with blood and whose scalp was covered with pale, festering wounds that unfortunately recalled the tuna flakes he'd had at lunch. He was on the verge of vomiting. A glimpse of a pair of wrinkled breasts and dark nipples through the open front of a prisoner's gown made him cover his mouth with his hand to hold it back. He heard someone crying, but couldn't tell who it was.

"Next you place the sheets of black and white sesame on top of each other. Then you roll them up—just as if you were making sushi rolls. You could even use one of those little bamboo mats if you like. Finally you take a sharp knife and cut slices to the desired width. What do you think? Easy, isn't it?" The commander spread out his hands and beamed as he brought his explanation to an end.

Just in front of them someone moaned in pain and toppled forward, hands on the floor to support his body. The long shadow of a soldier moving toward him made the man shake his head and whimper like a child. The soldier grabbed his hair and pulled him upright. Still held by his hair, he began desperately apologizing, yelling almost incoherently that he was sorry, as the soldier's nightstick came down at the joint of his shoulder.

"Hey, Kuroda, you all right? Looks like they're up to something down there." It was his colleague Tsuchiya outside his door. They'd been at college together, and Tsuchiya was now the deputy head of hematology. Kuroda had been dozing in his chair, sleeping off a double dose of tranquilizers. His head felt heavy and his body sluggish, and the strength had gone from his hands, leaving an unpleasant numbness in his fingertips. He got up and opened the door. "Ah, the color's coming back to your face," Tsuchiya said, stepping inside and taking his left wrist to check the pulse. Kuroda could have done this himself, but it felt reassuring to have another white-coated doctor do it. "It's still over a hundred!" Tsuchiya took a blood-pressure cuff off the shelf and applied it to his arm. The reading came out at 172 over 110—both figures almost forty higher than normal. He'd been dozing for over an hour, but he was still in a state of extreme tension.

Kuroda hadn't spoken to anyone about his experience at the Sea Hawk Hotel. The three patients with a suspected infectious disease, the insects, the prisoners—these were things he mustn't talk about, and that little tour of the detention facility was effectively a warning of what lay in store for him if he did. As soon as it was over, he'd run to a toilet and thrown up. One of the stalls was covered in blood, and a prisoner with hollow eyes was cleaning it up and watching him vacantly. Afterwards, when he staggered into the hospital, his white coat stained with vomit, Takahashi was there to meet him. Kuroda was still in the company of Pak and Heo, however, and had lied to his department head, saying that the hotel's ventilation wasn't working well and he'd started to feel queasy while examining a soldier with acute pneumonia. Pak and Heo had left after thanking them politely, and Kuroda had gone to his consultation room to rest.

"How's the nausea?" asked Tsuchiya. Kuroda tried to say it was better, but there was something stuck in his throat. He screwed up his face and pressed his hand to his neck, and a look of concern crossed Tsuchiya's face. Then he coughed, and a bit of vomit flew out. "I'll be okay now," he said, wiping his mouth with his handkerchief. Tsuchiya jerked his chin in the direction of the camp. "It looks like something's going on. Everyone's talking about it. The soldiers have all gathered in formation." It's the public execution, thought Kuroda. What with the shock of the detention center, he'd clean forgotten about the two wooden posts in the camp. "I'll be along in a moment," he said. He washed his hands and gargled at the sink, then put on a fresh white coat. His mouth still tasted sour.

Some of the medical staff had gathered on a glass-enclosed balcony at the far end of the outpatients waiting hall. It was north-facing, but on fine days it got quite a bit of sun, and it had an unobstructed view of the hotel and Dome. "Kuroda, are you all right?" Takahashi was standing in the middle of the balcony. "I had a nap," he said, making his way over to him and looking down at the encampment. In the rain, soldiers were still filing into the open space before a large tent. A helicopter marked NHK FUKUOKA was hovering just to the left of the hotel. Several soldiers were checking that the posts hadn't become loose in the rain, stamping down the earth around them, with two officers watching to make sure the things were straight and the sandbags in place.

The patients shouldn't be seeing this, thought Kuroda. The fifth to tenth floors were occupied by inpatients, and those in north-facing wards would effectively have a grandstand view of it all. Kuroda tugged at the arm of Takahashi's white coat and steered him away from the balcony. "They're about to conduct an execution by firing squad," he told him in a low voice. Takahashi gaped at him, brow creased in utter incomprehension. The media apparently hadn't reported this. "I think we should try to stop the patients upstairs from seeing it," Kuroda added, but Takahashi just blinked rapidly: "Did you just say, *execution*?" Kuroda's still felt sluggish from the tranquilizers, and the department head's slow reaction was irritating. "Two soldiers are about to be shot," he said, raising his voice.

But then he remembered that Takahashi hadn't had any direct contact with the KEF. It had taken Kuroda himself a few moments to grasp what he'd been told in the car earlier. These days you only ever heard the word "execution" in the movies or manga. And it was doubly hard to imagine it taking place before a great crowd standing in rows as if they were at morning assembly or an award ceremony. "Look," he said quietly. "There are two stakes set up in the clearing, with sandbags piled up behind them. They're about to shoot two of their own people." Takahashi went back to the balcony to check. In front of the serried ranks of soldiers were indeed two posts of slightly different heights, each within an arc of sandbags. Their purpose, once the image of people tied to them came into focus, was unmistakable. Takahashi's face turned pale. He was a good doctor, said to be the top man in Kyushu for treating tuberculosis with chemotherapy, but he seemed at a complete loss now.

Kuroda called Tsuchiya over and explained the circumstances to him. Tsuchiya listened wide-eyed and shocked, but when Kuroda said that they shouldn't let the patients watch it, he immediately saw what needed to be done, and rushed off, saying he'd get hold of the nursing manager. Next Kuroda took out his cellphone and called Koshida, the head of security. He could sense the jolt it gave him when he mentioned the word "execution." He explained, "I want you to take urgent measures to prevent the patients from seeing what goes on. Especially those on the North Wing, and the West Wing maternity and pediatrics wards—we definitely don't want any expecting mothers seeing it. There aren't any patients here, on the second-floor balcony, right now." Takahashi seemed to have finally grasped the situation and, still white-faced, was about to say something, but Kuroda held up a hand to stop him. "Even if we get all the guards together," Koshida was saying on the phone, "there aren't enough to cover the whole North Wing. Maybe we could announce it over the PA system."

But how would they word it? If they told people not to look, it would just arouse their curiosity. There were about twenty rooms on each of the six inpatient floors of the North Wing. Around eighty of them were for seriously ill people confined to bed and unable to get up without assistance, which left around forty other rooms. "Dr. Tsuchiya's already gone to the North Wing, so why don't you check up on maternity and pediatrics?" he told Koshida, and hung up. "Shall I call the other doctors?" asked Takahashi, but Kuroda thought it would be better to dispatch nurses to the wards. The sick were sensitive, and it might well alarm them to have doctors other than their regular consultants barging in. A call came from Tsuchiya's cellphone. "I've already talked to staff on the fifth floor, and I'm on my way to the sixth. Can you deal with the seventh?" Kuroda asked Takahashi to take the top two floors, nine and ten, and the pair of them headed for the elevator at a run.

The rain had eased up, and the pointed tip of the Sea Hawk Hotel was now shrouded in a low white cloud. A helicopter still circled overhead. The assembled troops stood waiting, their uniforms dripping wet. Seen from this distance, the two stakes looked the size of matchsticks. It was a bit like watching a game from the top row of the outfield bleachers in Fukuoka Dome. With Kuroda on the balcony were Tsuchiya and Takahashi, and another seven or eight doctors from dermatology, plastic surgery, and pediatric surgery. Several outpatient nurses and auxiliary nurses had also been there but had left after being told what was about to happen. Kuroda had no desire to see someone shot by a firing squad either. Yet even if he went back to the consulting room, short of packing his ears with cotton wool and pressing his hands over them, he would still hear the shots. And the sound alone would paint the picture in his imagination, and might be even harder to forget. "Are they really going to kill their own soldiers?" muttered Tsuchiya. Yes, and without even batting an eye, Kuroda thought but didn't say. Takahashi was taking deep breaths and swallowing repeatedly.

A group of officers, four women among them, came out of the hotel and exchanged salutes with those on parade. The officers then formed two rows on either side of the stakes, where they would have an unobstructed view of the proceedings. And then two men, their hands tied behind their backs, emerged from the large tent. Barefoot and stooped over, heads drooping, they were marched toward the stakes. They had been stripped of their uniforms and were in simple white T-shirts and gray pants. Each was flanked by two armed soldiers. "Sorry, I can't take this," Takahashi said, and left the balcony. Four of the dermatologists and pediatric surgeons joined him, shaking their heads. The condemned men reached the stakes. One pair of soldiers in gray uniforms untied their hands, then retied them behind the posts.

Kuroda glanced sideways at Tsuchiya and noticed that his eyes were brimming with tears. He remembered a movie in which a Jewish woman in a concentration camp was shot for just speaking up. She hadn't even been protesting. Just as the Nazis had done, the KEF violently stripped their detainees of everything they owned and then held them in submission by exploiting their natural instinct to survive. What would *he* do if any of his family were among those prisoners? That woman whose wrinkled breasts he'd glimpsed through the gap in her gown—what if she'd been his wife, or his mother? Surely he couldn't have kept quiet then? But what could he have done? Physical resistance would just have resulted in a vicious beating. He didn't know how to protest because he'd never before been in the position of being controlled by the threat of violence. But he had to keep thinking of a way, if he wanted to overcome the rage and impotence he felt.

The condemned men had been secured to the posts at the chest and waist, and were now being bound around the thighs. Eight soldiers with rifles lined up side by side facing them, several meters away. Kuroda had just decided he had to watch this execution through, however hard it was, when his cellphone suddenly rang. It was Koshida, from security. He'd just returned to the guardroom by the main entrance, he said, when Dr. Seragi rushed past him, heading for the clearing in the camp. Kuroda felt goosebumps rise on his arms. "Stop him!" he yelled, but Koshida yelled back: "I already tried!" Tsuchiya, who had heard this exchange, pointed outside. They could see a figure in a white coat passing through a gap in the hedge between the hospital grounds and the park. He must have rushed out the moment he'd heard about the execution. Dodging between see-saws and slides, he ran on, still wearing his hospital slippers.

Kuroda stood rooted to the spot in horror. Tsuchiya grabbed the cellphone out of his hand and shouted at Koshida: "Go stop him! We're on our way." Koshida started to say something back, but Tsuchiya cut the line and took Kuroda by the arm: "Let's go." But Kuroda couldn't move. His body simply wouldn't do what it was told. He didn't have the strength to face those people again. "Come on!" Tsuchiya tugged at his arm. You don't know what they're like, Kuroda thought. Tsuchiya gave him a last, baffled look, then ran for the elevator.

His white coat now splattered with mud, Seragi was nearing the killing ground. Koshida and another guard could be seen chasing after him, followed at some distance by Tsuchiya and several other doctors. Kuroda looked out over the park, the scene going in and out of focus with his own reflection in the rain-spattered glass. His mind was blank. He heard a voice inside him asking if it was okay to do nothing. His legs seemed to stir, but as soon as he tried to move it was as if a transparent barrier came down to block his way, and his nostrils filled with the stench of the detention center.

When Seragi reached the rear line of soldiers, he stopped running. He paused briefly, then started walking slowly through the narrow gap between the orderly rows of uniforms. His white coat stood out starkly against the khaki. The troops must have noticed him, though none of them moved a muscle. They were probably forbidden to break ranks, but they must have been startled at the sudden appearance of this old man all in white. Koshida and Tsuchiya, rather than squeezing between the rows, began to make their way around them. The two condemned men were now lashed securely to the posts. A gray-uniformed officer barked out an order, and the firing squad checked the breeches of their guns. When the line of eight marksmen raised their rifles, Seragi again broke into a run, cupping his hands around his mouth like a megaphone and shouting something. It was unclear what he was saying, but his voice was faintly audible even from where Kuroda stood.

One of the officers took a step forward and gave an order. Four soldiers moved to block Seragi, then surrounded him, hiding him from view. He tried to slip between them, only to be held back, with two of them taking an arm on either side and the other two grabbing his legs and lifting him off the ground. One of his slippers fell off. Tsuchiya, Koshida, and the others were stopped by several officers running toward them, weapons out, and raised their arms in surrender. Seragi was dragged over to them, passing in front of the four women officers. The old man yelled something at the top of his voice, but Kuroda couldn't tell if it was in Korean or Japanese.

The soldiers let go, and Seragi fell backwards, landing on his buttocks. An officer aimed his revolver at Seragi's head, but another—the one who appeared regularly on NHK Fukuoka—restrained him. The helicopter had come lower and was now hovering overhead, probably trying to film the figure of Seragi sitting there exhausted on the ground. Tsuchiya and the others helped him up and were brushing the dirt off his white coat when there was a short series of popping sounds, like a string of firecrackers going off. The shots echoed off the surrounding buildings, and even Kuroda standing on the balcony heard them quite clearly. The men tied to the posts jerked and slumped forward. The gray-uniformed officer moved quickly toward them and shot each man in the back of the head with his revolver. Kuroda watched as parts of their heads spattered around them. The officer stood rigidly at attention, then looked up at the sky and shouted something, whereupon all the troops saluted. And then, just like that, everyone dispersed. Tsuchiya and the others were making their way back, half carrying Seragi between them. At some point he stopped, wrenched himself out of their grip, and, removing his one remaining slipper, walked on, holding it in his hand. The two corpses were cut down, laid on wide wooden planks, and carried into the large tent. Kuroda left the balcony, telling himself he must try to wipe this scene from his mind.

# 9

# BON VOYAGE

*April 10, 2011*

S HINOHARA SAT CONCEALED in the undergrowth of the artificial jungle. The second hand of his watch ticked forward, and the date changed. It was midnight, the morning of the tenth, twenty-four hours since they'd slipped into the hotel. The only illumination was from the emergency-exit signs, and when he raised his head he could see dark Hakata Bay outside the glass walls. Tateno lay snoring softly nearby, amid a clump of tropical trees. He was wrapped in a green wedding dress he'd taken from a place in the adjoining shopping arcade that sold and rented formalwear. Shinohara looked up. The enclosure was shaped like a giant snail's shell, and the ceiling and all the walls were glass criss-crossed with a steel framework. Tateno awoke in his niche between the trees and looked around. He was wearing a black sweatshirt, black trousers, and black sneakers beneath his wedding-dress wrapping. "Why're you awake?" he whispered. "Not sleepy," said Shinohara, "but you go ahead." He showed him his watch. "Still an hour left?" Tateno muttered, and closed his eyes again.

Their strategy had been devised the night of Takei's burial at sea. Takeguchi's proposal for bringing down the Sea Hawk Hotel with special explosives had been so off-the-wall that at first no one took him seriously. "You've seen big demolitions on TV, where they make buildings implode, right?" he'd asked the group. "Well, how do you think they do it? They collapse the columns that hold the buildings up."

He displayed a kind of metal pipe with an odd profile, like an inverted M. "This is called a linear shaped charge, or LSC," he said. "You pack the interior with high explosives, and when they're detonated the pipe melts and bends, and the tip of this V narrows to a point and expels a jet of molten metal that travels at thousands of meters per second and can cut through anything in an instant. Attach these to the columns and set them off simultaneously, and you can bring down even the biggest, sturdiest building. But that's not all. By configuring the cuts properly you can actually make the building topple over, not just collapse in its own footprint. And you can decide which way you want it to fall."

The room had erupted in cheers, and even Shinohara had been impressed, though far from convinced. It was exciting to talk about bringing down a high-rise building, but it didn't seem realistic. The others too, after cheering, were now looking at Takeguchi with *No, but seriously* expressions. He smiled and said, "The problem with you all is, you got no schoolin'. You probably don't know anything about tank artillery either. Well, tanks nowadays are mounted with two types of guns. One fires normal rounds, for use against enemy troops, and the other shoots armor-piercing rounds. If you fire a normal round at a tank, it explodes on contact with the steel armor and doesn't do any harm to personnel. But armor-piercing rounds work on the same principle as this linear shaped charge. They have a V-shaped liner in the tip that's packed with a high explosive, and the instant the tip hits the tank it creates a metal jet that rips a hole in the armor, and the round proceeds into the interior before exploding and killing everyone inside."

"So why don't ordinary people know about these LSCs?" Kaneshiro had said. "I mean people who aren't bomb geeks? None of us have ever even heard of them before."

"Idiot!" Ishihara pointed an accusing finger at him from his rocking chair in the center of the Living. "So! You're not just a dinkydink who likes killing people but a dingalingdong who wouldn't know a blue alien babe from a dog licking your balls!" Takeguchi opened his mouth to speak, but Ishihara silenced him with a raised hand. Waving the Colt Government in the other and wriggling all over, he shouted: "Why is this stuff kept secret? You'd all better scour your brains and foreskins and bumfringe till you have the answer!" It was the gun Takei had been shot with and was still splattered with his blood but no longer loaded. "Ishihara-san, watch where you're pointing that thing," Kaneshiro said, making a face and leaning from side to side to avoid looking down the barrel. "Shut up," Ishihara said. "Don't be getting all uppity! Pushing out your lips like a disgruntled goldfish…" He swung the gun in an even wider arc, and Matsuyama, as if prompted by this sweeping gesture, raised his hand and said, "I know! Maybe they've tried to keep it quiet so terrorists wouldn't use it."

This answer seemed to satisfy everyone. Takeguchi said that professional demolitionists had stopped talking publicly about these devices long ago. Linear shaped charges were at the core of a conspiracy theory which held that the Bush administration had itself orchestrated the terrorist attacks in New York City during his presidency. Even Shinohara, as a small child, had thought it odd that those buildings should collapse like that just because planes had crashed into them. Some time after the second crash, the World Trade Center towers had dropped as if sliced in half. It all made more sense if you assumed that LSCs had been put in place and then set off by remote control.

But according to Takeguchi that scenario wasn't credible. It would be a massive undertaking to set LSCs in buildings of that size. The collapse had begun from the middle floors, and to set the charges on multiple floors in each of the Twin Towers, where tens of thousands of people were working day and night—it couldn't have been done, he said. "What about us, then?" said Ando. "That hotel isn't exactly small either." Fukuda handed Takeguchi a letter-size sheet of paper with a photograph of the Sea Hawk Hotel. Takeguchi stared at it and sighed. "No, it isn't, is it. And I don't know anything about architecture, so I've no idea how many columns there are, or where they're positioned."

Hino had then inserted his stone-bodhisattva face and peered at the photo. "When was this built?" he said. "It was already here when I came to Fukuoka," skull-faced Okubo told him, and Ando and the five Satanists nodded. "You're a Kyushu boy, right?" Sato said to Toyohara, who replied, "Pop-Pop, he told me that that hotel was there as long as he could remember, which means like the Taisho era or Meiji era or the Warring States period, I guess." Everyone had been particularly solicitous toward Toyohara since his accidental shooting of Takei, and now Fukuda patted his shaved head and said, "Very good." Felix got on the Internet and discovered that the hotel had been completed in the spring of 1995. "In that case, from the middle floors up it'll be steel frame," Hino said, "and for the lower floors a mixture of that and reinforced concrete." Lightweight steel frames had been developed in the early Nineties or so, he said, and had been used almost exclusively in high-rises ever since, being much more economical than reinforced concrete. Staring hard at the photo, he began to add up the probable columns. "One at the very front... Longitudinally through the building, ten or eleven per side... Four for the crossbeams..." He was like a middle-aged man counting the hairs in his comb. "Four around the elevator shafts, eight around the emergency stairway and service corridor... Basically, there should be about forty columns per floor."

"Can you tell the size of the columns," Takeguchi asked him, "or the thickness of the steel?" Hino peered even more closely at the photo, tilting his head to one side. "They'd probably be from a hundred to a hundred and twenty centimeters across, with a plate thickness of thirty millimeters or so," he reckoned. "You're sure they aren't filled with concrete?" Takeguchi asked. Apparently the LSCs had too short a range to slice through concrete or thick layers of metal. Linear shaped charges displayed their power to best advantage when used on buildings with hollow steel frames or on structures like steel bridges and smokestacks. "It's possible that the bottom four floors use reinforced concrete," Hino said, "but I can guarantee you that the columns are hollow from the fifth floor up." Fukuda handed another sheet of paper to Takeguchi, who pulled a calculator from his pocket and lay prone on the floor. He propped himself up on his elbows and mumbled as he made his calculations.

"If we target the four floors from the fifth floor up, and there are forty columns on each floor, here's how many we have to hit: all forty columns on the fifth floor, twenty on the sixth floor—just the ones on the side you want the building to fall toward—and on the seventh and eighth only the ones along the wall on that side, say ten columns each. That's a total of eighty columns, each of which has to be cut completely through from all four sides, both at top and bottom, which means eight LSCs per column. Eighty times eight is... We need to make six hundred and forty linear shaped charges. If we estimate the width of the steel plate to be twelve hundred millimeters, with a thickness of thirty millimeters, we'll need about five hundred grams of explosive for each LSC. Six hundred and forty times 0.5 is, what, three hundred and twenty kilos? How many twenty-five-kilo boxes of RDX did we have?" Fourteen, Fukuda told him. "That should do it, then," Takeguchi said, and climbed to his feet. "It's all right," he reported, beaming like a boy scout. "We *can* bring down that hotel." The Living echoed with cheers again, but Ishihara raised both hands to quell the premature celebration. Stroking his stubbly cheek with the barrel of the Colt Government, he stretched up in his seat to peer out the window. It was past two in the morning, but construction continued on the temporary Koryo barracks at the Odo *danchi*. You could see the lights of vehicles and the sparks of welders. The Koryos had every intention of finishing construction by the time their reinforcements arrived.

"Two questions," Ishihara said. "First, how do we go about setting the LSCs inside the hotel when the Koryos themselves are using it for their command center? And second, would knocking down the hotel really kill them all?" He stood up and called Ando over to stand at one corner of the carpet. He then had Toyohara and Okubo sit about a meter down either edge, so that they and Ando formed an equilateral triangle, and turned Ando to face Toyohara.

"An-an is the hotel, Toyo-toyo is the Dome, and Kubo-kubo is the hospital," he said, pointing at each of them in turn with the gun. "The enemy is camped out in the middle here. In order to flatten them all, we need the hotel to fall diagonally, like this." He pushed on Ando's left shoulder, making him tilt toward Okubo. "But that's not really possible, right?"

"You bring down a building the same way you chop down a tree," Takeguchi said, stepping forward and bending over to make a diagonal cutting motion at Ando's shins. "You cut all the columns on the fifth floor, half as many on the sixth floor—just the ones on the collapsing side—and a quarter as many on the seventh and eighth floors. To visualize it, think of an axe cutting into a tree." Ishihara nodded. "A notch in the building like Pac-Man's mouth, right? But my question is, the way you describe the cuts, wouldn't the hotel fall toward the Dome, miss most of the Koryos' camp, and fail to squash them all as flat as pancakes?"

Takeguchi and Fukuda exchanged wry smiles. Fukuda was acting as the assistant during this presentation. He knew all about DIY bombs made with household materials but deferred to Takeguchi when it came to high explosives. Shaking his head with some exasperation now, he walked over to the entrance, lifted one of the large wooden palettes there, dragged it back, and stood it on end in front of everyone. The palette was a rectangle about twice the size of a tatami mat, and it blocked Fukuda completely from view. No one had any idea what he was doing, and when Ishihara said, "What's up, Fuku? You gonna strain the river for floaters?" he didn't reply but gave the palette a nudge and let it fall forward. It toppled like a tree and slammed against the concrete floor with a terrific bang. A cloud of dust flew up, and those sitting closest coughed and spat and rubbed their eyes. "What the hell are you doing?" Yamada demanded, slapping the dust off his beige jacket with both hands.

Takeguchi stood next to the fallen palette with a small notebook. "This palette is 1.3 meters across and two meters long, thickness about ten centimeters, and it weighs less than ten kilograms. The Sea Hawk Hotel, according to my estimate, is about a hundred meters across, a hundred forty-five tall, and twenty-four deep, with a total volume of about three hundred and fifty thousand cubic meters and a total weight of about two hundred million kilograms, or two hundred thousand metric tons. The explosion of the charges themselves, at a radius of twenty-five meters, will produce a force of some twelve to twenty thousand kilograms per square meter. At fifty meters it's six to eight thousand, and at a hundred meters still two to three thousand. Three thousand kilograms per square meter is enough to break window frames and storm shutters. At eight thousand your eardrums are in danger of bursting and the pillars of wooden houses can give way, and at twenty thousand, people would be blown out of their shoes and wooden houses would be reduced to kindling—that's the power of three hundred and twenty kilograms of RDX.

"Next, let's discuss the seismic effects of the hotel collapsing." Takeguchi turned to a new page in his notebook. "According to my calculations, it will take about six seconds for the building to collapse completely. At a radius of a hundred meters, it will register from a hundred to a hundred and twenty decibels, which translates to a seven on the Japan Meteorological Agency's seismic-intensity scale, meaning it'll flatten virtually all wooden structures and cause buildings of reinforced concrete to break apart or list to one side. And then there's the wind pressure. In the direction opposite the collapse it will be about seventy kilos, and in the direction of the collapse two hundred and eighty. A wind pressure of seventy works out to an instantaneous wind speed, which is what the JMA use for typhoons, of ninety meters a second. No typhoon in Japan has ever recorded a wind speed of ninety meters. Even the biggest trees would be uprooted, and it would be impossible for a person to stay on his feet. For two hundred and eighty kilos the instantaneous wind speed is two hundred fifty meters per second. I have no idea what would happen to people and buildings in winds like that, and there's no data."

Takeguchi spoke in a detached, indifferent way, referring constantly to his notes. "That's mind-blowing," Tateno whispered, but all the talk about seismic intensity and typhoons still only added up to numbers for Shinohara—he couldn't grasp the actual forces involved. As Takeguchi was concluding his remarks, however, he threw in a couple of facts that made everyone's jaw drop. "Rubble would fly from the point of the collapse to a radius of about two hundred meters. We're talking clumps of concrete traveling at the unbelievable speed of a hundred to three hundred meters per *second*. A dense cloud of dust would billow out, also to about two hundred meters, and if you were in that cloud you wouldn't be doing any more breathing. So what I'm trying to say is, we're not going to flatten anybody much under the hotel itself. But you need to understand that unless you're an alien or something, if you're within a radius of two hundred meters of the collapse, it might be from the force of the blast or the seismic activity or the flying rubble or the dust, but you're going down."

Shinohara thought he could make out the faint sound of waves through the soaring glass walls. Someone had said that heavy rain was expected tonight, but it hadn't yet begun to fall. The fan-like leaves of a traveler's palm drooped over his head. The leaves were paler and thinner than those of the same palms in real rainforests, because the soil and air here were artificially treated and controlled. There was no draft because of the glass, and all the plants—the screw pines, the Chinese banyans, the weeping figs—stood there like sculptures, never waving or rustling. Colorful feathers littered the ground; the parrots had already been dead in their cages and beginning to decompose when Shinohara and Tateno arrived here. He got a bottle of Volvic water from his backpack and took a sip. In the past twenty-four hours he'd had nothing but some water and Calorie Mate bars, but he was much too on edge to feel hungry. Takeguchi had emphasized that they were all going to have to work hard tonight and that each of them should get plenty of food and rest. Shinohara was running on adrenaline, however.

It had been one thing to decide to demolish the hotel with LSCs, but how were they to make that happen? They had no strategy for getting the charges in place, and no one had any ideas. They had exhausted all their energy on Takei's funeral, and by the time Takeguchi finished explaining how the devices worked, Ishihara was nodding off in his rocking chair. Each time Kaneshiro nudged him back to consciousness, he would command Tateno or Toyohara or someone to bring him some more refreshment. He was drinking tequila. He would lick some salt, bite a slice of lime, throw back a shot, then gasp and stare at nothing with glistening eyes. Okubo suggested they postpone the meeting till tomorrow, but there was no time—once the Koryo reinforcements arrived, it wouldn't matter if the hotel got knocked down or not. Takeguchi said it would take two days to manufacture six hundred and forty LSCs, provided he could get ten volunteers to help him in the lab in Building E. Once they'd smuggled the charges inside the hotel, it would take seven to eight minutes to attach each one. Taping them to the columns would be easy enough, but first they'd have to strip away the decorative fabric or marble or wood veneers, and that could be time-consuming. He estimated they would need eleven hours to set all the charges. The question now was, how could they arrange for the Koryos to be elsewhere during all that time?

Shinohara's building mates Yamada, Mori, and Hino came up with the idea of releasing his frogs in the hotel. The frogs, they proposed, could be used to kill all the Koryos inside, after which they'd be able go in and set the charges. Kaneshiro had endorsed this plan, saying, "Those beasties of yours are more poisonous even than cobras, right?" Shinohara told them that dart frogs lose their toxicity when bred and raised by humans, but since the others clearly suspected him of just trying to protect his precious pets, he explained at some length. "The standard they use to measure toxicity is called the LD50, or medium lethal dose," he said. "The LD50 for potassium cyanide, taken orally, is ten milligrams per kilogram of body weight, so for a man of sixty kilograms the lethal dose would be 0.6 grams. The strongest poison in the world is made by the bacteria that cause botulism. It's approximately ten million times as potent as potassium cyanide: one gram of botulinum toxin is enough to kill seventeen million people. Dart frogs can't match that, but the venom of the most poisonous one is about five thousand times as strong as potassium cyanide, about two hundred and fifty times the venom of a cobra, about two hundred times sarin, fifty times sea-snake venom, eight times VX nerve gas, and five times stronger than blowfish poison.

"However. No one knows why exactly, but once the frogs are removed from their natural habitats—the jungles of Central and South America—they stop producing poison." Shinohara's eyes went unfocused as he spoke. He was picturing the frogs' homelands. He could call up vivid scenes from those rainforests wherever he was or whatever he was doing, not because he'd been there—he hadn't—but because he had envisioned them thousands of times. The home of a given frog, whether in Peru, Colombia, Ecuador, Panama, Costa Rica, Guyana, or Suriname, would be at the misty foot of some mountain range, where the air was heavy with moisture, and vegetation and trees grew thick in the humus soil—a paradise ruled by wild animals, birds arrayed in gaudy colors, and yet-undiscovered insects and bacteria. He could see water dripping from the tips of drooping leaves, a network of streams whispering over the moss-covered earth, and wild orchids blooming in every cranny. Tears welled up whenever he thought of the frogs' homelands, and his eyes were moist as he went on.

"Especially amazing is the *Phyllobates terribilis*, which lives where the Patia and San Juan rivers meet in south-west Colombia. Also known as the golden poison frog. One milligram of its poison can kill ten people. They come in three different color variations, or morphs: metallic mint or pale green, metallic yellow, and metallic orange. Of course, these guys too lose toxicity when taken out of their environment. There was a theory that their poison is made from the formic acid in the ants they eat, but a breeder in America imported some Costa Rican ants and raised them to feed his *terribilis*, and the frogs stopped producing poison anyway. I tried it too: same result. Which means the poisonous substance must be in the stuff the ants eat back home. Ants eat the meat of dead animals and insects and things, so now they think maybe bacteria are the root source of the poison, but there are so many types of bacteria that there's no way of telling which one it might be. So in the end it remains a mystery why these frogs lose their poison away from home. Nobody really knows.

"But let me tell you about *Dendrobates variabilis*, which I consider the most beautiful creature on earth. It's less than two centimeters long and can sit on your thumbnail, but its coloring is spectacular, with extreme variations depending on the angle of the light—a gradation from lime green to electric blue on the body, with legs that vary from electric silver to electric sky blue, and gunmetal black spots all over. *Variabilis* lives in the Huallaga River basin, at the foot of the Andes, between Tarapoto and Yurimaguas. The frogs are well protected there, because the wetlands are full of mosquitoes and gnats that carry viruses, and poisonous bugs and snakes, and the dense forests around them are home to boa constrictors and leopards. It's a kingdom barred to human beings. The ecosystem itself protects the frogs. The habitat of the golden poison frog too is so hostile to humans that not even the Colombian special forces, the Lanceros, will set foot inside it, which is why the Popular Liberation Army is said to have its base of operations there."

The others pricked up their ears at this last tidbit. "El Ejército Popular de Liberación?" Kaneshiro asked, enunciating carefully, and Shinohara said, "That's right." Kaneshiro nodded in a contented way and said, "So the guerrillas and the dart frogs are looking out for each other," and Ishihara, his cheeks red from tequila, murmured dreamily, "Wonderful, wonderful froggies!" Shinohara cleared his throat and continued. "In fact, the habitat of *variabilis* was the location of one of the base camps of the Sendero Luminoso in Peru, and a few years back some foreigners went to the Huallaga River basin to collect specimens and got themselves executed." Hearing this, Ishihara's excitement bubbled over again, and he rose from his chair waving the Colt Government and shouting, "Sendero Luminoso—the Shining Path!" Shinohara nodded. "An American pharmaceutical company once decided to catch tens of thousands of dart frogs, hoping to manufacture a new painkiller from the batrachotoxin they carry, but the plan fell through because of the guerrillas. Big drug companies can only catch frogs in Costa Rica and Panama, places like that, where it's not as dangerous."

"Well, we couldn't very well turn such precious creatures into weapons anyway," Ishihara said, and the others nodded in agreement. *No way. It wouldn't be right. But how cool is Sendero Luminoso? You think they ever use frogs to kill people?* The discussion rolled on, providing a brief period of relative peace and comfort. But having ruled out the frogs they were back to square one, and eventually the collective mood of exhaustion and anxiety reasserted itself. Kaneshiro came up with the rash suggestion that a team blast their way in and set the explosives while another team hold off the Koryos with Takei's weapons, but Ishihara quickly vetoed that, saying if he wanted to commit suicide he should do it alone. Everyone understood the strength of the enemy. In Daimyo 1-Chome a soldier with the Koryo Special Police had put two successive bullets into the head of his target, and it was said that a Koryo officer who'd been held hostage in Ohori Park, though suffering severe burns over his face and upper body, had punctured an SAT man's throat with a karate blow. You couldn't go head to head with people like that. "They're human beings too, though," Ishihara had said after a while. "There must be something they can't deal with, some point of vulnerability. Scour your skullcheese and skinflutes and figure out what that might be."

This artificial jungle had nothing remotely resembling the beauty represented by poison-dart frogs, Shinohara was thinking as he got up to pee in the shadow of the traveler's palm. He pointed the flow down the trunk of the tree to minimize noise. He was just contemplating whether to take a pre-emptive dump as well when the cellphone vibrated in his vest pocket. It was Takeguchi checking in. "All clear here," Shinohara reported, and Takeguchi said, "We start right on time, then, at one o'clock sharp," and clicked off. Not wanting to shit too near his own nest, Shinohara went behind one of the birdcages. There were four of these, surrounded by dragon trees, long-leafed figs, screw pines, giant upright elephant ears, and other exotic plants. The Koryos had cut the water supply, and some of the plants were already withering. But the way Shinohara saw it, simply putting them in this artificial environment was equivalent to gradually killing them anyway. The ground was laid with tile and brick for the convenience of visitors, confining the plants to limited areas. What little earth they had was covered thickly with white sand and polished pebbles to deter bacteria and insects. The plants consumed nutrients produced not by bacteria but chemical fertilizers and were sprayed regularly with insecticides.

They'd been brought from their native habitats to a completely different environment to be exploited, abused, and slowly murdered. It's like the assholes who raise reptiles, Shinohara was thinking as he lowered his pants. He kept dart frogs and arthropods but drew the line at reptiles. He was intrigued by the black mamba, which was said to be the world's most poisonous and aggressive snake, but he'd never kept a reptile and never intended to. In elementary school he had lived near a pet shop, and he'd often gone there to look at the tropical fish and tarantulas and scorpions and things. They had a lot of reptiles for sale too. Owning pets had become something of a fad, and many people who lived in small condos and apartments where you couldn't keep a cat or dog were raising lizards and tortoises. Certain species of tortoise with interesting designs on their shells had been so in demand on the Japanese market that they nearly became extinct. Shinohara bought scorpions and spiders at the shop, but it made his heart bleed to see an Egyptian tortoise in a case lined with sawdust, ramming its head against the glass wall again and again, or a big lizard like a tegu in a case so small it couldn't even turn around. But there were always people ogling the imprisoned turtles, snakes, lizards, and chameleons, and squealing about how cute they were.

If he were rich, he was pretty sure he'd buy up all the reptiles from importers everywhere and release them back into their natural habitats. And if he had his own police force and army, he'd just arrest all the importers. It was true that some species were in danger of extinction in their native lands as a result of war, poverty, and destructive development, but that didn't justify exporting them. Keeping reptiles as pets was, to Shinohara, the ultimate symbol of human self-indulgence. He identified with the tortoise ramming its head against the walls of its display case. People who thought it fun to keep tegu lizards in cases too small for them displayed a mentality exactly like that of his parents. "It's so cute!" they cooed as they fed the thing or gave it water or moved its case into the sunlight or warmed it with lamps. Even under the best conditions, lizards and tortoises never lived as long in captivity as in the wild; these people were slowly but surely killing the pets they found so adorable.

When he was a little boy, Shinohara's parents had dismissed his bouts of anxiety as nothing to worry about. The symptoms had first appeared when he was seven. In kindergarten, he had enjoyed playing with Lego blocks. He would lock the little pieces together to make houses, rockets, robots, and so forth, and his parents displayed these little masterpieces on shelves in the living room. But one day when he was in second grade, Shinohara took a pair of those kindergarten-era creations in his hands and suddenly began to panic. In order to see the things as rockets or robots, a sort of compact or agreement was necessary. Everyone agreed to recognize these little blocks, when stacked in a certain way, as something else. Within Shinohara's internal landscape, however, that compact had suddenly evaporated. All he could see were little plastic boxes with interlocking pegs.

From that time on, he often had spells during which the building blocks of reality itself seemed to come apart. He would experience, during waking hours, the twilight state everyone enters just before falling asleep. Memories of the past would arise at random—scenery and conversations, the voices and faces of parents, friends, teachers. If his mother, for example, was standing before him during one of these episodes, her face would become all pixilated and confused with the clock on the wall and the noise of the traffic outside and the world of imagination in his own head. There was a breakdown of the compact that linked his awareness to his senses. It was like looking at a completed jigsaw puzzle and only being able to see the individual pieces. Everything around him—the TV, a comic book, a box of cookies, his book bag, his desk, his milk glass—disintegrated into something unrecognizable. He would perceive his parents and little sister slipping farther and farther away, even as they sat in the same room talking to him, and would feel trapped inside a kind of membrane that separated him from his surroundings. When he tried to tell his parents what he was experiencing, however, all they would say is, "It's all right, son. Nothing to worry about."

About the time Shinohara entered middle school, a birthday party was held for his father, a national university professor who specialized in medieval European architecture. A lot of people were invited to their house in Setagaya, Tokyo, including some foreign diplomats who were acquaintances of his mother, a translator of French. After dinner with wine, his little sister played the cello. Sitting there, Shinohara found that he didn't know what that noise he was hearing was, or what that gourd-shaped wooden thing was, or who that was who was sawing away at it, or who these people were who'd gathered to watch, or what the objects they were sitting on were called, or what it meant to "sit," or what all these things had to do with one another. After a jolt of electrifying anxiety, he dashed up to his bedroom, where he took dozens of scorpions and spiders out of their cases and put them in two paper shopping bags. Returning to the living room, he walked up behind his mother and father, who were listening attentively to their daughter's recital, and dumped the bags over their heads.

When asked how a boy like him, growing up in such privileged circumstances, could be so dissatisfied and unhappy, he blamed it on the fact that his parents doted solely on his sister; but that wasn't really the problem. The problem was that no one understood the terror he felt on those occasions when the building blocks of reality began falling apart. He went through hell both at home and in school. Only when he was watching his scorpions and spiders catch and eat live bait, or when he was reading books about poisons, did reality remain reliably stable. His parents misunderstood this, however.

They believed the reason for his mental disturbance was that he was raising such bizarre fauna. They urged him to get interested in music, like his sister, or learn a foreign language or take up a sport, and they bought him a flute, Chinese-language tapes, and tennis gear. This was essentially the same as gazing at a stir-crazy turtle or lizard and calling it "cute." It was proof of an inability to see or consider things from the other's point of view. In middle school, Shinohara began getting serious about centipedes and millipedes, buying them over the Internet straight from their native lands. And if the Lego blocks of reality began to slip out of kilter, he would use his centipedes from Guyana or Myanmar to threaten and even assault classmates or family members.

He was still in middle school when he learned of a newly discovered, extremely poisonous type of centipede from Haiti. A Dominican supplier with whom he'd been dealing for several years suggested he place an order immediately, before they were banned from sale. Shinohara purchased a hundred specimens, which arrived along with the necessary CITES Certificate of Origin. These centipedes were so full of vitality that raising and breeding them was no work at all. Since there was nothing else he wanted, Shinohara spent all his allowance on his many-footed little friends, and with the help of some fake IDs even managed to rent a small room in the city to keep them in. What was so wonderful about these creatures was that you could hide them—the smaller ones, at least—almost anywhere. You could keep dozens of them in a small Tupperware container and even carry a couple in your wallet. Though Shinohara was placed in an institution during his second year of middle school, he made use of his centipedes to effect an immediate escape. His parents had him removed from the family register but paid him off with a fairly large lump sum, so he packed a suitcase with several hundred centipedes and hit the road. He was biding his time at a park in the city, unleashing a pet or two on the occasional homeless person, when he made the acquaintance of an old friend of Ishihara's, a man with a face like an alien, who encouraged him to head for Fukuoka.

Only after arriving in Fukuoka had he become interested in poison-dart frogs. The first ones he got his hands belonged to the species *Dendrobates amazonicus*. They were an entire cosmos in a package no bigger than the nail of his little finger. Just by looking at his frogs, or by making a vivarium for them, or breeding insects to feed them—just by being involved with them—Shinohara was able to connect with an unshakable reality. You could search the entire world, if not the entire universe, without finding many things as beautiful as these frogs. They carried their tadpoles around on their backs and raised them anywhere water accumulated, even in the creases of leaves, and they'd been surviving in the richest, most seductive, and most dangerous environment in the world—the tropical rainforest—since long before human beings ever saw the light of day. Their evolutionary adaptation hadn't involved tools or language but the poison they excreted through their soft, metallic-hued skin. Amphibian skin lacked keratin or scales, and the frogs excreted poison to protect them from harmful bacteria and viruses. They needed this powerful poison, and the unbelievably beautiful coloring that went with it, in order to survive in tropical jungles.

Maybe it was because he'd been eating only Calorie Mate, but his bowel movement hardly smelled at all. As he was buckling his belt, he peered into the cage of dead parrots and saw something moving inside. One bird's bloated stomach had ruptured, releasing a crawling mass of maggots. They were several times larger than the maggots of the fruit flies he bred for his frogs. At the all-night meeting after Takei died, when he had suggested they use flies and centipedes rather than frogs, the others had all looked at him as if he were delirious. "You think the Koryos are gonna run away screaming from flies?" Ishihara said, and began flapping his hands, hopping about and making a buzzing sound in an apparent imitation of a housefly. Shinohara said, "Hold that thought," and trotted over to Building H. He returned with two breeding bottles and a Tupperware container. Ishihara laughed when he saw the breeding bottles and said, "Shino! Where'd you get the co-eds' dill-dolls?"

They were plastic cylinders about three centimeters in diameter and twenty centimeters long, stoppered with little cylindrical sponges. When transporting them like this, Shinohara secured the stoppers with rubber bands. He held up one of the bottles, at the bottom of which was the medium where the insects laid and incubated their eggs. This one contained four-day-old fruit flies, feed for his larger dart frogs. He walked up to the rocking chair, held the breeding bottle in front of Ishihara's nose, and removed the sponge stopper. "Poo," Ishihara said, wrinkling his face and turning away in reaction to the smell that immediately filled the air. The medium was a fermented mash of banana, apple, cornmeal, and wheat mixed with apple vinegar and dry yeast. Shinohara turned the bottle upside down and tapped the lid on the arm of the rocking chair. What looked like gray powder fell out, landing on Ishihara's thigh and stomach and then seeming to bounce right off. In the next instant he was on his feet, babbling unintelligibly, his face coated with a second skin of flies the size of grains of sand. Kaneshiro, Takeguchi, Fukuda, and Yamada, who had all been sitting near Ishihara's chair, emitted a collective "Whoa!" and scrambled away on all fours.

Some of the flies seemed to be jumpers and others fliers, and collectively they moved like wind-whipped smoke. There was no telling how many hundreds or thousands of them there were. At first they remained clustered near the rocking chair, but as Ishihara and others nearby flailed about, slapping themselves and dancing spastically, the flies divided into several platoons to seek warmth elsewhere and soon peppered the faces and exposed skin of everyone in the room. "What the hell are you doing, letting those things loose in here?" Kaneshiro shouted, frantically trying to brush flies off his trouser legs. Flies had somehow found their way into Toyohara's Hawaiian shirt as well, and as he tried to unbutton it they began to congregate on his hairy hands and fingers, a sight that made him panic and jump up and down and squeal like a child throwing a tantrum.

Imitating the sound of an ambulance siren—*Pii-po! Pii-po!*—Mori had run to the kitchen and grabbed a can of cockroach spray. He aimed it at a platoon of flies, but because they weighed almost nothing the pressure of the spray merely pushed them out of range, and Matsuyama snatched the can away, saying it hurt his eyes. Miyazaki and Shibata covered their faces with their hands and complained that the little bastards were climbing right inside their mouths and noses and ears. "This other one," Shinohara said, pointing at the second breeding bottle, "contains crickets. Shall I let them out?" Ishihara aimed the Colt at him. "Don't even think about it!" he said in an unprecedentedly no-nonsense tone of voice. "What are you going to do about this?" he demanded, gesturing at the floor of the Living and the flies that carpeted it. "Where am I and I going to sleep tonight?" All but Shinohara were in something like a state of panic now, as flies continued to land on their cheeks and foreheads and necks and arms. They shook their heads and writhed about, slapping at the relentless pests, which were so tiny and light and agile that they couldn't be swatted, captured, or discouraged. "Seriously," said Ando, thrashing away. "What happens now? Will they go away after a while?" Smiling, Shinohara spread his arms and gazed happily at his open hands and the flies that covered each finger. "A small swarm like this will disperse and move on eventually," he said. "How long is *eventually*?" Ishihara shouted. He was stomping around in a frantic circle, trying to crush the flies underfoot, but the downdraft kept ejecting them from the danger zone just before the soles of his sneakers made contact with the floor. "Not to worry," Shinohara said. "They'll all be gone in a couple of weeks or so." Ishihara exploded with genuine anger now. "Two weeks, my ass!" he bellowed, and dragged the vacuum cleaner out from its corner.

*Take this, you little buggers… Suck you all down to a vacuumy grave…* Muttering under his breath, Ishihara hit the switch and wielded the tube like a fencing sword. "Touché," he said, as he sucked up a small gathering at his feet, and everyone cheered. A cloud of about twenty flies was orbiting his head, however, and apparently one of them found its way into his inner ear. Ishihara flung the tube aside and began rolling his head around on his shoulders, looking like a kabuki actor winding up for a dramatic pose, then tore at his hair and sank to his knees, crying, "I'm sorry! Forgive me! My bad! Someone open the windows!" Sato, Felix, and Matsuyama ran to do so. "See? We're opening the windows!" Ishihara told the flies. "Please leave. Please go away now!" Shinohara shook his head. "They're not going to go out there, where it's colder. Never happen. But if we make it colder in here—or much warmer, for that matter—they'll slow down a lot." Shinohara was removing the Tupperware container from his pocket as he spoke. The Satanist Orihara shouted, "Stop!" and moved forward in a crouch, as if ready to tackle him. "What've you got in there?"

Shinohara raised his free hand and said, "Back up. These guys are not to be messed with." He held the translucent container aloft. Something dark and squishy was wriggling around inside. "What is it?" Kaneshiro asked, but Shinohara put a finger to his lips to shush him, then took from his back pocket a pair of thick leather gloves such as welders use. He put them on and stood perfectly still, staring at the container as if to focus his attention. He glanced at Ishihara and the others nearby and jerked his chin to indicate that they should move farther away. No one was going to argue with him now. Nor did they doubt the rumors about him any longer—that he had driven two middle-school teachers to attempt suicide, or that he'd forced the head hoodlum in the institution to help him escape, or that he'd threatened a female probation officer with his bugs, stripping her naked and having his way with her. They all backed off slowly, gasping for breath and swatting at the flies that brazenly circled their heads and clung to their faces and arms. Shinohara was moistening his lips with his tongue as he stared at the Tupperware box. Finally he pried the lid open a crack and immediately turned the container around, so that the opening was facing away from him. After a beat, a reddish-brown thing about the thickness of a grown man's finger stuck its head out, then wriggled free and dropped to the floor. Shinohara quickly closed the lid and squared off to face the thing, which was about as long as a man's finger as well. Its reddish-brown body gleamed dully in the fluorescent ceiling lights.

"Is it a worm?" Yamada whispered, and Mori gave him a nudge in the ribs: "Dummy. He said 'flies and centipedes,' remember?"

Shinohara squatted down, with his gloved hands before him goal-keeper-style, and edged slowly forward to narrow the distance between himself and the centipede. At the instant the outline of his shadow reached the creature, it raised what appeared to be its head, reared back, and dived at his knee. It was like a spring flying out of a broken mechanism, a burst of released energy, and it flew at its target not in an arc but a straight line. Shinohara caught the centipede in his left-hand glove like a shortstop fielding a grounder. Then, after clamping the right-hand glove on top to keep the thing from escaping, he took hold of it with a deft twist of his right thumb and forefinger. Still swatting flies, Takeguchi, Okubo, Sato, and Miyazaki hesitantly moved closer, but when they saw the centipede's underside, with its countless wriggling legs, they stopped dead in their tracks and clapped their hands over their mouths. "See how it's changed color?" Shinohara said, displaying the thing's back. The reddish brown had indeed turned a bright crimson. "Does it hurt if they sting you?" Okubo asked. "They don't sting, they bite, and yes, it hurts like hell. And like scorpions and spiders, it's often the smaller ones that are the most poisonous." Shinohara held the ferocious creature up to the light, and everyone joined the wide semicircle around him—except Ishihara, Kaneshiro, and Ando, who were still brushing the flies from their faces and clothing and looking on sourly from some distance away. Toyohara had ripped off his Hawaiian shirt and was sweating heavily as he tried to extract the flies tangled in his bushy armpits. He alone was oblivious to the centipede; the others were eyeing it and its owner with a mixture of fear and hatred. The monster's creepy little yellowish legs were jointed and much longer than those of Japanese centipedes.

"They use those long, articulated legs to jump," Shinohara told them. "If you get bitten by one of these guys, you break out in a painful rash, often accompanied by fever and diarrhea." When he was in middle school Shinohara had tested his centipedes' poison by dabbing a diluted mixture on his skin, or licking it. Even when well diluted, the poison caused his skin to swell and redden and sting quite painfully; and after licking the stuff, his tongue went numb, his heartbeat quickened, and the muscles in his arms and legs began to ache. He'd been bitten just once, not long after being disowned and leaving home with more than five hundred centipedes in his suitcase. He had raised several generations by then, mixing supplements containing vitamins, minerals, calcium, and essential amino acids into their food, and occasionally a centipede with exceptional jumping ability would materialize. One of these had pounced on the back of his hand with startling speed and taken a bite. Shinohara pulled the thing off and crushed it underfoot, making sure that the head—or more properly the forcipules that secrete the venom—didn't remain embedded in his skin. If it had been one of the more common types of centipede and produced only histamine toxins, sucking the poison out of the wound would have been sufficient, but for a bite from this species he needed an extractor, a device that resembled a hypodermic needle. Fortunately he had one and used it promptly, but nonetheless his arm swelled up and turned dark red from elbow to fingers, and the muscles in his neck ached so much he could hardly move for two days.

"These guys have a poisonous hemolytic protein, in addition to the histamine toxin. In Haiti, where they're from, thousands of bite victims are hospitalized every year, and if they're babies or old or sickly, sometimes they die." Shinohara slammed the centipede on the floor and stepped on it. As it was being crushed it made a crackling noise, like thin glass breaking. "They're carnivores and can't coexist with any other living creatures, so unfortunately if one gets free you have to kill it."

"Shinohara, what's up with these flies?" Takeguchi said. "They all look the same, but some of them can fly and some only jump." Shinohara said that they were genetically engineered to be flightless, for use in experiments. "But when you breed huge numbers of them, a lot start to mutate back to being able to fly." Ishihara asked how many he'd just let loose. "I usually keep about two hundred in a bottle, but I packed in about twice as many to show you." How many did he have in total, then? "Well, they're too small to count, of course, but I've got about five hundred of these bottles, plus the large breeding jars, so, I don't know, half a million?" Both gasps and cheers met this announcement. "Half a million of these little fuckers?" Fukuda muttered as he watched the flies leapfrogging about on the floor, and Ishihara sighed and said, "Shino, you are amazing."

"Besides these, I've got two species of cricket, maybe about three hundred thousand all together. Never counted 'em exactly, of course. Then I have what we call springtails, which are about the size of a speck of dust—you can hardly even see 'em, let alone count 'em. I feed them to my red-backed dart frogs—*Dendrobates reticulatus*, one of the smaller species—just after they develop from tadpoles. And then I have bugs I don't feed to the frogs but just like to look at, like camel spiders, which live in deserts or savannahs. I've got a few hundred of those, I guess." And how many of these scary centipedes, Kaneshiro asked. "Well, they breed like crazy, and they're low maintenance. Not even extreme changes in their environment affect them much, and you can stuff 'em in Tupperware like this and they're fine—they just curl up together. I like these guys a lot and have a whole block of plastic cases packed with them, so I'd say, at the very least, about two thousand." Shinohara's face remained as smooth and expressionless as a hard-boiled egg as he said this.

"I think it could work." Takeguchi was grinning. "Just imagine half a million of these little bastards buzzing around you," he said, but Shinohara was quick to correct him. "We can't use them all. I need to save enough to keep the frogs alive." Everyone except Toyohara, who was still disentangling flies from his armpits and looked on the verge of tears, was suddenly enthusiastic. "The ultimate biological weapon," said Kaneshiro, and Matsuyama noted that "You can't shoot a centipede with an AK." Okubo said, "These flies are too small for even people from the land of starvation to catch and eat," and Mori made a joke about pinning Kim Il Sung badges on the centipedes to force the Koryos to bow down to them. But when Tateno wondered aloud how they were going to get these new weapons of theirs inside the hotel, everyone fell silent.

"How about having them delivered?" Orihara suggested. Postal and delivery services had resumed throughout Kyushu—a decision reached by the governors of the various prefectures on the island, rather than the national government—as well as distribution of gasoline, kerosene, medicine, and rice and other staples. Apparently all sorts of "gifts" were being delivered to the Koryos at the Sea Hawk Hotel. Afraid of being arrested or shot once the reinforcements arrived, many of Kyushu's wealthier citizens tried to curry favor by sending brandy and cigars; certain municipal officials sent samples of local specialties; and elementary-school classrooms sent posters they'd drawn with messages like NO WAR, PLEASE! on them. Jo Su Ryeon had mentioned on his TV show this morning that packages like these were first inspected and then stored somewhere in the hotel. However, Orihara's idea was summarily rejected by Ishihara, who was following a single fly around the room, squatting down to blow on it each time it came to rest.

"It's no good if they know the bugs came from outside," he said. "They'll just keep trying to shoo them back out. They need to think they're coming from *in*side the hotel, so the bugs can shoo *them* out." Shibata asked if maybe Felix couldn't come up with some fake ID cards to let them pose as workmen and bring in the bugs that way. With construction having started, workers for private firms were constantly calling at the Koryo camp, and large shipments of food and other supplies were being delivered. Felix said it would be easy enough to make the IDs, but they'd need to know which businesses had access to the hotel and how incoming cargo was handled. "What did I and I just say? It's no good bringing the bugs *in*!" Ishihara was on his hands and knees now, and blew on the fly again. "If you look closely," he said, "he's built just like any fly, only way smaller, and so cute, rubbing his little hands together. *Don't swat the poor fly! He wrings his wee hands! He pulls his wee pud!*" Ishihara punctuated his haiku with another puff of breath, and the fly leaped into the air, coming down a short distance away only after some impressive hang time. "Hey, Gonta!" Apparently he'd given the fly a name. "This time see if you can land on Toyo-toyo's nose!"

Hino had been watching this performance closely, but it was plain that he was thinking hard about something. Finally he took a step

519

forward. "I know!" he said, raising his hand like a kid in elementary school. "If we could get to the hotel's air-conditioning machinery, we could release the insects into the ventilation ducts."

When Shinohara returned to the traveler's palm, Tateno was vocalizing in his sleep: "*Koryo Weonjeonggun, mansae-e-e-e! Koryo Weonjeonggun, chwego-o-o-o!*" He woke himself up with the final extended vowel, realized he'd been dreaming, and went right back to sleep. We had it drilled into us, after all, Shinohara thought, smirking as he remembered the practice session with the Chief and Deputy Chief of the local Speed Tribe. To ask the Tribe for help getting into the hotel had been Fukuda's idea. There was a lot of equipment to transport: six hundred and forty linear shaped charges, cables and wires, weapons and ammo from Takei's collection, the insects, Hino's cutting and welding tools, Felix's electronic equipment, bottles of water, boxes of Calorie Mate protein bars. It all came to about eight hundred kilograms, or forty kilos apiece, if they split it up evenly. They could handle that. The problem wasn't the bulk or weight of the baggage but how to get it past the Koryos.

"Tonight—well, last night now, technically—our wimpy old boy Takei passed away. The cause of death was an accidental gunshot." Greeted point-blank with this news after being summoned by Ishihara at three in the morning, the Chief and Deputy Chief had stood before him stunned and speechless. The Chief, son of a building contractor in Hakata, was tall and slim, with a pompadour that preceded him by about four centimeters. His deputy, the sole heir of a well-known local maker of bean-jam buns, was seriously acne-scarred and not very tall but had the chest and shoulders of a bodybuilder. They both sported large-gauge rings in their eyebrows, black suits, and white satin turtlenecks, though when they rode with the Tribe they dressed in special uniforms that resembled those of the Nazi SS, with flowing white silk-blend scarves. These two were long-time fans of Ishihara and Nobue and had often come by to drop hints about joining forces—hints that were always ignored by their idols. The Chief led an organization of four or five hundred souls, and Shinohara had once asked Ishihara why he wouldn't let them join the group. Ishihara had said, "People like that are a snore. You and Hino, Tateno and Kaneshiro, An-an and Toyo-toyo and Yamada and Mori, the boy Satanists and Takeguchi and Fukuda and the rest, you're all hopeless scum, but you're *interesting*. Being around you for too long induces nausea, and none of you drink, and you're all completely loco in the coco, but one thing you aren't is boring. Speed Tribers beat up people they don't like and go up against the police or whatever. But you boys don't choose sides between rebels and regulars, good guys and bad guys, and you don't divide things into like or hate. Speed Tribers are just lonely—they're starved for love—but you boys are different. You're not particularly lonely and you're not searching for love. You can't be compromised or held to any social contract, because you never signed on. That's why no one likes you, but it's also why you can't be fooled. The Speed Tribe is easily swayed by the mojority, but you've already been rejected by the mojority. That's what makes you interesting."

As Ishihara addressed the two Tribal leaders, saying, "Now steel yourselves and pledge your cooperation in our fight," he pressed the barrel of the Colt Government against his right temple. Not knowing exactly what had happened earlier, and unaware of how much tequila he'd drunk, the scions of construction and bean-jam must have thought they saw madness in his eyes. They stood pale and frozen. Also present in the Living, in addition to Shinohara, were Hino, Ando, and Tateno. The rest were either in Building E, helping Takeguchi and Fukuda set up production of the LSCs or in their rooms snatching some sleep.

"Tell us this," Ishihara said. "Why do you guys tear around on bikes and stuff?" The Chief thought for a moment, looking up at the ceiling, then said, "Because we're pissed off at this rotten, stinkin' world." Ishihara opened his glittering, bloodshot eyes wide and glared at him. "No good," he said. "'Because we're pissed off'? That won't cut it. Isn't it really because you want to see this whole cesspool of a world painted black? To paint all the doors black, all the streets and roads and alleys and crosswalks black, all the traffic lights not red-green-yellow but black, and all the houses and schools and buildings and structures, the land and sea and sky—to paint 'em *all* black?" He was wriggling again, holding the gun in one hand, bending his free arm into a series of odd angles, and occasionally tearing at his hair.

All of which seemed to leave the Chief dumbfounded. Ishihara's way of speaking was always somewhat off, somewhat different from normal verbal expression. He had said "streets and roads and alleys and crosswalks"—words that overlapped in meaning but that his pronunciation tended to destabilize, distorting the various images they summoned and creating a sense of anxious anticipation in the listener. "That's right," said the Chief. "It's our favorite color. Our uniforms, our decals, our patches, they're all black." His cohort enthusiastically nodded confirmation. They were missing the point completely, but Ishihara wasn't just toying with them. He was seriously trying to communicate something. "Tell us this, then," he said, pointing the gun at the Chief's forehead: "What do you guys live for?" The Chief automatically took a step backwards. Ishihara parted his lips and flicked his purplish tongue in and out between his teeth. The Tribers looked at each other. It seemed they both wanted to speak but couldn't find the words.

"You live each day without even knowing what you're living *for*?" Ishihara shouted. He was walking in a circle, swinging his right arm forward as he stepped with his right foot and his left with his left. It was never possible to anticipate his next bewildering action or gesture. The Chief and his deputy drooped visibly. "If you don't know what you're living for, what makes you any different from the average geezer or salaryman or office worker or middle-aged drudge or civil servant? I'm only going to say this once. It's important, so prick up your ears and pucker the inner lips of your heart of hearts. What do we live for? We live to destroy. There are only two types of people in this world: those who scrimp and save little by little to build a breakwater or levee or windbreak or irrigation canal, and those who destroy the vested interests and the old system and the fortress of evil with enough emotion and inspiration and fervor and fury and desire and passion fruits to crack open everyone's skull and ring their balls like bells." Ishihara's cheeks were flushed, his hair was standing on end, and his eyes glistened and sparkled.

The Chief exchanged glances with his deputy again, then looked down at his boots and said, "Ishihara-san, if I could interrupt… Are you askin' us to help you fight these Koryos? We're honored, of course… Me, I'll be thirty-seven this year, and Koizumi here, he's thirty-three and got one foot in runnin' the family business now, makin' yuzu bean-jam buns and rice-cake balls and all, and as I'm sure you know, the Tribe nowadays, it's not like it used to be. We got a lot of part-timers now, you might say. A lot of the guys are settlin' in to steady jobs, we got a few carpenters and plasterers, even some who work in nursin' homes, and of course they can only ride when they're off work. And, but, listen, I saw the firefight with the Koryos the other day in Ohori Park, and, I mean, holy shit. I hate to say it, but there's no way we could beat those guys. As the boss of this Tribe, I took a vow not to do drugs or hit on the ladies, and if I used violence on a civilian I'd be out on my ass. But this is different. Just tell me what you need us to do. I'll bring at least a hundred men. I couldn't ask for anything more than to fight side by side with you." When he had finished his speech, his buddy said, "Boss! We decided long ago that we'd die together, didn't we? Bean-jam buns or no buns, I'm with you all the way." And the two of them clasped hands manfully.

"Thank you," Ishihara said, and stood still for a moment, facing them. "You've got the wrong idea, though. It's true that there's no way to beat the Koryos head to head. But tonight we've come up with an epic plan for wiping them out in one fell swoop without any of us getting hurt. I and I'll explain it all later, but it's something no one could have thought of but our roly-poly sunshine terror babies." He handed out a few sheets of paper on which some Korean words were copied out phonetically. "Let's start with a drill. Everyone repeat after me: '*Koryo Weonjeonggun, mansae-e-e-e! Koryo Weonjeonggun, chwego-o-o-o-o! Koryo Weonjeonggun, iptae shikhyeo-juseyo-o-o-o-o!*' Project from your diaphragm and your taint! Come on, all together now! You need to memorize this and teach it to your troops. Repeat it till it's second nature. '*Koryo Weonjeonggun, mansae-e-e-e-e! Koryo Weonjeonggun, chwego-o-o-o-o! Koryo Weonjeonggun, iptae shikhyeo-juseyo-o-o-o-o!*' He insisted that Shinohara, Tateno, and Hino chant and memorize it too. The only part they understood was the word *Koryo*, but Shinohara guessed that *Weonjeonggun* must be the same as *Enseigun* in Japanese—"Expeditionary Force."

Ishihara translated, looking quite proud of himself. "'Long live the Koryo Expeditionary Force! The Koryo Expeditionary Force is great! We want to join the Koryo Expeditionary Force!' That's what it means. After you get the Tribe together, you pick up the terror babies and circle the Koryo camp, the hotel, and the Dome chanting this as loud as—" The Chief gave a start and said, "You mean on the other side of the checkpoints? That's all controlled by the Koryos." Ishihara told him not to worry. "We'll alert the media, and they'll be there with television cameras. The Koryos aren't going to shoot Japanese civilians on TV. Also, make as many banners and flags as you can with the Koryo logo—that weird pagoda thing. Put red stars on your headwear and scarves too. No one's saying they're going to *welcome* you if you do that, but they won't suspect anything. They've got a hundred and twenty thousand reinforcements coming soon, and they won't want any trouble in the meantime. You know damn well they're laughing at this country, where nobody—not the government or the military or the police—offers any resistance. They'd never imagine that a group of civilians would try to infiltrate their command center."

He must have nodded off while curled up at the foot of the traveler's palm. Tateno woke him up, shaking his shoulder and showing him his watch: "Almost time." Shinohara stifled a cough as he sat up. This place was just a stone's throw from the enemy camp, and the walls were made of glass. Shinohara and Tateno had remained here, separate from the main team, to survey the Koryos' movements. At first they had concealed themselves behind a screw pine, then in a grassy area planted with peperomia, bowstring hemp, and peace lilies. This was where they had been when a Koryo officer suddenly materialized on the other side of the glass wall, no more than ten meters away. It was, in fact, the commanding officer, someone whose face they'd seen a number of times on TV. The Koryos weren't occupying any floors above the third—what was he doing up here? When he appeared just outside the glass, Shinohara and Tateno had hit the dirt. The officer was holding an umbrella and was accompanied by two other officers and what appeared to be a Japanese doctor dressed in hospital whites. Shinohara was unable to breathe for a moment; cold sweat rolled down his stomach. Later they estimated that the Koryos had stood out there for only ten minutes or so, but at the time it had seemed an eternity. "I can't take it," Tateno whispered at one point. "I can't take the tension." He covered his mouth with both hands and clenched every muscle in his body to stifle a scream. Shinohara too was close to panicking. Because of the glass and the rain it was impossible to hear what was being said outside, but the officer looked and pointed their way several times. Of course, the fact that the top brass was there with virtually no protection showed at least that the Koryos had no suspicions about intruders. But Shinohara only realized this later on, after calmer reflection.

"Fifteen more minutes," Tateno said now, looking at his watch. "Never slept in a wedding dress before," he muttered as he folded the thing up. He opened his daypack, which held some water, Calorie Mate bars, and forty boomerangs in an L-shaped leather case, and removed the case to inspect the weapons. The boomerangs were bound together at the grips in bundles of five, and the blades were protected with plastic wrapping. Shinohara had coated the edges of the blades with a paste he'd prepared by mashing together the fruit of the Japanese star anise—a tree favored by cemeteries—and sacred lily root, then adding the maxillipeds of centipedes. The berry of the star anise contains the neurotoxin anisatin, which works directly on the nerve cells, releasing a flood of the neurotransmitters that communicate excitement. This causes the muscles as well as the circulatory and respiratory organs to spasm, leading to paralysis and asphyxiation. The sacred lily root contains a component called rhodein, which also causes convulsions and paralysis.

"I wonder what Ishihara-san is doing right now," Tateno said. "It's hard to believe it's been only about twenty-four hours since we left." A picture of Ishihara's clock-stopping face loomed in Shinohara's mind.

It had taken two entire days to prepare for the operation. Shinohara had readied plastic sacks that would hold the flies and other live weapons, and separately packed up some extra culture medium for which he had a special plan. Tateno had gone to the lab in Building E, where he joined the team that ended up making four hundred LSCs the first day. Hino did a thorough check of his hand-held tools—electric cutters and breaker hammers, portable welding and cutting equipment, tanks of acetylene and oxygen. He seemed to be enjoying himself immensely as he lined the tools up in the hallway. "I always thought I'd use these to build a building," he said. "Not to bring one down." Okubo, Miyazaki, and Shibata set out to buy supplies and returned with nineteen oversized mountaineer's backpacks and ten smaller daypacks. The daypacks were for things that needed to be handled with special care, like Hino's tools, the hand grenades, the electric detonators, and the exploder.

Yamada and Mori had spent the entire two days helping make LSCs, stopping only for meals. It was a simple operation. They used a mechanical press to fold lead plates into the inverted M shape, then filled them with a gelatinous mixture of high explosives. "It's like spreading crusty old mustard or ketchup on a hotdog," Yamada said with a big smile. In addition to gathering and checking his tools and carrying them to Building C, Hino had studied the sketch of the Sea Hawk Hotel and managed to locate the central control room and the air-conditioning machine rooms. According to him, all air-conditioning and ventilation machinery used to be in the basements of high-rise buildings because they took up so much space and created so much vibration. But as the size of the machinery was drastically reduced over the years, builders began placing a number of independent machine rooms in high-rises—one on a low floor, one or more on the middle floors, and one near the top. This was more efficient than putting in ductwork that went from basement to roof.

Hino had zeroed in on the sixth and seventh floors, both of which had Japanese-style rooms on one side of the hotel only and expanded service corridors on the other. The air-conditioning machinery for the lower floors would be on the sixth, he was sure, and for the middle floors on the seventh. There would be another machine room higher up, but it wasn't necessary to find that one. All they needed access to was the stuff that regulated the air on the lower floors. The Koryos were using the main banquet hall, on the third floor, as their command center. Hino said that a room as large as that would have its own dedicated ventilation ductwork employing an enormous fan. It was his idea to release the flies directly into the duct that fed that fan.

The preparations had finally been completed on the night of the second day. What delayed them in the end was Shinohara's packing of the bugs. He had to wait till the last minute, so that they wouldn't use up all the oxygen in the vinyl bags. After making sure he'd set aside enough flies to feed his frogs for three days, he headed for Building C, where everyone was to gather. He put the plastic bags containing the insects into two hundred-liter-capacity backpacks that he and Tateno were to carry. These weighed almost nothing, so they would also carry daypacks with Hino's spare acetylene and oxygen tanks.

They had decided not to bring any weapons they were unlikely to use. That included all the sniper rifles. The only automatic weapons they took were the M16, the AK-74, and the sub-machine guns—the Uzi and the Scorpion. They also packed the FN and the Beretta, whose ammo was interchangeable. All of these weapons fitted into a couple of the large backpacks with room to spare, so they threw in the short-barreled shotgun and grenade launcher as well. The remaining fifteen backpacks were filled with LSCs, wiring, and the styrofoam they'd use when attaching the charges to the columns. Fukuda put the exploder and the remote-control apparatus in a daypack, which he carried cradled in his arms. On his back was a second daypack containing Felix's laptop and electronic jamming device, the late Takei's night-vision goggles and thermographic scope, and Hino's electric tools.

In the shadows between Buildings C and D, waiting for midnight, were five cars and three motorcycles driven by members of the Speed Tribe. Shinohara and the others were wearing black or dark-blue shirts or sweatshirts and black, rubber-soled sneakers, but the Tribe had prepared uniforms for them to wear over these—white tunics, like elongated happi coats, emblazoned on the back with the pagoda symbol the Koryos used. The trunks of the cars popped open to receive the large backpacks, and three team members jumped in each car, all holding daypacks. Shinohara, Hino, and Tateno, who were going to carry their bags to the air-conditioning machine room, would ride on the pillion seats of the bikes, so that they could spring instantly into action. Shinohara and Hino were told to climb on behind the Chief and bean-jam Koizumi, respectively, and Tateno jumped on behind another deputy, a guy who wore his long hair in a samurai-style *chonmage*. Hino's daypack held several gas cylinders for his cutting torch. He would use the torch to cut out the locks on any doors they needed to get through.

Toyohara had arrived a little late. Kaneshiro tried to get him to change out of his usual Hawaiian shirt, shorts, and sandals, but the Chief said there was no need for that—it was exactly the sort of outfit an off-duty Speed Triber might wear. Toyohara was also wearing a headband with something written in Hangul, and he had a short sword wrapped in cloth and strapped to his back. The sword became an issue, but Toyohara wouldn't be denied. He insisted he was fighting for Pop-Pop as well, and the others decided to let it go. There was something surreal about the figure he cut in his muumuu-like black shirt with its skulls-and-dragons motif, his shorts, his tattered leather sandals, and the samurai sword.

Perched atop the Chief's pompadour was a khaki DPRK People's Army cap, complete with an embroidered red star and a chin strap. He'd found it in a boutique in Tenjin. The two deputies wore headbands saying KORYO EXPEDITIONARY FORCE in both kanji and Hangul. Ishihara tried to get into one of the cars, but Kaneshiro stopped him. "Ishihara-san, please stay here and hold down the fort." Takeguchi and Ando nodded their agreement, as did Orihara and Okubo. Everyone was focused on this exchange. "Ya think?" Ishihara said, rolling his eyes this way and that. "Well, I and I *am* almost fifty, and still feeling the tequila from last night, and the old ears are ringing like fire alarms, so... Maybe I and I *would* just be in the way."

"It isn't that," Kaneshiro said, standing at attention. He had one of the daypacks reversed so that it hung against his chest. "All of us are really grateful to you for looking out for us all this time. Please stay behind and write a book about us. It doesn't matter if it gets published or not, but just tell our story. Will you do that?" Ishihara scratched his head in an embarrassed way and said, "We're not big on prose. Let's make it a poem, okay?" He looked around at everybody. "All right, then. Bon voyage. Or, as they say in English: *Habu a naisu torippu!*"

The cars and motorcycles departed one by one, moving slowly and quietly. All the vehicles had their mufflers hooked up. Just down the road, at the Odo *danchi*, construction was in progress on the barracks, and the thunder of unsilenced engines would only have drawn unwanted attention. They weren't likely to be attacked on the way, but if the convoy got stopped by the police and searched, it'd be all over. "Once we get closer," the Chief said to Shinohara, who was hanging on tight behind him, "we'll disconnect the mufflers and blast off." The Chief's ride was a vintage model. When Shinohara complimented him on it, he said, "You won't find one of these in your average used-bike lot." It was a lovingly restored 1970s Yamaha XJ-400. "I'm all right with dyin'," he said. "But I wouldn't ever want to wreck this thing."

As they were pulling away from Building C, Shinohara had turned to look back. Ishihara stood between C and D, quietly waving. It was too dark and too far to make out the expression on his face, but Shinohara imagined it to be his usual sleepy look. He was still badly hung-over and probably just waiting for them to move out of sight before hurrying to bed. No one who got sentimental in this sort of situation would have joined the group in the first place. Tearful farewells, endless love, unquestioning trust—all such things, Ishihara had taught them, were lies. He'd tried to climb into a car, but had he really meant to participate in the operation? Shinohara had once heard him say that he didn't mind dying but was scared to death of fear and pain.

Kaneshiro wanted Ishihara to write about them—did that mean he expected to die? They'd devised a detailed plan for infiltrating the hotel, but no one had said much about how they were going to avoid being hoist by their own LSCs. Once the charges were all set, they hoped to escape and head for the bay, where they'd position themselves behind a breakwater and set off the explosions by remote control—this rough outline of an exit plan was all they had. No one complained, however. No one here was the sort to look before leaping. Shinohara's take on death was similar to the Chief's. He didn't mind dying. He just didn't want to leave his dart frogs crying.

It was a humid night, with a ceiling of low-hanging clouds. As they approached the gasoline station where the rest of the Tribe were waiting Shinohara heard the roar of engines, so loud that it reverberated in his guts, and saw the sweeping cones of light created by criss-crossing headlamps. The gas station and the street in front of it were jammed with cars and bikes as far as he could see. Checkpoint C was visible from here. Some of the cars were mounted with searchlights, and the entire area was lit as bright as noon. Huge banners waved from car windows and flapped at the backs of bikes—some made up like the DPRK flag, some decorated with the Koryo pagoda symbol, even some inscribed KORYO EXPE-DITIONARY FORCE: FUKUOKA DIVISION. The banners were as much as four meters long. When the bike bearing Shinohara and the Chief arrived, the crowd erupted in cheers. "Must be three hundred rides here," the Chief muttered, surveying the scene. "More than I expected." Koizumi the bean-jam heir nodded and said, "Beautiful." The three eastbound lanes of Yokatopia Avenue were overflowing with vehicles as far as the Jigyohama 3-Chome intersection, and the noise was terrific. Checkpoint C was on the north-west corner of the intersection, the Hawks Town Mall on the north-east.

Koryo soldiers and some locals emerged from Hawks Town to see what was going on, and the soldiers at Checkpoint C already had their machine guns pointed this way and were working their cellphones. There were only three of them, but backup could arrive at any moment. Police getting involved would be the worst possible scenario. "It's time," the Chief said. He disconnected his muffler and told Koizumi to give the signal. Hino was on the back of Koizumi's bike, clinging to his pelvic bones with both hands. From either side of the engine protruded a shiny array of bugle-shaped horns. The deputy sounded two long blasts, like the shrieks of a heavy-metal singer, and the bikes and cars began maneuvering into formation.

When they were all in position, Koizumi cranked his siren again, just once. The passengers in all the cars leaned out of their windows, and the other deputy, the one with the samurai hairdo, counted off through a handheld loudspeaker—"Three, four! *Koryo Weonjeonggun, mansae-e-e-e-e! Koryo Weonjeonggun, chwego-o-o-o-o! Koryo Weonjeonggun, iptae shikhyeo-juseyo!*" Each time they shouted "*mansae*" they all raised both arms in the age-old "banzai" gesture. The bellowed chants and the howls of the horns and sirens split the night sky and echoed off the buildings. The sentries at Hawks Town and the soldiers at Checkpoint C were all looking this way wide-eyed, and Shinohara saw one of them smile. It must make even North Korean soldiers happy to hear the local citizens praising them in their own language. The Chief signaled again, Koizumi sounded his siren, and the convoy moved slowly forward until Speed Tribe vehicles filled the wide intersection.

"*Koryo Weonjeonggun, mansae-e-e-e-e!*" The chant went on. A taxi approaching from the direction of the special-needs school caught sight of the massive caravan, made a quick U-turn, and sped away. Koizumi got off the bike, turned slowly to face the checkpoint, silenced the mob with a blast of his siren, then picked up a loud-speaker to restart the chant. "*Koryo Weonjeonggun, mansae-e-e-e-e!*" he yelled, setting a slower rhythm. While that was going on, the Chief turned to Shinohara and said, "So, what happened to the media?" Ishihara's assertion that the Koryos wouldn't dare shoot because of the TV cameras had been nothing more than an expedient lie. "We're going to sneak into the hotel," Shinohara shouted into the Chief's ear, his nose nearly touching the pomade-smelling hair as he struggled to be heard above the engine noise and chanting. "If a TV camera caught us doin' that, and the Koryos saw it, we'd all be dead ducks," he added, throwing in a bit of Fukuoka dialect. The biker peered up at the cloudy sky and growled, "Oh yeah?" He seemed to be having second thoughts, which made Shinohara panic a bit. If the Tribe pulled out, the operation would fall apart before it ever got started. The Chief turned to face him, a deep furrow creasing his brow, eyes wide and intense. "Hell, I'm a man," he said. "The Chief of the Hakatakko Devils. Hang on, brother. Here we go." He drew a whistle from his pocket and gave a long, ear-splitting shriek on it. At this, Koizumi drove slowly up to the soldiers at Checkpoint C and blasted his siren. He pointed at his own chest, then pointed to the road beyond the checkpoint—*Can we pass?* The soldiers made no eye contact with him but shook their heads expressionlessly.

Koizumi placed his palms together as if pleading, then shouted, "*Koryo Weonjeonggun, mansae-e-e-e!*" and gave two short squeals with his siren. At that signal, a dozen or more cars and bikes began doing a high-speed zigzag up and down the half-kilometer stretch of Yokatopia Avenue between Checkpoint B and Checkpoint D, weaving a lace-like pattern at full throttle, racing their engines, waving their banners, and sounding their klaxons and sirens. Some of the bikes popped wheelies and the modified lowriders scraped the asphalt and spat sparks. It had to be an astonishing sight for the Koryos: the sentries at Hawks Town leaned out to watch, and even the machine-gun-toting checkpoint guards turned their heads to observe this array of colorful, glittering vehicles perform such intricate high-speed maneuvers.

There was a warmish onshore wind. The Chief carefully gauged his timing before blowing his skull-piercing whistle once again. The bikes and cars still in formation raced their engines, and the zigzag-gers slid to a halt with a great screeching of rubber. When all the headlamps up and down Yokatopia Avenue were turned toward the encampment, the Chief took the lead, bellowing like a bull as he roared across the avenue, with the rest of the vehicles—a hundred-plus cars and nearly two hundred motorcycles—peeling out en masse and blowing right through the three checkpoints into the occupied grounds. All of them were already inside the Koryo-controlled zone when a crackle of warning shots punctured the sky. The Chief led his division past Checkpoint C and straight down the highway toward the hotel and Dome, but more than a hundred vehicles had entered through different routes, breaching Checkpoints B and D as well as the two narrow streets on either side of the Chinese consulate and even the Hawks Town parking lot.

The Chief was still at full throttle as the Dome loomed up on their right and the road curved sharply to the left. He laid the bike so low that Shinohara's knee nearly scraped the asphalt. The long, narrow white lane markers blinked past at blinding speed, the wind in his face was so strong that he could barely keep his eyes open, and the trailing happi coat flapped and snapped violently behind him, as if trying to rip itself to shreds. He could see the Koryo camp on the left. Dozens of soldiers came out to the side of the road and looked on, AKs in hand. The bikes and cars that had taken alternate routes joined the main division in front of the Kyushu Medical Center, and the two deputies pulled up on either side of the Chief's bike. Hino and Tateno were plastered to the backs of Koizumi and Chonmage to protect themselves from the wind, and both were shouting with either excitement or terror—it was hard to tell if they were grin-ning or grimacing. Shinohara thought that the same was probably true of himself. Then the Chief's body seemed to stiffen. Ahead on the left was a group of Koryo soldiers. The soldiers raised their left hands, palm out, signaling them to stop, but the Chief didn't even slow down. Would they actually shoot? Shinohara heard the Chief shouting: "*Koryo Weonjeonggun, chwego-o-o-o-o!*" The deputies on either side were driving one-handed, with megaphones in their free hands, supporting the chant. Kaneshiro, Fukuda, and Ando were half outside their cars, waving DPRK flags and joining in: "*Mansae-e-e-e-e! Chwego-o-o-o-o!*" Could the soldiers hear it? Shinohara too was shouting at the top of his voice, and so were Hino and Tateno. At this point it wasn't even about trying to be heard by the Koryos; you had to scream something if only to keep the fear at bay.

The headlamps illuminated the faces of the soldiers beside the road. Their AKs were lowered, not trained on the riders. One face leaped out at Shinohara, a soldier who was smirking as if to say, *What a bunch of idiots*. And with that, Shinohara was assured that they weren't going to shoot. To them, this was just a laughable display by the lowest sort of dimwitted, decadent punks, who admired them and actually wanted to enlist. The Chief slowed the bike as they approached Checkpoint A, a bit past the entrance to the hotel, where he was going to make a hard right, and at that moment a number of bare-chested, off-duty Koryos, red-faced and clearly drunk, ran toward the convoy, shouting along: "*Mansae-e-e-e-e! Chwego-o-o-o-o!*" They pantomimed driving motorcycles and waving banners, and they laughed as they chanted and slapped one another's backs. Two soldiers stood smoking at the checkpoint, their AKs hanging slack as they watched the riders. Their guard was down. After all, they had yet to run into a single Japanese civilian who resisted or fought back. Shinohara prayed that they would continue to think of this as just a parade of idiots. *Sneer at us. Laugh at us. No need to be wary. We're here to deliver a special gift.*

The speeding horde turned right at Checkpoint A and followed the two-lane road, driving straight toward the sea for about a hundred meters before swerving hard to the right. With the jet-black waters of Hakata Bay on their left now, the road was a straight shot as far as Checkpoint E. The perimeter of the zone under Koryo control was a line that encompassed the Sea Hawk Hotel and the Dome, Hawks Town and the hospital, and the South Korean and Chinese consulates. Felix and Matsuyama had done a thorough study of the roads in the immediate area and discovered one spot that wouldn't be visible from any of the checkpoints. Adjoining the hotel on the opposite side was a glassed-in, steel-framed structure that protruded like a burl at the bottom of a tree. The steps that led up to it started at the sidewalk right next to the road, where the hotel blocked the view from Checkpoint A and the structure itself from Checkpoint E.

The Koryos had taken extra care to defend against infiltration from the sea, and the entire shoreline of the occupied zone was visible from Checkpoints A and E. To attack from the beach would have got you annihilated: the checkpoints were equipped with machine guns, and even if you got past them, soldiers and MAVs from the encampment would be all over you. But the terror babies' ploy had been improbable enough to work. The Koryos didn't see this mob as the enemy but as a loony fan club. After rounding the bend, the Chief slowed down, letting those behind roll past as he pulled up to the curb next to the steps. A different division, which had entered near Checkpoint D and taken the other way around the Dome, appeared from the opposite direction and roared past. The five cars carrying Kaneshiro, Takeguchi, and others, and the two bikes with Hino and Tateno on board pulled up to the curb behind the Chief. Trunks popped open and baggage was rapidly stacked on the sidewalk.

"If anything happens, I'll ring your cellphone," the Chief told Shinohara, and sped off the moment everyone and everything was unloaded. The two deputies and the cars all peeled off after him. Everyone shouldered a backpack, cradled a daypack in their arms, and ran at full speed up the steps. It wasn't easy negotiating the steps in the darkness, and there was a fair amount of stumbling, but they met no resistance. Kaneshiro reached the top first and checked to make sure the landing was deserted, then hissed for Hino. Hino, carrying only a daypack, ran past him straight for the entrance to the glass structure. Shinohara and Tateno followed with the extra acetylene and oxygen cylinders.

Shinohara's memory of what happened after they'd sped past the checkpoint and entered the occupied zone was a jumble. From the point where he climbed off the bike and ran up the steps with his backpack, his impressions seemed all the more unreal—all stop-frame or fast-forward. The entrance to the structure was a pair of big glass doors. Hino pulled out his cutting torch and attached the little one-liter tanks of acetylene gas and oxygen. He checked the sound of the gas escaping, lit a clear disposable lighter that had YOTCHAN'S PUB printed on it in black, and held the flame to the nozzle. It ignited with a satisfying *poof*, creating a wavering orange flame that Shinohara was worried the Koryos might see. But Hino immediately turned a valve and transformed the flame into a hissing, thin blue stream. "This is the sort of flame you need to cut steel," he whispered as he raised the torch to the gap between the doors, then sputtered: "What the hell?" He turned off the torch and pushed on one panel. It swung open to a black interior and smells of vegetation and decay. There was no sign of any human presence.

"Why would the Koryos leave it open?" Hino whispered. "What are they, a bunch of doodoo-heads?" Tateno muffled a laugh with a hand over his mouth, and Shinohara too had to suppress giggles that made his stomach muscles spasm. Knowing he mustn't make any sound only made it worse—his nervous system demanded laughter to relieve the tension. After the door swung open, Kaneshiro and the others streamed in, keeping low beneath their backpacks. Kaneshiro held a handgun at the ready. "That was fast," he said as he went past Shinohara. "The damn door—" He was unable to finish the sentence for fear of laughing again. It was only when someone said "Toyohara's not here" that Shinohara abruptly sobered up. Beyond the large, drooping leaves of some darkly silhouetted tropical plants was a shopping arcade. All the lights were off, so they decided to hunker down there for the time being. Toyohara's not here? Shinohara wondered where the hell he could be, but the first order of business was to establish a base camp. By the dim glow of emergency exit signs they walked along a corridor that curved to the right.

Ahead was the shopping arcade. The doors to all the stores were open. Goods and papers were scattered about in some of them. The salesclerks must have left in a hurry when news of the Koryo takeover of the Dome reached them. To the right was a rental shop for formalwear and a photography studio, to the left a cafe. On the tables in the cafe were half-empty glasses with straws protruding, unfinished cups of coffee, and plates with partially eaten slices of cake. The centerpiece of the rental shop's window display was a wedding dress and tuxedo designed with a Hawks motif. "What happened to Toyohara?" Shinohara asked, and Kaneshiro gave him an angry look and whispered, "Shut up." The lobby used by the Koryos was on this floor. And they couldn't be certain yet that even this arcade was deserted. They all walked slowly under their heavy loads, one hand to the wall, one noiseless step at a time. A sportswear shop; a clothes boutique; shops selling handbags, perfume, cosmetics; a variety store. At the first corner were a cake shop and a bakery, and in front of the latter was a large stainless-steel kettle full of raw cream with a layer of black mold on top. Then came a little shop offering fashion accessories; one with traditional Central and South America handicrafts; one selling Chinese teas and various bric-a-brac; and near the exit a caricaturist's table and chairs, under which lay the artist's renderings of an American actor and a Japanese politician.

After making sure no Koryos were in the arcade, they made their way back down the corridor to the formalwear shop, where they took off the backpacks. They were all breathing heavily, and many of them gulped down some water. Sweat beaded Shinohara's forehead and the bridge of his nose. He was about to ask Kaneshiro about Toyohara again when the cellphone in his pocket rang, making his heart nearly jump out of his mouth. Kaneshiro slapped him hard and said, "Turn the ringer off, you fool!" Shinohara tried to apologize, but nothing came out—his throat was so dry it had closed up. He could hear the biker Chief on the phone. Hino handed him a bottle of water, and he chugged it. "Shinohara here," he gasped. "Are you in?" the Chief asked. "Listen. One of your guys—the skinhead who's built like a weightlifter?" Shinohara said, "Toyohara, yeah," and asked where he was. "He's dead," the Chief told him. Shinohara put his hand over the mouthpiece and relayed this to the others.

It seemed that Toyohara had been so delirious with excitement that he forgot to get out of the car when it stopped at the bottom of the steps, but as the convoy was leaving the occupied zone he threw a tantrum and demanded to be let off. When they stopped and let him out, he unsheathed his katana and ran straight for the Koryo soldiers at Checkpoint D. One of the soldiers shot him in the knee with his AK, and Toyohara went down. As he did so, his injured wrist gave out, turning the tip of the weapon against his chest. He literally fell on his own sword, which ran him right through. Even the Koryos seemed stunned by this. The Chief had quickly turned his bike over to another member and dragged the body into one of the cars. Before they drove away, he pulled the sword from Toyohara's body, and "it was like openin' a spigot—blood just gushin' out." But Toyohara was already dead. "I'm sorry," were his last words, mouthed as he lay in the Chief's arms. "That skinhead was pretty weird," the Chief said, "but he done a helluva job." The way he saw it, Toyohara's performance with the samurai sword had deflected attention from the hotel. He went on to say that they didn't want to lead the cops back to Ishihara's place, so they'd take the body elsewhere. He also said they'd make sure Toyohara's family was contacted, if he had any.

"I know he's got a grandfather in Saga," Shinohara said, before realizing he didn't know the old man's name. Neither did anyone else. "It wouldn't be Toyohara Pop-Pop, would it?" somebody suggested but was ignored. Since the attack of giggles after finding the door open, Shinohara's nerves had gone numb and unresponsive. He was no more capable of being shocked now than he was capable of laughing. "We don't know his name or address, though," he said into the phone. No one even knew Toyohara's own given name, as it turned out. "I think it was Kensaku," someone said, but the others shook their heads. Satoru, Taro, Hitoshi—several guesses were put forward, but none of them rang a bell. "No worries. We'll take care of the burial," the Chief said, and clicked off. Shinohara just couldn't process the news or respond appropriately to it. They had broken inside enemy lines, and there was no room in this rush of sensations for sadness. They had too much to plan and think about right now. And it occurred to him that if he himself were to die, that too would scarcely cause a ripple at a time like this. One of eighteen remaining lights has been extinguished—it made no more impression than that. "I wonder who Toyohara was apologizing to," Yamada muttered, but no one ventured an answer.

Five of them—Hino, Tateno, Shinohara, Kaneshiro, and Fukuda—left in search of the air-conditioning-machine room. The rest were to lie low in the shop. "I know we've been over this several times, but remember," Kaneshiro told everyone in a whisper before leaving. "It's hard to tell because we entered from the rear of the hotel, but this is the fourth floor—the same floor as the main lobby, where the Koryos come and go. The lobby is just on the other side of that wall. Whatever happens, don't make a sound, and don't leave this spot till we come back for you." Kaneshiro and Fukuda stuffed their pockets with handguns and grenades and took the two daypacks with the acetylene and oxygen tanks. Hino carried another filled with four different welding and cutting torches, and Shinohara and Tateno shouldered the two backpacks full of insects. Leaving the shop, they walked down a dark corridor about two meters wide with the artificial jungle on either side. After they'd gone some distance they could see light leaking out from the gaps in the partition separating the arcade from the lobby.

The previous day Kaneshiro and Fukuda had handed out copies of their sketches of the relevant floor plans and told everyone to memorize them, but the layout of this hotel was incredibly confusing. Floors three to six, in particular, comprised a veritable labyrinth—you couldn't tell what was connected to what, or where. Viewed from above, the hotel tower was shaped like a ship. On the Dome side of the hotel proper was a structure about the size of a soccer ground, an annex that housed a complex of shops and facilities connected by a bewildering array of corridors and stairways and escalators and elevators. On the third floor, where the Koryos had their command center, were a Christian chapel, a Japanese-style wedding room, and a number of smaller banquet rooms. The fourth floor was the most complicated of all, with the shopping arcade, the artificial jungle, and dozens of restaurants, not to mention the main lobby and front desk on the other side of that partition. Adjoining the fifth floor was a members-only gym, and the sixth opened onto a large outdoor garden with Japanese and Korean restaurants. This was the top level of the facilities annex; from the fifth floor up there was only the smooth hull of the ship-shaped tower rising skyward.

The smell of decay came from a clump of benjamin and rubber trees in the jungle. There was an enormous birdcage there, and with no one to care for them the birds had quickly died. The dimly lit lobby was visible now beyond rows of pillars. It was one in the morning. Shinohara's view was limited, but he saw no sign that anyone was in the lobby. As they headed for the escalator that rose from the jungle, the headlights of a distant car swept over the glass doors of the lobby entrance, and the silhouette of a Koryo guard jumped into focus. His AK wasn't slung over his shoulder but held diagonally against his chest. He was standing just outside the big front doors. For Shinohara, it was like being in a safari park and spotting his first lion. There were two sets of doors with an air curtain between. "The inner doors probably have fire shutters," Hino whispered. Fukuda pointed at the entrance and said, "We could place the antipersonnel mines there, once all the Koryos are out."

There was a total of four birdcages in the jungle. The birds were all large parrots, and between the bars you could see them lying on the ground with bright red, blue, and yellow feathers protruding in every direction. The smell was the particular smell produced when maggots have hatched in dead meat. The escalator to the fifth floor wasn't moving. Kaneshiro and Fukuda took the lead, squatting on the escalator steps, hunched forward, and pushing themselves up backwards one step at a time, to keep the profiles of their backpacks beneath the railing. They had to take care not to be visible from the entrance, or from the fifth and sixth floor balconies overlooking the lobby, although the fact that the escalators weren't moving suggested that the Koryos weren't using those floors.

Shinohara had drunk a whole bottle of water while on the phone, but his throat was already dry again. He tried to form spit to swallow, but none came. Humping up the steps backwards, balancing a load that was nearly as big as himself, his back and buttocks and thighs began to burn. When they reached the landing, they saw that the fifth floor was in total darkness. Shinohara whispered to Kaneshiro that he was so parched he could hardly breathe. "Me too," Kaneshiro said, rubbing his throat; and Hino, Fukuda, and Tateno nodded. Some faint light from emergency exits filtered in, but it was too dark to see their surroundings clearly. They had all gulped a lot of water in the formalwear shop and thought that would do them, so they'd economized on weight by not bringing anything to drink. Only now did they realize how stupid that was. "Anyway, let's go on," Hino said, jerking his chin toward the darkness. "It's a health club for rich people. There must at least be some bottled water."

They were in the corridor that connected the annex with the tower of guest rooms. According to the floor plan, the fitness club was at the far end of the corridor, and if you turned right from there you entered the tower. The main elevators were in the middle of the tower, but the Koryos used those. The plan was to enter the fitness club, proceed to the pool area, exit through a door at the rear, and cross the patio garden to a stairway that led to the sixth floor. They felt their way along the wall and soon came to a heavy steel door. They couldn't see a knob or handle. Tateno caught his backpack on some sort of sign that protruded from the wall next to it and stumbled forward. He put his hand on the door to stop himself, and it swung silently open, so that he kept going and would have fallen on his face had Hino and Fukuda not grabbed his backpack from behind and held him upright. The lights of the emergency-exit signs dimly illuminated the lobby of the fitness club, which was littered with swimming suits, bathing caps, and scattered papers. The walls were adorned with what looked like ceremonial African masks of carved wood. "What's with those things?" Fukuda said in a low voice. The masks were spooky in the pale light.

541

Tateno found a brochure, and they followed its simple map to the locker room. Kaneshiro nearly took a tumble at the step where you were supposed to take off your shoes. Inside were distinct areas separated by narrow rows of lockers—washrooms, toilets, showers, baths, massage rooms, and what have you. It was a bit maze-like, but they finally found their way to the pool area. Dotted around the pool were jacuzzis of various sizes. Except for the emergency-exit signs, all electricity was shut down, so the water hadn't been circulating and was stagnant. Sticking out from the wall over one of the jacuzzis was an installation in the shape of tree roots, and the poles supporting the canopies were meant to resemble trees of the African savannah. Next to the pool was a glassed-in snack bar. Because the refrigeration was off, all of the bottled water and soft drinks were warm. They chose colas.

Beyond the pool was a glass door that led to the patio garden—a long, narrow, balcony-like strip of landscaping. This door too was open. Why didn't the Koryos lock the doors? It must be because there was no real need to, Shinohara decided. There weren't any Japanese who were going to try to break into the North Korean occupation army command center. Shinohara and the others crouched low, threading their way through the hedges and moving from bush to tree across ten meters or so of garden. The Dome loomed up right in front of them, like a gently rounded silver spaceship against the low clouds. There were two more jacuzzis out here and benches and deckchairs placed randomly about. Discarded towels and bathrobes lay scattered on the ground. At the far end of the garden was a flight of steps that would take them up to the sixth-floor level. From the bottom of the steps you could see Checkpoint E in the distance. They had to slip the backpacks off their shoulders, hold them tucked under one arm, and crawl up on their sides.

It wasn't easy dragging yourself up the steps on a bony elbow while hanging on to a huge backpack. Shinohara was reminded of the way poison worked its way into the body. It was as if the hotel were a gigantic organism and he a drop of poison. To do its work, poison first has to enter the body by being eaten or drunk or inhaled or injected. Probably the easiest route for it to take, however, was through an open wound. We are poison entering the Koryos' bloodstream through a tear in their flesh, he thought, struggling to ignore the pain in his elbow and legs as he crawled up the steps.

When he finally reached the landing, Fukuda was lying there on his stomach peering straight ahead and gesturing for him to stay down. Kaneshiro too was flat on the bricks, frozen. Shinohara opened his mouth, but Fukuda shushed him with a finger to the lips. Directly in front of them were hedges of azaleas and hydrangeas. Beyond these hedges was a landscape garden about the size of two basketball courts, bordered at the other end by a number of small old-timey Japanese buildings connected by covered walkways. There were white gravel paths in the garden, pines and plum trees, stone lanterns, and two ponds—one crescent-shaped and one kidney-shaped. Hino and Tateno reached the landing, and Fukuda signaled them too not to speak or budge. Kaneshiro crawled slowly backward until he was level with Shinohara. "Something's moving," he whispered. Peering through the azaleas into the dark grounds, Shinohara could indeed see movement near a stone lantern beside the crescent pond.

"Dogs," Kaneshiro said, keeping his head low. It was hard to make out in the dark, but yes, there were two dogs standing side by side, worrying something in the grass. "What are dogs doing in a roof garden?" Hino muttered beneath his breath. "*We* got in here," Fukuda whispered. "Even easier for them." Kaneshiro scowled and said, "In any case, they're dogs. If they see us they'll bark." Any sudden barking, and the Koryos would surely come to investigate. The dogs seemed to be tearing meat from something on the ground. Among the small buildings was a seafood restaurant with a fish tank. Maybe it wasn't so strange that stray dogs should find their way here to feast on the dead fish or whatever.

Fukuda suggested they go back and use the emergency stairway, but Hino shook his head. "Too dangerous. That stairwell's right next to the elevator hall." Kaneshiro was peering at Tateno. "Can you kill them with?..." Tateno tilted his head, gauging the distance, and said it was difficult because of the building right behind the dogs. "I'll give it a shot, though," he told him. Near the shrine in Meinohama where he collected insects, Shinohara had seen Tateno throw his boomerangs a number of times. When somebody used one in movies or manga, it would cut off the target's head or arm and come right back to the thrower, who would catch it in his bare hand. But Tateno had assured him that this was impossible: to try to catch a razor-sharp blade that was spinning so fast as to be a blur would be suicidal. The idea was to have the boomerang return and stick in the ground in front of you. Tateno took the L-shaped leather case from his daypack and extracted a bundle of boomerangs with blades about twenty centimeters long. "They could ricochet off the gravel," he whispered, "so I'll bring them back to this bush. You'd better go back down the steps."

Kaneshiro and Fukuda exchanged a doubtful glance, but when Shinohara mentioned that the blades were coated with centipede poison, they meekly retreated into the stairwell. Tateno selected two boomerangs, tested the feel of their grips, and removed the plastic wrapping from their blades. The grip ends had little grooves, and Tateno had spent hours winding them tightly with string. Each was slightly different from the other, and apparently he chose his weapons in a given situation instinctively, by feel. He licked a finger and held it up to test the wind, then rose to a crouch with the two boomerangs in his left hand and crept behind the azaleas. Shinohara was thinking it must be hard to home in on a target in such dim light, when Tateno suddenly stood up and made two successive slicing motions with his right forearm and wrist. There was a soft *whoosh*, and then another. "Did he throw them?" whispered Hino. Kaneshiro said, "Where'd they go?" Just then one of the blades glinted as it swept above the surface of the pond. It didn't look L-shaped but circular. The first boomerang passed about ten centimeters over the dogs' heads and then swung upwards. Fukuda shook his head and said, "Missed." Hearing the first one pass above them, the dogs reflexively looked up, and the moment they raised their heads the second one skimmed beneath their jaws.

One after the other, the boomerangs banked in front of the building and headed back this way in a pair of pretty arcs, finally embedding themselves in the azaleas in front of Tateno. Both dogs squealed briefly and made as if to scratch at their throats with their hind legs but then collapsed like unstrung puppets. Tateno carefully extracted the boomerangs from the bushes, where they had sheared through several large branches. There was no blood on the blades. Tateno wiped them down, quickly wrapped them in plastic, and put them back in the leather case. When Kaneshiro asked if the dogs' throats had been slit right through, Tateno just said, "The poison got 'em."

They crept across the garden in the shadow of the bushes and trees, then through the seafood restaurant to a corridor that led to the hotel tower. Guest rooms on the middle and upper floors overlooked the garden, so they hadn't dawdled to inspect the dead dogs, but there didn't seem to be any blood where they lay. Tateno said that if the cut was clean enough, sometimes there was very little bleeding. "If not for the poison, I'd have had to cut their heads off, or stick the blades in their hearts, to make sure they died."

Fukuda wondered aloud if it was all right to leave the carcasses lying there. Kaneshiro said the Koryos would just think the dogs had eaten something bad, and Hino smiled and said, "What if they ate the dogs? Would *they* die?" Shinohara said, no, they wouldn't, though it might give them the runs. He was pleased with his blend of star anise, *Rohdea japonica*, and centipede. Judging from the way the dogs had dropped, it was clear that the poison had worked directly on the heart. Kaneshiro asked Tateno if he'd thrown the first one too high on purpose, so the dogs would look up, at which he just smiled very slightly and said, "Secret." He wasn't excited or puffed up at having brought down his target but casual and matter-of-fact. Like a carpenter who'd just repaired a friend's bookshelf, Shinohara thought.

Fluorescent lights illuminated the elevator hall on the sixth floor of the tower. Kaneshiro and Fukuda checked it out, and once they were sure no one was in there, they signaled for the others to come. The four elevator shafts were in the center of the ship-shaped tower.

The rooms on the "port" side of them were in the Japanese style, with fancy names rather than numbers—*Cloud Grass*, *Willow Flower*, *Fragrance of May*, and so on—and across from *Crimson Camellia* and *Green Destiny* was a door marked PRIVATE.

This was unlocked, and beyond it was a room-service corridor, with shelves of tableware, a staff room, a storage area for cleaning equipment, shelves of toothpaste and razors and other amenities, four more elevators for service or emergency use, and an office. Farther on was another door that said AUTHORIZED PERSONNEL ONLY, behind which was a space lined with electric switchboards. Hino identified it as the electrical room and shut the door. They continued another twenty or thirty meters along the narrow corridor, between pipes and valves, until they came to a door with EMERGENCY GENERATOR on it, opposite which was yet another door, a gray one. A low rumbling emanated from behind it, and the concrete floor beneath them vibrated noticeably. There was no lock on the door, and Hino turned the handle and pulled it open.

It was cold inside. The room was deep and wide and filled with rows of gigantic, unfamiliar machines. They all looked the same to Shinohara, but Hino studied each of them and the control panel on one of the pillars, saying, "So that's the boiler... This is the air-conditioning unit," and so on, then stood in front of one machine about the size of a shipping container. "This is it," he said, and began preparing his equipment. The ventilator looked less like a machine than a prefab house made of thin sheet metal. There was a cylindrical fan housing in front, a big box of the same sheet metal at the back, and stacked in between were dozens of metal meshwork plates. Two square ducts protruded from beside the fan and one more from the big box behind it, and all were wrapped in silvery insulation. Hino laid his tools on the stainless-steel frame that lined the machine's base, then stepped up and began stripping insulation from the duct in the rear. He pried out each staple connecting the seams and gently removed the silver, cottony material, revealing the bare duct, which was big enough to have accommodated several bodies side by side.

Hino attached the hoses to the acetylene and oxygen tanks, hooked them up to the torch, and told Shinohara to be ready with the insects. He wanted to cover the hole up again as soon as the bugs were released inside. Apparently if the fan's output decreased for an extended period, the machinery would, for safety reasons, automatically shut down. Shinohara and Tateno opened the two large backpacks and with the help of Kaneshiro and Fukuda took out the vinyl sacks of flies, crickets, springtails, and camel spiders and the flat Tupperware containers filled with centipedes. "Wow," Kaneshiro muttered, turning his face aside as he lifted one of the sacks of flies. Into each long, narrow bag, the capacity of which was roughly a liter, Shinohara had put about ten thousand flies—close to the maximum number for that amount of air. The flies and crickets and springtails surged thickly against the inner walls of the sacks, looking almost like a milky liquid. Hino opened the two valves on the tanks and checked the numbers on the gas regulator. With the torch in his right hand, he called Shinohara over and pointed at a seam on the air duct. "I'll cut out a square from this seam down. As soon as I pry it open, bung in the bugs."

Hino continued to mutter as if to himself as he pulled out the YOTCHAN'S PUB lighter and ignited the torch: "With galvanized sheet iron, it's hard to get the flame right, so that it doesn't melt and stick back together." He turned the valve on the torch to transform the flame into a narrow blue stream, the tip of which he positioned diagonally against the metal, cutting through it as if it were paper. It took only a few seconds to cut three sides of the square. He then inserted a screwdriver into the uppermost gap and pried open a strip about the size of a sports tabloid. A low rumbling issued from the hole, inside which Shinohara placed one end of the first vinyl sack. He slit the end open with a box cutter and whispered, "Bon voyage." The flies billowed out in a cloud, like a giant dandelion disintegrating in the wind, and disappeared inside the duct.

There wasn't so much as a draft or breeze in the artificial jungle. Tateno had folded the green wedding dress into a small bundle, which he was now tying with string. Shinohara asked him what he was going to do with it, and Tateno said that after sleeping with the thing all this time he'd become attached to it and thought he'd use it for naps during the LSC-setting operation. "A whole day we've spent here," Shinohara said, looking up at the glass ceiling. If the hotel came down, this structure would be the first to be crushed. Not even a trace would be left of all these plants. If only he could use a place like this as a vivarium for his dart frogs—he'd had this thought any number of times during the past twenty-four hours. With this much space, he could recreate morning mists and evening squalls. He could spread moss and fallen leaves and make a system of circulating creeks. He could stock the place with small animals and birds, and maybe even a few large reptiles. In the abundant puddles and pools, the frogs would lay their eggs and carry their young around on their backs between the garish flowers, to bathe in the wells of neoregelias and tillandsias and other bromeliads.

But he couldn't help feeling that there was something unsound about even this vision of his, and in the end he always came back to thinking that this artificial jungle too needed to be destroyed. Hanging from the semicircular glass wall was a neon sign saying CAFE LUGGNAGG. The whole thing was meant to be a representation of some fictional South Pacific island paradise, a superficially recon-structed scene to give visitors a "tropical experience." Shinohara's actual vivarium, though much smaller than this, represented an effort to recreate the tropics from the inside out, so to speak, in that he gave priority to making conditions ideal for the raising and breeding of his frogs. This place, like so much in this world, was about faking it. Before coming to Fukuoka, everyone he'd ever met had been faking something, pretending to be something other than what they were. There were prototypes for the warm, loving family; the good, upstanding citizen; the fulfilled, happy life—and people tried to conform to those types, to fit themselves into those molds.

"Shall we?" he said, and they headed first for the lobby. Before beginning operations on the fifth floor, Takeguchi wanted to make sure that the noise they'd be making couldn't be heard from there.

When attaching the LSCs to the columns, you needed to leave a precisely gauged gap, which was referred to as the stand-off, in order to maximize the metal jet's cutting power. For thirty-millimeter-thick steel frames, the ideal stand-off was 2.5 centimeters. Takeguchi and Fukuda had brought hundreds of matchbox-size blocks of styrofoam to attach to the columns and serve as platforms for the LSCs. The columns were covered with cloth or marble or wood veneers that had to be removed in order to judge the stand-off correctly. Hino was in charge of cutting through the coverings, but he would need to use electric tools, which would produce noise and vibrations. They had to know if this work on the fifth floor would be detectable below.

The corridor leading directly to the lobby from the artificial jungle was blocked by fire shutters. Shinohara and Tateno walked back to the end of the shopping arcade and crossed through the office behind the front desk out into the lobby. The Koryos had evacuated the fourth floor that morning and locked all the entrances and exits, stopped the elevators, and closed the fire shutters. The shutters had been lowered on the entrance as well, and a powerful smell of fumigants was in the air. "Amazing that all the flies are gone already," Tateno said as they walked across the empty lobby. After sending the insects through the air ducts into the large banquet room on the third floor, Shinohara had released the remaining hundred thousand or so flies directly on the fourth, fifth, and sixth floors.

Most of the centipedes had gone into the banquet room, and after saving one containerful for emergency use, he'd scattered the rest in the fourth-floor lobby. These the Koryos seemed to have got rid of, but Shinohara had also prepared a quantity of powdered medium which he'd injected into the third-floor air ducts along with the flies. It hadn't been scientifically proven, but according to Shinohara's experience, flies tended to seek out and stick to the medium in which they were hatched and raised. Whenever he messed up and accidentally let a large number of flies escape, he would put the medium they'd been hatched in outside in the trash, and the next thing he knew they'd be gone. He was sure that the flies released on the higher floors would make their way down to the third. "You think they get homesick for where they were born?" Tateno asked him. He said he didn't know, but that he'd seen them distinguish between their own medium and another batch made of exactly the same ingredients.

The cellphone vibrated in his pocket. It was Takeguchi, asking him to go and stand in the men's room next to the express elevator. He made his way to the guest tower in the darkness. His eyes had become accustomed to the dim light from the exit signs, but no light at all reached inside the restroom. He switched on his penlight and reported to Takeguchi that he was in. "If you face the wall, you should see the bulge of a column in the right-hand corner. I'm going to cut through the covering on that column up here for about three seconds. Let me know how much you can hear or feel down there." A moment later there was a sound like a rain shower issuing from the ceiling above. Shinohara asked him to do it again and put his hand on the column. He heard the same faint noise and felt a slight vibration. "Well?" Takeguchi said. "It's all right," Shinohara told him. The Koryos were in the first-floor banquet hall now, and that had a two-story-high ceiling. There was little chance of their noticing anything.

"Good," Takeguchi said. "Come on up." The staticky sound of the electric cutter started up again. The operation had begun. Takeguchi had been laying out the wires to connect the LSCs since earlier that day, and that part of the work was now completed. *Eleven more hours*, Shinohara thought as he hurried across the lobby.

# 10

# TATTLETALE

*April 11, 2011*

O NOE CHIKAKO removed the additive-free waffle from the oven, poured some Japanese lotus honey over it, and put it on the table along with a few organic cherry tomatoes, fresh orange juice, and some Koiwai pasteurized milk. She was determined to feed her kids the healthiest food money could buy. Her daughter, Risako, had already eaten and left for school. It was apparently her turn to look after the school rabbit, so she'd had to leave early. Risako had just started her second year of elementary at Nishijin municipal, although ideally Chikako would have sent her to a private school. Nishijin was one of the best, but the standard of municipal education in Fukuoka had been steadily declining, and there was always the bullying problem, although it wasn't as bad here as in Tokyo and Osaka. Her hope was that in a few years she'd be able to send Risako to a private middle school for gifted kids.

Her son, Kenta, was pointing at the TV screen and saying, "Boats! Mommy, look, boats!" It was the NHK morning news. A nervous newscaster was announcing that the North Korean fleet had reached the border of the exclusive economic zone between Japan and Korea, and was now passing to the west of Takeshima, proceeding southwards. The South Koreans hadn't dispatched any of their navy and apparently had no intention of using armed force to stop the fleet from heading for Japan, and the US forces in Korea had issued a statement to similar effect. The screen switched to a shot of Japanese coastguard and naval vessels: sleek gray things with gleaming paintwork and names like *Chikuzen, Kunisaki, Genkai, Hayanami, Ariake, Kirisame,* and *Inazuma* visible on their hulls. Compared to these ships, the patched-up North Korean fleet looked more like a flotilla of refugee boats. Some of them were red with rust or listing heavily as they sailed. They were all being used as troopships, with some of the larger ones carrying several thousand men, many sitting on the decks huddled against the wind, now and then glancing up impassively at an NHK helicopter filming them. They would reach Japanese territorial waters in about four hours, the news anchor solemnly reported.

Kenta was glued to the TV screen, scraping honey from the waffle's lattice grooves and licking the spoon but otherwise leaving the food untouched. "Eat your tomatoes!" she told him, and pushed a piece into his mouth. He chewed, then went "Waah!" and dribbled sticky red juice down the front of his bib. Chikako turned off the TV and wiped up the mess. Kenta seemed to think she was cross with him and kept his eyes down, looking tearful. "It's almost time to go to school, so at least have a bit of milk," she said gently, but he recoiled dramatically at the word "school."

Chikako lived in a public-housing complex in Momochi, and Kenta's kindergarten was opposite Central Park in Nishijin. When traffic was light it was just a few minutes by car, but on Monday mornings the roads were always busier than usual, and she had to leave a little early. She put the cap with the kindergarten's logo on Kenta's head, eased his schoolbag over his shoulders, and pushed a handkerchief into his pocket, then led him toward the front door. But Kenta slumped to the floor, his arms hanging limply at his sides. Not again, thought Chikako. She'd hoped things would get better once he reached the last year of kindergarten, but she'd been too optimistic. For some reason or other, he'd started to hate going there.

She took hold of his hand and tried to make him get up, but he shook her away with surprising strength. Then he tore his cap off and lay down there in the hallway. "What's wrong?" she asked him, but he just said, "Not going!" and tried to shake himself free of his bag. "But what about Yoshi and Kimi and the others? They're all waiting for you." Taking him under each arm she picked him up and, holding him close, tried to reassure him as she left the apartment. Kenta struggled in her arms, then burst into tears. One of the neighbors, a housewife, was coming down the corridor and smiled at the crying child, commenting dryly, "My, we are in a good mood this morning!" Chikako gave her a brief "Good morning" and got into the elevator. This past week, everyone in the housing complex seemed different in the way they behaved toward her. It wasn't that anyone had been nasty, but they'd been rather keeping their distance.

Maybe she should have turned the mayor's request down. Her neighbors all knew that she'd been seconded from City Hall to the KEF command center. Following the incident in Ohori Park and news of the backup fleet setting sail, more and more people seemed eager to get in good favor with the KEF. Several of her neighbors had asked her about the execution on Saturday. Although she explained repeatedly that she'd been in the hotel and hadn't actually seen anything, they kept pestering her with questions like "It wasn't shown on TV, but I heard it looked like their heads exploded! Is that true?" or "Do you think they'll start executing local people too?" or "Are they going to hold lots of executions there from now on?" Then there were those who came with requests such as "I want to open a barbecue place near the temporary housing in Odo. Can you introduce me to the person I need to speak to in the KEF?" or "I once wrote a lot of bad things about North Korea on an Internet board. Can you fix it so I don't get arrested?" or "What qualifications do I need to work for the KEF?" and even some who wanted to donate things or make contributions. Nobody seemed to think the Japan Self-Defense Force was capable of attacking the fleet, which meant that by this evening the KEF's control of Kyushu would be sealed.

In the elevator, Kenta hung his head, sobbing. There were still some bits of tomato around his mouth. Chikako moistened a handkerchief with some saliva and wiped it clean. Kenta had hardly eaten anything for breakfast. The cherry tomatoes were from an organic farm in Shizuoka and cost a fortune. Risako had eaten half of them, but Kenta had only tried a mouthful. The waffles were handmade, and a pack of six cost eight hundred yen, while the fresh orange juice was two thousand yen for a liter bottle. Her health-food club gave a discount, but even so, with inflation the way it was, prices had doubled in the past year.

Her own breakfast had been the remains of last night's grilled fish, chopped up on top of a bowl of rice, and green tea, while the healthy stuff was for her children. Kids treated with care and affection early on had things better when they grew up, were generally liked, and had the kind of self-confidence that would go down well with prospective employers. Giving her kids good food was her way of showing how much she loved them. Things full of natural flavor didn't just help them grow, they were good for them mentally, according to one child expert, and she agreed. When Risako was born, she had joined an Internet mail-order health-food club that delivered things to her door every three days, albeit at a cost that was disproportionate to her salary as a local-government worker.

When her boss in the construction department had first sounded her out about a possible secondment to the KEF, he'd told her that she would be given an extra five thousand yen per day as an expense allowance. That was certainly tempting, but it wasn't the only reason she'd accepted. The mayor himself had summoned her to his office and said she'd been singled out as someone who could hold her own regarding the KEF and get the job done. And it wasn't about doing whatever they wanted, he'd said. "To begin with, there's the garbage and raw sewage of five hundred people in the camp to deal with. That's a major job in itself. But a bigger problem is what to do when the reinforcements arrive. I don't want them requisitioning land or buildings all over the city. As far as possible, I'd like to keep them in one place—in Odo. That's where you come in, Onoe-san.

I want you to use your powers of gentle persuasion on them."
Being told this by the mayor himself had tickled her pride. She'd
turned thirty-eight last year, and in the personnel reshuffle earlier
this month a female colleague of the same age had been promoted
to general manager. Whichever way you looked at it, that colleague
had been less capable than she was. She realized, to her dismay, that
her prospects had been affected by the divorce.

It had been three years now. Her ex-husband was still in hospital
and not paying anything toward the children's upkeep. Their marriage had been pretty much arranged by their parents, right from
their first meeting up to the wedding day. After graduating from
Kyushu University, her husband had gone to work in the Fukuoka
branch of a major printing company. He was dependable and
earnest, but weak-willed. Four years earlier, one of his friends from
university had set up an agency selling cosmetics in north-eastern
China, and had invited him to join it as sales manager. He had
dithered, not wanting to give up his job but reluctant to turn down
a request from a pal, but in the end he'd gone with the friend.
Unfortunately, the outfit had gone bust even before the Beijing
Olympics. To succeed in business in China you needed ample funds
and powerful connections as well as know-how, but his friend was an
amateur, unaware even that demand had dried up and that China
was in a credit crunch. He was typical of the many people and
companies trying to do business there at the time and getting burned.

As a business associate, her husband had to shoulder some of the
liabilities, and they had lost the condo on which they'd only just made
a down payment. He couldn't forgive himself for letting this happen,
and before long depression set in. He withdrew into himself, and
eventually was admitted to a hospital in the suburbs. It had been his
endless self-reproach, apologies, and grumbling that had made her
decide to divorce him. He kept saying, "I should never have left the
printing company! But I believed in that guy. If I hadn't listened to
him, we'd have been celebrating Risako's birthday in the condo. Why
didn't you stop me?" As far as she was concerned, he simply hadn't
quite understood that choosing one thing meant giving up another.

She listened in silence to his constant complaining, but it went on week after week, and finally she couldn't take it anymore. When she'd gone to get his signature on the divorce papers, her mother-in-law had said nastily, "A good wife doesn't leave her husband just because he loses his job. I guess you weren't trustworthy after all, were you, Chikako? You're not particularly nice or pretty, and not even from a good family, but we thought at least you'd be reliable—that's why we accepted the match."

Everyone had always told her she was reliable—she'd been at the top of her class in elementary school, on the student council in high school, and the only girl in her year to get a place at Kyushu University to study economics. And then she'd ranked second in the entrance exam for the City Council. New employees were given a number that was theirs until retirement, used for salary payments as well as things like the mutual-aid association, and Chikako's number was 95002. The first two digits signified the year; the first zero her job classification, office worker; and the last two digits her place in the civil-service exam. She'd always thought of herself as just an ordinary woman with no special talents, but that 02 had boosted her self-esteem. Which was why it had come as such a blow when a colleague had been promoted ahead of her. And the real reason she'd agreed to be seconded to the KEF was because the mayor's confidence in her had helped restore her pride.

Chikako had borrowed some money from the employees' mutual-aid association, got lucky in the lottery for public housing, and managed to protect her livelihood from the inflation that followed the freeze on bank accounts. Civil servants had been hard hit by inflation, and she'd heard of some female employees turning to bar work and even prostitution to pay back the loans they'd taken out for their kids' college education. There had been a number of suicides and cases of clinical depression. In the midst of all this, however, she had somehow managed to provide for her two kids. After some thought, she'd decided to change their surnames to Onoe as well. They were usually well behaved and no trouble, so it had come as a surprise when, shortly after New Year's, Kenta had burst into tears and refused to go to kindergarten. At first she'd thought it might have something to do with the way his sister treated him. Since about fall last year, she had started cracking down on her little brother, scolding and even hitting and kicking him for little things such as being untidy and dribbling on his clothes, or not putting his toys away, or watching too much TV. This violent side of her was something new, and very disturbing.

When she asked the kindergarten teacher about Kenta, she was told that yes, he seemed more withdrawn nowadays, but the signs had been there from the outset. Even when playing with other kids, he would suddenly burst into tears for no apparent reason. Chikako said nothing about Risako to the teacher. She had discussed her daughter's rowdy behavior with her parents, but they had dismissed it as a phase that would soon pass. She also confided in her former boss in the Ports and Harbors Authority, Mizuki Nobuyuki. He was the only person in the whole of City Hall she could go to for advice. "Children are surprisingly difficult," he'd said, starting out in typically long-winded fashion. Mizuki was exceptionally competent at his work. He was responsible for having initiated numerous business collaborations between government and the private sector in East Asia, and he'd worked hard to attract high-tech companies to the city's new industrial park on reclaimed land in Momochi.

"Kids can get stressed out about all kinds of things," he told her. "Like if their parents divorce, or have another baby. Some kids are good at expressing how they feel, but others aren't. Maybe you should be thinking along those lines." Of course, both Risako and Kenta must have been affected by the divorce, and Risako had begun positively to radiate unhappiness whenever she thought Kenta was getting more attention than her. Maybe Kenta's refusal to go to kindergarten was his way of expressing his own feelings.

Come to think of it, Chikako remembered something similar having happened to her, too. She'd been four years old when her little sister was born. Her sister had attracted all the attention as the pretty one, and Chikako had felt left out. The two of them didn't

557

dislike each other, but they never really got along all that well, and she clearly remembered that twinge of jealousy she used to get whenever the subject of her sister came up. She'd continued to feel that way even as an adult, and it was only in her thirties that she'd been able to recognize the source of these feelings—the emotional wound she'd suffered when her sister was born.

Children tried their best to adapt to circumstances, but perhaps it was inevitable that things would resurface sooner or later. "Kenta, let's both try hard together—Mama at work, and Kenta at school," she murmured soothingly, but the boy shook his head, sobbing. "I want to go to Granny's! Not school!"

Kenta was sitting in his child seat in the back of the car, stuffing his face with chocolate and smearing it all around his mouth in the process. Chikako had bought it for him at the convenience store next to the parking lot, and he had cheered up a little. He knew that sweets weren't allowed in the schoolroom, so he was trying to finish it before they got there. He wasn't even tasting it, just cramming it in, and Chikako couldn't bear to watch.

A car pulled up alongside them at a stoplight and the driver stared at her. On the windscreen of her Mazda Familia was a sticker issued by the KEF with PERMITTED VEHICLE written in large Hangul lettering. At first she had even had stones thrown at her, but the harassment had let up after the Ohori Park incident. Half the local residents had lost trust in the government as a result of that, she reckoned.

"How's the choccy?" she asked, but Kenta just nodded mechanically, his face expressionless. She reached over and stroked his cheek and then prodded it gently with her finger. He smiled briefly, turning his face away as if to say, "It tickles!" People who don't have children can never know just how soft a child's cheeks are and how good it feels to touch them, thought Chikako. She had never been all that fond of children, but when she first held Risako in the delivery room, she'd been amazed at the softness of her skin, and affection had welled up in her of its own accord. Right then and there, she promised herself to always take care of this child.

When Risako smiled for the first time, Chikako wondered how on earth she'd known how to do that when nobody had ever taught her. Life might be a mystery, but it wasn't all that complicated; it seemed to her that it was all in a baby's smile—and the warm, fuzzy feeling that smile inspires. In time she decided it was thanks to those soft cheeks, the comfort she got from them, that she could carry on raising her children. However exhausted she felt, however stressed out by office politics, she only had to touch their faces gently as they slept to feel calm and balanced. For the first time she knew what it was like to have her mind and her emotions in perfect alignment: it was a feeling of fitting neatly into the world around her.

Kenta's teacher had told Chikako he wasn't being bullied by the other kids or anything like that. She would know, since she was with them all through the day. "Kenta," Chikako called, looking at him in the rear-view mirror. "Mm," came the unenthusiastic response. "Next day off, how about taking a picnic to the beach?" He looked up and said, "What beach?" It's impossible to understand exactly how kids feel, Mizuki had told her, and advised her just to try and make things fun for the boy.

"Which beach would you like to go to?" she asked him, and he blurted out: "Where we saw those big boys flying like birds in the sky!" Last summer she'd taken the kids to Jigyohama, and they had spent the whole time watching some youths parasailing. Jigyohama was the beach overlooked by the Sea Hawk Hotel, in the area now controlled by the KEF, and was out of bounds to residents. "Got it," she said. "We'll go to Jigyohama." Kenta clapped his hands, beaming. If the backup fleet arrived this evening as planned, the KEF would be moving to Odo, which meant they'd probably lift the ban on access to the beach.

The kindergarten was next to a Baptist church attached to Seinan Gakuin University, in a well-heeled neighborhood with luxury condominiums and tree-lined streets. Chikako could see Kenta through the window of the playroom on the far side of the grassy grounds. He was sitting quietly on one of several chairs laid out in a semicircle, eyes downcast, legs dangling. On their arrival the teacher had taken his hand, and he'd gone inside without looking back. She'd felt relieved, but also a bit sad. She wished he could enjoy himself at school, and not feel lonely or bad about things. He would stay there until after lunch, when he'd be taken by the school bus to a day-care center near their apartment. "Good morning, Onoe-san!" Chikako turned to see some of the other mothers there. They were getting out of their cars and leading their children to the school gate, where the teacher was waiting for them.

They all had expensive cars. The new Toyota hybrid belonged to the wife of a young entrepreneur who ran a foodstuffs company; the deep red Nissan Skyline to the wife of the president of a local bank; the dark blue BMW to the wife of a section head at Sony Fukuoka; the deep green Saab to the wife of the owner of a long-established eel restaurant in Tenjin; and the cream Benz to the wife of a real-estate agent who'd developed some fancy property around Nishi Park. All five were married to men who had benefited from the present financial situation. "It's no joke," the bank president's wife told Chikako. "They've got to open accounts for a hundred and twenty thousand people, so my husband has been in meetings nonstop. He stayed over in a hotel all weekend." She had short hair with a red streak in the bangs, and was dressed in tight leather pants and jacket, along with boots. Finding herself surrounded by the five, Chikako sneaked a look at her watch. A quarter to eight—she could chat for fifteen minutes or so. Work wasn't supposed to start till nine, but the workaholic KEF officers always showed up half an hour early, and the City Hall staff were advised to follow suit.

"When they don't even come home, you never know what they're really up to," laughed Mrs. Foodstuffs, lighting a cigarette and blowing smoke through pursed lips. She had curly hair dyed auburn, and was wearing black tights, flat buckskin shoes, and a dark-brown knitted suit, with an orange shawl around her shoulders. The restaurateur's wife was in jeans and sneakers, but she was wearing what looked like a Prada sweater with mink fur trim around the collar and long diamond earrings dangling on either side of her face. Chikako couldn't even begin to imagine how much they must have cost. She also noticed the white leather Max Mara coat slung over the shoulders of the real-estate agent's wife. Chikako was the only one of them without dyed hair, and her gray suit, bought at a budget store that offered a forty per cent discount to City Hall staff, looked as cheap as it was. She didn't much enjoy chatting with these wealthy women, though she didn't actively dislike them. They at least respected her as a successful woman with an important job. All had married relatively late, only having kids after thirty, but they positively doted on their children. Chikako had read in some child-raising book that most young mothers went through a phase when their animal instincts took over, and being covered in a kid's various excretions didn't bother them at all. It must be true even for women like this, she thought.

Though the economic gap between them and her was obvious, they were all comrades in motherhood. And despite their general flashiness, they were too refined to meddle in other people's affairs—unlike her gossipy neighbors, for example. "It must be really hard on you now, Onoe-san," the real-estate agent's wife told her. Chikako agreed that it hadn't been easy. She was currently negotiating with the KEF, for example, about wharf space for five hundred ships. Thanks to the blockade on Hakata Port, it should be possible to fit them in, but the city wanted to limit them to the Okihama and Higashihama piers. They had already agreed that ten boats, each with a KEF officer on board, would be sent out to guide the ships into harbor. The young wives were impressed, and told her so.

"But what's going to happen now?" asked the Sony man's wife, twirling the key to her BMW around her finger. Everyone in Fukuoka was wondering the same thing, but nobody had an answer. The bank president's wife changed the subject: "I just downloaded the latest anime from Studio Ghibli and copied it onto a DVD. You can take turns borrowing it, if you like." Everyone clamored to be first, so they had to resort to "rock-paper-scissors" to decide the order. Chikako couldn't help thinking how tough they all were. They had no idea what was going to happen, but they knew exactly what their function was right now. Their kids still needed to be fed, bathed, dressed, and taken to kindergarten every day.

Chikako had already told them that the KEF had promised City Hall they wouldn't seize any land, property, or assets belonging to ordinary Fukuoka residents. But there was no guarantee that they'd keep that promise, and if they wanted to take your stuff, all they had to do was label you a criminal. No one knew how they would govern the city. The only thing she had learned for certain in the week she'd been assigned to the command center was something that should have been obvious: each North Korean was a unique individual. She often worked with a female officer in the logistics and supplies division by the name of Kim Hyang Mok, who was well educated, straightforward, and very hardworking. Chikako sometimes wondered when she ever got time to sleep. But then there was the hulking major Kim Hak Su, always in battledress, with that chilling look in his eyes. She'd been appalled by the abusive way he treated some of the people under his command; he frightened her so much that she now avoided all eye contact with him.

Once they'd settled the matter of the DVD, one of the women asked Chikako, with a worried look, whether there was any risk of the LNG tank in Higashihama being blown up if the fleet was attacked. Chikako said she didn't know. She couldn't very well ask any of the KEF officers about something like that. But after spending a week with them, she had to wonder whether they would really do anything that desperate; they struck her as surprisingly sensible. Kim Hyang Mok had done an incredible job of negotiating with local traders, and had been almost childishly delighted when she'd managed to get hold of some insecticides and antiseptics for virtually nothing after that insect outbreak over the weekend. A potential attack on LNG sites was effective as a threat, but it would be suicidal actually to go through with it.

To finish with, Chikako told the wives about the paper recycling. This was a story she'd actually heard from Ri Gwi Hui, a female intelligence officer. "Any idea how the resident codes and other personal information were leaked to the KEF?" she asked. "No—do tell us!" they said. "It's true that the general-affairs department handed over the codes in response to direct threats. But in fact for the last ten years Fukuoka has been exporting waste paper. We get lots of containers coming in from abroad, right? Well, there's no sense in sending any of them back empty, so we decided to export our waste paper. Southeast Asia is short of paper, so we send them ours to recycle. But here's the thing. At City Hall, for example, they're always going on about how we've got to economize, so we jot down notes or whatever on the back of used paper, without bothering much about whether it has any personal details printed on it. And since shredding everything would take for ever, it all gets exported for recycling."

The women were listening closely. "I was told that a lot of the paper shipped in those containers ends up in North Korea, and they have an army of people go through it page by page, checking for any useful information. There's a massive amount of personal information on all that stuff, not just from City Hall, but from banks and private companies too—and this was monitored for anything they could use when they invaded Fukuoka. Not only that, but I was told that the programming for the Juki Net is commissioned from private companies that subcontract most of the work to China and India, who in turn re-subcontract some of it to North Korea."

"Unbelievable!" said the Sony man's wife. "Who'd ever have thought they'd do that?" Chikako said she had to get going. After double-checking when her turn for the DVD was, she said, "Bye now," and started toward her car. The restaurateur's wife had parked her Saab right in front of Chikako's Mazda, and she walked along with her. "I heard something very strange from a young lady I know," the woman said, and lowered her voice. "She's married to the heir to the old bean-jam bun shop just down the road from our restaurant. He's over thirty but still involved in the Speed Tribe, and she said that over the weekend he and his friends helped a group sneak into the Sea Hawk Hotel—a group claiming it was going to topple the KEF. Mind you, this was over drinks, so I don't know if there's any truth in it." She ran her finger along the sticker with Hangul writing on Chikako's car. "I don't suppose anything happened at the hotel last weekend, did it?" Chikako shook her head and said, "No. Nothing in particular."

She drove alongside Central Park, then turned right before Fukuoka Tower to head for the command center. She had tried to find some music on the car radio, but all the channels were relaying the latest news of the North Korean fleet. On NHK 1, a well-known commentator on military affairs was saying something about the SDF's warships and fighter planes being among the best equipped in the world, capable of easily destroying this outdated fleet simply by launching missiles at it. All four of the Kongo class of Aegis destroyers had been dispatched to the Tsushima Island area. Even just one of them could probably sink most of the four hundred and eighty-seven ships so far confirmed. The original Aegis cruiser was designed to protect aircraft carriers from enemy planes, and although he didn't know why the Maritime SDF, which didn't have any aircraft carriers, needed such high-tech ships at a cost of a hundred and twenty billion yen each, the Aegis had not only a formidable capacity to process information but also attack power: multiple missile launchers, backed up by radar that could detect and follow over a hundred targets within a radius of four hundred kilometers. The Ground SDF had the Type 88 Surface-to-Ship Missile for coastal protection, and the data link with the Maritime SDF's P-3C planes had apparently been completed some five years earlier.

"What this means," the commentator coolly went on, "is that the SDF's latest equipment, designed for sophisticated electronic warfare, is now faced with an armada of the lowest-tech ships imaginable—ships that look as though they'll sink on their own, without any encouragement from us, and with zero ability to gather information or even to attack. The fleet is essentially defenseless, and, incredibly, they appear to be only checking each other's position and speed by eye. In other words, they don't have any radar, and most of them don't even have proper radio transmission. Yet sailing they are—and getting closer and closer. And we're just sitting with folded arms, watching. If that isn't ironic, then I don't know what is.

"We can't attack because the North Koreans are effectively holding the whole nation hostage through the occupation of one city and the threat to blow up LNG stockpiles around the country. But if the government was determined to block them from crossing the territorial limit, it could be over in a matter of minutes. To put it bluntly, these are little more than armed 'boat people.' It wouldn't even make sense to lay mines since they would probably line up ten or so ships and make a dash for it, the first ones getting blown up to let the others through—suicidal, but simple."

Listening to his comments only underlined how gutless the government seemed to be. It was the same kind of attitude her husband had. He hadn't wanted to leave his job, but he couldn't bring himself to turn down a friend's request. Similarly, the government didn't want the fleet to reach Fukuoka, but they couldn't risk any terrorist attacks. Choosing one thing meant sacrificing something else; so many people simply didn't understand this, and her husband was a perfect example of it. He'd probably been spoiled by that awful mother of his—or smothered by her, more like. The woman had pride and disappointment etched into the wrinkles on her face. "Do as I say and you can have everything; disobey me and you'll get nothing"—this was undoubtedly the sort of implied threat that she'd held over her son, impressing upon him that there was nothing to be gained from thinking for himself and making his own decisions.

This train of thought brought Mizuki to mind. About six months after her divorce, she had been out drinking with him when he'd suddenly made a pass at her. Chewing on a piece of chicken gizzard, he calmly said, "How about an affair with me?" Chikako respected Mizuki and was flattered, but he was married and had a couple of kids in high school. "You can't be serious," she told him. "I'm not pretty, and I haven't an ounce of charm." He admitted that there were plenty of prettier women. "But plenty are a whole lot uglier too!" he said, and laughed. She loved his smile so much that she wavered a bit, but in the end decided against the idea. She just didn't see herself in that kind of situation. When she told him this honestly, he'd taken it in good grace and carried on giving her advice and a listening ear just as he always had done. But every morning, looking in the mirror, she noticed the spreading crow's feet around her eyes, and the skin on her arms and legs was beginning to get flabby. She sometimes wondered what her life would have been like if she had taken up with him—yet she didn't regret it. She had promised herself that, whatever happened, she'd never harbor any regrets.

After she passed the Fukuoka City Bank and the Fujitsu Building, the Sea Hawk Hotel came into view, raising its thin blade into the blue sky. The building always looked so unstable to her. Peering up at it glittering silver in the sun, she recalled what the restaurant owner's wife had said about bikers helping an anti-KEF group to get into the hotel. Chikako had already left for home by then and hadn't actually seen anything herself, but it had been reported on the news the next morning that in the early hours a local Speed Tribe had entered the restricted area and circled the hotel, and that the KEF commander had called for security to be tightened up at the checkpoints. The woman's story was hearsay twice removed, so it was impossible to judge how much truth there was in it, and it was apparently something told over a drink or two. She decided to ask Mizuki later what she should do with that sort of information. Chikako slowed down to cross over Yokatopia Bridge and then stopped at Checkpoint A, greeting the familiar guard in Korean: "*Annyeong haseyo.*"

She parked on the bottom level of the first-floor parking lot. The Sea Hawk Hotel had no second floor because of the ballrooms' soaring ceilings, and the parking lot adjacent to the first floor was divided into lower, middle, and upper levels, to make the most of the space. When she got out of her car, Chikako strained her ears to see if she could hear anything from further down—screams, for example. The B2 lot was where those arrested were being held. Of course she had never seen the detention facilities with her own eyes, and the subject was taboo in the command center. But she had often seen people crossing the lobby as they were being taken down there. There had been a lot of familiar faces—a well-known doctor, for example, who ran a special nursing home for the elderly about which there'd been a lot of rumors, and a former member of the Upper House. A staffer from the tax department at City Hall, seconded with her, had helped the KEF draw up a list of those suspected of large-scale tax evasion.

She and her colleagues on secondment often talked at lunch or on the way home about what sort of place the detention center really was. The fact that none of them had actually seen it only stoked their curiosity. They couldn't discuss it at work, so they had to rely on things they'd gleaned from various KEF soldiers. *I heard they use a vise on people and crush their fingers... They say that after just a day in there, the prisoners look like ghosts... It sounds like a living hell...* Almost a hundred people had already been locked up, but they were all characters it was hard to sympathize with. There were a couple of women there, too. One was a legendary battle-ax in her fifties who employed women from all over Asia in a string of massage parlors she operated in the Nakasu entertainment district, while the other was a company boss in her forties who'd made a fortune smuggling aphrodisiacs and slimming drugs from China. The man in charge of deciding whom to arrest often checked with the seconded staff regarding the sort of reputation these people had, and tended to select only those that ordinary residents complained about. At any rate, they were supposed to be moving the detention center to Odo soon.

She went through several doors until she reached the escalator hall, then headed along the corridor to where the command center was now based. On entering the hotel, the smell of insecticide stung her nose. Were they still spraying? There had been a major outbreak of insects on the third and fourth floors on Saturday, and they'd moved their HQ downstairs. It seemed the neglected tropical plants in the cafe next to the tower of guest rooms had been to blame. That morning, when Chikako had gone to work, the fire shutters over the main entrance were already closed and the soldier on guard told her to go to the first floor, so she knew something must have happened. Things from upstairs had been piled in a first-floor banquet hall: large TV monitors, computers, telephones, bundles of documents and writing materials, crockery, sleeping cots, and a large number of uniforms, caps, and so forth. An engineer had been called over from the camp to weld shut all doors that had access to the third floor. Soldiers were brushing bugs off their uniforms, some in a panic, scratching at their hair or stripping down to their underpants. In the ladies toilet, Ri Gwi Hui, Ri Gyu Yeong, and Kim Sun I were changing into new uniforms. When she asked what had happened, she was told "Bugs! Everywhere!" The floors of the banquet hall and the bathroom were littered with the bodies of small insects of a type she'd never seen before. Work had been completely disrupted by the fuss, and documents had been scattered and lost.

Today, Commander Han Seung Jin, First Lieutenant Pak Myeong, and First Lieutenant Jo Su Ryeon were seated in easy chairs in the banquet-hall lobby discussing something, but they fell silent as Chikako approached. Pak returned her greeting and asked how preparations for the wharfs and anchorage in Hakata Port were going. Everything should be ready by three o'clock that afternoon, she told him. She always spoke Japanese with Pak, but could follow a simple conversation in Korean. She thought she'd heard them use the word for "quarantine."

She liked walking along the thick red carpet that ran from the lobby to the ballroom where she worked. The sweet smell of kimchi blended with the cigarette smoke that hung over the hall. All of the North Korean men were heavy smokers. Ri Gwi Hui's electronic-intelligence team had been expanded and was gathered in one corner of the room, tapping away at keyboards as they compiled a database in order to get resident-register numbers for the extra troops arriving shortly.

In another corner a seventy-inch TV screen was covering the deployment of SDF ships at Japan's territorial line and the F-15 Eagle fighter planes preparing to scramble at Kasuga airbase. But nobody was watching—they were all confident that no interception

568

would take place. The ballroom was about the same size as the gym at Chikako's middle school. Liza Minnelli and Whitney Houston had apparently performed here, and their photos were hanging by the entrance. Now it contained twenty or so desks laid out in three rows and partitioned off. There were about twenty officers permanently stationed here who were in charge of sections like Strategy, Intelligence, Propaganda and Guidance, Logistics and Supplies, Construction and Engineering, Medical Affairs, as well as the KEF Special Police and legal, financial, and transport departments. A number of rank-and-file soldiers under them were constantly coming and going, and more and more local traders were visiting in person too.

The meeting in the lobby must have ended, because Pak and Jo now came into the hall. Jo was steadily gaining a large fan base with his regular TV appearances. A senior officer asked him something as he came in and was told, "I'm going to NHK Fukuoka this morning to prepare for the afternoon broadcast—I'll be talking about the fleet's arrival, so I have to be sure to get it right." It was easy to see why this good-looking fellow was popular with women, but there was something about him that didn't quite click with Chikako. It wasn't just him, though—she felt the same way about all of them. She couldn't put her finger on it at first, but eventually realized that it was a certain grubbiness they all shared, which must be the result of a more general poverty and ignorance. There was an unsophisticated feel to even the slightest thing they did.

The women never shaved their underarms or facial hair, while the men weren't bothered if they smelled of sweat—in fact, they made it worse with a liberal use of cheap cologne. Chikako herself was from a provincial town on the border of Kumamoto Prefecture, and had grown up surrounded by people of similar personal habits. It had been when she came to live in Fukuoka City as a college student that she'd had her first taste of "culture"—in fashion, make-up, food, music. Even Jo and Pak had a touch of that grubbiness about them, and the others were worse. They also displayed an obedience that verged on servility, the flip side of which was a domineering attitude toward subordinates and a strong mistrust and dislike of outsiders. Looked at another way, of course, submissiveness might be regarded as sincerity and aggressiveness as strength, and mistrust and dislike of outsiders could also signal solidarity with your own group. How you thought about it depended on who you were.

The desks for seconded staff were next to the Logistics and Supplies section, diagonally across from Construction and Engineering. Her colleagues weren't in yet. When Chikako had first come to the command center accompanied by seven other people from City Hall, she'd been so nervous her legs were shaking, and a petrified colleague had muttered, "This'll be the end of me." On arrival, however, they had been greeted by the entire body of KEF officers, lined up and applauding as they were handed bouquets of flowers. The commander himself had presented the bouquets. Of course, it was the kind of performance the North Koreans were so good at, but Chikako had been both relieved and impressed. At City Hall, new staff members were just made to line up and listen to a long sermon on how hard they were expected to work. After this enthusiastic, flower-filled reception, on the other hand, the eight of them had immediately felt motivated to make themselves useful.

Chikako had just arrived at her desk, taken her laptop out of her bag, and was opening up a file when Second Lieutenant Kim Hyang Mok came over and said good morning. She was younger than Chikako, and always very polite to her. She was small, with a sweet face, and this morning she was dressed in civilian clothes instead of the usual combat fatigues. Her suit was plain, with yellow pinstripes on a gray background, but it looked good on her. She was probably due to meet a local trader. That was the only time she was allowed to wear anything other than a uniform.

"I am going out for a little while later this afternoon," she told Chikako, "so I hope it's okay if I leave the list for canned-seafood purchases until this afternoon?" Chikako asked whether she was going to Hawks Town to negotiate with shops there, but Kim said she had to go to the Kyushu Medical Center. It seemed she'd been told to settle the bill for treatment of the soldier wounded in the attack that had led to the public execution. It had nothing to do with food or clothing supplies, but Kim was responsible for all payments in yen. "No problem. It's just a matter of delaying the calls to the canned-food suppliers," said Chikako. "Thank you," said Kim, bobbing her head before returning to her desk.

Chikako looked at her watch. Ten-forty already. It looked as if the whole morning would be taken up with calls to contractors and City Hall. The mayor was out making arrangements to welcome the North Korean fleet, delaying the response from the finance department even further. First thing in the morning a call had come from the contractor laying the pipes for water, sewage, and electricity at the temporary accommodation. He wanted to know when they would receive the payment for materials. The work to make the elementary school and housing complex in Odo habitable had been contracted between local businesses and City Hall—in other words, it was being treated as a public-works project to be funded by the KEF. Chikako had initially thought she could check the payment dates by herself, but there were twenty-six contractors involved, with work being carried out at over three hundred points, and for each of these there were almost twenty documents, from estimates to orders and provisional contracts. These all needed further checking by the KEF, which meant they had to be translated into Korean. Her computer was already cluttered with purchase agreements on supplies of clothing, medicine, and food, as well as provisional contracts for the disposal of sewage and garbage. She was struggling to keep track of everything.

While she was waiting for a search to be completed of City Hall's database for the provisional contracts for laying pipes, Chikako got together the documents related to the quarantine inspection and health check of the hundred and twenty thousand people due to arrive at Hakata Port, and cast her eyes over the draft of a contract with a company to provide buses to transfer them all to Odo. Of course her colleagues were helping her, but Mizuki had specifically told her to be sure to personally check everything that involved financial transactions, and so she couldn't cut corners.

Whenever the mayor was out, liaison with City Hall broke down. Relations between the general staff and those on secondment were becoming increasingly strained. When she grumbled about this to Mizuki, he told her to grin and bear it, and that's what she tried to do. Many of the City Hall people disliked and feared the KEF, and there was also some jealousy toward the seconded staff, but the biggest problem was simply that there wasn't enough time to do everything. A city works project would normally take from three to four years from the initial survey to completion. The initial survey alone could take up to a year, after which a preliminary design was drawn up, along with projected costs for inclusion in the next year's budget.

This whole process had been skipped in the case of projects for the KEF. The size of the budget had not been specified, and there had been no time to submit it to the council. The very nature of city public works was that there could be no exceptions, and it had never occurred to her before that it was possible for someone like her, a mere manager, to bypass the section and department heads and discuss things directly with the mayor. Her first job for the KEF had been to negotiate with Japan Tobacco Fukuoka to scrape together a truckload of Seven Stars, and she had persuaded the mayor to arrange things with the finance department head. They had agreed, albeit with barely disguised displeasure.

Jo Su Ryeon had changed out of his uniform and was leaving the hall, no doubt on his way to the NHK studio, just as the strikingly tall Major Kim Hak Su came in. The other officers saluted nervously. The major strolled over to Commander Han's desk by the wall, and the two began discussing something, their faces close together. A tense mood descended over the room with Kim's mere appearance, as if everyone had suddenly become acutely aware of the fragility of life. Feeling shaken herself, Chikako remembered what she'd heard from the restaurateur's wife. She had to talk to Mizuki about that. She decided to call his cellphone. Just the thought of hearing his voice again was enough to bring a smile to her lips. She tried to avoid phoning him unnecessarily, not wanting to presume on his kindness. She gazed at the huge tapestry of the Mongolian invasions of Japan covering one wall of the hall as she listened to his phone ringing. Suddenly a woman's voice echoed in her ear. "Hello? Mizuki's cellphone here." Chikako almost dropped the receiver. "This is Onoe from the construction department," she said, conscious of a quaver in her voice. "Thank you for calling. He's in bed with flu right now, although he told me he would take any urgent calls." The woman must be his wife. "No, it's not urgent," Chikako told her, and hung up.

Her heart was beating so fast that her chest hurt. Her colleagues were staring at her with puzzled looks. The color must have drained from her face. It was the first time she'd ever heard his wife's voice. Of course she'd known he was married, but still it had disturbed her as surely as a stone sends ripples across a stretch of still water. She had not been to bed with Mizuki. They'd never even sung a karaoke duet together, let alone kissed. She had strictly forbidden herself from doing anything like that. So how come she'd been so flustered just at the sound of his wife's voice? Was she that fond of him? She began to feel annoyed with him for being in bed with flu at a time like this and, even worse, getting his wife to answer his phone for him. Her irritation brought up a lot of negative thoughts. Why had she really been chosen for secondment? All the seconded workers were senior staff in their thirties—nobody from management. It wasn't because they were especially capable that they'd been chosen; it was simply because sending management-class employees would have created more problems than it solved. Now that this had occurred to her, she was sure of it. It was a humiliating realization, and tears welled up in her eyes.

"Onoe-san, what's up?" asked one of her colleagues from City Hall. Partly to stave off the tears, she blurted out the story she'd heard from the restaurant owner's wife. "It's not a rerun of Ohori Park, is it?" he said, blithely referring to the possibility of the government again secretly sending in an SAT team. The very thought sent shudders through Chikako. It's no joke, she thought. If she were to die, Kenta and Risako would be orphaned. After looking around the room for a few moments, she mustered up the courage to approach Kim Hak Su.

He had finished his talk with the commander, and was now leaning against the desk smoking a cigarette. She stopped a meter away, and greeted him in polite Korean: "*Annyeong hashimnikka.*" He blew out some smoke, enjoying the Seven Star, and nodded slightly, his face expressionless. Come to think of it, it was the first time she'd ever spoken to him. She had always observed him from a distance, intimidated by his aura of brutality. Seeing him close up, her fear of him only increased. The skin from the corner of his right eye up to the temple was puckered in a deep, narrow scar. How on earth could you get a scar like that? She was wondering how to say "motorcycle gang" in Korean, when he told her she could speak in Japanese if she liked. His voice seemed to come from somewhere deep inside him.

"Last weekend... a motorcycle gang member... told his family... that he had helped... a suspicious group... sneak into this hotel," she said, enunciating the words clearly. "What was the gang member's name?" he asked. "I don't know." If she said his name, he'd probably be arrested. "I just heard a rumor," she said. "Where did you hear it?" Kim demanded. "In the supermarket near my apartment," she lied. "I overheard one of the customers talking about it."

The commander had also been listening to this conversation, cocking his head as if wondering what to make of it. Then he said something in Korean and Kim shouted "*Ne!*" and saluted. The commander had been speaking too fast for Chikako to understand, but she thought she caught the words for "arrest," and "attack." "Thank you for the information," Kim told her. "We'll take care of it," he added by way of dismissal. Then he picked up the phone and barked, "Send the 2nd Platoon to the hotel immediately!" He listened for a moment, and then yelled, "Fully armed, you idiot! Have them conduct a complete search of the hotel, starting from the top floor!"

Chikako went back to her desk. It occurred to her that what she'd just done amounted to tattling, like a child in elementary school telling the teacher, "That boy was cheating—I saw him!" If the people the Speed Tribe had smuggled in were a commando unit from the Japanese police or SDF, it would mean she'd just sold out some of her own countrymen—heroes come to confront an occupying army, no less. Perhaps the government thought that if they warned anyone locally, the information would leak out and the plan would fail again, as it had in Ohori Park. The country had a duty to protect its people, but that hadn't happened here in Fukuoka. On the contrary, they'd been cut off. Did a country like that deserve one's loyalty? Maybe they were planning to destroy the hotel to save the rest of the country. But just as happened in Ohori Park, lots of local people would be sacrificed—and if she herself was one of them, her kids would be left motherless.

Until a week ago, Chikako had just been one of the general public. A sudden change in circumstances meant that she'd now been relegated to a minority—it could happen to anybody at any time. The government knew nothing about a thirty-eight-year-old City Hall staff member with two children currently on secondment to the KEF, and why should they? She went back to her desk and ran her eyes over the documents lying on it, but the word "tattletale" kept weighing down on her. She reminded herself of Kenta's soft cheeks and tried to imagine touching them, but somehow the image of Kim Hak Su's thin, deep scar interfered.

# PRECIOUS MOMENTS

*April 11, 2011*

H<small>INO ADJUSTED HIS GRIP</small> on the electric cutter. The vibration of the tool made his hands and arms go numb, and he had to concentrate to maintain the correct pressure. He'd been stripping veneer from columns for about ten hours now, but it felt more like thirty. Sweat dripped from his forehead down the edges of his safety goggles, and his leather gloves were sodden on the inside and would need to be changed again soon. He'd taken a number of short breaks while Shinohara or Tateno or Ando tried using the cutter, but they didn't know the tool like he did, and he always had to jump back in after a few minutes to keep up the pace. When Hino's team lost time, the whole operation bottlenecked. Takeguchi's team was close behind them, setting the linear shaped charges. They attached a little styrofoam platform to each newly exposed steel surface, taped an LSC to the platform, then inserted an electric blasting cap and connected it to the detonator.

The columns were about two and a half meters from floor to ceiling, and each had to be cut at an angle in two places in order to blow out the middle fifty centimeters. It was necessary to remove a ten-centimeter-wide strip of veneer from each column surface before attaching the LSC. Hino drew cut lines with a felt pen, then made the cuts with the blade set to a depth of five millimeters. Shinohara used a hammer, chisel, and crowbar to remove the veneer between the cuts and expose the bare steel. At first Takeguchi had been drawing the cut lines, but after a few dozen columns Hino knew the proper height and angle without measuring and began doing it himself. The mark on the front of each column was parallel to the floor, but those on the sides had to be at forty-five degree angles and were trickier. The cuts on the lower half of the columns angled up and those on the upper part angled down. To make these he had to sit on the floor, bending to one side, or lean precariously from a stepladder. With the blade ripping through the stuff at sixty revolutions per second, dust billowed about him and particles and fibers clung to his sweaty skin.

They were just finishing up the column in Room 8033. Hino had already completed seventy-one columns and would have only eight to go after this one. All the rooms here on the eighth floor were regular guest rooms with large windows, and they had to take care not to be seen from outside as they worked. The ten columns to be severed on this floor were along the starboard wall, which faced the Dome. From the windows they could see Koryo sentries outside the stadium—three of them, standing about thirty meters apart. The curtains were opened a mere slit to allow Tateno to watch them with the binoculars.

The operation had begun on the fifth floor, where they had placed charges on all forty columns. There were no guest rooms on that floor but several restaurants, including a tea room for members of the fitness club. The columns there didn't have any cloth coverings, and a blade depth of three millimeters had been sufficient for the thin veneer, so Hino's job had been relatively easy. Windows had been fewer there as well, so that the sentries outside the Dome were less of an issue. But for Takeguchi's wiring team, which included Yamada, Mori, and all five Satanists, the fifth floor had been challenging.

Each of the eight LSCs attached to a column had to be connected to the detonation device, which was of a type known as an exploder or "hell-box." Takeguchi was laying out the wiring in such a way that even if one section was cut, the rest of the explosives could still be triggered. From the blasting cap embedded in each load of RDX there extended two wires coated in red vinyl—one positive and one negative. "These are called the detonator wires," Takeguchi had instructed his team. "The two cables coming from the hell-box are called buses, and the wires that connect the detonator wires to the buses are called auxiliary busbars. The three types of wires are of different thickness and colors, as you can see. The detonator wires are red, the buses yellow, and the auxiliary busbars blue."

He said they would employ both series and parallel circuits, and delivered a brief overview of the wiring diagram. "For our purposes, once the bus from the positive terminal of the hell-box is connected to the auxiliary busbar, we'll call that the positive bus. We connect the positive detonator wire from LSC number one to the positive bus. Then we connect the negative detonator wire from LSC number 320 to the negative bus. From there, we just connect the negative detonator wire from LSC number one to the negative bus; the positive detonator wire from LSC number 320 to the positive bus; and so on. LSC number two and number 319, three and 318, positive detonator wire and positive bus, negative detonator wire and negative bus, we just connect them all serially." He demonstrated the first two connections, taking questions and stressing the importance of getting the terminology right. "The terminology for explosives wasn't chosen by scientists but developed by pyrotechnicians and professional blasters in the course of doing the actual work," he said. "It'll make things go a lot smoother if when you hear the words 'auxiliary busbar,' for example, you immediately picture the blue wire that connects the detonator wire to the bus."

He designated the entire system of wiring on the fifth floor "Group Five," that on the sixth floor "Group Six," and so on. The wiring for each floor was fundamentally the same, he explained, but because the number of charges was different for each, it was necessary to use a certain device to provide consistent resistance levels. "This is a cement resistor," he said, holding up a small white box and explaining that the component itself was inside the ceramic case, embedded in cement. He had already calculated how many of these to use on the other floors to match the resistance level of Group Five, with its three hundred and twenty LSCs.

The exploder remained on a table in the Italian restaurant on the fifth floor, guarded by Kaneshiro and Okubo, who were armed with the Uzi, the FN pistol, and hand grenades. Takeguchi had constructed his hell-box out of metal plates, and it was about the size of a box of tissues. On top were three holes the diameter of small coins through which you could insert a metal handle to turn a switch. Beneath the holes were the words CHARGE, FIRE, and STOP, written with a felt pen. Above the switches were small pilot lights, and when the device was sufficiently charged, a green one came on. A black cable extended from a gap beneath the top plate and was connected at the other end to a cellphone charger. A blank email sent to the phone resting in the charger would supposedly turn it on, delivering an electric current to the exploder and triggering the blast. Hino didn't know a lot about electrical stuff and was impressed that Takeguchi did. But when he said as much, Takeguchi shook his head and told him, "A hell-box is a simple thing. You hook up a dry battery to a converter, turn up the voltage, accumulate the electricity in a condenser, and then release it into the cable all at once. I only know as much as I need to know to make bombs."

In the corridor outside Room 8030, Yamada, Mori, and the Satanists Sato and Orihara were connecting the red detonator wires to the blue auxiliary busbars. Using wire-stripping nippers and pliers, they first skinned about two centimeters of vinyl coating from the auxiliary busbar to expose the bare copper and three or four centimeters from the end of the detonator wire. Then, after reconfirming positive and negative, they connected the bare wires by hand, twisting the end of one around the other ten times or so, then using needle-nose pliers to crimp and secure the connection, and finally covering it all with electrical tape. The most important thing, Takeguchi reminded them several times, was to avoid mistaking positive and negative, and next was to make sure the connections wouldn't come apart even if accidentally given a tug.

Sato was surprisingly good at this. He handled the various pliers and nippers with delicacy and precision. He was also faster than everyone else, and he didn't make mistakes. Takeguchi asked him if he'd had any experience working in a blasting company. "Nah, I don't know anything about explosives," he said, his big eyes sparkling. "Besides, I'm only sixteen." Orihara, the de facto leader of the Satanists, said, "This guy always was good with his hands, even as a little kid." Back in the Lucifer Incident days, he said, they had shown the media a Satanic altar, a booklet in which the Devil's signs were displayed and decoded, and bizarrely shaped accessories the Devil had supposedly worn; and all of these things had been Sato's handiwork.

The charges yet to be set were stashed in the corridor. Of the six hundred and forty they'd brought along, less than seventy remained. There was still an hour left before noon, when the blast was scheduled. Plenty of time, thought Hino.

The hotel had been built to look like an ocean liner plowing toward Hakata Bay, and Hino referred to the "front" end as the bow and the "rear" (where the ground-floor tour bus entrance was) as the stern. "Forward" meant toward the bow and "aft" toward the stern. The main entrance to the hotel was on the starboard side, as was Fukuoka Dome, only about a hundred meters away. Along both of the forward corridors were narrowly spaced doors to single rooms. Felix and Matsuyama were in charge of unlocking the starboard doors by inserting an electronic device into each slot. Approximately every third room housed a column. On the eighth floor only the ten columns on the side toward which the building would fall were to be cut. On the fifth they had rigged all forty columns; on the sixth, ten in the service corridor and ten around the central elevator hall, for a total of twenty; and on the seventh the same ten as the eighth.

The seventh floor had Japanese-style guest rooms, and in the bow were the baths—one for men and one for women. These were large pools complete with boulders to evoke the atmosphere of natural hot springs, and the column there was inside the partition between the men's and women's baths. In the women's changing room, underwear and robes and towels lay scattered about, suggesting that the bathers had dropped everything and fled. But the boys had all been focused on the job at hand and no one fooled around inspecting the panties and bras or sniffing them or waving them in the air.

Stripping veneer from columns was the only thing on Hino's mind. Shinohara followed behind with his chisel, hammer, and crowbar, looking more like a real construction worker than a guy who raised frogs and flies and centipedes. Fukuda was placing homemade antipersonnel mines on the three emergency stairways between the third and fourth floors. The five Satanists were busy carving more styrofoam blocks to hold the charges the proper distance from the steel columns and setting the electric detonators, taking special care not to tangle the increasingly complicated network of wires. Takeguchi, whose eyes were now badly bloodshot, eventually left Sato in charge of overseeing the entire wiring operation.

Dawn had broken by the time they finished their work on the sixth floor, but none of them noticed. They had continued working with penlights, and no one was aware of the pale light seeping in through the slit in the curtains until Shibata looked up from the styrofoam he was cutting and said, "Whoa. Here comes the sun." Those who weren't working at any given moment, whether waiting for the others to catch up or taking a break, would hydrate with water or soda and eat Calorie Mate bars while studying how to operate the weapons. These included a sub-machine gun, two automatic rifles, two pistols, some hand grenades, the short-barreled Scorpion, the Franchi shotgun, and a grenade launcher.

Takei had left detailed memos regarding the maintenance and use of all the weapons, and they practiced the correct grip and stance for firing a handgun, the way to work the charging handle on an automatic rifle, and so on. Hino had pored over the shotgun and hand-grenade sections. The US army grenades Takei had bought were called M67s. They exploded on impact, which meant that you couldn't bounce one around a corner, for example, to get at an enemy.

The first column Hino had taken his cutter to was near the window in the Italian restaurant on the fifth floor, and he hadn't slept since. When he had first come to Ishihara's place, he'd slept like a dead man for days on end. At the construction site where he lied about his age to get a job, he had always slept well in the unfinished buildings of bare concrete after working all day, but the walls of the institution he was confined in just before coming to Fukuoka had smelled of new synthetic materials, and being unable to sleep there he'd gone off the deep end.

One thing Hino had never admitted to anyone was that he had always hated and feared mirrors. He would sometimes look at a mirror and find that he couldn't recognize the person it reflected. Even if no one else was in the room, he would begin to wonder if that was really his face—and if not, whose was it?—and end up panic-stricken. About a week after arriving in Fukuoka, he'd been walking through the Living, carefully blocking the big mirror from sight with a shielding hand, when Ishihara burst out laughing. "Hey, Vladimir Hinochinko, what the heck are you doing?" Nobody else was around, so he mumbled something about his fear of mirrors. "Well well well," said Ishihara. He stood in front of the mirror, pointed at it, and said, "Hinochinko, look in here from there. What do you see?" Reflected in the mirror, of course, was Ishihara's clock-stopping face. "I see *you*," he said, and Ishihara told him to come stand next to him and look. Hino was reluctant, but something about the man's voice and way of speaking seemed to drain him of his will, and he found himself standing before the mirror. "Looky, looky! Do you see two widdle faces?" Ishihara said in a creepy voice, as if hosting a TV show for toddlers. "Hinochinko, which of these two faces do you think most closely resembles your own? Not which one *is* you; that's not what I and I mean. When you look at this noble face here, like a Latin American freedom fighter turned genius poet, and then that round and pathetic face there that would be right at home on a little roadside stone bodhisattva, which would you say most closely resembles your own image of yourself?"

Hino couldn't help laughing, but he thought he understood more or less what Ishihara was saying: that nothing was certain, and that being unnerved by mirrors was perfectly normal. At least, that's the way it came across to him. Ishihara hadn't said there was something wrong with him or that it was loony to be afraid of your own reflection, he'd merely suggested a new way of looking at the problem. "It's definitely this one," Hino said, pointing at his own face in the glass. And ever since then, strangely enough, he'd been all right with mirrors. Whenever he did get anxious about what he saw there, he would think of Orihara's old-man face or Miyazaki's Moai statue face or Shibata's squashed and zit-covered face or Toyohara's big round skinhead face and realize that the one he was looking at was much more like him than any of those. It was from that point on that he'd begun sleeping twelve or more hours a day, as if making up for the sleep he'd lost in the institution.

Massaging his numb hand and arm, he wondered if all that hibernating had somehow been in preparation for this day. He walked out of Room 8033 and headed for 8036, where the next column was, with his team in tow. Felix and Matsuyama, who had already unlocked the door and left it ajar, were now in front of 8048, sticking the electronic master key into the slot. Felix looked across at him but didn't wave or say anything. He mechanically opened the lock, set the doorstop so it wouldn't close, and moved on.

Three blue lines ran parallel down the corridor's cream-colored carpeting. There were only two buses, connected to the exploder's plus and minus terminals, but the "negative bus" U-turned back on itself. To minimize the danger of getting the polarity wrong, Takeguchi had wrapped bands of white tape around the negative bus at intervals of about a meter. Sixteen red detonator wires from the column's eight LSCs snaked out from 8033 into the corridor. They looked like capillaries visible through translucent skin, reaching for the blue veins of the auxiliary busbars.

Seven columns remained, including the one here in 8036. When Hino stepped into the room, the clock by the bed changed from 11:09 to 11:10. It had been taking an average of five or six minutes per column, from veneer removal to connecting the wires. At this rate, they would probably finish well before the scheduled zero hour. Once their work was done, they were going to retrace the route they took to sneak in, leave through the Cafe Luggnagg exit, descend the steps, cross the road, run to the seashore, and take cover behind the breakwater. The breakwater was to the port side of the hotel, so if they got in the water and hugged the concrete, they should be okay, according to Takeguchi. The only problem was that while crossing the road they'd be visible to the guards at Checkpoint E. They would probably be shot at, but not even the Koryos were likely to hit anything from a distance of five hundred meters. Once they'd crossed, they would drop to the beach and out of the line of fire; and the moment they all reached the breakwater and took cover, Takeguchi would hit the switch on his hell-box by remote control, and it would all be over.

The column in 8036 was in the left-hand corner of the room. Tateno stood at the window, watching the movements of the sentries outside the Dome; Ando plugged in the hand-held electric cutter and readied the stepladder; and Shinohara stood by with his stripping tools as Hino drew the cut lines with a felt pen. None of them spoke as they worked. So this is what it's like to share a goal with other people and work together to achieve it, Hino thought as he turned the cutter on. Everyone who'd gathered at Ishihara's place, himself included, had always refused to follow orders from adults, had been categorized as mentally ill, and had attempted or committed serious crimes. All their lives they'd been told to reform, but none of them had ever even understood what the word meant.

Hino's teachers, the attendants at the institution, and other adults had always trotted out, like a mantra, the proposition that nothing was more precious than human life. Great numbers of people were being killed every day in the continuing upheavals in the Middle East, and tens of thousands of children were dying of starvation in Sudan and Ethiopia and other African countries. But these authority figures never spoke about the preciousness of *those* lives—apparently only the lives in their immediate circle counted. What were children supposed to make of people like that telling them how to live? Some, of course, simply knuckled under, but it wasn't because they'd concluded that the adults were right. They merely knew that obedience led to reward and rebellion to punishment, and they wanted to avoid the latter. The key was to find something you thought needed to be done and to do it, just as he and the others were doing right now. If you didn't have anything to do, if you merely accepted the advice of corrupt adults, obeying them and living the way they told you to, you woke up one day to find that your life was devoid of any excitement or pleasure. You lost hope and became homeless, or you searched for like-minded souls on the Internet and committed group suicide, or you resigned yourself to being a slave to the "grown-ups" for the rest of your days.

This room, 8036, was bigger than the others. According to the floor plan posted on the inside of the door, the rooms up to 8035 were all singles, and those aft of there were deluxe twins. Probably pretty expensive. Perhaps even the covering on the columns was meant to suggest luxury—the material was thick, with a long pile. Hino had to take even more care than usual, or fibers would get caught in the blade, making it slip. As with welding or cutting or chiseling, however, "taking care" didn't mean being gentle or slow. He had to grip both handles of the cutter tightly and then move decisively, cutting in one quick stroke. Bits of the material got in his mouth and nose, and he fought against the tickling in his throat. When he finished the first cut, he fell to his hands and knees and coughed violently. "Wanna rest awhile?" Shinohara said, lowering his crowbar. "No, I'm all right." Hino raised his head, and both Shinohara and Tateno burst out laughing. Shinohara touched his own upper lip and told Hino he was "leaking." A drip of snot, white with dust particles, was dangling from one nostril.

Ando went to see how Takeguchi and the others were progressing. On his return he said, "Looking good. Let's take five." Hino went to the bathroom to blow his nose, wash his face and hands, and put in some eye drops. Returning, he sat on the floor with the others.

They drank cans of oolong tea and Coke and Pocari Sweat from the fridge. "Hino's snot balloon reminded me of something that happened to me once," Ando said. "My father was a tax account- ant, and when I was maybe twelve, he said he wanted to treat me to some oysters and took me to this French restaurant, the only one in town. He didn't live with us, but about three or four times a year he'd take me out to dinner like that. So at the restaurant he ordered some wine and even poured some for me, though I didn't drink it, and I don't know if it was because we hadn't talked in a long time or what, but he was really nervous and kept guzzling this yellow—I mean, I guess you call it white wine.

"Anyway, he wasn't much of a drinker, and in the taxi on the way back he started feeling sick. He didn't want to barf in the cab, so he had the driver stop and got out and threw up. He crouched there for a long time, and finally I got worried and went to check on him. I'm like, Are you all right? and he's like, Yeah, sorry about this, or whatever, and he turns to look at me, and this big gray blob is hanging out of his nostril. I'm freakin' out, I'm like, *What the hell is that?* Well, what does it turn out to be but a whole undigested oyster, all covered with snot, just hanging there over his lips. And ever since then I can't even stand to look at an oyster, much less eat one."

Ando related this little reminiscence in such a heartfelt way that the other three felt obliged to stifle their laughter. Hino stood up and said, "Shall we get back to it?" Tateno grabbed the binoculars hanging from a strap around his neck and went to the window, where he immediately gave a strangled cry and dropped to a crouch, pointing the binoculars downward over the windowsill. "Koryo soldiers," he said. "They're coming in the main entrance." His voice was shaky, his face and fingers pale. "Nothing unusual about that," Shinohara said. "Their HQ's here." He stepped toward the window, but Tateno raised his right hand to stop him and began counting the soldiers. "One, two, three, four," he said. "Five, six, seven, eight. Yeah, but this is different. Nine, ten, eleven, twelve. They're running. Got weapons too. Thirteen, fourteen, fifteen, sixteen, seventeen, eighteen, nineteen, twenty, twenty-one…"

By the time he passed twenty, the blood had drained from the others' faces as well, and Hino began to feel as if he were trying to digest a golf ball. "Twenty-two... Ah! One of them just looked up this way. Twenty-three, twenty-four—another one looked up. Twenty-five, twenty-six... Twenty-six altogether." Tateno turned around. "They're all armed," he said. "It doesn't necessarily mean they're onto us," Hino said. "Anyway, let's finish the job." He was picking up his cutter when Fukuda poked his head through the open door and said, "You'd better come and look. The elevators are moving."

The elevators had been shut down since the Koryos relocated their HQ. Everyone except Kaneshiro and Okubo was in the elevator hall, watching the array of floor indicator panels. They had all brought arms with them: Mori the M16, Orihara the AK, Miyazaki the Scorpion light machine gun, Kondo the Beretta, Yamada the shotgun, and Ando the grenade launcher. But compared to the opposition, Hino thought, they were like monkeys showing up on the first tee with an assortment of golf clubs.

There was no access to the six express elevators, which skipped all the floors between three and seventeen, but the indicators showed that four of the six were moving. Tateno had counted twenty-six soldiers, all heavily armed, so they had probably boarded in groups of six or seven. It was obvious that the Koryos knew something was up.

"Why would they be onto us, all of a sudden?" Felix asked, expressing what everyone must have been thinking, then immediately came up with the correct response: "Well, no point in wondering about that right now." Takeguchi warned Kaneshiro and Okubo by cellphone. Kaneshiro said he'd be right up to join them, but Takeguchi vetoed that. "Whatever happens, you and Okubo need to stay with the hell-box. If the Koryos show up on the fifth floor, disconnect the device like I showed you. Cut the two auxiliary busbar extensions, positive and negative, and bring the box up here, making sure the wires don't get tangled."

Yamada was staring at the floor indicator panels. "What'll we do if one stops at this floor?" he said, his voice quavering. Sato told him that only the express elevators were moving, and they didn't stop at eight. As they watched, the moving elevators all raced to the top floor, the thirty-fifth, where they came to rest. "Shouldn't we finish our work, rather than stand here watching the elevators?" Mori said, but Shinohara kept his eyes on the indicators and said, "First we've got to figure out what they're up to."

Fukuda pointed out that in any case it would be best to retrieve the antipersonnel mines they'd set on the emergency stairways, and headed aft. There were three of these stairways—one fore, on the starboard side; one adjoining the express-elevator shafts, in the middle; and one aft, which led to the lobby. "Fukuda, wait," said Mori, and unslung the M16: "You want this?" Fukuda shook his head. "Nah. If I bump into those guys, no weapon's gonna do me any good." Ando was looking back and forth from the floor indicators to his watch, and Shibata asked him what he was doing. "They must be searching the place," he said. "I'm timing how long it'll take them to finish one whole floor."

The elevators began to move. Ando looked at his watch and said, "Approximately three minutes." They stopped at the next floor down from the top. "So they're searching one floor at a time?" Kondo said. Shibata calculated that at the rate of one every three minutes, they'd arrive here in about an hour and eighteen minutes, prompting Takeguchi to say, "Then we can finish in time. Let's get back to it." Tateno pointed out that they might change tactics and suggested that one person stay behind to watch the elevators, but Takeguchi was against the idea. "Fukuda's busy with the mines, and we're already shorthanded," he said. "We can't spare another man." But Ando took a step forward. "I'll stay," he offered. "Tateno's got the binoculars, and Shinohara's way better at stripping the veneer than I am. I might be more useful here."

Hino got back to work, wearing a towel over his nose and mouth like a bandanna. The shaggy coverings were still a problem; if he lost concentration for a moment, the blade slipped. Shinohara asked Tateno if anything was happening with the guards outside the

Dome. "There are just two of them now," he said. "And they're both talking on their cellphones." Still looking through the binoculars, he asked, "What about the bugs? Why aren't they afraid of 'em now?" Shinohara cocked his head to one side as he scraped off some old adhesive with the chisel. "Good question," he said. Hino thought the guys in charge must have decided that these twenty-six men were expendable. Even if the centipedes got them they'd hardly be missed, since a whole division was expected that evening. Tateno's cellphone vibrated. It was Ando, reporting that the Koryos had reached floor thirty-one. That seemed faster than expected, and Shinohara checked his watch. "They've completed three floors in only seven minutes and forty seconds."

"They're getting the hang of it," Hino said. His towel was already damp in front from his sweat and breath, making speech difficult. "After all, we're going faster than we were at first too." Shinohara, standing on the stepladder, inserted the tip of the chisel in a cut line, hit it with the hammer to pry the covering up, then shoved in the crowbar. He was spitting out dust and fibers and muttering to himself.

"They don't give a fuck. They're exterminators, is what they are. Anybody resists, they just kill 'em. They don't care who it is. It's all about getting rid of anyone who's different." He switched to the lower front of the column. Hino moved the stepladder to work on the upper right, then put the cutter down on the bed for a minute to massage his arms and wipe off the sweat with the sheets. The guests had left in a hurry, and the rooms were in disarray. At the forward end, they'd seen bloodstained sheets in a couple of the rooms and a used condom lying on the floor in another. The one right at the end of the corridor had a hot tub surrounded by large bow windows, with a green bottle sticking out of a silver wine bucket next to it.

The image of the bath and the bottle of wine stuck in Hino's head even as he took up the electric cutter again and climbed the stepladder. Had the guest in that room been alone? No, he was more likely to have had company. What would it be like to get into a tub like that with a naked woman and drink wine and look out at the city lights? While he was speculating about this, the blade of the cutter slipped on the shaggy covering and strayed from the line. He turned the thing off and repositioned it.

What was wrong with him? Was he tired? No, he decided—it was just that the Koryos upstairs were messing with his concentration. Shinohara was fighting the copious amounts of adhesive and cursing and muttering to himself: "Fuckin' Koryos. They can't stand to have someone around who isn't just like them. It's no problem for them if people die or get killed—enemies, allies, they don't give a fuck. Bugs, people—anyone who's different from them, or just in the way, gets exterminated."

Hino had never heard Shinohara talk this much; he was usually so cool and reserved. Why was he going on like that? And why were the bloody sheets and used condom and glassed-in hot tub weighing on his own mind? He'd never had thoughts intrude on him like this before. Tateno was peering through the binoculars he held in his right hand and holding the cellphone against his ear with the left, waiting for Ando's reports and muttering useless information about the guards: *They're looking up at the sky… They're having a smoke… They're talking… They're laughing.* The reason we're all acting weird like this, Hino suddenly realized, is because we're scared shitless.

Tateno relayed Ando's report that the Koryos had moved to floor thirty. They were definitely getting faster. And we, Hino thought, are so shook up that we've actually slowed down. He left the room, telling Tateno and Shinohara that he was going to have a word with Takeguchi, and they followed him. On the way they passed through the central elevator hall. Ando was there, watching the floor indicators, and when he saw them running toward him, he asked what was wrong. "I'll explain later," Hino said as they ran past. "Just stay here and keep watch, okay?"

Takeguchi's team had run into problems too. Miyazaki had mistaken positive and negative while connecting one of the detonator wires, much to the exasperation of the team leader, who was now checking all the wires one by one with Sato. When Hino said he wanted a word with him, Takeguchi gave him a dubious look and asked if he'd already finished his job. Hino didn't answer but explained what had just occurred to him. Yamada and Mori, the five Satanists, and Felix and Matsuyama, who had stopped unlocking doors and come to help with the wiring, laid down their tools to listen. "Right now we're so scared we're afraid to recognize it," he said, "and we're all trying to act calm. Me, I'm just about to piss my pants, but I'm afraid to admit it, and that's why I can't concentrate on what I'm doing. We're losing time, and suddenly we're making mistakes. At this rate, the Koryos are going to arrive before we're finished." Several of the others nodded, looking visibly relieved. Everybody seemed to be having a similar reaction. Takeguchi looked down at his feet. "You saying we should get out of here?" he said.

"Let me ask you one thing," Hino said. "You're the only one who can answer. If we stop work now and run for it, can you hit the remote control from the beach and bring the hotel down?" Takeguchi shook his head, and there was a collective groan of disappointment. Mori and Yamada looked at each other and said, "Damn," in unison. "We still have eight columns to rig. If we set it off now, it would probably just buckle at the eighth floor and lean over but not collapse." Takeguchi looked around at everyone after saying this. "They've moved to twenty-eight," Tateno reported. Hino asked Takeguchi about the antipersonnel mines.

"They're replicas of Claymores that Fukuda made. You put five cookies in a container that looks like a flat audio speaker, and shove in twelve hundred ball bearings. When it explodes, the balls rip the target to shreds. At three meters, they have a fan-shaped radius of four meters; at five, six meters. Set one off in front of an open elevator and you'll kill all seven or eight Koryos inside. But there's a problem. They're using four elevators, and we only have three mines. Fukuda made them for the three emergency stairwells, and he can't make another one because he hasn't got the ingredients. Besides, they're not going to be synchronizing the elevators to arrive at a floor at the same time—there's bound to be a lag of at least a few seconds. When they hear the first explosion, some of the others might take cover and survive."

591

"If there are any survivors, we kill them," Hino said. He looked at the others and added, "Don't get me wrong. I don't want to fight these guys. But we've done all this work, and now that we're this close, I want to finish the job. For us to concentrate on getting it done, we've got to decide what we're going to do. If we're going to fight them to the death, we need to be clear about that."

Everyone nodded agreement at the words "finish the job." None of them had ever worked as part of a team before. They'd never helped anyone or been helped by anyone in any sort of endeavor. They were all scared to death of the Koryos, but they wanted to see their project through. "Ah," said Takeguchi. "So that's what you're trying to say. Okay. Let's decide what we need to do when they get to this floor—how to fight them." He told Felix and Matsuyama to take over from Kaneshiro and Okubo on the fifth floor and send them up here. After receiving a brief explanation of how to handle the exploder, the two of them headed for the stairs.

"The one thing we have going for us is that the Koryos aren't expecting an ambush," Hino said, and Takeguchi, looking at the ceiling, added, "Here's hoping their guard is down by the time they reach us, after searching all those floors and not finding anything."

Fukuda's mines were just as Takeguchi had described them—they looked like flat speakers, covered with the same sort of mesh material. Each was supported by a low stand, had red cables extending from the rear, and was about the size of a looseleaf binder and only a few centimeters thick. Fukuda placed them in front of the doors to the lower-floor elevators. There were four of these, two on either side. He designated the forward elevators "A" and "B" and the aft pair, directly across from them, "C" and "D." On the stairways he'd rigged the mines with trip wires, but he had disassembled these and now connected each mine to a manual detonator. These were simple devices that consisted of two dry-cell batteries, a small converter, and a switch panel of sheet copper.

Two of the mines were aimed at elevators C and D, each positioned diagonally and a couple of paces away. A certain distance from the target was needed for the little steel balls to fan out and do their job, and the angle would prevent the Koryos at the front acting as shields for those behind. Fukuda had to set the third mine even farther back, where it could do some damage to either A or B. According to Ando, who'd continued to watch the floor indicators, the lag between the first elevator to move and the last varied from six to twelve seconds, and there was no pattern to the order in which they arrived.

After they had reached a consensus on the ambush plan, Kaneshiro and Fukuda remained with Ando in the elevator hall while the rest went back to setting the charges. Hino's team had started at Room 8027, which was located in the bow, and were working sternward toward the last room with a column, 8052. So far they had completed only 8033. Even if they continued at the pace they'd maintained till now, they probably wouldn't finish before the Koryos arrived.

If there were any survivors from elevators C and D, they would naturally try to head aft, where they'd find Hino and Takeguchi and the others at work and shoot them all down in about two seconds. Any Koryo survivors had to be driven forward, therefore, so most of the weapons were needed aft of the elevators. Kaneshiro dragged some mini refrigerators from the guest rooms and placed four of them side by side across the aft corridors. He then piled three more on top, and braced these makeshift barricades with sofas and chairs, to create a line of defense. He built three of these in all—one across the starboard corridor forward of elevator B and one each in the two sternward corridors, just aft of C and D. He decided to position Orihara with the AK behind line of defense B; Miyazaki with the light machine gun behind C; and to concentrate the rest of the firepower behind line D, which he proceeded to fortify with a second fridge-and-furniture barricade. He stacked the refrigerators two-high at the first of these, but added a third layer for the rear one, some four meters back.

Kaneshiro and Yamada positioned themselves behind the front barricade at line D with the Uzi and the Franchi shotgun. The idea was to kill any escaping Koryos with a barrage of gunfire at close range. Behind the rear barricade were Mori with his M16 and Ando with the grenade launcher. The difference in height between the two barricades meant that those in front could kneel and fire while those behind fired standing up. In the rear barricade they left a gap on one side wide enough for a single person to run through, so that if the front barricade was breached, Kaneshiro and Yamada could fall back. Shibata, on the wiring team, was entrusted with the FN, and Felix, who was guarding the exploder, had the other pistol, the Beretta. This was in anticipation of the worst-case scenario—the Koryos breaking through both barricades and reaching the center of activity. Orihara and Miyazaki had two hand grenades apiece, and the remaining nine grenades were placed behind the line D barricades—four at the front and five at the rear.

They hadn't loaded the weapons and spare magazines before bringing them here and had to do so now. It proved unexpectedly time-consuming, and Matsuyama and Felix were summoned back to the eighth floor to help. They brought the exploder with them and carried it to the last room, 8052, where they would stay to guard it. Tateno, too, took a break from the binoculars to help load a magazine for the Uzi. The little machine gun was made completely of shiny black steel and was surprisingly heavy, as was the magazine. Tateno took the bullets from cardboard packages and pressed them one by one into the rectangular magazine. Each time one went in properly, it made a satisfying *ka-chick* sound, like a hammer striking stone. In his notes Takei had said that unless you pushed until you heard that sound, it could cause a misfire. The Uzi magazine had what was called a double column, allowing for more bullets in a small space. When you shoved a round in, the previous bullet was pushed to the side and downward. There must be a powerful spring inside, Tateno said, and after inserting about fourteen rounds he announced that his thumb was killing him. The Uzi held thirty-two rounds, but he said he couldn't possibly do another eighteen. "I might need this hand later," he said with a scowl, and gave the magazine and bullets back to Kaneshiro.

Kaneshiro loaded the magazines with the speed and assurance of a pro. Hino guessed that he had practiced a lot with Takei. It seemed that the trick, when time was limited, was to load fewer rounds than the capacity. If the magazine held thirty rounds, for example, he would load only twenty-seven. Kaneshiro was wearing the form-fitting, dark-blue uniform of the GEK Cobra Unit from Takei's collection. They had all dressed in dark clothing for the night-time infiltration, but he alone had chosen a uniform and lace-up boots. Elastic held the material in at his wrists and ankles and waist, and the uniform did seem to provide excellent mobility. It had pockets for magazines and grenades, and lots of belt straps to hold weapons or equipment. Kaneshiro had a big combat knife in an ankle sheath, and he was also wearing a bulletproof vest. When Yamada saw the vest, with its pleated ridges, he said, "Can I have one of those?" He got no reply, but someone tried to console him by saying that the Koryos always aimed for the head anyway.

Since his arrival on the eighth floor, Kaneshiro's demeanor had remained calm even as he began preparations for the counterattack. For Hino and the others setting the charges, the aim was to bring down the hotel, but Kaneshiro seemed to have a separate goal of his own. In any case, the preparations went smoothly and efficiently under his direction, and once the lines of defense were ready, it was he who decided where to position everyone. "He's the real deal," Felix said, and Okubo agreed: "He's studied pretty much every book and DVD ever made about war and terrorism and stuff." Having trained with Takei using live rounds in the basement of Building E, Kaneshiro was the only one here who had actually fired a rifle or sub-machine gun; the others had only read Takei's handwritten notes. But he was so cool as he gave them instructions that they all seemed optimistic about their chances. No one was panicky. He pointed out that they would be shooting at very close range and convinced them that if they just held their weapons firmly and squeezed the triggers, they'd mow the enemy down. He said these things as if explaining how to snap a photo with his camera. His usual energy and intensity seemed accentuated a bit, but he showed no excitement, much less anxiety. He was like a baseball player at some north-country high school playing catch after the first thaw of spring.

While the others were building barricades and loading guns or setting antipersonnel mines, Takeguchi and Sato used knives and a crowbar to peel back about twenty meters of carpeting from either end of the elevator hall, and hid the auxiliary busbars underneath it. Sato was worried the mines might rip through the wires when they exploded, but Takeguchi assured him that the blast would be angled above the horizontal. All these activities took about twenty minutes, during which time the Koryos had moved down to floor twenty-one. Just thirteen floors away. Thirty or thirty-five minutes, Hino figured. But he had learned the trick to cutting the shaggy material—letting the wind from the blade form a part in the pile before pressing down—and that speeded things up considerably. His team managed to finish rooms 8036, 8039, and 8042 in exactly fifteen minutes.

When it was reported that the squadron upstairs had reached the seventeenth floor, the tension was palpable. Below seventeen, they would switch to the lower-floor elevators. With the mine detonators, the Uzi, and the grenade launcher at the ready, Kaneshiro, Fukuda, and Ando took up their positions behind the first barricade at line D. They had a clear view of the floor indicators from there. As soon as the Koryos reached the tenth floor, everyone but the people setting the charges would be summoned to their battle stations. Okubo and Shibata would be behind the rear barricade D, reloading magazines. When the Koryos left floor ten, Hino would turn off his electric cutter, to make sure they weren't tipped off by the noise.

With the door of 8045 open, Hino could see the elevator hall and lines of defense B and D. The Koryos were approaching at a pace of about two and a half to three minutes per floor. They would arrive here within twenty minutes, by which time the Hino and Takeguchi teams would have moved behind the rear barricade to 8050 or, hopefully, 8052. Hino had always had a recurring nightmare in which he found himself in a confined space, unable to move as a murderer slowly closed in. Now it was really happening. "Fifteenth floor," Ando reported. Hino could feel his heartbeat pound in the bone-dry walls of his throat. But strangely enough he was working faster and more efficiently than ever. It wasn't that the fear had waned—he was definitely still afraid. But knowing you were afraid was different from pretending you weren't. He may have been on the verge of wetting himself, but at least he knew what counter-measures they would take when the Koryos materialized. Even if you were terrified, as long as you were aware of it and had decided on a course of action, you could face the object of your fear head on. As he thought about this, he suddenly remembered his mother.

With dust flying around him and the towel bandanna sodden from spit and snot, Hino saw his mother's face—the face of the woman who'd stabbed his father to death, stabbed and seriously injured her own son, and then killed herself. He had never thought about her at all since that time and hadn't felt anything even when they told him at the institution that she'd committed suicide. But coming into focus in his mind's eye now was the image of her eating lunch with him in a neighborhood park when he was little. They'd bought box lunches at a convenience store. His mother always got the tofu chili, and he the hamburger steak.

His mother hadn't had anything to do, and as a result she was always seeing and hearing things she had no business seeing and hearing. Not realizing that the fear came from inside herself, she had blamed it on the building materials in their new house. It wasn't connected with the materials, of course: the object of her fear might have been anything—needles, the moon, shopping malls, high places, her own sweat—but as long as she believed it was something outside her, it was outside her control. Poor thing, she didn't even know there *was* any way of dealing with her fears. Hino had never felt sorry for his mother before. He'd never felt hatred or resentment either, but rather had buried all his feelings about her. And yet now, of all times, they had been unearthed in an eruption of sympathy.

He felt he could understand her now. Living had become such agony for her that she'd had no way of coping other than to stab those closest to her and then kill herself. With this feeling of sympathy, something deep in his gut seemed to melt and radiate a kind of warmth throughout his body. Waves of an emotion he hadn't known before surged up inside him, and tears accumulated at the inner rim of his goggles. His vision was blurred, and he couldn't see his own cut line. He took the goggles off and wiped his eyes with the knuckles of his leather gloves. Shinohara asked him what was wrong. "Nothing. Just got some stuff in my eyes," he said, and gripped the cutter again. *I'll avenge you*, he muttered under his breath. *Keep watching from hell. See what your son is going to do.* He pictured her sitting on the grass in the park, eating her tofu chili, as he inwardly repeated these words. *Just watch.*

They were nearly finished in 8050 when Ando popped his head in and said that the Koryos had left the tenth floor. "Fuckers," Hino said as he switched the cutter off. Shinohara said, "Shit! We're almost done." After this room, there was only the final one, 8052. "I reckon that's about the size of it, though," Hino muttered, remembering the old guy who'd taught him how to use arc welders and cutting torches at a construction site in Shinagawa. The geezer had used this expression habitually, always following it up with, "If things go too smooth in life, you end up dyin' before your time."

Still standing in the doorway, Ando asked if they could spare Tateno. "Kaneshiro says if he's not needed here, he should come help load the magazines." Tateno was already removing the binoculars from his neck when Hino said, "No, we need him here." He was going to object, but Shinohara silenced him with a small shake of his head. And just then Takeguchi, Sato, and Kondo piled in through the doorway, sideswiping Ando and nearly knocking him down. They had finished setting and wiring the LSCs in 8048, and now, without a word, they got to work on the column in this room. Their teamwork was so good now that it took them only about two and a half minutes to set charges on all five of the spots that Hino and Shinohara had exposed. Sato quickly connected the wires in the corridor, then came back to the doorway and said, "If you hear things heating up down the hall, just keep going. No need to worry about making noise anymore. Let's get it finished."

Hino nodded, but Tateno asked in an anguished way why he shouldn't go and help the others. He was nearly in tears. "They're going to shoot it out with the Koryos," he said. "What good am I here?" Shinohara told him to stay put and not worry about it. "But why?" Hino, plucking bits of material from the blade of the cutter, said, "Because this is the safest place. There's nothing wrong with resting while everyone's working their ass off, and there's nothing wrong with running for safety when everyone's shooting each other. Listen, Tateno. This isn't about anybody being a hero. We're here to do a job, not because we're all eager to die side by side. You don't have to obey Kaneshiro's orders. You don't have to obey anybody. A minute ago your thumb was killing you when you tried to load that magazine. You think you'll be any use reloading if some of the Koryos survive and it turns into an actual firefight? I mean, I don't know. Do what you want to do. If you really want to reload magazines, go. If you don't want to, don't."

Tateno slumped to a sitting position on the floor beside the window. Then they heard someone say, "Here they come." Hino scuttled to the doorway and lay prone there, alongside Sato and Takeguchi, looking up the corridor through the gap in the rear barricade at D. They heard the *ding* of an arriving elevator, and Sato whispered, "It's B." All was silent except for the mechanical whir of the door opening, and then a number of footsteps and the clatter of metal against metal. Lying on his stomach, his hands over his ears, Takeguchi turned a pale face toward Hino and mouthed: *It's a dud!* The Koryos' footsteps were coming this way but suddenly stopped. They must have reached the corridor and seen the mini-fridge barricade. Something was said, then shouted, in Korean and—*ding*—another elevator arrived. "That's C," Sato whispered, and two seconds later came a deafening roar and a shock wave that lifted them off the floor and seemed to turn their insides to jelly. This was followed almost immediately by a hurricane-force blast of scorched-smelling wind through the corridor.

599

Hino hadn't covered his ears and for a moment couldn't hear anything but a high-pitched ringing. He had in fact wet himself. But the sprinklers in the room and corridor had sprung to life, and everybody was getting soaked. Carefully shielding the cellphone, Takeguchi scooted back to the middle of the room, contacted Matsuyama in 8052, and shouted that he mustn't let the exploder get wet. Pointing, Kondo said, "What's that?" and when Hino peered up the corridor he saw Miyazaki with his back to them, one shoulder hanging at an unnatural angle. He was staggering forward with his hands outstretched, groping his way toward the elevator hall. "He's supposed to be at line C," Sato said. "What the hell's he doing?" Takeguchi said that he must have been wounded by the mine and lost his bearings.

Something more than just urine had exited Hino's body when he peed himself: the thing they called ego or soul or spirit or something. He didn't feel the cold water of the sprinklers as unpleasant, or as anything else. All he knew was that he had to get back to work. His ears were still ringing loudly, and he could hear only intermittently what the others were saying. He bent down with a grimace and picked up the electric cutter. He was about to switch it on when a hand stopped him. The egg-like smoothness of the face told him it was Shinohara, but he wasn't sure how he knew this person. "Not yet," Shinohara was telling him. "Not till all the elevators have arrived. We don't need to let them know we're in here cutting stuff up."

He couldn't grasp what Shinohara was saying. Water was still spraying vigorously from the sprinklers. His field of vision was distorted as if by a fish-eye lens. He went back to the doorway and leaned out, and in the distance he could see Miyazaki, covered with blood. His understanding of what was going on came down to two words: "explosion" and "Koryo." Explosion, Koryo. Because of one or the other, blood was oozing like melted ice cream from Miyazaki's shoulder and the top of his head. "What happened to the first group of Koryos?" someone asked. "They went back to the elevator hall when the others arrived," said a voice he recognized as Takeguchi's. "The mine got 'em." And then, over the ringing in his ears, he heard two consecutive *dings*. "Miyazaki's out there!" Tateno said, and Sato, diving to the floor and covering his ears, said, "It's A and D—two at once." Hino also got down and covered his ears, but the second explosion lifted him right up in the air and then slammed him back down face-first on the carpet. The shock wave threatened to squeeze his intestines out though his asshole, and the sprinklers rained sideways upon him as a sulfurous wind blew over his head and down the corridor.

He could hear Takeguchi saying, "Too many cookies in those things! They took out some of our guys too!" Tateno asked what had happened to Miyazaki. Sato's voice said, "Shouldn't there be flames?" Takeguchi said, "This isn't Hollywood," and Shinohara shouted, "Koryos!" Figures had appeared in the elevator hall toward which Miyazaki had been walking moments ago. Kaneshiro turned to the rear barricade at D and yelled, "Hand grenade!" and Mori rose slowly behind the mini fridges, like a child who'd been found out at hide-and-seek. He was winding up to throw his grenade when bright, tracer-like streaks raced toward him. His right arm separated from his shoulder and spun off on its own, and most of his midsection was ripped out in an explosion of blood. The green Koryo shadows moved jerkily, like broken marionettes. Kaneshiro was firing the Uzi nonstop. "What happened to Miyazaki?" Tateno kept chanting as he climbed to his feet. "What happened to Miyazaki?" Suddenly Ando staggered in through the doorway. A red chunk of someone's flesh had landed on his face and stuck there. "Get it off me!" he shrieked. "Somebody get it off me!" He was slapping hysterically at his own cheek, apparently oblivious to the hole in his neck from which blood was spurting in small parabolas.

Takeguchi said, "Let's get to it." Hino grabbed the cutter from a puddle on the carpeting and began crawling toward the next column. Tateno was in the corner. Right in front of him Ando, still slapping at his face, buckled at the knees and toppled to the floor. As he lay there twitching, blood from the hole in his neck crawled over the carpet like worms in grass. Hino stood as if mesmerized by the sight. He kept hearing a harsh, metallic keening, but he wasn't sure

601

if it was his ears ringing or bullets whizzing through the air. Only Takeguchi's "Let's get to it" had registered clearly.

At construction sites, you heard those words without fail at the end of the lunch break. Hino had always loved being part of the flow of workers heading back to their stations and enjoyed reuniting with his own section of steel frame or pipework, through which the blue flame of his blowtorch would soon be slicing like scissors through paper. He turned the cutter on. His spirit had left him along with his urine, but he could still strip veneer from columns.

Water continued to squirt from the sprinklers. The walls and floor were all wet, and the long-piled coverings were actually easier to cut through because of being drenched. Shinohara was waiting with crowbar, hammer, and chisel, but he laid the tools next to the column, then turned around and slapped Tateno's face, hard. "If the Koryos come, you kill them," he said, stripping the backpack from Tateno's shoulders and slamming it against his chest. "Got it?" Was he telling him to kill them with his boomerangs? Or just trying to get him to snap out of it? Tateno stood there like a sleepwalker, cradling the backpack and staring down at the stream of blood making its way from the neck of the now motionless Ando toward his own shoes. It was as if the tentacles of blood were alive and Tateno himself some sort of wooden object. The gunfight was still raging, and smaller explosions echoed through the low-ceilinged corridor and made the air itself seem to tremble. Hino heard Sato say, "Kaneshiro's the only one shooting," and then Takeguchi: "Shibata, Okubo, and Kondo are down."

He did the rest of the cuts in about thirty seconds. After watching Shinohara finish his bit, he turned to Takeguchi to say, "We're done." He unplugged the cutter and was heading out the door to move to 8052 when Sato, who was crouching there, grabbed his ankle and brought him down. "What're you, crazy?" Sato shouted right in his face. "There are still Koryos out there!" With a jerk of his head, he drew Hino's attention to Kondo, who was lying just outside the doorway. From under Kondo's arm extended a tube-like thing about the size of a child's finger, the exposed end of which was merrily spraying blood. It was an artery. Takeguchi and Sato crawled over to move Kondo's body and grab the bundle of LSCs he'd fallen on. Keeping low, they hurried back to the column at the room's far wall and got to work. Hino and Shinohara now crawled out into the corridor for a look. Behind the rear barricade, with its half-collapsed pile of mini fridges, lay Mori's body, about a meter away from his right arm. There was another corpse on top of him, but Hino didn't know who it was.

After he'd set fire to the reformatory, one of the attendants there had shown Hino photographs of charred bodies, and all he'd thought was that they looked like chocolate-coated figurines. But there was a distinctive atmosphere about dead people in real life. Something had leaked out of them. It wasn't just blood and fluids, or viruses or bacteria fleeing the host, and it wasn't the spirit either. Hino's spirit had leaked out of him a while ago, and he wasn't dead. What was it that had left these bodies? He was wondering about this as he crawled on toward the stern, when another explosion shook the entire corridor. The percussion went right through him, from the soles of his feet to the top of his skull, and a nauseating, sulfuric stench overwhelmed the metallic smell of the blood-saturated carpeting. The shock wave gave his insides another good squeeze, but no piss came out this time. Shinohara, his elbows red with carpet-blood as he crawled along beside him, explained: "Kaneshiro must have thrown a grenade." They were about half the distance to the doorway of 8052 when they heard Kaneshiro call out to them: "One Koryo coming your way!" Terrified, Hino turned to look behind him, but there was no one there. Realizing he must've meant the other direction, he turned back and caught a glimpse of a gun barrel, a green camouflaged sleeve, and a blood-soaked hand in the shadows of the sternmost emergency stairwell. The Koryo had circled around from the port-side corridor.

Kaneshiro switched from the Uzi to the M16 and was firing in three-shot bursts. Several of his bullets hit the fire extinguisher at the end of the corridor, attached to the wall behind which the Koryo was holed up. A large splinter of wood from the paneling lodged in Hino's shoulder as he lay there face down, and two of the bullets that ricocheted off the fire extinguisher banged one after another into the door to 8052. Matsuyama, mistaking the sound for someone knocking, opened the door a crack to look out and was met with a flurry of AK fire at short range. The Koryo then fired a second sustained burst that chewed into the door, causing it to swing wide open, rebound, and slam shut again. He pulled back into the stairwell until Kaneshiro stopped firing, then thrust the barrel of the AK out from the shadows. But before he could shoot, something exploded behind him, and as if propelled from a trampoline he did a high-speed twisting somersault, bounced off the door to 8052, and dropped heavily to the floor. "That's all of them," Sato said, stepping over Hino and Shinohara on the way to 8052. "All the Koryos are dead." Takeguchi, close behind him, yelled at them to get up and get back to work. They both jumped to their feet, grabbed their tools, and followed. The Koryo was sitting slumped against the wall next to the door, legs outspread. He was dead, but there were few visible wounds. Takeguchi explained that a grenade's shock wave can rattle your brain so hard it kills you.

There was a small bloodstain on Hino's shirt where the splinter of wood had pierced his shoulder, but it didn't hurt and he had full use of his arm. Matsuyama had fallen near the column, and he had to move him aside. His face looked like a pomegranate split in half. Hino picked up the cutter; Takeguchi had already drawn the cut lines. Felix had been hit by the Koryo's AK as well; he was bleeding from the chest and buttocks, and each breath was like the wheeze of a severe asthma attack. When they gently rolled him onto his back, they uncovered the exploder, wrapped in a plastic laundry bag. It wasn't clear whether Felix had been shielding the device with his body or merely happened to fall on it. Takeguchi wiped a few drops of sticky blood from the panel and inspected his hell-box. "It's alive," he said.

Orihara came limping in. It turned out he was the one who'd thrown the grenade from behind the Koryo. A bit of shrapnel had grazed his thigh, he said. As he tore open his trouser leg to apply antiseptic to the wound, he mentioned that Kaneshiro was using his knife on the dead bodies. Not knowing what this meant, they all ignored it and went about their work in a trance of concentration, with Sato checking all the lines to make sure none of them had been severed in the firefight. They were nearly finished when Tateno came into the room and echoed what Orihara had said. "Kaneshiro is doing something to the bodies." The sprinklers had finally stopped, five minutes after the first explosion. Hino looked around: Shinohara, Tateno, Sato, Takeguchi, Orihara. Apparently they and Kaneshiro were the only ones still alive and kicking. "How are we going to escape?" Sato said, trying to dry himself with a towel from the closet. Felix, on the bed, let out a rattling groan, and they all looked at one another: What do we do with *him*? Just then, Kaneshiro came bounding in. The M16 hung from his shoulder strap, and he held something cupped in his hands, half hidden by the handle of a combat knife clamped in the crook of his thumb. He had the air of a young girl carrying a bunch of freshly picked flowers.

"What's... that?" Takeguchi asked, his voice catching as he looked more closely at what might have been a batch of gyoza dumplings. Kaneshiro seemed puzzled by the question, then glanced down at his hands. "Oh, these?" he said. "Ears. Warriors always take the enemy's ears and string them into a necklace. I thought everybody knew that. Goes way back to the Romans, the Huns, up through the Zulus and the Viet Cong. You all go ahead and get out of here." He dropped his trophies on the floor, gripped the knife, and cut the cable to the cellphone charger. Takeguchi, his face red with rage, was about to pounce on him when Kaneshiro said, "No choice now but to set it off by hand, right? So hurry up. Get the hell out." Takeguchi glared at him. "You going to set it off yourself?" he said, and Kaneshiro nodded. "I'm staying here. Look at all this." He waved a hand at the carnage in the room and out in the corridor. "This is the world I've always dreamed of, and I've finally found it. Why would I go anywhere else? I'll take care of everything. It's my world, so I get to destroy it myself. If the Koryos come, I'll hit the switch immediately. If they don't come, I'll hit it in five—no, let's say seven and a half minutes. That should be plenty of time. But get going."

Why the time limit, Takeguchi asked, and Kaneshiro said, "Precious moments are precious because they're only moments." From the bed, Felix moaned something in a wheeze like escaping air. Tateno went to his side and bent down to listen, then reported that he was asking them to lay Matsuyama down beside him. One of them held the two parts of Matsuyama's face together as they carried his remains over to the bed. "I guess they were homos after all," Sato said quietly. When Tateno asked if they were just going to leave Felix there, Kaneshiro, who was taking his bulletproof vest off, said, "He's drowning in his own blood. He'll be dead in a minute."

Thinking the stairs would take too much time, they decided to use one of the emergency elevators to make their escape. These went all the way down to the garage in B2, which had an exit leading to the four-lane road that circled the hotel and Dome. "But the Koryos will see that the main elevators aren't working," said Sato, "and they probably heard the explosions. What if they send people up, find the charges, and cut the wires? I'll fuckin' shoot myself." Takeguchi patted his back and pointed at the exploder at Kaneshiro's feet. "Don't worry. To defuse a bomb, you always have to disconnect the detonator first, because some are rigged to go off when a wire is cut. Besides, we used what's called serial circuitry, so unless they cut one of the buses there'll be fireworks."

Kaneshiro was holding forth as the others prepared to leave. "I didn't get hit once. Not even on my vest," he told them, picking up an ear from the floor and poking a hole in it with the tip of his knife. "The mines never touched me, and not a single bullet so much as grazed me. All the great terrorists have been like that. Wyatt Earp, Napoleon, General Patton, Vo Nguyen Giap, Fidel Castro, none of them were ever hit." He then made a request. "When you get back to the warehouse, be sure to tell Ishihara-san to write about what happened here. In a poem or something." With what looked like a grimace of embarrassment, he said: "Okay. Seven and a half minutes from... now." He pushed a button on his watch and returned to opening holes in the ears.

The emergency elevators were in the service corridor, beyond the walled-off express-elevator shafts. Orihara, limping along with his bandaged thigh, held up his AK and said, "Anybody want this?" Sato took the weapon, saying he'd hang on to it for now. Takeguchi picked up a pair of hand grenades lying beside Mori's corpse, stuck one in his pocket, and handed the other to Hino. Testing the heft of the AK, Sato said, "This thing's surprisingly light." It was fully loaded, too—Orihara hadn't fired a single shot. Nor had Yamada fired his shotgun, or Miyazaki or Ando their weapons. They had all been felled by ball bearings or bullets before getting off a single round.

As they trotted along, Shinohara muttered, "Napoleon and Patton were terrorists?" Sato looked at Takeguchi. "I never heard of Nazis cutting off ears," he said. "Just putting people in gas chambers." Takeguchi shook his head grimly. "He's completely out of his mind, that guy," he said. Tateno said, "He was smiling a bit at the end, though, wasn't he?" and looked around at the others, but apparently none of them wanted to think about it. Kaneshiro's strange grimace may well have been an attempt to smile, thought Hino—at least, it was the nearest thing to a smile he'd ever seen on the guy. "It's true, though," Orihara said. "He was right out in the open, shooting away, and none of their bullets hit him. And when the mine went off, even though he was right next to Yamada, who got ripped to shreds, nothing touched him." Blood was beginning to soak the bandage on Orihara's thigh.

Takeguchi looked at his watch. "It's about twelve-ten. We'd better be at the breakwater before twelve-seventeen. If I know Kaneshiro, he'll hit the switch the instant his little alarm goes off." Shinohara looked at the bodies of Kondo and Mori lying in the corridor, then turned away scowling. "Don't tell me he mutilated our people too." Kondo had been shot in the side, Mori in the arm and lower stomach, and farther along Shibata and Okubo, both in the chest; and each of them was bleeding beneath the temple and missing an ear. Hino remembered Kaneshiro once saying, "There are no enemies or allies in this life. Just you and everybody else."

Slim cans of cola and Pocari Sweat had spilled out from a collapsed pile of mini fridges, and they excavated and guzzled two or three apiece. Hino accidentally grabbed a beer and was so thirsty that he downed half of it before realizing his mistake. He spat out what he could and tried to dilute the alcohol by draining a bottle of Evian, but as they hurried on he began to feel dizzy and when they reached the elevator hall he threw up. Tateno, Shinohara, and Takeguchi were sick as well, after seeing the bodies of Yamada and Fukuda and several Koryos there. Yamada and Fukuda had been near the second mine when it went off, and the damage was extreme. Yamada's head lay on top of Fukuda's severed leg, and Fukuda was face down in a pile of guts that had slid out of Yamada's ruptured belly. A number of the corpses had been ripped open, and intestines had sprayed over every surface, along with lots of putrid-smelling excrement.

The entire elevator hall had been blown out of kilter by the explosions and was littered with lumps of scorched plastic and steel, spent shell casings, body parts, and gore. The door to elevator B had been blown apart, and the bodies of several Koryos were plastered to the inner walls. The frameworks of A and C were twisted, the cars leaning crazily. The soldiers who'd been hit with the full force of the blasts were no longer recognizable as individual human beings. You couldn't even tell how many bodies made up the piles of torn flesh that lay soaking in pools of blood. At the pre-operation meeting they had discussed dressing in Koryo uniforms to make their escape, but there were no wearable uniforms here—nothing but bloodstained rags. All four elevators were permanently disabled. Even the button panels, vents, walls, and cables had melted out of shape.

Orihara had been alone at line of defense B when those green camos first appeared in the corridor. The Koryos had pulled up short the moment they saw the strange barricade and turned back to consult their comrades arriving in elevator D. The elevator hall was therefore jammed with Koryos when the first mine went off. It was the one set right in front of Orihara's line of defense, and the outer frame of the device blew back and slammed into his mini fridges. He saw the Koryos fall like bowling pins, then watched Miyazaki, who'd taken a few ball bearings in the face, wander through the elevator hall with his hands outstretched, as if he were "it" in a game of blind man's bluff. Miyazaki met the second explosion head on and burst like a balloon, his entire body erupting into little pieces that stuck to the walls and ceiling. Orihara said that with that explosion, the fridges and sofas had fallen on top of him, but when the shooting started he squirmed out and sprinted around to the port corridor, taking the long route to where Takeguchi and the others were. When he got to the stairwell at the stern, he saw the lone Koryo there, so he pulled the pin from a grenade and flung it as they'd been instructed to do. "If the first mine hadn't been a dud, you'd be dead too," Takeguchi said, but Orihara just blinked at him. He hadn't even realized that one of them didn't go off.

They passed the middle emergency stairway and entered the service corridor through a door marked PRIVATE. Inside they found a pantry with a sink and water heater, shelves stocked with disposable razors, toothbrushes, and other amenities, and enormous laundry baskets overflowing with dirty sheets and towels. Beyond these were the four emergency elevators, two on either side. A food trolley that had been on its way to a banquet lay toppled over, and broken bowls, dishes, and glasses littered the floor amid puddles of soup that had sprouted mold. Tateno, with his hand on an elevator door, wondered if it was working. The floor indicator wasn't lit. "They're emergency elevators," Hino said, opening a switch panel on the wall. "They're designed to work in any circumstances." He flicked the power to ON, then hit the DOWN button. A moment later the floor indicator lit up, and they heard the machinery start. "Won't the Koryos notice?" Orihara said. "These things only open on the service corridors, where they probably never even go," Hino said hopefully. The door took some time to open. He stepped aboard, and the others followed.

The interior of the elevator was stark, with a plywood floor and linoleum walls and ceiling. Hino pressed B2, the door closed slowly, and they began to descend. "What do we do if it stops at the first floor?" Shinohara said, and all eyes turned to the AK Sato was holding. "It's loaded, right?" Sato said, and Orihara nodded. "I didn't even shoot once." As they passed floor six, he said, "Sato, you've got to push the safety catch down or you won't be able to pull the charging handle." Sato moved the thing to full auto, pulled the handle back, and released it. "Whoa!" he said. "I saw a bullet!" The action made a metallic sound not quite like anything else, the sound of a powerful spring sliding through a narrow steel tube. Holding the AK at his hip, he said, "But if they fire back I'm not sure this one gun is enough." They decided that if the elevator stopped at the first floor, Sato would fire through the opening door as the others flattened themselves against the walls and Hino pressed the CLOSE button.

Takeguchi kept looking at his watch. Hino was doing the same, with one eye on the floor indicator. Above the door was a row of numbers, from B2 to 35, which lit up one at a time as they descended. When 5 came on, it was 12:12:20. Orihara had begun sweating heavily as soon as he entered the elevator. His leg must have been hurting a lot—he was bent over with a hand on one hip, grimacing. He'd said it was only a surface wound, but maybe it was worse than that. As 4 lit up, Hino became acutely conscious of a need to relieve his bladder again. He also noticed that everyone looked like hell. Their hair and clothing were wet, their shoes and the cuffs of their pants were soaked with blood, and even their faces and necks and arms were splattered with it. If they ran into any Koryos, they'd be arrested on the spot. If they resisted, they'd probably all be shot down where they stood.

When the light for 4 went out, Shinohara startled everyone with a sudden cry. "Shit!" he said. "I completely forgot about these other guys." He reached into his backpack, took out a Tupperware container, and held it up to the fluorescent ceiling light. "Don't be opening that thing in here," Orihara growled, wiping sweat from the bridge of his nose. "About half of 'em are still alive," Shinohara said, smiling happily. "They're eating one another." Tateno, who had been carefully wiping the blood off his hands, glared at the container full of centipedes and pulled his boomerang bag closer. Hino was thinking about the tools he'd left behind. The electric cutter, the welder, and the acetylene tanks had been too bulky and heavy to take with them. He'd acquired his equipment little by little over the years, being given some tools and stealing others, and he'd maintained and cared for it all this time. *I reckon that's about the size of it, though*, he thought. He'd just have to start a new collection.

"This elevator's awfully slow, isn't it?" Sato said, pursing his lips in a show of impatience. Hino reminded him that it was normally used for transporting carts full of food and things like that. He himself was focused on quelling the urge to pee. When they reached the first floor, where the current command center was, everyone pressed up against the side walls. Orihara was bent over in pain, sweat dripping from his face and neck onto the floor, and Hino wondered if he'd even be able to walk. The number 1 lit up and then went out, and Sato clenched his fist: "Yes!" Relief swept over them, but just as Tateno reached down to lend Orihara a hand, there was a *ding*. "What the hell?" Takeguchi said stupidly. "It's B1," Shinohara said, and Hino looked up in a panic as the elevator began braking. B1 remained lit.

With a high-pitched creaking of cables the thing came to a stop, and the door slowly opened to a figure in white. A woman in a doctor's smock was standing there looking down at a notebook in her hands. Behind her were three pairs of uniformed soldiers, each pair carrying a patient on a stretcher. Beneath her white coat, the woman wore a mustard-brown uniform with a red star on the collar. She stepped toward the elevator without taking her eyes off her notes, but when one of the men behind her shouted something she stopped and looked up, eyes wide and jaw dropping. Hino was hitting the CLOSE button so hard it hurt his index finger. There were six soldiers, but they were all carrying one end of a stretcher and couldn't reach for the pistols at their hips. Everyone on both sides of the elevator door stood there like wax figures. The woman raised

611

her eyebrows and muttered something in Korean, gearing up to make some kind of move, but Sato said, "*Annyeong hashimnikka*," and fired his AK. Three bursts of a jackhammer sound echoed inside the elevator and out. The doctor crumpled to the floor, holding her stomach with both hands, and the soldiers behind her dropped the stretchers and toppled backwards. Hino heard the heads and elbows of the patients crack against the concrete floor. The elevator door closed at a leisurely pace, the space narrowing as the smock's red stain expanded.

The elevator began to descend but immediately made the *ding* sound again and shook as it braked. Sato lowered the AK, accidentally brushing the hot barrel against Takeguchi's bare forearm and eliciting a cry of pain. Orihara was crouching on the floor. "You still got bullets?" he asked, reaching into his knapsack and pulling out another magazine. Sato took it. "That was too easy," he muttered, a troubled look on his face. "All I did was squeeze the trigger." Hino, having been right there, knew exactly what he meant. It was as if you could actually see the projectiles boring their way at impossible speed into the soft, white-clad human flesh. "I mean, did that really just happen?" Sato said. He looked almost tearful. Takeguchi, his own face red with tension, clapped him on the shoulder and said, "Hey, it was self-defense." Sato bit his lip. "It's not that," he said.

The elevator shivered again and stopped. Orihara groaned, and Tateno helped him up and lent him an arm. "When we get out of the elevator hall," Takeguchi said, "the exit is across the parking lot, to the left. Get ready to run all the way." Sato leaned out through the open door with the reloaded AK and looked up and down the hall. He gave the all-clear, and Tateno walked Orihara out first. Takeguchi trotted ahead to open the door to the garage for them and Shinohara. Hino entered the dim garage last, along with Sato, and nearly let out a scream. In front of them, in regularly spaced rows, perhaps a hundred human figures lay or sat hugging their knees on the bare concrete floor. They wore only thin cotton robes and rubber sandals. "Who are they?" Sato whispered, bug-eyed. Hino supposed that they were the "criminals" the Koryos had arrested.

612

Some were lying on their sides, a few face down, and the smell one associates with homeless people hung in the air. Beyond them a tour bus was parked, and next to it a pair of Koryo soldiers leaned against a concrete pillar, looking toward the exit. They were smoking, the gray cigarette smoke curling up toward the fluorescent light fixtures suspended from the ceiling. The pillars were spaced several meters apart throughout the garage, but only the center row of lights was on. In the semi-darkness, the hundred pairs of hollow eyes turned as one toward them. Hino forgot about having to pee.

Tateno half walked, half carried Orihara to the pillar directly in front of them. Takeguchi joined them in its shadow, while Hino, Sato, and Shinohara quickly took cover behind the next one down. Shinohara whispered that three or four Koryos had just run up the emergency stairs. They must have heard the gunfire on the floor above. As soon as they caught a glimpse of the bodies outside the elevator, they'd realize what was going on and head back here. On the wall near the exit was a digital clock showing 12:13:40. Takeguchi crept over to Hino's pillar. "We'll throw the grenades at the bus and run to the exit when they explode," he said. One of the Koryos leaning against the pillar next to the bus had an AK hanging from a shoulder strap; the other had a pistol on his hip. They seemed to be waiting for something as they smoked, their attention still directed toward the exit. From Hino's pillar to the bus was about twenty meters, with most of that space filled with rows of prisoners. From the bus to the exit was another twenty meters.

"Can Orihara make it?" Hino whispered. He was obviously in no shape to run. Though he said he'd just been grazed by the grenade flak, clearly it was worse than that. But Hino knew that Tateno was upset about what had happened to Miyazaki and Felix and wouldn't hear of leaving Orihara behind. "When I give the signal, we heave the grenades," Takeguchi said, and Hino nodded, though the thought of contributing to more bloodshed made him sick to his stomach. He had never seen anything as repulsive and disturbing as the scenes upstairs. "Psst. Hey," someone hissed. Hino and Takeguchi both gave a start and peered out around the pillar.

Lying on his side in the first row of prisoners, a man with a shaved head said, "You're Japanese, right?" The men around him, hearing this, began whispering amongst themselves. "Can't you help us?" the skinhead said, then held out his hands. "Just look." The flesh on the back of them was flayed, and the fingers were bent at weird angles. "You must be SDF, right? I didn't do anything wrong, and look what they did to me. I've got a family!" As he whispered all this, he was inching toward them on his elbows, his broken fingers flopping. Several others began edging this way as well, with a pleading look in their eyes.

"They're coming toward us," Takeguchi said, the blood draining from his face. "I'll put a stop to that," Shinohara said. He took out his Tupperware container, removed the lid, and sailed it into the middle of the block of prisoners. The container flipped over in mid-air, and the centipedes dropped like rain. The skinhead screamed and rolled on the floor, apparently bitten, and then several other prisoners began shrieking and thrashing about. The two guards crushed out their cigarettes under the toes of their boots and shouted something.

"Now," Takeguchi said in a soft voice, and backed up two steps. The pillar was big enough to hide the four of them easily, but he had to step out to the right of it, bringing his arm back in a wide arc. The Koryo with the AK spotted him and raised his weapon. Takeguchi's arm whipped forward, and just as he released the grenade, two dry *pocks* resounded through the garage. His head jerked backwards twice and he fell at Hino's feet. The upper-right quadrant of his head was missing. Seeing this, Sato scowled, his cheeks flushed red, and he leaped out to the left of the column firing his own AK and shouting, "Motherfuckers!" just as the grenade exploded against the windows of the bus.

The force of the explosion dislodged several of the light fixtures from their chains. Sato shielded his eyes and spun back behind the pillar. Nudging aside the body of Takeguchi, whose blood continued to surge over what was left of his face, Hino was suddenly seized with a raw fury that robbed him of all self-control. As he threw his grenade at the bus, the rear of which was already a ruin, he was clearly visualizing the carnage that would result. One of the prisoners had crawled up to his pillar, mumbling something, and now reached out to grab hold of Hino's leg. Sato hit the man with the butt of his rifle and Shinohara kicked him in the chest, knocking him back on his ass and making him wail like a siren. His voice was immediately drowned out by the second explosion, which lifted him sideways briefly and brought another light fixture crashing down nearby. "That's it for the Koryos. Let's go," Shinohara said, and ran for the exit. Sato, shouldering the AK, tried to get one arm under Takeguchi to lift him to his feet. "He's dead," Hino said, pulling him away. Sato gaped back at him for a moment, then turned and ran. Hino helped Tateno support Orihara, lending a shoulder on the other side, and the three of them followed.

It was even darker now that so many lights were broken. Some of the prisoners reached out toward Hino and Tateno, begging to be taken along. Orihara's bandage was saturated with blood, his thigh swollen and purple, and with each step he gave a small cry of pain. Shinohara stood at the revolving door by the exit, gesturing for them to hurry. Fear took hold of Hino again as they pressed on, and he wondered how he'd managed such a murderous rage just now. The rage had filled him like gas injected into a balloon. Right then I could have killed anyone, he thought—a woman, an old man, a kid. One of the Koryos was propped against the half-burned bus in a daze, his arms hanging helplessly at his sides, and the other was face down on the floor and motionless. Dead prisoners littered the floor well into the interior of the garage. They could see the steps just outside the exit. At the top of the steps they should find the four-lane road, and beyond that the beach.

Hino stumbled over a fallen light fixture, and a prisoner lying nearby grabbed hold of Orihara's leg. Tateno was about to kick him in the face when he realized it was a woman. Her cotton robe was ragged, exposing her breasts and crotch, and her eyes were wild. She was flapping her lips, trying to say something, but both edges of her mouth had been slit open, and she couldn't form words. Hino tried to kick her hand away, but another prisoner had already tottered over to cling to Orihara's torso. A third grabbed his arm, and now a swarm of them was converging on him. Orihara gave an anguished moan as he was pulled back and to one side, slipping out of his companions' grasp, and he screamed when his wounded thigh hit the floor. One after another, prisoners straddled or crawled over him, as if pantomiming a gang rape. They must have thought that by holding on to him they could stop the other two as well. "I'm out of here," Hino said. Tateno looked back at Orihara, now barely visible beneath the wriggling mass of figures, and whispered, "Forgive us," before he too made a dash for the exit.

Outside, they saw the road right in front of them. Beyond it was the elevated expressway, and beyond that a pine grove, the sky, and the sea. They were on a brick sidewalk lined with tall, vase-shaped shrubs. Men were running this way from Checkpoint E, to the right. Sato ran up the steps and out into the road. There he stopped, pointed his AK at the soldiers, and pulled the trigger, but the magazine was empty. He threw the weapon down and sprinted for the bay. The enemy were maybe two hundred meters away at this point. One stopped and raised his own rifle, and the now familiar *pock-pock-pock* sound punctured the air. These were warning shots, but the next burst ricocheted off the asphalt at Sato's feet. They were aiming low in order to disable and capture, Hino thought. It'd be better to die than to end up like one of those prisoners. There was no point in zigzagging since the fire was from the side, so they made a beeline across the divided four-lane road. Straight ahead, just beyond the road, they would reach the expressway overpass and the shelter of its huge pillars. Hino was thinking of those TV commercials in which impossibly happy young people run toward the sea, whooping it up with friends or sweethearts, when ahead of him Shinohara caught a bullet in the ankle and went down.

He stopped to help him up, stooping to wrap Shinohara's right arm around his own shoulders. Tateno took the other arm, and the three of them ran on as bullets skipped off the potholed asphalt in front of them, Shinohara dragging one foot and leaving a smeared trail of blood. They had just reached the center divider when they saw Sato slip into the shadow of the overpass and jump down to the beach. "We make too good a target like this," Shinohara said. "Leave me here. I can't even feel my leg." Tateno shook his head. "What about the bugs and frogs?" he said, and Hino said, "Yeah, those fuckin' things. Without you, they'd die." Another bullet keened off the asphalt and Hino felt something hot and sharp pierce his hip. He assumed he'd been shot, but he managed to continue hobbling along at the same speed, and neither of the others noticed anything. In the distance behind them, a loudspeaker at the Koryo camp crackled to life and spat out an announcement in Korean. Craning his neck to look back, Hino saw soldiers spilling out of their tents, preparing their weapons, and falling in, as three MAVs rolled this way from the far side of Checkpoint A.

*Are you watching?* he muttered to the mind's-eye image of his mother. *You see all the rats panicking?* The gunfire ceased once it was clear that the targets were heading for the beach, where the Koryos knew the sea would block their escape. They were out of breath by the time they reached the sand, and running was even more of a struggle here. Ahead, Sato was already crawling under an enormous shelf of concrete where the beach bordered the foundation of the road. "There's no time to reach the breakwater!" he shouted. "Take cover here!" With his left arm supporting Shinohara, Hino couldn't see his watch and had no idea how much time was left. They stumbled to the shelf, dived to the sand, and dug in behind Sato, who was already wedged in as far as he could get. Blood was flowing from Hino's hip and soaking into the sand. Shinohara saw this and gasped: "Hino! You got hit?" Everything below his waist had gone cold, and suddenly he couldn't feel anything at all down there. His elbows and chest hurt from crawling over the wet sand, but it was as if his lower half had been disconnected.

*Hino! Hino-san!* The voices grew smaller and smaller. It was like being left on a riverbank as people called his name from a receding boat. *Is this all death is?* he asked himself. There was nothing scary about it. Others would come along to take his place. Being with the

617

Ishihara group had taught him that no one is indispensable, that someone somewhere could always replace you. People who think that they alone are the be-all and end-all must freak out when facing death, he thought, but any further thoughts dissolved unformed into a vast darkness, like the bottom of the deepest lake. He was sinking toward it, spiraling like a slowly falling leaf, and just as he was about to touch down, there was an unearthly roar and a shock wave that split the lake floor apart. Registering the shock even in his unfeeling hip and legs, Hino sank into the depths that had opened below.

# WINGS OF AN ANGEL

*April 11, 2011*

I N A DREAM KIM HYANG MOK finds herself making her way down a sloping road near the village she grew up in. The landscape around her is covered with snow, and in the dim light she has to take care over each step. A large black automobile is approaching from behind. What is such a fancy car doing on this twisting mountain road? Some part of her knows she's dreaming. The dazzling headlights make it impossible to see the driver or passengers, but the car appears to be of Japanese make. It pulls to one side, as though trying to pass her, but either because the road is too narrow or someone inside wants to talk to her, it merely slows down. The twin beams reach toward the distant mountains, illuminating their jagged outline against the dark sky. She hears a voice calling to her, but it's too faint for her to make out the words. "What did you say?" she asks in Japanese, but then remembers: the rabbits! She forgot all about the quota she's been assigned. She has to catch at least three rabbits during the winter and bring the pelts to school. The meat will go to the trapper, so she mustn't fail.

Hyang Mok turns toward the mountains, the car headlights pointing the way. She's holding the wire snare that one of her older brothers made for her, with a loop at the front end. Along the way, on top of a hillock, she sees the house she was born in. She looks down and notices that she is barefoot. She will have to stop by and put on some shoes; otherwise she'll never make it to the mountains. When she steps into the earthen-floored entrance, the whole family is lined up there waiting for her, all standing in a row just outside the pitch-dark kitchen. Even her two older brothers are there—they must be back from military service. She asks them if they've seen her shoes, then asks her mother and little brothers as well, but no one answers. The smell of burning pine twigs comes from the heated *ondol* floor. She can't see her father, even though she was sure he was standing there with the others. Perhaps he's gone off somewhere, she thinks, but then remembers that he's been dead for some time. When she at last finds her shoes, it turns out they're both for her right foot. She hears a voice saying: "Hurry!" It's that man. He appears from behind her mother, slips past her, and runs out into the darkness, urging her again and again: "Hurry! Hurry!"

Hyang Mok awoke earlier than usual, at 5:30. Her heart was pounding. Some decisive event had occurred, and there was somewhere she must go—and go immediately. She'd never experienced such a disorienting sensation before. She didn't usually dream—or, rather, forgot her dreams the moment she awoke. Even back at home in her village, let alone after joining the army, she'd rarely slept more than four hours. She would drop off the instant she settled under her covers and leap out of bed the instant she awoke; she never had time for dreams. And yet now she'd dreamed for three nights running. And the same person had appeared each time—a Japanese man. The first night he had simply been there, but the second time he'd tried to say something, and this time she'd understood: he was telling her to hurry. The voice was neither harsh nor gentle, but urgent. And yet she'd had no shoes to wear. She must have taken them off somewhere. "Hurry!" the person had said. "Never mind about left or right or even whose shoes they are. Just go!" Sensing that if she didn't catch up with the man, she'd never see him again, she dashed out after him barefoot—and that was the point at which she awoke.

Lying there, she was aware of an oppressive and unfamiliar feeling in her breast, a mixture of sadness and joy. It was like blending two different oil paints and ending up with a new and unexpected color. Nothing like this had ever happened before, but it wasn't as if she could tell anyone about it. She could hardly confess that she was dreaming of the same Japanese man every night, seeing him not only in her dreams but in her mind's eye just before falling asleep, or that she found herself deep in thought about him even during the day. She lingered in her cot, wrapped in her blanket, wondering why she was so obsessed with this person. Now as before, she found no answer.

Her three bunkmates—Ri Gwi Hui, Kim Sun I, and Ri Gyu Yeong—were still asleep. Being careful not to wake them, Hyang Mok untangled herself from her blanket, got out of bed, quietly slipped into her uniform, and went to wash her face. On the morning of the ninth, the mess hall and the officers' sleeping quarters had been shifted to the first floor, along with the command center. The men slept in the smaller ballroom, which also served as the canteen, while the women had the Maple Room. This was one of five banquet rooms, all lavishly furnished and named after trees: Katsura, Laurel, Oak, Elm, Maple. The command center was directly across from them, in the big ballroom named Argos, which resembled in sheer scale the Revolutionary Museum, and had crimson carpeting and six enormous crystal chandeliers.

Light was leaking into the lobby from the command center; several officers had been working all night. The convoy of ships carrying troops from the Eighth Corps was now well on its way, under the command of rigidly anti-American figures like Vice-Marshal Ri Cheong Yeol and General Kim Myeong Hyeon, both of whom had often been mentioned in those persistent rumors of a *coup d'état*. This was a critical time in the operation. Pressure was on Japan to reopen foreign consulates, which might force the government to abandon any attempt to retake Fukuoka and would be a persuasive fait accompli for international recognition of the KEF.

China and southern Korea in particular were actively working, through private corporations in Fukuoka, to get the consulates reopened. From their point of view, the blockade of Hakata Port was a crucial concern; losses for the past week alone were easily on the order of hundreds of millions of yen. It was also reported that with the blocking of the northern shipping lanes connecting Shanghai, Busan, Fukuoka, and Seattle, America's West Coast high-tech industry had been badly affected and was thus expected to use its considerable muscle to lobby Congress in the same cause.

But economic factors would be far from the minds of Ri Cheong Yeol and Kim Myeong Hyeon, who thought of the US and southern Korea as the Republic's mortal enemies. Winning these hardliners over would require first of all the cooperation of China. Secondly, military discipline had to be improved and a model for Fukuoka's ongoing administration outlined; and thirdly, they had to show that the city was firmly under the thumb of the KEF. With that aim, Han Seung Jin intended to explain that major criminal elements had been arrested and their assets seized, and to underline how accommodating City Hall had been in helping them secure supplies and arrange for construction of the new barracks. Han had assigned to the mayor the task of mobilizing several thousand citizens to greet the troops as they made their landing. First Lieutenant Jo Su Ryeon had also issued an appeal to that effect on his NHK program.

The imminent arrival of another hundred and twenty thousand soldiers filled Kim Hyang Mok with a mixture of reassurance and dismay. Until now, five hundred had endeavored to uphold the values of the Republic; now those same values would permeate the city. She washed her face in the bathroom and adjusted her clothing. She still wasn't used to getting hot water from the tap. One faucet was blue, the other red, and if she turned the latter, she had to be careful not to scald herself. And yet by using both in a balanced mixture, she was assured of a constant supply at just the right temperature. With no running water in her small village near the harbor town of Ranam, it was the children's task to go every morning to a stream several hundred meters away. She had two older brothers and one younger. According to the household rule established before she was born, a child was obliged to help carry water from the age of five. Hyang Mok adored her older brothers, who, like their father, were tall and good-looking. She and the two of them would get up in the morning, go to the stream, wash their faces, return with the water, and pour it into a vat on the earthen floor. Her brothers carried large buckets, she a smaller one.

It was not an unpleasant chore. In the summer, they would also catch fish, and from the winding mountain road there were glimpses of the sea. Beyond the stream was a sweet-smelling orchard with apples, pears, and bitter oranges. But what she enjoyed most was chatting with her brothers as they walked along. Once, when she had just turned five, she asked why it was their job to fetch water, and the younger of them told her it was to ease the burden on their parents, who had to work from early morning till late at night. The older one said that when their mother was thirsty or their father wanted some tea or to wash his face and shave, he was glad he could be useful. They said there was nothing better than making their family happy. They also mentioned the Great Leader, who had constantly said that seeing the people of the Republic content filled him with a joy beyond all personal pleasure. And this too inspired them.

In the winter, when the temperature sometimes fell to twenty below zero, scooping up water meant first breaking through the frozen surface of the stream. That job belonged to Hyang Mok's brothers, and she was told to remain on dry land. They would carefully check the thickness of the ice and then, using a sharp stone, gouge out a hole and lower their buckets, holding on to the attached cord. Their fingers would promptly turn purple and go numb. And yet despite the cold, the pain, and the effort involved, it never occurred to them to hate the job. They would sometimes slip and slide about, as if they had real skates on their feet, or eat the frozen oranges that had fallen down from the orchard onto the ice. The fruit would melt in their mouths, the blend of tartness and fragrance more delicious than any sherbet.

Just being with her older brothers was pleasure enough for her. On winter days, they wrapped their socks in plastic as insulation, and when hers broke, resulting in chilblains and chapping, they cut their own wrappings in half for her. Over the plastic they wore cotton-lined cloth shoes, which they then bound with twine. All she had to do now was close her eyes to remember the village's crisp winter air; their ragged shoes, endlessly patched and resewn; and her brothers' grinning faces. The eldest was doing military service on the DMZ; the younger was a first lieutenant in the Third Artillery Corps. For them the idea of hot water coming straight out of a faucet would no doubt be hard to imagine. She wondered what they would think of her being in Fukuoka.

She wet her hair a little with some of that hot water, then ran a white plastic brush through it. The brush, included among the hotel-room amenities, was clean, lightweight, and pleasant to use, and it could be folded in half and carried about. She had had some compunction about borrowing hotel property, but after being informed by a City Hall employee that the brush was disposable, she'd consulted with other female officers and finally obtained the permission of the deputy commander. She stood in front of the mirror that covered the entire bathroom wall as she brushed her hair. She had never liked her face, thinking it made her look willful or impudent. She'd grown up being told by everyone around her that she was pretty, but that never made her happy; it was as if she were being told to be seen and not heard. To be "pretty" or "cute" was in the male mind synonymous with "knowing one's place." Besides, she didn't think of herself as pretty. Her eyebrows were a bit too thick, her forehead was too broad, her nose was on the flat side, and her face was as round as the moon.

Still, there was one feature that she did like: her eyes. Their contours were distinct, the corners pointing neither up nor down, and they suggested an uncompromising and independent nature. It was this that pleased her. From the time she was a child, her family and neighbors alike had said that she never whimpered or gave up. And now in this far-off place she had the self-confidence to endure whatever lay in store. She was unlikely ever to see her brothers or her village again, and the thought brought a stab of pain with it. But there was no room in her present duties for any sentimentality. Nor must she allow silly thoughts and dreams to distract her emotionally. There was a lot to do, and the work itself would help her forget about the person that was so much on her mind.

She passed the Oak Room on her way to the command center. This was the room in which, until yesterday morning, the bodies of Captain Choi Hyo Il and the other men killed in the Ohori Park shoot-out had been. It was common knowledge that there had been a difference of opinion higher up as to whether they should be interred according to Korean custom. Back in the Republic, particularly in the countryside, traditional ways in this regard had persisted, not in defiance of the Party, but simply out of adherence to an older convention.

In her own village, Hyang Mok attended many such funerals, from early childhood on. Her father, a physician, had been among those ethnic Koreans in China who had fled to the Republic during the Great Proletarian Cultural Revolution and was thus a critic of traditional practices. Her mother, on the other hand, a distant relative of the Great Leader's mother, Kang Ban Sok, was a staunch supporter. When Hyang Mok was still small, even before she started to help with fetching the water, the chief engineer at the local coal mine died suddenly of a stomach ailment. It was a small-scale mine, with only about thirty workers, two families of which were also returnees from China. Her father's clinic included an isolation ward for patients with contagious diseases still in the incubation stage, but he also made house calls. On his return from the miners' barracks one day, he informed his wife of the man's death, and she set out for the funeral with her daughter. As their house was located on a hill, they had not gone far before they could see the relatives of the dead man on the roof of the barracks, waving his clothing and wailing: "*Aigo! Aigo!*"

As they walked along, her mother told her about the three souls a person has. When somebody dies, she explained, one soul stays on

in the memorial tablet and another in the grave, while the third goes
to the next world—a place Hyang Mok was now hearing about for
the first time. She asked where this "next world" was. "On the other
side of this one," her mother replied. "'The other side'?" she asked
again, and her mother pointed at a flat stone, about the size of a
human head. "Tell me what you see there," she said. "I see moss,"
the girl replied. "But you can't see what's underneath it, can you?"
her mother continued. "No one can say what's on the bottom of
the stone, whether it's wet or has weeds growing there, whether it's
also covered with moss or with little bugs. But we know that it *has*
another side. The next world is like that."

The miners' barracks, consisting of four long, high-roofed buildings
made from old railroad ties, mine timber, and corrugated iron, stood
on a hill overlooking the mineshaft. Inside, they were partitioned into
spaces about half the size of Hyang Mok's own living room, each
inhabited by an entire family. Her mother pointed to the deceased's
house, where a blue plastic sheet had been spread in front of the
sliding door. On it were three bowls of corn-and-rice meal, some
shriveled pumpkins, and three pairs of plastic sandals. Hyang Mok's
mother noted that traditionally the footwear was supposed to be
made of woven straw, but as the village produced neither rice nor
barley, this wasn't possible. The food and sandals were apparently
intended to be used by the three envoys charged with taking the soul
of the deceased to the next world. There, ten judges would examine
him to determine whether, according to his conduct on earth, he
should be sent to heaven or hell, a subject about which they were
already well informed from spirit sources of their own.

Hyang Mok's mother approached the entrance and stood among
the other mourners. And then, to the girl's astonishment, she suddenly covered her face and burst into tears, wailing "*Aigo!*" too.
Family members were serving liquor and plates of fish, and many of
the men were already drunk. One of them was even vomiting in a
ditch out back. Hyang Mok was surprised to see that they all seemed
to be in high spirits. Some had spread out a sheet of paper and sat
down to gamble at cards. Others were laughing or telling jokes. Of

course, neither the family nor the chief mourner was indulging in any of this. Hyang Mok would later learn that the guests' behavior was meant to distract the survivors from their grief.

At dusk the pallbearers lit some crude handmade lanterns and bore the coffin away on a plank, as the accompanying crowd sang for the repose of the departing soul. The door-sized plank was decorated with wild flowers and red and blue streamers. The pallbearers, close male friends of the deceased, were so drunk that the coffin came close to falling off as it tilted this way and that. One of them joked: "If we drop 'im, he might come back to life!" The coffin was lowered into a grave dug halfway up a nearby hill, and then covered with branches. *Soju* was poured over the branches, and each member of the family tossed in some dirt. When the burial ceremony was over, the pallbearers shouldered the plank and went back to the house. There the women pretended to break the three bowls of corn-rice and to discard the three pairs of plastic sandals; then, seeing the empty plank, they burst into a new round of wailing. Such was the tradition that Hyang Mok had known.

Funeral traditions varied widely by region, but common to all was the consumption of alcohol in large quantities by the male guests. This became an issue here at the camp, in relation to the burial of the three bodies in the Oak Room. When Hyang Mok objected that providing drink for five hundred soldiers would be both too costly and undisciplined, voices were raised. "No alcohol?" a senior officer exclaimed. Even Kim Hak Su, despite all his concerns about maintaining discipline, complained that a funeral with only water or tea was not a Korean funeral. How would it be then, she asked, if each soldier were given a can of Kirin beer? The plan was approved, with her further stipulation that as the item could not be paid for out of her section's budget, it should be deducted from each man's food allowance. Ri Hui Cheol expressed amazement at Comrade Kim's frugality, in a way that made everyone laugh.

Seen off by nearly five hundred soldiers, each raising a can of beer, Choi Hyo Il and the other two fallen comrades had been borne away in an MAV. They were buried on a south-facing slope in a hilly and sparsely populated section of Higashi Ward, far from any shrines, temples, or houses.

In the canteen that had been set up in the smaller ballroom, Hyang Mok made do with a simple breakfast of tea and a pine-nut cookie. Black tea, ginseng tea, cookies, and bread, as well as apples and other fruit, were always available. At lunch and dinnertime, rice, a main dish, soup, and kimchi were served. The main dish was typically reheated canned fish; in the soup was *wakame* seaweed, pork, or vegetables with miso. After breakfast, she made her way to her desk in the command center. Snoozing on the sofas to one side were those assigned to all-night duty. Only two of the chandeliers were lit. As there were no windows, some artificial lighting was needed even in the daytime.

Later she would have various meetings with representatives of food wholesalers, large-scale retailers of electrical goods, and wholesalers of cooking utensils, and she'd need to go over the numbers first. With the new troops about to arrive, she was wrestling with so many different problems that it made her head spin. Particularly troubling was the fact that most of the officers, including the commander and his deputy, were much more interested in political and military concerns than in money matters and tended to take lightly the sort of funding challenges that she and Ra Jae Gong, her colleague in the financial section, faced every day. At present, a soldier's daily food allowance was slightly below three hundred yen; for officers, it was ten yen more. They had been able to stick to these amounts because of the cheap rice, warehoused and then forgotten, that had been discovered with the help of City Hall. Even if these figures remained feasible, however, the daily outlay for the main force would come to thirty-six million yen.

So far the funds seized from major felons came to over thirty billion, part of which Ra Jae Gong had put to various uses, even investing in Western hedge funds. Working with him, Hyang Mok had become something of an expert on hedge funds, investment management, and the art of moving money around. The fact remained, however, that feeding the newcomers for just three days would cost a hundred million yen. Simple arithmetic suggested that even thirty billion would, at that rate, be gone in less than three years' time. Moreover, when the cost of clothing and medical care, along with temporary housing, electrical appliances such as rice cookers, eating utensils, and writing materials, was taken into account, it seemed likely that the seized assets would be depleted within the year. Since the end of the previous week, the number of those arrested had dropped: it was not as if there were millions of well-heeled undesirables waiting to be fleeced. In addition, with the American and Chinese consulates likely to be reopened, the ongoing confiscation of funds would become more problematic. And even Ra Jae Kong's wizardry had its limits.

The commander and his entourage were apparently of the opinion that the new arrivals should be put to work locally. Yet all members of the Eighth Corps were trained combat soldiers and had probably never so much as tilled a field back home. What's more, interaction with the local business sector made it clear that there was already a surplus of workers in Fukuoka. Han's group had also decided to disarm most of the newcomers, despite concerns about the willingness of the military hardliners to go along with the idea. Disarmament was likely to be a condition set by the Americans, the southern Koreans, and the Chinese for the reopening of their consulates. One proposal for raising money was to sell the decommissioned weapons; another was to impose a tax on citizens to pay for the KEF's efforts to maintain order and security. These were rejected, however, because of the prospect of fierce opposition to such measures.

After consulting Ra, Hyang Mok felt that the best that could be done was to arrange for the troops to receive Japanese-language lessons and occupational training, in order to be farmed out as cheap labor. Training would take between three and six months. In the meantime, it was essential to shave every yen possible off the price of items to be bought in such vast quantities—even T-shirts and socks.

\*

By 7:00 a.m. there were more people present at headquarters, and all the chandeliers were lit. The large television screen in a corner of the ballroom was showing state-of-the-art warships and fighter planes in readiness for action, but nobody was paying much attention. No one believed that the SDF would engage in combat with the ships. Earlier that morning, the Cabinet Secretary had declared that the government was still calling for cooperation from the US and its forces stationed here, and urging the UN Security Council to denounce these acts of aggression. A TV announcer went on to say that there had been no signs of sabotage at any of the country's liquefied-natural-gas facilities. Under pressure from the media and various interest groups, including the opposition parties, an initially reluctant government had stepped up surveillance and banned the public from an area of five kilometers around all storage sites. But with twenty-nine such installations and more than a thousand kilometers of pipeline, it would be impossible to protect the entire LNG infrastructure. The implausible idea that any attempt to stop the incoming ships would result in terrorist attacks on LNG tanks was treated as fact by the media and fully exploited by the KEF. Han Seung Jin made the following declaration at a press conference.

"We are regular troops, neither guerrillas nor terrorists. We are very much opposed to terrorism. The fact of the matter is, however, that unless you surround the soft targets, which your gas tanks and pipelines are, with impenetrable concrete barriers, you will not be able to ward off attacks. All it would take would be a long-range anti-tank rocket fired from outside the perimeter. Hitting one of those large sites would be easy. A trained soldier would hardly be needed: with a few minutes of instruction, even a child could do it."

Why had the Japanese media jumped to the conclusion that these would be prime targets? Lieutenant Pak Myeong of the operations section had his own explanation: most people here were looking for a justification for the blockade and an excuse for not attacking the KEF, and the threat of sabotage suited this purpose perfectly. It reflected the weakness of individuals and groups seeking a way out in the face of a crisis. As any excuse would do, they were sure to find one. Pak added that while it was easy enough for those standing outside Japanese society to recognize this attitude, there was little awareness of it on the part of those on the inside.

As she was going over the list of companies with which arrangements had already been made regarding provisions for the arriving troops, Hyang Mok was summoned to the reception area by the deputy commander, Ri Hui Cheol. She left the hall and made her way to the Katsura Room, which served as reception. Ri and Major Kim Hak Su were there, going over the security plan for the main force's temporary barracks. They asked her how many truck deliveries of clothing and fresh and processed food would be made daily, and she replied that the tentative figure was around forty. She had saluted and started to leave the room, when Kim called her back. Sitting on the sofa, he slowly turned his broad shoulders and looked at her. "Are your plans for securing food provisions going well?" he asked with a smile. "If there's any problem, you can always come to me." This was an officer feared by all, but for some reason he was always exceptionally nice to her.

Some of her colleagues had gone so far as to tell her that the major regarded her as a kind of daughter or younger sister. But the honor of being noticed by such a high-ranking superior was tempered by a vague sense of dissatisfaction at not being fully recognized as a fellow officer. He was absolutely typical of the DPRK male—the mere fact that she was a woman made him look down on her. His attitude was not one of deliberate disrespect or discrimination. His instinctive assumption was that she was sweet but a bit weak and so needed looking after. "For the time being," she told him, "we've got enough to last three weeks." The major gave her a satisfied nod, then asked her to do a favor for them. Could she go to the Kyushu Medical Center that morning and pay the hospital bill for Corporal Song Jin Pal, who was to be released in the evening. The tab would be repaid from the Special Police budget, but it would be a big help if she could take care of it in the meantime.

At the mention of the hospital, she faltered for a moment, her eye fixed on a painting on the shiny wall of a woman on horseback galloping between the trees in a grove. "What's wrong?" the major asked. "Nothing," she replied, shaking her head. "I could have a couple of security guards take you," he said. "That won't be necessary, but could you please write a memo concerning the deduction from the police budget?" Kim exchanged a smiling glance with Ri. "You're certainly efficient," he remarked as he handed her the signed chit. "Are all women from your part of the country like you?"

Her heart was still beating fast. She had never imagined that she'd be going there, where *he* worked. But if she let this chance go by, there surely wouldn't be another, particularly if headquarters was moved out to Odo. She had first seen him on the day the two men were executed. Dressed in hospital whites, he had burst out of the hospital, heading through the rain toward the camp's assembly area. As she stood there watching him approach, she felt tension building up inside her. Nobody, whether an officer or an enlisted man, was in the least looking forward to the impending event, and now this white-coated figure had come along to stir her conscience and stifle her breath.

The thin, elderly doctor had passed between the rows of soldiers. The security guards hesitated to restrain him, both because of his apparel and obvious profession and because of his age. Though under orders to allow neither spectators nor the media to witness the execution, they'd never expected anyone like this to show up. No Japanese individual had ever dared to confront the KEF on his own. Moreover, the whole contingent was drawn up, with the firing squad ready to proceed. Waving his arms, his mouth set tight and his rain-soaked hair plastered to his forehead, he trudged straight on through the mud that speckled the hem of his hospital coat and turned his white sandals brown. The commander stared in disbelief as the man moved closer through the ranks and, making a megaphone of his hands, shouted again and again for them to

"Stop the murder!"—first in Japanese, and then in broken Korean: "*Sar-in mallida! Sar-in mallida!*"

The condemned men, tied to the posts and blindfolded, turned their heads, straining to understand the commotion. Even those resigned to death might start getting their hopes up from a sudden shift in mood like this. Would it be called off? Hyang Mok had seen other men about to be shot grasping at such straws, frantically trying to free themselves and begging for mercy. When Major Kim ordered the man's removal, the guards surrounded him, lifted him onto their shoulders, and carried him over to a few of his colleagues who had come in pursuit. As he was being borne away, he passed directly in front of Hyang Mok, standing next to Kim Sun I and Ri Gwi Hui. The small white name tag attached to his breast pocket caught her eye. She recognized the three Chinese characters—"world," "good," "tree"—but didn't know how to pronounce them in Japanese. As soon as he had been lowered to the ground, shots from the firing squad rang out. The major, as instructed, then reached for his Tokarev and gave each of the writhing men the *coup de grâce*. At that moment, Hyang Mok felt as though a thorn had lodged in her throat. As a member of the railway police on the Chinese border, she had witnessed other executions without any such reaction; it had to be the old man's protest that brought it on. She stood watching in the rain until, surrounded by his colleagues, he had returned to the hospital. "Comrade Kim," called out a soldier in charge of the cleanup operation, "don't catch cold."

The two corpses were untied and lowered onto plywood boards. While they were being taken away, she noticed a solitary sandal lying in the mud. Looking around to be sure that nobody was watching, she picked it up, without knowing why. That night, as she was falling asleep on her cot, the old doctor rose into her mind, and at dawn he reappeared in a dream. And yet her preoccupation was still a mystery to her. All she knew was that she wanted to meet him.

She returned to her desk in the big hall and went back to work but couldn't concentrate. She stared blankly at the names on the bilingual list. "Someone's on the line," said Kang Cheol, her immediate subordinate, who was sitting across from her. The call was from the director of a food wholesaler. She began with her usual flattery, saying how much everyone had enjoyed the sesame liquor they'd recently received. "Ah, glad to hear it," came the reply. As they turned to business, she thought she'd be able to put the hospital out of her mind. The director, whose name was Yoshimoto, told her about some supplies of shellfish, sardines, and bonito, informed her he had a batch of instant noodles and curry that were past their sell-date, and brought to her attention a quantity of ham that was being stored in a Hakata Port warehouse.

For some reason, the word "ham" made her heart skip a beat. She knew she'd heard it before, though at first she couldn't remember when or where. "Ham?" she said. "Yes, from China. We got it two years ago, lots of it, from Guangzhou, but it doesn't sell here: too salty. It wound up in our warehouse on the Hakozaki Pier. We'd be happy to let you have it cheap." Hyang Mok asked what exactly ham was. "It's a kind of cured pork," she was told. And suddenly a long-lost memory resurfaced. It was uncanny: perhaps the recurrent dreams about the hospital doctor had plowed up the field of her past, allowing these memories of her father to spring up.

One day during her first year at the local People's School, her father had presented the family with a large, cylindrical chunk of meat: "This," he said, smiling, "is called *ham*." He normally didn't talk much, and only rarely laughed, so the family was surprised, even worried, by his cheerful mood. "Yes, this is pretty special," he declared as he laid the object on the table. That afternoon an old woman, a returnee from Japan, had apparently come to the hospital where he worked, asking to be examined for pain in her knees and abdominal discomfort. The woman had left Japan some forty years before, staying first in Pyongyang but then settling in this mining area, after being more or less sent into exile. She said she hadn't a single *chon* to pay him with, then abruptly reached down and lifted her skirt.

"I nearly fell out of my chair," he said with a burst of laughter. The old woman had been sent some parcels by relatives in Japan, but she was now down to the last item of any value, and this she had tied under her skirt before slipping out of the house. She'd had to resort to this scheme, she said, because her son and daughter-in-law thought she spent too much on herself. The flesh-colored ham, he said, had looked at first like the stump of a third leg.

Hyang Mok fell silent for a moment. "Hello? Lieutenant Kim? Can you hear me?" the man shouted into the receiver. "I was thinking about the ham," she replied. "Could you bring a sample here to headquarters this evening?" He agreed, and she ended the call but sat at her desk with a lingering smile. "Good news?" asked Kang. "He said something funny," she answered, and stood up. Her face had tightened again as she moved toward the exit, feeling annoyed with herself for getting distracted.

It was still a bit early, but she decided to change into civilian clothes, thinking that doing so, along with arranging her hair, might help her calm down. She returned to the Maple Room and opened the wardrobe shared by all the women officers. This big piece of furniture, made of a fine-grained, unvarnished wood, had been on display outside the grand ballroom, as a sales sample. Apparently parents bought such gifts for their newly-wed children. The amount shown on the tag was 1.8 million yen. She was astonished at the price, as were her roommates; they had counted and recounted the zeros. The tag still dangled from the door handle. A gray suit was hanging next to a T-shirt, jeans, and a spare uniform. The store where she had bought the suit had provided the clear plastic bag in which it was wrapped and the white plastic hanger—a novelty to her. She brushed her hand over the surface of her cot to remove any dirt or dust before taking the suit from the bag and laying it down.

Only Hyang Mok among the female officers was authorized to dress in civilian clothes and then for the sole purpose of meeting and negotiating with company representatives. Along with the cut-price suit, she had bought two white blouses, four pairs of stockings of the kind that you wore like pants, and a pair of low-heeled boots. She'd not worn a skirt since her days as a pupil in the People's School, and she had never before pulled nylon stockings over her legs. They had a pleasantly smooth feel, and though they were so thin as to be virtually invisible against the skin, they were surprisingly warm. She had given a pair to Ri Gwi Hui, who told her she got cold sitting in front of a computer all day.

She took off her uniform and the T-shirt she wore underneath and ran her arms through the sleeves of the blouse. It was as plain as a man's shirt, but it had a touch of the feminine about it, with a roundish collar and buttons that looked vaguely like seashells, and Hyang Mok was particularly fond of it. She couldn't say the same about the underwear, however. She remembered how she and Gwi Hui had protested when given these flimsy things during their training for the occupation of the Dome. Even now she disliked the shape and color: they made her feel like a streetwalker. And yet, as she and Gwi Hui admitted to each other in frequent conversations on the subject, they were actually quite pleasant to wear.

The fabric and tailoring of the gray suit was so smooth that merely touching it with her fingertips gave her pleasure. If she pressed her face against it, there was the smell of high-quality cloth. As a child, she had been given a sweater her mother had made from the wool of a sheep they'd bought in the free market. There wasn't enough for all four of the children, but her older brothers had willingly let their little sister have priority. She had enjoyed watching them and their mother shear the sheep in the spring light, its bleating reverberating through the valley as the wool fluttered down like clumps of dandelion fluff. Put into a pot and cooked to remove the grease, with the water being allowed to boil away three times, it was placed on a board to dry before being carefully combed, then stretched out and wound onto the spindle of the spinning wheel. The sweater her mother knitted for her was bristly and heavy, and when she put her arms through the sleeves, it had an animal smell. But it was wonderfully warm.

She remembered the feel of that sweater as she adjusted her collar and skirt in front of the wardrobe mirror. The front of the jacket seemed to be lacking something, so she added a silver necklace that the manager of a clothing store called Gap had given her. Once she had put a small comb in her hair, her dress preparations were complete. On a page from a notebook lying on the table she wrote the three characters of the doctor's name, then took from her own personal drawer in the wardrobe the sandal she'd been keeping there. She shoved it into her leather shoulder bag.

Hyang Mok informed the woman on loan from City Hall that there would be a delay in the purchase-order form for the canned seafood. At ten o'clock she met the head of a company dealing in plastic chopsticks and spoons. With the declining birthrate, the number of children in Fukuoka had diminished drastically, and there was a huge surplus of utensils like those the man brought to show her. These were unacceptable, however: they all had cartoon figures on the handles. At ten-thirty she and the doctor Heo Jip moved to the Laurel Room, now set aside as a special meeting place, to talk with the head of sales for Medicina, a pharmaceutical wholesaler. Other commercial negotiations were usually conducted with the participants sitting on sofas in the lobby, but Medicina was virtually the only wholesaler of its kind in Kyushu and thus relatively impervious to bargaining, which was why their people were given special treatment.

The executive, a man named Ninomiya, was a mild-mannered chemist in his late forties—and an unrelentingly tough negotiator. The ongoing shortage of medical supplies that had come in the wake of the blockade, and the upcoming arrival of hordes of soldiers who'd had a storm-tossed voyage, made the KEF's needs all the more urgent. As he sipped the ginseng tea he'd been served, Ninomiya examined the list provided by Heo Jip and compared it to the inventory recorded in his laptop.

Heo Jip's lack of Japanese meant things had to be translated, which was made difficult and tedious by the large number of technical words and phrases involved. With constant reference to a dictionary acquired in Fukuoka, Hyang Mok struggled to explain such terms as diuretics used to treat malnutrition-caused edema, quinolone

637

antibiotics used against enterococci, and beta blockers used to treat high blood pressure. As there were many new medications unavailable in the Republic, and as those required were in any case in short supply, the discussion dragged on. The most commonly used items such as antibiotics, analgesics, antiseptic lotion, nutritional supplements, digestive medicine, antipyretics, eye drops, and sticking plaster were particularly scarce. In the end, only a fifth of the hoped-for supply could be purchased, and at a higher-than-expected cost. Ninomiya explained that while, strictly speaking, the arrangement was contrary to Japanese law, the company would cooperate out of humanitarian concern.

While they were still in conversation, they heard the sound of army boots and jangling equipment. An SOF platoon led by Second Lieutenant Pak Il Su entered the lobby carrying AK rifles and Scorpion sub-machine guns. Major Kim Hak Su was issuing orders in front of the elevator, but the glass partition made his words difficult to hear. Finally the soldiers split into groups and boarded four of the elevators. "What's all this?" Ninomiya asked, and Hyang Mok said she thought it must be a training exercise. Heo Jip got up and opened the door to ask Kim what was going on. The latter, aware that an important meeting was being conducted in the special reception area, made a point of entering the room and politely greeting Ninomiya before explaining in Japanese that they had received a report of some "vermin" on the loose and were thus conducting a precautionary patrol. "Vermin?" said Ninomiya. "Yes," said Kim Hak Su, with a laugh. "Nothing to worry about. Just some little rats!"

When the meeting was over, Ninomiya, knowing that Hyang Mok was on her way to the Kyushu Medical Center, offered her a ride in his car, saying that he too was going there to make arrangements for the delivery of supplies. With her superior's permission, she accepted the offer. Would she need an armed escort? She said that wouldn't be necessary but was told to take along a pistol. She requisitioned a Soviet-era PSM, a lightweight weapon used on special assignments, and placed it in her shoulder bag.

Ninomiya drove his large white automobile up to the entrance to the reception hall, got out, and opened the door for her. The name of his firm was painted on the side in blue letters. As he started the engine, he explained that the company president had given the enterprise a Spanish name because he was keen on the paintings of Picasso. The leather seats had a pleasant smell. The sea, sparkling in the late morning sun, came immediately into view as they drove off. Hyang Mok remarked on the beauty of the scene, and Ninomiya gave her a quiet smile and nodded in agreement. As they passed the checkpoint, she extracted the memo from her shoulder bag and asked him whether he knew a physician by the name that was written on it. He took it in one hand, glanced at it, and replied: "Yes, Dr. Seragi," saying that he was well known and respected in the area but that he also had a reputation for being somewhat stubborn and something of a lone wolf. He was usually, she was told, in the immunology office on the third floor.

*A lone wolf.* When she heard this expression, it occurred to her that Seragi might in some ways resemble her own father. She knew that after having suffered horribly as an ethnic Korean during the Cultural Revolution in China, he had fled to the Republic all by himself, and in other respects as well he was a solitary man. A specialist in cholera, he had almost no friends and made no effort to socialize. Welling up from inside her came an image of him pressing his hands together above the water that she and her brothers brought each morning and mumbling some sort of prayer, then donning his hat and going off to the clinic, lunchbox and satchel in hand. She had no memory of him ever playing with her, or reading her a story. Just once, he had spent an evening fishing with her and her oldest brother. They spoke little and caught nothing, but it was an evening she'd never forgotten.

Fathers in the Republic, particularly in rural areas, were still deeply imbued with the feudalistic, patriarchal attitude of days gone by. But Hyang Mok's father did not rule over his family with fussy authority, or scold them, or punish them with beatings. He was, to be sure, rather brusque with them, but as her mother once explained, he was simply a very serious man, and terribly shy. Maybe he just didn't know how to relate to children. But they, for their part, were in awe of their father. They knew that he could read medical texts in German and Russian and was fluent in Chinese as well.

"I'll let you out here, and drive on to the parking lot." Ninomiya opened the door for her and said goodbye. By the entrance to the hospital was a guardroom, where an older man dressed in a navy-blue uniform greeted her and immediately ushered her in, presumably because he'd seen her get out of a car with the Medicina logo. She nodded and gave him a little smile as the large glass door slid open. The lobby was as big as the hotel's, with a soaring ceiling. A number of senior citizens were sitting in front of the outpatient counter waiting to be called. In her wallet Hyang Mok had, in addition to some cash, an ID card containing various information including a resident code, a civilian health-insurance number, and an account number for a local bank. This had been issued only to her and a few other officers. She could go to the counter, show her card, state her business, and pay the bill, all in a few minutes.

But if she made the payment first and then asked to see Dr. Seragi, her identity as a KEF officer would already be known to the hospital. Having tried to stop the execution of the two soldiers, he was likely to be hostile and might tell the receptionist to say that he was out of the office or in a meeting, and that would be that. With the arriving troops, she was bound to be busy helping to set things up in the temporary barracks and wouldn't get another chance to come here. She looked at her watch. It was still several minutes before noon. If she talked to Seragi for a quarter of an hour, paid the bill, and then returned to headquarters, it shouldn't be a problem. Leaving the reception area, she crossed the lobby and nipped into the elevator just as the doors were closing. "Which floor?" an elderly man clutching an IV stand asked her. "Three, please," she replied with a slight bow of her head.

It was such a large hospital that one could easily lose one's way. Hyang Mok got off on the third floor. There were rooms running right and left, and she couldn't even guess where the one she was looking for might be. The linoleum floor had a mirror-like polish, and the entire corridor was spotless. Hyang Mok asked a passing nurse for Dr. Seragi's office. Asked in turn what her business was, she replied that she had an appointment with him at noon to discuss a possible lecture. The nurse told her in a precise but friendly way that she should turn right in front of the dispensary; his office was at the end of that corridor. Walking on, Hyang Mok noted with some nostalgia the faint smell of medicine and disinfectant, and the peculiar atmosphere of a place populated by sick people and those caring for them. Her father's clinic had been an old wooden structure with antiquated equipment and couldn't be compared to this. But the feeling of the place had been very much the same.

She passed a group of doctors outside the dispensary, nodded to them, and walked purposefully on, head held high. From the gist of their conversation, she guessed they were on their way to lunch in the cafeteria. It was not long before noon; she could only hope Seragi was still in his office. She turned right and continued on past a conference room, a kitchenette, and the orderlies' room, and then came to the offices. There were five of these, separated by recessed, floor-to-ceiling windows. The sign on the first door said MEDICAL ENGINEERING RESEARCH OFFICE; then came KINETIC IMAGING, CARDIOVASCULAR PHYSIOLOGY, and ORGAN PRESERVATION AND TRANSPLANTATION. The last office was long and narrow and situated next to an enclosed balcony that looked out onto the hotel, the Dome, and the KEF camp. The sign, in both English and Japanese, read IMMUNOLOGY RESEARCH OFFICE. On the door at eye level was a card indicating that the doctor was in. Her heart was beating faster, and she took several deep breaths before knocking. "Come in," said a voice inside. Her pulse further quickened, as though her heart might pop out of her mouth. What was she trying to do? She was acting on her own, without any authorization. The thought of being taken into custody by the Japanese police or SDF made her look in her shoulder bag, just to make sure the PSM was there. If that happened, she told herself, she would end it then and there.

641

As she was about to knock again, the door opened. Seragi stood before her, a puzzled expression on his face. "Who are you?" he asked. When she said she wanted to speak to him, she got a sharp look from behind his glasses. Again he asked: "Who are you?" His voice was soft, but he made no move to let her in. Her imperfect Japanese, she realized, probably told him that she was Korean. "My name is Kim Hyang Mok. I am a second lieutenant in the Koryo Expeditionary Force." At the mention of the KEF, Seragi stared at her, frowning, then looked to see whether there was anyone behind her. "You're alone?" he asked, and when she nodded, he moved aside to let her enter.

Three of the walls were lined with bookshelves. In the middle of the room was a large desk, and outside the window was the balcony, beyond which she could see the hotel and the camp. Seragi didn't offer her a chair, and he himself remained standing, arms folded. He left the door open. He looked smaller and older than he had when she first saw him. Physically he was quite different from her father. But now that she was seeing him face to face in his doctor's apparel, she understood why he had appeared to her in her dreams and why she had come to see him. The shock of the realization made her feel as though she'd walked out of an *ondol*-heated room into subfreezing air. She sat down in a chair in front of the desk. She knew she should say something but found herself speechless. She heard Seragi's voice as though from a great distance: "What do you want?" Still seated, she reached into her shoulder bag, took out the PSM, released the safety catch, and thumbed back the hammer. The metallic sound of the spring was unmistakable in the quiet room. Clearly alarmed, Seragi moved toward the door. "I'd like you to stay," said Hyang Mok. "Are you here to shoot me?" he asked. Hyang Mok shook her head and reached into her shoulder bag again to produce the white sandal. "I wanted to return this to you."

Adjusting his glasses, Seragi came forward and took the sandal from her, though still apparently unaware that it was his own. He alternately looked at it, then at her, evidently baffled by this gesture.

Then, seeing his own name written faintly on the instep, he looked at her again, as though remembering the execution, and took a deep breath. "Why did you bring me this?" he asked her. "I thought you might need it," she replied. Seragi stepped to the door and glanced up and down the corridor before closing it.

Holding the sandal in one hand, he slowly crossed the room and sat down in his high-backed swivel chair across from her. The outline of his white coat was silhouetted against the light from the window. On his desk she saw a notebook PC, photographs that appeared to be of his family, various books, and memos. There was also a strange object: a stuffed baby chicken with black wings, sitting on a stand inscribed with the word *Chimera*. Seragi noticed that she was staring at it and explained: "It has this name because it represents an organism containing genetically different tissues. The wings are those of a quail. Early on in the embryonic development of the chick, part of its neural tube is replaced by that of a quail, and that's why the wings are black. But the chick dies soon after hatching. It becomes paralyzed, unable to move its wings or walk, and finally weakens and gives up the ghost. Its immune system rejects the quail's nerve cells, you see."

As he spoke, Seragi placed the sandal on his desk and, as if speaking to himself, wondered again why she had gone to the trouble of bringing it to him. "My father is a physician; he too values the things he works with," she said, then realized that she'd been speaking in the present tense. "I'm sorry," she continued, "my father is no longer alive." It was while on duty as a railway security guard at a tunnel near the Chinese border that she'd heard he was seriously ill. Her commanding officer had received a telegram and given her temporary leave. The next morning she headed for home, first taking the train and then getting a ride in a charcoal delivery truck. Her father was very weak, having contracted pneumonia, and he died soon after her arrival. As she had sat at his bedside, he'd brought his face close to hers to convey two final messages. The first was: "Wish I could have gone fishing with you again." The second was: "Love and cherish your children."

"Love and cherish your children." She turned the words over and over now in her mind, words she had long since buried inside her. She felt she should say something to avoid further confusion, but her throat was too dry and her voice too hoarse. When Seragi poured her some coffee from a pot at the window, she nodded her thanks and finally managed to ask him why he had made his protest at the execution. He poured some coffee for himself, silently held the cup in both hands as though to warm them, and then gazed out of the window. Beyond the glass pane and the balcony lay the campground. The lunch hour had just begun, and soldiers were gathered around steaming pots on folding tables. "Let me tell you a story from long ago," he said. "During the war, I witnessed many executions in your country. It's not as if everything we did in your country was evil. We built roads and dams; we carried out irrigation and draining projects. But we did terrible things too. As a boy soldier, I couldn't do anything to stop the executions, but it also wouldn't have occurred to me to try, because I didn't see anything wrong with it."

The walls were all lined with books. There were bookshelves next to the door and others on both sides that reached the ceiling. The strange little bird perched atop the desk had been so skillfully stuffed that it looked as if it might cheep. The sugarless coffee was bitter but had a delicious aroma. Hyang Mok was barely following what Seragi was saying. "I was fifteen at the time. I didn't know anything. I wasn't so much a monster as an ignoramus. But there's nothing worse than ignorance. After we were all repatriated, I began to have disturbing dreams. And when I got back to school, I began to realize the significance of those executions. It's now been nearly seventy years, and the scenes still come back to me in my sleep. At the age of eighty-three, I know I could die at any time, but I've got no stomach for a new set of nightmares."

He stopped speaking and looked at Hyang Mok's hands. She was still holding the pistol. It wasn't him she wanted to shoot, but herself. She couldn't do it here, though; that would only cause trouble for everyone. She'd have to do it somewhere else—put a bullet through her throat, or through her head. "Love and cherish your children," her father had said to her as he lay dying. She had forgotten those words, and gone on living as though nothing were wrong. Staring down at the pistol in her hand, she told Seragi: "I killed my own baby." She looked up to see his silhouette shifting in the chair, but against the light she couldn't make out his features clearly. After her father's death she had left the railway job and returned home, where she married a man who worked as a technician for a cannery near the sea. A child was born in 2002. The village, too small to benefit from Chinese black-market supplies, had been suffering from a long-term famine. Price controls had collapsed, so that rice and corn now cost hundreds of times more than they had just a few years before. The immediate cause of her father's death had been pneumonia, but his weakened condition had been the result of malnutrition. They had killed the sheep that had provided the wool for Hyang Mok's sweater and sold the meat on the free market. Her mother had gone with her brothers into the hills in the hope of collecting firewood to exchange on the market in Ranam for eggs and honey, but other villagers had already done the same, and not a stick remained.

Hyang Mok's husband was a serious and resourceful person. He used split bamboo staves to bring running water into their house from upstream, and he taught himself how to manufacture soap from acorn ash. The food shortage worsened after the birth of their child, and he was tempted every day to steal cans from the factory, where sardines and codfish were being processed for cat-food exports. But the factory was run under the watchful supervision of the Fourth Corps of the People's Army, with military trucks being used to transport both the raw materials and the final product. By the time the baby was able to hold its head steady, Hyang Mok no longer had any breast milk, forcing her to feed the infant the juice from mashed corn, but corn, to say nothing of rice, became increasingly hard to come by.

Her husband used to stay up all night making soap to sell on the free market, burning acorns, filtering the ashes through hemp cloth, and mixing them with powdered pieces of ordinary soap. The result was a foamy liquid that he then bottled. The trouble was that a better-quality Chinese soap was already available, so that he was obliged to sell what he'd made for next to nothing, with much of it finding no buyers at any price. Hyang Mok's mother and her brothers sold the family furniture on the Chinese border and with the money bought some corn, selling half of it in Ranam and keeping the rest for the family. They used only a bare minimum of crockery and bedding and auctioned off the old doctor's books and medical equipment. The last thing to go was the oil-paper cover on the *ondol* floor, which they peeled off and sold. Finally, when there was nothing else that could be exchanged for money, Hyang Mok remembered having gone to the coast with her siblings years ago to collect shellfish. Braving the cold of the autumn sea, she waded in but found that even that source of food had been exhausted. When she suggested going into the hills to trap rabbits, her mother laughed: they had long since vanished, she was told, along with the pheasants, turtle doves, wild ducks, bamboo partridges, and other birds.

When winter came, the villagers resorted to cutting down the trees in their orchard in order to keep warm. At one time Hyang Mok had often gone into the hills in search of medicinal herbs, but now only conifers such as pine and cedar remained on the largely denuded hills. With the first snowfall, a public execution attended by the entire village took place in front of the miners' barracks. Her husband was shocked to see that the two condemned men tied to the posts were fellow workers at the factory, who had been caught stealing cans. After that he seemed to become utterly dispirited. He told her that some workers drinking together had been overheard by soldiers complaining that there was "plenty of fish for foreign cats but none for us," and were beaten within an inch of their lives. Shortly afterwards he left home, going off to look for work across the Tumen River in China. He returned once, carrying a sack of wheat flour, but then left again, this time for good. There were various rumors: some said he had drowned crossing the river; others said that he'd been apprehended and executed by Korean border guards, others still that he was living with an ethnic Korean woman in Yanji. The truth of the matter remained unknown.

One wintry day Hyang Mok's mother and brothers came by to take her into the hills to strip bark off the pine trees, which the villagers were beginning to eat, cutting into the trunks with a sickle and then pulling with their hands. The bark didn't peel easily, and their nails would get broken and bloody. Once they got the stuff off, they took it home and used a sharp stone to scrape off the tough outer layer and the sap. They soaked what remained in a bucket of water overnight, then put it in a pot and boiled it for hours in sodium bicarbonate. Washed once, it was left to dry in the shade for another forty-eight hours, before being beaten with a round stone in a hemp sack. Finally, they would mix the sticky powder with wheat flour or corn and eat it. The pine fibers were tasteless and virtually indigestible, causing the abdomen to swell. This is what began to happen to Hyang Mok's undernourished one-year-old, who'd grown too weak even to cry. The powdered pine bark seemed to relieve the baby's hunger, but it went largely undigested and was excreted more or less whole. Hyang Mok had to pick fibers out of the infant's rectum.

One day, after chewing on the pine fiber herself to soften it further, she gave the child a small mouthful, but it was now so weak that it couldn't swallow, spitting it all out. And when Hyang Mok finally managed to force some down, the baby began to writhe about, its small belly gurgling, its intestines bulging under the skin, and the accumulated gas swelling its entire midsection. The fibers had blocked the digestive tract. With the death of her father, the village had no doctor, so there was nothing that could be done. That evening, its belly swollen like a balloon, the infant died. Mothers locally used to gently tap their babies on the belly to lull them to sleep, rather than rocking them in a cradle. Seeing her dead child's monstrously swollen tummy, Hyang Mok thought she'd committed a sin that not even her own death would expunge.

"This was foolish of me," she said to Seragi. "Coming to see you and telling you this can't take away my guilt. I'm sorry for intruding.

It was foolish." She had failed to honor her father's wish. Far from loving and cherishing her child, she had killed it with her own hands, and then tried to escape that reality. Seeing Dr. Seragi there at the place of execution in his white coat, she had remembered her father and was forced to confront the crime she'd tried for so long to conceal from herself. The irony was that if she hadn't come to Kyushu, she might never have come to grips with this reality; her duty to the Republic had always taken precedence. Moreover, there were so many others who had lost children to starvation that the sheer horror of it all had eased what should have been any human being's most heartbreaking loss.

She returned the PSM to her shoulder bag, feeling ashamed of imposing on this man and taking up his time. Seragi remained in his chair, staring at her. The hotel beyond the window stood like a knife plunged straight into the earth. Suddenly she saw white smoke coming from the windows of one floor. An instant later she heard the sound of a small explosion. Seragi turned around to look. Reaching for her phone, she called Ri Hui Cheol. There was more smoke from the same floor—the eighth—and then the sound of a second explosion.

"We haven't been able to contact the reconnaissance unit and don't know what's happened," Ri calmly reported. "It's not clear whether there's been enemy infiltration or an accident. A Japanese worker has reported that it might be a gas leak. We've called the police and the fire department. They're on their way." He ended the call, and she decided to take care of the hospital bill and return to headquarters. There was no reason for her to stay here any longer. She should have died, not the child. That alone was now clear. "You must excuse me, Doctor," she said, getting up and heading for the door, but he stopped her, saying, "Wait a moment." He went to a shelf against the wall and pulled out an old book. "Do you know any English?" he asked. "A little," she said. "Then you should be able to read this simple story by Hans Christian Andersen. There's a story called 'The Angel.' Let me just read you the beginning for now. 'Whenever a good child dies, an angel of God comes down

648

from heaven, takes the dead child in his arms, spreads out his great white wings, and flies over all the places that child had loved in life. Then he gathers a large handful of flowers, which he carries up to the Lord, that they may bloom more brightly in heaven than they do on earth. And He presses the flowers to His heart, kissing the one that pleases Him best and bestowing on it a voice, that it may join the choir in hymns of joy.'"

Seragi offered her the book. Taking it with both hands, she bowed her head: "*Arigato gozaimasu.*" On the torn, reddish-brown cover was the title: *The Red Shoes and Other Tales.* Seragi's reading had moved her almost to tears. But what exactly was an "angel"? She remembered hearing about them, but her impression was hazy. "They come from the next world," he explained, stretching out his arms and adding: "They have wings." Hyang Mok smiled at the gesture, wondering where the white-winged angel had taken her own child. It had been only a year old and knew only the village area. Had the angel taken it to the orchard or the stream? To her mother's house, or the foothills where rabbits and pheasants lived? When she imagined the baby folded in those white wings and flying through the sky above her village, she felt her frozen heart begin to thaw. And with that warming came another suppressed memory from her youth. She had always wanted to help the many children in her village and surrounding areas who had lost their parents and become homeless beggars. It had been her dream one day to set up an orphanage back home, when her military career was finished. Whatever happened to that dream, she wondered.

The sound of sirens came from somewhere in the distance. Fire trucks were no doubt on their way. Seragi's hands were resting on the windowsill as he looked out over the campground. The loudspeakers were announcing something, but the closed windows made it difficult to hear. "What are they saying?" he asked. Hyang Mok approached the window and, standing next to him, looked out. "'There are a number of intruders,'" she said, interpreting the last words of the announcement: "'They are on the run.'" MAVs could be seen driving along the streets in the vicinity. The elbow of her gray suit brushed against his white coat. He was a kind man, she thought, as she put the book he had given her into her shoulder bag. Perhaps she should mention the orphanage idea to him.

"Doctor," she said. And just as Seragi turned to her, thick clouds of dust burst horizontally from the base of the hotel, billowing out like the jets of smoke at a rocket launch, giving the high-rise a skirt of swirling soot that enveloped the entire base of the building. There was a sharp popping sound, as cracks appeared in the glass of the balcony windows, and a second later they heard the roar of an explosion that shook the earth. Hyang Mok immediately covered her ears and crouched down. Amid the smoke, glass shards flashed and glittered in the sunlight. Troops in the campground were frantically trying to escape the flying debris, some crawling under tables, and the stretch of water beyond was seething, with overlapping waves breaking against the seawall. Seragi had fallen to the floor on his backside, but he reached for the windowsill and pulled himself up beside Hyang Mok to look out.

Smoke, borne by the sea wind in their direction, parted to reveal a great black cavity toward the base of the hotel. Hyang Mok experienced a strange sensation: her field of vision seemed to rotate clockwise, as though she herself were falling to the left. As she watched the glass snail-shaped structure near the bottom disintegrate, she realized that the whole hotel, still maintaining its knife-like shape, was toppling over. There was a deep rumbling, followed by a quick, fierce wind that made the trees reel and sent paper trash and garbage whirling up into the air. Through the windows they could hear the crack and crunch of collapsing steel, quite as though a giant had stepped on a pile of dead wood, sending bits flying as far out as the now white-capped water. Fishing boats were turning and making for the open sea.

The roof of the fourth floor's covered entrance was crushed and its pillars catapulted into the campground tents, tearing them to shreds and mowing down the poles to which the loudspeakers had been fastened and on which KEF flags had been hoisted. Dozens of soldiers lay prostrate on the ground either already dead or trying to escape the windblast. An MAV flipped over, skidded across the road, smashed into a pillar supporting the elevated expressway, and burst into flames. The wall of the Dome was battered and pushed inward, opening a big gap beneath the silver roof. The tremors were so powerful, like waves rolling through the entire landscape, that Hyang Mok was lifted right off her feet, then instantly dropped down again. The shock of it shot up her spine from her tailbone to her brain. She grabbed onto the window frame for support and screamed, if only to keep from fainting. Seragi too was shouting something, but she couldn't hear him over the deafening noise. The Medical Center continued to bounce and sway. It felt as if its girders were askew and the floor and ceiling on the verge of collapsing.

Above the length of the fallen hotel a mushroom cloud was taking shape. The burgeoning smoke looked literally like some furiously multiplying fruit or fungus. It grew until it enveloped and concealed the campground, the Dome, and the waters beyond, and now rose to fill the sky, turning day to night. Debris flew through the darkness at ferocious speeds, flattening whatever lay in its path. In a trice the warped walls and the roof of the Dome across the way resembled tin plates riddled and shredded by machine-gun fire. Soldiers who had taken shelter in the shadow of a water tower simply disappeared, swept away by chunks of concrete the size of oil drums. Sections of steel and pieces of concrete collided and rained down on the hospital like meteorites, delivering a series of powerful jolts. A small black shadow appeared amid the smoke and instantly grew to the size of a refrigerator: part of a girder spinning toward them. It smashed into the next room to their left, causing the wall on that side to burst apart and collapse. The glass was pulverized, the window frame twisted out of shape, and big cracks opened up in the pillars and ceiling. The bookcases had fallen, strewing their contents on the floor. Seragi was holding his right leg, his face distorted with pain—apparently he'd twisted his ankle. Hyang Mok reached under his arms and pulled him away from the window toward the center of the room, though it wasn't easy going, with the toppled furniture and bits of broken glass and wall plaster littering the floor. She shoved him between the protruding legs of the capsized desk, then crawled in after him.

Shards of glass and fist-sized stones continued to pour down, and now a car-sized concrete mass was hurtling toward them. A moment later it made impact, and the balcony was gone, shorn right off by it. The air in the room was so thick that they couldn't keep their eyes open. "Doctor, can you get up?" Hyang Mok shouted into Seragi's ear, but he could only reply with a weak shake of his head. The door had been ripped off its hinges, and the room might collapse at any moment. She draped his arm around her shoulder. Her mouth and nose were filled with fine particles of concrete and glass dust that got in her eyes, making them flood with tears.

Seragi's glasses were broken. He had a cut at the corner of one eye, and the side of his shirt was stained with blood. Hyang Mok took out the book he had given her, put it in an inner jacket pocket, and tossed the shoulder bag aside. In the haze of the smoke-filled room, she covered her mouth and nose with a handkerchief and tied the ends around the back of her head, before struggling over the jumble of books and plaster toward the door. Looking back, she could just see that the view outside was different now. The sea had turned a muddy brown, and a low-lying cloud of dust hung like mist over the land below. The Dome was flattened and unrecognizable. A section of its silver roof lay in the parking lot of Hawk's Town, wavering eerily in the wind.

The campground had become a mountain of rubble, and the KEF headquarters was no more. It was unlikely that anyone had survived. Had the Japanese government launched the attack? Was it the Americans? In any case, the Koryo Expeditionary Force had been wiped out. With no hostages, the main body of soldiers would be forced to turn back. And yet, strangely enough, Hyang Mok felt neither grief nor despair. This destruction, she thought, was the wrath of heaven, bringing all things back to their beginning. She had no doubt that she herself would be arrested and put to death. And she had no fear of that punishment: she deserved it, for letting her own child die. Still, she had to rescue this doctor. If she could get him to the other side of the hotel, he should be fine.

Outside the windows in the corridor, she saw that the white dust enveloping the camp was being dispersed by the sea wind and carried skyward. Maybe this is what it looks like, she thought, when an angel spreads its great white wings.

## EPILOGUE 1

*April 14, 2011*
*Akasaka, Tokyo*

S ANJO MASAHIRO was considering the night's playlist while he
filled the espresso machine. It seemed that quite a few of his
regulars would be along earlier than usual this evening. Even a few
from the various ministries had emailed that they were coming. He
supposed they'd all want to get his take on the KEF story. He turned
the TV on to watch the news, but it was still showing endless shots
of the ruined hotel, and a series of idiots calling themselves experts
were trotting out their useless theories, so he turned it off again.

Sanjo had asked a number of his government contacts whether
or not US special ops had been brought in to blow up the hotel,
but nobody knew anything. It had been one hell of an explosion,
yet there were surprisingly few civilian casualties. The hotel had
collapsed in the direction of the Dome, which acted as a shield, and
the blast and wreckage hadn't reached all that far. But the Kyushu
Medical Center, overlooking the camp, had been hit hard. Altogether
there had been a hundred and eighty-seven civilian fatalities and
numerous injured, most of them patients, but some medical staff
as well. Still, it was an extraordinarily low number, considering
the mountain of rubble the hotel had left behind. It was lucky the
hospital hadn't collapsed too.

The North Korean fleet had refused to believe that the KEF in
Fukuoka had really been wiped out and had encroached ten nautical
miles into Japanese waters despite warning shots from the SDF, so

654

that tensions remained high for a while. According to the Ministry for Foreign Affairs it was only after Beijing threatened to send in submarines that they finally withdrew. The bodies of most of the KEF lay deep under the wreckage, making it impossible to confirm the exact number. The officers in the hotel had received the full force of the blast, and though pieces of them were found, there were no DNA samples or dental records to identify them. Six KEF engineers had been working in another location and had escaped the collapse of the hotel, but on returning to the ruins of the encampment they'd all apparently committed suicide, to avoid being taken captive. One staff officer alone seemed to have survived—the handsome Lieutenant Jo. He'd been recording his broadcast at NHK at the time, and was currently being held by Fukuoka prefectural police. The government and the National Police Agency in Tokyo were demanding that he be handed over, but the city authorities had yet to comply.

All the people under arrest by the KEF, as well as all the City Hall staff on secondment, had perished. The question of just who had planted the explosive devices remained, however. Many of the foreign news agencies were claiming that the Japanese government had been behind it, and the Cabinet had neither confirmed nor denied this. But it had to have been America, thought Sanjo, as he looked through his vinyl collection on the shelf. US Special Forces must have planted the explosives, then detonated them by remote control. There were so many unanswered questions, though. Wouldn't it have been to America's advantage to have the rebel army stationed in Fukuoka? That would have kept a check on military expansionism in Japan. America would then probably have sent, say, ten thousand troops to Kyushu as a UN Peacekeeping Force. Even if war had broken out, there would have been a need for weapons and materiel, and firms supplying the military would have made a bundle. And since the KEF was a rebel army, it wouldn't have damaged relations with North Korea or necessarily antagonized China. Still, even if the attack was carried out by, say, the Navy Seals, it must have been backed by the Japanese.

*

The first customer to arrive was Tom Kai from the Ministry for Home Affairs. When Sanjo pointed out it was only seven-thirty, Kai said he'd left work early since there was nothing to do. Fukuoka City wasn't giving them any information, so they were all just twiddling their thumbs. Fukuoka had evidently lost all trust in the central government.

"I really feel like listening to some Wes Montgomery," said Kai. Sanjo selected 'Full House.' He dropped the needle onto the record, and they both listened in silence for a while. You didn't get guitar playing like that anymore. Montgomery's technique of simultaneously thumbing the same note on two strings an octave apart was brilliant. There were plenty of other guitarists who played octaves, of course, but it all originated with him. Jazz had once been a real movement. Not anymore. Now it only lived on in old recordings for devotees. Youngsters like Kai, who'd never heard jazz in its heyday, had no idea. "That's Wynton Kelly on piano, isn't it, Sanjo-san? Wasn't he still with Miles Davis at the time of this recording?" Sanjo said that yes, he probably was with Miles then, but privately he thought, so what? Wes Montgomery couldn't read music. His octave technique was probably just something he'd hit upon and then developed, because he liked the way it sounded and felt. Playing jazz and being up on jazz were two different things.

At least Kai wasn't talking about the hotel's collapse. Up until just yesterday he'd phoned and emailed Sanjo repeatedly, asking who he thought did it. It was hard to believe it could be the government, since not even the top brass in the ministries seemed to know anything. Overseas, the Japanese government was praised for presumably bringing in a domestic commando unit. Resolving a crisis like that with a loss of fewer than two hundred civilian lives was deemed a great success. If, however, the government had not in fact been involved, Sanjo believed that Japan was going to sink even lower than it already had. Kai and other bureaucrats he knew acknowledged that government officials didn't seem to have any intention of investigating what had really happened. Nor did they seem interested in sending any fact-finding missions to interview local officials or ordinary citizens. They couldn't get around the fact that they had imposed the blockade, but as always they tried to avoid facing up to unpleasant realities.

Real life was full of troubles and problems. Post-war Japan had avoided facing up to reality by depending on America for protection. Countries like that refine their own society and culture as they cruise along with a false sense of reality, but eventually they lose their drive and decline. Part of Sanjo was sad that the KEF had been wiped out, since their presence in Kyushu would have forced Tokyo to get real. Sooner or later there was bound to have been open conflict with the KEF. The US and China would have been drawn in, and it could have developed into a mini-world war, with Kyushu as the battlefield. As far as Sanjo was concerned, it might have been a whole lot more interesting had they stayed in Fukuoka, though this sort of nihilistic curiosity would probably have soon worn off.

The door to the bar opened again. More bureaucrats, probably, or some fairly well-heeled people who'd come to down expensive wine or cognac as if nothing had ever happened. Just one thing still bothered Sanjo: what had happened to all that money taken from the "criminals"? There must be a considerable sum sitting in a private bank account somewhere. Who was going to get their hands on that? Still mulling this over, he called out a professional-sounding "*Irasshaimase*" and went over to greet his customers.

*May 5, 2014*
*Sakito Island*

S ERAGI YOKO had taken a train from Fukuoka to Huis Ten
Bosch Station in the city of Sasebo, and had then got on a bus
headed for Sakitojima, an island linked to Kyushu by several bridges.
A doctor who had trained under her grandfather at the Kyushu
Medical Center had opened a clinic there, and still scrupulously
sent midsummer and year-end gifts of fresh sea bream, abalone, or
lobster. Today he was holding a small celebration at his clinic, and
Yoko had been invited in her grandfather's place.

The seaside town sparkled in the sunlight. Azaleas were in full
bloom along the road, and a pleasant breeze came through the bus
window. "Perfect weather, innit?" said the old lady sitting next to
her. They both spoke the same Kyushu dialect, but her accent was
slightly different. "And the azaleas are lovely," said Yoko in return.
The old lady was reading a women's weekly magazine that featured
a close-up of a woman anchor from NHK Fukuoka named Hosoda
Sakiko. Hosoda was a prominent supporter of the sole surviving KEF
officer, who was in Fukuoka Prison. Under the KEF occupation, the
officer had his own TV program at NHK Fukuoka, and his good
looks and his way with words had earned him a lot of female fans.
Even now, three years later, Hosoda continued to correspond with
him and to visit him regularly.

Jo Su Ryeon had been recording his program when he learned that
the Sea Hawk Hotel and the KEF camp had been destroyed. On

hearing that the six remaining engineers had committed suicide, Jo turned himself in to the police. The government declared him an enemy of the state, but the local people—both KEF sympathizers and detractors alike—had opposed their demand that he be handed over. All the government had ever done for them was cut them off; it hadn't offered any help or even tried to negotiate with the KEF, so why should they cooperate?

Hosoda Sakiko was at the forefront of those opposing Jo's transfer to Tokyo. "Yes, he has to face up to his crimes. All I'm saying is that the investigation and trial should take place here in Fukuoka," had been her line, and she had attracted many other supporters. In time, Jo had come to symbolize the antagonism between Fukuoka and central government, and neither the city nor the prefectural police had shown any inclination to turn him over. Eventually, the government had stopped referring to it, though they hadn't officially dropped their demand. Jo had been tried in the Fukuoka District Court in double-quick time, and was sentenced to life imprisonment. Some sympathizers even said that this was too harsh, given that it wasn't a murder or kidnapping case. Others held that he was in the safest place possible: having been involved in a covert foreign plot, his life would always be in danger on the outside. It seemed that with Hosoda's encouragement, Jo was spending his time improving his Japanese and writing fiction and poetry.

Japan's economy had continued to shrink, and the country was still isolated internationally. With the end of the emergency, the Cabinet had resigned en masse, and the ruling Japan Green party had won the subsequent general election by a narrow margin, although their power base had since been even further eroded. Unemployment was approaching ten per cent, and other economic indicators were no better. At least the hardline militarists had been silenced, albeit probably only temporarily. The KEF episode had brought home to the nation that Japan could not deal with a major crisis without a relationship of mutual cooperation with America and the rest of Asia. Even so, no fundamental sense of urgency was reflected in the new government's policies. Relations with the US and China had not thawed, and the Cabinet had failed to introduce institutional reforms in order to tackle the severe recession and social disorder. The year before, a UK economics magazine had run an article headed "Sun Setting on the Land of the Rising Sun," which seemed to sum it all up.

Kyushu, in contrast, had been greatly changed by the experience. It had taken action on such matters as food self-sufficiency and the environment. Administrative reforms were implemented that included reducing public works, and a five-year plan had been drawn up to eliminate the need for dependence on governmental subsidies and local tax allocations. The prefectural government had left its offices in Fukuoka and dispersed to seven regional towns, and the number of municipal workers had been halved, while more effort was being put into economic collaboration and trade with East Asia.

A couple of years ago, students had been invited from all over Asia to spend a year in twenty-three cities and towns around Kyushu, in an event titled "A Thousand Years of Asian Wisdom." Almost two thousand of them came to partake in discussions with local residents and businesses on how best to revitalize provincial towns. The towns they stayed in began to attract more visitors, with the students themselves becoming a useful human resource linking these towns with other countries in Asia. The unemployment rate in Kyushu was five per cent lower than in the rest of Japan, and the birthrate also stopped declining. A fair number of people who had left Kyushu now returned home, while others from different areas were beginning to move there.

There were four bridges joining Sakito to the mainland. Each had its own character, and all were set in spectacular scenery. Yoko had often visited the place, but she never tired of the combination of little bays and an azure sea. In the Edo period, the island had prospered from whaling, while in the late nineteenth century it had become famous for its seabed coal mines, and the hilly area along the coast with the remains of miners' housing had been turned into a commemorative park. These days the island was just one of a number of places in Kyushu whose mainstay industry was its saltworks, producing special mineral salt and mineral water for sale on the mainland.

After its mines were closed, Sakito had stagnated. The bright side of this was that it retained a good deal of untouched scenery, and the vista from the Mining Memorial Park over the port and the central town and public offices was wonderful. The low eaves of houses were visible around the gently curving bay, beyond which the hills drew their green contours against the backdrop of the sea. Along an unusual beach of flat bedrock known as "A Thousand Tatamis" was a promenade stretching for about three hundred meters, from which you could enjoy the sea breeze and a view of the smaller islands in the offing. At low tide you could cross over to one of these, which had a pretty lighthouse and abundant fish swimming in its waters.

Yoko got off the bus at the town hall and started walking up a steep, narrow path. A sweet scent hung over the trail from the azaleas on either side, and halfway up, an open lot was covered with nodding poppies. After a few minutes, she began to sweat and removed her cardigan. The clinic, together with a childcare facility, was in a spot from which the ocean could be seen in all directions. Yoko walked around the back of the daycare center into the courtyard, and peered through a window. Today was Children's Day and they probably had a special program, for through the glass she saw seven or eight local kids sitting inside, and a woman who was reading a book to them. This was a former Koryo Expeditionary Force officer who had been adopted by Yoko's grandfather. She'd been in the Medical Center at the time the hotel was blown up and had saved his life, helping him out of his office moments before the ceiling came down. A lot of people had died, and the resident-codes system had been so muddled up by the KEF that it hadn't been all that hard to register her as his newly adopted daughter. Since she was well known among the traders in Fukuoka, however, he had quickly arranged for her to stay with his former student on this island.

Yoko's grandfather had retired from the Medical Center, but was still involved in research into autoimmune diseases. At the grand old age of eighty-six his legs were getting weak and it was hard for him to travel, so he only came to the island once a year now. The woman noticed Yoko and waved at her. Her name had been Kim Hyang Mok, but Dr. Seragi used one of the Chinese characters of her name to make the Japanese name Kaori, or "fragrance," by which she was now known. When Kaori was alone with Yoko, she always talked about home. "I expect I'll live a long time, the air here's so good," she'd say, her eyes sparkling. "But one day, when the Korean Peninsula is united again, I'll go back to my village. And I'll build an orphanage."

Yoko pointed at the clinic to indicate where she was going. Kaori nodded, and carried on reading the story to the children. She was earnest and sweet, and the Seragi family were all fond of her. Yet there was something unfathomable about her. "Yoko-san, do you realize you could occupy this whole island with just ten soldiers?" she once said when they were talking together, and it was hard to tell whether she was joking or not. When Yoko told her grandfather this, he reminded her that Kaori had no intention of becoming Japanese. She was only hiding out here.

But who had blown up the hotel? Kaori was always bringing the subject up. It hadn't been either the SDF or the US Army. Both countries had made official statements to that effect to the UN Security Council and the foreign media. There had been all kinds of speculation as a result: fingers were pointed at the South Korean SOF, at a European mercenary group that had claimed responsibility on its website, at an American counter-terrorist organization, and so on. Kaori herself seemed to think that Kim Jong Il had used his intelligence agents to wipe out the KEF. The hardline admiral and key officers in the backup fleet had all apparently been purged after returning to North Korea. Kim Jong Il had thus been able to eliminate the biggest obstacle to North Korea-US collaboration and eventual unification with the South. But nobody seemed to have any clear idea who could actually have set the charges. It was a puzzle that would no doubt be talked about for a long time to come.

*June 13, 2014*
*Meinohama*

I WAGAKI DECIDED to drop by the warehouse again. He didn't want to go to school, and he didn't have anywhere else to go. A strange group of older dudes were living in one of the abandoned warehouses in Meinohama. He'd first met one of them, a guy named Tateno, at an event last summer on Nokonoshima Island. It was a so-called Activities Fair, featuring lessons in various sports and hobbies—diving, kite-flying, body surfing, clam digging, beach volleyball, futsal. The man was offering boomerang lessons but not getting any takers. He didn't talk much or joke around and basically came across as sullen and weird, and the kids at the fair tended to choose more on the basis of the instructor's personality than the activity itself. But something about this character appealed to Iwagaki, and he had spent the entire day throwing boomerangs.

As he entered the warehouse, a man in a wheelchair, someone called Shinohara, was just rolling off to his room. Iwagaki greeted him, but he merely stared back with a *You again?* kind of look. Iwagaki didn't mind being ignored like that, though. He liked it that the people here didn't try to play up to kids the way most adults did. Shinohara supposedly raised hundreds of frogs with insanely colorful skin, but Iwagaki hadn't seen them yet.

He was in the second year of middle school now, but he had lost all interest in education when he was in kindergarten. That year, on Christmas Eve, the teacher had told the class that the local fire brigade was bringing a real live reindeer for them to see. When it turned out to be a pony with plastic antlers attached behind its ears, Iwagaki began shouting: "That's not a reindeer!" The teacher lost her temper when she couldn't get him to stop saying this, and he ended up having to leave the school. Since then, he had gone to class only sporadically, and he'd stolen money from his parents and run away any number of times.

Tateno was having a cup of tea in the room everyone called the Living. When Iwagaki said hello, he glanced up indifferently and said, "Hey." Looking around, Iwagaki noticed that they weren't alone: an old man lay asleep in a rocking chair, as still as a wax figure. There were a lot of stories about this character, whose name was Ishihara, and the group around him. A friend of Iwagaki's who was in the local Speed Tribe had told him that, according to rumor, it was these guys who'd brought down the Sea Hawk Hotel three years ago. A lot of them were supposed to have died in the operation, but since they hadn't had resident codes, nobody knew who they were. Iwagaki had once asked Tateno if the rumor was true, but all he'd said was, "Don't be a fool."

A powerful-sounding engine roared to a stop outside, and in a minute another man walked into the Living. He was carrying a heavy cardboard box. Exchanging greetings with Tateno, he sat on the sofa and put the box down at his feet. This guy, Sato, was relatively young. Ignoring Iwagaki, he addressed the sleeper in the rocking chair, telling him, "I brought the booze." The old man twitched at the word "booze," and his eyes popped open. It was weird, but the whole atmosphere of the room seemed to change when those eyes emerged from that wrinkled face.

Sato was taking bottles of various shapes and sizes out of the cardboard box and lining them up on the floor. Ishihara stood up and walked unsteadily into the kitchen, returning with a glass and some ice. "Shall we start with vodka, then?" he said. He filled his glass with the clear liquid and drained half of it before smacking his lips and beaming: "That's goooood." Shinohara, who must have heard this, came wheeling out of his room. "How's business?" he said to Sato, as he propelled himself toward the sofa. "Not bad," the other answered. Sato managed a string of beauty parlors and nail salons in Tenjin and Nakasu, and drove a silver Porsche. He was said to be something of a genius with his hands, and his "nail art miniatures" had caught on big time. These consisted of finely detailed paintings, or abstract strips of color that under a magnifying glass turned into lines of text.

His own left thumbnail was brightly painted, and Iwagaki screwed up his nerve and asked if he could take a closer look. Sato gave him an impatient glance, then thrust out his thumb and said, "Knock yourself out." The names were written in kanji, reading from left to right. At the top were two green lines that on closer inspection turned out to be a series of surnames: YAMADA MORI MATSUYAMA OKUBO FUKUDA. The third line was red and the characters a bit bigger: ORIHARA KONDO MIYAZAKI SHIBATA. Next came another thin green line: ANDO FELIX TAKEI TOYOHARA. Then another thick red one: HINO TAKEGUCHI. And at the bottom, in very small black print, were the two kanji for KANESHIRO, followed by tiny katakana script reading KORYOS.

Why were some names bigger than others? Did "Koryos" mean that rebel army from North Korea? Sato was beginning to look restless, so Iwagaki decided not to ask any questions. Tateno, after telling him not to be a fool, had made it clear that it wasn't cool to ask people about things they themselves didn't bring up first. While the old man drank his vodka, the other three sat on the sofa silently sipping oolong tea and Pocari Sweat. They didn't smoke or listen to music or watch TV or look at magazines. From an ordinary point of view, they didn't seem to be enjoying themselves at all. But the man named Tateno had also taught Iwagaki something about the concept of "fun." Fun wasn't about whooping it up and goofing around in a crowd. It was about just spending time with people who mattered to you.

All four sat there quietly as time ticked by. There was nothing oppressive about the silence, but Iwagaki somehow began to feel that he was intruding and decided to leave. When he excused himself, only Tateno gave him a little wave. After opening the door, he turned back and asked, "Is it all right if I come again tomorrow?" The old man looked over at him.

"You're free to do as you please," he said.

# AFTERWORD

THOUGH SET mostly in the spring of 2011, this novel was first published in May 2005. I spent a year and a half writing it, in my getaway in the mountains of Hakone, after three years of research. Preparations included a series of interviews in Seoul with some twenty refugees from North Korea. Seoul plays host to a whole community of escapees, and their cooperation was invaluable to me.

I was interested not so much in how my informants had escaped as in what their daily lives had been like in the North. In the case of former members of the military, I focused on the training they received and the equipment and weapons they used. Most of the escapees still have family in North Korea. When I pressed them for specific details about the geography of their hometowns, some became wary, suspecting me of working for Japanese intelligence.

Conducting these interviews was exhausting. Concepts of life, country, politics, society, and so on are so different from the paradigms we take for granted in democratic nations, that my informants often couldn't even make sense of my questions. Particularly difficult for me to understand was the interconnection of the Workers' Party, the government, and the People's Army. The more I probed into it, the more the separate chains of command seemed to be entangled, and the less I could see who had the actual authority to decide things.

The Anti-Aircraft Corps stationed in the capital, Pyongyang, for example, are reportedly among the elite of the People's Army. I was told that in addition to a commanding officer, however, the corps have a member of the government over them as well, and that both issue commands. When I asked if the government representative had a military rank, the man I was interviewing eventually confessed that he had no idea what I was talking about. What I finally came to see, in any case, was that the party, the government, and the army were basically all one, with the person named Kim Jong Il at the top of this three-sided pyramid.

The dictator was never as universally respected in North Korea as his father, Kim Il Sung, but the picture that emerged from the interviews was of a crafty and extremely cautious man. What I gather from having read a pile of material in Japanese and interviewing former members of the Politburo is that by 2004 Kim Jong Il had already established the basic outline for the regime that would rule after his death. It involved a collective leadership centered around his younger sister's husband, the reformist Jang Sung Taek (briefly mentioned in "Prologue 2"), and it presupposed the support and cooperation of China.

Last year, the crafty dictator died, and his son Kim Jong Un was selected as his successor. Presumably there has been no change of plan, however: the son will be propped up and guided by the group surrounding his uncle Jang Sung Taek, with China's backing.

This English translation is the result of a collaborative effort by Ralph McCarthy, Ginny Tapley Takemori, Charles De Wolf, and their editor Stephen Shaw. As the author, I feel incredibly fortunate to have had such a talented and dedicated team working together on the book. Ralph, Ginny, Charles, Stephen: thank you!

RYU MURAKAMI
*February 15, 2012*
*Yokohama*

## Pushkin Press

Pushkin Press was founded in 1997, and publishes novels, essays, memoirs, children's books—everything from timeless classics to the urgent and contemporary.

Our books represent exciting, high-quality writing from around the world: we publish some of the twentieth century's most widely acclaimed, brilliant authors such as Stefan Zweig, Marcel Aymé, Antal Szerb, Paul Morand and Yasushi Inoue, as well as compelling and award-winning contemporary writers, including Andrés Neuman, Edith Pearlman and Ryu Murakami.

Pushkin Press publishes the world's best stories, to be read and read again. Here are just some of the titles from our long and varied list:

---

### THE SPECTRE OF ALEXANDER WOLF
GAITO GAZDANOV

'A mesmerising work of literature' Antony Beevor

### BINOCULAR VISION
EDITH PEARLMAN

'A genius of the short story' Mark Lawson, *Guardian*

### TRAVELLER OF THE CENTURY
ANDRÉS NEUMAN

'A beautiful, accomplished novel: as ambitious as it is generous, as moving as it is smart' Juan Gabriel Vásquez, *Guardian*

### BEWARE OF PITY
STEFAN ZWEIG

'Zweig's fictional masterpiece' *Guardian*

**THE BREAK**

PIETRO GROSSI

'Small and perfectly formed... reaching its end leaves the reader desirous to start all over again' *Independent*

**FROM THE FATHERLAND, WITH LOVE**

RYU MURAKAMI

'If Haruki is *The Beatles* of Japanese literature, Ryu is its *Rolling Stones*' David Pilling

**BUTTERFLIES IN NOVEMBER**

AUÐUR AVA ÓLAFSDÓTTIR

'A funny, moving and occasionally bizarre exploration of life's upheavals and reversals' *Financial Times*

**BARCELONA SHADOWS**

MARC PASTOR

'As gruesome as it is gripping... the writing is extraordinarily vivid... Highly recommended' *Independent*

**THE LAST DAYS**

LAURENT SEKSIK

'Mesmerising... Seksik's portrait of Zweig's final months is dignified and tender' *Financial Times*

**BY BLOOD**

ELLEN ULLMAN

'Delicious and intriguing' *Daily Telegraph*

**WHILE THE GODS WERE SLEEPING**

ERWIN MORTIER

'A monumental, phenomenal book' *De Morgen*

**THE BRETHREN**

ROBERT MERLE

'A master of the historical novel' *Guardian*